Exile

EXILE

A Novel

RICHARD NORTH PATTERSON

LARGE PRINT PRESS
An imprint of Thomson Gale, a part of The Thomson Corporation

Detroit • New York • San Francisco • New Haven, Conn. • Waterville, Maine • London

The text of this Large Print edition is unabridged.
Other aspects of the book may vary from the original edition.
Set in 16 pt. Plantin.

LIBRARY OF CONGRESS CATALOGING-IN-PUBLICATION DATA

Patterson, Richard North.
Exile / by Richard North Patterson.
p. cm.
ISBN-13: 978-1-59722-417-8 (hc : alk. paper)
ISBN-10: 1-59722-417-0 (hc : alk. paper)
1. Jews—California—Fiction. 2. Palestinian Arabs—California—Fiction.
3. Terrorists—Fiction. 4. Large type books. I. Title.
PS3566.A8242E95 2007b
813'.54—dc22 2006034927

ISBN 13: 978-1-59413-222-3 (sc : alk. paper)
ISBN 10: 1-59413-222-4 (sc : alk. paper)
Published in 2007 in arrangement with Henry Holt and Company LLC.

Printed in the United States of America on permanent paper
10 9 8 7 6 5 4 3 2 1

For Alan Dershowitz and Jim Zogby

For Alan Dershowitz and Jim Zogby

In wartime, truth is so precious that she should always be attended by a bodyguard of lies.

—WINSTON CHURCHILL

PROLOGUE
THE MARTYRS

Gazing at the white-capped aqua waters of the Mayan Riviera, Ibrahim Jefar struggled to imagine the act that would end his life: the righteous murder, far from home, of the man who led the enemy of his people, the hawk-faced architect of his sister's shame and grief.

Ibrahim and Iyad Hassan, who directed their actions and would join him in death, were living in suspension, awaiting the directives that would transform their anonymity to honor. Their temporary refuge was the village of Akumal, sequestered in a strip of beaches on the east coast of Mexico. Once the area had been peopled by Mayans, whose disappearance had left behind the ruins of pyramids and temples; now it was the playground of rich foreigners, sport fishermen and snorkelers, drawn by a reef system that offered coral of rich and varied hues and a plethora of vividly colored tropical fish. Their white stucco villa was one of a string of such places, sheltered by coconut palms, built into black rock ledges at the edge of the Caribbean. To Ibrahim, used to the desolation of his homeland, it was beautiful and alien, as disorienting as the aftershock of a dream.

They had existed here for a week. Each morning, as now, stiff breezes drove away the early clouds and exposed a rich blue sky, which met the deeper blue of the ocean. Sunlight summoned forth the slender women in string bikinis who snorkeled and swam and walked on the beach nearby, filling him with desire and shame. He turned from them as he did from the pitiless sun.

To Ibrahim, in their heedlessness and privilege, these tourists symbolized those who had shamed his people, the Zionists who used America's weaponry to occupy their remaining lands and strangle them in a web of settlements and roadblocks, cementing their exile with the glue of poverty. He thought of his sister, sweet and scared, who once had trembled when the bombs fell, before the soldiers drove all reason from her brain; of his father, whose profitable accounting practice had shriveled to bare subsistence; of their ancestral home in Haifa, now possessed by Jews, its beauty known to Ibrahim only through photographs; of another image, this one of bombed-out wreckage in the refugee camp in Jenin, beneath which lay a corpse whose sole marker was a shattered pair of gold-rimmed glasses. "Terrorist" the Zionists had called him.

No, Ibrahim thought — a martyr, and my friend. But it was Salwa, his sister, who fueled his wavering resolve in this place too far from home.

Their journey here had begun in Ramallah, on the West Bank. Using their own passports, they drove to Amman, then flew to Paris, Mexico City, and Cancún. There they had rented a car in Iyad's true name, driving to the villa selected by the unknown authors of their mission. Ibrahim was unused to this freedom of travel — a clear highway without checkpoints or soldiers, running for miles in a straight line.

They were free here, Ibrahim thought now, a bitter irony. Neither had a criminal record; both spoke fluent English. They were in Akumal for the diving, they said on the few occasions in which they needed to say anything, and then proceeded to do nothing but await their fate in luxury. The conceit of this refuge was that no one with their actual mission would choose such a place: they were rendered inconspicuous by the sheer incongruity of their presence, and the indifference of vacationers bent on their own pleasure and distraction.

And so they kept to themselves, unnoticed save by a housekeeper who spoke rudimentary English and did what little cooking and cleaning they required. Their plans, Ibrahim felt certain, were beyond anything that life had led this simple woman to contemplate. The only Jews she had ever known were no doubt rich Americans — like, by the evidence Ibrahim had sifted from photographs and books, the absentee owners of the villa — and probably she did not even know what they were. For now, at least, he and Iyad seemed safe.

Yet Ibrahim was both frightened and sad. The dream state of this respite made him feel small, the puppet of unseen forces. He tried to imagine once more the pride of his friends, the admiration of strangers for whom, in death, he would enter into history. But here, in Akumal, this vision lacked the vividness it had had in Ramallah. Instead it seemed somehow juvenile, the fantasy of a boy who had placed himself in an action movie with which he had killed some idle afternoon.

Their only contact with reality was Iyad's cell phone. Ibrahim was not allowed to answer it: Iyad would retreat to a corner of the villa, speaking Arabic in a low voice. His terse comments afterward made Ibrahim feel patronized, a child fed by his parents some rehearsed and edited version of a grown-up conversation held behind closed doors. It was this, he supposed, that made it even harder to imagine Iyad Hassan taking orders from a woman.

But this woman, too, was surely only a conduit, the instrument of other men who shared their vision. In the end, they and their faceless masters were all servants of their people, and of God.

Ibrahim checked his watch. Inside, he knew, Iyad was finishing his extended prayers — head bowed, eyes squinting tight, deepening the premature lines of a face too careworn for a man who, at twenty-four, was only two years older than Ibrahim himself. Sometimes Ibrahim believed that Iyad had known everything but doubt.

Sometimes he wished that Iyad had not chosen him.

He could not envision paradise. He could experience what martyrdom would bring him only in earthly imaginings of the Ramallah that would persist after his death, peopled by ordinary citizens whose pleasure it was to recall Ibrahim's sacrifice while living out their ordinary lives — in a land, he could only pray, transformed by his act. He would never know the unborn children who, Iyad had assured him, would feel pride in the mention of his name, study his photograph for the markers of bravery. The pieces of his ruined body would find no grave at home.

This place was his oasis, and his prison: he was a hostage to time that dragged with agonizing slowness, waiting for the phone call that would propel them into action. So yet again, he sat on a stone bench atop a rocky ledge where waves struck with a low thud and shot spumes of white into the air, dampening his face and bare chest with a cool mist. The sandy space between the rocks and the villa was thick with palms; the pounding surf filled the air with a ceaseless watery static. The villa itself was bright and airy, and in the sheltered front garden was a swimming pool. Ibrahim could not imagine that anyone lived like this — except the Zionist settlers, the red tile roofs of whose houses resembled the roof of this villa, or, he thought with fleeting disdain, the eminences of the Palestinian Authority, once his nominal leaders. But from the evidence of the photographs, this was the home of a bearded American Jew and his skinny wife, grinning maniacally at the camera in a parody of the vacationer's escapist glee. On their coffee table was a picture book entitled *A Day in the Life of Israel,* a catalog of Zionist achievement, schools and cities and deserts bursting with green orchards and bright fruits and vegetables. Still, what Ibrahim saw as he leafed through the pages was his grandfather dying in a refugee camp, a small wizened man with a gaze at once nearsighted and faraway, the look of decades of wretchedness and dispossession. There was no book with a picture of his grandfather, he thought now; the old man had died as he had lived, seen only by his family.

Remembering, Ibrahim felt his eyes mist with grief and anger. The world weeps, he thought, at the death of a Jewish child. But there is no press coverage of dead Palestinians, unless they die killing Jews; there was no notice of his sister, or the daughter she would never hold, by a media obsessed with Jews blown up in cafés and restaurants by those brave few who chose to emerge from the faceless squalor of their camps, seeking to make their enemy suffer as deeply as did their people. And yet, though Ibrahim respected their courage and understood its purpose, he could not easily conceive of taking women and children with him to their doom. He must be grateful that he had been sent to kill a man.

This man, the face of Israel.

Ibrahim had known that face since childhood, as long as he had known Israeli soldiers and overcrowding and humiliation; that even dogs, but not Palestinians, were allowed to bark; that the real terrorists were not only the Jews but the Americans; that when a Jew dies, the president of the United States weeps in sorrow. He had known all this, and done nothing. Until the day when he looked into the eyes of his sister, now as dull in life as they would someday be in death, and knew that he must redeem his honor . . .

Something heavy struck his back. Flinching, he heard the bomb's percussive pop, stiffened against the explosion that would tear his limbs apart. Then he saw, rolling to a stop, a half-ruined coconut that had dropped from the tree behind him.

Wanly, Ibrahim laughed at himself — a displaced Palestinian on a verdant patch of Mexico, with imaginary bombs falling on him from a palm tree.

Before the trauma of Salwa, he had laughed more often, even in the worst of times. He wondered if what he saw on Iyad's face had entered his soul without touching his own unmarked face — this sense of having felt too much, of a despair deeper and older than his years. On television, at home, he could see beautiful people from all over the world, as free and happy as the half-naked women on the beach at Akumal. But that television set, all he possessed besides a few books and clothes and a college degree from Birzeit without a future he could see, filled him with a sense of his own nothingness. He would sit in his international relations class, furtively admiring Fatin of the light brown eyes and seductive smile, and know that nothing was all he had to offer her.

Even this sojourn was a tribute to their facelessness. That they were in Akumal instead of western Mexico, Iyad informed him, was a change of plans, a fluke of racism and oppression. Self-appointed American vigilantes had begun spending their idle hours patrolling the borders of Arizona and New Mexico, hoping to snare Mexican illegals scurrying across. Those who had planned their mission did not want them caught by some white people's hunt for brown invaders they could not tell from Arabs.

Americans, and Jews. When Iyad had first approached him, he had recited a sermon he had heard from a radical imam. Wherever you are, the holy man had said, kill Jews and Americans. He who straps a suicide belt on his children will be blessed. No Jews believe in peace; all are liars. Even if some piece of paper is signed by Jews and Palestinian traitors, we cannot forget Haifa, or Jericho, or Galilee, all the land and lives the Zionists have stolen from us, the day-by-day degradation into which the occupiers grind our faces. " 'Have no mercy on the Jews,' " Iyad repeated. " 'No matter what country they are in. And never forget that Jews are the sword of the United States of America, the enemy who arms our enemy.' "

This recitation left Ibrahim unmoved. He had heard it all before, countless times; hearing it again gave him the dull sensation of being rhythmically pounded on the head with a bag of sand. Then he thought of Salwa . . .

Once more, Ibrahim flinched.

Tensing, he heard the second discordant ring of Iyad's cell phone, carrying through the screen door of the villa. The ringing stopped abruptly, followed by the sound of Iyad's voice.

Ibrahim closed his eyes.

For minutes he was still. Then, with a sense of foreboding, he heard Iyad's footfalls in the sand, felt his shadow block the sun.

Raising his head, Ibrahim looked into his companion's gaunt face. Then, as before, he thought that God had given Iyad too little skin to cover his bones.

"She called," Iyad said. His monotone had the trace of disdain that Ibrahim found so discordant, given the exactitude with which he carried out her directives. "This is our last night in paradise on earth. The next will be far better."

Two afternoons later, driven by a lean, cold-eyed man they knew only as Pablo, they rode in a van headed toward the border. Crossing would be no problem, Pablo assured them in surprisingly good English — thousands did it every day. Although not, Ibrahim thought, for such a reason.

Pablo left them a mile from the border. Stepping onto the parched earth, they began to walk in the sweltering heat. Turning, Iyad watched Pablo's van disappear, then ordered, "We leave the cell phone here. And our passports. Everything that names us."

These few words, Ibrahim found, sealed his sense of foreboding.

He emptied his pockets. With the care of a man tending a garden, Iyad buried their passports under a makeshift pile of rocks.

An hour later, sweat from their trek coating his face, Ibrahim saw the metallic glint of a silver van driving toward them across the featureless terrain. Ibrahim froze in fear. With preternatural calm, Iyad said, "We're in America. The home of the brave, the liberators of Iraq."

The van stopped beside them. Silently, its dark-haired young driver opened the door, motioning them into the back. In English as fluent as Pablo's, he said, "Lie down. I'm not getting paid to lose you." To Ibrahim, he looked more Arabic than Hispanic. But then, he realized, so had Pablo.

When the man told them to sit up, they were in Brownsville, Texas. He dropped them near a bus terminal with nothing but what he had given them, the key to a locker inside.

The terminal was nearly empty. Glancing over his shoulder, Iyad opened the locker. The brown bag they found held a credit card, three thousand dollars in cash, car keys, a binder, two American passports in false names, and California driver's licenses. With mild astonishment, Ibrahim gazed at his photograph, encased in plastic, and discovered that his new name was Yusuf Akel.

"Let's go," Iyad murmured in Arabic.

Expressionless, he led Ibrahim to a nondescript Ford sedan with California license plates, parked two blocks away. Iyad unlocked the passenger door for Ibrahim.

"We have seven days," Iyad said. "We'll drive until it's dark."

It was June, late spring, and the days were long. Tasting the last saliva in his dry mouth, Ibrahim got in, knowing he would not sleep for hours, if at all.

Iyad drove in silence. Ibrahim riffled through the

binder. It contained a sheaf of maps, detailing a route from Brownsville to San Francisco. On the final map of San Francisco were two stars scrawled with a Magic Marker: one labeled "bus station," the other beside a place called Fort Point.

Closing his eyes against the harsh sunlight, Ibrahim tried to summon an image of San Francisco, the end of his life's journey.

Part 1
The Hope

1

Until Hana Arif called him after thirteen years of silence, and he knew whose voice it was so quickly that he felt time stop, David Wolfe's life was proceeding as he had long intended.

Except for the spring of Hana, as he still thought of it, David had always had a plan. He had planned to excel in prep school as a student and at sports, and did. After college, he had planned to go to Harvard Law, and he had. He had planned to become a prosecutor and then enter politics, and now he was.

That this last was proceeding even more smoothly than he could have hoped was due to his fiancée, Carole Shorr, who, though not planned on, had entered his life at least in part because her plans meshed so well with his. Now their plan was the same: marriage, two children, and a run for Congress, which continued the more or less straight line of David's life since his early teens, when he had realized that his dark good looks, wry humor, and quickness of mind were matched by a self-discipline that wrung every last particle out of the talents he possessed. Only once — with Hana — had nothing mattered but another person, an experience so frightening, exhilarating, and, in the end, scarifying that he had endured it only by clinging to his plans until they became who he was. It was a sin, David had come to believe, to be surprised by your own life.

This conclusion did not make him callous, or disdainful of others. The experience of Hana had taught him too much about his own humanness. And he knew that his self-discipline and gift for detachment were part of the mixed blessings, perhaps intensified by Hana, passed down by his parents — a psychiatrist and an English professor who shared a certain intellectual severity, both of them descendants of German Jews and so thoroughly assimilated that their banked emotions reminded him of the privileged WASPs he had encountered when his parents had dispatched him from San Francisco to prep school in Connecticut, with little more sentiment than he had come to expect.

All this made him value and even envy the deep emotionality of Carole and her father, Harold — the Holocaust survivor and his daughter, for whom their very existence was to be celebrated. So that this morning, when he and Carole had selected a wedding date after making love, and her eyes had filled with tears, he understood at once that her joy was not only for herself but for Harold, who would celebrate their wedding day on behalf of all the ghosts whose deaths in Hitler's camps — as unfathomable to Harold as his own survival — required him to invest his heart and soul in each gift life gave him, of which his only child was the greatest.

So David and Carole had made love again. Afterward, she lay against him, smiling, her breasts touching his chest, the tendrils of her brunette curls grazing his shoulder. And he had forgotten, for a blissful time, the other woman, smaller and darker, in his memory always twenty-three, with whom making love had been to lose himself.

Thus the David Wolfe who answered his telephone was firmly rooted in the present and, blessedly, his future. He was, he had told himself once more, a fortunate man, gifted with genetics that, with no effort on his part, had given him intelligence, a level disposition, and a face on which every feature was pronounced — strong cheekbones, ridged nose, cleft chin — plus cool blue eyes to make it one that people remembered and television flattered. To his natural height and athleticism he added fitness, enforced by a daily regime of weights and aerobic exercise.

His current life was a similar fusion of luck, self-discipline, and careful planning. That morning, upon reaching his clean and sparely decorated law office, David had flipped his desk calendar, looking past the orderly notations of the lawyer and would-be politician — the hearings, depositions, and trial dates of a practice that commingled civil law with criminal defense; the lunches, evening speeches, and meetings of civic groups that marked the progress of a Democratic congressman-in-waiting — and lit on the wedding date he and Carole had selected. It would be an occasion. Harold Shorr would spare no expense, and this served Carole's interest in a day that combined deep celebration with an opportunity for David's further advancement in the Jewish community that would become his financial base in politics.

This was fine with David: Carole's penthouse was a focal point for Democratic and Jewish causes, and he had become accustomed to Carole filling dates with social opportunities both onerous and interesting, the latter represented by the dinner Carole was hosting that evening for the Israeli prime minister, Amos Ben-Aron. This one of Carole's many dinners promised to be particularly intriguing. Formerly an obdurate hard-liner, Ben-Aron was now barnstorming America to rally support for his controversial last-ditch plan to achieve peace between Israel and the Palestinians, with whom it had too long been locked in a violent and corrosive struggle — about which, as it happened, David knew a little more than he could have admitted to Carole without inflicting needless wounds, or reopening his own.

Dismissing the thought, David gazed down at his wedding date. Perhaps the prime minister, David mused with a smile, would agree to serve as their best man. No doubt Carole had considered this; in her reckoning, David's only flaw was a shortfall of Jewishness. Not that this was obvious: a gentile former girlfriend, studying David's face after lovemaking, had remarked, "You look like an Israeli film star, if there is such a thing." Then, as now, David had no idea; he had never been to Israel. No doubt Carole would change this, as well.

Still light of spirit, he had just looked up from the calendar to his view of the San Francisco skyline when the telephone rang.

He glanced at the caller ID panel. But the number it displayed was a jumble that made no sense to him — a cell phone number, he supposed, perhaps foreign. Intrigued, he answered it.

"David?"

Her voice, precise and soft at once, caused the briefest delay in his response.

"Yes?"

"David." The repetition of his name was quieter yet. "It's Hana."

"Hana," he blurted. He stood up, half out of reflex, half from shock. "What on earth . . ."

"I know." She hesitated. "I know. I mean, it's been long."

"Thirteen years."

"Thirteen years. And now I'm visiting here. San Francisco."

David managed to laugh. "Just like that."

"Not exactly. Saeb is relentlessly tracking Amos Ben-Aron, pointing out the manifest defects and incongruities of this new plan of his — perhaps more sharply than our American hosts are happy with."

She said this as if it were logical, expected. "So you two are married."

"Yes. And we — or I — decided it was time for Munira to see the United States." This time it was Hana who laughed. "I'm a mother, David."

There was something in the timbre of her laugh that David could not define — perhaps simply the acknowledgment that she was not the young woman he had known, the lover he might still remember.

"It happens," he answered. "Or so I'm told."

"Not you?"

"Not yet. But I'm getting married in seven months. According to the conventions, children follow." Temporarily, he lost his place in the conversation. "So how is it, being a parent?"

This time it was Hana who seemed, for a moment, distracted. "Munira," she answered dryly, "is my own parents' revenge. She's bright, willful, and filled with the passion of her own ideas. Sometimes I think she will never imagine that *I* was such a person. Or experience the kind of amusement, pride, and chagrin a mother feels when she looks at her daughter and sees herself."

Though he had begun to pace, David smiled a little. "So she's beautiful, as well."

"Beautiful?" The word seemed to take Hana by surprise. David recalled that she had often seemed unaware of her own impact — at least until she looked at him and saw it in his eyes. "Oh," she added lightly, "of course."

With this, neither seemed to know what to say. "This is all right?" she asked.

"What?"

"To call you."

"Of course. I'm glad you did."

She hesitated. "Because I thought we might have lunch."

David stood still. "The three of us?" he asked at length.

Another pause. "Or four of us, counting your wife-to-be."

She tried to infuse this with a tone of generosity, including in her proposal a woman she did not seem to have expected.

"How *is* Saeb?" David parried.

"Much as you would recall him. We are both professors at Birzeit University, near Ramallah — it's been some time, you may recall, since the Israeli army last shut us down. Saeb is still brilliant, and still angry. Perhaps angrier than me now. He's just as committed to Palestine, but more radical. And very much more Islamic." She stopped there. *Is it such a good idea,* David wanted to ask, *to put Saeb and me at the same table once again?* But to question this would be to intimate that to Saeb, and perhaps to Hana, David occupied the lingering psychic space that Hana did for him. Then she spoke again.

"Perhaps you're right," she said simply, answering the question he had not asked. "You are well, David?"

"I'm well. Very." He felt a brief twinge, his last memory of Hana. "And you?"

"Yes. Enough." Once more she sounded hesitant, perhaps rueful that she had called. "And you've become a trial lawyer as you wished?"

"Yes."

"And a good one, I am sure."

"Good enough. I've yet to lose a case — mainly because I spent all my career until last year as a prosecutor, and prosecutors try the cases they can win. Now I'm a defense lawyer with my own practice — me and one associate — working as tribune for the mostly guilty. So I'm overdue for a loss."

"I hope not, if only for the sake of your next client." Her voice softened again. "Your fiancée, does she have a name?"

"Carole. Carole Shorr."

"What does she do?"

"Good works, mainly. She has a master's degree in social work. But her father's quite wealthy, so she's found her way into causes she cares deeply about — raising money for the Democratic Party, chairing the board of a group that combats violence against women and children. A lot of time put into Jewish charities and promoting ties between Israel and the United States." He paused briefly. "Without, I might add, despising Palestinians. All she wants for Israel is a stable peace, and an end to killing."

Hana was briefly silent. "So," she said gently. "A nice Jewish girl, and a rich one at that. Things often end up the way they're supposed to, I think."

There was a moment in time for me, David thought, when "supposed to" did not count. Had it ever been like that, he wondered now, for Hana? Then he heard his own silence.

"So here we are," he said. "I'm happy about Munira. If there was ever a graduate of Harvard Law School who should downstream her DNA, it's you."

After an instant, Hana laughed briefly. "Then congratulations to us both, David." Her voice abruptly sobered. "Though I worry she has seen too much on the West Bank, too much oppression, too much death. I can feel her growing too old, and too scarred, too quickly. The Zionist occupation has been criminal — generation after generation, they are always with us. Ben-Aron most of all."

David did not respond.

Hana paused, seemingly uncertain of what to say next, then retrieved a note of warmth. "I'm glad to know you're well. Take care, David."

"And you."

"Oh, I will." A last moment of hesitation. "Good-bye, David."

"Good-bye, Hana."

Slowly, David put down the telephone, his morning utterly transformed.

2

From the moment David Wolfe first saw Hana Arif — igniting that incandescent spark that, for him, never died despite all his efforts — she was bound to Saeb Khalid in ways more profound than David could then conceive.

It was February, and he was marking time. In three months, he would graduate from Harvard and begin the law career he had been planning for so long. Grades no longer worried him; a job in the District Attorney's Office for the City and County of San Francisco awaited, and David was allowing himself the rare luxury of indifference. And so, on a bleak winter evening in Cambridge, David found himself hurrying to the law school with his friend Noah Klein, late for a discussion among a moderator and four students — two Jews and two Arabs — about the Israeli-Palestinian dilemma.

Ordinarily, this subject would not have diverted David from watching the Celtics game on television. But Noah wanted company and, over dinner, David had allowed that it might be amusing to watch their classmate Marcus Goodman — a devout Orthodox Jew from Brooklyn of almost comical sincerity — take up the cudgel for the Jewish homeland. When they entered the lecture room, David spotted Marcus at one end of a table with their Israeli classmate Ruth Harr, separated from two young Palestinians by the moderator, a bearded professor of constitutional law. But what drew David's attention was the Palestinian woman scornfully interrupting Marcus's assertion that what she no doubt considered part of her homeland, the West Bank of the Jordan River, was, in fact, a "biblical and immutable grant of land from God to the Jewish people —"

"Since when," she inquired, "did God become a real estate agent?"

There was scattered laughter from the audience packing the room. Still standing, David struggled to suppress a smile at Marcus's discomfiture. And then he realized that the woman was now contemplating David himself, the conspicuously late arrival, with an appraisal at once leisurely and disdainful. Himself no stranger to pride, David coolly returned her gaze, allowing his amused expression to linger. How long, he silently asked her, do you want to keep this up?

"Let's sit," Noah murmured. "There are two places over there."

They sat, comfortably distant from the panel, and David began to study the woman in earnest.

It was worth his time. She was slim and startlingly pretty — a full mouth, sculpted face, black hair pulled back at the nape of her neck, intense dark eyes — the type of olive-skinned beauty, accented by gold earrings and red lipstick, to which David had always felt a chemical attraction he both savored and distrusted. But as the discussion continued, what engaged him even more was her vividness in debate, an arresting quickness of thought and speech accented by a vibrant animation. Nothing about her was inscrutable. Not the swift, sardonic smile that showcased white, perfect teeth, nor the look of displeasure with which she regarded her antagonists — head tilted, eyes narrowing in skepticism, and the full line of her mouth depressing slightly, as though to restrain some biting interjection. For David, it was as though the others faded to black and white, and this woman emerged in Technicolor.

She was a first-year law student, David discovered from the program, and her name was Hana Arif.

"In 1947," Hana was saying to Marcus Goodman, "the United Nations recommended the partition of my homeland, Palestine — then controlled by the British — into a Jewish state and a Palestinian state.

"My grandparents were farmers in the Galilee." Her tone became muted with sorrow. "That was all they knew. They did not understand that they must pay for a Holocaust perpetrated by Europeans by giving up their home, based on a Zionist program of colonizing our lands that began before Hitler was even born. They failed to see why it was unfair for Jews to live as a minority in a Palestinian state, but fair for half the Palestinian people — like those in their own village — to be converted overnight into an Arab minority in a Jewish state of the outside world's creation —"

"What would have changed for them, really?" Ruth Harr interrupted. "They should have stayed and learned to live with Jews in peace. By leaving they created their own tragedy."

At this, the slight young man sitting beside Hana — Saeb Khalid, a graduate student in international relations, the program told David — placed his hand lightly on her arm, a signal that he wished to intervene, to which she, somewhat to David's surprise, assented. Turning to Ruth, Saeb's fine poet's face became a mask of anger, and his first words were choked with emotion. "My grandparents' lives were *your* grandparents' creation. Your soldiers drove us out, destroyed our villages. At Deir Yassin, the terrorist organization Irgun — founded by your prime minister, the great peacemaker Menachem Begin — slaughtered over two hundred and fifty Palestinian men, women, and children, who were stripped, mutilated, thrown into a well, or simply murdered.

"As Hana said, our grandparents were simple people. But they understood death well enough —"

"And so do we." Ruth straightened in her chair, her own dark intensity mirroring Hana's. "Don't equate your history with ours. And don't pass off anti-Semitism as a quaint eccentricity of Europeans — although the Spanish Inquisition, the many bloody pograms carried out by the Russians and the Poles, and Hitler's Teutonic efficiency make for a truly impressive list. Three times in the 1930s, your people slaughtered Jews in Hebron. Your grand mufti of Jerusalem was Hitler's Arab friend, a partner in their common passion for exterminating Jews."

Good, David thought.

"And the grand mufti," Ruth concluded, "was nothing if not the authentic voice of Islam. Why else did the Arab nations invade Israel in 1948?"

"How," Saeb inquired with fearful politeness, "do you invade something that does not exist? Who made Israel a country? Your 'invasion' was, in truth, a failed war of liberation — the liberation of Palestinians from a Zionist program of expulsion. You could not have your 'Jewish democracy' with more Palestinians than Jews. You needed to be rid of us, by whatever means at hand." The young man paused, biting off his final words. "But you will never be rid of us for good. Not *all* of us."

His deep-set eyes flashed with warning. There was about him, David thought, a molten anger deeper than Hana's. Though this smell of the visceral was galvanizing, it left David disheartened. When, he wondered, could these two peoples leave their histories behind?

As if to answer him, Hana spoke in more level tones: "It is generations since my grandparents fled what you call the State of Israel. They died in the squalid refugee camp in Lebanon where their children — my parents — still live. Saeb's parents died there as well, murdered by Christian militia in a slaughter condoned by Menachem Begin and Ariel Sharon. Now the rest of our land, including the West Bank, is occupied by the Israeli army."

At this, Marcus Goodman spun on her. "The West Bank is a center of terrorism —"

"*You* talk of terrorism." Saeb's tone was acid and accusatory. "Israel was conceived in terrorism. It is drenched in terrorism. The Jewish Irgun brought terrorism to the Middle East. They bombed and killed the British until the Brits could stand no more, and then deployed more terror to expel us from our land. And then their henchmen killed still more of us in the Lebanese stinkhole that confines us.

"If we are terrorists, it is because we must be. Perhaps killing is all the Jews have left us."

The silence of the audience suddenly felt stifling. Marcus and Ruth were zealous advocates, David thought, but Saeb Khalid spoke from raw experience. It was fascinating, and more than a little frightening.

"Let us hope," the moderator intoned, "that the Oslo Accords, paving the way for the return of Yasser Arafat and the Palestinian Liberation Organization to land now occupied by Israel, will provide an alternative to violence. And, with that thought, I'd like to thank the audience, and our panel . . ."

"You go ahead," David murmured to Noah. "I think I'll stay for a while."

David lingered, watching Hana from the edge of the scrum of law students who had gathered around the panelists for further inquiry and debate. She was smaller, he saw, than the impression created by her intensity. In private conversation her manner seemed to soften, the directness of her gaze leavened by attentiveness and flashes of humor. She appeared a different species from Saeb, who had about him the air of a prophet, a man too consumed by his vision to make allowances for others. David had no desire to speak with him. His only interest was in Hana.

At length, David angled through the crowd until he stood in front of her. Around her neck, David noted with curiosity, was a simple necklace on which hung what appeared to be an old brass key. Her upward gaze held the same disconcerting directness she had trained on him before. "You found all this amusing, I noticed."

Once again, David resolved to stand his ground. "Not terribly," he answered evenly. "Death is not amusing. Nothing about your history amuses me. You simply caught me admiring your gifts. And I'm way out of sympathy with anyone, even my friend Marcus, who thinks that God has punched his ticket."

This elicited a first, faint smile. "God gave us the land as well. He just forgot to leave the deed."

David glanced again at her necklace. "The key you wear," he asked, "what is it?"

"The key to my father's home. In Galilee."

"In Israel," David amended gently. "Have you ever seen it?"

Still she held his gaze. "No. Nor has my father, since he was seven. When my grandfather took a mule and cart and packed up his family and all he could take from the home he had built with his own hands. Including this key."

David shoved his hands into the pockets of his jeans. "Listening tonight, I found myself wondering where each of you thought history began. Does *your* history begin in 1947?"

"Don't patronize me," Hana answered crisply. "I know the Jewish narrative, all too well. And don't sell our history short. My history begins with the thousands of years we occupied the land that you call Israel."

David smiled. "I happen to be Jewish, as you might have guessed. But if I recall my Middle Eastern history course, what *I* call Israel — a strip of land on the Mediterranean — was occupied thousands of years ago not by Arabs or Jews but by Philistines. Gentiles, in short. So I suppose I could make a case for the Philistine Liberation Organization." He held up his hand, fending off the irritation flashing through her eyes. "I don't mean to make light of this. I'm just trying to point out that the past is a black hole. There's no way to resolve it."

"That's no reason to forget it —"

"I'm not suggesting amnesia. Peace would be enough. An end to killing."

At this, Hana glanced at Saeb, who was speaking with two law students. David sensed that she, like him, had just discovered that Saeb was furtively watching them. Seemingly disconcerted, Hana turned back to David. "With all respect," she said dismissively, "I think you have much to learn."

"And time to learn it." David steeled himself to make a suggestion that — unique to this woman among all the women he had known — he found surprisingly difficult. "I'd like to talk with you some more."

For an instant, Hana looked genuinely startled. Then she stared at him so deeply that, it seemed to David, she believed that she could gaze into his soul. "Perhaps lunch," she murmured at last. Glancing at Saeb again, she added softly, "Somewhere less incendiary."

David felt a tingle of surprise. This was nothing, he assured himself, a small distraction from the tedium of a last semester, the way station to his certain future.

"Lunch," he said, and their private history began.

3

For Ibrahim, San Francisco was a cool gray purgatory.

It was the sixth day. He stood on Ocean Beach, the edge of America, his back to their seedy motel across the four-lane road. For all he knew the dense, swirling fog in which he stood stretched, like the ocean, to Asia. The dull tan of the beach merged with the featureless gray water, which vanished in the mist. A bleak depression seeped into his bones like the dampness of the air. He could not believe that this misery was summer.

There was no one on the beach but the two of them. Ibrahim folded his arms against the cold, staring into nothingness as Iyad, perhaps a hundred feet away, called her on his cell phone.

She had a system, Iyad had explained. All communications were through phones with local numbers, avoiding the American spy agencies that monitored international calls. Every two days, she would order him to discard the phone and direct him to a new one, purchased for cash by one of her faceless helpers. Only she would know the cell phone number; she would call Iyad on the new phone, giving him fresh instructions and the number of her latest unregistered phone. Her system, Ibrahim knew, was that used by drug dealers and arms smugglers — or, under the Israelis, by the Palestinian resistance. She was clever, Iyad conceded, or at least well schooled.

Ibrahim tried to imagine their conversations. By a strange mental trick, Ibrahim sometimes fantasized that it was his sister — whose mind, in reality, was as dark as ruined film — who issued such precise instructions. Perhaps the stress was eroding his own reason.

Ibrahim shivered, miserable in the cold, against which his polo shirt provided no cover. In the distance, Iyad flipped his cell phone shut and shoved it in his pocket. For a moment, he, too, gazed at the water, as if absorbed by what he had heard. Then he walked toward Ibrahim.

Standing close, Iyad spoke in Arabic — softly, as though his words might carry in the mist. They would drive to the Greyhound station marked on the map. Taped to the back of a men's room toilet in the last stall to the left would be a key to another locker. Inside they would find a new phone, a last safeguard against detection, for the instructions that would bring about their deaths.

"God willing," Iyad said in the somber tones of prayer, "the enemy will die with us. Tomorrow."

The telephone rang in David's office, startling him from the past. This time the voice was Carole's, and he understood how completely a single phone call had effaced the thirteen years since Harvard.

"Dad wants to take us to lunch. To celebrate." Her voice was a fusion of warmth for Harold Shorr and concern that David understand. "I told him you'd love that. Is it okay?"

David did not exactly love it. Outside of politics, he avoided lunch dates — he did not like to fall behind, losing control of his day. Glancing at his watch, he realized that an hour had already been lost to memory. The day remaining was a full one: a meeting with United States Attorney Marnie Sharpe — who loathed him — to discuss a high-end bank robbery carried out by his patently guilty client; a conference with a medical expert in a complex, and regrettably fatal, case of medical malpractice. Carole knew these things, even as she knew that his workday would be cut short by her dinner for Prime Minister Ben-Aron, for which she had extracted David's pledge to arrive a half hour early.

So he was mildly annoyed that, whatever her excitement, Carole had placed her father's enthusiasm above the pressures of his own workday. But knowing this made him feel petty. And though he could never replicate Carole's deep bond with her widowed father, he understood it. In his own more restrained way, David loved and admired his father-in-law-to-be and, he was forced to admit, suspected that the attachment of father and daughter exposed an emotional deficiency in David himself.

Like Carole, David was an only child. There the similarities ended. He rarely examined his own past or spoke of his now-deceased parents — indeed, he avoided it. But Carole's childhood, intertwined with her fierce love for Harold Shorr, was such a richly remembered presence in her life that, to David, it seemed more vivid than his own.

Some memories he knew by heart. That every Sunday Harold, a graceful skater, had taken her for ice-skating and hot chocolate. That he could fix any toy she broke — the doll's arm might be funny, but now she could scratch her back. That father and daughter learned Hebrew together. That her parents never argued over Carole except once, in Polish, about whether she could watch TV past nine o'clock.

But there were other, darker memories. That, after coughing, Harold flinched as though remembering those days and nights in Auschwitz when the Nazis might shoot him for being sick. That he carried within him a deep silence that could consume him for hours. That Carole sensed that each new day was a surprise because no one wished to kill him.

It was this that infused her memories with so much meaning. Harold Shorr's consuming quest was to give Carole a better life, one of warmth and safety. Her wedding would be the culmination of his most cherished, most wistful dreams.

So when David responded to her question, his tone was one of wry affection. "Lunch? Of course I'd love it. You knew that even before you didn't ask."

Hanging up, David smiled. Once more, he found himself reflecting that though Harold's wounds touched both father and daughter, Harold had wrested from a horror he could not fully articulate the cocoon of goodness that defined who Carole was. And then, sadly, David thought again of a twenty-three-year-old woman, dark and lovely, whose wounds he could never heal, and she could never quite transcend.

4

It was during their first lunch that David sensed the vulnerability beneath the articulate fierceness Hana Arif presented to the world.

At Hana's suggestion, they met at a Chinese restaurant off campus, notable for its lack of clientele. As Hana glanced around the restaurant, empty save for a professional-appearing man and a pretty, much younger woman who looked as furtive as her companion, David realized that Hana feared being seen alone with a man — especially a Jew. It was a feeling of otherness David seldom had.

"Why," he inquired mildly, "am I feeling like a secret agent? Is one of us not supposed to be here?"

The question seemed to deepen her unease. "It's not like I'm a prisoner," she said. "But I *am* Muslim, and Saeb and I are to be married."

For an instant, David felt a foolish disappointment. Casually, he asked, "Was that your decision?"

Almost imperceptibly, she stiffened. "I'm not a prisoner," she repeated. "But there are conventions. Within reason, I try to respect them. Saeb wouldn't understand this lunch, and it's not important that I make him."

David sifted the conflicting intimations of this answer: that David himself was unimportant; that, nonetheless, she was committing a small act of defiance which caused her real discomfort. "How has it been for you?" he asked. "Harvard, I mean."

David watched her ponder the question, and then, it seemed, conceal Hana the woman behind Hana the Palestinian. "We feel isolated. There are fifteen Arab students at the law school, and not all of them care for Palestinians. And so many of our classmates are Jews —"

"Yes," David said. "We're everywhere."

She regarded him with a smile that did not touch her eyes. "Perhaps you think I'm anti-Semitic."

He returned her smile in kind. "I wouldn't know."

After a moment, Hana shrugged. "At least you don't assume I am. But if I say I don't like Zionism, people think it means I hate all Jews.

"My torts professor, a Jew, saves the hardest questions for me. The day after the debate you saw, another student came into that class, sat beside me, and put a miniature Israeli flag on the desk in front of him." Her voice became both weary and sardonic. "I suppose God had made that desk another grant to the Jewish people. But that day all I wanted was to sit in class and learn whatever I could." Pausing, she shrugged again, her voice softening. "I didn't start the Holocaust, and I don't deny that it happened. But the American Jews I meet are completely ignorant of the history you would like me to set aside. Sometimes I think Jews are so consumed by anti-Semitism that they can only see their own suffering and loss, not that of others."

David repressed his first rejoinder — that Hana's

plaint, even were it true, could be turned back on itself. "Of course," he parried. "That's why so many Jews joined our civil rights movement. For that matter, it's why I asked you to lunch."

Eyebrows raised, Hana gave him a penetrant look. "Yes," she said, "why did you?"

"Because I was curious about you. Why did you come?"

"Because I was curious about why you asked me. Though I expected that you saw me as some mildly exotic novelty, like encountering a chinchilla in one of your petting zoos."

At once, David grasped the deeper truth beneath her cleverness: her facility with words and images concealed an isolation far deeper than she chose to confess. Only candor, he decided, had a chance of piercing her defenses.

"When I met you," he said, "I saw a particular woman. A beautiful one, which never hurts. A woman who might despise me for what I am. But also one with a life so different from mine that I wanted to know more about it. Besides, as I said, I have the time."

She studied him. "So why not ask Saeb?"

"Because he's not a beautiful woman."

Hana laughed, a clear, pleasing trill free of rancor that took him by surprise. "And because," David finished, "with all respect to your fiancé, I don't think ten lunches in a row would make the slightest difference to him."

A young Chinese waiter arrived to take their order. When he left, Hana was gazing at the table with a veiled look of contemplation. "So," she inquired at length, "what do you want to know about me?"

"To start, what you envision as your home."

"We have no home," she said bitterly. "The refugee camp is an open sewer, a burial ground." She paused, draining the disdain from her voice. "Our home is in the Lower Galilee. It's built on a hillside, surrounded by the olive trees my grandfather planted, with a system of pipes and drains that capture the rainwater and channel it, and a cistern for the house. The house itself is stone. Its ceiling is reinforced with steel beams, and there are four rooms — a room to gather in, and bedrooms for my father and my uncles, for my aunts, and for my grandparents. There is no kitchen. My grandmother cooked outside, and they ate from plates they shared —"

"How can you know all this?"

Hana's face softened. "My grandfather described it for us, countless times, before he died. Stone by stone, like Flaubert described the village in *Madame Bovary.* But my grandparents' village was real, not imagined."

David wondered about this — what memory embellished, time destroyed. "And Saeb?" he asked.

"Is from the same village. Not literally, of course — in 1948, our parents were children. But their memories are as vivid as my grandfather's."

Perhaps their memories *are* your grandfather's, David thought but did not say. Instead, he inquired, "How did you come to Lebanon?"

Hana summoned a smile that signaled her forbearance. "Another accident of the history you have so little use for, and of people who have little use for us. After hearing of the massacre at Deir Yassin, my grandparents fled to Jordan. So did hundreds of thousands of Palestinians. The war in 1948 brought still more, as did the war of 1967. But all those Palestinians challenged the power of

King Hussein. And so the Jordanian army shelled our camps, and drove our fighters into Lebanon." Her voice held quiet anger. "From which, as a by-product of the cleansing operation Saeb mentioned, the Israelis forced Arafat and the PLO into exile in Tunis, claiming that their acts of 'terror' threatened northern Israel.

"Now they are gathered on the West Bank, still occupied by Israeli soldiers. My parents still wait in Lebanon. Only Saeb and I were able to leave for the West Bank, and then the Zionists closed Birzeit University before we could study there. And so," Hana continued with a smile that was no smile, "with the help of the refugee agency of the United Nations, Israel's creator, and some scholarship money, we washed up on the shores of America, the openhearted patron of those who displaced us. Where I carry on my people's struggle by engaging in foolish debates with those whose notion of Arabs comes from the novel *Exodus,* and who see our history as a western in which Israel is Jimmy Stewart and Saeb and I are Indians." Hana caught herself, summoning a bitter smile. "You asked. But perhaps you did not wish for an answer quite so comprehensive."

"I did ask," David said simply. "And you exaggerate."

To his surprise, her smile became more wistful than resentful. "I wish it were so. But I've learned to hope for nothing."

"And Saeb?"

"Has his own history." She looked briefly down again, pensive. "I'm not ready to talk about him, David."

Surprised by the tacit intimacy of his name on her lips, David tried to decipher what lay beneath her answer, and then the waiter appeared with steaming plates of beef chow mein and cooked vegetables. Serving them both, Hana said, "So I've become this contradictory person, a semiobservant Muslim leftist. Not because I embrace the Communists but because only the left seems determined to give us what we want."

David sampled the chow mein, more flavorful than the paucity of customers would suggest. "Which is?"

"A homeland. Our land returned to us. If Jews want to live among us, they can. But not in a Jewish ghetto called Israel, one that oppresses and excludes us."

"There are negotiations going on," David objected. "Arafat and Prime Minister Rabin already have agreed to let the PLO take over the civil governance of Gaza and the West Bank. A start toward your own country."

"We'll see," Hana answered with weary resignation. "More likely our children will someday have the same discussion. And it will be as academic to your child as it is to you."

David did not know what moved him next. He had always lived the circumscribed life of the American upper classes — professional parents; privileged friends; elite schools. The women he had dated, though of varied personalities and, at times, neuroses, were of the same class, with similar aspirations comfortably supported by similar families. But this woman had passion and experiences David Wolfe had never encountered, and it seemed to draw from him his own small spark of rebellion.

Whatever it was, he reached out and covered her hand with his. "Not academic. Not to me."

For a long time, she gazed down at his hand on

hers, though she made no move to withdraw it. "This is complicated." Her voice was soft, muffled. "You have no idea how much."

"Then tell me."

"I'm pledged to Saeb." She drew a breath, still looking down. "I'm Muslim. Wherever my home will be, Muslim women do not have men who are not Muslim. Let alone a Jewish man.

"There are rules. Women represent the honor of their family, as I represent mine." She looked up at him, eyes clouded. "That I even let you touch me stains their honor."

"But not yours, Hana. We're people, you and I."

She shook her head. But still she did not move her hand. "We can't afford to be. *You* can't afford to be. The price could be too great."

David gazed into her dark eyes, filled with uncertainty and even fear. Then he gave an answer that, when he recalled it later, seemed as blithely, blindly American as it must have seemed to her. A statement invincibly David Wolfe at twenty-five in its ignorance of pain.

"I want to see you, Hana, as often as you'll let me. I'll take my chances with the rest."

5

With an underhand flip, Iyad tossed his old cell phone into the swift, powerful current of San Francisco Bay. "Perhaps years from now," he said in chill tones, "they'll find it in Hawaii. Long after our people retake Jerusalem and dig up what pieces they had left of him to bury."

They stood at Fort Point, the foot of the massive concrete pillars beneath the Golden Gate Bridge, an orange-painted span that jutted above them into the fog creeping from the ocean through the narrow passage to the bay. Ibrahim's sense of living a surreal nightmare deepened; he felt like an automaton, being moved to ever more alien locations by someone who did not even acknowledge his existence. How had he come to be in this place, he asked himself, with this man, on the eve of his death? He knew nothing but what Iyad deigned to tell him — that their enemy was coming; that the woman would soon place the weapons of destruction in their hands.

But how? So many hated their quarry that he lived in a steel cocoon, guarded by a handpicked elite chosen from the Zionist army, ruthless men with reflexes for killing. Standing in this place unarmed, his only link to humanity a laconic, hate-filled zealot, Ibrahim felt as naked as Salwa before the insolent soldiers . . .

He still could see the checkpoint, clear as yesterday — it stretched for miles, cars and trucks backed up in a relentless heat that baked the parched earth and asphalt. His sister lay in the back seat of the car, belly swollen and face contorted in agony, her flowing skirt pulled up around her waist to expose what a brother should not see. "Please, God," she kept pleading, "please don't let us die."

Eyes shut, Ibrahim had grasped her hand. Now Salwa lived, her mind as empty as her womb.

Iyad's new cell phone rang.

"Don't be cute, David." Marnie Sharpe used her most caustic tone. "Don't tell me this bullshit trick doesn't have your fingerprints all over it."

They sat in the United States attorney's corner office in the federal building: Sharpe at her desk, David facing her in a chair that was none too comfortable. Sharpe and David had a history, and now they were playing it out.

The year before, Sharpe had asked for, and promptly received, David's resignation as an assistant United States attorney. Their problems had begun with rancid chemistry. David sometimes found the vagaries of law amusing; little amused Marnie Sharpe. She had carried into her mid-forties a humorless single-mindedness, Spartan habits, and no known passions save for her personal vision of justice, as inviolate as a family might be to someone else. When he had worked for her, David had tried to imagine Marnie Sharpe making love to anyone, man or woman, and failed utterly. The label for Sharpe he settled on was "armadillo."

They could have survived this. Marnie was a

good lawyer, and in his better moments David could work up sympathy for anyone who needed a carapace so thick. But the death penalty had done them in.

Sharpe believed in it; David did not. He had refused to seek it in the murder of an eight-year-old girl by a child molester who had himself been sexually abused and tortured by his father and who was, David knew, borderline retarded. After David's resignation, his successor, following Sharpe's instructions, had sought and secured a death sentence. Asked by a reporter to comment, David had not restrained himself. "This murder was a sickening tragedy. But were I Ms. Sharpe, I'd reserve the death penalty for men smart enough to know what dying means."

This sealed their mutual dislike. To Marnie Sharpe, David Wolfe put his own rarified sensibilities above the law; to David, the U.S. attorney did not admit, even to herself, that her zeal for the death penalty was intended to endear her to those who dole out federal judgeships. That he was now a defense lawyer worsened their dynamic, allowing David to use the one gift in his toolbox Marnie did not possess: the imagination to exploit the ambiguities of a legal system that Sharpe saw as a blueprint. Throw David Wolfe into a legal thicket, and what he saw were escape routes.

All of which had led to the gambit that brought them together now: the chance to frustrate Sharpe in the interests of a client who, but for David, might be on his way to an extended term in prison. But lurking beneath this was a purpose just as serious: David's absolute conviction that Marnie Sharpe should never wield the power invested in a federal judge, as deep as her own belief that he should never be a congressman.

"I'm not here to be chastised," David told her calmly. "In fact, I'm wondering why I'm here at all."

She shot him a look of irritation. "We have an eight-million-dollar Brinks robbery. Your client was caught. All he had to offer was 'The Mafia made me do it.' "

" 'Or they'd kill me,' " David amended. "Raymond thought *that* part was important. So do I." He spread his hands. "It's a first offense, and you're charging Ray Scallone with everything but planning 9/11. He's a tool —"

"He's a goon who threatened a security guard with a Saturday night special. He needs to be off the street."

David shrugged. "So let's work out a deal or try the case."

"Why should I cut a deal? I suppose because someone, not from our office, leaked to the press that we — which is to say the FBI — were investigating whether the Mafia was connected to this robbery. We weren't investigating any such connection —"

"Then you should have —"

Sharpe spoke over him. "But after Channel 5 reported this so-called Mafia connection, the FBI started to investigate the possibility. Then, coincidentally enough, *you* demanded access to all the records of its investigation, claiming that they were vital to Scallone's defense."

"They *are* his defense," David said. "After all, you *did* catch him with the money. So why didn't you just turn over the records?"

"There *are* no records that would help Scallone," Sharpe retorted. "There *is* no evidence that the

Mafia threatened anyone. But now you've filed a motion to dismiss the entire case, claiming that you can't put on a proper defense without knowing why the FBI launched an investigation of what turns out to be vapor — just as if you didn't know." She paused, fixing David with a gelid stare. "Any sane judge would use this motion to line their cat box. Any judge who was still breathing would have wondered who the source was for this serendipitous 'leak.' But you've lucked into 'Kick-'Em-Loose Bruce' Myers, the last hemophiliac on the federal bench."

David shrugged again. "Beats a necrophiliac, I suppose."

This tacit reference to the death penalty caused Sharpe's eyes to narrow. "You know what's happening here, David. And so do I."

"I'm hoping so," he responded blandly. "I'm willing to discuss a plea if you are."

Sharpe sat back, considering him in silence. David took this for what it was: a concession that, however distasteful, cutting a deal might be preferable to what Judge Myers might do with David's motion. "Based on what, dare I ask? Your bogus motion?"

"No. Based on a mutual respect and our common dislike of overprosecution." David smiled faintly. "Except in death penalty cases, of course. We'll save that for another time."

An hour later, David left the federal building, hurrying back to his office to meet Carole.

He should be satisfied — whatever grudge Marnie Sharpe might hold, he had done his job as a lawyer. But the confrontation left a sour residue, a toxic admixture with the emotions stirred by

Hana's call. Perhaps, he thought, it was the memory of his own fallibility, the painful lesson, first learned through Hana Arif, that the consequence of his actions might be far different than he intended, or even imagined.

It's just a case, he told himself — not a love affair. The only consequences, if any, would lie in his next case against Marnie Sharpe. He would deal with it then.

6

Within moments of entering his office, Carole Shorr stopped talking about their wedding, cocked her head as though recalibrating her sense of David's mood, and abruptly asked, "How has your day been? You seem a little distracted."

David was forced to smile. Carole was very good at reading others — including, in many if not all ways, David himself. But this was not the right occasion for unvarnished truth. "Why shouldn't I be?" he answered amiably. "We just set a date. I'm getting married in seven months, at the age of thirty-eight. In a huge wedding. I'm both too old and too young for that sort of thing, and suddenly I'm on the conveyor belt to fatherhood. Which I find a little daunting."

Carole grinned, good humor restored. As if seeing her for the first time in days — which, given the events of his morning, did not seem that far off — David found himself studying the woman he soon would marry. Carole had a full, curvaceous figure, wavy brown hair, and a pretty, wholesome face, complicated by the deep brown pools of eyes whose almond shape carried a hint of Eurasia, once prompting David to suggest to her that some female Polish ancestor had been ravaged by a Tatar passing through her village. Though her expression was habitually pleasant, it had a resolute cast, suggesting the planner and organizer she was. The Carole Shorr School of Management, David once told her, was what America truly needed.

"The world," she had amended cheerfully. "If only I had the time."

Certainly, Carole Shorr managed her slice of the world with consummate practicality and efficiency. She was smart and socially adept, with an assertive charm that made people like her and, more often than not, do what she wanted. She leavened her determination with a warm, sometimes lightly flirtatious manner, mixed with humor. All this added up to a gift for knowing the influentials of the Jewish community, the Democratic Party, and, at times, the larger world, without the sharp elbows or avidity that would have made her a figure of sport or envy.

All of which made her indispensable to David. Beyond this, only he was privileged to know that she was sexy not just in manner but in fact, with an openness that had, at first, surprised him. And only he saw Carole's vulnerability — a deep desire to be needed, to be cherished and respected by a partner she knew to be her peer.

"Oh, I know," Carole told him now. "It's *so* hard being a guy." Glancing at her watch, she picked up her purse and stood. "Don't worry, I'll take care of everything. Including having the babies."

David snatched the suit coat off the back of his chair. "Good. I'm best at delegation."

"Just do your part. Sort of like you did this morning." Abruptly, her expression became more probing. "So what *did* happen between then and now? Something."

David opened his door, waving her past his secretary's empty desk. "Have I mentioned that you are a remarkably perceptive woman? Relentlessly so."

Carole laughed. "As soon as we're married, I promise to change. Until then you'll have to put up with my sensitivity to your moods."

They reached the elevator to the parking garage. Pushing the button, David said, "You'll remember I was meeting with Marnie Sharpe."

"It didn't go so well?"

The elevator opened. Carole stepped inside, then David. "Given that she hates me," he answered, "it never goes well. I got what I wanted. But not before Marnie accused me of leaking to the press some fiction about an FBI investigation, then exploiting it to knock years off my client's sentence."

"And did you?"

David smiled. "Of course. But it still hurt."

Carole gave him a dubious look. "Isn't that unethical?"

"Not to me. And it's certainly not illegal." Pausing, he spoke more seriously. "First, I believe Raymond's story, though a lawyer believes clients at his peril. Second, the FBI *should* have investigated. Truth to tell, I didn't know *what* the FBI was doing. I only knew what they *should* be doing. Sharpe wouldn't listen to me. So I decided to encourage the FBI by other means." David smiled again. "Any lawyer can succeed with an innocent client. The guilty require imagination."

Carole gazed at him with a bemusement. "To a simple girl like me, David, you sometimes sound immoral. I see this glint in your eye, and for a minute I'm not sure I know you."

The elevator door opened to a cavernous underground garage. "Don't feel alone," David consoled her blithely. "My mother never knew me. Not that I knew *her*, either.

"But seriously, Sharpe deserved it. She overprosecutes, and she loves convictions more than truth. Lawyers should be forced to take a Rorschach test before we allow them to be prosecutors."

They found Carole's green Jaguar convertible — British, not German, she had emphasized to David. She inserted her key in the ignition, then turned to him again. "Can we talk for a minute? Dad will understand if we're a little late."

"I thought we *were* talking."

"Deploying words isn't always the same as talking." She gazed at the dashboard, gathering her thoughts. "Listening to this story, I wonder about your defending criminals — okay, alleged criminals — two years before you run for Congress."

"Even if I think they're innocent?"

"Even then, unfortunately. You'll probably get by with this case — at least Ray Scallone didn't murder that guard. But you're already on the 'wrong' side of the death penalty issue."

"Most voters in my district," David objected, "don't *like* executions."

"Maybe not. But some do. Most *Californians* do, and they elect U.S. senators."

David smiled at this. "Aren't we getting ahead of ourselves? Why not president?"

"The first Jewish president?" she answered briskly. "It's about time."

"I thought you were about to say 'semi-Jewish.' Anyhow, criminal law is what I like."

Carole touched his hand. "I know. And the Jewish part we can work on. But sometimes, it feels like you think you're immune to disaster, or even hurt, as if God's given you a pass."

That David knew better, and that a single phone call had reminded him of why, was not something he cared to discuss. "I don't feel immune," he told her. "No matter what you think of my charmed life."

"Not just charmed," she countered softly. "Detached."

"Don't you mean 'in denial'? I know it still bothers you that my parents were Jewish in name only. They barely mentioned the Holocaust, or Israel. They were patrons of the symphony, the opera, and the ballet who preferred a life of intellect and refinement to one of feeling or group identity —"

"They *had* an identity, David. They were German Jews, American for three generations. We were Polish Jews, immigrants, the kind your parents would find embarrassing. We even talk about body functions."

David smiled at this. But the difference, he understood, went deeper than his parents' tastes in music, or that her parents' refrigerator had been crammed with beets and homemade soups, or that Jewish holidays were strictly observed in her family and perfunctorily noted in his. It was that Harold's family had vanished up the stacks of Hitler's camps, impelling Carole to remember, even to live for, men and women she had never known. As she had once mordantly put it to David, she was "suffering from secondhand smoke." It left her with a profound sense of tribal loyalty coupled with an indefinable foreboding that lay beneath her air of confidence and good humor, a sense that mischance must be avoided, not courted.

"We're certainly a pair," David said now. "You and I."

Carole smiled a little. She knew what he meant,

David suspected. Carole was determined to order the world as she wished it to be, the better to fend off doom. But, like Harold, she had a certain reticence — the sense that power was better exercised in private, in ways less conspicuous than was David's inclination. So her public ambitions were for him, a melding of their temperaments and needs.

David smiled back at her, appreciating how comfortable he felt with her. Like Carole, he wanted children; it was easy to imagine her as a mother, one of the many ways in which he thought of her with confidence and warmth. If he sometimes watched Carole with the eyes of a partner rather than a lover, David knew that this was his way: between Hana and Carole no woman had truly touched his heart, and he had stopped believing that he would find a love that could wholly erase the past. He had loved without constraint only once, and it had brought him such misery that he was determined never to endure it again.

"We *are* a pair," David reaffirmed with a quick grin. "Our son will have his bar mitzvah, our daughter her bat mitzvah. And we'll make them go to Hebrew school until they hate us both."

Accepting this concession with a look of satisfied amusement, Carole turned the key in the ignition. "I can hardly wait to tell Dad about Hebrew school. He'll be thrilled."

They pulled out of the garage into the sunlight, David watching Carole's hair ripple in the breeze of a cool summer day. *So,* Hana had said, *a nice Jewish girl, and a rich one at that. Things often end up the way they're supposed to, I think.*

Years before, David thought, she had tried to tell him.

7

Hana looked around herself as if she had stepped through the rabbit hole.

It had taken several long telephone calls before Hana had agreed to meet again, this time in the only place where no one could see them: his apartment. It was a warren off Harvard Square — a living room with a couch, coffee table, television, desk, and computer; a cramped kitchen with a table that seated two, a bedroom with a queen bed, a dresser, and the racing bike David used for exercise in the spring and fall. Dressed in blue jeans and a sweater, Hana stood in the middle of the living room, unsure of whether to stay or go.

"It's all right," David said gently. "You're safe with me. Or from me, if that worries you."

"It's just that this is so strange. Being here."

"I'd gladly take you out to dinner. You know that."

"I can't though. You know *that.*"

David considered her. "Do I? I don't know anything but what you've told me."

Hana smiled a little. "Were you Arab, you would know without my telling you."

"Were I Saeb, you mean."

A flicker of emotion — guilt, David thought — surfaced in the dark pool of her eyes, causing him to regret his last remark. "I can learn, Hana. Really."

"Why is that so important to you?"

"I'm not sure yet. I only know that it is."

She gave him a look of cool appraisal. "Perhaps I'm something you can't have," she said at length. "And so you'll want me until you do."

David shook his head. "Right now, all I want is to cook dinner. And all I need from you is your company."

She followed him to the kitchen. David had set the table — white dishes, two wineglasses, bright cloth napkins, a candle in a brass candlestick holder — and laid out the veal cutlets, soaking in a marinade of his own invention. As though for something to say, she inquired, "Did you cook at home? Your parents' home, I mean."

"Not really. The housekeeper did, mostly. My mother's passion is for English literature, not cooking."

"And you have brothers and sisters?"

The question reminded David of how little they knew of each other, the gaps between his instinctive sense of her and the accretion of fact and detail through which people learned — or thought they learned — who another person was. "No," he answered. "I seem to have exhausted their interest in playing life's genetic lottery." He nodded toward an open bottle of cabernet sauvignon. "I usually sip wine while I cook. But I'm guessing you don't drink at all."

Hana hesitated. "I do, a little," she told him. "When I'm not with Saeb, or girlfriends who might disapprove."

He poured some for her. "Then taste it, if you like."

She hesitated, then took a sip. "It's good, I think. But then how would I know?"

David gave her a sideways glance. "What you think is all that matters. Only wine snobs care about knowing. In California, some people devote their lives to it."

Hana smiled, as if she found this inconceivable. "Americans — even your indulgences take on such importance. You would think no one was starving, here or anywhere." She took another sip of wine. "That's much of what makes America dangerous, I think — this self-absorption that keeps so many of you so strangely innocent. Sometimes America is like a large puppy, all big paws and floppy tail, that runs through the living room breaking the glassware and knocking things off tables, too happy discovering all it can do to care about the damage. Except that your living room is the world."

The metaphor made David laugh. "I've got such a lot to atone for."

Hana gave him an indulgent smile. "It would take a lifetime. Your annual day of atonement — Yom Kippur, is it? Repentance on the installment plan will not be enough."

"Even if I can cook?"

"That remains to be seen." Her tone became teasing. "Another thing about Americans is they're overconfident. They're not used to letting outsiders grade their performance."

"Go ahead. My ego's not that fragile."

"Maybe not about cooking. But all men are fragile, somehow."

Smiling, David resolved to focus on the cutlets. When he looked at her again, she was freeing her hair from the band at the nape of her neck. Luxuriant and black, it fell across her shoulders. But when she saw him gazing at her, she seemed embarrassed, as though they had been caught at something.

"I was thinking your hair's beautiful." He paused a moment, searching for some conversational escape route. "At home, do you cover?"

"At times. For religious observances, or when I'm with women who are older."

David turned the cutlets. "It seems a waste."

Hana moved her shoulders, the smallest of shrugs. "That's just what's done. But when I do it here, men seem to notice me even more. So it rather defeats the purpose."

How much was she aware, David wondered, of the power her beauty had on him? "Dinner's ready," he said. "You can grade me afterward."

They ate without haste, sipping wine, talking both of small things and the world as they saw it. "Then you have no religion?" she asked.

"Not in the way you do, though I'm culturally Jewish, which is something I take pride in. They keep on killing us, and yet we do far more than survive — we invent, write, discover, build, create. And no matter what you think, Judaism, at its best, is a tolerant religion — we don't proselytize, and we've learned enough about suffering and oppression to notice others who are suffering and oppressed.

"But the history of religion, at its worst, is the story of mass murder. Why have other religions roasted Jews on spits for two thousand years? Why do Jews and Arabs hate each other now? It's hard to think of all that and raise your eyes to heaven. Sometimes I think it's man who created God in his own image — murderous and narrow."

Hana gave him a long, thoughtful look. "What lies between your people and mine," she said finally, "is more than some bloodthirsty God, or the Torah and Koran. It's history and land. It's people's stories — among many others Saeb's. And mine."

"But don't you think if it were left to you and me, we'd find some way to resolve all that?"

"I wonder. Anyhow, it's not, and never will be. This is so much bigger than two people."

Gazing at the table, David smiled a little but said nothing. "What is it?" she asked.

"I was thinking of what Bogart said to Ingrid Bergman at the end of *Casablanca.*"

Her own smile was a flicker. "This isn't a movie. You can't rewrite the ending."

"Then perhaps I'm as American as your puppy. But I believe in people writing their own endings."

Hana looked into his face, her eyes shadowed with an emotion that David could not quite grasp. "Dinner was good," she said at last. "We should be happy just with that."

"What were you thinking?" David asked. "Before."

Briefly, she looked away, and then directly at him. "That I'm afraid of what else I might want from you. And of what you want from me."

At first he had no answer. Then, impulsively, he stood, taking her hands, gently raising her from the chair so that he could look into her face. "What if you're not just 'something I can't have'? What if I end up wanting all of you?"

For a long moment she was still, eyes locked on his, and then she rested her forehead against his shoulder. He felt, or perhaps imagined, a tremor running through her. "Only that?" she murmured.

"So much more than I can give you. All I could ever give you is an hour at a time, until I can no longer stand it."

David could smell her hair, fragrant as fresh-cut herbs. "You make it sound like torture. Don't you think we should find out?"

"Not just torture . . ."

She did not finish. As his lips grazed her throat, he could feel her pulse beating, then felt the warmth of her body against his.

Their kiss, at first gentle and tentative, did not stop at that.

David reached beneath her sweater, tracing the slender line of her back and shoulders. When he slowly raised her sweater, she held her arms up to help him, a kind of surrender. Her eyes did not leave his.

She wore no bra. David felt himself quiver with wanting her, and then saw that her eyes were filling with tears. Softly he asked, "Is this all right?"

"Yes." Her voice was tremulous. "This once."

David kissed her nipples, her stomach, then unfastened her belt. Wordless, he slid her clothes off, then his. They leaned against each other, still silent, caught between doubt and desire.

"We'll be all right," he murmured.

Taking her hand, he led her to the bedroom. Hana's fingers curled around his.

Filled with a haste he fought against, David drew down the bedcover. Rain began to spatter his dark window.

Together they slipped into the bed, warm skin on cool sheets, her breasts resting against his chest as they looked into each other's faces. He allowed himself to savor the surprise of touching her, of her touching him where she wished.

"No rush," he whispered. "No rush." And then the rush was hers.

When he was inside her, she stared up into his eyes, as though to read his soul. Then it was all feeling, her hips rising to take him, their bodies moving together slowly, then more quickly, her soft cries his only guide.

With the first tremor of her body, Hana cried out his name, the damp tendrils of her hair pressed against his face.

Afterward they lay facing each other, quiet and warm, rediscovering each other in the light from David's kitchen. Time passed like that, new lovers content with wonder.

"Perhaps *this* is why I came," she said at last.

David felt unsure. "To make love with me?"

"More than that. Perhaps I thought you could help me escape myself."

"And can I?"

Her eyes were troubled. "Not for long, I think. But at least here I'm allowed to look at you."

"Here? The first time you saw me your eyes reminded me of burn holes. Like if you stared at me long enough, I'd turn to ash and bone."

This made Hana smile. "Then I must tell you about Arab women — at least Palestinian women, or Jordanians or Lebanese. We're allowed to look at men in public, as long as we employ the appropriate stare of hauteur to cover the fact that we're interested. I saw you were attractive, so I allowed myself to look at you with as much contempt as I could muster, for as long as I dared."

David laughed at this admission. "You certainly fooled me."

"Yes. And look how well it worked."

David kissed her. And then, with less fear but no less desire, they began to find each other again.

Only later, sipping coffee at his kitchen table, did Hana glance at her watch.

"Are you afraid?" David asked.

A shadow crossed her face. "It's not what you think," she answered. "Another myth about Arab women is that we're subservient. Perhaps Saudi women. But in my culture, the sole imperative is never to confront men with what would shame them. Or shame you."

"And for men?"

"It's different. For example, if an Arab man sleeps with an American woman, it's no problem. But it's understood they will marry one of us."

Her tone of matter-of-fact acceptance took him by surprise. "Nice to have the double-standard codified."

Hana shrugged her shoulders. "It is true that Arab men have a streak of paternalism and misogyny — like many Israelis. I hope someday we can progress to the state of social relations in America, where men are hypocritical about their chauvinism, and even slightly embarrassed."

Though he smiled, David would not be deflected. "And what do you hope for from Saeb?"

"More openness," Hana said flatly. "Including for our daughters, should we have them."

This casual acknowledgment of her future wounded him. As though sensing this, she touched his face. "I am sorry, David. But that is how it is."

"That may be. But I don't know *why* it is."

"Is that so important?"

"I think so, yes."

Hana closed her eyes. "There's so much to it,"

she said at last. "Our fathers were cousins, our mothers second cousins. When we were eleven, our fathers began discussing that we should marry —"

"That can't be what you really want."

"Because I'm here, with you, in secret?" Hana drew a breath. "It's true that Saeb would be consumed by my betrayal. With a Jew, yet never with him."

Astonishment slowed David's answer. "Sleeping with me is one thing," he said at last. "Marrying Saeb is another."

"And why is this your concern?"

David spread both palms in a gesture of bewilderment and frustration. "Oh, I don't know. Perhaps because in my hypocritical culture, it's women who are supposed to sentimentalize sex, and men who compartmentalize it —"

"And so this means nothing to me," Hana cut in. "How little you *do* understand." Her voice adopted a tone of weary acceptance. "Marrying Saeb is about far more than an arranged marriage, the traditions of a village culture. The wisdom of our fathers' pledge lies in the things that have made us who we are. That we are Palestinian. That Saeb more than matches me in intellect and ambition. All that, and, yes, history.

"History is not just that our parents were born in the same village. It's how the Zionist victory shaped the narrative of all our lives. Because they came from Galilee, our parents fled to Lebanon. Saeb's parents married at the refugee camp of Tel Zaatar — mine at the camps of Sabra and Shatila. The cesspools of their exile, crowded, dirty, ridden by disease." Her voice held quiet anger. "At first my family thought we were the lucky ones. Because when civil war broke out between the Lebanese

Christians and Muslims, the Christian militia — the Phalange — surrounded Tel Zaatar and rained rockets on our people's homes.

"It took sixteen days for them to tire of this. When they were through, the Phalange burst into the camp and began slaughtering the men. Saeb, the oldest child, was only eight. So he, his mother, four brothers and sisters survived, although their home was rubble. But now they thought *they* were lucky — Saeb's father was looking for work in Beirut when the siege began, and could not get back to die —"

Hana paused abruptly. "When it was done," she told David, "the Phalange rounded up the women and children, drove them in trucks to the border of West Beirut, and told them to start walking.

"Saeb's father was searching for his family. When he found them, Saeb has told me, tears rolled down his face." Her voice was toneless now. "Their refuge was my birth place — Sabra and Shatila. Two camps side by side, run by the United Nations — thousands of Palestinians crowded into one-story concrete buildings with corrugated roofs and bare bulbs hanging from the ceilings. Saeb's family found a place near ours, in a squalid corner named after their village, but where the only olive tree grew in a barrel filled with soil my parents had dug up from their garden.

" 'He who is not interred in his own land,' my grandfather always told me, 'has had no life.' But we buried him at the camp, with his chickens and goats and pitiful olive tree the only remnant of the life he knew — a farmer with nowhere to farm, part of a faceless mass that, to Americans, is at most an object of scorn or pity. This is the place where our parents decided we should marry."

The last was said with a casual bitterness that, David knew, bespoke a far deeper anger. "Perhaps," she finished in a softer tone, "you begin to understand. But you cannot truly understand unless you know what the Jews and Christians did to us at Sabra and Shatila. By marrying me, Saeb is honoring the wishes of a dead man."

David poured more coffee for both of them. "Tell me about what happened at Sabra and Shatila, Hana."

For a time she gazed at him over the rim of her cup. Then, quite softly, she began speaking.

8

In the summer of 1982, when Saeb was fourteen years old, Israel invaded Lebanon, asserting the need to protect its borders from the freedom fighters of Arafat's PLO.

Saeb's family had little to eat. His mother helped support them by sewing and baking; after school, Saeb would sell the sweets she made. Their home had four small rooms — a bath and kitchen combined; a living room, where his parents slept; a bedroom for Saeb and his brothers; another for his sisters. No one thought of privacy — that was a Western concept. Saeb's world, and Hana's, was as constricted as their hopes.

But the outside world was close at hand. At five o'clock one morning, Hana awakened to the terrible scream of Israeli F-16s over the rooftops of Beirut. The fearsome planes, a gift from the United States, flew well above the fire from the PLO's hand-cranked antiaircraft guns and shoulder-fired missiles. Hana could still feel the concussive shock waves of bombs exploding; see the skies afire with orange-red flares; hear the cries of her mother, brother, and sister as her father rushed them into the living room, lying with their faces pressed against their tattered carpet. Watching Hana tell this story now, David saw her eyes filling with reflexive terror.

"That was the beginning," she told him.

For two months, the Israelis bombed Beirut and the camps. By day there were burials at Sabra and Shatila, while children played in the craters made by Zionist bombs. The only way Arafat and the PLO could end this devastation was by agreeing to leave Lebanon for Tunis.

And so the Americans brokered a peace, promising the civilians of Sabra and Shatila — who feared both the Zionists and their brutal allies, the Lebanese Christian Phalange — that they could live in peace by disdaining violence. Numb, the twelve-year-old Hana could not grasp what the Israelis wanted — a last chance to kill more freedom fighters before they reached their exile. That was why, Hana insisted to David, the great general Ariel Sharon required that those PLO fighters still at Sabra and Shatila remain there. Saeb, her intended husband and older friend, divined the trap before she did.

"Saeb no longer believed in peace," she explained to David. "He had seen the Phalange at Tel Zaatar."

And then the leader of the Phalange, Bashir Gemayel, was killed at his headquarters in Beirut.

The Israeli army surrounded the camps. "Under the rules of war," Hana said, "the Zionists were responsible for our safety. Only later did we learn that Sharon wanted the Phalange to do his work for him."

On the night of September 16, she explained, the Phalange streamed into the camp with machetes, rifles, and submachine guns, going from house to house. Watching from the surrounding rooftops, Zionist soldiers fired bright orange flares to light the camp. Then Hana heard the gunfire starting.

As she said this, David took her hand.

"They shot us in our streets and homes," Hana told him in a monotone. "My favorite aunt, Suha, my mother's sister, saw Phalange militia herding women and children into a truck, and risked her life to report this to an Israeli guard post at the edge of our camp. For days we did not know what had become of her."

Only later, after Saeb told her of finding Suha, did Hana learn what had become of *him.*

That first night, three Phalange gunmen battered down the door of Saeb's parents' home.

His family huddled in the darkness of their living room — Saeb's father, mother, two brothers, and two sisters. Through the open door, Saeb heard a neighbor woman scream. His twelve-year-old sister, Aisha, clutched his hand. His mother began to pray.

When his father stood in front of her, the leader of the Phalange shot him in the chest.

"No!" his mother cried out. "Please, not my children —"

A second man shot her. As she crumpled beside her husband, her killer ordered coldly, "The rest of you — on the floor."

Frozen by horror, Saeb lay against the concrete, still grasping his sister's hand. One by one three gunshots shattered the skulls of his two brothers and youngest sister. Teeth clenched against his own death, he felt Aisha's terror as his.

From above them, Saeb heard a soft voice say, "You two must be lovers."

They lay there, waiting for death. "Get up," the man said.

Trembling, Saeb stood, pulling Aisha with him.

The man shined a flashlight in his eyes. Saeb could not see faces. From the darkness, a hand reached out to touch his sister's earring.

"Gold or zinc?" the same voice asked.

Leaning against Saeb, Aisha could barely speak. "Zinc."

"Leave her," Saeb pled, the words raw in his throat. "Shoot me — I don't care. But let my sister live . . ."

"Live?" the man said roughly. "You give me an idea."

Brutally, he jerked Aisha from Saeb's grasp, directing her to a corner with his flashlight. "Over there. And watch that you don't step on your mother."

As Aisha stumbled to where she was told, the outer circle of light caught their father's outstretched hand. Instinctively, Saeb stepped forward, then felt a gun against his temple.

The man pressed the flashlight into his palm. "Hold this on her," he ordered.

Swallowing, Saeb did so. In the light his sister's eyes were like those of a hunted animal, fearful and uncomprehending.

"Strip," the man told her.

"No," Saeb protested. "No . . ."

"Bitch," the man snapped at Aisha. "Show us everything or I'll shoot him in the balls."

Watching her brother's face, Aisha did as she was told.

Saeb turned away. *"Look at her,"* another man ordered. "Keep the flashlight on her or she'll die."

Watching his naked sister, so fragile and so pretty, Saeb felt the sweat run down his face. "Lie down," the first man told her. "Spread your legs for us to see."

As she did this, Saeb closed his eyes with her, a reflex. The gun nudged his head, a warning to watch her shame. Aisha cried out; Saeb saw the naked man enter her roughly, the gold cross around his neck falling across her stricken face.

Let her die, Saeb prayed. The man on top of her grunted his satisfaction.

As though transfixed, the second man who held the gun to Saeb stepped forward, leaving Saeb to watch what the man would do to Aisha.

Squat and mustached, he mounted her. In the glow of the flashlight, Aisha stared at her brother, tears running down her face. As the gunman pushed inside her, she mouthed a last silent word:

Run.

Dropping the flashlight, Saeb bolted for the door.

Behind him a Phalangist shouted. A bullet grazed Saeb's shoulder as he ran into the murderous night, his body shaking and his heart beating wildly. Running through unlit alleys he knew by instinct, he stopped only to vomit.

He made it to the headquarters of the Red Cross. For three days he hid with other refugees, eating nothing, speaking to no one. When the Phalange banged at the door, a doctor, risking his life, ordered them to go away. Saeb hoped only to die.

To his mild surprise, the Phalange went away.

"This was toward the end," Hana explained to David. "The Americans began to protest. The Zionists decided the Phalange had gone too far, and ordered them to leave. The situation was under control, a Zionist general told your special envoy. His reply was useless outrage. That's the best we got from America, protector of human rights."

When the last of the Phalange was gone, Saeb wandered the camp alone.

He found one small miracle: though Saeb's neighbor, nine months pregnant, was killed by a bomb, a doctor had delivered her baby alive. But the camp was filled with bodies and rubble, from beneath which rescuers extracted more ruined corpses. Saeb saw a line of dead men at the foot of a concrete barrier — fourteen, he counted — blood and bullet holes spattering the wall beneath the bloody letters "PLO." Perhaps it was a mercy that Aisha had been buried with his family beneath the ruins of their home.

"I imagine you were playing football," Hana said to David. "Your football starts in September, yes? If so, this is not your fault. But maybe you can understand why Saeb has so little interest in having lunch with you.

"Saeb is scarred forever. It was not just what he saw, or how he feels about Zionists, or the Phalange, or America. It's how he feels about himself for running. And for living."

Saeb found her aunt Suha, a few strands of hair beneath a pile of debris. Her hair was red, Hana said, distinctive; Saeb knew her from that.

David struggled to imagine this. "And the rest of your family?"

"Survived. It was Saeb who lost all his family." Hana stared into her coffee cup. "Two thousand people were killed. Some by rockets, some with bullets, some beheaded with machetes. In Israel, there was a great demonstration in the streets, protesting this atrocity. A commission of inquiry followed, and Sharon was reprimanded. Yet he remained in the cabinet, accepting no blame. It seems that only the conquered are prosecuted as war criminals. The victors get promoted.

"What remains to us is a camp now built on corpses, filled with refugees the world has forgotten." Her voice was soft with irony. "But Saeb and I are lucky — America gave us scholarships, to study the rule of law. And now I find myself with you." Pausing, she gazed past David, as though speaking to herself. "What is becoming of me, I wonder, to tempt myself with no good end."

David was silent. After a time, he reached again for her hand, more tentative than before. "Nothing's becoming of you, Hana. It's just that you don't love him. What you feel is compassion and obligation."

Even to David, the words sounded trite, inadequate. Hana looked away. "I'm his family," she said flatly. "The woman his father wished for him. And, yes, I wish it too."

A sadness stole through David, both from Saeb's story and Hana's words. Hana's shoulders slumped with weariness. "Can I sleep here?" she asked. "On your couch, just for an hour or so. I'm too tired to leave right now."

Unable to decipher her emotions, he could only nod. "I'll get a blanket for you."

David turned off the living room lamp.

He sat in the kitchen, drinking coffee, watching her sleep in the darkened room. A half hour passed. Then he saw her blanket stirring, heard her muffled cry as she awakened.

He went to her. "What is it, Hana?"

She hunched forward, her elbows resting on her knees, the fingertips of one hand touching her forehead. "A dream," she said in a monotone. "Only a dream, one I've had many times before."

David sat beside her. "Tell me."

She stood in Saeb's home, alone. Though in the dream the Phalange had not destroyed the house, its rooms were empty. On the wall were photographs of Saeb's murdered family — his parents, brothers, sisters.

Hana's eyes were drawn to Aisha's face.

As Hana watched, Aisha stepped from the picture, her body materializing from nothing. She was as Hana had known her, pretty and chastely dressed.

"Could you bring me a glass of water," the young girl asked politely. "Then please take me to my brother."

Hana went to the kitchen. But when she returned, Aisha had vanished. The place for her photograph was bare.

Awake now, sitting with David, Hana shook her head. "The same dream, always. I never know what becomes of her."

It's all right, David might have said to another woman. *You're safe here, with me.* That he could not say this to Hana did not yet tell him that he, David Wolfe, was no longer safe with her.

9

The spectacle of Stonestown shopping center stunned Ibrahim with its opulence.

He stood with Iyad in the vast parking lot, beside the rental car they would abandon there. A two-story monolith a quarter mile long, Stonestown contained a supermarket, a department store, several restaurants, and every imaginable purveyor of shoes, books, clothes, candies, cosmetics, sports equipment, compact discs, and artwork. Streams of cars and SUVs eased in and out of the lot. Ibrahim tried to grasp the vast entitlement of people for whom such opulence was second nature. He felt negligible; his birthplace — the refugee camp at Jenin — seemed as distant as another planet. He could not believe that those who drove the cars, women mostly, had ever conceived of such a place, or cared what their Zionist allies had inflicted on his sister.

"It's so big," he murmured to Iyad.

The derisive half-smile on Iyad's face confirmed the banality of what he had just said. "Yes," Iyad answered. "And Americans are so smug and pompous and stupid. They have no purpose, no soul, no values except to consume and pay someone to keep them amused. To them, the world is a video game. That is why we will win."

That was right, Ibrahim believed — the West was corrupt, and believed in nothing but preserving its privilege and power, and that of the Jews controlling the instruments of entertainment that consumed their money and drugged their minds. But Ibrahim envied Iyad's grim serenity. There lurked within Ibrahim a tinge of envy: to shop and spend and go to movies sometimes seemed more blessed than the privilege of killing and dying with which Iyad had favored him.

Iyad pointed toward a towering light, intended, Ibrahim supposed, to illuminate a section of the parking lot at night. "It should be *there,*" he said.

It was — a nondescript white van, parked at the base of the pole. As before, Ibrahim wondered at the invisible network that caused cell phones to appear, lockers to hold cash and credit cards and false identification, and, now, had materialized a van big enough to house two motorcycles. Opening the door, Iyad found the ignition key beneath the floor mat on the driver's side.

A second key, small and shiny, was taped beneath the seat.

As Iyad held it up the key glinted in the sunlight. "Our key to paradise," he said.

The North Beach was a bright, well-appointed restaurant amid the bustle of the city's historically Italian section. It was Harold Shorr's favorite meeting place; the energetic maître d' shepherded them to Harold's corner table with a sense of occasion suitable to the children of a potentate. Beaming, Harold kissed Carole on the cheek, then took her face in his hands. "Our family goes on," he said in a voice accented by his native Polish, "far away from that miserable village."

David could only guess how much their marriage meant to Harold. Of six children and their parents, all but he had perished in the Holocaust — Carole was their future, the only one of her kind. Turning to David, Harold clasped his shoulders and pressed his forehead to David's. Deep feeling was hard for Harold to articulate — he was better at showing than expressing. But there was no missing the amplitude of Harold's joy; in this man's bear hug, David felt a warmth he had seldom shared with his own father.

"Seven months," Harold told them in mock chagrin. "Why so long?"

David grinned, setting aside the events that had shadowed his morning. "It'll take that long for Carole to make out the guest list."

"So you're complaining? That means more gifts for you." As they sat, Harold clasped his only child's hands in his. "At last a wedding," he added with a smile, "for your mother, at the Temple Emanu-El."

This was said lightly, but there was an undertone of rue and remembrance — Carole's mother had died the previous year, still pursued by the indelible fears of sixty years before. "We had to negotiate the wedding contract," Carole answered with a self-mocking smile that took in David. "All the ways in which David promises to be satisfactory. You know me, Dad — leave nothing to chance."

Harold spread his arms in an elaborate shrug that said that men and women must be patient with each other. "I hope," he told Carole, "that you made a few promises of your own. Maybe one unplanned day each month."

Harold surely knew his daughter, David thought. Fondly, he regarded the man, two years ago a stranger, who had become so central to his life.

At seventy-six, Harold Shorr had a high forehead, receding iron-gray hair, a full mouth and strong chin, and deep-set brown eyes beneath eyebrows that arched to punctuate his remarks. He was stocky but not fat, with shoulders that seemed hunched to bear weight, or resist pressure. On his face, watchful and expressive, often played a faint smile that, to David, betrayed a hint of melancholy.

There was also a shyness that, David thought, bespoke a deeper reticence. Part was a lack of education mixed with an immigrant's sense that his speech was halting and inelegant — even though Harold's vocabulary was apt and his command of American vernacular keen and flavored with humor. Far deeper was his fear of calling too much attention to himself, imprinted a time long ago, when to be invisible might be to live another day. That Harold had raised so accomplished and confident a daughter was, to him, a constant source of pride and wonder.

So the Shorrs' smiles conveyed that they were part of each other's journey in a way few families could grasp. Watching, David was aware of a bond that belonged to them alone. Its depth came from something within Harold that he had never expressed to David — in this particular, as in others, Carole had spoken for her father, fulfilling her imperative that David comprehend them both.

Carole was four, she had told David, when she had first recited the numbers on his wrist.

They were sitting at the breakfast table. *Eight,* she said with a child's precocity and pride, *three, five, seven, one.* Encouragingly, Harold recited the numbers with her.

Her mother had turned away.

■ ■ ■ ■

Though she did not know why, from early childhood Carole sensed that the numbers held a mystical power.

Her parents never spoke of this. But she knew that the adults who gathered in their home often wore such numbers, and no one else did. Perhaps, Carole reasoned, only people not born in America had numbers. But those same people sometimes switched from English to Yiddish when Carole was present, speaking in somber voices about something they did not wish her to know. When she saw her classmates' grandparents, she realized that there was no one old in the lives of those with numbers. Then a family friend carelessly left an album in her parents' living room — opening it, Carole found the photograph of a bearded man hanging from a gallows in a public square, surrounded by men in uniforms who gazed up at him, indifferent or even satisfied. And she began to wonder what the absence of grandparents had to do with speaking Yiddish, and why her parents never spoke of being children.

These questions came more swiftly. After temple one day, walking her to the corner store for candy, her father shrank back from a neighbor's tethered dog; though he tried to laugh about it, Carole realized that Harold, who admitted no fear, feared dogs in a way she did not grasp. Then came the unseasonably warm day when her father decided to take Carole and her friend to Baker Beach.

She had never seen her father in a swimsuit. When he peeled off the running suit and exposed his torso, Carole saw to her horror that his chest and arms and legs were crosshatched with raised white scars. Though her friend Arlene seemed not to notice, Carole was bewildered and ashamed.

That night Carole pointed to the tattooed numbers. "Can you take them off?" she asked.

Harold's expression combined melancholy and faint reproach. "And make another scar?" he asked gently. "As you saw today, I already have scars enough."

Now Carole was quite certain — something terrible had happened that her father would not tell her.

It was Carole's mother who broke the silence.

Rachel Shorr was not like other mothers. It was more than just her accent. It was the way Carole's father looked after Rachel; the way she feared leaving the house without him; the way she avoided speaking to mothers who were not Jewish. To know that the world frightened her own mother troubled Carole still more.

One night when she was seven, Carole and her parents went shopping just before Hanukkah. They walked through Union Square; though Carole knew little about Christmas, the bright lights strung on trees and lampposts entranced her. Turning to her mother, she saw Rachel's lips trembling, heard her speaking to Harold in Yiddish.

Harold put his arm around her shoulder. "We'll go," he told her quietly.

Her father drove them home; her mother would not drive. From the back seat Carole asked, "What's wrong?"

She did not expect an answer. To her surprise, her mother almost whispered, "It was the Nazis."

The word seemed to carry the totemic power of the numbers. "We still were in the Warsaw ghetto,"

Rachel continued softly. "My older cousin Lillian and I sneaked out of our old neighborhood, scavenging for food to fill our stomachs. But the streets were too bright — it was all the lights from the gentiles' Christmas parties, the lights on their trees. When we ran away, the Nazis caught Lillian in an alley.

"The day before was her eleventh birthday. I never saw her again."

In the darkness of the back seat, Carole understood that the Nazis had killed her mother's cousin. And then her mother said, "If Israel ceases to exist, Jews will perish."

That night Carole could not sleep.

She knew that Israel was the homeland of the Jews. She remembered the teacher at Hebrew school collecting money so they could plant a tree in Israel. She envisioned the Israel she'd seen in pictures, a place of blossoming deserts, purposeful men and women. But she had not known that Israel was linked to her own fate.

If Israel ceases to exist, her mother had said, *Jews will perish.* At some point during that long, sleepless night, Carole decided that she must not let this happen.

When she was twelve, Carole got her teacher's permission to write a report on the Holocaust.

After dinner she told her father. "Will you help me?" Carole pled.

Harold shook his head. "Why?" he asked. "You know how to use the library. You read faster and better than I can. You're much too old for such help."

The answer was so unlike him that Carole fought back tears.

Harold looked down, shame-faced. "I know what you're asking," he said, reaching for her hand. "Perhaps, someday, I will learn to write it down for you."

A few weeks later, Harold enrolled at San Francisco State, to take a course in writing.

One night, Harold began writing in his study. Carole saw him emerge gripping a spiral notebook, his face pale and abstracted. He barely seemed to notice her, said nothing about this new pursuit. Only later did she hear him sobbing in the bedroom he shared with her mother.

Still Harold kept on writing.

On the first day he let Carole read what he had written, the door closed to her own room, she wept for all of them.

David Wolfe was the only other person who had read it.

Even a half century after the events Harold Shorr had described, so simply that their horror spoke for itself, David found them as difficult to imagine as to read.

Harold was eleven years old when the German army came to the Polish village of his birth. For many Poles, it hardly seemed an invasion. Sometimes Harold could barely distinguish between the soldiers and his Polish neighbors — both were in the cheering, laughing audience the night the soldiers rounded up the Jews for a "comedy show," forcing the rabbi to slaughter a pig, his wife and children to canter and neigh like horses. Yet when a half-mad teenager, wild-eyed and famished, sought refuge with their neighbors, Harold's father would not believe his story about the Germans forcing him to bury his parents alive.

On Yom Kippur in 1942, three soldiers from the SS broke into their home. In front of his terrified wife and children, the Germans held a gun to their father's head. Then they herded the family to the cobblestoned square at the center of the village. More angry then frightened, Harold wondered what sport would highlight the latest "comedy show," and what role the Nazis had reserved for Isaac Shorr.

At the center of the square was a gallows.

The man whose picture you saw in the album, Harold wrote, *was your grandfather. No one dared cut him down.*

They packed Harold in a cattle car with his mother, brother, and sisters. His sister Miriam was forced to shit in a bucket, weeping with shame, as others turned their faces. But by the time they stopped for good, the stench that stayed in Harold's nostrils came from their rabbi, dead of a heart attack.

Huddled with his family and their neighbors beside the tracks, Harold blinked in the sunlight.

A German officer with a death's-head insignia on his visored cap directed each Jew into one of two lines, left or right. Looking about him, Harold saw at once that, though hungry, he and eleven-year-old Yakov were sturdier than many. Languidly appraising them, the officer pointed his mother and sisters to the left, Harold and Yakov to a section called "Quarantine." There, as Harold flinched with pain, a smirking corporal tattooed a number on his wrist.

Comparing their tattoos in a daze, Harold and Yakov found themselves standing outside in a barbed-wire compound with other men and boys, some of whom had been there longer. "If we're to be with our mother and sisters," Yakov murmured, "why do they separate us?"

Nearby, a prisoner laughed harshly, then pointed to a distant section of the camp, where black smoke issued from the chimney of a nondescript building.

"See that smoke?" the man said. "That's your mother and sisters. In time, the Jewish people will be nothing but smoke and ash, until there is no one left to say prayers for our dead."

Harold was too stunned to pray, or even to weep. Mute, he held Yakov in his arms.

They put us in the coal mines, his diary continued. *In the mines I learned the names of men who died, and then the men who came after, and died after that — like generations of the dead whose lifespan was measured in nine months. But Yakov and I lived on.*

There was only one reason: I had a second job at night, cleaning the kitchen for the Germans. From this place I stole bread, for Yakov and for me.

I did not share it with the others. The shame still burns inside me. I watched as others died in our miserable barracks, stacked with corpses-in-waiting.

One night the living ate the dead.

It was several days before David continued reading.

You wonder why I fear dogs, Harold had written. *Let me explain.*

I tried not to steal too much bread. I was too afraid the Germans would notice, and that Yakov and I would die in the mines. So I stole just enough to keep us living one month more, then another.

But Yakov was dying as I watched. His eyes sunk in his head, his body bent like an old man's. One day in the mines he fell to his knees, sobbing. I pulled him up before the Germans saw this, and felt how light he was.

I loved Yakov. I loved him for himself — sweet-natured and unquestioning — a boy who followed his older brother like a puppy. And I loved him because he was all I had of my father, mother, and sisters, the only sign outside myself to say that they were real. I could not let him die.

The Germans caught me stealing an entire loaf of bread.

It was night. They took us out in the prison yard — Yakov and me. Then they made a circle of soldiers with their snarling dogs on leashes, and turned the flashlights on us.

It was cold, and Yakov was trembling worse than I was, sobbing like the frightened child he still was. The Germans saw the spots of pee on the pants of his uniform and started laughing at him.

One of the guards spoke in German and then the dogs came for us.

I jumped on top of Yakov, to protect him. But there were too many dogs. Their teeth ripped through our ragged uniforms and tore at my chest and arms and legs. While I fought them, I could hear Yakov screaming beneath the pack of dogs, which were tearing him apart.

The soldiers saved me so I could watch my brother die. I can never forget Yakov screaming until he was a carcass without a face, and they made me clean him up.

After that, death was all I had to wish for.

Instead, the Germans ran away.

Harold was too weary to wonder why. He did not know what year it was; he knew nothing about the war. He knew only that his tormentors had fled.

The surviving Jews huddled in the camp. One man with a will to live led them into the woods. When the Americans found them, Harold was delirious.

The Spam they fed him gave him diarrhea. He could no longer eat normal food; in the hospital they forced him to wear diapers. For days he could not speak.

When Harold awakened from his long twilight, he was put in a camp for displaced persons. He could never return to Poland. He had no family, no country, no past to resurrect or future he could imagine. His only identity was a number, his inner landscape a gift from Adolf Hitler. He had seen the worst that men could do.

When Carole finished reading the journals, she told David, she had gone to Harold and said that she loved him more than life.

Tears had filled his eyes. "Please," he told her with a wistful smile, "not more than life."

"It was strange," Carole told David later. "At that moment, I knew that the most important thing that would ever happen to me had happened before I was born."

Now Harold raised his glass to them, filled to the brim with rich red wine. David saw the tattooed "8" appear above his shirtsleeve.

"L'chaim," Harold said.

Raising his own glass, David thought of Hana's key.

Both Harold and Hana were marked by history, he reflected — as were Carole and Saeb Khalid. David did not compare the ways; to him, the horror of Harold Shorr's suffering was reinforced by the terrible deliberation of its authors, repeated six million times. But Saeb's family was as dead to him as Harold's. And the question he had asked Hana thirteen years ago still lingered in David's mind.

Where does history begin?

For Harold Shorr, history began on the day the Nazis killed his father — the same day, David knew, that it began for Carole. For Hana, the date was the flight of her family in 1948 — as with Carole, she was marked by events she had never witnessed. But for Saeb, as for Harold, history truly started with the murder of his family at the hands of gentiles — and, Saeb would insist, Jews. Thinking of another lunch long ago, his only meeting with Saeb Khalid, David found himself wishing, for Hana's sake if not his own, that Saeb could have come to terms with his own past.

10

It was one of those moments after making love, when Hana seemed to slip away from him. She remained tantalizingly close, her back against his chest, the nape of her neck moist and warm as his lips grazed her skin. And yet her face was turned from him; David knew that her eyes, though he could not see them, were troubled and abstracted.

"What is it?" David asked.

She drew a breath. "Saeb wishes to have lunch. With you, and me."

Startled, David stiffened, propping his head on his palm. "You must be joking."

"No."

"How did *that* happen? We've never even spoken. Unless I'm missing something, he doesn't know that I exist. Let alone about what we've just finished doing."

Hana turned to him, sheet around her waist, her breasts uncovered. She was so beautiful that it silenced him.

"I told him we'd begun to talk — at law school, between classes or at the cafeteria. That you're interested in what's happened to us." She hesitated, then said, "A lie is more persuasive if it contains a little truth."

The ambiguities of Hana's psyche, oscillating between guilt and its absence, unsettled David further. "Why take the chance of mentioning me at all? Unless," he added with sudden hope, "you're getting ready to tell him the undiluted truth."

"No," she said flatly. "Not that."

The swiftness of her response deepened David's hurt. "Then what other, smaller truth did you tell him?"

"None. Only that I've come to like you, and that you're not like other Jews."

This stung him. "No," he said harshly. "I'm hardly Jewish at all."

Hana touched his arm. "I didn't mean that as it sounded."

"Like an anti-Semitic cliché, you mean? Unlike most of us, I'm not cheap, either, or obsessed with money. No wonder your fiancé is dying to have lunch with me — I'm that rare Jew any Arab would be proud to know. If not to sleep with."

"Please, David." Her eyes implored him. "Please, I'm sorry."

David rolled on his back. "God help me, I'm sounding like some neglected woman, someone you're fucking on the side. Which is true, I guess."

"Not the way you say it — even without the sexism. I told you, the first time we were like this, how it is for me." She hesitated, then asked quietly, "So is this the day that I stop coming here?"

The fear of losing her, David found, was as strong as the hope that she would keep coming back until she found that she could not stop, and was forced to confront what that might mean. "Lunch with Saeb," he said at last, "is not a good idea."

There was a subtle change in her expression, a softening, as though she was relieved that he was edging back from the precipice. "But how could I say no to him? At least without acting like I'm hiding something important."

"And aren't you?"

For minutes after, he pondered his own question, the disturbing ways that Hana's half-truth to Saeb suggested the depth and complexity of their connection — her need to speak to him of David, yet her willingness to dissemble. Hana lay her face against his shoulder.

They were to meet at a Lebanese restaurant in Cambridge — Saeb's selection. It was seedy and a little dark, its quiet broken by taped Middle Eastern music discordant to David's ear, the words as alien as a muezzin's call to prayer. David felt on edge, his mood soured by his being forced to play the part of prospective Jewish friend to a betrothed Palestinian couple, complicated still further by his desire somehow to gain from this charade at Saeb's expense.

When Hana arrived with Saeb, she was composed but distant. David felt as though he were watching her through glass; she sat across the table, but did not touch him. Saeb's handshake was perfunctory and soft.

"We're glad you came," Hana said pleasantly, as though to an acquaintance.

Amid the awkward small talk with which they began, David tried to focus on Saeb Khalid.

He was slight, much smaller than David; though his motions were fluid and graceful, there was nothing of the athlete about him. His face was an intellectual's, slender and fine-featured. But what captured David's attention were Saeb's eyes, the principal source of his undeniable charisma. Dark and liquid, they seemed at once deeply human and terribly wounded, suggesting a mind both troubled and intuitive. Knowing what had happened to his family, David felt an awkward sympathy — this was a man to whom lasting damage had been done, living with an aftershock that must permeate his soul.

But it was the intuitive quality that David found unnerving. Saeb was no fool, David felt certain, and he was vigilant against hurt or humiliation. His manner seemed to vacillate between reticence — intensified, David suspected, by an aversion to David himself — and a desire to find out why this American Jew might interest Hana, and therefore pose a threat to him. The one thing David did not feel from him was the simple curiosity of one human being about another.

"So," Saeb said, "you're about to graduate, Hana says. That leaves so little time to know you."

Intended or not, this double-edged remark put David more on edge. Hana would not look at him. Lightly, David answered, "It's the only thing I mind about graduating."

"What will you do?"

"Go back to San Francisco, work as a prosecutor. And you?"

Saeb's smile was brief. "That's a little more problematic. A master's degree in international relations might entitle me to teach. But where? The Zionists do not seem very anxious to let me return to my actual home."

"Israel, you mean?"

Saeb's eyes flashed briefly, and then he covered this with a briefer smile. "So they call it. How have your people, David, come to live in our land, and we live in camps or exile?"

When David glanced at Hana, she looked away. "For Jews," he answered, "our history is the history of exile, a history two thousand years long. But land is only land. My homeland is some city in Germany, I suppose, though my ancestors would have been murdered had they stayed there. So I guess my parents' homeland is San Francisco. They seem to like it quite a lot."

At this, Hana's eyes widened in unspoken warning. "Not Israel?" Saeb interjected with mock surprise. "Then why were we so badly inconvenienced?"

"I don't dismiss what happened to you," David answered calmly. "A people was dispersed. But land doesn't make a people; people make a land. That land could be the West Bank —"

"Which is occupied by the Zionist army. If Jews can remember two thousand years, forty-five years is not too long for Palestinians to remember. Do you expect me to forget all that's happened to us?" Saeb paused, and his tone became quietly insinuating. "Or do you require Hana to remind you?"

All at once, David sensed the second agenda beneath Saeb's question, even more visceral than the first. Hana folded her hands, staring at the table. "After I came here," Saeb continued as though nothing were amiss, "I researched how your media reported the massacre at Sabra and Shatila. The *Washington Post* was typical. Mainly they interviewed American Jews, allowing them to agonize about how Jews could have countenanced such acts." His tone became quieter. "Even our deaths were about Jews and their feelings. No one thought to ask *us* how we felt about women and children being raped and slaughtered. We were, as always, faceless. Because Jews write the story."

Facing Saeb across the table, David fought to curb his temper. Fueling Saeb's dislike, he told himself, was the shame of watching his family massacred and his sister raped, a humiliation that would follow him to the grave. Now, in front of Hana, he was facing an unscarred man she liked, and might even desire. Suddenly, David felt a disturbing mix of envy and superiority. *Do you wonder if I'm sleeping with her?* he wanted to ask Saeb. *Or is despising someone like me simply as hardwired in your psyche as distrusting Jews?*

It was good, David supposed, that lunch arrived.

Hana served the dish of spiced lamb and onion and rice to Saeb, then David, then herself. "So here we are," she ventured in a mollifying tone. "And you are right, David — all of us have our histories. But now it is we Palestinians who suffer. The deaths we remember are of family we knew. Our memory of dispossession is fresh, and new memories grow day by day." Her voice lowered; for the first time, David saw something in her eyes like an apology, a plea for understanding that was more personal than political. "You must realize how raw this is for us."

David gazed at her openly. With a doubleness he intended, he asked her, "Then what is the way out for us?"

Saeb covered Hana's hand, a proprietary gesture that — David felt certain — was intended more as a message to David than to signal Saeb's desire to speak. "There is no 'way out' for 'us,' David. In the end, only one of 'us' survives."

And for *us?* David wanted to ask Hana. Instead, he paid for lunch.

It was the last time he had seen Saeb Khalid.

11

Ibrahim sat with Iyad in the van. "What now?" he asked.

"We wait."

Ibrahim had been waiting all his life. Waiting for Arafat; waiting for the Zionist occupation to end; waiting for his oldest sister's first child to be born, for the joy of being called uncle. Waiting for the soldier to acknowledge their desperate pleas to let them take his sister to the hospital. Now in fear and frustration, he was awaiting a woman's permission to become a man.

Perhaps, somewhere in this city, she waited also, for her own permission to deliver their final instructions. From whom these would come, Ibrahim did not know.

Restless, he watched the shoppers driving in and out of the parking lot. There was much left to do; less than twenty-four hours remained, and yet Ibrahim and Iyad were without the means of destruction, still ignorant of where or how to kill him. Ibrahim tried to restrain himself from checking his watch, and could not; by this time tomorrow he should be well beyond doing such a thing.

One thirty-seven.

Iyad's cell phone rang.

■ ■ ■ ■

Basking in the warmth of the occasion, Harold and Carole lingered over coffee as David swiftly checked his watch.

He could relax, he told himself. There was still a comfortable hour before he met with the expert witness in his somewhat grim malpractice case, time to enjoy the company of his future wife and father-in-law. And now even his new timepiece reminded David of how much he valued this man, and had come to understand him.

The watch was a Piaget. A few moments before, David had remarked on it. "Then have it," Harold said, and took it off his wrist.

"Good Lord, no, Harold. It's yours, and it's way too expensive."

Harold smiled. "And, for me, a waste. I was going to put it in a safe. Such a fancy watch feels wrong to wear in public, just as I can never imagine a Holocaust survivor flaunting a hundred-foot yacht. As for watches, I can remember all too well when I measured time in days, not hours." Firmly, Harold took David's wrist and slipped on the thin gold piece of art. "It is my nature," he said softly, "the one the Germans gave me. You have no such inhibitions, nor will your children. Pass it on to your first son with his grandfather's love."

He stopped, embarrassed by his own sentiment, even as he sometimes seemed embarrassed by his hard-earned success as a real estate developer. But his hand remained on David's wrist — as so often, David thought, Harold's hands spoke for him. As though to cover this moment of emotion, Harold turned to Carole, saying in a fondly chiding tone, "And so I will see you both again tonight, when you force me to listen to this man Ben-Aron. Perhaps you wish me to sing 'Beautiful Dreamer' as he speaks."

David shot Carole a swift grin. Though a liberal in American terms, in Israeli politics Harold favored the most adamant skeptics about the Palestinians as partners in peace. Amos Ben-Aron had long been just as obdurate. But his selection as prime minister had changed him — despite the increasing sway of Hamas, pledged to the destruction of Israel, Ben-Aron now argued that as many Palestinians as Jews desired peace, and that Israel must work with the opponents of Hamas to establish a viable Palestinian state in the territories controlled by Israeli soldiers.

"Wishful thinking is not a plan," Harold continued. "Ben-Aron has begun thinking about the Palestinians like a man kidnapped by terrorists: it is intolerable to believe that they mean to kill him, so he imagines that they're holding him captive because they like his company." Turning to David, he asked, "And do you agree with me?"

"Nope," David said flatly. "Even granting the rise of Hamas. Because you've omitted Palestinians from your list of human beings."

Harold accorded David a wry smile. "And what do you know of Palestinians?"

"Something. I knew a couple in law school." David paused, toying with his coffee cup. "Let's start with where we agree — that Israel's survival is a moral imperative. But it was always way too facile to call Israel 'a land without a people for a people without a land.' Granted, the Palestinians were living in the place to which Jews have the deepest connection, and where British domination had left the Arab populace without a government of their own.

But, geopolitically, it was an arbitrary act, with all the injustice an arbitrary act creates. So now Jews and Palestinians are stuck with each other —"

"David," Harold protested, "these 'human beings' strap belts of explosives on their young people and send them to blow up Jews. They hate us — especially Hamas."

Briefly, David thought of Saeb Khalid. "Some do. Others don't. But their grandchildren, we can hope, will have more to live for than killing us. It's in our interest to help them."

Harold clasped his hands. "I'm a realist, David. Life has taught me that this Palestinian state you hope for is less likely to be a palliative than a haven for Hamas terrorists. They do not want us there, and never will.

"Perhaps you know that, after college, Carole wished to live in Israel. She'd fallen in love with an Israeli. But I put her off, pleading her mother's health, playing on the guilt of a loving only child until her relationship died out." With palpable reluctance, he faced his daughter. "For this manipulation, I'm sorry. But I was afraid. For all my talk of sacrifice, you were dearer to me than Israel."

Carole took his hand. "You were pretty transparent, Dad," she said in a husky voice. "It wasn't because of Mom I didn't go. It was because of you." Inclining her head toward David, she added with a smile, "And it's all turned out okay."

"Yes. It has." Turning to David, Harold said, "You are all I could have wished for, Carole. And neither of you should be dragging an old man's fears behind you like an anvil." Summoning a smile, he said, "I love you dearly, David, almost as much as my own daughter. Enough, even, to break bread with Amos Ben-Aron. Our last, best hope of peace."

12

It was past five o'clock when David arrived at Carole's tenth-floor penthouse in Pacific Heights, and white-jacketed waiters were already setting six round tables for eight in the spacious room she reserved for events of particular importance.

Entertaining with a purpose was central to Carole's life, and the apartment she had chosen served it well. Eighty years old, the brick building carried an elegant flavor of the 1930s, with a doorman, a generous foyer, and an old-fashioned elevator, which, although it wheezed a little, had carried David smoothly to Carole's door. Her apartment had the hardwood floors, crown moldings, and high ceilings more common to a time of luxuriant construction. The rooms were spacious, and the furniture carefully chosen and arranged, creating space for guests to mingle and more intimate places for them to sit in small groups. The living and dining areas shared the same floor-to-ceiling view across San Francisco Bay to the gold-brown hills of Marin County; as David watched, the last glow of sunlight faded on the deepening blue water, and sailboats had begun tacking toward their moorings.

He heard the click of Carole's heels behind him, and then she put her hands on his waist. "Meeting okay?" she asked.

"Good enough. My defendant the doctor has some problems. But that's what expert witnesses are for."

"Some days," she admonished him with a smile, "you sound a little cynical about your clients."

David turned to her. "Just not sentimental. That's a lawyer's big mistake."

"I'd just hate you to be sentimental," Carole rejoined. Giving him a quick kiss, Carole went to the dining room and began arranging the place cards.

David glanced at the television, tuned to CNN. "At this hour," Wolf Blitzer was saying, "Israeli prime minister Amos Ben-Aron is arriving in San Francisco, the last stop on a trip aimed at rallying American support for his highly controversial peace initiative . . ."

On the screen, Ben-Aron was disembarking from a jumbo jet, surrounded by men in suits who appeared to be security guards. Though the camera was far away, Ben-Aron was easy to spot. Silver-haired and erect, he was slighter than the others, and his brisk, purposeful stride bespoke the general he had once been. David felt a keen anticipation: he looked forward to meeting this man and hoped they could talk in private.

The picture changed to an angry, chanting crowd of demonstrators, one of whom, David saw, carried a placard showing Ben-Aron with Adolf Hitler's mustache. "Earlier today in Jerusalem," the anchorman continued, "an alliance of Orthodox Jews staged a massive protest against Ben-Aron's new proposal. At stake, they believe, is the future of Jewish settlements on the West Bank, the putative site of a Palestinian state advocated by Ben-Aron. For many Israelis, a Palestinian state is necessary to a lasting peace; for some, like these demonstrators, it is a betrayal of God's grant of the West Bank — the biblical Judea and Samaria — to the Jewish people . . ."

Since when, David remembered Hana inquiring, *did God become a real estate agent?* He could not help but smile at the memory.

On the screen, a bearded man appeared against a backdrop of rocky, barren hills, accompanied by Wolf Blitzer's voice-over. "A few extremist settlers, like Barak Lev, the American-born leader of the controversial Masada movement, centered in the Israeli settlement of Bar Kochba, are making some very troubling pronouncements . . ."

David stopped smiling. Lev was young and lean, with the black gaze and slow, insistent intonations of a prophet pronouncing judgment on the unrighteous. "Like Adolf Hitler," Lev said to the camera, "Ben-Aron wants our biblical land to be *Judenrein* — free of Jews. His Palestinian partners, Hitler's heirs, have no identity beyond the hatred of Jews, no culture beyond the murder of Jews. This 'homeland' he proposes for them is the base they will use to exterminate the Jews of Israel . . ."

In close-up, David saw, Lev's eyes seemed dissociated, his gaze intent on his own inner vision. "This will not be allowed," he intoned. "As God struck Hitler dead, so, too, will He strike down Ben-Aron."

Carole came in to watch with him. "As I recall," David remarked to her, "Hitler put a bullet in his own brain. But I suppose God works in mysterious ways."

"This man's bughouse," she said flatly. "He doesn't speak for Israelis — he's the minority of a crazy minority of dead-enders."

Still watching, David put his arm around her shoulder. "Near Bar Kochba," the newscaster was saying, "several dozen settlers threw rocks at soldiers seeking to remove two mobile homes inhabited by squatters. A right-wing member of parliament protested the prime minister's plan to dismantle allegedly illegal settlements — like Bar Kochba — by reading the names of settlers 'marked for expulsion by the traitor Ben-Aron.' Outside, demonstrators with sleeping bags prepared to fast until, they say, Ben-Aron reverses course.

"Ben-Aron's challenge is to demonstrate, despite the rise of Hamas and the turmoil roiling Israel, that he can somehow deliver what most Israelis want: security, then a lasting peace with a people that many distrust, and even fear."

David kissed Carole on the forehead. "Congratulations," he said. "This should be a truly exciting dinner."

"But the controversy," the newsman's voice-over continued, "has followed the Israeli prime minister to America. Today, in San Francisco, a spokesman for Palestinian opposition groups characterized Ben-Aron's peace plan as a 'sham.' "

Though David should have expected it, his first glimpse of Saeb Khalid startled him.

Saeb stood in front of the Commonwealth Club, where Ben-Aron would speak at noon tomorrow. Crow's-feet creased the corners of his eyes, and the fine angles of his face were concealed by a well-trimmed beard, which made him appear harsher than the tormented man with whom David had shared the subtle poison of their lunch. Unlike Barak Lev, he spoke with the confidence of an intellectual who — whatever his Muslim beliefs —

was firmly grounded in his version of fact.

"First they took our land," Saeb was saying. "Now Ben-Aron offers us a 'homeland' on the West Bank that is one-fifth of what we had. He offers nothing to the refugees in Lebanon whose families were slaughtered at the direction of Israel — certainly not a return to the land from which the Zionists expelled us . . ."

"They *can't* return," Carole said flatly.

Unsettled, David watched, disturbed by the complex of emotions — jealousy, compassion, sheer male competitiveness — that Saeb could still arouse in him. "Where was Ben-Aron the peacemaker," Saeb inquired acidly, "when they slaughtered us at Sabra and Shatila? And now he proposes to remove a pitiful few settlers among the many who will remain to burn our crops, destroy our greenhouses, and use our water for their swimming pools." Saeb's voice hardened. "The settlers will remain, and so will their injustice. And Ben-Aron's 'peace plan' will keep Israel's fingers around our throats, strangling the life out of our people . . ."

"Who *is* this guy?" Carole interjected. "He's scary."

"He's damaged."

Carole turned to him in inquiry. "I knew him a little," David added, "at Harvard."

"You were friends?"

A lie is more persuasive, Hana had told him, *if it contains a little truth.* "Saeb and I could never be friends. Then, or now."

"Because you're Jewish?"

"And because I'm me." Abruptly, David switched off the remote, banishing Saeb Khalid from Carole's living room as he had once wished to banish him from Hana's life.

■ ■ ■ ■

A week after the lunch with Saeb, David came home to his apartment in Cambridge, tossed his spiral notebook on the couch, then stopped abruptly.

Beside the notebook was Hana's bright cloth purse.

He had not seen her since the lunch, nor had she returned his calls. With a glow of excitement, he walked quickly to his bedroom.

She stood with her back to him, her head bowed. Though she must have heard his footsteps, she did not turn.

"Hana . . . ," he began.

Facing east, Hana was lost in the Muslim ritual of prayer. In that moment, more profoundly than when she gave voice to it in words, David felt the distance that divided them, even when they were skin to skin.

For minutes he stood behind her. Then, without turning, she raised her head, and began to silently undress.

When she had finished, she faced him. They did not speak. She made no sound until, lying beneath him, she cried out — whether in pleasure or anguish, David could not tell.

Palm cradling her face, David spoke first. "I thought I'd never see you again."

"Yes. I thought so too."

"And so?"

Hana spoke softly, almost sadly, as though she had looked into her soul and seen its weakness and desire. "At first, you were an indulgence — an attractive man from a different place. My own small rebellion. But now you are inside me.

"I imagined you — how *I* would feel — how *you* must feel. Like I had rejected you for Saeb. It's so much more complex than that, and I had no way to tell you, except to be with you." Hana touched his face. "And, yes, I wanted you. We have so little time — just as Saeb said. Though I pray he never knows how precious that time is to me."

Though her last words disheartened him, David tried to smile. "You make it sound like I'm about to be executed, and this is your last conjugal visit."

She did not return his smile. "When you're obtuse like this, I *know* we are from different places. You have no idea of my world — how complicated it is, even among ourselves —"

"You're talking about politics," David cut in. "That's not about us."

Briefly Hana shook her head, regarding him with melancholy fondness. "You are so American, David. At times much more American than Jewish. An Israeli would not say that to me. But to Americans, the world is America. If you have fantasies about a life together, it is an American life, where I leave the messy past behind and realize my full potential as a woman." A corner of her mouth turned up. "In America, of course. Where else are such things possible?"

This stung him. "I'm not that simpleminded, Hana. I'm just not blind. I watched you at lunch — you're different with Saeb than with me. *You* didn't choose him — your parents, and his tragedies, chose you. I may have started as a 'small rebellion,' some sort of emotional jailbreak. But the reasons for that are not so small."

Hana turned on her back, gazing at the ceiling. "I don't need you as my psychiatrist. I know what my resentments are, even what my fears are — that, as a woman, I may not achieve all I wish. But that is all the more reason for women to try within our own culture, not someone else's. Our people have so many challenges, and they need all of us —"

"But what about *you?* What about *your* days and nights? Maybe you can give Saeb what he wants — as a wounded man who needs to heal, or an Arab man who needs more adoration than I do. But who do you want to wake up with?" David felt his anger and frustration break loose. "Who? Look at me, dammit."

Slowly, Hana turned her face on the pillow and looked into his eyes.

"I see you as a woman," David said more evenly. "And as a Palestinian. But I don't see you as an emotional prop. You listen to me; I listen to you. We respect each other. And we sure as hell *want* each other — more than either of us has wanted anyone. We can overcome the things that divide us, because they aren't about us as people. But I don't think you can ever overcome being with the wrong person —"

"How can you know what is right?" she answered with quiet vehemence. "How can you know so much without living my life, knowing how that feels. We've had three months —"

"And I already know you. Better than Saeb Khalid ever will."

"Do you? David, how can you?"

Laying his curled finger against the warm skin of Hana's throat, David could feel the soft, insistent beating of her pulse. "Tell me this, Hana. Will you ever want Saeb the way you want me?"

After a moment, Hana closed her eyes. Her only answer, David found, was when she touched him, wanting to make love again.

Now, standing with Carole in her living room, David tried to purge the image from his mind.

Tense, Ibrahim waited for the traffic light to change, permitting Iyad to drive out of the parking lot and take the wide street marked "19th Avenue" to wherever the woman had directed him.

Between them lay their map and a list of numbers written down by Iyad as he had listened on his cell phone. To Ibrahim they were indecipherable, as were the means by which they would kill their enemy.

Why was the street so empty, he wondered, and then he heard the distant wail of sirens pierce the silence.

Involuntarily, Ibrahim flinched — they must be coming for him and Iyad, he felt certain. Iyad's fingers tightened on the wheel. As the sirens squealed, moving closer, Ibrahim hunched in his seat.

A bank of policemen on motorcycles suddenly filled the empty street, cruising in tight formation. Flanked by more officers, a black limousine passed, the first of a procession of identical limousines with tinted windows, like the opaque glasses of a blind man. On their aerials flew the blue-and-white flag of Israel.

"Seven limousines so far," Iyad murmured. "Bulletproof, reinforced with armor."

Three more followed. Only the eighth had clear glass windows. Through the motorcycles, Ibrahim spotted a man with the profile of a hawk, staring straight ahead.

Him.

The last car swept by, followed by more policemen on motorcycles.

Ibrahim watched the motorcade recede with a sense of awe. Even the slow fade of the sirens seemed to diminish him.

How could they accomplish this? he wondered in despair. And who, besides God, would be able to design a plan that would succeed?

13

From the moment Amos Ben-Aron arrived at Carole's dinner party, David watched him with considerable fascination.

As a budding politician, David had learned how to work a room, combining his good looks and easy smile with a quick wit that helped establish a rapport. But the flinty charisma that distinguished Amos Ben-Aron made David feel synthetic. He was strikingly fit for a man of sixty-five — small and wiry, with piercing blue eyes, a bald head, and skin drawn tight across his sharp features. Though he seldom smiled, his eyes locked with those of whomever he met, signaling his complete attention and, on occasion, glinting with a somewhat wintry humor. He had the look of a leader: sufficient to himself, used to being listened to and obeyed. He did not seem like an easy man to defy.

David said as much to Danny Neyer, Ben-Aron's young spokesman, as they watched the prime minister meet wealthy Jewish influentials of varying political inclinations. "Yes," Neyer said, with an ironic smile. "From the outside you would think that Amos Ben-Aron never knows doubt. But up close he's a man beset on all sides, who believes that he can never bring about peace if he betrays a moment's weakness or uncertainty. It wears on him."

David was struck by the contrast between the prime minister's burdens as a leader and the more trivial necessity of engaging Carole's guests. At the moment, Ben-Aron was gently detaching from Dorothy Kushner, a woman in her early fifties whose bright blond hair, too smooth skin, and bottomless social avidity betrayed the anxiety of a former beauty who feared that something terribly important might happen without her. Then, as though Neyer's purpose had been to mark David for his boss, Ben-Aron began wending toward their spot near the windows, a subtle minuet in which the prime minister was interrupted, but never diverted, from his apparent mission of meeting David Wolfe, a guest's courtesy to his hostess.

Finally they were face-to-face. At close range Ben-Aron looked older, his pale skin like parchment. But David experienced his force at once, the sense that — though Carole's living room was filled with those vying for a private word — David had his complete attention. "So," he said, shaking David's hand with a quick, firm grip. "I understand you've an interest in entering politics."

David smiled. "Would you advise me to?"

Ben-Aron's eyes glinted with arid humor. "That depends on what you want to accomplish. I wouldn't recommend it merely as an exercise. Though there are those who thrive on it.

"Your President Clinton was one such man. Do you remember the famous White House handshake between Prime Minister Rabin and Arafat, when the world thought all things were possible?"

"Sure."

"I was present," Ben-Aron continued with the practiced air of a politician proffering an inside story, "and there was so much more to that handshake than the mere fact that Rabin could not bring himself to smile. When Yitzhak came to the White House, Clinton took him aside and told him he'd have to shake hands with Arafat. This was to be expected. But for Rabin, Arafat was a murderer, a terrorist, and a practiced liar — which pretty well summed up his talents. Finally, Yitzhak growled, 'I'll shake the bastard's hand. But I refuse to let him kiss me.'

"Clinton was a genius," Ben-Aron continued with a smile. "Before the ceremony he actually practiced standing between the two adversaries, holding them far enough apart so that Arafat could grasp Yitzhak's hand but would have to lunge to kiss him. The onlookers applauding the historic handshake never suspected that your president was practicing jujitsu. Or," he finished wryly, "perhaps it was *Jew*-jitsu."

David laughed. "I didn't know the story. But it's been a while since I thought that peace would be nearly as easy as that handshake looked."

"You didn't trust Arafat either?"

David shook his head. "It was more than that," he said seriously. "I knew some Palestinians in law school, including one who turned up on television this afternoon. His grievances go very deep — not just his parents' flight in 1948, but their deaths at Sabra and Shatila. Both of which he never forgot, and mentioned again today."

Ben-Aron studied him with sharpened interest. "Sabra and Shatila," he said in a lower voice, "was a tragedy, both complex and brutally simple. I should know — I was there. As I'm sure your friend was also at pains to mention."

"Yes. He was."

Ben-Aron's chest seemed to rise and fall in an involuntary sigh. "Before Sabra and Shatila, Lebanon was a base for PLO terror attacks against Israel. And Arafat was resolved to turn West Beirut into what Stalingrad was for the Russians in World War II — a place where his fighters could wage a war of attrition. So Sharon determined to pulverize every PLO stronghold from the air.

"At least three hundred people died, many of them civilians. But Sharon got what he wanted: Arafat agreed to leave for Tunis." Pausing, Ben-Aron grimaced. "For some of us it was enough. For others, it was not — there were at least two hundred armed PLO at Sabra and Shatila, and this was our chance to kill them before they left.

"On a pragmatic basis, I could not disagree — Arafat's men might someday kill us if we did not kill them. But the bombing had hurt our international reputation and Lebanon was conveniently torn by Christian-Muslim strife. So it was decided to ally with the Christian militia, the Phalange.

"I was a colonel then, on the general staff. I knew what the Phalangists were — they would kiss your wife's hand, then cut her throat. And they were inflamed by the murder of their leader, Gemayel." The movement of Ben-Aron's shoulders implied his resignation. "To this day I don't know whether Sharon and the others were certain what would happen. But for my part, I warned my superiors that these murderers would slaughter Palestinians without discrimination."

Now Ben-Aron spoke so quietly that David strained to hear, though his gaze remained unflinching. "They did not listen. When it was done, I entered the camp. And I found children who had been scalped, men who had been castrated, women who had been raped before their throats were slit.

Among the survivors were children with arms or legs gone, others with their minds gone. If I cannot forget this, how could your Palestinian?

"But what he forgets is the response to this horror in Israel. Four hundred thousand people took to the streets to demand a public inquiry. Our Prime Minister Begin tried to counter this horror by invoking the one million children sent to the ovens by Nazis, as though unleashing the Phalange had spared us another Holocaust. But the public would not rest until he gave them their inquiry.

"Though Sharon and the others were reprimanded, some still call it a whitewash. But what country, besides Israel, has faced such threats to its survival and yet worked so hard to preserve the rule of law? And what country has faced more hatred and demonization by our enemies, more stereotyping as murderers and racists?"

"I know that," David said. "All too well."

"I'm sure you do. But now there is our presence in the West Bank, more hatred building every day." To David's surprise, the prime minister reached out to touch his arm. "When I was a young boy in Jerusalem, living under British rule, I idolized my father. One day, after the Irgun blew up the King David Hotel, he was stopped for questioning by British soldiers. Perhaps they thought my father was a terrorist — perhaps he *was* one, I do not know for sure. But I never forgot those soldiers slapping and humiliating my father. And from that day on, I hated the British." To David, Ben-Aron looked suddenly weary, and somehow older. "Now I think of all the hatred since, so deeply planted, awaiting us all in the fullness of time. The moment for peace is swiftly passing."

With that, Ben-Aron turned, standing straighter,

ready to greet the next stranger.

Before David could begin circulating, Danny Neyer reappeared. "So what did you think?"

"That he's remarkable." Glancing about the room, David picked out several men, all young, whose faces he did not know. "And that you seem to have a lot of security."

A shadow crossed Neyer's face. "Not as much as at home. When I was at university, such a thing was unthinkable — Jew killing Jew. Then a right-wing Jew made Rabin pay for that famous handshake with his life." Neyer contemplated his glass of soda water. "Now I'm feeling that it could happen to Ben-Aron."

"Is that a real possibility?"

"More so every day, I think. He's become a lightning rod — to the far right, he's betrayed both the settlers and God's plan for Israel." Neyer paused, looking about them. "Between us, David, the Shin Bet — our FBI — says that as many as two hundred people very much want to kill him. Amos Ben-Aron has been to a restaurant only once since taking office, and not with friends or family. He's too afraid some fanatic will take a loved one with him. So a night like this is as close to normal as he's allowed."

"Then I wish I'd taken less of his time."

"If he hadn't wished to talk, he wouldn't have." Neyer gave David the briefest smile. "From what little I could tell, he might even have liked you."

14

At dusk, Iyad and Ibrahim reached a fenced-in compound south of San Francisco.

The sign above the gate read "Safe Guard — the place to store what you can't afford to lose." From the ill-lit guardhouse emerged a young Chinese man in a security officer's uniform.

Presenting his driver's license, Iyad tersely spoke a number: "Thirty-four." The guard went inside to consult a computer screen. Then he came back out, returned Iyad's license, and waved the van inside with bored indifference.

No one else was there. Stepping from the van, Ibrahim saw rows of metal boxes the size of moving vans. The lowering dark made them look like steel sarcophagi.

With a flashlight, Iyad walked among the giant containers until he found the one with "34" painted on its door.

Across a metal handle was a giant padlock. Iyad fished the paper from his pocket. "Hold the flashlight," he ordered. "And read these numbers aloud."

As Ibrahim did this, Iyad carefully turned the dial on the padlock with each number, right, then left, then right again, until Ibrahim had recited the last number.

With one quick motion, Iyad jerked open the padlock. Then, glancing over his shoulder, he slowly pulled the handle. The door opened with a low metallic creak, and the flashlight in Ibrahim's hand cut the darkness inside.

Ibrahim could scarcely comprehend what he was seeing. Wires coiled in one corner, wooden boxes without labels. Against the rear wall of the storage container leaned two motorcycles with the lettering "SFPD."

Swiftly, Iyad motioned Ibrahim inside, closing the door behind them. Even with the weak light, Ibrahim felt entombed.

At his feet was a large suitcase. When Iyad flipped open its metal snaps, Ibrahim saw helmets, motorcycle boots, blue uniforms with gleaming silver badges. Above the pockets, stitched in gold, were the words "San Francisco Police Department."

Who, Ibrahim wondered, could have managed this? Instead he murmured, "What's in the boxes?"

With equal quiet, Iyad answered, "Plastique. They seem to have done well."

Ibrahim could no longer repress his curiosity. "Who?" he asked.

Iyad shot him a sharp glance. "Strangers. It is not our business to know. No one will. I am sure the locker has been rented by a man who does not exist. Whoever came here left no fingerprints. And everything we see here has been bought with cash . . ."

"Even the police license plates?" Ibrahim inquired.

"Stolen, I assume. We will never know *that* either. And once we are finished, the U.S. authorities will never find this locker. All they will find is one dead end after the other." Iyad gave him a belated look of impatience. "Must you play the child? Only children ask so many questions. It is enough for you to die with him."

And with you, Ibrahim thought, a moment of despair gripping his heart.

The evening flowed as Carole had planned, Ben-Aron seated beside her, the chatter floating in the air from the tables of eight, their intimacy promoting conversation. By Carole's arrangement, David sat between Stanley and Rae Sharfman. It was a shrewd choice — Stanley was a power in the community, an ardent promoter of his chosen Democratic candidates; Rae, his bubbly wife, was harmlessly susceptible to David's charm. Now and then David or Carole caught the other's eye: in their individual ways, each was hard at work, and they would not compare notes until the last guest had departed and her kitchen clattered with the sounds of caterers cleaning up.

Toward the end of dinner, Carole stood, signaling her readiness to speak. David saw Harold gazing with wonder at a daughter who seemed to have such an effortless public presence. "As most of you know," she began, "and some at considerable cost, this is not the first evening I've entertained here. This evening, however, is free of charge — the prime minister assures me that he seeks no lower office."

David, a tacit subject of this jest, began laughing with the others. "But this is a remarkable evening," Carole continued, "for a far different reason. Our guest is an extraordinary person — a decorated hero in three wars, the grandfather of six children, the leader of a nation cherished by us all, and a seeker of peace in a time when even the hope of peace is hard to find." Carole flashed a smile at Ben-Aron. "In fact, I've told him he should not seek much peace from *you.*

"He has come to address your concerns, whatever they may be. That, too, is an extraordinary opportunity for all of us who care so deeply. It is a privilege to welcome all of you and, especially, the prime minister of the State of Israel, Amos Ben-Aron."

Amid warm applause, Ben-Aron stood, briefly embraced Carole, and waited with a half smile until the applause died down, replaced by the intent gazes of his listeners. "Thank you, Carole — for opening your home to me, and assembling so many important friends of Israel. Perhaps regrettably, I have repaid you by encouraging your fiancé to enter public life. As for the rest of you," he added, provoking general laughter, "this may be your last free dinner until David enters Congress."

It was deft, David thought — with the right mix of warmth and humor, Ben-Aron had honored Carole by blessing David's ambitions. "But I know that Carole is right," the prime minister continued. "My life in politics has taught me that the only thing more difficult than fighting against our enemies is taking questions from my friends." Amid knowing chuckles, he promised, "Nonetheless, I shall do my best.

"First let me say this much. I know that those we must make peace with are riven by contending forces. Some have sent their sons, and even their daughters, to kill our sons and daughters. But I believe that we are strong enough to find a better way — in which Israelis, and the great majority of Palestinians, will work toward a day when our grandchildren live as neighbors." Pausing, Ben-Aron gazed soberly about the room. "And so, your questions."

Sitting beside David, Stanley Sharfman raised his hand. Before Ben-Aron could point to anyone else, Sharfman demanded, "Israel gave away Gaza and all it got in return was more terrorism from Hamas and Hezbollah. How can you consider giving the West Bank back to people like Hamas?"

"I don't propose to give it away," Ben-Aron retorted. "But our occupation of the West Bank is, in the long run, untenable. To persist in keeping the populace of the West Bank under our control means either that we will cease to be a democracy or — if we seek to incorporate three million Palestinians — will cease to be a Jewish state."

Sharfman blinked; for all of his concern for Israel, David detected, this quandary had never occurred to him. "Now," Ben-Aron continued forcefully, "we find ourselves mired in the horror of a continuing intifada, where terrorists murder us on buses and in cafés. So to fight the suicide bombers, we strangle the Palestinians as a whole with checkpoints manned by frightened young soldiers who, at times, wind up abusing or even killing the innocent.

"I do not suggest that we have become like terrorists — suicide bombing is infinitely more terrible than whatever we do to thwart it. But hour by hour, a Jewish soldier at some checkpoint creates another enemy." Fixing Sharfman with his unwavering gaze, Ben-Aron finished, "The vicious cycle of the intifada is bleeding the souls of Jew and Arabs alike. No military solution is clear, none is just, and none, in the end, will leave Israel any safer —"

"But what about the settlements?" David recognized the man speaking as Sandy Rappaport, an insurance broker steeped in right-wing Israeli politics. "Beginning in 1967," Rappaport continued, "Israel asked its bravest citizens to serve as buffers against invasion by settling on West Bank. Then we permitted Arafat and his armed men to live there, too. Now it seems like you'd abandon the next generation of settlers to placate terrorists like Hamas who revel in the murder of our people —"

Ben-Aron held up a hand. "I didn't start the settlements. I don't tolerate murder. I only deal with the consequences.

"Today the problem's plain enough. The settlements require a large number of Israeli soldiers to protect a relatively small number of settlers. Far from being a bulwark, they have become a national obsession — the focus of our political life and a drain on our public finances. Those are facts. And a rationally drawn border cannot include indefensible outposts peopled by fanatics, like the Bar Kochba settlement of the Masada movement. So must we continue to defend them?" Bluntly, Ben-Aron concluded, "We cannot. A handful of religious zealots should not dictate our actions. Especially when there will be no peace or stability in the Middle East as long as the problem of Israelis and Palestinians exists, and every malefactor in the region can exploit this conflict for reasons of their own."

This will not be allowed, David recalled the settler saying. *As God struck Hitler dead, so, too, will He strike down Ben-Aron.*

The atmosphere in Carole's dining room was taut now. "I *don't* favor unilateral concessions," Ben-Aron continued. "We must give up land for peace, not land for nothing. As for what we must resolve, the status of certain settlements is one of three main issues. The second is the status of Jerusalem; the third is the Palestinians' so-called right of return to the land that is now the State of Israel." Ben-Aron paused, surveying the room. "As to all these issues," he said flatly, "perhaps the biggest barriers to peace are the myths that animate too many Jews and Palestinians."

At the corner of his vision, David saw a bearded man — an Orthodox Jew of Harold's acquaintance — frown with disapproval. "*Our* great myth," Ben-Aron continued, "is that God gave us exclusive rights to Jerusalem and, beyond that, the West Bank. *Their* great myth is the 'right of return' — the inalienable right of all the descendants of refugees who fled in 1948 to come back and overrun us." Ben-Aron looked directly at his hostile Orthodox listener. "These myths will kill us all.

"First, our myth. God did not dedicate the land we love as a killing ground for religious rivals — that concept should have died with the Crusades. It is not for us to keep it alive. As for *their* myth," he added with a swift, ironic smile, "we must help them let it go. We cannot accept our destruction, or countenance the idea that Israel was born in a state of sin.

"For our part, we must acknowledge some hard truths of our own. In 1948, the Arabs did not leave simply because they could not imagine governance by Jews. There was a war. Many Arabs were frightened — Jews overran Arab villages, expelled the families who lived there, blew up their homes to prevent them from coming back. This is hardly unique in world history. But it *is* a fact.

"In short, we must recognize each other's histories in order to transcend them." Ben-Aron smiled briefly. "Tomorrow, at the Commonwealth Club, I will make my own modest proposal as to how we can begin."

For the first time in thirteen years, David Wolfe began to feel hope.

Beneath the police uniforms Iyad found another map of San Francisco.

Kneeling, Ibrahim saw three lines carefully drawn in pen, leading from downtown San Francisco to the airport. Softly, Iyad said. "He must take one of these."

But which route, Ibrahim wondered, and how would they know? *When* would they know? But the hard cast of Iyad's face kept Ibrahim from asking.

In the dim illumination of the flashlight, Ibrahim and Iyad stripped, trying on the uniforms of two San Francisco policemen.

To Ibrahim's surprise, his uniform fit perfectly. And so, it appeared, did Iyad's, the disguise complemented by his air of authority. More clearly, Ibrahim found himself able to imagine their success.

At least, he told himself, he would die to serve a purpose, at a moment of his choosing. Or God's.

When Carole touched his sleeve, signaling her willingness to end the questioning, Ben-Aron briefly shook his head.

"But who will be your peace partner?" Sandy Rappaport demanded. "For years the Palestinian Authority was controlled by Fatah, whose original leader, Arafat, never outgrew his role as a terrorist. Now Fatah's decrepit leadership must cede power to Hamas. If the Palestinian Authority could harness terrorists, that would be one thing. But they can't. Or won't."

A fair point, David thought. Ben-Aron acknowledged this with a brisk nod before answering, "There are terrorists, and there are terrorists. The Al Aqsa Martyrs Brigade, the militant arm of Fatah, has committed terrorist acts. But Al Aqsa is fighting for its *own* country — while they think it's perfectly okay to kill Israelis on the West Bank, many don't favor killing us in Tel Aviv." Ben-Aron permitted himself a wintry smile. "You may not deem this a hopeful sign, or Al Aqsa a possible component in combating terror. But consider our alternatives.

"The first, and worst, is Hamas." Abruptly, Ben-Aron's smile faded. "Most of the suicide bombers who come to Israel are Hamas. Those in the vanguard of Hamas mean to destroy us, and they are patient men. And now they dominate the Palestinian legislature. Their next goal is simple: to finish supplanting Fatah as leader of the Palestinian Authority."

Sandy Rappaport, David observed, looked as grim as the prime minister. "Imagine," Ben-Aron told him, "a fundamentalist Islamic state on our doorstep, sixty miles from Tel Aviv. That is the nightmare I wish to prevent —"

"How?"

"Israel cannot accomplish that alone. The leader of the Palestinian Authority, Marwan Faras, opposes violence. But we need more from him than noble sentiments. We need a Palestinian leadership willing — and able — to crack down on terror, end corruption, deliver services to its people, and stop the torrent of hatred that turns suicide bombers into heroes." Ben-Aron spoke slowly and emphatically. "If Faras can promise Palestinians what they most want — freedom from occupation — then perhaps his people will turn away from Hamas. Then the militants of his own party, the Al Aqsa Martyrs, might become the means through which Faras can control Hamas. Or, perhaps, Faras can eventually engage Hamas in the serious business of creating a society that works for Palestinians in the land where they now live.

"I need him; he needs me. Israel and the Palestinian moderates need each other." Sternly, Ben-Aron surveyed his listeners. "If we fail, our sole alternative is Hamas."

When David raised his hand, Ben-Aron looked relieved. "Yes, David."

David felt others turn to stare at him, not only as the questioner but as Carole Shorr's fiancé, the congressman-in-waiting. "You seem to be suggesting," David said, "that the greatest threat to peace is religious fundamentalism — or, perhaps, fundamentalist extremism. Could you amplify that point?"

"Gladly," Ben-Aron responded. "But first let me distinguish between fundamentalism and religion.

"Fundamentalism is certitude — it's ideology, not religion. Hamas and our extremist settlers share a common dialectic, the absence of doubt. They are cousins of the American Christian fundamentalists who believe that the Jews and Arabs must annihilate each other to bring about the Second Coming.

"I, for one, would rather we not play our part."

Though the dry remark drew chuckles, Ben-Aron continued without pause. "This is a very serious thing. There are Jewish fundamentalists in Israel who say that I am betraying God. It is this absolutist God, interpreted by a madman, who made the peacemaker Yitzhak Rabin into a traitor worthy of death. And the chance for peace died with him.

"Extremists learned this lesson well. If Jewish extremists destroy a Muslim holy site with a rocket, they could destroy *this* chance of peace. The same is true if Palestinian religious extremists blow up a school filled with Jewish children. The Middle East is like a bomb, and fanatics on both sides are forever looking for the fuse."

"What about extremist regimes such as Syria or Iran?" David asked. "How do we control them? And won't they keep on fomenting violence in order to prevent peace?"

Though this question underscored for Carole's guests David's grasp of geopolitics, his concern was real. "Yes," Ben-Aron answered promptly. "And the most dangerous are the mullahs in Iran." He jabbed an index finger into his open palm, emphasizing each point. "They are extremist *and* they are fundamentalist. Their intelligence services are powerful and skilled, with tentacles around the world. They help Hamas recruit Palestinians, and enlist Israeli Arabs against us. They wish to change the balance of power in the Middle East. That is why — and do not doubt this — they are building a nuclear bomb until they become the dominant force.

"As an ideological matter, Iran wishes to eradicate the State of Israel. As a practical matter, Iran needs violence between Jews and Palestinians to divert the world from its nuclear ambitions. Which, once realized, are a mortal threat to Israel." Softly but emphatically, Ben-Aron finished, "Israel can stop suicide bombers — by themselves, they cannot destroy us. But one nuclear warhead could do that very well. We must deal with Iran, our greatest threat, which is why I am so determined to give peace between Israelis and Palestinians this one last chance."

As David had hoped, his question — and Ben-Aron's answer — seemed to drain the antagonism from the room. "Given all of these enemies," Dorothy Kushner asked with obvious worry, "do you fear for your own life?"

"Fear?" Ben-Aron gave her a faint smile. "Those who wish to kill me are like customers in one of your ice-cream parlors — on a busy day, you have to take a number.

"I have no wish to die. But I cannot add more days to this waning life by making myself safer at the cost of lives much younger than mine, either Israeli or Palestinian." With a shrug of fatalism, Ben-Aron finished. "I've given much of my life to keeping Israel alive. What will all that have meant if I cannot leave it safer?"

Quickly, Iyad opened the wooden box of plastique.

Wrapped in newspaper, the explosives looked like greenish blocks. Iyad placed one in Ibrahim's hand.

It was eerie, Ibrahim thought, to hold the instrument of his own destruction.

"Very light," Iyad said in a conversational tone. "Easy to use."

Taking the block from his hand, Iyad pointed to the motorcycles. "See those saddlebags on each side of the rear tire? Pack them with these and it's enough to do the job, even on an armored car. All you have to do is get the wiring right."

Ibrahim tried thinking of his sister.

Kneeling over the box of plastique blocks, Iyad casually tossed one over his shoulder. Startled, Ibrahim failed to catch it before it clattered on the metal floor.

Laughing softly, Iyad said, "They are very stable — they do not detonate by themselves. That is what the wires are for."

Within minutes, Iyad had rigged a toggle switch to the handlebars of a motorcycle, then drawn the wires from the switch back to the saddlebags. The black wires, the color of the motorcycle, were virtually invisible.

"It's really very simple," Iyad said with satisfaction. "Anyone can learn to do it."

Before he left, Ben-Aron drew David Wolfe aside.

"This was an honor," David said.

Ben-Aron smiled wryly. "For me, as well. Although, at times, I was reminded of your President Lincoln's story about the politician who was tarred, feathered, and ridden out of town on a rail. 'But for the honor of the thing,' the politician said, 'I'd have passed it up.' "

"They're frightened for your country, Mr. Prime Minister."

"Aren't we all." Ben-Aron touched his shoulder. "I didn't say so tonight, but we need more involvement from your government. There are interests who want America to stay on the sidelines, not involved in the process of making peace. That could be fatal." Leaning closer, Ben-Aron gazed at David with new intensity. "You can be a part of this, David. When your time comes, I hope that you will help us."

Briefly squeezing David's shoulder, Ben-Aron turned away, kissed Carole on the cheek, and left, surrounded by his security detail.

From the window, David watched the street below. With the lights of police cars swirling, David saw the motorcade begin to move, headlights cutting the darkness, slowly turning a street corner like a giant serpent before it disappeared.

15

In the darkness of the compound, Iyad backed the van to the door of the storage container.

Ibrahim opened the rear doors. Swiftly, they began loading the van — first the boxes with their uniforms and helmets, then the extra wires. After this, sweating in the cool night air, they hoisted the motorcycles, rigged with wires and plastique.

As they left the compound, the guard looked up from his magazine and gave them a perfunctory wave. Heart in his throat, Ibrahim waved back.

To David's surprise, Harold Shorr emerged from the kitchen with a snifter of Armagnac and sat heavily in the overstuffed chair that was his favorite. This was unusual; Harold seldom took an after-dinner drink, and it was his practice to leave Carole and David to themselves after a social evening.

Briefly, David glanced at his fiancée. "Well?" he said to Harold.

Harold broke off his contemplation of the crystal snifter, looking up at David with a pained smile. "The 'right of return' is a 'myth,' didn't he say? Something that can be wished away like a fairy tale told to children. But they've nurtured that myth for sixty years by staying in what they still call 'refugee camps.' It's just another way of saying 'Jews are not wanted here.' Just like we weren't wanted in Germany, or Russia, or Poland." Harold cocked his head toward Carole. "To what place would we return? The Polish village where I come from, now empty of Jews?"

A look of understanding passed between father and daughter, touched with melancholy and, in Harold's case, a trace of bitterness. "You are young," he said wearily. "I am not. And I am tired from watching our history repeat itself. My parents would not believe the Germans would kill them until they did. Now it's the Palestinians — a few steps forward, a few steps back. Another handshake, another truce, then another Palestinian blowing up Israelis to prove that none of it matters.

"Forever, there is hope given, hope taken away. Now we have Hamas." Harold mustered a smile. "I am sorry, David. But I have little hope for Amos Ben-Aron."

After Harold had left, David stood gazing out Carole's window at the lights of the Marina District, the dark pool of the bay.

Behind him he heard the sound of Carole's bare feet. "Can you stay the night?"

"Of course."

In the bedroom, they undressed, wordless, and slipped into bed. Carole pressed her body against his.

Gently, David kissed her forehead, a signal that he wished to sleep.

But he found that he could not. Harold's last remark, underscoring his loss of hope, resonated with a memory David could not quite place.

At last it came to him. It was a weekend with

Hana, near the end. *You are free to hope for us,* she had told him. *But I am not free to hope with you.*

When Saeb flew to Chicago for a three-day conference of Palestinian students, enabling Hana to steal away, David was elated.

They drove to New Hampshire in David's secondhand convertible, Hana's dark hair flowing in the wind, Bruce Springsteen and Tom Petty providing the soundtrack. "Normal," David said with a grin, "this is what it could be like — normal." Not even Hana's delphic smile could dampen his exhilaration.

They stayed in a bed-and-breakfast at the foot of Green Mountain. Saturday morning, David brought her breakfast in bed, croissants and coffee and orange juice. Still naked, Hana hungrily consumed her first croissant. David thought he had never seen anything more charming.

"Normal," he repeated.

Her mouth full, Hana could only raise her eyebrows.

"I could do this every Saturday," David said.

Hana finished swallowing her last bite. "Do what?" she inquired with a smile. And so they had made love again.

Later, they left to take a hike; Hana had never stayed with a man, and David, who had learned to read her restlessness as apprehension, chose to distract her rather than argue that they were safe. After all, hiking was normal, too.

The trail up Green Mountain rose at a steep angle through dense pines, causing Hana to pause for breath, or to drink from David's bottle of water. Finally, they reached a promontory of rock weathered by wind and rain. The afternoon was temperate — light breezes, the mild sun of a New England spring — and the view went on for miles.

"Beautiful," Hana whispered.

It was. The wooded sweep of hills and valleys was so vast that it seemed less to end than to vanish on some far horizon. Amid the woodlands they could see only a few clearings for farms or hamlets marked by steepled churches; after the Civil War, nature had begun reclaiming the land, overtaking civilization as the energy of man moved west. David related all of this to Hana.

"So much land," she observed. "So easy to leave it, if you think there will always be more. Sometimes, I think, land explains so much about a people."

"It does for Americans," David answered. "There was always someplace else to go, a sense of things never running out. In the end it's an illusion. But if a people's illusion lasts long enough, it can shape who they become."

Hana gave him a look, the hint of a challenging smile in her eyes, as though she knew he was also referring to the illusions of Palestinians. But she chose not to engage in a debate. After a time, she said simply, "Thank you for bringing me here. This hill, this place, the inn with breakfast for me, in bed. I will never forget it."

David felt the impulse to speak overcome his instinct to be silent. "This is what life could be like for us. Free to go where we want, do what we like. Free to grow together without always watching the clock."

Pensive, Hana gazed at the woodland before them. "Free," she said, as though listening to its sound on her lips. "Such a simple word to you. You're an individual — obligated to no one, little more concerned about being Jewish than being right-handed. Satisfying your own desires is the simplest thing; you want something, so why not have it." She held his hand tighter, as though to remove any sting from her words. "You're so American, complete within yourself. Sometimes, with you, I feel like this girl — happy, almost carefree. Then I look at you again, and you seem so innocent. And I feel as though I'm a thousand years old."

In profile, she seemed wistful, or perhaps resigned. "You're twenty-three, Hana. And our time is running out. I graduate in a month —"

"Don't, David. Please."

The last vestige of restraint deserted him. "If there were time, I'd be endlessly patient, just letting it all spin out. I've got that in me. But we don't have time. We have to deal with this now — it's way too important to treat this like a college student's summer romance, doomed to end when the girl goes back to school —"

"But that's all it can be." She turned to him, speaking in an urgent voice. "Don't you see? With you I'd be constantly pulled from one side to the other, looking for a balance I could never find. What keeps us apart is so much bigger than we are. To my family, I am Sabra and Shatila, and you would be the murderer —"

"I'm not a symbol, for Christ's sake. I'm a person. Am I a murderer to you?"

"No." Hana paused, then added quietly. "But you are the man who's killing me inside. I want to be with you, David — to talk with you, listen to you, argue with you. And, yes, sometimes I desire you so much it feels like what I'm made for. Which is crazy. Because I'm more than a woman who wants a man.

"In my culture, family defines us. You never understand that. For you, it's easy — you're just you. You have no deep ties to your parents, and your parents seem to have no ties to their history or religion. But when your children ask about your family, and where you come from, what will you tell them?"

"Nothing," David replied. "They'll never ask, because the question would have no meaning for them. I can't imagine a child of mine falling in love and asking me, 'What would the Wolfe family do?' "

Hana shook her head, as though losing all hope that he would ever comprehend her. "To you these are stupid questions, really not questions at all. You're not really a 'Wolfe,' you're only 'David.' But not me. Before I came here, my mother said, 'Please do not love anyone in America. It would only cause you heartache.' Too late for that. But what she was also saying is that I'd also cause *them* heartache. And that I can never do."

With these last words, Hana's pain became his. "Then how can you do *this?*"

"I lie." Her tone became detached, almost matter-of-fact. "We're a shame culture, not a guilt culture. We worry about our name, our image, our honor in the eyes of others. But not what we do in private. I know Palestinian women from good families who go abroad and have affairs. But they never talk of it at home, and their family never knows. I don't need to tell my family about anything but Saeb."

When they returned to Cambridge, she got out three blocks from her apartment. David watched her walk away.

This is insane, he thought.

He headed toward graduation like an automaton, measuring his days as they passed too quickly, one after the other, toward the moment he had come to dread. On some nights — hastily stolen from Saeb or her studies — they would lie in bed, looking into each other's faces, bodies damp with lovemaking. They spent minutes without speaking, David running his fingers along her spine. He could no longer imagine his life without her.

One evening they watched *Casablanca* together, and David found himself hoping that Ingrid Bergman's choice of her husband, freedom's dutiful savior, over the man she loved would feel as miserable to Hana as it did to him. But when he said as much, Hana answered simply, "Ingrid Bergman was not her husband's partner. I will be."

"Are you so sure?" David challenged her. "I've only met Saeb once, and already I know how damaged he is. I'm not sure he even sees you."

"We're all damaged," Hana answered evenly. "Tell me, David, do you wish to live on the West Bank?"

The suggestion of a life together, however rhetorical, gave David hope. "I don't think I'd be welcome there. But you could practice law in America. Or teach."

"*I* don't feel welcome *here.* And it's not my country. It's the country of the powerful, Israel's chief ally, without which my grandfather would still be living in the land his parents left to him." Slowly, she moved her hand from his. "You know that I have feelings for you. But you forget how I feel about your country. And mine."

She left without making love with him, her face and body expressing too much misery to stay.

▪ ▪ ▪ ▪

The next night she came back. They made love swiftly, intensely, as if to dispel what both had said.

"Stay the night with me," David implored her.

"I can't. You know that."

"Because of Saeb," he said flatly.

"And because of me." She sat up in bed, tears filling her eyes. "You still think you understand me. But you can't understand that I've made a deal — let me give myself to this man for a few precious weeks, and I'll follow the rules for the rest of my life.

"At least let me take this moment, I tell God, and maybe the next, and I'll promise to pay You back. Knowing that every moment brings me that much closer to never seeing you again."

Her voice was suffused with anger. "You wonder if I love you? All right, David, I love you. And if you loved me more you'd wish I didn't.

"I think of the life I might have with you, but that we can never have. The happiness I have with you carries inside it such sadness. Maybe that makes our lovemaking more intense, more precious. But there is such pain —"

"There's pain either way, Hana," David interrupted gently. "Don't you think you'll feel pain two weeks from now, if you decide to never see me again? You can't get out of this without hurting someone. Especially yourself."

She turned from him. In a muffled voice, she said, "I've promised Saeb."

"Promised him what? A wife who doesn't love him?" He grasped her by the shoulders. "Look at me, Hana."

For an instant, he felt her tremble. When she

turned to him, she looked wounded, as though it hurt to see his face.

David's voice was thick. "I want a life with you. I want you to come with me to San Francisco."

Her expression was stunned, almost uncomprehending.

More quietly, he said, "Marry me, Hana."

She bowed her head. She seemed unable to speak, or even move. The tears running down her face were her only answer.

16

A little before noon the next day, Carole and David walked from David's office to the Commonwealth Club, on Market Street; at least ten blocks of Market were barred to automobiles, and the street was lined with barricades, police officers, and members of the Secret Service, distinguished by the sunglasses that concealed who the agents might be watching.

Angry demonstrators, Jewish and Arab, united only in their loathing of Amos Ben-Aron, pressed up against the barricades.

"A lot of security," Carole noted in a worried tone. "They need it."

David nodded. "Make it daunting enough and the Lee Harvey Oswalds of the world may decide that it's the wrong day to enter history." He pointed to the rooftops of the three- and four-story buildings. "There'll be sharpshooters on the rooftops, and security all over the auditorium. No way the U.S. government is losing Ben-Aron on *its* watch."

"It's sad to be afraid like this," Carole observed. "But still not as bad as Israel. Since the bombings started, you get frisked at shopping malls."

Her remark, and the demonstrators, were a reminder of the virulent hatred that made peace so difficult to imagine. But David felt lighter of spirit than he had since Hana's call. The spring day was crystalline; David, responsive to weather, hoped it might auger a fresh season between Israelis and Palestinians. As they entered the Commonwealth Club, he remarked to Carole, "I hope whatever Ben-Aron has to say matches people's expectations."

With that, they took their place in line, waiting to pass through the metal detectors.

Feigning the authority of the police officers who manned the barricades, Ibrahim and Iyad cruised down Market, stopping at the corner of Tenth Street. This was his route to the airport, Iyad had explained, the one shown on the map. Once more, Ibrahim wondered at the knowledge of those who had planned for them to join the forces deployed to protect their enemy. They had entered the zone of protection unimpeded; to Ibrahim's relief, the real policemen remained focused on their duties.

Last night he had not slept, roiled by anxiety and painful images of his sister. Today he felt resolute, yet strangely disoriented. With his face covered by the helmet and plastic mask, Iyad resembled a Zionist soldier in riot gear; among the onlookers lining Market Street, Ibrahim saw demonstrators denouncing Israel as the oppressor of his people. The path to martyrdom seemed so open that it stunned him. When four motorcycle police officers sped by, taking up positions on the first block of Tenth Street, Iyad murmured, "It is just as she promised."

Ibrahim said a silent prayer. In little more than an hour, should they succeed, they would no longer walk on earth.

■ ■ ■ ■

Within minutes, David knew they were hearing a remarkable speech.

The crowd of five hundred listeners, San Francisco's civic elite, seemed to sense this, too; even considering the anticipation that greeted the prime minister's words, underscored by the presence of cameras from the major news networks, they were uncommonly still.

"The epic story of Jews," Ben-Aron said, his voice measured and strong, "repeated by our prophets and poets over hundreds of years, called for us to reclaim the land of Israel. Today, Palestinians speak of their historic destiny to reclaim this land as their own. And both stand on the shoulders of those who came before. Consider Jerusalem. Jews were living there before the Bible was written, Muslims since the dawn of Islam. But too often each of us is blind to the story of the other . . ."

When does history begin for you? David remembered asking Hana. It seemed clear that Amos Ben-Aron intended to transcend the question.

"There are Jews," Ben-Aron continued, "so consumed by the tragedies of three thousand years that they cannot see the suffering of Palestinians. There are Palestinians so blinded by the suffering of sixty years ago that they cannot acknowledge the suffering of Jews. Today Palestinians call the date of Israel's founding the 'day of catastrophe,' marking it with the moment of silence with which we, on our Day of Remembrance, recall the victims of the Holocaust. Today Palestinians chafe under the occupation by Israeli soldiers, while Israelis fear death at the hands of Palestinian suicide bombers.

"Enough." Standing straighter, Ben-Aron surveyed the audience. "To the Palestinian people, I say, 'I know your history. You, like we, have suffered and died. You, like we, have been displaced and dispossessed. Your history is our history. Yet you the victims, and we the victims, have been pitted against each other in one of history's cruelest ironies . . .' "

As David turned to Carole, her eyes shone with expectation. "Enough," Ben-Aron repeated. "It is time to build a future for our children. Our history must not be their destiny; their destiny cannot be still more death . . ."

Pulling the cell phone from his jacket, Iyad listened intently.

Ibrahim tried not to react. But when Iyad shoved the phone back into his jacket, his mouth was a grim line, his air of self-possession gone. "That was her," he said. "They've changed the Zionist's route."

Listening, David lost track of time. "After forty years of war," Ben-Aron continued, "this is the truth I wish to tell to Palestinians. As a Jew, it hurts me to live in a world where my people's safety is not assured. It hurts me to live in a world where nations question our value as human beings. I would like not to worry about children who seek honor by killing Jews. I would like not to wonder if there will be a safe place for my grandchildren . . ."

And so, David thought, would Harold Shorr. When he glanced again at Carole, David knew that she was thinking the same thing.

"That is what I would like," Ben-Aron said more quietly. "And this is what I ask of you. I ask you to recognize our right to exist. I ask you to reject violence. I ask you to help us leave your land by spurning those — such as Hamas — who would kill us in our land. I ask that you offer those willing to abandon terror — such as the Al Aqsa Martyrs Brigade — the chance to enter your security forces as a bulwark against terror."

This, David thought, was risky and extremely clever: by suggesting that the Al Aqsa Martyrs might become the linchpin of the Palestinian security forces, Ben-Aron was hoping to pit them against Hamas, dividing two major groups of Palestinian militants while risking still more anger from the Israeli right. "I ask you to work," Ben-Aron continued, "toward a society that meets the needs of its own people rather than feeds their anger at my people. A society, in short, that will be our partner in peace.

"In return, this is what I offer you."

As Ben-Aron paused, David felt a quickening of hope.

"An end to suffocating checkpoints," Ben-Aron continued, "arbitrary arrests, and petty humiliations. A negotiation of fair borders that provide for *our* security and *your* prosperity. A program of compensation to the descendants of Palestinian refugees. A dismantling of illegal settlements. An agreement that Jerusalem will be an open city, the capital of both of our nations. An effort to help build an economy that promises your young people something better than a martyr's grave. And, at last, a country of your own."

Once again, Ben-Aron's gaze swept the audience. "I also offer you these truths," he continued soberly. "That we as Jews accept our share of responsibility for the violence that caused your grandparents to flee; for the needless slaughter of Sabra and Shatila; for the soul-grinding pressure of your daily lives. That all of us — Palestinian and Jew — are responsible for who our children become. That it is our common responsibility to prevent them from making our land a common grave. That it falls to all of us — Palestinian and Jew — to replace the cult of death and suicide with the promise of peace and dignity. And that you, the Palestinian people, must do your part by rejecting the witches brew of hatred and revenge offered by extremists like Hamas."

At that moment, David wished he could turn to Hana Arif and tell her, *We can do this. Or, at least, our children can.*

"Which brings me," Ben-Aron continued, "back to the claims of history.

"None of us can resurrect the past. None of us can return to a time or place that vanished sixty years ago. But for those whose lives are more past than future — those Palestinians born in what is now Israel — we can offer a return." The prime minister's voice softened. "Not the *right* of return, but the chance, if they wish it, to return to where they lived before the birth of Israel . . ."

Surprised, David tried to imagine the emotion of a man and woman he had never met, Hana's parents. To return might be heartrending, an end to dreams. And yet this dream had consumed their lives, and Ben-Aron was willing to acknowledge this.

"They," Ben-Aron concluded, "like me, are old. And I, like they, have an old man's dream — to sit beneath an olive tree and watch our grandchildren play, free of history's burden. Let this, the best of our dreams, speak to the best in all of us."

■ ■ ■ ■

Abruptly, Iyad spun his motorcycle in the direction of the Commonwealth Club. "Fourth Street," he said to Ibrahim. "We must hurry."

Hitting the accelerator, Iyad sped back toward where they had come from, pausing only to throw his cell phone in a curbside trash container. Ibrahim followed, his prayers obliterated by panic, the blast of Iyad's motorcycle, the vibrations of his own.

17

Outside the Commonwealth Club, David paused, too captured by the moment to rush back to his office.

He stood with Carole amid the crowd at the corner of Market and Second Streets, gazing at the police barricades, the unwonted emptiness of the street itself, the line of black limousines awaiting Ben-Aron. "I'd like to watch him leave," he said. "Let's find a better vantage point."

He led her through the crowd toward where Fourth Street ran into Market. "When I was in the DA's office," he explained, "I knew the cop who ran Dignitary Protection. Sometimes they'll change routes; if they're really worried, they might even use a dummy motorcade. But from here there are only three direct routes to the airport — down Fourth, Sixth, or Tenth Streets to Highway 101. If we stand at Fourth, we're sure to see them passing."

They found a place behind the barricades at the corner of Market and Fourth. With a practiced eye, David studied the policemen on motorcycles waiting along Market as it ran toward Tenth, the barricades blocking Fourth Street. "I'd guess they're going down Tenth Street."

Carole took his hand. David scanned the onlookers lining Market Street: a cluster of young

Jewish men in yarmulkes; a few Arab students whose signs called for an end to occupation; a bearded derelict with a shopping cart and the dissociated look of a man wandering in a daze; mothers and children waiting to experience history; a trim young man in sunglasses whose expression of tensile alertness marked him as a Secret Service agent. On the roof of a sporting goods store, David spotted a man with a sniper rifle, and then his attention was caught by two motorcycle policemen speeding toward them from the direction of Tenth Street.

As if on cue, a team of uniformed police opened the barricades blocking Fourth Street. Abruptly, the two cyclists swerved onto Fourth, their Harley-Davidsons careening sideways. They stopped a few feet down the block, brakes screeching, one stationed on each side of the street. Beyond them, David saw more policemen and barricades lining the one-way street toward Highway 101.

"Those two motorcycle cops," David said. "Something's happening . . ."

Carole shot him an apprehensive look. "Trouble?"

"Just caution, I think."

From near the Commonwealth Club came the whine of police sirens, the sound of the motorcade starting up; just beyond Fourth Street, more police pushed steel barricades across Market, sealing it off. To David, this symmetry of sound and movement expressed a certain majesty.

The motorcade came toward them now — a phalanx of six more police officers on motorcycles, followed by the limousines in close formation, perhaps six feet apart.

"Which car is Ben-Aron's?" Carole asked.

Almost sinuously, the motorcycles turned in unison down Fourth Street, passing in front of David and Carole.

Ibrahim watched the policemen glide past him, marking the final moments of his life. Across the street, Iyad hunched over his motorcycle, preparing to give the signal. "I'll go first," he had instructed. "Count to three, then follow. Even if they shoot me you'll blow him straight to hell."

Through clenched teeth, Ibrahim murmured his sister's name, a kind of prayer. He could find no words to speak to God.

The first limousine turned the corner. Peering vainly at its opaque windows, Carole murmured, "I don't think we'll be able to see him."

The second limousine slowly passed, then the third. These, too, had tinted windows; inside, David knew, rode aides and Secret Service agents and members of Ben-Aron's security detail. The two sharpshooters on the trunk of the fourth limousine scanned each side of Market Street.

"Here he comes, I think."

As the next limousine turned down Fourth Street, the sharpshooters braced themselves. From each side, the two motorcycle policemen who had waited there joined the motorcade. David trained his gaze on the limousine gliding around the corner.

Its windows were untinted. Leaning across the barricade, David peered into the rear seat and saw the prime minister raise his hand, half wave and half benediction, the brief moment passing with his limousine.

As David and Carole watched, the two policemen slowed their motorcycles until Ben-Aron's limousine slipped between them.

To his right, Ibrahim saw the driver glancing out at him with surprise. But from the car ahead, the sharpshooters still watched the crowd for signs of danger. Heart racing, Ibrahim awaited Iyad's signal.

Iyad edged his motorcycle closer to the limousine, slowing so that he was beside its rear window. *"Please,"* Ibrahim implored him, *"let it be done."*

Still Iyad gave him no sign. From the passenger seat, the aquiline face of Amos Ben-Aron seemed to stare into Iyad's eyes.

A jolt ran through Ibrahim like an electric current. In a reflex of resolve and panic, he pressed the toggle switch that would end this man's life, and his . . .

Nothing happened. Ibrahim's fear turned to disbelief.

At that moment, Iyad veered toward the limousine.

David's disbelief lasted a split second — the instant it took for a bullet ripping through the assassin's head to spew blood and brains into the air. Then a thunderous explosion shook the sidewalk beneath their feet and shattered the windows behind them.

Ben-Aron's limousine erupted into flames, hurling glass and metal and body parts outward in slow motion. Carole's scream filled David's ears; reeling from the concussive blast, he pulled her close to him. His eyes recorded images his mind could not comprehend, a kaleidoscope of horror: a severed arm; the misshapen carcass of the limousine melting into a grotesque tomb; one of the assassins sprawled in the gutter like an oversized rag doll. David knew only that Amos Ben-Aron was dead, his dream as shattered as his body.

Trembling, Carol could make no sound. David pressed her face to his chest so that she could not see the images filling his soul with horror.

Dully, Ibrahim felt the blood soaking his tattered uniform. Helmet gone, his head lay on the concrete, which had scraped his face raw.

Was he alive? He must be. But he comprehended nothing of what had happened.

All around him he heard keening, the ululations of grief and revulsion. *I will meet the Prophet, surely I will meet the Prophet.* Darkness overcame him, a wretched sob of anguish dying in his throat.

18

At five o'clock, David and Carole at last returned to her apartment.

They had spent the intervening hours as involuntary prisoners, answering the questions of two FBI agents while the police and other agents sealed off the scene, picking through debris and the charred pieces of what had once been human beings. It seemed that there were three victims beyond Amos Ben-Aron — two men in the prime minister's limousine and their murderer, whose body had simply disappeared. The second assassin had survived, at least for the moment; paramedics had laid him on a stretcher, head lolling to one side, and rushed him to a hospital with sirens blaring. Numbly, David had tried to comfort Carole; save for her halting answers for the FBI, she had said little. Now David sat with her on the couch where, the night before, Harold Shorr had deprecated a dead man's hope of peace.

Nothing made sense — not the unearthly quiet of a tenth-floor penthouse, the evening sunlight of a pristine day, the memory of Amos Ben-Aron speaking in the next room. David felt suspended between reality and the hazy remnant of a nightmare.

Carole looked five years older. "I was thinking of

Anne Frank," she said tiredly, "what she wrote in her diary: 'In spite of everything I still believe that people are really good at heart.' Despite what happened to my father during the Holocaust — to all of them — I try to. But not now."

When the telephone rang, it was David who answered. "Are both of you all right?" Harold asked.

"As much as we can be."

"I know." Harold's monotone bespoke unutterable weariness. "It seems never to end — our history, this murder of Jews. Who were they, David?"

"I don't know. The man they carried away looked Arab."

"Arab," Harold repeated softly. "This much we know — suicide bombing has come to America. To kill a Jew who believed he could make peace with Arabs."

Though David was seared by what he had witnessed, the bitter resignation he heard came from Harold's wounded soul, cauterized but never healed. "Please come over," David told him. "It's good for us to be together."

Silently, the three of them watched television.

David imagined the world reverberating, the shock waves of the explosion he had witnessed spreading outward in concentric circles. From Washington, the president expressed the nation's shame and anger and resolve, pledging "America's commitment to find and punish the authors of this evil, however long it takes." The president of the Palestinian Authority, Marwan Faras, looking shrunken and defensive, decried "the heinous murder of this man of peace." The president of Israel joined throngs of Jews praying at the Western Wall; a spontaneous gathering in Tel Aviv swelled to a hundred thousand people. Across America, mourners gathered outside Israeli consulates; on CNN, commentators and statesmen invoked the murder of John F. Kennedy and the horror of America's first suicide bombing — its unspeakable slaughter, its foreignness, its resonance with the terror of 9/11. The mystery surrounding the assassins only deepened David's sense of a cosmic disturbance, history forever changed.

"You think they knew the route?" Harold asked.

"It seemed so. More than that, I think they knew the route had changed."

"What does that mean?"

"That someone told them — maybe by inadvertence, maybe not." David sipped his scotch, feeling the anesthetic warmth of alcohol. "Somehow they got uniforms, motorcycles, and explosives, infiltrated the cops, and ferreted out where Ben-Aron was going. Whoever planned this was more than lucky — they were sophisticated and determined."

Carole's cell phone rang. Reluctantly, she reached into her purse. "Burt?" she said, leaving David to wonder why his chief political consultant was calling at such a time. "Yes," Carole went on, "it's terrible. And yes, he's here."

She handed David the phone. Burt Newman spoke quickly, as if the act of speech was taxed by the minute. "Sorry to bother you at Carole's. But Channel 2 wants you for the *Ten o'Clock News*."

"What on earth for?"

"The Ben-Aron assassination. The producer wants somebody with political insight and legal experience, preferably as a prosecutor, to walk people through what's happening here. You're perfect —"

"Burt," David said emphatically, "I met the man.

I *saw* what happened today."

" 'Saw'? You mean literally saw, as in you were there?"

"Yes."

"That's even better. You're four people in one: acquaintance, eyewitness, politician, ex-prosecutor." Pausing, Newman continued in a more somber tone. "I'm sorry, David. But that's an hour of airtime somebody's going to fill — a hundred thousand dollars' worth, for free. And no one can accuse you of grandstanding —"

"Maybe grave robbing."

Carole turned to watch him. "You're preparing to run for Congress," Newman rejoined. "The murder of Amos Ben-Aron is as big a news event as this city is ever going to see, and you — David Wolfe — can speak to all of its dimensions with the seriousness it deserves. Besides, at least a quarter million people will be watching. Do you want them listening to some blatherer or you? More to the point, do you want to go to Congress? If the president of the United States can suck it up on television, so can you."

This was surreal, David thought, a heartless joke. And it touched a certain discomfort with one aspect of his own ambitions: the need for exposure, the no-man's-land between real and synthetic, sincere and self-serving. When he no longer knew the difference, he would become a nowhere man. "I'll call you back," he told his handler.

Getting off, David explained what Newman wanted. "How can I possibly do this?" he asked.

Harold lay his head back on the couch, eyes closed, dropping out of the discussion. "Because everything Burt said is right," Carole answered. "If something happened to Dad — no matter how sad it was — wouldn't you say something about him if a news station asked you to?"

"Why don't I just say it now, while Harold can still hear me?"

Carole shook her head. "David," she said tiredly, "what you do is up to you. But you're not like some narcissist on reality TV. You care about Amos Ben-Aron and what he stood for."

David put down his drink. "Give me the cell phone," he said at length. "But I won't do the eyewitness stuff. I can't."

It was a night for alienation.

The set of the *Ten o'Clock News* was at once glitzy and antiseptic, reminding David of a motel for business travelers, one he could not wait to leave. And though he liked the anchorwoman, Amy Chan, their dialogue felt like an out-of-body experience, that strange moment at a cocktail party when David, utterly detached, discovered himself listening to his own responses as though they came from someone else.

"In our lifetime, Amy, there are only a few leaders we call great — Martin Luther King, Nelson Mandela, maybe Lech Walesa in Poland. The tragedy is that in a year or so, we might have been adding Amos Ben-Aron. Now we're left to hope that his death doesn't mean the end of hope, the beginning of more bloodshed."

The anchorwoman nodded gravely. "That brings us to the legal and investigative aspects. The FBI has a man in custody. What happens next?"

"Let's start with the crime." He was on surer ground here, David found, his prosecutor's reflexes kicking in. "This is a triple murder — moreover, the murder of a foreign official and the murder of the Secret Service agent are both federal crimes. That means the investigation and prosecution will fall under the jurisdiction of the Justice Department and, locally, the United States attorney. Marnie Sharpe is a capable, experienced prosecutor — my bet is that she will help direct the investigation and try any prosecution herself. She's already under tremendous pressure — everyone is, from the president on down. The outcome of the investigation may change the history of at least two peoples, Israelis and Palestinians —"

"The president," Chan noted, "is committing massive resources."

David felt the camera staring at him from the shadows beyond the set. "An Israeli prime minister under our protection was murdered on U.S. soil. That means that the FBI, the Secret Service, and the CIA will be working with Israel's external security organization, the Mossad, and the Shin Bet, Israel's equivalent of the FBI. They'll also be working with the subunit of the Shin Bet that provided personal protection for the prime minister.

"The FBI will take the lead — they'll set up a command center in San Francisco, no doubt run by a counterterrorism expert, and interrogate every cop and Secret Service agent involved in protecting Ben-Aron —"

"Even the Israelis?"

David hesitated. "That's delicate. To be blunt, there's the possibility of a security breach — theirs or ours. In the worst case, it was deliberate. Given the political situation in Israel, that's potentially incendiary. The Israelis might want to handle their own people and conduct their own inquiry.

"Whatever the case, the investigation won't be confined to the United States. The list of people who wanted to murder Amos Ben-Aron starts in the Middle East. He knew that himself, very well. So the intelligence agencies of both countries will be working all their sources in the region." David paused again. "But potentially the best source is lying in a hospital bed. The second suicide bomber."

Chan's brow knit, a pantomime of puzzlement intended for her audience. "Why would someone willing to be a human bomb talk to the FBI?"

"That's a fair question. But another one is, Why is he still with us? Suicide bombers aren't supposed to survive." David felt his field of vision opening, and imagined himself as Marnie Sharpe. "Right now he's all we've got — the only one who may know where his orders came from. If he tells what he knows, it could blow this case — and, potentially, the Middle East — wide open.

"First, they want his handler. Then they want to follow this up the chain, right to the top. So whatever they can do to him — short of torture, that is — they will."

"Such as?"

"Under federal law, killing a foreign leader is publishable by death. So they'll charge him with capital murder. They may also threaten to extradite him to Israel, the only tactical problem being that Israel doesn't have the death penalty. They might even try to scare him with what they call 'extraordinary rendition' — sending him to a foreign regime that *does* use torture."

"That happens?"

"Sure — particularly since 9/11, though we don't like to talk about it. If this man's smart, he'll know they're bluffing: we can't ship him to the Saudis with all the world watching. The one thing I'm sure of is that he won't be getting a good night's sleep. Assuming that he recovers enough to answer questions —"

"Or chooses to."

"Yes. But he can't conceal who he is, or where he's from. That much we'll find out by ourselves."

"And when we do?"

There were many responses to this, David thought. But the one he chose surfaced from deep within his own past. "We hope he isn't Palestinian," David answered simply.

19

The producer at Channel 2 was so delighted that she invited David back. And so began the daily television appearances that David described to Carole as "the TV Stations of the Cross."

On the morning of the third day following the assassination, David entered the greenroom at Channel 2 and encountered Betsy Shapiro, the somewhat starchy and imperious senior senator from California who — through her long friendship with Harold and Carole — was David's political patron. Seeing David, Betsy awarded him a perfunctory embrace and smile. A businesslike woman, Betsy often gave the sense of having been interrupted by some unwelcome surprise; today, dressed in her senatorial uniform — suit, silk blouse, pearl necklace — she seemed focused on the interview to come. Senator Betsy Shapiro was always prepared, and she measured her words with precision.

"I guess you're here to talk about Ben-Aron," Betsy said tersely. "Be careful with it, David. You were good the other night. But raising the possibility of Israeli complicity in a security breach is not what most Jews want to hear. And if it's true, it'll tear Israeli society apart —"

The young producer of the morning news burst into the greenroom and switched on the television.

"Sorry, Senator. But there's an announcement on CNN."

Marnie Sharpe stood at a podium, surrounded by reporters, microphones, and cameras. To David, her tension was apparent: though she usually spoke without notes, she read from a prepared statement, her voice much flatter than normal. "As of this morning," she began, "we have conclusively identified the surviving assassin in the murder of Prime Minister Amos Ben-Aron. He is Ibrahim Jefar — a Palestinian national, a citizen of the West Bank city of Jenin, and a student at Birzeit University in Ramallah . . ."

"Shit," David murmured.

"Mr. Jefar and his coconspirator, Iyad Hassan, traveled from the West Bank to Mexico using their own passports. From there they entered the United States illegally, where Mr. Hassan rented a car under an assumed name, and the two men proceeded to San Francisco." Sharpe paused, as though burdened by the weight of her next words. "Except to report that Mr. Jefar himself is in good condition, we cannot confirm any further information at this time. But our intelligence services believe that Mr. Jefar is affiliated with a Palestinian terrorist group, the Al Aqsa Martyrs Brigade . . ."

Shapiro puffed her cheeks, slowly expelling air. "That tears it. If this assassin were Hamas, it would be bad enough. But Al Aqsa is an offshoot of Fatah, Faras's party, Ben-Aron's last hope for a viable peace partner. Like Ben-Aron, Faras had even proposed that Al Aqsa give up armed resistance and join his internal security forces. Now this pits him against Israel *and* Al Aqsa."

David's gaze returned to the screen. "This," a CNN analyst was saying, "may severely jeopardize any chance of a negotiated peace . . ."

" 'May'?" Betsy Shapiro waved a disdainful hand in the direction of CNN. "I'd lay odds we're getting a hard-liner as Israel's next prime minister. But *any* leader who wants to survive will cut off contact with Faras, retaliate militarily against Al Aqsa, accelerate building the security fence, and declare the Palestinian Authority responsible for Ben-Aron's assassination. And that can only destabilize Faras and further strengthen Hamas. If someone had designed a plan to destroy all hope of peace, they couldn't have done better."

It was this thought, taken literally, that stuck in David's mind.

By five o'clock that evening, though the embattled Marwan Faras had swiftly repudiated the Al Aqsa Martyrs Brigade, Israeli warplanes had screamed down from the sky above the refugee camp at Jenin, demolishing a home in which, the Israelis asserted, members of Al Aqsa were hiding. Palestinian claims of civilian casualties swiftly followed, laced with vitriol from the leaders of Hamas.

Watching television with Carole, David could not help but wonder what Hana Arif and Saeb Khalid were feeling, and how this might affect their future and that of their daughter. The lives of millions of Palestinians had changed, he feared — adding a generation, perhaps more, to all those held hostage to six decades of hatred. "We're watching a tragedy," he told Carole.

"What else could Israel do?" she inquired simply.

Her tone implied the rest: the "tragedy" was the murders she and David had witnessed, not the reprisal that followed. After a time Carole said, "There's a memorial service in Jerusalem for Amos

Ben-Aron. We should go, David."

The comment, David sensed, held multiple meanings: that it was not only important politically but important to Carole, sealing David's connection to Israel.

"I'll do my best," he answered, then rushed off to Channel 2.

Only when David arrived did he hear, from Amy Chan, that Ibrahim Jefar had been transferred from the hospital to a detention center, and had retained a lawyer from the federal public defender.

"Our sources," Amy told him on camera, "say that the lawyer, Peter Burden, has initiated discussions with the U.S. attorney. What might those discussions be?"

David sat back. "In one sense, Jefar holds all the cards — he's the only one who may know for sure who recruited them, who helped them, who handled them, how they breached Ben-Aron's security, and how they could come to a strange city and acquire all they needed to pull of this assassination."

"Seems like that makes him invaluable as a witness," Chan said. "He's the survivor who wasn't intended to survive."

"Sure. But this man helped kill the prime minister of Israel. Marnie Sharpe's not free to cut a deal — I'd be shocked if any potential deal wasn't first vetted at the White House. The most Jefar can aspire to is a life sentence in a safe place, maybe with the possibility of parole — a brief window of freedom between old age and death, in a world that has forgotten to despise him." David's tone was sardonic. "He's free to hope, I guess. After all, he's only twenty-two.

"As for the prosecutor," David continued, "the

aggressive approach is for Marnie Sharpe to tell Jefar's lawyer that his client has one day — and one day only — to tell the government what he'd say in court without having it used against him. But if Sharpe and his lawyer make a deal and then Jefar's testimony about the plot is different from the *basis* for that deal, Sharpe can use his admissions to convict him.

"It's called 'Queen for a Day.' This particular game has only one rule: tell the truth or die." David paused for emphasis. "There won't be a lot of trust here. A decent defense lawyer will demand a deal in writing. And Sharpe is going to want corroborating evidence — something that says Jefar's telling the truth. If she goes to trial and Jefar changes his story, he'll immortalize her as a fool. Even sending him to the death chamber won't compensate for *that*."

Ibrahim sat in a sterile room facing his lawyer, a skinny, bearded man who seemed more like a teacher than a fearsome advocate. "It's remarkable," the lawyer had told him on their first meeting. "Not only did you not succeed in dying, but you came out with nothing but scrapes and burns. So now you get to choose again."

Ibrahim was alone, cut off from all he had known, denied the honor of death. A miasma of nothingness descended on him. He was staring into the void of an afterlife he had never imagined, in the company of strangers — including this man who spoke to him of cooperation, of making his own situation better, of living with air to breathe instead of dying. His soul felt more shattered than his body.

"They know nothing," the lawyer was saying.

"Suppose, just for argument, that you were recruited on the West Bank. Suppose you start your story there. Whatever you tell me, I can't tell anyone unless you let me."

Ibrahim rubbed his temples. He could not bring himself to eat; his stomach was empty, and the hunger fed a pulsing headache, which made him feel nauseous. "I never talked to her — it was always Iyad."

"How did they communicate?"

"Cell phones, always new ones — he'd throw the old ones away. One time he borrowed mine. His wasn't working, he said."

"When was this?"

"The day before we killed the Jew, I think. It was one of the phones he threw away."

"What number did Iyad call?"

Ibrahim struggled to remember. "At the motel, there was a piece of paper with a telephone number. I saw him memorize it."

"What happened to the piece of paper?"

"I don't know." To Ibrahim, the sound of his own voice seemed to come from a great distance. "He threw that away, too, I think."

Ibrahim's lawyer smiled. "You're lucky," he said. "They found a slip of paper in the trash. If they showed it to you, would you know if it's the one?"

Dully, Ibrahim nodded. "I think so, yes."

"And those places you described — the bus station, the shopping mall, the storage container. Would you recognize them?"

Ibrahim shook his head. "I don't know where they are. Like that storage place — all I know is it was somewhere off a highway . . ."

"They think they've found it." The lawyer smiled encouragingly, a teacher prompting a student.

"Can you remember the number on the container's door?"

Ibrahim closed his eyes. The images were like slides — the gate; the guard . . .

"Thirty-four," Ibrahim ventured. "I think it was thirty-four."

"Good." The lawyer took off his wire-rimmed glasses, wiping them with a handkerchief. Softly, he inquired "How would you like to get out of this alive, Ibrahim?"

20

Abruptly, David's television appearances tapered off: the Justice Department and Marnie Sharpe had gone completely silent — there were no leaks from the investigation, no hint of where it might be headed. David was not certain how to interpret this blackout, but it eased the juggling of commitments necessary for attending Ben-Aron's memorial service. And so, three days before he was due to go, he arrived at his office at seven-thirty, hoping to catch up on his work.

When the phone rang, shortly before eight, he was certain that his caller must be Carole.

"David?"

He felt a moment's surprise — it was as though Hana had pervaded his thoughts until, finally, she had known to call him. Quietly, he asked, "How are you?"

"All right. And you? I've been watching you on television — you are very good, and you look well. But you seem sad to me."

"I saw him die, Hana. That's some of it. I also feel like our lives — yours and even mine — won't ever be the same."

"Yes — sometimes I think that, too."

"So why haven't you gone home? Too dangerous?"

Hana hesitated. "Not that. Your government's holding our passports."

"Why?"

"I don't know. But they have something called a material witness warrant. They want to question us about Ben-Aron's assassination."

David sat up straighter. "You and Saeb?"

"And Munira, too." Hana paused again, then said more urgently, "It's absurd, I know. But I may need to see you."

David touched his forehead. "As a lawyer?"

"Yes. Also as a friend, I hope."

David settled back in his chair, acutely conscious of the passage of time, Hana awaiting his answer. "We were once more than friends, as I recall. Or was it less?"

In the silence, he imagined her intake of breath. "I am sorry, David. But I never lied to you."

"No. I suppose you never did." Glancing at his watch, David asked, "Would Saeb be coming with you?"

"Not for this. It's been stressful enough . . ."

Her voice trailed off. David stood, gazing out the window. "I'm not sure that I can help you. But you do need someone, it seems."

"Thank you, David." Relief flooded her voice. "I did not know what you would say."

When Hana hung up, David closed his eyes, still holding the receiver.

Two nights before his graduation from law school, Hana had come to his apartment.

At first she had said nothing. As though possessed by emotion she could not express in words, she had kissed him with impetuous fury and, as she had never done before, began unbuttoning his shirt, her lips sliding down his stomach. David felt the beating of his own pulse, the shiver of desire. Then, for the first time, she took him in her mouth.

David raised her face to his. "No, Hana. I want *us*."

Eyes closing, she nodded. He led her to the bedroom. She undressed swiftly, turning away as though she could not face him.

"Look at me," he said. "I want to see you."

Turning, she looked into his eyes, slipping out of her jeans. When she was naked, Hana asked softly, "Do you see me now, David?"

Suddenly he was afraid to ask why she had come. She took his hand, drawing him down beside her on the cool white sheets.

His lips moved across her nipples, her stomach, seeking the most intimate part of her as she murmured his name, over and over, "Please, David — yes . . ."

When he was inside her the murmurs became an urgent cry, her hips thrusting against his. Her body was taut, insistent; their lovemaking became frenzied, all barriers shattered, two people as one and yet, David sensed at the edge of his consciousness, separate in their own need. Her last cries became a shudder he felt against his skin. "God," she said in a voice suffused with pain. "The price of you . . ."

He chose to hear this as the crossing of her psychic bridge, the decision to be with him. "It'll be all right," he said after a time. "My parents will be here tomorrow. You can meet them — they can't help but like you, I know . . ."

She turned from him, burying her face in the pillow. Then she gave the smallest shake of her head, as though completely spent. "I can't."

For a long time she lay prone, silent. David could

only wait, fearful of her response. He guessed, but was not sure, that Hana was crying.

When she turned to him, he saw that this was true. But her voice was clear and quiet. "I'm going back to Lebanon, to marry Saeb."

David could not comprehend this — their lovemaking, then her words, as cold to him as a death sentence. "You can't, Hana. It's not human. You've been in prison so long you can't believe you're free."

"Free," she said with sudden anger. "You keep using that word, 'free.' Don't you see — I am Palestinian, you are American and Jewish. To marry you would deny everything I am. In our culture we don't just marry a man. We marry his family, his history, just as he marries ours.

"No one asks you who your parents are. But among my people, the first question is, 'You are the daughter of whom?' I could never replace my family, or betray them — it would be like cutting off a limb." Her voice quickened, the sound of emotions bursting their bonds. "I would be a traitor in their eyes, the wife of an enemy, making them carry my shame to the grave. They've always been my source of love —"

"What kind of love," David snapped, "cuts a daughter off from it? What about loving you as much as they love themselves? Maybe even enough — though this must be hard for you to imagine — to care about whether you're happy?"

Hana stood abruptly, staring at him in anger. She began to dress. Then, perhaps because she saw the depth of his pain, she spoke more quietly. "This is not a drama of Montagues and Capulets, a story of blind adults and clear-eyed children in love. My parents are Palestinian."

"That can't be all that matters to you."

"*You* matter to me." Suddenly her voice broke. "I love you, David. I think perhaps I will always love you. But there are so many things that tell me, in the deepest part of my soul, that I must be with Saeb. Please, try to understand. No man by himself could heal the pain of losing my family. Not even you."

She turned from him, pulling on her sweater. In the turmoil of his emotions — anger, desperation, disbelief — David felt the last vestige of self-control slip away. "You say you love me," he said tightly. "But do you know what's even worse? The empty life you're running to."

Hana whirled on him, eyes alight with resentment. But then something akin to fear seemed to dull her outrage. "Good-bye," she said in a hollow voice.

David reached out for her. "Hana . . ."

She turned from him, rushing to the living room. In the instant it took for her to close his front door, she vanished from David's life.

David graduated from law school in a trance, acting out the pleasure his parents had come to see. He never spoke of Hana; they never knew that she existed. He could not bear for her to be as vivid to others as she would always be to him.

David and his parents flew back to San Francisco. Later, when he saw his father's photo of him, smiling as he received his diploma, David could not recall the moment.

21

Sitting across from Amy Chan the next morning, David sipped freshly roasted coffee from a mug emblazoned "Channel 2." One of the virtues of living in San Francisco, David reflected, was that even TV stations had good coffee. But his mood was bleak — images of Ben-Aron's death filled his mind, and the day's news featured still more death, the murder of three Israelis near the settlement of Bar Kochba.

"We understand," Amy Chan said to David, "that you'll be attending the memorial service for Amos Ben-Aron."

The question caught David by surprise — the information must have come from Burt Newman. "Yes," he answered simply.

Chan clearly hoped for more. "You were friends."

"Better just to say that I admired him." With that answer — which others would take as modesty — David knew, to his profound discomfort, that he had made himself sound more important to a dead man than he had ever been in life.

"Let's turn again to his tragic murder," Chan was saying smoothly. "According to sources inside the investigation, Ibrahim Jefar has begun proffering scraps of information through his lawyer. If you were Marnie Sharpe, how would you determine whether to believe him?"

"Besides corroborating evidence? She can ask him to take a polygraph —"

"Those aren't admissible, right?"

"Not in court. And it's a gamble for the prosecution — if he names a coconspirator, that person's lawyer may be able to obtain Jefar's answers." David shrugged. "But what'll keep Marnie up at night is the fear that he's still lying, or covering something up. A polygraph's better than nothing."

Ibrahim began pacing — the tiny room felt stifling, and they would not let him exercise. In a tentative tone, his lawyer said, "Sharpe says she needs to give you a lie detector test —"

"I am not a liar," Ibrahim snapped.

The lawyer watched him closely. "Perhaps she just wants to know that you're willing to take it. But I can't promise you she's bluffing."

Ibrahim turned to him. "So?"

"So," the lawyer answered coolly, "unless you think you can pass it, I strongly advise we tell her no."

Ibrahim folded his arms. "I tried to kill my enemy, and myself. I am not afraid of a test."

The room they used was bigger than where Ibrahim met with his lawyer; it held a laminated table with room for his lawyer, Marnie Sharpe, an FBI agent, and a laconic polygraph examiner. Ibrahim did not like being wired to a machine whose instruments measured his honor as a human being, or the way this examiner asked questions: toneless, persistent, probing for inconsistencies.

"You were a member of Al Aqsa?" the examiner asked.

"Yes. I told you that."

"Did you get your instructions from Iyad Hassan?"

"Yes."

"Did you discuss the plot to kill Ben-Aron with other members of Al Aqsa?"

"No. Again, no."

Expressionless, Sharpe and the examiner watched as the paper spooled, bearing marks Ibrahim could not see. "And you never discussed the plot with anyone but Iyad?"

"No. As I said, it was a matter of operational security."

"And Iyad gave you your instructions?"

"Yes."

"And did he receive instructions from someone else?"

"Yes."

"Did you speak to that person?"

"No," Ibrahim said impatiently. "Listen to my answers."

The examiner did not react. "Did Iyad tell you who that person was?"

Ibrahim felt clammy. Now, when it was too late, he found himself reluctant to answer.

Marnie Sharpe scrutinized him like a specimen on a slide. Ibrahim remained silent.

"Let me repeat the question," the examiner said. "Did Iyad tell you who that person was?"

Ibrahim bowed his head. "Yes," he said at last. "The same woman who recruited him. The professor from Birzeit."

Part II
The Labyrinth

1

With a quiet knock on his office door, Hana Arif reentered David's life as swiftly as she had left it.

She paused on the threshold. Beneath the flowing dress she was still slim, her carriage straight and proud, the sense of kinetic energy at rest still present. Her eyes remained brown pools, but somehow older, their fires banked. Her face had aged but subtly — her skin was perhaps closer to the bone, and when she smiled at him, the first hint of lines appeared at the corners of her eyes. To David, she had the beauty that only time can bring, reminding him that this had happened outside of his awareness, and that he knew nothing about who she had become.

"So," she said wryly. "Now you are my lawyer."

Standing, David managed a smile of his own. "You're free to hope."

"I said that once, didn't I." She came to him quickly, standing on tiptoe to give him a chaste kiss on the cheek, leaving a small tingle of electricity on David's skin. "You look wonderful, David — even better than on television. Time has been good to you."

David smiled again. "I exercise," he said lightly.

Hana gazed at him, silent, then scanned his office as if searching for something to do. Walking to his bookshelf, she studied a framed photograph. "This is Carole?"

"Yes."

Head tilted, Hana appraised her picture. "A good face, I think — warm. But smart-looking. More than a nice Jewish girl."

"Nice Jewish girls," David answered, "were never my obsession."

"No. As I remember, you had no ethnic requirements."

There was irony in her tone and, perhaps, the hint of an apology. When she turned to him, plainly disconcerted, David motioned her to the couch. "Tell me about your visit from the FBI."

She sat a few feet from him, ankles crossed, regarding him with quiet gravity. "Before we start," she said, "I am very grateful to you for seeing me. And it is very good to see you, David. There isn't a day I haven't thought of you." Amending this with a smile, she added more lightly, "Or, at least, a week. My life has been rich with incident."

David did not return her smile. "So it seems. How does Saeb feel about you coming here?"

Hana straightened her skirt, her expression pensive. "Ambivalent, at best. But not so ambivalent about the vagaries of the American legal process in the wake of Ben-Aron's assassination." Hana angled her head, making eye contact again. "We both watched you on television, and it's clear you know the system very well. And it's not as though we have a list of local lawyers passionate to help us."

"I imagine not. Given Saeb's political leanings, I'm surprised our government let him come here."

Hana shrugged. "Saeb has no record of violence — merely violent opinions. It is not like admitting a friend of Osama Bin Laden." Briefly Hana looked away. "We are not terrorists, David. Nor are we wealthy. We have little money for lawyers."

"We'll worry about that later. Though I'm wondering who paid for your trip."

"We're also not destitute," she said with a note of defensiveness. "But our trip was sponsored by a broad coalition — Palestinian opponents of the occupation, representatives of the refugees in Lebanon, university professors, even European peace activists. People who believe that our story remains untold in America, and that we Palestinians remain stereotypes — terrorists or victims, never ordinary people —"

"Ibrahim Jefar," David interjected, "made Saeb's mission a little tougher. And he's from Birzeit, where both of you teach. Did you or Saeb know him *or* Iyad Hassan?"

David's abruptness seemed to wound her. "So, it's on to business," she said more coolly. "As for me, I checked to see whether either were students of mine, and no. Nor can Saeb recall ever having met them. Birzeit has several thousand students, and one does not befriend them all." Her tone became quietly angry. "That leaves Munira — twelve years old — as the plotter in our midst."

David walked to his desk, picked up a legal pad and pen, and went back to the couch. "Who contacted you from the FBI?"

"A man named Victor Vallis came to our hotel. Do you know him?"

"No. He must be out of Washington." David wrote down the name. "What did Vallis say?"

"That he had a material witness warrant, and we could not leave America. He wanted to question us right away. When we said we wanted to consult a lawyer, he took our passports. Then he said he wanted to meet with us, and Munira, on Thursday."

Three days from now, David noted. "Did Vallis indicate why he wanted to question you, or their basis for keeping you in San Francisco?"

"Not specifically." Sitting back, Hana folded her hands. "We're Palestinian, we teach at Birzeit, we oppose the occupation, and we followed Ben-Aron to San Francisco. Isn't that enough?"

"Maybe. But tell me more about the current state of Saeb's politics. And yours."

Hana gazed at her hands. At length, she said quietly, "We should start with where you and I left off, David. The dawn of the Oslo Accords, the harbinger of peace. We were going to have a country, remember? Instead the Israelis doubled their settlements, confiscated more lands, and divided us into Bantustans isolated by Israeli security roads, and checkpoints that can turn a twenty-minute drive home into a three-hour nightmare. Unemployment rose, per capita income dropped —"

"What about the first intifada," David cut in, "all the suicide bombers beginning in 2000 —"

"After years of Israeli occupation," Hana retorted. "Creating more suicide bombers by the day, and destroying any pretense of Zionist morality." Pausing, Hana spoke more evenly. "Saeb would argue that Arafat was of little help. He imported a group of PLO fighters who became the privileged class, profiting from monopolies, patronage, and corruption instead of building a real government that served its people. Arafat governed — to the extent he had the will or power to govern at all — out of his back pocket. So between them, Arafat and the Israelis helped create Hamas, while Israel catered to a fanatic minority, their settler-zealots. Based on their collective legacy, our children can look forward to nothing but violence.

"I will tell you a story, David. A friend of mine was making a documentary about the children in a refugee camp outside Ramallah. The day I went with her she was filming young boys who'd saved up money to taxi to a checkpoint and throw stones at Jewish soldiers." Recalling this, Hana gazed into some middle distance. "They passed through two checkpoints to reach a third — barren, without shade, the heat shimmering off the asphalt road. Why, I asked a boy Munira's age, did they travel to this place?" Abruptly Hana turned to David, as though striving to convey what she had seen. "He was very thin, with large brown eyes — sensitive-looking, as Saeb had been at that age. His answer was that the Israeli soldiers had not shot anyone at the other checkpoints, but had killed his best friend's brother at *this* one. And I understood that this boy, barely able to comprehend death, was hoping to be killed."

To David, her tone conveyed the weariness of someone who had seen such things since childhood, and now was seeing them through the eyes of another generation of wounded children. "I asked," Hana continued, "what he wished to be when he grew up — a doctor, or perhaps a scientist? He gave me a look of incomprehension — if he lived long enough, growing up to him meant killing some Israelis when he died." Hana gazed out the window at David's view of the Golden Gate Bridge, but she did not appear to see it. "I despise the men who turn children into human bombs — one sees no 'leaders' of the resistance sending their sons to die. But this boy was a tragedy in the making. Even Ibrahim Jefar will have a story."

"I somehow doubt I'll work up any sympathy for Jefar."

"Perhaps not. But now I find myself remembering how you and I would talk of the Holocaust, of Jews living with a collective memory of violence. I worry about my people in this way — to be the subject of violence distorts the soul. And yet the Israelis themselves still cannot acknowledge the poison of their occupation."

"This poison," David interrupted, "how badly has it affected Saeb?"

Hana sat back, choosing her words. "Differently from me," she said at length. "I, too, am sick to death of Israel and Israelis. But I would accept a two-state solution *if* — and I sincerely doubt this — the Jews were willing to give us a viable country.

"Saeb has no doubt they never will. For him, Jews drove his grandparents out of Galilee, planned his parents' slaughter, and now occupy the place that Israel calls our 'homeland' — imprisoning us with or without cause, humiliating us at checkpoints in front of our own children, killing other children who throw stones." Pausing, Hana studied her hands, and David sensed within her a quiet sadness. "The Zionists have defined Saeb for himself. It shames him to have been studying in America instead of resisting on the West Bank, just as it shames him not to have died trying to protect his sister, even though he was just a boy. Sometimes he mocks himself as a 'rhetorician — the great theorist of struggle.' "

David set down his legal pad. "I don't know about the U.S. attorney, Hana. But if I were Marnie Sharpe and knew what you just told me, *I* might want the FBI to question Saeb."

Hana looked into his eyes. "I'm Saeb's wife," she

answered simply. "I've known him since we were children, and *we* have a child now. In his heart he may have wished Ben-Aron dead. But if Saeb were involved in killing him, I believe that I would know."

David studied her. "When you first called me," he reminded her, "you told me that Saeb had become much more Islamic. Tell me what you meant."

Silent, Hana contemplated his question and, David guessed, her marriage. "That is something," she responded, "that I've considered a great deal. And I've come to believe that much of it has to do with Munira."

"How so?"

"I'm not quite sure. But for a man, male authority — to demand the respect and obedience of one's children — is a hallmark of our culture. And yet Palestinian children see their fathers treated like cattle by teenage Jewish soldiers." Hana raised her head. "One weekend, we were stopped on the way to a wedding — Saeb, Munira, and I. Two armed Israeli soldiers forced Saeb to get out of the car and remove his shirt and belt. He stood there in the sun, looking frail between these strapping soldiers in combat gear as they joked about God knows what.

"I glanced into the back seat. Munira stared at the soldiers with such hatred that I was glad *she* did not have a gun — this girl, eleven years old. And yet I think what she hated most was not the soldiers but her own confusion at witnessing her father's impotence." Hana's tone bore the weight of a crucial memory, sifted and resifted. "When Saeb got back in the car," she went on, "I tried to pretend that things were still normal. Neither of them would speak.

"So I think there is this disturbance in their relationship, and that Saeb now looks to Islam as a way of restoring his proper role as a father — just as he has come to believe that it is Islam, and not Marxism, that will restore our dignity as Arabs. But that is a difficulty in our marriage, because I am Munira's model of a woman. Saeb wishes her to cover, and asks that I do. He forbids her to spend time with boys, and presses me not to socialize with men." Briefly, Hana looked down. "And he wishes to arrange her marriage, as our parents did for us."

David chose not to comment. "And you?"

"I wish for a more secular society, and a more secular home." Hana gazed at him directly. "For Munira, I want the best education and a good career — even to study in America, perhaps. And I want her to have reasonable independence."

"More than you had?"

Hana's gaze didn't waver. "Perhaps," she answered softly. "There still are things she doesn't yet know to want."

What those things might be, Hana's tone suggested, was not open for discussion. "Munira," she continued, "has her *own* ambivalence about me. For several years I was a consultant to our peace negotiators, spending nights away. Munira resented that — more than once she told me that when *she* grew up, she would never leave her children.

"One night she even managed to blame *me* for the occupation. At three A.M., soldiers broke down the gate outside our apartment building in Ramallah, locked us inside the building, and searched each apartment door-to-door. Munira was badly frightened. But when they had left, she screamed at me, 'If you're such a great peace negotiator, why are the Jews still here?' "

Quiet, David contemplated the distance between them — the ways in which Hana had been redefined by marriage, motherhood, and thirteen years of living he could only try to imagine. "You said Munira was scarred by the occupation. Is that what you meant?"

Hana gave a quick shake of the head. "I meant much more," she answered. "As a child she would awaken to the thunder of the Israelis shelling the homes where people they called terrorists lived. For a brief time she wet the bed again. And since she saw Arafat's compound reduced to rubble, she's had great trouble sleeping.

"If she grows up whole enough, there is hope. Women can advance in our society — even now, twenty percent of our legislature are women. But Munira must somehow heal, and decide for herself what kind of woman she wants to be." Hana's smile was fond but fleeting. "The name Munira means 'radiates life' — it was my expression of hope for a baby girl. My hope for her now is that this turns out to be so."

"And what does 'Hana' mean?" he asked. "I never knew."

" 'Serenity,' " Hana answered. "And satisfaction. As in contentment."

They both let the remark linger. "If it's any source of reassurance," she added with a smile, "Saeb means 'always truthful.' A good name for a prospective client."

"No doubt. Which brings me to whether Saeb — or you — has had any association with what the Israelis so impolitely call 'terrorist groups.' Starting with the Al Aqsa Martyrs Brigade."

Hana's smile vanished. "I don't have a membership card in Al Aqsa — or Hamas, Hezbollah, or Islamic Jihad. I don't ask others if *they* do. But it's impossible to teach at Birzeit and not know students or colleagues affiliated with Al Aqsa or Hamas — even if you aren't sure which ones. So if these two students were Al Aqsa, that would be no surprise.

"About Saeb, I have no reason to believe that he plays with matches — or people who carry out violence. But I would say that he has great sympathy for Hamas. They embrace Islam, principally to emphasize that they are not corrupt and will not be diverted from ridding us of Israelis."

"Including the ones in Israel?"

"Yes. That's another reason Saeb admires them."

"But not you."

"But not me." Hana looked into his face. "I'm so tired of it, David. I won't deny distrusting Amos Ben-Aron. But his death will mean more suffering and bloodshed — more Palestinians than Israelis, I believe. Still, it will do great harm to us both.

"You asked me once where history begins. I know that it did not begin in 1948, or at Tel Zaatar, or Sabra and Shatila. I know now that we must tolerate Israel as our neighbor. But we can have no real future without dealing with the past. In that way, Ben-Aron was right — there is no sense in telling my stateless parents, trapped in Lebanon, that the West Bank is their homeland. Israel must give my parents their dignity, and my daughter a country of her own. So that is what I wish for — more vainly than ever, it seems now."

Silent, David wondered if they would ever be closer to that day than when he and Hana were lovers. "So," she said abruptly, "the FBI. I know we can refuse to talk to them. Should we?"

"That depends. Someone needs to talk with the U.S. attorney, find out whatever she's willing to say. Which may not be that much."

Hana hesitated. "I know," she said at length, "that helping us would not be a popular course for you. I even worried about coming here — for all I know, the FBI is following me."

"For all *I* know. But I could hardly turn you away."

Hana seemed to study him, trying to read his meaning. "Then you believe me?" she asked hopefully. "You will help us?"

I want to believe you, David thought. *And I wish you had never come.* Every instinct he possessed, personal and professional, filled him with unease.

"Perhaps with the FBI," he answered. "Not if it goes further."

Hana summoned a tenuous smile. "With your advice," she said with more assurance, "there's less reason that it should."

Her relief, David found, only deepened his disquiet. "Are you *that* sure about Saeb?"

"As I said, he is my husband —"

"That much I know. Though I'm less sure what that tells me about Saeb Khalid. I seem to remember disagreeing about his character before you chose to marry him."

Hana gave him an enigmatic look. "I remember, David. I've forgotten very little."

For a time, David could only gaze at her. "I've always wondered," he said at last, "why you married him so quickly."

Hana looked down. "I had to, David. You and I were destroying me."

Abruptly standing, she murmured a brief goodbye, touching him on the wrist with cool fingertips. Only after she left did he realize that her scheduled interrogation fell the day after the memorial service for Amos Ben-Aron.

David's misgivings, already acute, deepened at Marnie Sharpe's response. "You're really giving up your new career as commentator," Sharpe inquired over the telephone, "to help these Palestinians?"

"Hana Arif is a friend of mine." David strove to maintain a tone that sounded matter-of-fact. "From law school. This is strictly a one-time engagement. The FBI is holding her, her husband, and her daughter as witnesses. She's asked me to advise them. Before I can, or can even know whether I can help them both, I need to know the nature of your interest."

Sharpe took a moment to answer. "We're interested in quite a lot," she said brusquely. "We want to know what they did here, where they went, who they met, who they spoke with on the telephone, and what they know about Ibrahim Jefar and Iyad Hassan."

"What does Jefar say?"

Sharpe ignored this. "So if *you* want to know about the husband and wife, they're decidedly 'people of interest.' As for Munira Khalid, she's the *daughter* of two people of interest, so that makes her of interest, too. More than that I'm not prepared to say. Except this," Sharp finished tersely.

"Until now, I never took you for a fool. Why this woman is of such concern to such an ambitious man eludes me."

With that, Sharpe got off, leaving David to wonder what Sharpe was not yet telling him.

2

Carole's expression — level gaze, lips slightly compressed — betrayed her effort to avoid inflaming a serious quarrel. "This makes no sense to me," she said evenly. "None."

They sat in Carole's apartment: David in his tuxedo, Carole in a black evening dress, ready to attend opening night at the opera, a modern restaging of *Don Carlo*. Instead they were running late, evidence, at least to Carole, that this discussion could not wait. "They were friends of mine," David tried again.

"*She* was your friend," Carole amended. "Who you haven't seen — or thought about, as far as I know — for thirteen years. Suddenly she's more important than Amos Ben-Aron."

"Ben-Aron's dead," David said flatly.

"With Hana Arif's assistance, for all you really know." Pausing, Carole added, "Of all cases, why touch one so disturbing to so many people? Starting with us, I thought."

"They're professors, Carole. They have a twelve-year-old daughter. This may be nothing more than Marnie Sharpe casting too broad a net. Everyone — the media, the Justice Department, even the White House — is desperate to know who planned the assassination." David spread his hands. "The

FBI simply wants to interview them, that's all. They don't have a lot of money, they want to take their daughter home, and they're worried about being Palestinians in a post-9/11 America intent on atoning for the murder of a Jewish statesman in a city where they happened to be."

"They didn't just *happen* to be here. I saw Saeb Khalid on television, remember?" Catching herself, Carole spoke more softly. "Of the two of us, you're the one who plays the cynic. This is the first time I've ever thought of you as naive. How can you just blow off this memorial service — as my fiancé, as a man who wants to enter politics, and as a human being who met and admired Ben-Aron? All for a couple of Arab anti-Semites who despised him."

Watching her, David had the odd sensation of doubleness: in his heart and mind, Hana Arif and Carole Shorr had resided in different places — one a searing memory, the other his settled future. Now, within hours, they had collided, disturbing his sense of psychic balance. "It *is* important," David tried to temporize. "You're important. But I'm the only lawyer in San Francisco that Hana knows. I also know that Hana Arif does *not* hate all Jews."

Carole gave him a troubled look. "And you learned all this by knowing her in law school."

David felt a stab of guilt. "Is that really so absurd? Look at us now. Every few months we'll meet two of our friends for dinner and have a four-sided conversation, where each of us says whatever little we care for three other people to know. In law school, at least we had a little time —"

"Time for what, David?" Carole's tone was pointed. "You're talking about everything but

Hana Arif. Tell me, please, how you got to know this woman so well that you'd just import her into our lives, confident that she couldn't possibly have been involved with the terrorists who murdered Ben-Aron."

This was so like Carole, David thought — her evenness, her persistence, her quiet perceptiveness. *We were lovers,* part of him wanted to acknowledge. But he could not. "Every now and then," he said, "you meet someone whose character you grasp at once. I felt that the night I met you."

"We're lovers," Carole protested. "We're getting married. You've had two years to confirm your first impression. How can you compare that to someone you knew at law school?"

He was stumbling, David thought, hitting one false note after the other. And yet the truth, he rationalized, would cause more hurt than his well-intentioned dissembling. "There's no comparison," he assured her. "I'm just asking you to trust my judgment.

"I just spent two hours with Hana. She's a mother now, and she's sick to death of killing. She knows that Ben-Aron's assassination is as much a disaster for Palestinians as for Jews — bigger, maybe. It looks to me like Hana and her family have been caught up in the riptide."

"Even her husband?" Carole asked.

Though it went to the heart of his uncertainty, her question about Saeb was a welcome diversion from Hana Arif. "Carole," David said firmly, "if I had a concrete reason to believe that Saeb *or* Hana know anything about what we saw on Market Street, I wouldn't touch this. That holds true tomorrow, and the next day. Not just because the case would be political plutonium, but because I couldn't sleep at night."

Carole appraised him — unsatisfied, he thought, but reluctant to go further. "All right," she said with a tone of resignation. "Maybe Dad will go with me to Israel."

The following morning, David drove Carole and Harold Shorr — both unusually quiet — to the airport.

Entering David's office, Saeb Khalid shepherded his wife to the couch, his manner protective, even proprietary. Although they sat together, David noticed — or perhaps wished — that Hana seemed distant from her husband.

Saeb's handshake had been perfunctory; moving closer to Hana, his gaze at David was wary and unsmiling. Then, to David's surprise, Saeb said quietly, "You are good to help us. Especially me, who you barely knew."

That was gracious enough, David thought, although the remark could have been double-edged. "After the three of us finish talking," David said to Saeb, "I'll have to speak with you in private, as I did with Hana. At least I'll know — at least as much as I can — that there's no conflict between the two of you."

"As in conflict of interest?" Saeb inquired with an indecipherable smile. "I think I understand. But I can tell you right away that I know nothing. Having studied the pictures of Iyad Hassan, I believe now that I may have met him — though where or how I cannot resurrect. As for Ibrahim Jefar, nothing. Which is what I know about the murder of Ben-Aron."

This response, at least, was mercifully free of cant. Quickly, David cataloged the changes in Saeb

Khalid. Though, as on television, the beard made the contours of his face seem harder, his liquid eyes remained sensitive, and his small frame was even slighter, conveying a frailty at war with his fierceness of spirit. "Let's turn to what you're dealing with," David said. "Right now, no one knows that Sharpe and the FBI are looking at you. But they're under enormous stress — hour after hour of television, front-page article after article, pressure from the White House, the Department of Justice, the State of Israel, and the Jewish community in America, with the rest of the world — particularly the Arab countries — looking on. That's their dilemma, and it's yours. Because it colors whatever they decide to do."

Though Hana shot her husband a look of concern, Saeb's expression remained impenetrable. "Ibrahim Jefar is talking," David continued. "That much we know. But Sharpe's got the investigation locked down tight — no statements, no calculated leaks. So we can only guess what Jefar's saying, or where the government is going with it.

"Sharpe wants you for a reason, and we don't know what it is. But to succeed she needs a whole lot more than Ibrahim Jefar. She needs to nail down who gave Jefar his orders, and who conspired to kill Israel's prime minister." Gazing at Saeb, David kept his voice clipped, factual. "So let me be plain, at the risk of being insulting. If Jefar knows anything that can implicate either one of you, that person should consider shutting up, at least with the FBI. Of course, that would bring you greater scrutiny. But if they already know you're involved, lying can make it worse. There's no point in cooperating unless the truth is helpful."

Saeb's eyes narrowed. "That's admirably direct."

"And?"

"I've nothing to hide from your authorities. Nor does Hana."

To David's ears, the last remark was ambiguous — it could be taken as a statement of confidence or as an order to his wife. Hana said nothing; in Saeb's presence, she seemed to recede, perhaps deferring to his complex feelings regarding David.

"Then let's talk about Munira," David suggested.

Saeb held up his hand. "There's no reason to discuss Munira. I will not have my daughter bullied by your government."

"That's up to you," David said, then quietly amended, "and Hana, of course. But we still need to talk about Munira's situation. They've already taken her passport, so they can keep her here as long as they keep you. What they can't do is make her talk." David looked from Hana to Saeb. "Nonetheless, I'd like to talk with her myself."

Saeb folded his arms. "If she's not talking to them," he answered, "why is it necessary that she even meet you?"

Hana, David noted, watched her husband carefully, seeming to suppress a frown. "Not 'necessary,' " David answered. "But preferable. You asked for my advice, so I'm giving it to you. Were there ever a trial, for *any* reason, the government could force her to testify, and whether we allow her to meet with the FBI has some strategic pros and cons.

"The cons are that she's twelve years old. You — or Hana — don't have to be hiding something to worry about carelessness, or thoughtlessness, in a child being interrogated by adults. But every question the FBI asks, of anyone, tells us more about what they're thinking. Munira may even know something that turns out to help one or both of you." David looked toward Hana. "I'd also like to get some sense of her maturity."

"Munira," Hana asserted with a quick glance at Saeb, "is highly intelligent, and quite mature. I see no problem with her meeting you."

A moment's irritation flashed in Saeb's eyes, and he placed a hand on Hana's arm. "If you must speak with her," he told David, "I must be present. As her father."

"As her father," David answered, "you might influence what she has to say. I'd hope to achieve some sort of rapport, if only to see how Munira reacts when she's not with either one of you. That will also help me advise you about the FBI. After that, the three of you can decide what Munira should do."

Slowly, Hana nodded. Though silent, Saeb looked even more resentful — an Arab man in America, dealing with another man he disliked, in a treacherous realm the other man had mastered. Turning to Hana, David asked, "Have you gathered up everything I've asked for?"

"Whatever we have," she answered. "Cell phone records, credit card slips, hotel receipts, and the documents from our rental car — mileage, even the amount of gas we used." Frown lines appeared on her forehead. "I hope all that won't be necessary."

"I hope so, too. But if the FBI tries to reconstruct every day you spent here, I'd like to have done that first."

Staring at the carpet, Saeb remained quiet. "Saeb," David said with a fair attempt at wryness, "let's visit without Hana for a while. You and I have some catching up to do."

■ ■ ■ ■

Alone with David, Saeb made no attempt at social niceties. "Let's get this done," he said.

"Why don't we. Starting with whether you really want me to represent you."

Saeb shrugged dismissively. "That was Hana's notion. But I'm sure you're more than capable." His tone became quietly caustic. "Though if innocence counts for anything in the murder of this great man, any lawyer would do nicely."

David sat back. "I admired Amos Ben-Aron," he said curtly. "Remembering that will make this easier on us both."

"All right." Saeb spread his hands in a pantomime of openness. "To you, he was great. To me, he's just dead. But I had nothing to do with that —"

"Do you have anything to do with the Al Aqsa Martyrs Brigade?"

"No. They profess to believe in a two-state solution. I do not. My sympathy is with Hamas."

"Including suicide bombers?"

"Including suicide bombers. Especially the martyr who died with Amos Ben-Aron — as distinct from this coward who lived to talk." Saeb fixed David with an adamantine stare. "To me, killing Ben-Aron was an act of resistance. If it also kills this phony peace plan, the better for my people."

David felt his jaw tighten. "I appreciate your candor. But you'll want to skip the editorials when you tell the FBI you're innocent. Your enthusiasm for murder might confuse them."

Saeb accorded him an icy smile. "Are *you* so sure you wish to represent me?"

"I'm doing this for Hana — we both know that.

And, I suppose, for a twelve-year-old girl I've yet to meet, but whom Hana plainly loves. Right now I'm clinging to that."

Saeb regarded him inscrutably. "All right," he said at length. "This much I owe you. I don't know these men. I don't know who helped them. I know nothing."

"Who proposed your trip here?"

"I did, although it was Hana's desire to come with me, and to bring Munira. The purpose of my sponsors was simple: to expose Ben-Aron's peace plan as a fraud, shrouded in noble rhetoric and his generous grant of geriatric return." Saeb gave an elegant shrug that conveyed both helplessness and disdain. "Perhaps in America, exposing Zionist hypocrisy is a crime all by itself. Other than that, I am completely without guilt. And so is Hana."

David cocked his head. "And you know about Hana because . . ."

"Because she actually mourns Ben-Aron's death, if not the man himself." Pausing, Saeb stared into David's eyes. "You knew her once — very well, I sometimes think. Can you imagine her as the mastermind of a suicide bombing? I cannot."

David met his stare. "What I can imagine, and what I know, are different."

"I know no more than you do. Perhaps less."

Saeb's comment, though delivered in the flattest of tones, nonetheless carried the same curious resonance, another intimation of double meaning. "Where were you," David asked, "when Ben-Aron was murdered?"

"At the hotel, with Munira. I'd listened to his speech on CNN. I was making notes for a statement of my own when they broke in to say that he'd been killed."

"And Hana?"

"Was shopping, she told me — she did not care to watch him. I watched only so that I'd be able to refute him." A spurt of anger suffused Saeb's face and voice. "By dying, Ben-Aron has trapped us in this wretched country. I'm ready for my family to leave."

For the moment, David had heard enough. "So am I," he answered softly. "For all our sakes. But first I want to meet Munira."

3

The next morning, when David arrived at their simply furnished suite in a hotel three blocks off Union Square, he was surprised to find Saeb and Hana watching coverage of Ben-Aron's memorial service.

For a time, David watched with them. The service was held on Mount Herzl; the president of the United States and then the president of Israel spoke of Amos Ben-Aron's service in war and his quest for peace. To David, his life and death encapsulated the fears and hopes of a people who felt always on the precipice of tragedy. David searched the crowd for Carole and Harold; instead, the camera panned to Ben-Aron's rival and apparent successor, Isaac Benjamin, whose thinly veiled opinion was that this memorial service captured the futility of compromise. In the hotel suite, no one spoke — Saeb, Hana, and David entertained their own thoughts, until the silence was broken by the distant crack of a sonic boom.

Startled, Hana glanced at David. "Fleet Week," he explained. "The navy does it every year — warships in the harbor, the Blue Angels flying jets in close formation just above the rooftops. Kids love it."

Saeb raised his eyebrows, mouth framing an

ironic smile. *The same jets,* David imagined him thinking, *with which Israel terrifies our children.* But all he said was "What a fortunate country you are."

David turned from the screen to Hana. "Where's Munira?" he asked.

Hana nodded toward a closed door. "In her room. I'll get her."

Hana opened the bedroom door, leaving it ajar. David heard the sound of two female voices, one higher than Hana's, murmuring in Arabic. Then Hana emerged, followed by an adolescent girl.

Unlike her mother, Munira covered her hair with a black scarf. Incongruously, she carried a boom box, which emitted the faint sound of a man singing, in Arabic, what might have been a love song. Hana said, "This is our daughter, Munira."

At the brief nod from her mother, Munira extended her hand, according him the touch of her fingertips. Her face was stronger than Hana's, he saw at once; though she had the same bright eyes, her chin was cleft, her nose more prominent. She would not become a beauty like her mother, but her looks were arresting and might, in time, become uncommonly striking, even imperious. That she would be taller than Hana was already clear, though she half-disguised this with a slump. Her gaze at David was filled with a deep reserve.

Smiling, he said, "I've looked forward to this. Back when I knew your parents, I couldn't have imagined you."

"Nor could we." Though Hana interposed this lightly, it was awkward, an obvious attempt to ease David's way. "Munira is our good fortune."

The subject of this exchange did not alter her expression. Glancing at Saeb, David asked, "Is it okay if I take Munira for a walk?"

"If you must," Saeb answered grudgingly, looking at his watch. "I shouldn't think you'd need much time."

Without responding, David turned to Munira. "Shall we go, then?"

The girl glanced at her father, as if for a cue. Briefly, he nodded; as though in mimicry, she gave David her own barely perceptible nod. Glancing at Hana, David caught a fleeting look of melancholy he could not interpret.

Gingerly, he shepherded Munira out the door.

Ten minutes later, when David found a bench for them in Union Square, Munira still had not spoken.

What to do, David wondered. In his awkwardness, he recalled that park, Union Square was where Carole, as a child, had first confronted the subject of the Holocaust. Now David sat with a Palestinian girl, head covered, as she listened to a boom box playing plaintive songs in Arabic.

"Who's the singer?" David asked.

Munira gazed at the shoppers passing in the noonday sun, affluent men and women on their way to Saks Fifth Avenue or Neiman Marcus. "Marcel Khalifa," she said at last. "Do you know him?"

"I'm afraid not."

"He's famous," Munira amplified with a touch of impatience. "He's even come to America."

David struggled for conversation. "What's this song about?" he asked.

Munira frowned. "It is the story of a Palestinian man who falls in love with an Israeli woman. 'Between her and my eyes is a gun,' he is singing — though he loves her, they are separated by hatred.

So marriage between them is impossible."

Gazing at Hana's daughter, David felt an inescapable sadness. "Do you think that?"

"Yes," she answered with quiet vehemence. "I could never be with a Jewish man."

The only Jews she had ever seen, David supposed, were soldiers. "I'm a Jewish man," he answered gently. "I'm also your parents' friend."

For the first time, she looked at him, her curiosity peering at him from beneath long eyelashes that he had not noted before. "Is that why you're helping them?"

"Yes. And you, I hope. So does it matter to you that I'm Jewish?"

Turning from him, Munira pondered the question with a look of deep contemplation, the first finger of her left hand resting against her cheek. Something in the gesture was familiar, David realized — surely from Hana, though he could summon no memory to confirm this. But the intensity of her expression was so like her mother that it briefly swept away the years. "No," she finally answered. "Not if you are a friend to both of them."

"I am."

Again, while David could not quite define it, Munira's sideways look of skepticism elicited a faint memory, though its origins eluded him. "What was she like?" the girl asked abruptly.

"Your mother?"

"Yes."

David paused to consider what attributes to choose, how familiar with Hana to seem. "She was very smart," he answered. "And confident — one of the best arguers I ever met. Sometimes it was hard for me to keep up with her."

Munira watched his face. Quietly, she asked, "She was also beautiful, you thought?"

"What do you think?"

"She's my mother," Munira answered with a faint, admonitory undertone. "She did not cover, did she?"

"No."

"Did she smoke, or drink, or go out with boys?"

Was this a twelve-year-old's curiosity, David wondered, or was she gathering data to argue on her own behalf? "When I knew your mother, Munira, she was already engaged to your father."

For a moment, Munira's look of inquiry persisted: not only was she bright, David perceived, but she seemed sensitive to nuance, perhaps from interpreting her parents' reactions to each other. With the same abruptness, she said, "My father doesn't wish me to see boys until I'm married."

David shrugged. "I'm not anyone's father, so I don't know what to say. But he's probably trying to save you a little trouble, or maybe hurt."

"Then why does my mother refuse to cover?"

Contemplating his answer, David watched a pigeon strut across the grass in front of him, puffing its chest out like a middle-aged plutocrat on his private beach. "Because, as a modern woman, she thinks differently. So do I, actually. But that's neither bad nor good. I guess that's why your mother hopes someday you'll study here — to learn more about how different people think."

"I already know what Americans think," Munira answered sharply. "They think we are nothing. So they arm Israelis to kill us. At Jenin, the Jews came with American warplanes, the F-16s, bombing women and children." The girl's fists balled, and her voice became strident. "We will never forgive the Jews, and we will never forgive America."

Though she suddenly quivered with life, so much like Hana, David could find no pleasure in it. He remembered Hana's story of the checkpoint, the two soldiers humiliating Saeb as his daughter's eyes filled with hate. "So," David ventured, "why do you think our government wants to question all of you?"

Munira folded her arms. "Because my father's a Palestinian patriot."

"All *I* know," David began, "is that they're investigating the assassination of Israel's prime minister."

"For *this,*" Munira countered contemptuously, "my *parents* are to blame? Two professors from Birzeit?"

"No one seems to be taking credit." David looked into the girl's eyes, seeking trust. "Please understand, Munira, to Americans — as well as to Marwan Faras — this is a terrible thing. Ben-Aron came here under the protection of the United States government, to speak out for peace between Jews and Palestinians. Now our government is responsible for finding out who killed him, and they're looking for information anywhere they can.

"I don't think for a moment that your mother, or your father, had anything to do with this. Once the questioning is done, I don't think the investigators will either. My job is to get this over with, so that you can get back home. So can I ask you what I think the FBI would ask?"

Narrow-eyed, Munira stared at the well-dressed passersby as though studying her parents' enemies. In her silence, the plaintive crooning of the singer filled the space between David and her. "All right," she said curtly. "My mother explained this."

David chose to adopt a tone of mild curiosity. "Then maybe we can just talk about your time in San Francisco, before the murder. How was it?"

Munira shrugged. "All right, I guess."

"What did you do?"

"She made me go a lot of places — the university at Berkeley, a restaurant where we watched some seals, a round tower where we looked out at the prison on the bay."

David could not help but smile at the girl's passionless recitation of her mother's efforts to string together sites of interest. "Alcatraz?" he asked.

"Yes. Also a bus trip through the city, and a ride on a ferryboat."

"Was that okay?"

Munira shrugged again. "I missed my friends. There was barely time to talk to them on the cell phone — my father has strict rules about that. Sometimes I was feeling like their prisoner."

David made a mental note, as a prospective father, to go light on family trips. "I suppose you were always with your parents — at least one of them."

Munira considered this. "Mostly my mother. Sometimes my father was busy, speaking out about the Zionists."

"Did you go sightseeing every day?"

"Yes. She made me."

He could piece much of this together, David thought, through credit card records and parking receipts. But the only specific interval he knew to focus on began shortly after one P.M., when the two suicide bombers, dressed as policemen, had rushed to Fourth Street as though alerted to a change in Ben-Aron's route. "During the prime minister's speech," David asked, "do you remember where you were?"

"Yes," Munira said flatly. "Watching television with my father. We listened to the Zionist's lies."

"Was your mother there?"

"No. She was out shopping."

"Why didn't you go with her?" David inquired lightly. "Shopping sounds like a lot more fun than listening to Zionist lies."

Munira did not smile. "She didn't ask me. So I stayed."

"Did you want to go?"

Reflecting, Munira brushed back a strand of hair that had escaped from her scarf. "I don't remember. She was in a hurry, I think."

The implications of the answer, at least to someone less friendly, troubled David. "Did she say that?" he asked.

"No. She was there, and then she just decided not to watch with us."

It was better not to push this, David decided. "Do you remember —"

Abruptly, Munira stood, a sudden look of panic in her eyes. David was instantly aware of the air around them, vibrating with the roar of jet planes. Turning to him, Munira cried out, "They're bombing us . . ."

David reached for her. The panic that seized her body made her tremble uncontrollably, even as she flinched from the touch of a man she did not know. Then the planes were directly overhead — the gleaming metal bellies of six fighter jets in tight formation nearly grazing the rooftops of department stores with a deafening scream. Crying out, Munira collapsed into his arms, her scarved head pressed against his face.

"It's okay," he murmured. "It's okay. That's just a

bunch of our fighter pilots, showing off. It's supposed to make us feel safe."

Though Carole was calling from Jerusalem, her voice was clear. David leaned back in his chair. "How are you?" he asked.

"Sad," she answered in a somber voice. "People here seem wounded. The whole country is numb. It's a little like I imagine Europe on the verge of World War II — a state of siege, where no one believes that what's going to happen will be good."

"And the service?"

"Very moving. Especially Ben-Aron's daughter, Anat, speaking of his dream of peace. But I didn't know whether to think that she was noble or just forlorn."

She sounded a little forlorn herself, David thought. "How's your dad?"

"Depressed. We both are."

In her voice, though toneless, David imagined hearing a faint reproach. "Is there any talk," he asked, "of a breach in Ben-Aron's personal security?"

"Some," Carole answered. "You know the press here. But the government has a lid on whatever it's investigating."

"Yes. I suppose that's no surprise."

Carole was momentarily silent. "How are your new clients?"

"All right." David hesitated. "To me, the most remarkable part was talking with Munira, their daughter. By the end, I wanted her to escape."

"From what? Her parents?"

David pondered this. "From everything," he answered.

4

The next morning's *New York Times* punctuated its coverage of Ben-Aron's memorial service with the ugly consequences of his assassination: a deadly suicide bombing at a fruit market in the Israeli coastal town of Hadera; the lethal shooting by Israeli soldiers of two alleged Al Aqsa militants outside Ramallah; a declaration by Iran's new president that Palestinians should now help "wipe the Jews off the map of our lands." On page 4, David noted, the *Times* reported the silence of the Justice Department regarding its massive investigation into the circumstances of Ben-Aron's murder, although the FBI, CIA, and Secret Service were tugging at all potential threads of information, in America and the Middle East. As to whether and how Ben-Aron's security had been breached, the Americans and Israelis were conducting separate inquiries — Israel had withdrawn its personnel from the United States, limiting the Americans to interrogating the police and Secret Service agents involved in Ben-Aron's protection. Amid all this, with little sense of how any of it might touch on the Khalid family, David and his most ambivalent client had a private meeting with the FBI in an interior conference room of the San Francisco Federal Building.

To David's surprise and concern, the FBI had asked to interview Saeb first, and then Munira, reserving Hana for last. Across the conference table, David and Saeb faced Victor Vallis, a special agent from Washington, and Ann Kornbluth of the San Francisco office. David knew Kornbluth, a plump, bespectacled, and extremely meticulous investigator renowned for her photographic memory and mastery of detail. Vallis — a bulky red-haired man with a shrewd, seamed face — was, according to a friend of David's in the Justice Department, the FBI's leading expert in counterterrorism and, as such, the agent in charge of this investigation. The fact that Sharpe had assigned the lead agent to these interviews deepened David's sense of having entered a dark room where unseen pitfalls lurked. He could only hope to divine them from the agents' questions.

The session started with Vallis's recitation of the criminal penalty for false statements to a federal officer. Hands folded in front of him, Saeb listened impassively, his contemplation of the ceiling evincing his disdain. When the questioning began, Saeb, as David had urged, listened carefully, pausing to consider his answers. What mattered, David had told him, was not his eagerness to appear helpful but the content of his responses. Choose your words, David had advised — don't guess, don't speculate, don't conjure up an answer for the sake of giving one. All of which suited Saeb's essential attitude: distaste for this interrogation, and for the agents who conducted it.

No, Saeb told them, he did not know either of the assassins — at most, he might have met the dead one. No, he was not associated with "any group that you call terrorist." No, he knew nothing about the assassination of Amos Ben-Aron. No, he had no purpose in coming to San Francisco other than refuting the prime minister. His itinerary was an open book — speeches and meetings with the media that he had no problem enumerating. All this he offered in an uninflected tone that suggested boredom and a complete lack of interest in engaging the agents in human terms. Vallis asked most of the questions; Kornbluth took meticulous notes. An hour into the session, David was no wiser as to the agents' intent.

"In your calls to and from the media," Vallis asked in a matter-of-fact voice, "did you use a cell phone or the hotel phone?"

"Cell phone."

"One, or more than one?"

"Only one."

Vallis glanced at the legal pad in front of him. "Is the number 972 (59) 696-0523?"

"Yes."

"Do you have international cell phone service?"

"Yes."

"So any cell phone calls you made in San Francisco would be reflected in the records for that same number."

"Yes."

Though David covered his reactions by scribbling notes after every response, this line of questioning — focused on cell phone use — began to trouble him. "Do you own a computer?" Vallis asked Saeb.

"Two."

"Where are they?"

"One is in my office, at Birzeit. The other is a laptop I carry with me."

"Do you use them both to word process?"

Saeb studied his hands. "Only the computer in my office."

"That's an HP desktop."

It was not a question. Briefly, Saeb met Vallis's eyes. What struck David, as it must have struck Saeb, was how much the FBI already knew. "Yes — an HP."

"Does your wife also have an office?"

"Yes."

"And her own HP desktop?"

"Yes."

Without changing expression, Vallis seemed to watch Saeb more closely. "Does she ever use your computer, or you hers?"

Saeb hesitated. "She may have used mine — I can't recall. I have no memory of using hers."

Kornbluth looked up from her notes. "What was your wife's purpose in traveling to the United States?"

"To accompany me. And to show Munira your country."

"Whose idea was that?"

Saeb paused. "To begin with, Hana's. But only after the groups I've already enumerated suggested that I shadow Ben-Aron. She had nothing to do with that."

This was Saeb's most expansive answer — the reason for his elaboration, it seemed to David, was to make clear to the FBI that his wife's presence in America was accidental, or at least derivative of his. And it suggested that Saeb, like David, had begun to sense that the FBI's focus might be his wife.

Kornbluth adjusted her glasses. "When did she decide to come?"

"We decided," Saeb corrected. "Mutually, about

three days after Israel announced Ben-Aron would be touring the United States."

"When did she know that his itinerary would include San Francisco?"

Saeb's eyes briefly flashed. "It was public information," he said in a slightly defensive tone. "*I* knew it. So did anyone who cared."

Vallis briefly glanced at Kornbluth. "During your time in San Francisco," he asked, "were you aware of your wife's movements?"

"Generally," Saeb answered. "We discussed what she might do — we arrived only a day before Ben-Aron. But I had my work."

"How often were you apart?"

Saeb gave a shrug of irritation. "Much of those two days. I did not keep a time sheet."

"When you were apart, where was your daughter, Munira?"

"With Hana, I believe. Almost always."

"What did you understand they were doing?"

"Sightseeing." Pausing, Saeb added with mild sarcasm, "I am sorry, they did not tell me what they had for lunch."

Vallis did not change expression. "Or dinner?"

"Dinner we ate together. Both nights."

"And you and your wife also slept together?"

Saeb's eyes flashed. "Of course."

"And Munira?"

"Slept in her room."

"On either night," Kornbluth interjected, "between midnight and four A.M., did you make or receive any telephone calls?"

With this question, David knew at once there was a problem — he felt as if Marnie Sharpe had just walked into the room. "No," Saeb answered flatly.

"You're certain."

"Yes. That is too late to call anyone, at least in San Francisco."

"Did anyone call you?"

"I told you, no."

Vallis leaned forward. "Did anyone call your wife?"

"No."

"How can you be certain?"

Saeb sat straighter, as though insulted. "Because we sleep together. A call to Hana would awaken me, as would a call *from* Hana to someone else. I heard no such calls."

"Could Munira have called someone?"

Saeb folded his arms. "Again, no."

"If she sleeps in another room, how would you know?"

The question, David saw, seemed to unsettle Saeb Khalid — his eyes froze, and his expression seemed to harden. "She is a child," he answered curtly. "I am her father. We have strict rules about her use of cell phones."

"Does your wife also enforce those rules?"

"Yes." Saeb's tone was adamant. "About this, we are agreed."

"Does your wife have her own cell phone?" Kornbluth asked.

"Yes."

"One, or more than one?"

Saeb hesitated. "I know of only one."

"In your family, Mr. Khalid, who pays the monthly bills?"

"I do."

"So you are aware of how many cell phones your family has."

"Of course."

"Does Munira have her own cell phone?"

"Yes. That is," Saeb added brusquely, "she had one. Through carelessness, she lost it."

"When?"

"I'm not sure. Perhaps in San Francisco."

"Have you replaced it?"

"No. One does not reward a child's carelessness." Saeb looked from Vallis to Kornbluth. "At least I do not."

"Was Munira's cell phone number 972 (59) 696-9726?"

"Yes."

Kornbluth looked up from her notes. "Where does your wife keep her cell phone?"

Saeb considered this. "In her purse, I suppose. I know of no set place."

"Do *you* ever use her cell phone?"

Saeb stroked his beard. He had begun to look tired, underscoring the frailty of his appearance; whatever strain he was feeling, David thought, he did not seem to have much stamina. "We are husband and wife," he said with annoyance. "If a battery goes low, or only one of us has a phone, such a thing might happen. I suppose that makes us co-conspirators."

Quickly, David placed a hand on Saeb's arm. "Mr. Khalid is tired," David said to the agents. "He's here voluntarily, to answer your questions. But it might help us both if you explained the purpose of all this minutiae about cell phones."

"We're almost done," Vallis responded in a clipped tone. Turning to Saeb, he asked, "Do you know your wife's cell phone number, Mr. Khalid?"

Saeb glanced at David, who shrugged. "Of course," Saeb answered.

"And what is that number?"

With sibilant precision, Saeb recited, "972 (59) 696-0896."

Kornbluth, David noticed, did not need to write down the number. "Are you familiar," Vallis asked, "with the cell phone number (415) 669-3666?"

Saeb's eyes narrowed in thought. "Whose number is that?"

Vallis did not answer. "Did you ever call that number, sir?"

Saeb stared at him. "415," he answered, "is a San Francisco area code. I called reporters, they called me. I did not memorize their numbers. If I called that number, *sir,* even if it is not recorded on my cell phone itself, in due course there will be a record. Do not ask me to perform feats of memory."

"Do you have your cell phone in your possession?"

"Yes. At the hotel."

"On the day Ben-Aron was killed," Kornbluth demanded, "do you remember your movements?"

Saeb gave her a measured look. "There were none."

"Please explain."

Saeb's voice became a drone of weariness. "I got up, ordered from room service, read the newspaper, placed several calls to colleagues in the West Bank or to the media, awaited the prime minister's speech, watched the speech, began drafting my responses, and heard the announcement that he was dead. All in our hotel room."

"Where was your wife?"

"At breakfast, with me. Then she took Munira on a ferryboat, I believe."

"How long were they gone?"

"I took no notice. They were back before noon."

"Did you expect them back?"

"I had no specific expectations."

"Did they watch the speech with you?"

Saeb hesitated. "Only Munira."

"Not your wife?"

"No."

"And where was she?"

Absently, Saeb rested the fingertips of his left hand against his temple. "Shopping."

"Do you know where she went?"

"Not specifically."

"When did she go out?"

"I'm not sure. If Ben-Aron's speech was at noon, a little before."

"Before she went out," Vallis asked, "did she make or receive any phone calls?"

Saeb spread his hands. "I don't know. I had other things to do than constantly observe her."

"When she left, Mr. Khalid, did she have a cell phone with her?"

"Mr. Vallis, I did not search her purse. So I truly cannot tell you."

The last two questions put David's nerves on edge; they focused, as had David himself, on the time period within which the assassins may have learned that the motorcade had changed its route. But, despite Saeb's disdain for the agents, he was proving a skilled witness — he listened to the questions, did not guess, and his answers were precise and careful. That the interrogation contained some unseen risk to Hana seemed as clear to him as to David.

"Did you discuss," Kornbluth inquired, "why she didn't stay for Ben-Aron's speech?"

"Yes. She didn't care to hear him."

"Did she say why?"

"She didn't have to." Saeb's voice was cool. "We

are Palestinian. For all our lives we have heard such speeches — new plans, fresh promises, peace about to bloom like roses in the desert. The pretty words of statesmen drenched in the blood of our people no longer give us hope."

"Should there be a trial," Vallis asked abruptly, "will you waive the marital privilege with respect to Hana Arif?"

David stifled his surprise. "In what context?" he asked.

"To keep his wife from testifying. The privilege belongs to him."

"That's true with respect to Hana giving evidence against Mr. Khalid," David countered. "But in the reverse situation, the privilege would belong to Ms. Arif. In either case, I would advise them not to waive any privilege in a vacuum."

Vallis turned to Saeb. "Is that your position, Mr. Khalid?"

"I will follow the advice of my counsel," Saeb answered with a touch of defiance. "But as far as I'm concerned, neither my wife nor I need any privilege. Our only crime was to come to America."

Vallis glanced at Kornbluth, who shook her head. "That's all we have for today," Vallis said blandly. "But before you go, we'll want to get your fingerprints."

Startled, David asked, "What's your basis for *that* request?"

Vallis produced a document from a manila folder and slid it across the table. "A subpoena from the federal grand jury."

The subpoena, David saw at once, called for fingerprints from Hana as well as Saeb. "I want to see the United States attorney," he demanded. "Right now."

■ ■ ■ ■

Marnie Sharpe sat behind her desk, arms folded. "*You* know that subpoena's valid."

"What I *don't* know," David snapped, "is something you're obligated to tell me under the rules of the Department of Justice: whether one of my clients, or both, was a target of your investigation at the time you invited them here."

"I told you," Sharpe said imperturbably, "both are 'persons of interest.' Whether one or both is a 'target' has yet to be determined."

"Bullshit. I just sat through two hours of interrogation. Any first-year lawyer would know you're sitting on something very specific, and using it to try and nail one or both of them. Which makes at least one of them a target." David made no effort to conceal his outrage. "You're walking close to the line, Marnie — in fact, I think you've crossed it. If you'd been straight with me, I might have thought a lot harder before I agreed to bring Khalid in. And now I'm not at all sure I'll allow you to interview his wife."

"You're not a virgin, David — far from it. The line between people we're looking at and the ones we think we may indict is often imprecise, and changes from moment to moment." Sharpe steepled her fingertips. "I'm not prepared to say that Hana Arif is a target in the assassination of Amos Ben-Aron. But there are questions we want her to answer. It's her choice, and yours, as to whether she cooperates."

In silence, David considered her. Beneath Sharpe's apparent coolness, he felt sure, was a prosecutor even more desperate for an indictment than he had imagined: she had chosen to dissemble, short-circuiting her obligation of candor to a witness in jeopardy in the hopes of a swift breakthrough. "I'll discuss it with Ms. Arif," he said at last, "in light of your assurances. And my assessment of their value."

"And Munira Khalid?"

"Is their daughter, not mine. I only know what I'd do."

Sharpe stood, signaling the end of their meeting. "Then let me know about Hana Arif — soon. This won't keep."

Saeb and Hana were waiting at David's office. Saeb's stare at David was an accusation without words; Hana's eyes were filled with doubt and worry. Saeb's fingertips bore the stains of an FBI inkpad.

David looked from Saeb to Hana, still absorbing that the truth might be far worse than he knew. "Sharpe misled me," he said. "I don't like the feel of this — all the questions about cell phones and computer use, the fingerprints. They couldn't get that warrant without showing at least some basis for it. They've got something specific, maybe from Ibrahim Jefar, maybe elsewhere. But we've got a lot of thinking to do, and little time to do it."

Saeb held up his hand. "First, Munira. I won't have her abused by your gestapo."

David glanced at Hana. "I understand," he said to Saeb, "and I don't want to risk putting Munira in the middle of something where she's terrified, or feels responsible if this goes badly for one or both of you. All I can say on the other side is that the more they ask Munira, the more we learn about what they might ask Hana."

"No," Saeb snapped. "That's like the parable of

the four blind men groping at different parts of an elephant. You can tell us this elephant is a wall, if you wish, or a rope. But not at Munira's expense."

David ignored the not-so-veiled insult. "Hana?" he asked.

Hana looked down. "I am worried. I would like to know what they are thinking. But Munira must come first."

"So I tell Sharpe no?"

"Not just no," Saeb said. "Tell her to go fuck herself."

David raised his eyebrows at Hana. Slowly, she nodded. "You may quote my husband, and say it comes from me."

David tried to read her face — in a few brief hours, the specter of her possible complicity had become real, casting a new and unflattering light on his decision to represent her. The fear that had crept into her eyes could be fear of the unknown, or an awareness of guilt. "Do *you* wish to meet with them, Hana? Sharpe intimates that you're not a target. I think you may be."

Hana looked at him steadily. "If you think that, then refusing them can only make this worse."

David shrugged. "Only if you're innocent."

A trace of hurt surfaced in her eyes. "I *am* innocent, David."

Perhaps only David heard the vibrato in her tone, a plea deeper and more intimate than that of a client. At the corner of his vision, David saw her husband glance quickly from his wife to him.

"Then you and I have work to do," David said to Hana. "Alone."

5

Relentless, David grilled her — cell phone calls; credit card slips; taxi receipts — reconstructing, hour by hour, her two days in San Francisco. Her only extended time alone, roughly an hour, coincided with Ben-Aron's speech.

"Why didn't you watch it?" David asked.

Hana clasped her hands in front of her, drawing her shoulders in; to David, she looked smaller, more disheartened. "Many reasons. Perhaps the greatest was that I did not want to be with Saeb."

"Why not?"

"Because I knew what I would hear from him — the hopelessness, the hatred." She looked into David's eyes. "I do not blame him. But such words have been the subtext of my life. That day I could not bear it."

David studied her, unsmiling. "That day, of all days. So why not take Munira with you?"

"To avoid a quarrel. Saeb would have insisted that she stay. Not to hear Ben-Aron but Saeb himself, to serve as audience for his loathing of the Jews."

David did not comment. For another twenty minutes, he tried to pick apart this hour of her life, movement by movement. At the end, he said, "Everything I've asked you, the FBI will ask. If what you've told me includes a single lie, they will know it."

The skin over Hana's cheekbones flushed. "When you knew me, David, did you think I was a liar?"

"I *knew* you were. If nothing else, you lied to Saeb."

Hana did not respond. After a moment, she sat straighter, her voice brittle and resolved. "All right. I am ready for these people." She did not ask again for David's belief, or even for his sympathy.

An hour later, Kornbluth set a tape recorder on the table in front of her, then switched it on. Vallis's legal admonitions, though rote, now sounded ominous: that they were agents of the FBI; that Hana's statements could be used against her in a court of law; that falsehoods could be the basis for a criminal charge of perjury. Did Hana understand this?

"Yes," she said without emotion. "I am a graduate of Harvard Law School."

Vallis watched her face. "Do you advocate violence against the State of Israel?"

"No."

"Have you ever done so?"

Hana placed a finger to her lips. "I suppose I may have said such things, when I was younger. Sometimes I may have felt them. But I truly cannot recall."

The agent took a second tape recorder from beneath the table. "What's *this?*" David asked.

Vallis pushed a button. From the tape recorder emerged a thin but angry voice: "If we are terrorists, it is because we must be. Perhaps killing is all the Jews have left us."

David felt a coldness on his skin. The voice was

Saeb's; the words, he recalled, were spoken at Harvard, on the night David first met Hana Arif.

"Do you recognize those words, Ms. Khalid?"

"Yes. They are my husband's, many years ago."

She seemed calm enough, David thought. But he was not — the tape had resurrected the past, underscoring the tenuousness of David's position now. "Do you agree with that statement?" Vallis asked her.

"Then, or now?"

"At any time."

Hana's voice was uninflected. "Then, perhaps. Not now. I am tired of killing."

Vallis placed a picture in front of her: a bearded man, clearly Arab, whose dark, intense eyes stared from a face so thin it could have belonged to an ascetic or a vagrant. "Do you recognize this man?"

"Yes."

"From where?"

A hint of sour amusement played on Hana's lips. "The first page of the *New York Times.* I believe that is Iyad Hassan, who no longer resembles his picture."

She was angry, David realized — perhaps at having been the subject of surveillance, perhaps at David himself. "Have you ever met Iyad Hassan?"

"As a professor, I meet many people. I have no specific memory of meeting this one."

David turned to watch her. *You're being too chilly,* he tried to convey without words; *remember your reasons for being here.* As though hearing his admonition, Hana's expression softened a bit.

"You are certain you've never met Mr. Hassan?" Kornbluth prodded.

"Not certain, no. All that I can tell you is that I have no memory of meeting him."

"At any time?"
"At any time."
"What about cell phone conversations. Did you ever speak to Mr. Hassan by cell phone?"
"Not that I recall. I don't know why I would have."
"Specifically, while in San Francisco, *this* month, did you ever speak to Hassan?"
Hana raised her eyebrows, glancing at David. "In San Francisco?" she asked in an incredulous tone. "No, definitely not. That I would remember." Hana's voice became cool. "I do not know this man. All that I'm saying, in an effort to be precise, is that I can't swear that I've never met him."
"What is your personal cell phone number?"
"972 (59) 696-0896."
"Did you ever give that number to Mr. Hassan?"
David tensed; despite her denials, the questions suggested that the FBI had reason to believe she knew Hassan, and their precision was meant to establish grounds for perjury. "No," Hana answered firmly.
"Again," Vallis asked, "you're very certain of that?"
"Yes."
"Did you ever write down this cell phone number for anyone?"
Hana looked both cornered and bemused. "I believe not, no."
"Not even for your husband or your daughter?"
"This is a new cell phone, bought perhaps a month ago. Saeb and Munira programmed the number on their phones. I had no need to write it out for them."
David watched the tape spinning, recording Hana's answers. Choosing his words with care, Val-

lis asked, "Did you ever, at any time, print the number 972 (59) 696-0896 on your HP desktop at Birzeit?"

Hana stared at him as though trying to comprehend the question, its specificity apparently troubling her as much as it did David. "Do you mean did I print this number on a piece of paper, using the computer and printer in my office?"

"Yes."

Hana turned her palms upward, a gesture of bewilderment. "Why would I do such a thing? My handwriting is clear enough."

"Please answer the question. Did you ever print your cell phone number for anyone on a piece of paper, using the computer and printer in your office?"

"I did answer. I have no memory of doing that, and can't imagine why I would."

Someone had done so, David was now sure. Were it Hana, her only motive would be to avoid writing it in her own hand, the one way she could deny having passed the paper on herself — assuming she had left no fingerprints. Now Kornbluth pursued this line of questioning. "Who else, besides your family, has that number?"

"Only a few friends and colleagues. Most of whose names and cell phone numbers, I believe, are programmed in my cell phone."

"And you still have that cell phone?"

"Yes."

"Did you use that phone in San Francisco?"

"Yes."

"For what?"

"To call Saeb or Munira, if we were in different places."

These questions, at least, were ones that David

had prepared her for. As David had earlier, Vallis asked, "While in San Francisco, did you call anyone else?"

"Mr. Wolfe," Hana said casually, "our friend from law school. Also restaurants and tour providers. I think I called a taxi company, to take Munira and me to the ferryboat. Those calls will show up on my cell phone records." She thought for a moment, then added, "Also, I called my parents."

"Where do they live?"

Briefly Hana compressed her lip. "At a refugee camp in Lebanon, Shatila."

"What is your parents' number?"

Hana recited it. Kornbluth glanced at Vallis, then asked, "During your time in San Francisco, did you make or receive any telephone calls between midnight and four A.M.?"

"I did not, no."

"Did your husband or Munira?"

"Were it to or from Saeb, such a call would have awakened me. As for Munira, she no longer has her own cell phone. She lost it, and we have yet to replace it."

"Does Munira borrow *your* phone?"

"No. Munira lost hers here in San Francisco, where or how I do not know. I need one, and do not want for her to lose mine, as well."

This time it was Vallis who glanced at Kornbluth, indicating his desire to intervene. "Are you familiar with the cell phone number (415) 669-3666?"

It was the identical question that Vallis had asked Saeb. "No," Hana answered, just as she had answered David. "I am not familiar with that number. If it is one I called, or the number of someone who called me, I cannot place it."

Vallis leaned forward. In a new tone, cold and

clipped, he asked, "Did you ever discuss with anyone the assassination of Amos Ben-Aron?"

Hana sat straighter. "Before it happened, do you mean?"

"Yes."

"If you mean that he might be killed, yes, I believe I've discussed that possibility."

"With whom?"

"With friends, or colleagues at Birzeit. His murder has long been a matter of speculation."

"Did you ever discuss with anyone the *means* by which Ben-Aron might be assassinated?"

"Means? Yes, in the sense that I thought he might be killed by his own people — the fanatic Orthodox, perhaps, or settlers who feared he'd 'sell them out,' in their twisted way of thinking." Hana sat back, looking at both agents with an air of weariness. "Why don't you just ask me if I know anything about the murder of Ben-Aron beyond what the public knows?"

Kornbluth turned to Vallis, then back to Hana. "Were you," she asked, "involved in any way in planning or carrying out the assassination of Amos Ben-Aron?"

"No," Hana said. "Certainly not."

"Did you ever advocate the murder of Ben-Aron?"

"No. What I felt about him was distrust, not hatred." Hana's voice rose slightly. "I do not advocate murder — not of Israelis in their markets or buses or cafés, or of their prime minister. Many years ago I stopped believing that such violence served any purpose but to continue this endless cycle of death. And it is clear to me, as it must be to any sane person, that no good can come of this."

"Where were you," Vallis asked, "during Ben-Aron's speech?"

Despite her rehearsal with David, Hana hesitated. "Wandering. Alone."

"Where?"

"Around the area of Union Square."

"Why didn't you watch the speech with your husband and daughter?"

Hana gazed at the table. "I just didn't feel like it. I have heard too many speeches."

"Did you tell your husband you were going shopping?"

"Yes."

"Did you?"

"No. I found I didn't feel like shopping, either."

"Did you go into any stores?"

"No. Not that I recall."

"What did you do?"

"As I said, I wandered. I have no specific memory of where."

Even if true, David knew, the answer was regrettable, creating a vacuum during what might be a critical time. "Did you speak with anyone?"

"No. At least not that I remember."

Kornbluth folded her hands in front of her. "Did you have your cell phone with you?" she asked.

"I think so. Yes."

"Did you have in your possession any cell phone other than the one you've already identified?"

Hana blinked. "No."

"Are you certain?"

"Yes."

"Did you, while 'wandering,' receive a cell phone call from anyone?"

Hana's eyes narrowed in apparent thought. "I believe not, no. I can remember none."

"Did you place any calls to anyone?"

"No."

"You're sure of that," Vallis cut in.

"Very."

"Why are you so certain, Ms. Arif?"

"Because I had no wish to talk with anyone." Her voice was soft. "Do you ever reflect upon your life, Mr. Vallis? That is what I was doing."

The answer seemed to give the agent pause. "Reflecting about what, in particular?"

"Many things. Most of them personal, and of no concern to you."

"Did you also reflect on Amos Ben-Aron?"

"Only in the sense that I was tired."

"Of Prime Minister Ben-Aron?"

Hana gazed at him directly. "I would say more tired of feeling bound to Israel, since I was old enough to know that I was born in a refugee camp, and not a home." Her voice became quieter. "Why am I here, talking with you? Why does my daughter have nightmares of bombs and soldiers?

"I will answer your questions as long as you like. But we will be that much closer to being dead, and for what?" She turned toward David, her eyes filmed with tears. "I have done nothing. That is all I can tell you. Whether you believe that is not for me to say."

After that, the FBI took her fingerprints.

Shadowed by foreboding, David drove her to the hotel. Except to respond to his questions or comments, listlessly and briefly, Hana did not speak. By the time David stopped the car, she had been silent for some minutes.

"If you hear from the FBI," he said, "call me."

Without responding, Hana opened the car door.

When she was halfway out, she paused, turning to him with a long look he could not decipher. "Good-bye, David. Thank you for what you've done."

Before he could answer, Hana Arif was gone.

6

Long after their lovemaking was finished, David still held Carole close to him, as though to grasp anew a reality he had felt slipping away from him.

They lay in the bedroom of David's Spanish-style flat in the Marina District. It was late Friday afternoon, a day removed from Hana's interrogation. Though Carole had been gone only since Tuesday, David felt that in those three days he had lived another life, one in which he had lost his footing — afraid for Hana, fearful of who she might have become, reliving a past he had thought sealed off forever but that he now could not stop reexamining — even as he posed as his familiar self. Less than two weeks ago, Carole had embodied the sanity he strove for — grounded, clear-eyed, rational — in which the passion he had once felt for Hana was subordinated to a vision of the future rooted in what, David believed, was a love consistent with his essential nature. What he felt now was an eagerness to reembrace that life of stability, never again to be engulfed by emotions he could not control. So he clung to Carole's essential goodness — her warmth, her sanity, her practicality — with the fervor of an unfaithful but chastened lover.

Another woman, David knew, might have accepted this as an unexpected gift, her fiancé's surprise at valuing her more than he knew. But Carole drew her face back from his, appraising him with a look that held the curiosity of a woman deeply attuned to a man and his complexities. "Are you finished with them now?" she asked. "The Palestinians?"

"Yes. I did what little I could for them."

Something in his tone seemed to catch her ear. "Are they in trouble?"

"I can't talk about what happened with the FBI. But now I'm on the other side of it." David touched her face. "Eleven days ago, we set a wedding date. That night we met Amos Ben-Aron; the next day we saw him blown to pieces. Ever since then we've been shell-shocked, or separated. My idea of therapy is to get up tomorrow, put on our running shoes, jog along the bay to that coffee shop at Fort Point, eat a bagel, walk back, read the paper, and figure out what movie we want to see. I'll even cook dinner for you. And on Sunday, after the talk shows, we can start on the guest list for our wedding." David kissed her, as though to draw Carole into the mood he craved. "Normal," he finished. "If we just start acting normal, maybe we will be."

"You're right." Abandoning her look of inquiry, Carole nestled the crown of her head against his shoulder. "We've both been through a lot."

Grateful that she could not read his thoughts, David tried not to worry for Hana — caught in the ambiguities of her marriage, stuck in limbo in a country not her own — even as, in David's mind, she oscillated between innocence and guilt. They had been so young, he thought, heedless of the fact that their lives, like their parents', would come to bear the fingerprints of time, defined by decisions made, or not made, in ways they could not imagine. And so it was understandable, he supposed, that as he lay with Carole, his thoughts drifted from Hana to Munira. He felt Carole breathing more deeply, the whisper of sleep to come.

The telephone rang. Drowsy, Carole asked, "Do you need to get it?"

The illuminated dial of his alarm clock read 5:45 P.M. "This is what I get for playing hooky," David said. Reluctantly, he answered.

He heard a recorded message click on; for an instant, cursing the omnipresence of telemarketers, he was ready to hang up. "Hello," the voice said. "You are receiving a call from an inmate at a federal prison facility. You may press 1 to accept, or say 'yes.' To decline the call, you can press 2, or simply hang up."

David sat up straight, clearing his head — only a client would be allowed to call collect. "Is something wrong?" Carole murmured.

David pressed 1. "David? I am sorry, but I have no one else to call." Hana's voice was tight, fearful. "I've been arrested for the murder of Amos Ben-Aron."

"Jesus." David struggled to suspend his own emotions. "Okay. Tell me what happened, step by step."

"The FBI came to arrest me — Vallis, the woman agent, and two others. They searched our hotel room, took our laptops and cell phones, turned everything upside down. Munira was so frightened —"

"Did they arrest Saeb?"

"No — they're still keeping him here as a material witness. Please believe me, I've done nothing wrong. I don't know why they've arrested me."

Marnie Sharpe does, David thought. She wouldn't have done this without being sure of her grounds, and getting clearance from the attorney general — perhaps with the knowledge of the president. This was not simply a criminal prosecution: it was America's statement to the world that its system of justice worked, and that it would find and punish those responsible for killing Amos Ben-Aron. That Sharpe had not informed him of the particulars or accorded him a chance to bring his client in suggested not only the absence of usual courtesy but her desire for surprise, the better to seize whatever evidence Saeb or Hana might possess.

"Where are you?" David asked.

"At the federal detention center." Hana paused, then asked anxiously, "Will you come?"

David was very still. "I'll be there," he heard himself say. "Just stay calm. Don't talk to anyone about anything important."

David put down the phone. "Who was that?" Carole asked.

David touched her bare shoulder, a request for quiet, and reached for his remote. On the screen, Marnie Sharpe stood behind a podium, Victor Vallis at her side. "The five-count indictment," Sharpe was saying, "spells out the government's allegations that Hana Arif helped to plan and execute the assassination of Amos Ben-Aron — resulting in the murder of the prime minister, Ariel Glick of his protective detail, and Agent Rodney Daves of the United States Secret Service."

Carole sat back, as though recoiling. "Oh my God . . ."

"First," Sharpe read, "the indictment alleges that Hana Arif is affiliated with the Al Aqsa Martyrs

Brigade, a Palestinian terrorist group opposed to the State of Israel." Though Sharpe spoke clearly, her face was pale, an intermittent stammer betraying her nervousness in the glare of worldwide scrutiny. "Second," she continued, "that Ms. Arif recruited the assassin Iyad Hassan, a student at Birzeit Univeristy and member of Al Aqsa, who in turn recruited the assassin Ibrahim Jefar.

"Third, that Ms. Arif provided directions to the assassins by cell phone calls to Mr. Hassan, beginning with their route from Birzeit to San Francisco, their movements on the day of the assassination, and the means — uniforms, motorcycles, explosives, and the route of the prime minister's motorcade — necessary to carry it out."

"All that by herself?" David asked aloud.

"Fourth," Sharpe went on, "that in furtherance of the assassination, Ms. Arif conspired with other individuals, currently unknown, inside and outside the United States." Sharpe looked up from her notes, continuing with greater confidence. "In securing the indictment of Hana Arif, the Department of Justice relied on information provided by Ibrahim Jefar, as well as physical evidence that corroborates his account. No promise was made in exchange, other than that the Justice Department will consider Jefar's cooperation, *after* the trial of Ms. Arif, in determining what penalties to seek in exchange for his plea of guilty."

"No death penalty," David said. "That's the deal."

"The investigation," Sharpe concluded, "is ongoing. Much work remains before we can know the full dimensions of the conspiracy or the means by which the conspirators acquired the information necessary to effect it. But with this indictment we are taking the first step toward complete accountability. The world community should be assured that our government will commit its full resources to the apprehension and prosecution of every individual — no matter where they may be found or seek to hide — responsible for this crime against three people, the State of Israel, and the security of the United States."

"She killed him," Carole said in a thick voice.

When David turned, Carole's eyes were filled with horror and disbelief. "I don't know that," he answered.

It was all that he could find to say. Like an automaton, he began to dress. "Where are you going?" Carole asked.

"To the federal detention center."

"That call was from *her?*" Carole leapt out of bed, heedless of her nakedness. "Don't you understand what she's done?"

Fumbling, David buttoned his shirt. "I don't understand anything about this."

"Then how can you go out there?" Her voice trembled. "You're Jewish, David. You *knew* Amos Ben-Aron."

"I also know Hana Arif." David struggled for words. "I didn't know what this was turning into, Carole. But I'm still her lawyer. Before I get out, I have to find her another one."

"You could have told her that on the telephone."

"She's *frightened.*" He caught himself, trying to frame a plea for reason. "Her daughter's frightened, and they've got no one. I can't just pull a blanket over my head before there's someone else ready to take over."

Lips parted, Carole stared at him, wounded and uncomprehending.

"I was stupid," he said. "Now I just need to get out of this with an ounce of self-respect."

He quickly kissed her forehead and, though she remained still as a statue, left.

David drove across the Bay Bridge, its lights flickering in the blue-gray of dusk, heading toward Danville. He knew the route by heart; he drove by reflex, his mind trying to process the drone of commentary over NPR — that the physical evidence included phone calls and fingerprints; that the indictment did not explain how Hana Arif could have known Ben-Aron's route in advance. Then he pulled out his cell phone and, driving one-handed, called Marnie Sharpe's office.

Victor Vallis answered. "Victor," David said brusquely, "this is David Wolfe. Give me Marnie."

There was a moment's delay. He heard Vallis speaking in an undertone, then Sharpe came on. "Yes, David."

"I'm on the way to Danville. I won't bother complaining that you didn't call. Just tell me what's in the indictment, and make sure I get in to see her."

Sharpe's tone was somewhere between chill and disbelieving. "You're still representing her?"

"Only until I hand it off. But I'm asking now, not then." David slowed the car, gliding onto the right-hand lane as a stream of headlights sped past him. "As I heard your statement, you don't allege that Jefar ever talked to her himself."

"That's right."

"So exactly how does he know *who* was handling Iyad Hassan?"

"Hassan told him — several times. And Jefar knows Arif on sight." Sharpe hesitated and then added, "You know the hearsay rules as well as I do,

David. Jefar's testimony against her is admissible at trial."

"Maybe, maybe not. But you didn't indict her on the secondhand word of a failed suicide bomber. What's your corroboration?"

"We found a piece of paper with her cell phone number on it," Sharpe answered, "with Hassan's fingerprints *and* hers. Hassan's cell phone showed a call to that same number, a little after midnight on the day of the assassination."

David felt a stab of dismay. "So you recovered Hassan's phone?"

"Yes. From a garbage can along Market Street."

"Let me get this right. You have one call to Hana's phone from Iyad Hassan. Is that his *only* call to her number?"

"Yes."

"I assume Hassan called other cell phone numbers, and received calls from other numbers. Including on the day they blew up Ben-Aron."

David heard the silence of thought, Sharpe weighing her obligations. "That goes beyond the face of the indictment, David. Your fortunate successor will no doubt file a discovery motion, and we'll give him or her whatever we're obliged to. By then, I would think, you'll have resumed your pursuit of elected office."

She had told him all she was required to. David thanked her and hung up, driving faster now, the commentary on NPR receding to the margins of his consciousness.

The federal detention center was institutional and modern, a featureless two-story complex on an old army base. For David it was like checking into a hospital: clean, sterile, and entirely unwelcoming.

The one new feature was the media gauntlet outside, a swarming cadre of reporters, photographers, and technicians with minicams. Driving past them, David had the uncomfortable sensation of not wanting, for once, to be recognized.

David parked, presented his credentials at a guard station, and passed through a metal detector. Within minutes a U.S. marshal had ushered him through the large room with tables where families could visit the incarcerated. Beyond that were several doors with wire-mesh windows, so that those meeting in the rooms behind them could be observed but not overheard. Through one of the windows, he saw Hana at a Formica table, hands folded in front of her, head bowed as though in prayer.

She wore the red jumpsuit reserved for those accused of the worst crimes and subject to the highest security; the jumpsuit was too large, and she seemed lost within its shapelessness. Thinking of Hana as he had first seen her — proudly arguing the Palestinian cause, poised on the cusp of her people's future, and her own — David found the sight both painful and difficult to believe.

The marshal opened the door, letting David inside.

Hana stood at once, hope flickering in her eyes. She started to reach for him, then stopped — at most, David was her lawyer, she seemed to remember, and she had forfeited the right of intimacy long ago.

He stood gazing at her, the table between them. "Are you okay?"

She summoned a wan smile. "Such a foolish question. But one cannot rehearse for moments like this, where there is nothing good to say. You and I learned that thirteen years ago."

David sat across from her. He could not shake off the surreal image of the two of them locked in a room with tile floors and cinder-block walls, monitored by an armed guard. "When can I see Munira?" Hana asked.

This concern, at least, was familiar. "Every day," he assured her. "There are family visiting hours when you can meet her and Saeb in the room outside. A guard will watch, and you're not allowed to touch. It's also best to talk softly — the guards tend to eavesdrop. But at least you'll get to be with her."

Hana touched her eyes. "Assuming I want her to see me like this. But I guess I have no choice. That's the worst of this, I'm already finding — to be her mother and yet not be, with no way to comfort her."

Her pain was so palpable that David could not believe that she would ever risk imprisonment. But he knew to his sorrow that Hana, whatever she might feel for someone, could be subject to passions that superseded love.

"Where are they holding you?" he asked.

"In a cell — one bunk, a small desk, not much light. Worse than a college dorm room. But they say the exercise yard's quite airy." She shook her head, dismissing this wan attempt at levity. "What will happen to me now?"

David glanced around the room, scrubbed bare of personality. "First I have to explain something. Whatever I say here, whatever you say, remember that someone may be listening. I know there's an attorney-client privilege. But under the new antiterrorism provisions, the government can put together a team of people to monitor our conversations — anyone not connected to the prosecution. The rationale is that they're looking for conversations in furtherance of an act of terror.

"As of now, Hana, you're a suspected terrorist. Your coconspirators are unknown, the pressure to identify them unprecedented. I don't trust the government to be overly nice about your rights."

Hana's eyes clouded. She gazed about the room, as though seeing anew the prison that might become her life. "You can call your lawyer, collect," David went on. "But phone calls are subject to eavesdropping, as well. As for calls to Munira, Saeb, or anyone else, husband them with care. You get three hundred minutes a month, fifteen minutes at a time — if you use the whole fifteen minutes, that's four to five calls a week. And the government can listen to those, for sure. As for calling your parents, I'm afraid you won't be able to." David spoke more softly. "I'm sorry to be so blunt. But for your own protection, and even sanity, you need to know the rules."

"Can't you get me out of here before the trial? I must be with Munira."

"Your lawyer can try to get you bail, but he won't succeed." David kept his tone dispassionate. "This is a potential death penalty case. And there's no bail when the victim's Amos Ben-Aron. The only quick way out is extradition to Israel."

"Will they do that?" Hana asked in alarm.

"They might — that's out of your control, and it's a Catch-22." David paused, pained at watching her absorb the depth of her dilemma. "This is a lot, I know. How much of it do you want to learn right now?"

Hana squared her shoulders. "All of it."

"Okay," David said slowly. "Israel doesn't have a death penalty, except for 'crimes against the Jewish people' — in essence, Holocaust-related mass murder. On the other hand, a defendant may have more rights here. As an accused Palestinian terrorist, I'd choose to be tried in America. Even after 9/11."

Hana crossed her arms as though hugging herself against the cold. "Go ahead."

"The worst case," David went on, "would be if you're tried in America for the murder of the Secret Service agent, tried in Israel for the murders of Ben-Aron and Glick, then sent back to America for execution." Forcing himself to play out his role as a lawyer, David looked into Hana's face. "I'm not saying you're guilty, but Sharpe is convinced you are. The point I'm making is this: if you know something more than you've told me, anything at all, you need to think about giving it up."

Hana closed her eyes. "Have you said it all now?"

"Yes."

"So now it's my turn. I have nothing to 'give up.' That's the problem with being innocent. I don't care what they say, and I don't care who's listening." Her eyes snapped open, and she spoke clearly, to the walls. "So hear me, whoever's out there. What kind of terrorist mastermind passes out her cell phone number? What master of subterfuge takes midnight calls from a suicide bomber using her own cell phone, then saves it for the FBI?

"I have no connection with Al Aqsa. I don't know those men." She paused, then spoke more softly. "I know you're doing your job, David — I asked you to. So let me tell you who I've become in the years since you believed I was worthy of becoming your wife. I'm a mother. A mother who loves Munira far too much to let Saeb raise her without me. To stay with Munira, I might murder Amos Ben-Aron. But

I would never risk abandoning my daughter."

They stared at each other across the table, as intensely as they had as lovers. Quietly, David said, "Then I'll find you a good lawyer."

"Not you?"

The question carried hurt and challenge and also, David sensed, desperation. He felt his need to answer overcome his fear of being overheard by eavesdroppers. "Not me," he responded, "for so many good reasons that it's hard to pick the best one. But here are a few. I'm not objective. I used to be your lover. I knew Ben-Aron, and saw him die. I heard you advocate violence more than once. The U.S. attorney despises me. So, by the way, does your husband — whose help your lawyer will need.

"But here's the best one, as far as I'm concerned. In the last year, I've sat across a table from ten other people almost as scared as you. But looking into their eyes, let alone defending them, didn't tie me up in knots. That's the kind of lawyer you need —"

"One that doesn't give a damn?"

"No," David answered. "One that doesn't need you to be innocent. I lost that the first night we made love."

Hana did not look away. "Was it the first night, David?" she asked, her voice as soft as his. "Or the last?"

David kept himself from answering. The deepest reason, he knew, lay not in their first night or their last but in the life he had built since then, after wanting nothing more than a life with Hana Arif.

"I'll find you a good lawyer," he repeated.

7

Cell phone held to his ear, David reached the foot of the Bay Bridge, framed against the glittering backdrop of San Francisco's Financial District at night, its high-rises shadowy outlines of varied shapes and sizes. "With whose money," Mark Sacher was asking, "is anyone supposed to defend this woman?"

David imagined his legal mentor in the criminal defense bar — silver-haired, urbane, and seemingly imperturbable — addressing him with the quizzical expression that, in Sacher, passed for astonishment. "Not hers," David answered.

"Too bad. Because I can't see legitimate Arab-American groups raising money to defend her. No one will, at least no one with whom I'd want to be associated. But that's not the worst problem, David — not to me, at least." Sacher paused, and then chose total candor. "If Arif were a drug dealer, no problem. Instead she apparently made Amos Ben-Aron the first victim of a suicide bombing in America, less than an hour after he gave a speech that I, as a Jew who cares for Israel, had waited for a decade to hear. There's no way I could defend her with the commitment she's going to need.

"This case will be huge and difficult, the ultimate

high-profile defense of an alleged terrorist. But that's why it's such a problem for you." Abruptly, Sacher's tone became avuncular. "I appreciate that you knew these people in law school and that, as lawyers, we're all supposed to believe she should have the best defense. But many people in this community — including *our* community — won't care about that. And lots of *those* people are the ones you need to finance your entry into politics.

"Frankly, I don't know *who'll* defend her. As long as *someone* does, I don't much care. Neither should you. Dump it on the federal public defender if you have to, David, but don't derail your life."

David heard a click on his cell phone, signaling an incoming call. "I've got to go," he told Sacher. "Please, think about a lawyer. The public defender's just not up to this."

Hitting another button, David said, "Hello?"

"Are you insane?" Burt Newman's speech was even more rapid than normal. "Just tell me you've got an evil twin who's doing this, or maybe that you forgot to take the lithium that keeps your two personalities together. Anything."

Filled with apprehension, David glided into a lane of cars stopped at one of the toll booths at the entrance to the bridge. "What's happened?"

"You tell me. Thirty minutes ago I was the political consultant to the Jewish JFK. Then I turn on the news, wanting to hear about this terrorist they've busted, and some beat reporter tells me you're representing her. So I call your place, get Carole — damn near in tears — and find out it's true."

David lowered his window, passing three dollars to the attendant. "It's Sharpe," he said. "She must have leaked it to the media."

"Surprise. So Sharpe screwed you — I don't give a fuck. Welcome to the big leagues, pal." As David accelerated, starting across the bridge, Newman continued unabated. "Until tonight, everyone was on your side. The state's senior United States senator. The congresswoman whose seat you want, ready to announce that the term she's about to win will be her last. Harold and Carole, with her golden Rolodex. The city's high-end donors, lined up to help you preempt a primary fight. In two years plus, you were waltzing into Congress with unlimited potential."

"I'm getting out of this, Burt —"

"The first Jewish-American president," Burt continued talking through him. "The one who could make us all proud. It wasn't unthinkable, David. Not with the country's largest state behind you, and all the money you'd need to get off the ground. At least *I* dared to think it. What's unthinkable is what you're doing now."

David reached the first span of the bridge, the city looming larger in his windshield. "What do you suggest I do?"

"It's good that you still care. I was hoping you would, so I've already drafted a statement. Want to hear it?"

"Sure."

"Here goes: 'Like every decent American, I grieve the loss of Amos Ben-Aron, a man I knew and deeply admired. And, like every American, I expect our government to conduct a full and impartial inquiry into the terrible circumstances of his murder.' That's the preamble, David. Still with me?"

"Yeah."

"Here's your escape hatch: 'Hana Arif is an acquaintance from law school, as is her husband, Saeb Khalid. Before any charges were brought, and before I became aware of the circumstances alleged in the indictment, Ms. Arif and her husband asked me for advice. In light of those charges, I will help Ms. Arif obtain a lawyer to give her the defense that our system accords everyone, regardless of the crime with which they are charged. As soon as I have done so, my obligation to the legal system will be over, and my brief involvement in this matter at an end.' " Grimly, Newman added, "That's the very best I can do."

David flashed on Hana sitting in a stark white room, shoulders sagging as he said, *I'll find you a good lawyer.* "Sounds good enough," he forced himself to say.

"Then I'll get it out tonight," Newman said with obvious relief. "And have your assistant refer all media calls to me. Let's keep your name beneath the fold, okay?"

"Suits me," David said, and took the exit ramp for the Marina District.

Carole was sitting at his kitchen table wearing a robe, sipping black coffee, Newman's press release in front of her. Without preface, she said, "You've talked to Burt, I guess."

David sat across from her — an eerie echo, to him, of his meeting with Hana Arif. "Yes. As promised, I'm getting out."

Carole's dark eyes, her most expressive feature, betrayed the doubt and worry behind the mask of patience she was trying to maintain. "It's really not about that. I know you — at least I think I do. But there's something here I don't quite get."

Feeling both sympathetic and defensive, David asked, "What's that?"

"Your concern for this woman, and even her child."

"It's not that hard," David temporized. "Hana stands to lose her life; Munira stands to lose her mother."

"Just who *is* she to you, David?"

Briefly, David exhaled. "I told you."

"Did you? Then look me in the face and tell me that what you've already said is all there ever was."

David gazed into her face, so familiar and now, on his account, so troubled. "I can't," he said finally.

Carole seemed to flinch. "You were lovers."

"Yes. Only for a few months, at the very end of law school." David felt as uncomfortable at this confession as he sounded. "Saeb never knew. No one did."

Carole turned from him. "My father tried," she said at last. "But sometimes he couldn't help remaining hidden, going somewhere no one could reach him. So when I met you, I was used to that — conditioned to it, maybe. I told myself that your distance, and what I sometimes felt was a lack of passion, didn't mean that you weren't warm. Just as the essence of my father is warmth, not distance." Her voice was parched, its note of reproval seemingly directed at herself. "You were so pleasant, so smart. And I knew about your parents — that they'd left their mark, as mine did. None of us are Adam and Eve, I told myself. But I never thought that how you are with me could be about some other woman."

David felt shaken. "Have I really been that bad?"

"Bad? I wouldn't love you if I didn't believe you

had the capacity to love. But in all the time I've known you, I've never seen you do anything reckless, or even unconsidered."

"No?" David tried to smile. "Not even with Marnie Sharpe?"

Carole faced him. "Tell me this. If Hana's husband was in trouble, this man that both of you deceived, would you help him?"

"No."

Carole glanced away, as though it hurt to look at him. "You loved her that much."

At first, David could say nothing. "It's done," he offered softly. "However you want to characterize it, it's done."

"Is it?" Tears stung Carole's eyes. "From her picture on the news tonight, she's stunning. For all I know, you and she rewrote the *Kama Sutra* between classes."

"Enough, Carole. This goes nowhere."

"Oh, it's gone *somewhere.* It's gotten us here — you at the federal detention center, me wondering about my peasant girl's body, and which piece of you is missing." Carole stood, hurt filling her voice. "Damn you, David. It must have broken your heart to find out what she's done."

"I don't know what she's done," David burst out. "I wish I did — it would have spared me hurting you and hating myself for it."

Carole watched his face. "You are *so* lost, David. You can't accept the truth, and you're not even sure where you belong."

"That," David said with real anger, "is not fair. I grant you, this has shaken me to the core — you flatter yourself that you knew someone, and then suddenly something happens that causes you to question everything you believed about them, even things you knew about yourself. But that makes me human, not lost. And it's absurd to think the answer is just to tell myself I'm Jewish, and move on.

"Okay, you're not the first woman I ever loved. Sorry. I'm not your first guy, either; some paragon of Israeli manhood beat me to it. The difference is that Hana came back to haunt me in a truly spectacular way, and not by any choice of mine. For *that,* I'm sorrier than you know. But at least let me get my balance —"

The telephone rang. Instinctively, David glanced at the phone on the kitchen wall, reading its ID pad. "I'd better get that," he said tiredly. "It's your dad."

"Let me, David."

Carole stood, taking a moment to pull herself together, then answered with a fair show of calm. "Yes, Dad. I know."

Listening, Carole gazed at the floor. "I understand," she said at last. "I feel that way, too. But you know David — he has principles of his own, and we love him for it. In fact, we're kind of in the middle of this right now, sorting it out, or else I'd put him on. But no one disagrees — David can't defend this woman, and doesn't want to. It's a matter of finding a quick and graceful exit."

Hearing Carole calm her father, preserving peace among the three of them at whatever cost to truth, David felt a deep sadness. Carole said good-bye to Harold and hung up the phone. "You were more than graceful," David said gently. "Thank you for that."

Carole shook her head. "Two hours," she said sadly, "and it's killing him. Both of us, really.

"We *are* Jewish, David. Dad and I are Americans by choice. But we're Jewish just because we are.

That's how the world's always seen us, and always will. No matter how hard he tried, my father would never understand your relationship with Hana Arif."

David went to her, holding her close to him. "Can you?"

Though Carole did not hug him, she allowed him to rest her face on his shoulder. "I'll try. But you have to help me, David. It's like you can't find your way out."

"There's a way out," he tried to reassure her. "Burt's releasing the statement tonight."

"And then what?" Carole asked softly.

Silent, David held her close.

8

The next morning's newspapers suggested that Newman's triage was working. It was Hana's stricken mug shot that drew the eyes. While both the *San Francisco Chronicle* and the *New York Times* mentioned David's involvement, each reported that it was temporary, his name a footnote in the columns of newsprint devoted to the charges against Hana Arif. And by the evidence of David's office voice mail, he had drawn a field of applicants to serve as Hana's lawyer — although, in David's disheartened estimate, all but one were too young, old, desperate, alcoholic, inept, radical, or obsessed with the spotlight to entrust with a defense so arduous and demanding. The exception, Max Salinas, filled David with unease; a devoted leftist, Salinas often put the cause — as defined by his sense of drama — ahead of his client. But however quirky, Salinas was experienced and skilled, and David was in no position to dismiss him out of hand. So he drove to Washington Square, where Salinas, a man of the people, liked to sip espresso on a wooden bench and watch the denizens of the park read Lawrence Ferlinghetti, toss Frisbees to their dogs, or nap beside the grocery bags that contained their sole possessions.

Salinas himself was easy to spot — a short, squat

man with a sloping belly, a shrewd Aztec face, and silver hair drawn back in a ponytail. He regarded David from his bench with the jaded scrutiny of the proletarian for the haute bourgeois. But Salinas also had not forgotten, David was quite sure, the nerve-racking trial in which David, then a prosecutor, had secured for Max's cocaine-dealer client an extended stretch in prison.

David sat down next to him. "Yeah," Salinas said without preface, "I can see why you don't want *this* one."

"Give the class struggle a rest, Max. She needs somebody good, which is why I'm here. Let's try to make sense of this."

Salinas shrugged. "Simple enough. There's two ways to defend her: technical or contextual."

"Meaning?"

"Technical is the same old song and dance — burden of proof, reasonable doubt, guilty until proven innocent. Taking the indictment, it goes like this: what Hassan told Jefar about Hana Arif is hearsay, and one slip of paper with fingerprints and a cell phone number, and a single call to that same number, doesn't prove conspiracy to murder beyond a reasonable doubt. That's where you start, but it's not enough."

"Agreed. So what's your context?"

Salinas eyed a spindly Chinese man leading a small group of seniors in a somewhat arthritic version of tai chi. "That fascist you used to work for needs a conviction. Her masters, from the president on down, need a body to sacrifice on the altar of the State of Israel and Amos Ben-Aron. Your law school friend is ready-made — Palestinian, allegedly associated with terrorists, a professor in a university filled with radicals from Al Aqsa and

Hamas. Never mind that the Zionists have been butt-fucking the Palestinians for the last three generations."

"Is that part of your summation? Or just a paraphrase?" When Max looked at him in annoyance, David added, "Seriously, how do you turn that into a defense?"

"By not running from the fact she's Palestinian. People don't know their story. So let the jury hear it: dispossession, massacres in refugee camps, and now the occupation — Jews stealing their land and water, keeping their kids in prison without trials, and generally squeezing the life out of three-plus million Palestinians." Salinas's body began to twitch with energy. "Sharpe lays out the official, government-approved white man's version of history. And then we lay out Hana's."

David examined the grass at their feet. "And then what? Listening to you, I'm almost ready to kill somebody myself. But how do you get all that into evidence? If I'm Marnie, I object like hell. Unless she decides you're making her case for her."

"Meaning?"

"Meaning that you may persuade twelve jurors that Hana had a motive." David glanced at Max sideways. "If the jury pool were confined to San Francisco — nonwhite, nonaffluent, and so liberal that the Green Party outpolls Republicans — you'd have a shot. If anyone can make Ben-Aron the oppressor and Hana the victim, it's you.

"But this case is in federal court. Unless you get a change of venue, the jury pool will come from the entire populace of northern California, including white folks, conservative retirees, ex–military officers, and citizens who still believe that our government tends to prosecute the guilty."

"I can turn them around. Not that many people are *that* brain-dead anymore."

"Maybe. But what your defense implies, without saying so, is that this is a case of justifiable homicide — or, at the least, that the jury should consider Hana Arif as much a victim as Amos Ben-Aron. Given his image as a peacemaker, that's a stretch. Throw in a dead Israeli security guy and a murdered American Secret Service agent with three kids under ten, and you're taking a real chance."

Salinas folded his arms. "So," he said, "you and I disagree. No surprise there, either — we come from different places. But ask yourself what choice you've got. This woman has no money, the public defender's overworked, most lawyers who are any good won't touch an impoverished female terrorist, those that want her will likely have my politics but not my tools, and *you,* David, need to get away from Hana Arif as quickly as you can."

That last remark rankled David, and also troubled him. "So what do you suggest, Max?"

"Let me meet with her." In profile, Salinas's lips formed a somewhat wintry smile. "She's the one they're going to execute, not you. Let her decide."

David tried to imagine Salinas and Hana, facing each other in the bare white room. "I'll talk to her," he finally said.

Nodding, Salinas sat back, gazing across the street at the ornate white marble Church of Saints Peter and Paul, an airy, stained-glass gem built on the sweat of the city's first Italian immigrants. "I read where you're getting married," Salinas said. "The society pages gave it quite a spread."

"I didn't know you read them."

"Only when I run out of things to dislike," Salinas answered. He pointed at the church. "Did you know that's where Joe DiMaggio married Marilyn Monroe? A real prick, DiMaggio."

David promised to get back to him.

The fifteen-minute drive to Senator Betsy Shapiro's Tudor manse in the enclave of Presidio Terrace seemed to cover miles of psychic distance. That he was responding to her urgent message, left while David met with Salinas, increased his sense of disquiet.

Betsy sat in her living room — decorated in the Chippendale style, redolent of New England, which David had also found curious in the home of his Jewish parents, Betsy's friends. But Betsy, like his parents, had good taste, as well as the good sense not to adorn her walls with portraits of horses, bloodhounds, and British gentry riding to the hunt. The senator herself, in slacks and a silk blouse, was as informal as she allowed herself to be except with her closest friends.

"Dumb," she told David after the housekeeper had brought tea in china cups. "Truly, colossally, dumb."

It was less a condemnation than a statement of fact. "Granted," David answered. "I didn't know what I was getting into."

"So I surmised from your artfully worded press release." Betsy's tone became arid. "Although you were aware, as I recall, of who the victim was. I hope by now you've found a lawyer for her."

"I'm still working on it."

"Then let me encourage you to work harder." Betsy took a sip of tea. "The immediate political damage is obvious. But there are more subtle pitfalls that you may not have grasped. Have you ever been to Israel?"

"No."

"I visit there quite a lot, for reasons both professional and personal. I also serve on the Foreign Relations and Intelligence Committees. I can't discuss classified information, and I don't claim to know — at least prior to our inevitable congressional investigation — who, besides the two assassins and Arif, may have murdered Amos Ben-Aron. But I do have a certain perspective.

"That his murder stirs the deepest passions of our own Jewish community is, again, obvious — I'd be shocked if you haven't confronted that in your family-to-be. But my deeper concerns only start there." The senator raised her eyebrows in admonition. "A week or so ago, on television, you floated the idea of a breach in Ben-Aron's personal security. I cautioned you about it then, and for good reason: I believe that it happened."

At once, David felt his lawyer's instincts surface. "Why?"

"Because thus far — and this is between us — the FBI and Secret Service can't find any deficiency in our procedures. Nor can they find any cop or agent with serious financial problems, or with some grievance with Israel or Ben-Aron. And yet, as you seem to have detected, his route to the airport *did* change at the last minute, and the bombers changed their location *before* they could have observed the changes occurring — as Ibrahim Jefar's story suggests." Shapiro pursed her lips, as though tasting something sour. "Maybe they were lucky. But it creates the real possibility of an inadvertent — or deliberate — breach on the Israeli side."

"Can the Justice Department find out?"

"Not easily. At least for now, whatever the Israelis are doing is buttoned up tight — for their own good reason." Shapiro paused, then continued in the pointed tones she used for recalcitrant witnesses and feckless bureaucrats. "Your suggestion goes to the heart of Israel's internal conflicts. The right wing, including the settler movement and those most rabidly anti-Palestinian, is using the assassination to gain and hold power. The only way I can see for the opposition to fight back — the moderates, the left, the peace movement — is to find a way to blame the Israeli right for Ben-Aron's assassination.

"If that happens, the accusation itself could tear Israel apart along the fault lines of its very fractious society — left versus right, secular versus Orthodox, settler versus nonsettler. And those same fault lines will divide friends in our own community — people like Harold Shorr on one side and me on the other, with anger overtaking reason."

"I can see that."

Betsy stared at him. "Good. Because you do not want to be part of provoking that. It would damage you politically, losing you friends you'll never get back. And for what? Hana Arif? I don't see how that helps her."

Carefully, David sipped his herbal tea. "Let me suggest a possibility. If there was a deliberate breach on the Israeli side, then someone potentially within our reach holds the key to what happened, and who was behind it —"

"Either Arif conspired to kill him," Betsy interjected sharply, "or she didn't. From the prosecutor's perspective, who else may have helped to kill him doesn't matter. At least until Arif tells us who they are, assuming that she can."

"So Sharpe will say," David responded. "But if this is more than a Palestinian plot, it holds a funhouse mirror to Sharpe's narrative. At the very least, one has to wonder what possible connection there could be between Hana Arif and the people guarding Ben-Aron."

"I'm trying to discourage you, David, *not* intrigue you."

David shrugged. "I can't help thinking like a lawyer."

Shapiro put down her cup. "It's time to start thinking like a congressman. So allow me to widen your field of vision. This case affects one of our country's most vital interests: its relationship with Israel, and the rest of the Middle East. The White House, State Department, and Justice Department are all under enormous pressure. Do they prosecute Arif here or ship her to Israel? If her lawyer opposes extradition and wins, does some terrorist in, say, Chicago hold schoolkids hostage with a dirty bomb unless we set her free? And what does Israel do then?"

David had considered none of this; now he did, dismayed. Pressing her argument, Betsy leaned forward. "And how would a lawyer oppose extradition if Israel demands it? By saying Israel can't give her a fair trial? If you were her lawyer, David, you'd definitely want to emphasize *that.*" Shapiro's tone became openly sarcastic. "And if you win and she's tried here, Sharpe will go for the death penalty. Or maybe — given that she's a dangerous prisoner to have in *anyone's* custody — Israel will *want* the Justice Department to keep her, and kill her. Sharpe would be happy to oblige — if the case works out, she writes her own ticket.

"In either scenario, you'd get to oppose the death penalty — another highly popular maneuver, especially in a case involving terrorists. In the meanwhile, all the politicians in our party, your would-be colleagues, will be bending over backward to placate Israel and its supporters. You'd be a pariah —"

"Betsy," David interrupted softly, "I'm handing over the case."

"To whom?" The senator paused, moderating her tone. "I know you say that, David. I believe you mean it. But you haven't yet, and I worry, because I can't for the life of me understand why you ever touched this in the first place. So out of an abundance of what I hope is needless caution, let me finish.

"You're living in an America redefined by its fear of terror. For you, defending Hana Arif would be the gift that keeps on giving, with consequences that will reverberate in your life long after you're on Social Security. Assuming there's any left."

The monologue had left David slightly shell-shocked. But beneath Betsy's vehemence, he knew, she intended a kindness: the preservation of his future — in politics, and with Carole. "Thank you," he said simply. "I appreciate your taking all this time."

"Consider it my wedding gift," she answered with the slightest smile. "I'm sure that Carole has all the china and crystal you two will ever need."

Driving to his office, David found that the two conflicting conversations — one with Salinas, and the other with Betsy Shapiro — echoed in his mind, forming and re-forming in a plethora of confusing patterns, reason colliding with emotion, the only constant his repeated image of Hana alone in a cell. Then he reached the office and found two messages from lawyers he respected, both turning down her defense, and an anguished one from Harold Shorr.

9

David found Harold Shorr at the head of the broad dirt path winding along the bay between the St. Francis Yacht Club and the foot of the Golden Gate Bridge, where Harold chose to take his daily constitutional. The afternoon was atypical of summer in San Francisco — breezy, crisp, the sky electric blue — and bikers and runners, the healthy young people the city drew like a magnet, passed them in both directions. But Harold trudged heavily, his hands thrust in his pockets, eyes fixed on the path in front of them. David knew that hard emotions, hurt or anger or disappointment, were painful for Harold to express: whatever he was feeling now seemed lodged in his throat.

At last, Harold spoke. "Forgive me," he said softly. "I promised myself never to intrude in your affairs, or come between you and Carole. But I'm afraid for her, and for you."

David turned to him. "It'll be all right, Harold. Really."

"Will it?" Harold gave him a sideways glance of appraisal. "Carole wouldn't tell me. But between you and this Palestinian woman, I think, there is something more than Harvard Law School."

David felt a profound discomfort. "Was," he amended. "I'm just trying to stay right with myself.

As a lawyer, and as a man."

"And as a Jew, David?"

"I didn't know that they were different."

Harold emitted a weary sigh. "As a Jew, you have no right to such innocence."

David chose not to answer. Harold's steps quickened, as did his speech, rising with emotion. "As a Jew, you've chosen to help a murderer of Jews, this Arafat with breasts."

"I'm finding her a lawyer, Harold. Was I just supposed to run away?"

"Run away?" Harold stopped in his tracks, speaking to the ground at David's feet. "You have no idea of what the world is like. In America, you've seen nothing. They hung my father in the public square. The worst thing that ever happened to your father was to be excluded from some private club. And even then, he had his own club — the safe world in which you were born, filled with books and music. The world of the German Jews until Hitler broke their windows —"

"And slaughtered them like dogs," David cut in sharply. "Because the Nazis had no rule of law." In a more level tone, he added, "No doubt the people you saw die at Auschwitz remembered they were Jews, all too well. But only a society that gave them rights could have saved them from the ovens."

"Hana Arif," Harold snapped, "is not a Jew."

"The rule of law is for everyone. In any other context, Harold, you'd be the *first* to see that. Why have Jews in this country always fought for minorities? Because they know the cost of denying people rights — no matter who they are — better than anyone. And it starts well before the government begins rounding people up." David paused, searching for an analogy. "Why did Alan Dershowitz help defend O. J. Simpson?" he asked. "Not to strike a blow for spousal abuse but to vindicate the rule of law. Surely you still know the difference."

"So now you presume to lecture me from a civics book." Harold looked into his face. "You risk your future, and my daughter, for such abstractions, all for a woman who seeks to drive a stake into the heart of Israel. And then you tell me, as a Jew, that I should feel pride in you.

"I cannot. Non-Jews will scorn you as a pathetic seeker of attention, so intent on self-promotion that you will take on any cause, even of an assassin who despises us. As for our own community, some may see great principle in defending the murderer of Amos Ben-Aron. But more will see you as naive or worse — a traitor."

"I'm not defending her, dammit. But if I wanted to, I wouldn't take a poll to find out if I should." David fought to keep his voice low. "Or seek anyone's permission — even yours. It's my job, and no else's, to decide what kind of man I am."

They stood facing each other, oblivious to the joggers swerving to avoid them. Harold's face was etched with pain. "Let us sit," he said finally. "Fighting with you makes me tired."

This was Harold's way, David knew, of stepping back from the precipice. "It's been a long day," David responded. "This is making me tired, too."

They found a bench in the partial shade of two wind-blown pine trees and sat, gazing at the white-capped expanse of the bay, the gold-brown hills of the Marin headlands. Harold hunched forward, elbows on knees, hands clasped in front of him. "Do you truly not understand," he asked, "that this woman is poison to us? Your defense of her is a denial of self, and of our history. Israel is our refuge."

"Not Carole's," David answered softly. "Her refuge is America."

"Where this Hana of yours has now brought us suicide bombers. This crime endangers America, and guarantees the killing of more Jews. As an American, or a Jew, you must shun this woman."

"And as a lawyer?"

Harold turned to him. "Are you the only lawyer in America? You're certainly not a doctor in an emergency room, where only you stand between Hana Arif and death, with no time for moral choice. Let some other lawyer do it."

"I will — I just have to find one. So why are we even having this conversation?"

Harold contemplated the question. "Because this is more than civics," he said finally. "It's not just legal abstractions that drew you into this, but a woman. And what you do because of her can't be predicted — as I never would have predicted that you'd take the risks you have so far. Knowing, as you must have, what that might mean for you and Carole." Tears came to Harold's eyes. "I'm her father, David. And you're hurting her. You, of all people, who she's trusted with her heart."

At once the anger drained from David. "I'm sorry, Harold. Please believe that . . ."

"I love my daughter more than life. Perhaps you cannot love her quite that much. But more, I hope, than this woman you're hurting her for."

"Do you doubt that?"

Harold turned to him. "Why else do you make me worry for her? Have you stopped to think that because of what you've done already, someone may seek to do you harm?"

"What do you mean?"

"What you may be bringing to our door is more

than hurt, or even shame." Harold's voice was rough. "When I left the Nazis behind, I swore that no one would make me cower again. But then I had the child I had prayed for to the God I no longer believed in.

"For myself, I fear nothing. But I can never escape my fears for her — that is why I did not wish for Carole to marry her Israeli. But it is *you* who has made me most afraid. Not only for her heart, but for her life." Harold looked into David's eyes. "In Israel, there are fanatics who would have gladly murdered Ben-Aron. Here there are extremist Jews every bit as angry, in a country that protects their right to arm themselves like terrorists. Do you think that they will choose to kill you in a manner that keeps my daughter safe?"

Gazing at Harold, David felt the gulf between them: the instinctive fear of enemies was as embedded in Harold's psyche as the first human's fear of snakes. "Carole," David told him, "is precious to me. All I've been hoping for is peace of mind. I'm sorry that I've shattered yours."

Harold shook his head, speaking slowly and sadly. "At my own wedding, there was no one from my family, or my childhood, to share our happiness. And so I've imagined Carole's wedding, surrounded by the people who have watched her grow, a community of Jews who love her. I've imagined her children, my grandchildren, with her strength of mind and heart, unscarred by all I saw. They would be our future, a vindication of all that happened in my past.

"And they would be *your* children, David — smart like you, confident like you, not afraid of anything." Harold brushed his eyes, then looked away. "I have loved you as you are — as a son, and as the man my daughter deserves. I beg you, do not take this from me."

When David tried to answer, the words caught in his throat.

"Wait," Barry Levin said over David's cell phone, "you're asking our office to take on the defense of Hana Arif — the supposed linchpin of a conspiracy of unknown dimensions — in the murder of Israel's prime minister?"

The head of the federal public defender's office sounded annoyed to be called at home on a Saturday afternoon. "Isn't that what your office is for?" David asked.

"In theory. But there's some up-front ethical problems, a potential conflict of interest. We're already representing Ibrahim Jefar, the chief witness against Hana Arif. Even if Arif chose to waive a conflict, a judge might bar us from representing her." Levin's tone was blunt. "Frankly, David, that would be a favor to us, and to her. We're overwhelmed as it is: too many cases, too few lawyers, way too small a budget. I'd only take this case if someone made us — unless Arif chooses to plead guilty, we can't give her anything close to what she's going to need. They're arraigning her on Monday, right?"

"Right."

"Then the best I can hope for, in the interests of all, is that someone else is standing next to her."

With that, the chief federal public defender went back to playing with his kids.

10

That evening, after placing three more calls to out-of-town lawyers, David kept his word to Carole by preparing dinner. Their meal was subdued; David felt Carole trying to avoid expressing the tension she so clearly felt. By the time they went to bed, lawyers from Las Vegas and Los Angeles had turned down Hana's case, citing her inability to fund her own defense. "With Michael Jackson," one remarked, "it was only little boys. And no one good would have tried that case for nothing."

Though silent, both Carole and David were unable to sleep. The next morning, gently kissing her, David slid out of bed. "I'm going for a walk," he told her. She did not ask him where, or why.

His path took him through Fort Mason, to the end of a pier jutting into the bay. Until he reached it, he allowed his mind to wander from person to person — Carole, Harold, Hana, Munira, Saeb, Betsy Shapiro, Max Salinas, and even, to his surprise, his own father and mother. His questions were at once momentous and banal, the stuff of moral choice and a thousand dormitory bull sessions.

David did not doubt that the answers to these questions might define his future, and that of others. That he had to consider them at all filled him with misgivings and, at times, a deep resentment of Hana Arif — he had offered her a life with him, and instead she had returned to disrupt the life he had worked to build without her. The evidence against her, while fragmentary, was damning. Yet the David Wolfe who had loved her, against all reason, could not accept that she was capable of murder.

That she was capable of lying, and perhaps untroubled by it, he knew well. But he kept recalling what she had said to him two nights ago: *To stay with Munira, I might murder Amos Ben-Aron. But I would never risk abandoning my daughter.* Though David had never been a parent, this had the resonance of truth.

I love my daughter, Harold had told him, *more than life. Perhaps you cannot love her quite that much. But more, I hope, than this woman you're hurting her for.*

Sitting at the end of the pier, David pondered his choices.

A lawyer who insisted on Hana's innocence would have few options. The nature of the evidence did not admit the possibility of mischance. Either Hana was an architect of terror or another architect had created a design that might condemn her to die in prison, from old age or lethal injection.

Were he a congressman but Hana dead, could he tell himself that he had acted rightly?

To hand this case to a capable lawyer would, perhaps, allow for peace of mind. Even setting aside the costs to David, the doubts he had expressed to Hana were compelling — there might well come a moment, fatal to her defense, where his emotions would distort his judgment. But Max Salinas was not the answer. And in the absence of a better alternative, David also knew his own strengths. He was a talented and creative trial lawyer, ready for this challenge, and he understood Sharpe and the system better than most. The fact that others would despise him would not in itself be a deterrent — were it not for Carole and his ambitions, he might well take the case.

So there it was — yet wasn't. Because he had already paid too high a price for loving Hana Arif.

Did he still? Such a feeling was absurd — at most, surely, he loved his memories of a twenty-three-year-old woman he once had thought he understood. As for the woman in prison, thirteen years a wife and mother, he would believe in her at his peril. *So let me tell you who I've become,* Hana had implored him, *in the years since you believed I was worthy of becoming your wife. I'm a mother. A mother who loves Munira far too much to let Saeb raise her without me.*

Restless, David plucked the cell phone from the pocket of his windbreaker.

On its voice mail was a message from a former colleague living in Manhattan. His own practice was jammed with trials, his friend explained; his new marriage, he added dryly, was something he could not abandon for the pro bono defense of a Palestinian terrorist accused of murdering the prime minister of Israel.

David found himself gazing at the cell phone in his hand. *What kind of terrorist mastermind,* Hana had asked, *passes out her cell phone number?*

Once again, his lawyer's instincts quickened. *If there was a deliberate breach on the Israeli side,* he had told Betsy Shapiro, *then someone potentially within our reach holds the key to what happened, and who was behind it.*

Putting away the cell phone, David began his long walk home, trying to untangle principle from passion, wholly uncertain of what lay ahead.

"It would just be for the arraignment," David said slowly. "Until I can find somebody who's qualified to defend her."

"You won't." Sitting in David's living room, Carole spoke softly; what betrayed her was the look in her eyes, filling with hurt and disbelief. "Do you love me at all, David? Or my father?"

David's mouth felt dry. "Of course. But if I do this, neither of you is going to die. If I don't, Hana Arif may well. Maybe there's no living with you if I take this case. But how do I live with myself if I don't? This isn't about who loves who the most."

"Isn't it? Then why defend her?"

"Because something's just not right here, and she deserves a decent lawyer —"

"You and she were *lovers*. You can't cloak this in being a lawyer — you're my fiancé, we have a life together. Now all that feels like it was a script someone else had given you to read." Carole stood, her voice choked with feeling. "I think you're still in love with her, like in some Hitchcock film about obsession, *Fatal Attraction* in reverse. You'd throw away our life just to get her out of jail."

"That's not fair," David interrupted in a low voice. "This isn't you, Carole."

She sat down, imploring now. "Then tell me, please, what about me isn't enough for you? I feel like you've seen your long-lost love, and now you're looking at what you've had to settle for — me."

"I didn't go looking for this."

"No. *She* came looking for *you*. And Amos Ben-

Aron." Carole's voice rose. "I'm afraid for you, too — that she'll destroy you. You'll be like the walking dead."

Sitting beside her, he put his arms around her. "I still want our life . . ."

She pulled away. "Then it can't include Hana Arif, or the life we'll lead will be the one she'll leave you with. No politics. No community to call your own. No sense of who you are, or what limits that imposes. David Wolfe, the wandering Jew." Her voice filled with anguish. "Does what happened to my father mean nothing to you? Do you even have a conscience?"

David felt the pain cut through him. "I have a conscience. Like it or not, it's telling me I'm not just some Jewish prototype to be plugged into a slot."

"I have a conscience, too," Carole shot back. "And the deepest part of it remembers seeing the best hope of Israel blown into a thousand bloody pieces. By this woman you're defending." Tears sprang to Carole's eyes. "You can't love me and do this for her. You can't even love yourself."

Abruptly, she turned away, face in her hands. David reached for her. "We've both said way too much, Carole. We need time to work this out."

"There won't be anything left to work on." Carole turned to him, eyes still moist, voice drained of all emotion. "I love you, David, more than you can ever love *me*. I thought that I could live with that. But now I *know* way too much. Please, at least let me keep my dignity."

Heartsick, David watched her leave, taking the life they had made with her.

In the white room, David sat across from Hana. It was strange — he felt as lost as she must. Softly, she said, "I thought I might never see you again."

"So did I."

Hana hesitated. "And your fiancée? How does *she* feel?"

"What makes you ask?"

"Two nights ago, when you gave all the reasons you could not help me, her name never passed your lips. Even then, I couldn't help but notice the omission."

David sat back. "Carole's not germane to this discussion."

Hana gave him a probing look. "I think perhaps she is. Do you love her?"

"Yes." Despite his deep instinct of reserve, David felt the sudden need to talk. "She's very smart and very warm. I trust her. Sometimes I think she cares more about what happens in my day than in hers."

Stopping himself, David felt a fresh wave of remorse — he was still speaking in the present tense of someone he had lost, barely aware that he had lost her, unable to grasp how changed his life would be. Hana studied his face, as if seeing him anew. "And before Carole, you never wished to marry?"

"No. I kept wanting to feel more than I was able to."

For a time, Hana was silent. In a tentative voice, she asked, "Did I do that to you? Did I truly hurt you that much?"

David felt a flash of anger — at her, and at himself. "Enough of this, Hana. I'm your lawyer now. You'll have to be content with that."

Hana looked away. When she looked back at him, her voice was clear. "I have asked too much of you, I realize now. I was scared, and had no one but you to trust." She paused, then finished quietly: "Quit the case, David. They can appoint another lawyer."

"Not another like me, I'm afraid — not without money. No one I tried wants this."

Hana mustered a slight shrug. "All that the system requires is a lawyer good enough to lose without becoming an embarrassment. We learned that much at Harvard. And I heard you the other night, well enough. You don't believe you can win."

David looked into her eyes. "Did you do this, Hana?"

For a long moment, she gazed back at him in silence. "Part of me," she said at last, "would like to tell you yes. Then, at least, you could just walk out of here, perhaps retrieve the life I sense you're losing. But no, David, I did not conspire to assassinate Amos Ben-Aron."

Once more, David reflected, he was in danger of losing himself with Hana Arif — this time, as her lawyer. He thought of Ben-Aron's last seconds of life, and all that he was giving up to help the woman who might have killed him.

"Then let's talk about the arraignment," David said.

11

To David, the morning of Hana's arraignment felt jumbled and disorienting, a blur in which he struggled to suspend his disbelief.

He climbed the steps of the federal building through a gauntlet of minicams and reporters, keeping his eyes straight ahead, ignoring their shouted queries about why he had chosen to defend Hana Arif, the cacophony of angry demonstrators — more pro-Israeli than Palestinian — screened off by a wall of U.S. marshals. The only mercy was that Hana would not face them: the marshal's office was bringing her up in an internal elevator from the garage, the end of a trip in which her truck was convoyed by motorcycles and police cars and media, helicopters overhead, an eerie echo of the motorcade for Amos Ben-Aron.

David entered the cavernous marble lobby. A relative oasis of civility, its access to the upper floors, the venue of the federal courts, was controlled by metal detectors and security guards. When David took his place at the end of a line of reporters shuffling through security, a woman from Channel 5 tried to question him; a U.S. marshal, recognizing David from his days as a federal prosecutor, whisked him through security and into an empty elevator. By the time he arrived on the nineteenth floor, David understood, more clearly than before, that he was no longer David Wolfe as he defined himself — he was the lawyer who, inexplicably, had chosen to defend a terrorist.

More reporters waited for him to exit the elevator. Had the choice been David's, Saeb and Munira would have been with him; as David had argued to Saeb, this would remind those reading the paper or watching film clips that Hana had a husband and daughter. But Saeb had demanded that David arrange their private entry through the garage, sparing Munira the attentions of "a pack of media jackals"; wasn't it enough, Saeb had inquired acidly, that David insisted that she watch her own mother being charged with murder?

And so, brushing off questions with a synthetic smile, David hurried down the tiled hallway, the reporters' footsteps clattering behind him. He entered the airy but sterile courtroom of the judge who — assuming Hana was not deported — would either accept her plea of guilty or preside over a trial most jurists would gladly avoid.

The courtroom was full, lined with marshals along the walls and at the end of the aisle bisecting five rows of lacquered wooden benches. In the first row, Saeb and Munira sat between two more marshals. "Don't make her cover," David had implored. "I want Americans to look at her and imagine their own daughter." To which Saeb had responded tersely, "She is *not* their daughter." The girl David saw now wore a loose-fitting black dress that concealed all but her hands and head, covered in a black scarf. But no dress could conceal the girl's desire to disappear; no head scarf could obscure her fear.

David went to them, giving Saeb a swift, sharp

glance, returned in kind, then inclined his head toward Munira. The hollow of her eyes was smudged with the soot of sleeplessness. "Is my mother coming?" she asked.

David nodded. "Soon. I've arranged for you to see her, after the hearing. At least for a few minutes."

Silent, Munira tried to absorb the fact that any contact with her mother would be doled out at the sufferance of strangers. Despite his own anxiety, David felt desperately sorry for her; while the legal process was second nature to him, it must be as alien and confusing to Munira as the events for which her mother now stood accused. Remembering her fright at the Blue Angels, her belated shame at having clung to him, David found himself helpless to reassure her in Saeb's presence. "We'll talk later," he told father and daughter, and went to the well of the courtroom.

By the prosecution table, Marnie Sharpe and her red-haired deputy, Paul MacInnis — a dedicated career prosecutor who could no more imagine defending Hana Arif than wearing a tutu to court — huddled with Victor Vallis and a slight, balding man whom David did not recognize. When David approached, Sharpe interrupted their conference with a brisk nod in his direction. "Unbelievable, David. I'd no idea you were such an idealist."

Her voice carried a tinge of paranoia — that David could only be acting from some concealed motive she had yet to ferret out. When David merely shrugged, his own nerves too jangled for witticism, Sharpe turned, touching the stranger's shoulder, and said, "This is Avi Hertz, David. Among other things, Avi's representing the government of Israel as an observer."

What the "other things" were, David could only guess. As they shook hands, David asked politely, "Are you from your attorney general's office?"

"Yes." Hertz's somewhat elfin expression was countered by blue-gray eyes as cool as those of an actuary calculating David's lifespan. "For the moment."

Shin Bet, David guessed, or perhaps Mossad. "I may have some requests of the Israeli government," David told him. "Should I bring them to you?"

Hertz's face showed no surprise, and his tone was neither welcoming nor defensive. "By all means," he answered. "Ms. Sharpe knows how to reach me."

Before David could respond, Hertz glanced swiftly toward the raised bench from which Judge Taylor would preside. But instead of the judge, Hana emerged through the rear door to the courtroom, another U.S. marshal at her side.

It was her first appearance in public — at David's request, the marshal's office had allowed her to wear a blouse and simple, flowing skirt. She paused, searching out her husband and daughter. Her focus was on Munira, her small smile intended to assure the girl that her mother was unafraid. Only after a glance at Saeb, far more sober and opaque, did she take in the crowded courtroom and, finally, David himself.

The marshals shepherded her to the defense table. When David moved to her side, she did not look at him. "I am sorry," she murmured.

"For what?"

Head bowed, Hana did not answer. *"All rise,"* the judge's courtroom deputy called out. The spectators stirred to their feet, and Judge Caitlin Taylor strode briskly to the bench.

Drawn by lot from among fourteen eligible judges, Taylor was new to the court, and David had never appeared before her. Her early reputation was in keeping with her appearance: slender and patrician, Taylor had long brunette hair and a pale, sculpted face accented by wire-rimmed glasses that lent her an air of scholarly precision. A former corporate litigator with a keen mind and a decisive manner, she was nonetheless a mystery. She had little background in criminal cases, and there was little to suggest how she would bear up under worldwide scrutiny — "the judge in the murder trial of Hana Arif," her obituary might well begin — or how she might react to the complex strategy unfolding in David's mind.

Taylor's performance would be a question of character as much as intellect. Notorious cases, David knew well, magnified a judge's strengths and weaknesses, exposing arrogance, vanity, or indecisiveness, rewarding coolheadedness, prudence, and a steady internal compass. The one thing that David now knew was that Caitlin Taylor intended to take charge from the outset: eschewing the usual procedures — arraignment before a magistrate — the judge had chosen to preside herself.

"You may be seated," Judge Taylor began in a calm, clear voice. "The matter before us is *The United States of America versus Hana Arif.* Will counsel please enter their appearances."

Standing, Sharpe did so, introducing Paul MacInnis. When David said simply, "David Wolfe for defendant Hana Arif," Judge Taylor raised her eyebrows — no stranger to politics, she seemed as puzzled by his presence as Sharpe was, though in a more neutral way.

"Before we proceed," Sharpe interjected, "may I be heard on the subject of Mr. Wolfe's role in these proceedings?"

Seemingly as surprised as David, the judge turned back to Sharpe, her expression instantly alert. "You may."

Sharpe spoke with staccato swiftness, to David a sign of nerves. "When the assassination occurred, your honor, Mr. Wolfe was standing at the corner of Market Street and Fourth. Not only did he witness the suicide bombing at the heart of this case, but he gave a statement to the FBI." With a brief glance at David, Sharpe continued: "For that reason he may be a percipient witness at any trial, and disqualified from serving as counsel to Ms. Arif."

As the judge turned to him, David was buffeted by conflicting emotions — the certainty that Sharpe desired to be rid of him; the unwelcome but deeply tempting thought that she might have handed him the exit from his dilemma that he could not bring himself to take; the uncomfortable sensation that his far deeper connection, to Hana herself, might somehow be discovered. He was acutely aware of Hana watching his reaction. "Mr. Wolfe?" the judge prodded. "Do you wish to withdraw? Or, put another way, should you?"

David tried to distill his thoughts. "Your Honor, Ms. Sharpe has at least a hundred other witnesses, an alleged confession by Ibrahim Jefar, and, I suspect, a videotape of the assassination itself. Is she suggesting that she needs my help to prove that Amos Ben-Aron was killed?"

Though her expression did not change, the angle of Judge Taylor's look toward Sharpe suggested challenge. "Of course not," Sharpe answered with asperity. "But this is a case of international importance, with many unanswered questions. Our investigation is ongoing and wide-ranging. No one knows what detail may prove to be important, or who can give it to us."

Sharpe was perilously close, David thought, to a subject he doubted she wished to touch on but that might well account for Avi Hertz's presence — the assassin's apparent foreknowledge that the motorcade would change its route. "What is at issue here," David responded, "is not the fact of three deaths but who planned them, and whether — in reality — Ms. Arif played any role at all. About this, I have no more personal knowledge than Ms. Sharpe.

"Meanwhile, Ms. Arif is entitled to counsel of her choice. Nothing that the prosecution suggests is sufficient to deprive her of that choice."

Judge Taylor steepled her fingers, resting their tips against her chin. "I agree," she said after a moment. "If you decide to list Mr. Wolfe as a witness, Ms. Sharpe, get back to me with reasons transcending 'barely plausible.' Until then, I'm allowing him to proceed as counsel." Turning to Hana she said, "Ms. Arif, do you understand the nature of the charges against you?"

Hana stood straighter. "I do."

"And do you, indeed, wish Mr. Wolfe to represent you?"

Hana seemed to hesitate. "Yes," she said more quietly. "I do."

For a moment, the judge studied her. "All right," she said to David. "Your client is charged, among other things, with violating 18 USC 1116, murder of a foreign official in the United States. Do you require a reading of the indictment?"

"We do not, Your Honor."

"Is the defendant prepared to enter a plea?"

"To each count of the indictment," David answered, "Ms. Arif pleads not guilty."

There was a stirring behind them, the incipient excitement of the media at a story to come, a trial to report, with its promise of drama and surprises. Feeling his own misgivings, David saw Hana briefly close her eyes.

"Very well," the judge said calmly. "Do you wish to be heard on the subject of bail, Mr. Wolfe?"

"We do," David replied. "Until these proceedings end, Mr. Arif's husband and daughter have no passports. They are not going anywhere, and Ms. Arif desires to be with them." David turned, nodding toward Munira. "Ms. Arif's daughter is twelve years old. Seeing her mother arrested was traumatic enough; living without her is far worse. Given that Ms. Arif no longer has a passport, and that her family is being detained, there's no need for the government to separate them."

"Ms. Sharpe?"

"The assassins," Sharpe said dryly, "did not require passports to enter the United States. This defendant does not require one to leave it. And her motive to ignore the niceties of our immigration laws is obvious.

"As the indictment spells out, she has been named by Mr. Jefar as the director of a plot to assassinate Amos Ben-Aron planned by the Al Aqsa Martyrs Brigade, of which the incidental victims were two men with families — one American, one Israeli — and the ultimate victim the prospect for peace between Israelis and Palestinians." Now Sharpe spoke with greater confidence, hitting her stride as she framed her case for the media. "Our century is young yet. But it is fair to say that this is the most notorious murder this nation has suffered since the assassination of President Kennedy, representing a conspiracy the dimensions of which are not yet known. Further, we believe that Ms. Arif holds the key to exposing unknown others — perhaps many others — responsible for this heinous act.

"The United States cannot acquiesce to bail for a defendant with so much potential information to give, and so many reasons to escape — especially where we may seek the death penalty. With all respect, Your Honor, bail would be unprecedented."

"I agree," the judge said promptly. "Ms. Arif's request for bail is denied."

Next to him, David saw Hana deflate, her shoulders sagging under the weight of days and nights without Munira, the invocation of a sentence that would separate them forever. Glancing at Munira, David now wished that she had not come. "The court will hold its first pretrial hearing in thirty days," Taylor continued. "At this time, I will expect the defense to address its need for discovery from the government, and to hear both counsels on the subject of a trial date."

"Your Honor," David said, "may I respectfully suggest that the court hold that hearing outside the presence of the media or the public."

"For what reason?" Taylor asked with obvious surprise. "If there's any case where the justice system needs to be transparent, this is the one."

David steeled himself for controversy. "Ordinarily, Your Honor, I'd agree, but my discovery request of the government may well touch on sensitive matters of national security and international relations, including information protected by law. To spell them out in public would not serve anyone's interests."

For the first time, Taylor looked wary. "Ms. Sharpe?"

Sharpe shot a look of concern toward Avi Hertz. "For the reasons outlined by the court," she told the judge, "I'm reluctant to shut the world out. But I can't know what tactics Mr. Wolfe may be pursuing, or where he proposes to lead us. Until I do, I can't respond."

"Nor can I." The judged hesitated, consulting her own instincts. "For the moment, Mr. Wolfe," she directed, "we'll proceed as you suggest. File your discovery requests under seal seven days prior to the hearing. Ms. Sharpe will respond within three days. I'll take matters from there." Looking from Sharpe to David, she finished. "Thank you both. I'll see you in thirty days."

As Taylor stood, leaving as quickly as she had entered, the courtroom filled with the sounds of repressed excitement — the crowd rising, reporters speculating to one another, notebooks whispering shut, Sharpe putting away her notes while adopting an expression of studied blankness. In this brief cocoon of privacy, Hana turned to David, with a look of sadness that was somehow intimate. "Thank you," she said softly.

David tried to smile. "First you're sorry; now you're grateful. For what?"

"The same thing, David. You." Then the marshals came for her, leaving David to ponder this alone.

12

The crowd of onlookers began to dwindle, the tension leaking from the courtroom. Catching Sharpe's eye as she was preparing to leave, David said, "Why didn't you just call me before trying to have me booted?"

She regarded him with a gimlet stare. "Because I don't trust you. Why this death wish, I keep wondering. Are you *that* put out with me?"

"Don't flatter yourself, Marnie."

"Perhaps it's just a matter of national security." Sharpe eyed him for another moment, then shrugged. "Anyhow, you're here at Taylor's sufferance — at least for now. So let's try to be civil." With that, the prosecutor walked away.

Hana was waiting in a small room, guarded by two marshals. Though the room was suffocating in its own way, she and David were sealed off from scrutiny, and from reporters determined to interrogate him before he was prepared to advance his own agenda. "You look worried," she said.

"It's nothing much — just a little chat with Sharpe. She wants me gone from this case."

Hana considered him, and then surprised him by mustering the briefest smile. "You were once a witness to much more than she imagines. Given the rest of this morning, I suppose I should be grateful for the nature of her objection."

Perhaps, in her misery, Hana was searching for distraction. But David did not reply, or even smile. His disquiet was too deep, both at the impact of their past on his present and at the suspicion, unwelcome but ineradicable, that Hana Arif knew how to pull the strings of his emotions.

Her smile faded. "I'm sorry. Something more is troubling you."

"Several somethings. Saeb, among others."

Hana searched his face for meaning. "If you're asking how he feels about you representing me," she said finally, "what choice does he have? I'm more concerned about Munira." Her voice softened. "I've no right to ask for favors, even for my daughter, on top of everything you're doing. But I hope you'll help her through this — perhaps explain the process, reassure her as much as you can.

"She will feel her father's powerlessness as acutely as at that Israeli checkpoint. You, at least, can give her hope."

Slowly, David nodded. "I can try. But with Munira, I may be a little out of my depth."

Hana summoned a faint smile. "Somehow I doubt that." Abruptly, her expression became serious. "A last favor, then — could you occupy Saeb for a moment? I'd like to speak with her alone."

David felt his own emotional reticence, a deep aversion to being drawn, against his instincts, into a familial dynamic he did not fully understand. "I'll manage," he said at length. "Munira aside, Saeb and I need to talk."

The relief on her face was palpable. "I am very grateful, David. How I can repay you, I really do not know."

■■■■

It was jarring, David thought, to have Saeb sitting where, moments before, there had been Hana.

She had been still, soft-spoken; her husband seemed restless, even agitated, his fingers drumming on the Formica table. "If there's a trial," David began with studied dispassion, "we could be living with each other for quite a while. The strain will be considerable — neither of us knowing what will happen, and me forced to make decisions with consequences no one can predict.

"I respect your feelings — Hana is your wife, Munira is your daughter. But I'm Hana's lawyer: any hope she has of an acquittal depends on me. You and I will need to coexist."

Saeb's fingers stopped moving. "You think, perhaps, that I'm not grateful for your intervention."

"It's crossed my mind."

"Then I should say it," Saeb said slowly. "I am grateful — and humiliated. We have no money to pay you."

Was this truly at the heart of his antipathy? David wondered. Except when Saeb was angry, David found his expression difficult to read. "I am hoping," Saeb continued, "to raise money from the groups who sponsored my trip here."

David shook his head. "Money's not my worry, Saeb — my circumstances are comfortable." Saying this, David realized that relying on his largesse might further scrape Saeb's wounds. "As for the groups who sent you," he added, "to say we have a massive public relations problem is an understatement. Part of my job will be to make Hana's case in the media — Americans are already so familiar with the evidence against her that a change of venue wouldn't help. Taking money from anyone perceived to be anti-Israel, let alone a group that espouses violence, would make things infinitely worse."

"Then *I* am the problem," Saeb said with sudden heat. "*I* am the one who does not shrink from violence. Your government will try to make her guilty by association." Saeb stood, agitated, looking as though he wished to pace. "Hana's innocent — she buried her militancy at Harvard. The only explanation I can give you is that my enemies have framed her."

David looked at him in surprise. "What enemies? And why?"

Saeb crossed his arms, seemingly offended by the challenge. "The whys are clear: to get back at me, and to point suspicion at a woman who can't trade her life for information about whoever else was involved."

"Then why not just frame *you?*"

"I can't know everything," Saeb answered with impatience. "But Hana did not materialize these motorcycles and explosives. How could she be the planner when Munira and I were with her nearly all the time?"

"That much we agree on." Pausing, David waited for Saeb to calm. "It's one reason," he continued, "why Hana may need you as a witness. And why you owe it to her — as a witness and as her husband — to say nothing more to anyone about Amos Ben-Aron, the State of Israel, suicide bombings, the Palestinian diaspora, Sabra and Shatila, this prosecution, or anything else that will inflame America's post-9/11 sensibilities. If that makes you feel like a eunuch, so be it. There'll be plenty of time for free expression on the other side of a jury verdict." David's tone cooled. "As Hana's lawyer, I'll give your theory every consideration — I don't want her to die for someone else's crime. Your job is to ensure that she doesn't die for you."

Saeb sat down again, hands folded in front of him, staring into David's eyes. "As you wish, then," he answered tonelessly. "As a Palestinian, I'm used to having my life controlled by others."

"As an American," David retorted, "I'm not. So I don't enjoy it now. But it seems we have a common interest — your wife, and your daughter."

"Yes. So it seems." Saeb let the comment linger, then asked, "This issue you raised — national security. What exactly are you after?"

"I can't tell you, I'm afraid. Obviously, you're no longer my client — I can't represent a prospective witness, or anyone but Hana —"

"I'm her husband," Saeb protested.

"I think we're clear on that. But Sharpe could cross-examine you about anything you learn from me. So this is where you start to trust me."

Saeb considered this, then shrugged. "As you say."

"I do." David glanced at his watch. "There's not much time left. Before they take her, Hana wants to be with you alone. I'll do my best to distract Munira."

Saeb hesitated. "For a moment," he said grudgingly. "I don't want you upsetting Munira. Forcing her to come here was damaging enough."

Sitting across from David, Munira was a portrait in misery, the black of her dress and head scarf starkly outlined against the bare white walls. "Will they murder her?" she asked.

How could he best speak, David wondered,

across the gulf of gender, age, culture, and religion to this traumatized girl afraid of losing the mother she had so recently resented, and who now must experience this as guilt? Her only consolation, in Hana's absence, would come from a father whose own trauma was sealed long ago. Her only knowledge of the legal system would be what David chose to tell her.

"No," David answered gently. "In America, being charged with a crime doesn't mean you're guilty. We don't just 'kill' the innocent."

"The Zionists do," Munira said vehemently. "Or they arrest people for no reason, lock them up in prison without trials. They, too, say that we have 'rights.' But it's all a lie."

Though heartfelt, the speech had a curious pseudoprecocity, like a catechism memorized by a child. "Whatever you believe about the Zionists," David told her, "I'm asking you to believe in me, just as your mother does. Do you think maybe you can?"

Munira looked down, unable to respond. "I don't lie," David said flatly. "There *will* be a trial — that was what the hearing was for. Did the judge seem fair to you?"

The girl's eyes flickered, regarding David with surprise, perhaps at being asked for her opinion. Then she shook her head, less in demurral than confusion. "Americans hate my mother. On television they call her 'terrorist.' " The girl hesitated, then asked, "Do *you* believe her?"

So much for never lying. "Yes, Munira. I do."

The girl looked at him more closely — for an instant, David had the uncanny sense that she intuited more than she could articulate, knew him better than was possible. He was reminded of her mother's keen intelligence, her swift perception, perhaps nascent in Munira. "For the jury to find her guilty," David continued, "the prosecutor has to prove her case beyond any reasonable doubt. If she can't, the court will set your mother free. I'm determined to make that happen."

Though Munira's long lashes covered her half-closed eyes, David thought he detected a brief glimmer of hope. "How long will it take?" she asked.

"I'm not sure yet. Six months, maybe."

Though this estimate was optimistic, Munira looked crestfallen. "Six months," she repeated dully.

David guessed at her imaginings — of an alien hotel room in an alien city, of a silent, brooding father, of a mother taken from her for reasons she still could not understand. "You can see her," David promised. "She hasn't gone away."

Not yet, he saw Munira thinking. Tears surfaced in her eyes.

"If you like," David said softly, "when your father's busy, I'll take you to see her myself."

The black cloth around her neck pulsed, perhaps with the effort of choking back her grief. "Can I see her alone again?"

"Yes," David promised. "I'll make sure of it."

Driving away from the courthouse, David watched a clump of demonstrators chase him in the rearview mirror. "Self-hating Jew!" a bearded man shouted. "You'd sell your mother to Heinrich Himmler!" This was merely a down payment, David supposed, on what was sure to come.

Briefly, he thought of decisions made, or not made — of the life he had wanted with Hana, the life he had lost with Carole. And of regrets he could not allow himself to feel, or to share with either woman.

Enough, he told himself. There was much to do, and a man he had to see on a matter of national security.

13

In the thin sunlight of a foggy summer day, David met Bryce Martel at the head of the Tennessee Valley Trail. Ahead, the broad dirt path wound through a narrow valley in southern Marin County, ending where a blue-gray surf flowed into an inlet between low, jagged cliffs.

Though a WASP aristocrat by background, Martel, a classmate of David's father at Columbia, had shared Philip Wolfe's interests in art and music. Beyond that, the two men's paths had diverged: Philip Wolfe became a psychiatrist; Bryce Martel had occupied a series of vaguely described governmental posts until, at the end of his career, he'd emerged as a leading antiterrorism analyst, perhaps the harshest critic of an intelligence apparatus that he described as "almost as self-serving and incompetent as the politicians who abuse it."

This apostasy had earned Martel a dignified exile at the Hoover Institution at Stanford. David's faded childhood memories of Martel's visits with his father, spent debating such things as the merits of twentieth-century symphonic music, were refreshed by Martel's faithful attendance on Philip Wolfe as he slowly died of inoperable brain cancer. David, realistic enough to know that — even under the best of circumstances — he would never pierce his father's emotional carapace and comprehend his inner thoughts, was grateful for Martel's calm acceptance of death, and for the unexpected chance to learn more about his father's life. Martel seemed to understand this; every few months, over a superb meal in one of the few restaurants whose wine lists were sufficiently imaginative to please him, he and David still talked about matters old and new. "Your father became a psychiatrist," Martel once told him, "because, like many psychiatrists, he wished to understand himself. But whatever he discovered, he did not wish to share. Including how he felt about being a Jew."

Now, to his surprise, David needed Martel for another reason: to help untangle what promised to be a complex, even byzantine, case.

In his late sixties, Martel remained trim, with salt-and-pepper hair, a keen, weathered visage, and bright green eyes still too sharp to require glasses. He liked the outdoors, as his well-worn hiking outfit — pure New England in its scuffed boots, faded khakis, and well-worn flannel shirt — suggested. Besides, he'd added casually, it was best for David to talk with him where others would find it hard to listen.

"They're tired of me," Martel said with weary acceptance, "but they'll be all over you — looking for radical ties, clues about who else planned Ben-Aron's assassination, anything that explains why you took this case. It's a puzzle to them, David. Which, in these perilous times, also makes you their target."

Martel's tone suggested that it was also a puzzle to him, but he was too polite, or respectful of human complexity, to ask. "Whose target?" David asked.

"Your own government's. Not to mention the Mossad. You can reasonably expect to have your home and office phones tapped, along with Harold's and Carole's, and anyone who works with you on defending Hana Arif. And, of course, everyone's cell phone conversations will be overheard."

"By the Mossad?"

"In a heartbeat. The Israelis have sleepers in almost every embassy. In America, they recruit people who can get them sensitive information, or they dig it up themselves." Martel stuck his hands in his pockets, trudging steadily along the trail. "You still may think of yourself as David Wolfe, the future congressman you were last week. But to our government, and Israel, you're the lawyer for a terrorist who's shaken both countries to the core. They want to know the same thing *you* do — who's behind the murder of Amos Ben-Aron. By now, you're no doubt under surveillance.

"Your only advantage is that they may think you're too naive to know that. So you can have a little fun — stage conversations to mislead whoever's listening until they don't know true from false." Martel smiled thinly, his eyes on the horizon. "I know it sounds like something from a book for boys. But it's as serious a thing as you'll ever face, carried out by serious people. So don't say anything indictable."

More than anything Martel had said, the last remark shook David badly. "I feel like I just stepped through the looking glass."

"Never doubt it. Especially given your belief that the leak in Ben-Aron's security came from the inside. That's yet another reason you're causing such excitement: our government believes it, too. Our people want to know what Hana Arif knows, and you want to know what they know."

"Hana swears that she knows nothing."

Martel turned to him, his expression neutral. "We'll get to that toward the end. Your first problem is penetrating what we — and the Israelis — are doing to find out.

"On the American side, the CIA is running traces on the two assassins, Arif, her husband, and anyone else who pops up along the way. They're tapping all their assets, and any foreign intelligence agency they can pump for information. But the FBI and Secret Service are coming up with very little to suggest that the Secret Service or SFPD was the source of any leak."

"That leaves the Israelis."

"So it does, and they're not talking. But there's certainly precedent for it, and not only the assassination of Rabin. Do you remember the Colosio assassination?"

"Vaguely." David fished out his sunglasses; the sun, attempting to penetrate the fog, had begun to hurt his eyes. "Wasn't he a candidate for president of Mexico?"

Martel nodded. "Some people in his own party didn't like him. For whatever reason, he was shot dead at a campaign rally, amid a crowd of more than a thousand people. A videotape showed that one of his security men stepped back, almost on cue, an instant before the assassin pulled the trigger. Somehow the shooter escaped in the chaos. No one was ever prosecuted — not the assassin, nor anyone in Colosio's security.

"Israel isn't Mexico — the Shin Bet and Mossad are all over this. But the possibility of a betrayal from the inside, and the vulnerability it suggests, is extremely sensitive — at least until the Israelis find out what really happened." Martel brushed back a windblown forelock. "Whatever the answer, your Mr. Khalid is right about one thing. Even if she's guilty, Hana Arif is merely one piece of an extremely complex puzzle — a meticulously planned, well-executed plot conceived by people with a sophisticated grasp of geopolitical cause and effect. People who understood the effect not only of killing Ben-Aron but of doing it on U.S. soil: that America would stop pushing the peace process to compensate for its own sense of responsibility to Israel."

The more Martel explained, the more daunting David found his task, so far outside the normal reach of the legal system. "And who might those people be?"

Martel laughed softly. "The Al Aqsa Martyrs Brigade, of course. Isn't it obvious?"

"Not to you, I suspect."

"Not to Al Aqsa, either. Two of their alleged leaders have denied it on the Internet — although given that the Israelis have killed a number of them, and driven the rest so far underground they can't come up for air, it's hard to know who speaks for them. So we're left to conjecture why a group allied with Fatah, which is barely hanging on to the presidency of the Palestinian Authority, would do something so potentially fatal to them both." Martel stopped, breathing in the sea-scented air as he surveyed the rolling hills around them. "Al Aqsa's name is derived from the famous mosque in the Old City of Jerusalem, symbolizing the Islamic fundamentalism that scares the hell out of most Americans. But its genesis is really quite parochial — Arafat funded it so as to create a militant rival to Hamas, which was already threatening his authority." Pausing, Martel lifted his eyebrows. "It's not that Al Aqsa isn't sincere — they've certainly carried out suicide bombings. But the first suicide bombing in America? Unless I've missed something, Al Aqsa has no infrastructure here."

"Meaning?"

"That Jefar and Hassan may be Al Aqsa. Perhaps Arif, as well." Turning to David, Martel stopped walking. "But if they are, they needed help from others — on the inside, breaching Ben-Aron's security; on the outside, providing support and equipment for the assassins. Both are beyond Al Aqsa's capacity."

"Who then?"

Martel's eyes glinted. "Well, it *is* the Middle East, and the victim *is* Amos Ben-Aron. There are Muslims, Jews, and even Christians who wished him dead — a rainbow coalition of hatred. As one example, are you familiar with a Jewish settler from Brooklyn named Barak Lev, and something called the Masada movement?"

David nodded. "I saw him on CNN, suggesting that God might want to kill Ben-Aron Himself."

"People like Lev sometimes try to help God along. Which brings me to fundamentalist Christians. You've heard of the Rapture."

"Vaguely."

"The Rapture was concocted by a couple of fundamentalist preachers. They took disparate passages from the Bible and wove them into a narrative that has captured the imagination of millions in these lunatic times." Martel shook his head in wonder. "Its outlines are simple, if bizarre. Once Israel has occupied its 'biblical lands' — meaning, among other things, your client's erstwhile home

— legions of the 'Antichrist' — Muslims, we are to assume — will attack the Jews, triggering a showdown in the valley of Armageddon, an actual place on the West Bank. The Jews who have not 'found' Christ will burn; the true believers will be lifted out of their clothes and transported to heaven, where, seated at the right hand of God, they'll get to watch their opponents suffer plagues of boils, sores, locusts, and frogs for years of tribulation."

"Are you sure this isn't a documentary on contemporary American politics?"

Martel chuckled. "In a way, it is. The Rapture is one reason our fundamentalists have made common cause with Jewish settlers. For the craziest among them, a war with Islam in the Middle East is not to be feared but welcomed, with Israel as the canary in God's mine shaft. None of which, as you'll recall, warmed the heart of the late prime minister."

David lapsed into silence, thinking again of Ben-Aron's clarity of vision, and of his own moral confusion at defending the accused murderer of a man he deeply admired. "Granted," Martel continued, "it's hard to imagine these Bible-bangers carrying out his murder. But it does suggest the depth of unreason, from all sides, so uniquely attached to the Middle East — including the conflict between Palestinians and Jews.

"So let's turn to the Islamists." They began walking again, Martel's eyes trained on the sparkle of distant waves. "As I said, I'm skeptical about Al Aqsa. I'm less so about Hamas, their rivals who now predominate the infrastructure of the Palestinian Authority. They're the ones bent on pushing Jews into the sea. And, unlike Al Aqsa, they have a presence in the United States — including so-called charities that, our best people believe, funnel money to their terrorists at home.

"As for what Hamas would stand to gain, we're watching it happen. The peace plan they deplore has blown up. Their rivals for control of the Palestinian Authority, Faras and his Fatah party, have been destabilized and discredited. Their rival for street cred among the armed 'resistance' groups, particularly Al Aqsa — who both Faras and Ben-Aron were reaching out to — is being eradicated by the Israel Defense Forces —"

"Back up," David interrupted. "Are you suggesting that Jefar might be Hamas?"

"I'm raising the possibility, David, that very little about Ben-Aron's assassination is what it seems. So let me spin this out. In theory, Hamas could supply the infrastructure to support this suicide bombing; they have access to a network of radical Palestinians, students and otherwise, who might be able to help lay the framework. Some aspects, like acquiring police uniforms, might be easy enough to do." Martel turned to him again. "But consider the range of what the indictment suggests the assassins needed: false IDs, credit cards, explosives, stolen motorcycles, a van bought under an assumed name. One wonders if all that wouldn't tax even the brightest students at Berkeley. Which, to me, squarely raises the specter of Iran."

Despite himself, David managed to laugh. "The Iranians. How could I forget?"

"You shouldn't. Ben-Aron didn't — he was all too aware of Iran's encouragement of Hamas and the Hezbollah, which led to the last conflict in Lebanon. And you no doubt saw that its new president suggested wiping Israel off the map. Unpleasant as that seemed to some, it was merely a restatement, in more unvarnished form, of Iran's essential foreign policy —"

"But could they murder Israel's prime minister in America? And would they? It seems like a terrible risk."

"As to 'could,' yes. In Argentina, in the early nineties, the Iranians bombed the Israeli embassy and a Jewish day-care center — never formally proven, but a fact. And they have an extensive operation in the United States, including Iranian émigrés."

Martel paused for a moment, staring out at the beach, strewn with driftwood and sea-worn rocks. "As to 'would,' " he said finally, "I agree that it's a risk. Their secret intelligence service would have to believe not only that they would succeed, but that their operation would prove to be impenetrable. A good start is their assumption that the two obvious potential sources of information, the suicide bombers, would, in fact, commit suicide. Or, at least, one would *think* the Iranians thought that.

"I'll return to that conundrum in a bit. As for motive, Iran would need a truly compelling reason. But the radicals and mullahs who run the secret intelligence service are the keepers of the flame, the vanguard of the Islamic revolution. Along with Syria, it's Iran that helps finance terrorist groups in the Middle East — including, we believe, Al Qaeda. It's Iran that is developing nuclear weapons. It's Iran that most despises Israel and that, more than any outside country, tries to instigate acts of violence that will force the Israelis to respond in kind."

Reaching the edge of the sand, Martel stopped. "The Iranians," he said, "are far more ambitious than the Syrians, who themselves blew up one of *their* antagonists, the former prime minister of Lebanon, by jamming a Beirut manhole with explosives. Why should America be immune, I can imagine the Iranians asking themselves. But what perplexes me, among many other things, is this: how on earth could the Iranians penetrate Ben-Aron's security?"

David's mind was reeling. "A moment ago," he told Martel, "you said that one would 'think' that the planners meant both assassins to die."

Martel gazed at the water, mica flashes of sunlight on blue waves. "That troubles me," he finally answered. "If you know what you're doing, it's hard to botch a suicide bombing. The plastique should have blown Jefar to paradise in little pieces."

"And so?"

Martel drew a bottle of red Bordeaux from his knapsack, nodding toward a weathered log wedged into the sand. "Describing the labyrinth," he said, "is the easy part. Let's have some wine and try to figure out where you are. A lot more may depend on that than the future of Hana Arif."

14

Stripped of bark, the redwood log had washed up on the gray-brown sand that marked the reach of high tide. The two men sat, sipping Bordeaux as they gazed at the water, the surf softly dying a few feet away.

"Start with the breach of Ben-Aron's security," Martel said. "It's remotely plausible that the breach was not internal — that someone working with the assassins intercepted a communication about the change of route. But that would have required luck and equipment of considerable sophistication, and there seems to be no evidence of the latter. So you have to assume a leak on the Israeli side.

"That means more than angry extremists like the Masada people — the plotters would need someone on the inside whom the Israelis, an extremely careful lot, mistakenly believed to be reliable. But the suicide bombers were ordinary Palestinians." Martel paused to sip his wine, savoring the conundrum. "So how do you connect such seemingly irreconcilable elements? And who's capable of doing so?"

"Guilty or innocent," David responded, "Hana's not the answer to your question. Whoever set this up is watching from the shadows. Meanwhile, I'm starting with two threads: a possible leak on the Israeli side, and the certainty that the assassins were Palestinians. All I can do is try to pull each thread and see what I unravel."

Martel nodded. "One thread at a time, David. The security team for Ben-Aron had an inner circle — the detail leader of our Secret Service and the leader of the Israeli team. They would have met well in advance, exchanging information about threats to Ben-Aron, carefully mapping out a city-by-city itinerary that allowed them to put the security in place well before his arrival — leaving flexibility, however, for last-minute changes of route."

"Who would have made that decision?"

"The American detail leader, minutes before it happened. He'd tell the Israelis and the head of Dignitary Protection from the SFPD, and they'd communicate with their respective people. Which means that someone on the inside would have had to tip off the handler, who then called Iyad Hassan, in an extremely short period of time. All without being detected." Martel turned to David. "Which is why the FBI questioned Arif so closely about her whereabouts, and why her responses are so problematic."

David studied an abalone shell, its shades of variegated pearl. "So the change of route was transmitted to a small group of Americans and Israelis. All of whom were in San Francisco, and none of whom knew in advance."

"Yes. So there actually are two threads — the Americans and the Israelis. But our interests and theirs are different. The Israelis want any breach to be our fault; we want it to be theirs. And while we're clearly to blame for letting two phony policemen join the motorcade, an Israeli may be to blame for enabling them to assassinate Ben-Aron."

"Just how far will we, and the Israelis, go to find out what happened?"

Martel pondered this. "Ordinarily, our intelligence people would consider dipping into their antiterrorist bag of tricks. Given a free hand, we've 'rendered' terrorist suspects to countries like Egypt to be tortured — one time, we put a suspected Al Qaeda operative in an airplane at Guantánamo and flew him around for a while, threatening to land in Cairo until he started talking. Or we might use 'black sites' maintained by the CIA in places like the former Soviet Union, where suspects just disappear.

"But none of that works here. The 'suspects' would be well-placed American and Israeli security officers — we can't just torture or 'disappear' them. And if our government used something overtly untoward to extract a confession and you didn't like its contents, you'd be complaining that it was . . ." Pausing, Martel shrugged. "What's the metaphor?"

"Fruit of the poisonous tree."

"Exactly. So given that, and the worldwide scrutiny attendant to this particular assassination, our government will proceed with care. Though Jefar might not have believed that with respect to him. Which may help explain his confession."

"And the Israelis?"

"May be more ruthless. Though they'll certainly have limits — Israel has a contentious press, and considerable respect for law. The problem for the prosecutor, and for you, is that the Israelis will proceed in secret. The day-to-day investigation will be run by their attorney general's office, an extremely professional bunch. They'll utilize Shin Bet and the

Mossad, of course. And they will *not* be sharing leads and raw intelligence with our government, and certainly not with you. Particularly if it suggests that one of their security people is tied to the assassination . . ."

"The reason being?"

"Reasons: the integrity of the investigation, fear of exposing internal vulnerability, and the political volatility of the question. Israeli political factions are sharply divided — depending on the answer, governments could rise or fall, and the course of Israeli politics change entirely. By raising this, you'll be tossing matches on a vat of kerosene." Martel spoke more quietly. "Having become a bit of a pariah myself, I can't say I envy you. Your decision to defend this woman may have consequences that are as unpredictable as they are unpleasant."

David silently contemplated his sudden isolation. "So here's how what you're telling me plays out," he said at length. "I go to the judge and demand access to the fruits of our government's investigation — *and* the Israelis'. Sharpe may have to give me what our government comes up with. But she has no power to make the Israelis give me anything. If they refuse, she's stuck between me and them — I'll claim that I need what the Israelis have to give Hana a fair trial, and Sharpe will say that she can't get it."

"What does that buy you?"

"Other than a lot of outrage? If I'm very lucky, a way into Israel's investigation, or a possible way out of this for Hana."

"Guilty or not."

David shrugged. "Guilty or not. All I can do, as you say, is toss the match."

Martel smiled faintly. "That's why I'm savoring our talk. Lawyers and spies develop the same qualities: a deep curiosity, a passion for truth, an understanding of betrayal, and an appreciation of moral ambiguity. The elements of human nature."

Even before this, David reflected, he could not imagine explaining such as conversation to Carole.

"In any event," Martel went on, "Avi Hertz is here to watch you, not help you. As you suspected, he's ex-Mossad, as tough and resourceful as he needs to be. His only interest will be in protecting Israel — by keeping its secrets, if need be, while trying to help Sharpe pressure your client into a confession."

"But if she doesn't confess," David answered, "his interests and Sharpe's may not be quite the same."

"The 'keeping secrets' part, you mean. You have some ideas, I suppose, about playing one side against the other?"

"Yes."

With another smile, Martel considered this. "Let's move on to the Palestinians," he said after a time. "What do you know about Hassan and Jefar?"

"Very little."

"They're where you start, of course, along with the context that can move a normal-seeming man to become a human bomb.

"Generalizations are dangerous. But it's almost certain that one, or both, will have a story. Though their families don't seem to be talking, we know they're both unmarried. But that doesn't mean that there aren't people they love deeply. In the lives of Palestinian suicide bombers, one often finds some humiliation — to them, perhaps, or a member of their family — that they attribute to the Israelis."

Sadly, David thought of Munira, watching the Israeli soldiers shame her father at a checkpoint. "Quite often," Martel continued, "there's much more than shame involved. There's a tragedy — perhaps the death of someone they loved, where they felt helpless to prevent it from occurring."

David cocked his head in inquiry. "What role does Islam play?"

"It varies — every religion has the capacity to be used for good or ill." Martel poured more wine. "Have you ever studied photographs of lynch mobs in the South?"

David shook his head.

"In many of them, the white men gazing up at the black men they've just hung are wearing suits. They'd just come from church, you see — in *their* minds, they were killing the sons of Ham, the inferior race mentioned in the Bible." Martel paused, clearing his throat with a phlegmy cough. "In the case of these particular suicide bombers, religious passion can serve as glue for their more temporal frustrations: certainly Hamas invokes Islam in its various exhortations to violence. But few of us crash airplanes into buildings just to get to heaven that much quicker.

"To me, all the stuff about seeking paradise is overblown." Briefly, Martel smiled. "Personally, I find the idea of deflowering seventy virgins both dreary and exhausting, and it utterly fails to address the sexual aspirations of *female* suicide bombers. But my central point is that suicide bombers are driven by hopelessness, anger, and the desire to free their land from some sort of occupation, real or perceived. In short, you should look for what happened to Jefar and Hassan — or what they *hoped* would happen — here on earth."

"And their handlers?"

"Are a different breed." Martel gave David a probing look. "I gather that, at one point in your life, you knew Hana Arif fairly well. Or, at least, thought you did. Obviously, I can't speak to her personal attributes. But the ideal handler has a unique ability to project his or her ideology, and a keen understanding of how to motivate others to sacrifice themselves to achieve the handler's ends. In three words: articulate, charismatic, and manipulative."

"Only two of them describe Hana. Articulate and charismatic."

"Not manipulative?"

David shrugged. "Not unless I'm being manipulated."

Eyebrows raised, Martel turned to the water. "It takes a certain gift, David, to make an act of self-destruction seem rational, even desirable. One has to be skilled at identifying, and then ensnaring, those people who are susceptible. But as I say, I don't know Hana Arif."

For a time, David, too, gazed at the Pacific. Then he said, "Her husband claims she's being framed."

"Does he? That's interesting. Did you ever read *Bodyguard of Lies*?"

"No."

"You should. The book's subject is an elite group set up by Winston Churchill and British intelligence prior to the Normandy invasion. Its entire purpose was to persuade Hitler and the Germans that the Allied invasion of Europe would begin not at Normandy, but Calais.

"Their tactics were quite inventive. As one example, they lifted the corpse of a young man from the morgue, put him in uniform, secreted supposedly classified information about the Calais invasion in his pocket, and floated him ashore in occupied France. In short, they painstakingly created a mosaic of lies for the Germans to assemble, creating the illusion of detailed military planning." Martel's voice changed tenor, becoming meditative. "Among the cruelest aspects of this deception was that the British fed their allies in the French resistance the same false information. So that when the Germans captured and then tortured them, some bravely died to protect a falsehood. And others broke, just as the British hoped, telling lies they thought were true in order that they might live."

It took a moment for David to comprehend the story. "Ibrahim Jefar."

"Yes. Why did Jefar survive, I keep asking myself." Martel paused. "Perhaps he was just lucky, or unlucky. Or perhaps his unwitting role was to tell the 'truth.' Like the French, he can pass a lie detector test, or name your client if someone shoots him full of sodium pentothal. All he seems to know is whatever Hassan told him."

David pondered this. "That leaves the fingerprints and the cell phone call."

"It does." Martel studied David closely. "You're after the husband, I assume."

"Of course. Who better to get a paper with her prints on it, or borrow Hana's cell phone as she slept?"

"Does he suspect that?"

"I'm not sure."

Martel laughed softly. " 'Oh, what a tangled web we weave,' " he quoted, " 'when first we practice to deceive.' The question is, Who's deceiving whom

— or themselves?" Abruptly, all humor vanished. "How badly, David, do you want it to be Khalid?"

David did not flinch; nor did he answer. "You said this was the Middle East. The surface of this story is too neat — the one apparent defect in a flawless plot is that Jefar can give them Hana's name, with just enough evidence to set her up for lethal injection. If she knows nothing, Hana becomes the perfect cul-de-sac."

"Then you've also considered the other interpretation."

"Yes. Saeb's guilty, and so is she. The intimations of marital stress are just an act."

Martel nodded. "With one more element," he added slowly. "The suspicion, on her behalf or his, that you want to believe it."

"There's only one problem with that thesis, Bryce. For Hana to be guilty, she would also have to be inexplicably careless. Which brings me back to Saeb."

Martel squinted into the failing sun. For a long time, he did not speak. When he did, it was in the tone of a man continuing another conversation, one of far longer standing. "Your father," he told David, "was good company, in his intellectual way. I became quite fond of him. But he spent his life observing the lives of others, until he became an observer of his own.

"In my own work, I've learned to keep a distance. But your father's detachment was more innate. It had nothing to do with whether, as a son, you deserved better. Your father was a cold man because he was a frightened one — of himself, I always thought, and of facing his own emotions." He turned to David, his face expressing more concern than he had ever allowed himself to show. "You have enough courage, it seems. But I never quite believed in the life I saw you living, not that you were bad at it.

"I don't know what's making you do this. But don't treat this case like it's a card trick you're performing — an act of pride, or another chance to be clever and creative. Your reasons go way deeper than that." Pausing, Martel rested his hand on David's shoulder. "Whatever they are, David, learn from them. That may be all this very hard experience will ever have to offer you."

15

That night, David could not sleep.

The world he had constructed so carefully for himself was disintegrating. He had received a curt phone call from Burt Newman, firing him as a client and pronouncing his career in politics "as dead as Adolf Hitler"; that one he had expected. More difficult were the calls and messages over the past few days from friends of his and Carole's, ranging from compassionate — "Are you okay?" — to condescending — "Have you thought about Carole?" — to shrill and self-involved — "How can you do this to us?" Equally depressing was the call from his law school friend Noah Klein, regarding his decision to defend Hana; though Noah tried to be tactful, he spoke to David as though he must have suffered a nervous breakdown. David's only distraction from the telephone was the media onslaught, stoked by the White House, Israel, and the terrible consequences of the crime itself, exemplified by the Israelis' systematic war against Al Aqsa. The weekly newsmagazines typified this: all three featured photographs of Hana on the cover, one bearing the caption "Professor of Terror?"; all sifted her personal history at length — from her radical statements at Harvard to the mundane surface of her current life — for clues to why she might have become a terrorist. *Newsweek*'s sidebar traced the history of female suicide bombers; *Time*'s focused on David's "inexplicable" decision to defend her, quoting anonymous "friends" and "acquaintances" regarding David's stunning "fall from grace," so bewildering in a man of "such obvious ambition."

Lying awake, David wondered if Marnie Sharpe could be counted as a "friend" or merely an "acquaintance." Time passed with merciless slowness — minutes, and finally another hour, marked by the red illuminated numbers of his alarm clock. Again and again he thought of Carole. But the absence of any sound in his bedroom confirmed that she had vanished from his life.

The next morning, while the private firm he had hired secured his office against wiretaps and surveillance devices, David met Angel Garriques and Marsha Kerr in the park near the Palace of Fine Arts.

The morning was cool but clear. They sat on the grass with croissants and a thermos of coffee, looking across the duck pond at the ornate dome, which reminded David of a bandshell built by Romans at the height of architectural decadence. Angel was a young ex–public defender whom David had hired three years before for his shrewd instincts and quick intelligence; Marsha, a fortyish professor at the University of San Francisco, was David's former colleague from the U.S. Attorney's Office, an expert in litigation involving foreign governments and classified information. As David's only associate and the new father of twins, Angel was in no position to object to representing Hana Arif; Marsha, meanwhile, was intrigued by the complexities of extracting highly sensitive information from two governments, and she also liked the handsome hourly rate at which David would be paying her. In both cases, David reflected, the morality of lawyers, so counterintuitive to the rest of the population, was helpful: that the guilt or innocence of a client, or even the horror of what she might have done, was secondary to ensuring that the system worked for everyone. That this ethic also served to cloak ego and amorality was, in David's experience, less remarked on by the tribunes of the law.

For a time, they dissected the case against Hana. Angel stroked the dark beard he had grown to age the sensitive brown eyes and round, lineless face he considered embarrassing for a seasoned trial lawyer. "We don't have much to go on," he concluded. "The usual defense is that the prosecution's evidence is deficient. But that doesn't seem like enough here. If we don't come up with something more, like who did what Hana's accused of doing, we're in trouble."

"But who?" David asked. "Unless we can name him, and back it up with evidence, we'll lose the jury. And Hana may lose her life."

"I assume," Marsha said, "that the FBI questioned Khalid about all that."

"Sure. What they got was 'I don't know about the slip of paper'; 'I never touched her cell phone'; 'I was watching CNN with my daughter.' None of which, even if true, rules him out as a coconspirator with Hana. But that possibility doesn't help us."

Marsha brushed back a strand of graying hair. "Why would Hana disguise her handwriting by typing out her cell phone number, then leave prints on the paper she'd typed on? And why pass out an international cell phone number?"

"If the evidence is phony," Angel added, "who planted it?"

"Have you talked to Munira?" Marsha asked David.

Pondering the question, David felt the last swallow of coffee jangling his nerves. "Not since the arrest. And it's tricky. Saeb is even more protective than Hana, and Munira's torn between them. Plus, she's twelve years old. How do I ask if her father made a suspicious-sounding phone call while they were watching CNN?"

"Suppose you liked her answer," Marsha said. "Arif's the client, not her daughter."

"It's not that simple," David rejoined. "I can't just put a twelve-year-old on the witness stand with half the world watching, hoping she'll incriminate her own father. Do I explain that I want to nail Saeb *before* she's sworn in? Or just exploit an already traumatized adolescent and hope it all works out?

"Either way, the jury would despise me. And if she takes down one parent, or both, how will she live with it?" David stopped himself, continuing in a softer tone. "If Munira blurts out something that convicts Hana instead of Saeb, I'd descend from callous to stupid."

Marsha put down her coffee. "I don't mind callous," she said coolly. "Especially when the *alternative* is being stupid."

He needed her expertise, David knew, and his internal conflicts were affecting his judgment. "As you say," David agreed, "Hana's the client. But I can't imagine her wanting me to put Munira on the stand."

"What do we need to go after Jefar?" Angel asked David. "If Hana's innocent, he's a liar."

"Unless he's just repeating what Hassan told him. As for what we know about either of them, it's not much. In the end, I'll probably have to go to the West Bank and try to track down more information." Against his better judgment, David took another sip of coffee, hoping for a lift. "Part of *our* case has to be that Sharpe's ignoring what matters most: who planned the assassination, and who supplied the equipment to carry it out? In particular, who leaked the change of route?"

"All good questions," Marsha responded. "But we can't just ask the government for everything they've got. All we're entitled to is information that might exculpate Arif, or at least might be 'material to the defense.' If what we want is classified, they can also withhold the 'sources and methods' they used to get it, even if they're helpful to us — otherwise, the argument goes, defense lawyers like us would dry up the government's sources, maybe even get American agents killed. As for the Israelis, anything they give us is voluntary. Of course, they won't volunteer a thing."

"In other words," Angel said, "we're fucked."

David glanced at Marsha. "Some of us, Angel, might consider that an opportunity."

Marsha laughed softly. "You're planning to blackmail the United States attorney, aren't you? Or, more accurately, 'graymail' her."

David shrugged away the phrase. "Hana's entitled to a fair trial. At least in theory, that means we should get any information that could help establish her defense. If the United States or Israel refuses — for whatever reason — then they're ensuring that Hana's trial won't be fair. That's our bottom line: fair trial or no trial."

Angel looked from David to Marsha. "Won't Sharpe just give us whatever she has? Otherwise, it's prosecutorial misconduct."

"That's certainly why she'll want to," Marsha answered. "But Sharpe's interests may differ from those of the intelligence agencies of either country, whose *own* interests may be at odds with each other's. The debate over 'who lost Ben-Aron' is central to Israel's leaders, and to ours. At least for now, Israel doesn't want to reveal that Ben-Aron's security detail may have included a traitor. So the Americans may be monitoring — to put it bluntly, spying on — Israel's internal investigation." Pausing, Marsha tossed the last scrap of her croissant to the duck that had been circling her. "The United States wants to redeem itself in the eyes of the Israelis, not to mention the world, by convicting Hana Arif — and, through Arif, by cracking open the conspiracy. But the president and our intelligence agencies have another interest, which is very different from Israel's. So if David can show that an Israeli mole set up Ben-Aron, the White House, in contrast to Sharpe, might consider that a favor. The Israelis won't."

Watching Angel try to absorb this, David sympathized: in a week he had morphed from a prospective congressman to the lawyer for an alleged terrorist, pitting his own government against an ally that had lost its leader in the bombing David had witnessed. He turned again to Marsha and said, "Tell Angel about the *Achille Lauro.*"

Marsha smiled faintly, a cynical crinkling of her eyes. "The *Achille Lauro,*" she began, "was a luxury liner boat-jacked by a terrorist network run by a man named Abu Abbas. The CIA was pretty sure

Abbas was hiding out in Egypt — though Mubarak, Egypt's president, assured them that he was moving heaven and earth to find him. The CIA had doubts. So the CIA and the Israelis redirected their intercept capacity and overheard our friend Mubarak's aides arranging Abbas's departure. Instead of expressing our government's disappointment, we simply forced Abbas's plane to land in Sicily." Marsha took a final sip of coffee and poured the remnants on the grass. "Now our intelligence people may be doing the same thing to the Israelis, hoping to learn whether someone in Ben-Aron's security detail helped kill him.

"If our intelligence agencies succeed, David may be entitled to know. Then it's the Americans who have a problem — they may not want the Israelis to know that they have this information, or how they got it. How *that* gets resolved is well beyond Sharpe's pay grade."

Angel looked bemused. "How would it all play out?" he asked Marsha.

"Hard to say. In 1988, Congress passed a law requiring the CIA to name the former Nazis it had recruited. But for a good while the CIA interpreted that law to exclude disclosure of the fact that its payroll included five associates of Adolf Eichmann, who planned Hitler's extermination of six million Jews. I suppose they thought that a bit sensitive for public consumption. There may be several reasons why our intelligence agencies won't just drop their files in David's lap."

"But in the media," Angel argued, "Hana Arif is the new face of terrorism. If I were Sharpe, I'd claim that the government knows nothing that discredits its case. Then I'd accuse *us* of jeopardizing national security to free a terrorist assassin, and

David of being her sleazebag left-wing lawyer. She'll prejudice the judge, turn the media against us, and poison the jury pool."

Angel, David saw, had begun to perceive the hidden costs of defending Hana Arif. But what made his prediction so depressing was its prescience. "That's why I want that hearing closed. But just as an exercise, try assuming Hana's innocence."

"I am," Angel said defensively.

"Good," David responded. "Then she's been framed. She's the victim of a conspiracy about which the Israeli and American governments may have information we can't get. And both governments have a bewildering variety of interests that trump any deep concern that Hana may be executed precisely because she *doesn't* know who plotted the assassination." David looked intently at Angel. "We're Hana's lawyers. So we may have no choice but to make our government — and the Israelis — choose: give Hana what she needs, at whatever risk, or risk Judge Taylor throwing out the case."

"How could she?" Angel said. "The victim is the Israeli prime minister."

David felt fatigue fraying his equanimity. "It's a long shot, I agree." He paused, and when he spoke again to Angel he was also speaking to himself. "And it's certainly not a crowd-pleaser to make Sharpe fight for Hana's rights, or put at risk the pleasure of facilitating her execution. But if we lose, it's Hana who will do the dying. We only have to live with the result."

16

By the time David reached his office, his secretary, Anna Chu, was referring media calls to the public relations firm he had hired for the duration of the case. Anna, a sharp, middle-aged woman who knew David well, asked what to do when the inevitable hate mail started to arrive. On the theory that he might learn something helpful in selecting a jury, David decided to read it. Then he closed the door to his office and listened to the voice-mail messages that had come in overnight.

There were several more from people he knew, none supportive. The doctor in his malpractice case had found another lawyer; Stan Sharfman, who had sat next to David at Carole's dinner for Amos Ben-Aron, had withdrawn his financial and political support; Senator Shapiro simply left her private cell phone number, though in a tone so chill that David dreaded calling her. The absence of any message from Harold Shorr reminded David of his obligation to place another call he had no heart for.

After deleting the last message, David leaned back in his chair, closing his eyes.

This was his life now. He had to wall off his emotions and husband his personal resources, or he would be no good to Hana or himself. That meant relying on the habits of a lifetime: plenty of exercise and sleep, coping with chaos by listing his priorities, then addressing them with a rigor that, at least, conferred the illusion of control. The first thing, he concluded, was to confront the mental undertow that would erode his concentration until he called Betsy and, especially, Harold.

The talk with Betsy Shapiro was mercifully brief.

"You must know why I called," Betsy said. "I can't support you for Congress now. Neither can the mayor." Her voice was polite but cool, indifferent to his reasons. "I'm sorry, David, but you don't come back from defending the murderer of Amos Ben-Aron. Any effort to justify yourself would only be demeaning."

Harold made things easier — he refused to take David's call, leaving him to wonder whether this refusal stemmed from anger or from hurt, and whether the hurt was more for Carole or himself. But no answer could lessen David's guilt.

The mail, when it came, offered him another incentive for self-preservation.

After directing Angel to research their argument against Hana's extradition, David read the letters, some anonymous and some not, that Anna had left on his desk. The only buffer was their sameness:

Dear Lying Jew (remember that I'm Jewish):

Why are you trying to get a Jew-killer off? May you and this Arab murderer fuck each other and die of AIDS . . .

Another said, more painfully: *Your hands are dripping with the blood of a man who sought peace for the Jewish people, and all those who will die because of his murder. I hope to see you suffer a slow and terrible death from cancer . . .*

And another: *Anyone who sides with a murderous Arab slut who killed a defender of Israel is a self-hating Jew, as bad as Hitler . . .*

Sometimes the theme was David's greed: *As a Holocaust survivor, I am ashamed that you are a Jew who sells out other Jews for money. You fulfill the stereotype of a greedy Jew, and I therefore declare you not Jewish . . .*

Or: *You're a shyster who would send his mother to the gas chambers for a fee . . .*

Or: *I am a Holocaust survivor, and you make me think of the Jewish collaborators in the ghetto of my native city of Lodz. Except you do this not to live, but for Arab dollars . . .*

David did not read the last few letters. "Throw these out," he told Anna, "and any like them. And don't let Angel see them. We've got too much else to think about."

David drove to the federal detention center.

The conversation with Hana began with what would become their pattern: an emotional reticence punctuated by ambiguous silences, which both could blame on the fear of eavesdropping. To David, it became like watching Hana through glass; she seemed untouchable and poignant, except when he wondered if she was a liar and a murderer.

Today, the subject was extradition. "I don't know what the Israelis are going to do," David told her. "But unless you want to be tried in Israel, we need a strategy to head that off. You know the considerations. We may have better access to government files in the United States. But Israel has no death penalty."

Hana folded her hands in front of her. "What an irony *that* would be," she said. "Hoping for the Zionists to save my life by imprisoning me in the land they stole from us, until at last I die of natural causes. The final humiliation, so interminable."

David studied her. "Worse than death?"

"More certain." Hana looked up at him. "I do not believe for a moment that the Israelis will give me a fair trial."

Though her fears were understandable, there was too much history, David knew, for her to separate distrust from reason. "I'm not sure you'll get a fair trial here," he answered.

"Nor am I. But at least there is you, David. Perhaps the only Jew who does not hate me."

David mustered a smile. "That's not my only qualification, I hope."

"No," she answered softly. "There are many other things. Such as courage. Even locked away, I know what this has cost you."

David chose not to answer. Discussing his personal misery with Hana, who had caused it, would cross the boundaries he had drawn for himself. As though seeing this, Hana looked away.

"About extradition," he told her after a time, "it's your decision. But I could never counsel you to risk your own execution. Not just for your sake, but Munira's."

Turning, Hana held his gaze. "This is all about Munira, David. Dead or in prison, I could not be her mother. A trial in America, I think, is my only chance to influence who my daughter becomes. Or even hold her in my arms."

Her feelings about Saeb as Munira's father, David sensed, were implicit in her answer. "All right," David said at last, "I'll do what I can for both of you."

"About extradition," Sharpe told him a week later, "I still don't know what the Israelis want. Neither do they, I think. For myself, I want to keep your client here."

They sat in her office — this particular mission, David had determined, could best be performed in person. With as much dispassion as he could muster, David asked, "Because we have the death penalty?"

"Among other reasons," she said, her tone as clinical as David's. "That can't surprise you. If Arif wants to save her life, you know what she can do."

David kept his expression blank. "Hana insists there's nothing she can give you."

"Too bad." A note of annoyance crept into Sharpe's voice. "In her position, she should consider being a little more forthcoming."

"Being innocent," David responded, "keeps Hana from finding a life sentence quite as enticing as you'd think. It also accounts for her inability to help you."

"There's time yet," Sharpe said. "As you know, I don't decide whether we seek the death penalty — I merely recommend. In this case, our office's recommendation will be to seek it. If you have something more compelling than the usual — that she's a mother, or has never before murdered a prime minister — you should address it to the attorney general, asking to appear before the committee of the Justice Department that makes the final decision." Sharpe's tone became arid. "You might explain why directing a violent act that guarantees another decade of violence, perhaps thousands more dead Jews and Palestinians, fails to qualify Ms. Arif to die herself. Telling *me* that is a waste of time."

"Then I won't bother," David answered. "But I have something else for you."

Removing Hana's demand for information from his briefcase, David passed it across Sharpe's desk. As she began to scan it, a subtle freezing of Sharpe's expression betrayed her anger. She placed the document to one side with a curious fastidiousness, as if ridding herself of a dirty tissue. "Very detailed. The Chinese would probably like this information, too. Or perhaps Osama Bin Laden."

David closed his briefcase. "I hope you don't start saying that in public. I'd have to ask for a gag order, or perhaps a change of venue."

Sharpe contrived to smile. "Don't worry, David. I'm saving it for the judge."

For the first two weeks after the arraignment, David confined his public comments to rote recitations of Hana's innocence — that she was a mother, that she had no connection to terrorists, that the evidence against her was anomalous — while waiting for the flood of publicity to recede. It barely did. Then, on the morning after a female suicide bomber, also a mother, killed twenty wedding guests at a hotel in Amman, Jordan, David consented to grant Meredith Vieira's request for an interview on the *Today* show.

It was harder than it looked, David decided, to sit alone in a TV studio, talking to the eye of a television camera while an interviewer's voice squeaked through his earpiece. Vieira was well-prepared; she began by repeating, and challenging, David's prior statements on Hana's behalf. "The ranks of terrorists," she said, "include mothers, fathers, brothers, and sisters. It's not hard to conclude that your client agreed to enter this plot because she never expected Jefar to survive, and because her own life was not at risk."

The same thought had occurred to David, many times. "Then why," he countered, "is there absolutely no evidence that Hana Arif is affiliated with Al Aqsa — or any group that carries out acts of terror? You don't just walk out of a classroom, Meredith, and set yourself up as the handler of two assassins."

"Maybe that could explain why — if the indictment is correct — your client made the mistakes she did."

"Then it would be a real mistake," David responded swiftly, "to make her the linchpin of an assassination plot, wouldn't it? It's hard to believe that people smart enough to make the components of a complicated conspiracy disappear without a trace would entrust it to an amateur."

Abruptly, Vieira shifted course. "You're opposing extradition to Israel. Do you believe that Israel's justice system can't treat your client fairly?"

David considered his words. "I have great respect for Israel, and for its system of justice. But Hana Arif is a Palestinian, accused of conspiring to kill Israel's prime minister. The charge against her resonates with sixty years of bitter history, many deaths on both sides, and the fact that the Israeli populace has itself suffered from suicide bombings for far too long. Under these circumstances, no people, anywhere, could be expected to view Hana with dispassion.

"Why ask that of the Israelis, when there's no fairer system of justice anywhere than in America?

This is where Hana should be tried."

Beyond the camera, David saw Vieira's image on a split screen next to his, her eyes expressing curiosity and compassion. "A last question," she said. "Many people around the country, David, wonder why you've taken on her defense. You seem to have forfeited a promising future in politics, you have no public record of affinity for the Palestinian cause, you admired Prime Minister Ben-Aron, and you are, yourself, Jewish. Is it simply that you knew Ms. Arif in law school?"

Briefly, David paused, marshaling the answer he had so carefully rehearsed. "It's not simply that I once knew Hana Arif — it's that I *believe* her. Just as I believe that the case against her makes no sense.

"Believing these things, what else could I do? The essence of American law is the presumption of innocence. As the historic victims of prejudice, discrimination, and worse, Jews know that better than anyone."

David paused, gazing into the camera as if it were the eyes of a juror. "I'm reminded of the words of a German pastor who died in one of Hitler's concentration camps: 'First they came for the Communists, and I didn't speak up, because I wasn't a Communist. Then they came for the Jews, and I didn't speak up, because I wasn't Jewish. Then they came for the Catholics, and I didn't speak up, because I was a Protestant. Then they came for me, and there was no one left to speak on my behalf.'

"I'm no martyr — just a lawyer. But, for Hana, the principle is the same. And, unlike Nazi Germany, in America she gets an advocate to speak on her behalf."

On the monitor, Vieira nodded, and then she thanked him through his earpiece.

This interview, at least, bought Hana some better publicity, and David a few approving phone calls — two from members of San Francisco's Jewish community — amid the litany of abuse that filled his voice mail. But the message that most affected him, from Carole, was waiting for him at home.

He had not talked to her since the day she'd walked out; hearing her voice again, David felt an instant of hope. But the familiar softness of her tone was no harbinger of peace, only of her profound disappointment and distress, her painful connection to a man she could never live with but from whom she was not yet free. "You make me sad," her message said. "I'm even sad that I can't help you. But your comparison of this woman to Hitler's victims was offensive, your claim that Israel can't treat her fairly even more so.

"Please, David, get your mind off Hana Arif long enough to look at yourself in the mirror. Not for me — it's too late for that. For your own sake."

Erasing the message, David was seized by the desire to call her. But he could not, any more than he could expose his loneliness to Hana. He and Carole were finished.

17

The undiminishing avalanche of publicity, repeated daily, made David's life still harder, even as it reinforced the mass assumption that Hana Arif was guilty. But another source of distress for David was how little access he had to Munira. Saeb kept her in isolation: though Hana saw her daughter every few days, they were never alone, and by the end of Hana's first month in detention, David had seen the girl only in passing. Saeb now controlled Munira's life.

The passage of a month brought David and Marnie Sharpe back before Judge Taylor in the closed hearing he had sought — the two lawyers and the judge met around an oval conference table in Taylor's chambers, the only witness a court reporter who transcribed the proceedings. By the judge's orders, the transcript, like David's papers and Sharpe's response, would be filed under seal, unavailable to anyone. Dressed in a black business suit, Taylor sat at the head of the table. The depth of her concern was as tangible as the tension between David and Sharpe.

"Before we deal with the information sought by Mr. Wolfe," the judge asked Sharpe, "will there be any effort to extradite his client?"

"No," Sharpe answered dryly. "Mr. Wolfe is getting his wish. The government of Israel has decided to leave this prosecution in the hands of the United States."

David tried to assess the complex dynamics that informed this decision: Israel's desire not to hold a dangerous prisoner; its hope of avoiding David's demand for information; Sharpe's intention to use the death penalty to pressure Hana into a confession. "All right," Taylor said to David. "You've asked for quite a lot of information from the United States government — much of it extremely sensitive — to which Ms. Sharpe takes great exception. Let's hear your argument."

David tried to strip his request to its basics. "The essence is plain enough. We're entitled not only to information that exculpates Ms. Arif but to anything that is material to our defense." David paused for emphasis. "Our defense, Your Honor, is that Ms. Arif was framed by whoever conspired to murder Prime Minister Ben-Aron. Anything the government has regarding the assassination may help us develop that thesis. Therefore, Ms. Sharpe should provide it."

"That's certainly succinct," Taylor said crisply. "Especially considering that you're asking for the sun, stars, and moon. Ms. Sharpe?"

Sharpe spoke rapidly, an edge creeping into her voice. "The court is right. Mr. Wolfe is not merely asking for materials generated by the FBI to support this prosecution. He wants files from the CIA and the Secret Service; records of our government's continuing inquiry into the assassination; any communications on that subject between the United States and Israel; and the fruits of the surveillance he imagines we're conducting inside Israel itself. Not only is this request ridiculously overbroad, but it seeks highly classified information — including the sources and methods the government uses to gather intelligence vital to national security.

"In short, Mr. Wolfe has concocted a defense in order to justify the attempted blackmail of our government. If any lawyer can do this, and drag our secrets into court, then America's investigative and intelligence agencies might as well close up shop —"

"We surely don't want that," the judge said with a note of irony. "Not after 9/11. So what *is* Mr. Wolfe entitled to?"

"Our evidence regarding Ms. Arif," Sharpe answered promptly. "Period. Whoever else may have conspired to murder the prime minister, the case against Arif is simple."

"Too simple," David retorted. "The question of who plotted to murder Amos Ben-Aron goes directly to whether Ms. Arif was involved or whether the plotters set her up. The prosecutor's driving lack of curiosity excludes any inquiry into who actually planned the assassination, who provided the materials to support it, and whether the plot involved one or more Israelis responsible for protecting Ben-Aron."

"This court is not the Warren Commission," Sharpe protested. "It is not the forum for a massive inquiry into every conceivable aspect of this murder — no matter how irrelevant to Ms. Arif. Mr. Wolfe is curious about everything but the case against his client."

David kept his eyes on Taylor. "Which comes down to Ibrahim Jefar," he said sardonically. "Taken at his word, he has no firsthand knowledge as to any of these questions, or even about Ms.

Arif. I could cross-examine him all day, and he couldn't help me. And yet, in Ms. Sharpe's view, Jefar's story entitles the prosecution to withhold anything that could be useful to my case." David felt a surge of real anger. "If other branches of the government — including the CIA — have what Ms. Arif needs to mount a defense, they should give it to her. This so-called blackmail is nothing more than an insistence on justice."

The judge raised her eyebrows, then abruptly asked Sharpe, "Is there any middle ground between your rather narrow sense of obligation and Mr. Wolfe's presumed desire to dismantle our intelligence apparatus?"

The phrasing of the question seemed to put Sharpe off balance. In a grudging tone, she answered, "I'm prepared to ask the FBI and our intelligence agencies for any information potentially exculpatory to Ms. Arif — excluding the sources and methods used to gather it. But that's as far as the law requires us to go."

" 'Exculpatory' according to whom?" David asked her. "Does that include information regarding a breach in Israel's protection of its own prime minister?"

"Not unless it relates to Ms. Arif."

"How can you know that it doesn't, Marnie?"

Judge Taylor held up her hand, demanding silence. "You should worry about that, Ms. Sharpe. I do. I appreciate the sensitivity of what Mr. Wolfe is seeking, much of which may not end up helping Ms. Arif.

"But this is a case where — for once — it's no exaggeration to say that the world is watching us. If you withhold information that becomes material to Ms. Arif's defense and that fact emerges later, any conviction could be thrown out. Unless Ms. Arif is no longer with us, which would create a somewhat larger problem." Leaning forward, Taylor admonished Sharpe. "Threats to national security are not confined to leaking secrets. A real or perceived injustice, approved by this court, would not only tarnish this country's image but might provoke fresh violence, here or overseas. I won't be part of that. And I won't let you be."

Surprised, David realized that the weight of Judge Taylor's responsibility was working in Hana's favor. "So here's my order," Taylor continued, speaking slowly and clearly. "The government will produce to the defense any materials in its possession that may exculpate Ms. Arif, or that relate to the assassination of Amos Ben-Aron. With respect to information that is classified or impacts national security, Mr. Wolfe will review it under the following conditions:

"First, the documents will be maintained in a secure room supervised by the FBI.

"Second, Mr. Wolfe alone can see them, and only after the FBI grants him a security clearance." Turning to David, she said, "You can't remove them, copy them, take notes regarding what they contain, or reveal their contents to anyone — not your employees, cocounsel, members of the defense team, or the media, and certainly not Ms. Arif." She paused, adding incisively, "Any violation of those conditions, Mr. Wolfe, will be treated as criminal contempt — and worse.

"Third, if you wish to use these documents in court or discuss them with your client, you will file a request under seal. Unless and until I grant your request, these conditions stand." Turning to Sharpe, she said, "You can delete information about the sources and methods used in gathering intelligence. Otherwise, it is your responsibility — and you should be very clear about this — to ensure that our government errs in favor of inclusion."

Elated, David attempted to control his expression, even as he saw Marnie Sharpe strive to repress her frustration and surprise. "Next," Taylor said to David, "you have a similar request for the government of Israel. Please explain what this court can do about *that*."

The sudden coolness of Judge Taylor's tone suggested that she had granted Hana Arif all the favors David could expect. "What the court can do," he answered, "is order our government to make this request on behalf of Ms. Arif —"

"Your Honor," Sharpe cut in, "you've already given Mr. Wolfe access to information that may jeopardize our relationship with the Israelis. Now he proposes to compound the damage by compelling us to troll for whatever the *Israelis* have, no matter how harmful to their own internal security. The only limit on such irresponsibility is this court."

Turning to David, Judge Taylor asked, "What exactly *do* you want?"

David steeled himself. "Access to materials generated by Israel's internal inquiry and depositions of the Israelis charged with Ben-Aron's protection."

"On what grounds?" Taylor demanded.

"We suspect that Ben-Aron was set up by a member of his security detail. If so, that person knows much more than Ibrahim Jefar, such as the true identity of the handler."

"Are you sure you really want an answer, Counsel?" This question, disturbing in itself, betrayed Taylor's root assumption — that Hana Arif was guilty. Catching herself, she hastily added, "As Ms. Sharpe pointed out, you're treading on ground more suited to the secretary of state than defense counsel."

"As defense counsel," David answered, "I propose to proceed under the same conditions already ordered by the court, and for the same reason: to obtain a fair trial for Ms. Arif."

"This is *truly* cynical," Sharpe objected. "In the guise of seeking a fair trial, Mr. Wolfe is contriving to make this prosecution so costly to the national interest that we cannot pursue it. His tactic is not the least bit subtle: force the government to dismiss the case, or set up his own motion to dismiss it."

"Only if there's a basis," David responded calmly. "And the only basis would be if the United States or Israel sits on information that could establish Hana's innocence. I've got no hope of getting anything from Israel. Under the Mutual Legal Assistance Treaty, *you* do. Ask for it, Marnie, and then you've done all you can."

"And when the Israelis refuse, as you expect they will, I'll have set up your motion to dismiss." Sharpe turned to the judge. "Just how transparent must this get?"

Watching Taylor's expression, David stifled a response. "Enough," the judge snapped, "from both of you." Facing David, she still spoke sternly. "Whatever Israel might do is academic. I've given you broad access to whatever our government has. Before I compel Ms. Sharpe to reach into the guts of the Israeli government, Mr. Wolfe, find out if what I've given you provides some better basis for it." Her concluding words, though softer, were definitive. "Six weeks after Ben-Aron was murdered in our city, I have no desire to further inflame our relationship with Israel."

However annoyed she was, Taylor had given him a basis for renewing his request; that this had occurred to Sharpe was apparent from her narrow-eyed contemplation of the table. Satisfied, David said, "Thank you, Your Honor."

"Oh, you're welcome," Taylor answered. "There's one more thing you *are* entitled to: a trial within sixty days. I take it that you'll pass on that."

David smiled. "Please."

"Then we'll revisit a trial date in four weeks' time, when I will have another hearing in the cozy confines of these chambers." With a far more grave expression, she said to Sharpe, "A final question. In the event of a conviction, will the government seek the death penalty for Ms. Arif?"

"That's our office's recommendation, Your Honor."

Taylor simply nodded. "I thought as much."

In the hallway, Sharpe and David walked together, bonded, despite their antagonism, by their experiences as Judge Taylor's supplicants. "A good day for you," Sharpe remarked in her flattest tone.

"Some days are. Just not that many."

Sharpe stared straight ahead. "You know, David, I thought that trick you played on behalf of Ray Scallone defined your low point as a lawyer. But your performance today had a kind of tawdry grandeur. The temptations, I suppose, of your moment on the world stage, in such a worthy cause as Hana Arif."

"My only temptation is to let that pass," David

answered. "But you and I have a history, and it's about to get much longer. So let's try to put this in perspective."

Sharpe stopped, facing him. "Go ahead," she told him, though her tone was not inviting.

"You and I don't like each other," David said, "and I don't like the death penalty. But I don't doubt that you believe in what you do.

"None of this is personal, and I didn't particularly enjoy our morning together. But I got what I wanted, for now." Pausing, David looked at her intently. "An execution after a fair trial is the law. If you win, that's what you're entitled to seek. But without a fair trial, it's not an execution — it's murder. I don't want our government to murder Hana Arif."

After a moment, Sharpe gave him a dubious smile. "You make it sound so simple. And you know so well it's not. You're far too clever for that."

"And so?"

"We'll find a way to live with each other, until one of us comes out on top. Other than an acquittal, that's what you want, isn't it? Just in case you need me."

Without awaiting his answer, she walked away.

18

In theory," Bryce Martel told David over the telephone, "whether the Justice Department accepts Sharpe's recommendations on Hana Arif won't involve politics. But that's nonsense. The White House will find ways to put its fingers on the scales."

"How so?"

"Oh, the president might ask the attorney general for a 'briefing.' There's no doubt the national security adviser is in constant contact with the Israelis, and concerns about foreign policy, national security, and homeland security will all weigh on the decision. Ultimately, this isn't about the life or death of Hana Arif. It's about our relationship with Israel, protecting foreign leaders on American soil, and punishing and preventing acts of terror. None of which helps your client."

David could not disagree.

Two days later, David flew to Washington. But in the event, his appearance before the committee of the Justice Department felt like ritual, Kabuki theater stripped of meaning.

They met in an ornate conference room in the wing dedicated to the Criminal Division, a throwback to the era when public buildings aspired to majesty. David recited his arguments against the death penalty for Hana Arif. The committee members listened politely; the chairman, a gray-haired civil servant, questioned him with dispassion, as though this were a routine case. For David, this dissonance with reality confirmed that the decision would be made elsewhere, were it not already made.

In the car to the airport, David placed a call to Saeb. "I want to see Munira."

"For what reason?"

"To prepare her." David waited a moment. "They're going for the death penalty, no question."

"Was there ever?" Saeb's voice was emotionless. "What do these bureaucrats of death have to do with Munira?"

"I promised Hana," David said, "that as the case moved forward, I'd explain matters to Munira. At least as best as I can."

"No need. You can explain them to me, her father. Then I will talk to her about whatever is appropriate. This is how a family should be."

David paused, striving for calm. "Saeb, I don't ask you for much. But this is one promise I'm keeping. Consider it my fee."

It was only after speaking that David recognized how inflammatory this was. In a brittle voice, Saeb said, "So this is how you choose to remind me."

"Let's not quarrel about it," David answered coolly. "I can be at your hotel by six o'clock."

Without responding, Saeb hung up.

When he arrived at their suite, Saeb opened the door. Munira sat on the couch, again covered in black, looking expectantly at David.

"I have told Munira," Saeb said coldly, "that I

wish for you to speak to her. But she is tired. Please make it brief."

Saeb's pretense of command was impressive — from his tone of voice, he could have been speaking to a servant. "Thank you," David said politely.

David and Munira sat in the hotel's somewhat shabby restaurant, drinking tea.

Matter-of-factly, Munira said, "My father does not like you. And you do not like him."

David tried to smile. "What makes you think that?"

"I watch you."

"At Harvard," David ventured carefully, "I knew your mother better. Now he's your father, and protective of you."

Munira gave him a searching look. "And of my mother?"

The ambiguity of the question, which could be understood to intimate a connection between David and Hana, made him even more tentative. Perhaps it was nothing; perhaps he overrated the perceptiveness of an adolescent girl. Or *this* girl, at times so like Hana in her acuity. "He worries for her," David answered. "We all do. Sometimes that affects us in different ways."

Munira considered this, her long lashes half-covering her gaze at the table. "Why did my father wish for me to see you?"

"I wished it also. Do you mind?"

Munira hesitated, then shook her head. Gently, David asked, "How has it been for you with your mother away?"

Eyes still downcast, Munira shook her head again, but much more slowly, a gesture as eloquent as speech. "What do you do, Munira?"

"They sent me books to study, from my school in Ramallah. There are assignments. When I'm done, my father tells me to study the Koran." Munira's voice grew quieter. "Except when I can see my mother, that is all."

The utter loneliness she evinced, the image of this child in a prison of her own, where the slow passage of time was a punishment, stirred David's deepest sympathies, even as it also evoked her mother. "When you visit her, how is she?"

Munira's eyes closed. "I can't really talk to her — my father's always there. They do not even let me touch her." The girl's voice grew husky. "Sometimes, it is like she is already dead."

For a moment, David remembered his father's final illness: Philip Wolfe withdrew within himself, a skeleton without the power of speech, his death certain, the only question its day and hour. David could still recall the visit when his sense of helplessness became the wish for death to come.

"I won't let your mother die," he promised Munira.

Two weeks later, Marnie Sharpe held a press conference.

David watched in his office. "The Department of Justice," she began, "has determined to seek the death penalty in the prosecution of Hana Arif . . ."

That afternoon, at Sharpe's invitation, David returned to her office. "I guess you're going to tell me how Hana can cheat death."

"Why don't we make a modest beginning," Sharpe answered. "With her husband."

In his surprise, David laughed aloud. "Surely that's your theory," she continued imperturbably. "Who else could have 'framed' her — the hotel maid? We agree on one thing, David: there's a genuine possibility that Khalid was involved. If so, why not let Khalid take her place?"

"By orphaning her daughter? Hana trades Saeb's life for a life in prison. Then it's all a question of who Munira gets to bury last." David shook his head. "Even assuming Hana's guilty, you've got a fairly perverse sense of their family dynamics."

Sharpe did not smile. "I want whoever planned this. Someone's going to tell us. Khalid may be your client's only chance to live. After that, he can make his own decisions."

"To repeat, Marnie — Hana knows nothing. Even if Saeb is involved in this, she can't help you."

Sharpe sat back, as though stymied by the gulf between them. Then she reached into her desk and produced a typed document of several pages. "Read this," she said.

"What is it?"

"The report of our polygraph test on Ibrahim Jefar." She slid it across the desk. "As you know, I don't place much stock in these. But our examiner is as good as the FBI has, and he gives Jefar straight A's. I watched the test. Jefar's either a sociopath, a gifted liar, or what I firmly believe him to be — a tormented and confused young man who did not expect to be alive to take a polygraph, and chose to tell the truth."

David scanned the report, and then reread selected passages with greater care. Mercifully, Sharpe could never enter it as evidence. But David knew that she felt what he, as a prosecutor, would have: that Hana's accuser was telling the truth.

"Talk to your client," Sharpe said.

19

"So," Hana said softly, "they wish to kill me. How do they do this? I would like to know."

What did she want from him? David wondered. He decided to be as dispassionate as possible. "There's a death chamber at San Quentin. They strap the inmate to a bed and run two IVs into his left forearm to inject potassium chloride. That's all, really."

"Very clinical," Hana said. "Clean — not like a bombing." She paused, then asked, "I suppose there is an audience."

"Yes. State officials. There are places for members of the victims' families, if they care to come. And for the family of the prisoner."

"I would not have them see this — Munira and Saeb. As for the others . . ." Her voice trailed off, and then she looked at David. "Of all the conversations we might have had, this is one I did not imagine."

For a moment, David waited to speak. "Sharpe wants to make a deal. Information for your life, the name of others involved in killing Ben-Aron. Saeb, perhaps."

"Why not Muhammad himself?" Hana asked in an ironic tone, then inclined her head, watching David. "About Saeb," she said more quietly, "what is it that Sharpe thinks I must know?"

"What *do* you know, Hana?"

Their eyes met, and Hana looked away. "I have thought about this," she said quietly. "Many hours. Who did this to me, I wonder."

"Saeb?"

"So you have thought this." Hana closed her eyes. "He could have, I know. But there are easier ways to disguise his role, and I am his wife. Why would he do this?"

"You tell me."

After a moment, her eyes opened. "Do you wish me to lie? To do to Saeb, or anyone, what has been done to me?" Her voice filled with resignation. "I am innocent, David. I have no one to betray."

"And nothing to tell me? Sharpe's looking at your history — statements that suggest you favor violence. And whether Saeb does."

"There's a difference between us, David. Also between who I was when you knew me and today. In only a few years there will be three generations of Jews born in Israel, who will grow up speaking Hebrew like their parents and grandparents. It is all they know, like the Galilee was all *my* parents and grandparents knew. What are we to do, eradicate them all or simply turn them into refugees? And where does it end?" Hana shook her head, her expression rueful. "I wish there were no Israel. But if I do not ask myself these questions now, what kind of person would I be?"

"And Saeb?"

"Saeb was defined when he was fourteen. He lost everyone; I merely lost an aunt. From that, I could perhaps imagine him becoming a suicide bomber — our young people have seen too much, and they feel so little hope. But to exploit them? It is morally bankrupt."

"Is that what Saeb believes?"

Hana folded her hands. "I've told you, David. If Saeb consorts with so-called terrorists, I do not know it. Just as I told your FBI I know nothing about Ibrahim Jefar. Let alone why he's lying."

"I'm not at all sure he is." David paused. "They gave him a lie detector test, Hana. He passed it."

Her reaction was almost undetectable, a slight movement of her shoulders that made her seem smaller. "I see."

"Sharpe believes him, and she dismisses my theory that you were framed as an excuse to meddle with our intelligence agencies and the Israeli government. That's why she's so comfortable asking for the death penalty."

Head bowed, Hana said nothing.

It was time to confront her, David thought. "There *is* one thing you can do."

"And what is that?"

"Take a lie detector test. Just as Jefar did."

For a moment Hana was silent. "And the risks?"

"There's only one. That you won't pass."

When Hana did not answer, David felt tension tightening his chest. "It would have to be done here," he went on. "So Sharpe will know we've tested you. She'll leak that to the media. If I can't say you've passed . . ."

Still Hana did not look at him. With a calm he did not feel, David continued, "If you do pass, Sharpe may want the FBI to test you. But this at least might give her pause. And I can use the test results with Judge Taylor to justify going after the Israelis, and to tell the media Sharpe is prosecuting an innocent woman."

David omitted the rest — that another use of the test was to force a guilty client to face reality. Or that, far more than he wished, Hana's answer mattered to him. Like David, she seemed hardly to breathe. "In law school," she said at last, "we learned that these tests are little better than witchcraft. The guilty can pass, the innocent fail. It won't matter to this prosecutor."

"So you won't do it."

"No, David, I will." She looked up at him then, eyes shiny with tears. "Because it matters to you."

David told her nothing about how the test worked, what the examiner would do to arouse her fears, or that it was fear that made the test so useful. He recognized this as a form of ruthlessness in himself, less as a lawyer than the man who wished to know if Hana had betrayed him. That he was also betraying Hana he understood too well.

They met with the polygraph examiner, a rotund former FBI agent with an avuncular demeanor, in a room that, though larger, was as white and featureless as the one where Hana and David consulted. The examiner, Gene Meyer, sat across from them, his machine on the table. He began by trying to engage her in seemingly random small talk while he assessed her reactions. Hana's responses were perfunctory, her manner indifferent. Abruptly, Meyer asked, "Have you had enough sleep, Ms. Arif?"

"Under the circumstances."

"Then let me explain how the test works. When I ask you a question, three needles will record your reaction as a roll of paper runs through the machine, sort of the way doctors measure how our heart is functioning. So this machine is not

the lie detector. You are."
"And how is that?"
Hana spoke with an air of boredom, as though she did not have sensors stuck to her wrists, her thumbs, and, beneath her jumpsuit, near her heart.
"When we lie," Meyer continued, "our bodies react in ways that betray us — changes in breathing, heart rate, even the amount of perspiration on our skin. You don't like to lie, do you?"
"That depends," Hana answered. "But usually not."
Meyer glanced at David. Only David knew, from long ago, that what passed for chill indifference could be anger Hana was struggling to restrain.
"Then let's try something." Meyer fished a deck of cards out of his pocket and spread them on the table. "Pick one."
Hana did this. When she picked it up, David saw the queen of spades. "I'll name every card in the deck," Meyer said, "from ace to deuce, and ask if that's the card you drew. Your job is to answer no to every question — even when the answer is yes. Do you understand?"
"Completely. With every card but one, I am to tell the truth. Once, I lie. And then you will see how good a liar I am."
Meyer's amiable pretense had begun to slip. Turning on his machine, he said briskly, "That's the idea, Ms. Arif. Is the card you're holding an ace?"
The paper began unspooling. "No," Hana answered.
"Is it a king?"
"No."
"Is it a queen?"
Briefly, Hana paused. "No."

She did not change expression with this answer, nor with the answer that followed. Impassive, Meyer watched the graph unfold in front of him. "Is your name Hana Arif?" he asked.

"Yes."

"Are you married to Saeb Khalid?"

"Yes."

"Do you have a daughter named Munira?"

"Yes. And I'd like to be with her again someday. So why don't you ask about what I'm supposed to have done."

Meyer's eyes narrowed. "Do you recall ever meeting a man named Iyad Hassan?"

"No."

"Within the last six months, have you spoken by telephone to Iyad Hassan?"

"No." Hana leaned forward. "Let *me* suggest a question, Mr. Meyer: Were you involved in the assassination of Amos Ben-Aron?"

David felt himself tense. Meyer stared at her, then repeated the question.

"No," Hana answered calmly. "But for the sake of completeness, perhaps you should ask if I was aware of any plan to kill him."

When Meyer glanced at him, David nodded. It took all the discipline he had not to watch the needle. "Before the death of Amos Ben-Aron," Meyer asked Hana, "were you aware of a plan to kill him?"

"No." With the same indifferent manner, Hana sat back. "Now I will answer your other questions."

They were numerous and detailed — whether Hana had typed her telephone number on a piece of paper; whether she had received a cell phone call on the night before Ben-Aron was killed; whether she had ever spoken to Ibrahim Jefar;

whether she had made any cell phone calls between the beginning of Ben-Aron's speech and the bombing. The pattern fell into a rhythm that David found hypnotic: two voices, one asking damning questions, the other answering "No"; the faint scratching of three needles on paper. Watching it unspool, David felt perspiration on his forehead.

Hana did not look at him. It was as though she had forgotten he was present.

When Meyer was done, he was silent for a time, studying the roll of paper. "How do you think you did?" he asked Hana.

Hana shrugged. "I suppose it depends on how good the machine is. Or you are."

Meyer looked up from the paper. "Can you think of any reason why you wouldn't have passed?"

"I'm sorry. That's not something I can answer with yes or no."

Slowly, Meyer smiled. "You passed, Ms. Arif. Not a twitch. Except on the queen of spades."

David inhaled. Turning to him, Hana spoke with a quiet that betrayed a deeper emotion. "So now your questions are answered, David. Except, of course, whether I have a conscience. For that, no machine can help you."

20

Her eyes slit in concentration, Marnie Sharpe read the report of Hana's polygraph examination. When she had finished, her tone was weary. "Some women could drown their babies in a bathtub and pass a test. *This* one may well be a sociopath."

"As opposed," David asked, "to the psychopathic human bomb you've chosen to believe?"

"Jefar intended to die. His story makes sense. There's evidence to support it that implicates Arif." Her tone became sardonic. "But this test does suggest that you might want to call her as a witness on her own behalf. She may have the same mesmerizing effect on a jury that she had on this machine. And, it seems, on you."

"Meaning?"

Sharpe considered him. "You're better off when you don't believe," she said evenly. "When a case is just a chess game. Arif's got you off balance."

Nettled, David held his temper. "This kind of thing won't help us. I could as easily say that you're an overambitious prosecutor with a make-or-break case, feeling so much pressure that you'd rather convict the innocent than no one."

"And you *will* say it, I expect. Sooner or later."

"Only if you force me," David answered. "The first day I joined this office, your sainted predecessor, Bill Kane, drilled it into me that I had an absolute obligation to ascertain the truth, to act with fairness and integrity and leave nothing to chance. And never to bring charges against anyone who I didn't absolutely believe was guilty. So is that still the standard, Marnie? Or is 'less than certain' okay when the victim's the prime minister of Israel?"

Sharpe took a sip of her tea, gazing at David over the rim. "What are you proposing?"

"That maybe we're both right — Hana's telling the truth, and so's Jefar. The difference is that Hana *knows* the truth, and Jefar just knows what Hassan told him."

Sharpe shook her head. "That makes no sense. Why would Hassan lie to someone who was going to kill himself?"

David shrugged. "Why did Jefar's motorcycle not blow up?"

"Accident," Sharpe answered dismissively. "Your theory piles coincidence on top of an incongruity: that Arif was framed for no reason, by a man about to die. At least give me some plausible human motivation that would lend this notion credence."

With unerring aim, Sharpe had illuminated the flaw in David's logic. "I can't yet," he conceded.

Sharpe's smile was skeptical. "And Ms. Arif has no idea, of course."

"No. Nor do you. As far as I can tell, you're prosecuting Hana without a clue about how the assassination was put together, or by whom. Shouldn't that bother you a little?"

For a moment, Sharpe seemed to contemplate the swath of morning sunlight on one corner of her desk. "Our investigation is far from over. In the meanwhile, what would you have me do? Issue a public apology and ship Arif back to Ramallah?"

"Not before you give her your own polygraph," David said calmly. "Take a chance, Marnie. Hana's even willing to sit for the same examiner you used on Ibrahim Jefar."

Sharpe raised her eyebrows, an expression of surprise tinged with distrust. "There *are* conditions, of course."

"Just one: that if she passes, you'll dismiss the case. If you come up with more evidence, you can always refile."

Sharpe shook her head emphatically. "Kick her loose because she can pass a polygraph? No way. I wouldn't test her even if your proposal weren't absurd." She jabbed a finger at the report in front of her. "For whatever reasons — which might be prior training or sheer heartlessness — we already know Arif can pass a polygraph. If she passed yours, I can only imagine your next performance on the *Today* show."

Abruptly, frustration broke through David's patience. "This is something out of Kafka," he snapped. "You tell me Jefar passed a polygraph, then say that Hana passing one means nothing. So now we're on the conveyor belt, moving toward the trial of a woman you can't be sure is guilty." His speech became staccato. "Maybe you'll convict her. Maybe you'll even get the death penalty. But based on the evidence as it stands, will you have the nerve to show up when she's executed?"

Sharpe's eyes were as opaque as shuttered windows. "It seems we're at an impasse. 'Based on the evidence as it stands,' it'll take more than polygraphs and rhetoric to keep me up at night. Tell your client to think a little harder."

■ ■ ■ ■

That afternoon, in an airless inner room provided by the FBI, David began reviewing boxes of documents produced by the prosecution.

The boxes were jammed with useless paper reflecting the government's desire to be inclusive, or merely to waste hours of his time while honoring Taylor's order to a fault. But any clues to a broader conspiracy were missing; the multitude of witness statements, though capturing the horror of the assassination, added little to what David already knew, and the report of the medical examiner was sickening but not enlightening. When David pointed this out to Sharpe, she answered, "This is a 'rolling production.' You asked for a lot, and we can't give you everything all at once. Especially given the breadth of your proposed defense: Palestinians and Israelis, all mixed in together."

For days on end, David remained a prisoner, eating takeout, culling dross until late at night, always getting up to run before daylight, shower, and return for another day of captivity. On occasion, when he caught a meal with Angel or one of the few friends he retained despite his defense of Hana and his breakup with Carole, he felt like a gopher emerging from its hole, blinking in the light after a very long winter.

After one such lunch, Sharpe called him on his cell phone. "We just got something you'll want to look at," she said. "I don't see that it helps your client. But given your imagination, I'm sure you'll think of something."

The document, David found, was a preliminary report by the FBI regarding its inquiry into the circumstances surrounding Ben-Aron's death. Its literary style was familiar: a mix of bureaucratic jargon, awkward sentence structure, and an overuse of the passive voice. Unknotting his tie, David scanned it for several minutes before a passage stopped him:

> Regarding Saeb Khalid, no evidence has been found that links him to the events under investigation, although statements have been discovered suggesting his advocacy of violent acts concerning Israel.

Two pages further, David found an account of the FBI investigation into the background of the assassination. As a catalog of frustration, the summary had a certain eloquence:

> The operation appears highly professional. The explosives used were stolen, perhaps from a military base. The provenance of the police uniforms is not yet known, although such can be acquired on the Internet. The motorcycles were purchased by unknown men, apparently of Middle Eastern origin, whom agents have not been able to trace. The storage container bore no suspect fingerprints except for those of Hassan and Jefar, nor did the remaining motorcycle. Hassan's and Jefar's driver's licenses were forgeries of high quality, their credit cards obtained under false names and mailed to post office boxes. No other suspicious persons known to have entered the United States before the assassination seem implicated at this time.
>
> The absence of leads may be interpreted to indi-

cate a well-planned conspiracy "rolled up" by highly skilled operatives of a number and origin currently undetermined.

David paused to reflect on Bryce Martel's conjecture, then read on:

> At this time, no further evidence has been found to link Hana Arif to the events under investigation. Telephone calls on the cell phone used by Hassan were made to cell phones purchased for cash, also by a man appearing to be of Middle Eastern origin. These cell phones have not been found or traced to any individual. Also, although Ms. Arif has associated with persons known or believed to be members of the Al Aqsa Martyrs Brigade, Hamas, and, in one instance, Islamic Jihad, it is unknown whether she is affiliated with any such groups.

What about Al Aqsa itself? David wondered. Reading on, he found a partial answer:

> Since the assassination, Al Aqsa has sustained heavy losses due to Israeli military operations, including attacks on cars and the destruction of safe houses used by purported members. While elements of Al Aqsa have denied involvement in the assassination, this may be attributed to fear of more such reprisals as have already occurred. However, our intelligence agencies are doubtful concerning a substantial presence by Al Aqsa in the United States.

David found no speculation on who the conspirators might be. But the next-to-final page caused him to sit up.

At 1:10, the detail leader ordered that the route to the airport take Fourth Street instead of Tenth Street. The detail leader states that this was a routine precaution. He conveyed this order by secure telephone to the members of his detail, and also to the leader of the Israeli security contingent and the head of Dignitary Protection for the SFPD, who then transmitted the same instruction to the people under their direction.

These new instructions were completed by 1:16. At 1:22, according to a tape from a security camera at a store on Market near Tenth Street, Hassan is shown receiving a call on his cell phone, and then hurriedly leaving his location.

It is possible to conclude that the telephone call alerted Hassan to the change in route ordered by the detail leader. Moreover, the telephone number of the caller shown on Hassan's cell phone is the same unknown cell phone number of the person who called Hassan in the last two days before the assassination. Jefar states that a map left for them in the storage container, but destroyed in the explosion, delineated in ink the original route on Tenth Street that was chosen three days before, as well as two alternative routes.

Taken together, these facts suggest that the original route, as well as the change, was conveyed to Hassan in a deliberate breach of security involving one or more persons informed of the plan. Our inquiry indicates that this information was confined to members of the Secret Service responsible for protecting Prime Minister Ben-Aron, as well as those police and Israeli security personnel with similar responsibilities.

A preliminary inquiry addressed the possible complicity of members of the Secret Service or San Francisco police. This inquiry has included extensive questioning of every such person involved, polygraph examinations, a review of financial, telephone, and cell phone records, credit card charges, and other investigative steps, including wiretaps and electronic surveillance. However, no facts have been discovered suggesting possible involvement by any such person or persons.

The final page, surprisingly terse, told David what he wished to know:

Two days after the assassination the Israeli government ordered all security personnel involved to return to Israel. A liaison officer was provided by Israel to facilitate communications regarding these events. At this time, however, we are unable to pursue the possibility that a member of the prime minister's security detail breached the arrangements designed for his protection by the Secret Service.

David sat with Bryce Martel on a wooden bench near the carousel at the San Francisco Zoo, watching children riding the painted hand-carved animals that glided up and down to blaring calliope music. With the summer sunlight on his face, Martel watched the children with a smile that mingled pleasure with regret. "Some of those wooden animals," Martel remarked, "are almost as old as I am. On the rare occasions when my grandchildren come to visit, they seem to like this. Certainly, I do."

Aware that Martel's relationship with his only daughter had been stunted by divorce and secrecy, David let his father's friend reflect for a time. Then Martel turned to him and said, "You wish to know more about the Israelis. Specifically, their security people. I assume that you've got something more that suggests they've sprung a leak."

"Yes."

"All right. The group assigned to Ben-Aron is the Special Protective Unit. They're the elite, almost all of them ex-military. In Israel, unlike here, military service is almost universal, a matter of national survival. So the pool of applicants is of a very high quality. The vetting is intense, and once you get the job, you lose all expectation of privacy — you're subject to routine polygraphs and surveillance.

"The Israelis leave nothing to chance: they fly their leaders in goverment planes so the security people can carry guns, and the planes themselves have antimissile systems." Removing his glasses, Martel cleaned them with a crisp white handkerchief. "For this to have involved a member of Ben-Aron's security detail would be almost unthinkable. Worse, even, than when Rabin was murdered by an extremist Jew."

"But is it impossible?"

"It's hard to imagine the Special Protective Unit taking in a traitor." Martel put on his glasses again, briefly fiddling with their stems. "What seems somewhat more plausible is a current member going off the tracks — whether because of money or, perhaps, a religious or political conversion that revealed to him that he was protecting an enemy of the Jewish people. Even then, I don't know how long such a person would be able to go undetected."

"Could this group be infiltrated by an extremist?"

"Would members of the unit *know* extremists? Sure. As I say, they're all ex-military — the Israeli army has its share of ideologues. But recruiting one?" Martel resumed watching the merry-go-round. "Still, you clearly don't think it's the Americans."

"No."

Martel pondered this. "Even within this very select group," he said at last, "one can make distinctions. Ben-Aron would have had three layers of protection — the inner perimeter, those literally closest to him, and therefore the most senior; the next most senior, the middle perimeter; then the outer perimeter. The inner perimeter would include only those in whom the Israelis had placed unshakable faith. As seniority declines, your thesis moves from the unimaginable to the merely difficult to conceive."

"Then what's your advice?"

"If *you're* considering this, the Israelis certainly are — that's why they pulled their agents out of the U.S. Obviously, you have to take a run at them." Martel smiled wryly. "My own sense, I regret to say, is that your chances of meeting any of these people are dimmer than your prospects of entering Congress. But if the Israelis put all of them in a lineup and told you to pick one, I'd choose someone young."

"The outer perimeter, in other words."

"Precisely." Turning to David, Martel concluded, "To kill Ben-Aron, you'd have had to be close to him. But to betray him, you only needed to know about his change of route. From there, all that's required is a cell phone, and complete indifference to your future. And, of course, a reason."

21

The Israeli consulate occupied a reconfigured mansion a few blocks from Carole's penthouse, its high ceilings and decorative moldings a remnant of affluent San Francisco from the days before the federal income tax. But the office given Avi Hertz seemed barely wider than it was tall, furnished only with a desk, two chairs, and a telephone. He waved David to a chair with no effort to ingratiate, bringing to mind Martel's admonition: "Avi Hertz has dedicated his life to one thing: the survival of the State of Israel. How he deals with you will be determined by that, and nothing else." Though his elfin face had a trace of humor, his laconic speech, economy of movement, and impenetrable gaze suggested the self-discipline through which Hertz had become the human equivalent of a one-way mirror, absorbing much while betraying nothing.

With a slight gesture of his left hand, Hertz indicated the letter on his desk. "I have read your letter, Mr. Wolfe. Reduced to its essence, you seem to want any information our government has about Hana Arif, Saeb Khalid, and the assassins of our prime minister. Including any supposed lapses in his protection, and culminating in sworn depositions of anyone in his security detail who was present when it happened. Or was there something more?"

Hertz's uninflected tone made this catalog sound preposterous, even to David. Determined to be as opaque as Hertz, he answered, "Nothing more."

"You understand the difficulties, of course."

David shrugged. "I understand my client's difficulties. Consistent with my obligations to her, I'll try to accommodate yours."

Hertz tented his fingers. "The principal difficulty," he said finally, "is that you see your interests as primary, and the interests of Israel as subordinate. In your conception of reality, we become an arm of your investigation — the Attorney General's Office, the Shin Bet, even the Mossad all working on your behalf."

"I only want whatever helps my client," David answered, "subject to the same conditions the judge imposed to protect my own government. There's a place where our interests intersect: your government is interested in much more about the assassination than the case against Hana Arif, and in order to defend her I need to learn much more."

"Was that haiku?" Hertz inquired. "Or merely a paradox? In either case, our inquiry into our prime minister's death involves the most sensitive matters. It must be built slowly and with great care. What is at stake for us is much larger, and more concrete, than your speculations on behalf of a single client —"

"Tell me this," David interrupted bluntly. "Does the government of Israel believe, or at least suspect, that someone in the prime minister's security detail was complicit in his murder?"

Hertz's expression did not change. "I am authorized to tell you," he said, "that we have found no information that would tend to exonerate Ms. Arif."

"Or implicate her?"

For the first time, Hertz's tone betrayed impatience. "If we had such evidence, we would immediately inform your government. Which, as I understand your system, would be required to provide it to you.

"That is not our situation. We have no evidence that Arif did not do exactly what she's charged with — conspire to assassinate Amos Ben-Aron. And no evidence that she *did,* beyond what is already known to you."

"Nothing more?" David kept his tone polite. "She didn't, for example, buy motorcycles or steal explosives?"

Hertz's gesture, an upward turning of palms, suggested that the question was too absurd to answer.

"So who did?" David prodded him. "Not Al Aqsa, surely."

Hertz touched the crew-cut bristles of his thinning hair, then gazed silently at David. "Now you are over your head," he said finally. "And well beyond the scope of your defense."

"That's not for you to say," David answered. "Which is why we have a judge."

"Which is why you're here," Hertz rejoined. "To cement your predicate for whatever legal tactic you're pursuing." The disdain behind his words was apparent. "I do not begrudge you your priorities — you are, after all, a lawyer. But only that, and for a woman accused of helping to do Israel great harm. We have many such enemies, and much larger priorities with which you do not seem concerned. I can only ask that you attempt to comprehend them."

David let his own annoyance show. "I've had this conversation before, with Sharpe — the same condescension, the same lofty references to national security, the same invocation of grand 'priorities.' My job is to make sure Hana Arif isn't swallowed by everyone else's 'priorities' — geopolitical or, less grandly, the merely political.

"The question of whether an Israeli chosen to protect Ben-Aron conspired to help kill him could cause your government great trouble, perhaps even determine which forces within Israel hold power. And it also bears directly on whether Hana was part of a larger design, or its victim. About which, I suspect, your government may already know more than it is saying." David paused to choose his words with care. "I know that this is delicate, especially if someone in Ben-Aron's security detail facilitated a suicide bombing planned by those who want Israel to disappear. Perhaps there'll come a time when your priorities, and mine, will require some accommodation."

Hertz took the time to weigh David's words, absorbing both their substance and the unstated threat they were intended to convey. "Your letter says you plan to visit Israel," he said simply. "Consistent with our interests, we will help you if we can.

"To repeat, we have nothing that would exonerate Arif." His voice, though softening, betrayed a buried anger. "We remember the Holocaust well, Mr. Wolfe. We are not in the business of murdering the innocent because they are not ours. Or protecting the guilty because they are."

"So," Hana said gently, "now you are at odds with

the Israelis. And still you do not speak of your fiancée."

It was David's first visit since the polygraph examination, and he felt more at sea than before: to his doubts about her innocence and his fear of being manipulated to some ruinous end, the examination had added a sense of guilt about mistrusting her. He had no heart to speak of this, nor to engage her sympathies by intimating what he had sacrificed to help her. "How many times in our relationship," he asked, "have you begun a sentence with 'So'? And what percentage of those sentences have caused me some discomfort?"

Hana's lips had the trace of a smile, though her eyes did not. "So," she persisted, "Carole is no longer your fiancée."

"That particular sentence," David answered, "proves my point."

Hana's eyes met his. "I am sorry," she said quietly, "and ashamed. I discover that being charged with murder has created a peculiar narcissism. 'Will he help me?' 'Will he understand how much I need him?' And, yes, 'Will he believe me?' "

She paused, looking down for a moment. "I was angry at you, David. Then I considered how much defending me must be costing you. For thirteen years, you remained in my heart and mind the David you were to me at Harvard. You had the right to expect more contemplation of what I've done to your life as it really is. Or was."

Though touched, David steeled himself against his own emotions. Evenly, he said, "You have a family, you've been charged with a capital crime, your face is on the cover of *Newsweek*, and you have a few concerns about who will raise your daughter. I have no expectations of you."

"Perhaps you should." To his surprise, Hana reached across the table, resting her hand on his wrist. "I want to be a friend, if it is not too late."

Instinctively, David glanced at the window, to see if a guard was watching them. Seeing this, Hana withdrew her hand.

"And your fiancée," she asked at length, "is that beyond repair?"

"It would seem so."

"Because of me," she said tonelessly. "And now the Israelis are unhappy with you as well."

"Yes. But that, at least, is relevant to your defense."

With veiled eyes, Hana absorbed this tacit rebuff. "Then tell me."

"There's a conflict," David began, "between your rights and what the U.S. and Israel perceive as their national security interests. How the U.S. and Israel define those interests may also conflict: to maintain this prosecution, our government may want the Israelis to cooperate with *me* more than the Israelis want to."

"Which makes Sharpe's position more difficult?"

It was easier, David discovered, to speak to Hana as the lawyer she once had been. "It could," he answered. "As a first resort, she'll say that her case against you is a straightforward murder prosecution, made remarkable only by the identity of the victim — in essence, that I'm using Ben-Aron's identity to expand the case in a way that threatens the interests of both countries but has nothing to do with your innocence or guilt. And I've got only two means of leverage against the Israelis themselves: to pressure them through the media and, with Judge Taylor's assistance, through Sharpe."

"Do you have any grounds for that?"

"I think so." David considered how to describe where matters stood. "The Americans, Israelis, and you are all part of a three-way Catch-22. But we've got a chance of putting the Israelis to a choice: either they tell me what they found out about Ben-Aron's assassination — however painful, and wherever it may lead — or they jeopardize Sharpe's ability to maintain a case against you."

Hana tilted her head, gazing into his face. "At what cost to you, David?"

"How do you mean?"

She paused to choose her words. "You live in a frightened country — not the one that existed when we met. I have seen myself in the magazines: I am an alien creature, like Bin Laden, and what I am accused of makes Americans fear for their children and the world they will live in. Just as, for years, I have feared for Munira.

"Now you, who are Jewish, are tampering with those same existential fears in the Israelis — worse, you're suggesting that their enemies are not just Palestinian but, perhaps, Jewish. This must be part of what happened between you and Carole." Her voice was gentle. "And so I cannot help but wonder, amid all this, just how you are living."

David summoned a deflective smile. "On Chinese takeout, mostly."

"At least say this much," Hana asked quietly. "Does Carole know what we were to each other?"

"Yes," David answered. "Does Saeb?"

Hana looked down, then shook her head. "Never in words."

For a long minute, they shared a silence. Then Hana looked up at him. "I would like to see Munira, David. Without her father if I could. It has been too long."

Another moment passed, and then David nodded. "I'll try to arrange it," he told her.

22

In the face of our government's allegations," Larry King asked, "why do you believe so strongly in the innocence of Hana Arif?"

For weeks, David had weighed the need to pressure the Israelis against the risk of antagonizing Judge Taylor. Now he sat in a semidarkened room at CNN's San Francisco outpost, trying to project sincerity into the glass eye of a camera; on a TV monitor to one side, King's mouth, by virtue of a three-second delay, had stopped moving even though his voice still sounded in David's earpiece. "Ms. Arif passed a comprehensive lie detector test," David answered. "She denied any knowledge of the Ben-Aron assassination, the assassins, or the acts she's accused of committing. The polygraph showed her answers to be truthful.

"I took these results to Marnie Sharpe, the United States attorney, and offered to make Ms. Arif available for another examination, conducted by the FBI. Ms. Sharpe refused my offer." David paused, then added firmly, "Hana Arif is being sacrificed on the altar of political expedience — quite literally, if she's executed despite this new evidence that she's been framed. And Americans, Israelis, and the world will still know nothing about the conspiracy to murder Amos Ben-Aron."

On the monitor, David's mouth was still moving as King asked, "Do *you* have an opinion as to who could have planned such a horrific act?"

David had prepared his answer with care. "At this time, Larry, I'm not free to tell you everything I know or suspect. But I believe that the prime minister's death resulted from a deliberate leak to the assassins that his motorcade was changing routes. That's why they were on Fourth Street, and that's why they were able to kill him.

"There's no evidence I'm aware of that the leak came from the Secret Service or the San Francisco police." For a moment, David hesitated. "That leaves the Israelis. Unfortunately, Israel has refused to share with the defense, or even the United States government, what its own investigation has uncovered.

"In short, the United States is prosecuting Ms. Arif while ignoring that she's passed a lie detector test, and Israel is refusing to address whether one of its own people may have helped murder its prime minister —"

"Are you saying," King interrupted, "that the Israelis *and* the Americans are perpetrating a cover-up?"

"What I'm saying," David demurred, "is that my client's guilt or innocence may cease to matter. That could be fatal both to Ms. Arif and to any chance of determining who murdered Amos Ben-Aron."

"For which, you're claiming, Israel's at least partly to blame."

"The Israeli people have suffered a great tragedy," David responded in clipped tones. "I'm hoping their own government won't compound it. The judicial murder of an innocent woman is contrary to the precepts on which Israel was founded — not only as a refuge for a persecuted people but as a beacon of justice in a region that has known too little." David paused, choosing his next words with care. "The murder of John F. Kennedy haunts us still. Now a conspiracy of unknown origins has murdered Amos Ben-Aron and, quite possibly, the chance of a lasting peace. That's what this trial must concern. For the United States to execute Hana Arif, based in part on Israel's silence, will haunt at least three peoples: Americans, Israelis, and Palestinians."

On the monitor, King's face was grave. "That's a fairly dire warning, David Wolfe. What's your solution?"

David kept his expression composed, his voice calmer than he felt. "If the Israeli government doesn't cooperate with the defense," he answered, "we will ask Judge Taylor to dismiss our government's prosecution of Hana Arif."

Driving home, David listened to Sharpe's message on his cell phone. Her tone was icy. "You've crossed the line," she said. "Before Judge Taylor decides whether to kick this case, she'll have to decide if you defied her order."

The call did not surprise him. But Sharpe's words were a depressing reminder of the controversy — not to mention hatred — his tactics would provoke.

As he pulled into his driveway, he saw that the windows of his living room glowed with light.

David searched his memory. Turning off the lights before leaving his flat was so habitual that he could not recall having done so. Using the automatic garage door opener would announce his presence. He parked his car on the street.

Walking softly, David climbed the darkened steps to his front door, the key in his hand. Turning the lock with a soft click, he eased himself into the alcove.

The light of his standing lamp caught Carole's startled face.

She was waiting on his sofa. Belatedly, David felt the gooseflesh on his skin, followed by a small rebirth of hope. "Should I be glad you're here?" he asked.

"I watched you tonight." Carole's voice was muted. "I hope *she* was allowed to see you. So impassioned, and so convincing. So much better than the man she made the mistake of marrying."

Deflated, David heard the depth of Carole's torment; she was unable to be with him, yet not able to let go. Now she had watched David deploy his gifts on behalf of a woman she both despised and envied, to challenge a country that she cherished.

"I had no choice," David said. "The media requires excess, and what I said is true enough. Whatever I may feel, lawyers don't have the luxury of divided loyalties."

"What *do* you feel, David?"

David sat on the arm of his sofa, a few feet from the woman he had planned to share his life with. "Except at night, when I'm alone, I try to detach myself. So that all I do is think, not feel."

"Perhaps that's how you prefer to live." Though composed, Carole looked away. "I ask myself, now, whether you're unknowable. To others, and to yourself."

This struck close enough to home that David felt both defensive and misunderstood. "This is *hard* for me, Carole. Do you really think I'm not in touch with that? I keep trying to follow my own conscience as a lawyer and a man, always wondering where the two collide."

"And Hana?"

"I wish I'd never met her," he said flatly, then wondered if this were wholly true. "I wish she didn't need my help. I wish you and I were still living the life we had, and that I didn't lie awake questioning my own motives and decisions." His tone grew softer. "More than anything, I wish I'd never hurt you. Or found out what you were capable of saying to me — worse, thinking about me — when I violated your sense of what it means to be a Jew."

Carole shook her head. "That's not fair, David."

"Isn't it?" David asked. "It's ironic, actually. 'You're so American,' Hana told me years ago. 'To you the individual is all that matters.' Maybe so. To *me*, both of you are so branded by two peoples' collective history that you've lost some part of yourself. But only one of you is accused of murder. And there's a decent chance she's innocent —"

"And that frees you to disparage Israel," Carole interrupted. "After all, Jews and Palestinians are mirror images of each other, just like Hana and me. Isn't that what you believe, David? The same tragedies, the same loss, the same blindness."

"Sabra and Shatila weren't Auschwitz," David snapped. "Just as the tragedies of Jews and Palestinians aren't remotely similar. For my purposes, they don't have to be. If six million Palestinians had died, rather than Jews, that wouldn't make watching the rape of his sister and the murder of his family more damaging to Saeb Khalid. Or Hana more deserving of a lawyer."

"Then what is it, David. That Hana was your lover?"

"Yes," David answered simply. "I loved her once. Years later, I loved you. But I couldn't trade her life for your approval. All of our lives have someone's fingerprints on them. Having loved her didn't mean I couldn't love you, and defending her doesn't make me a self-hating Jew." David's voice became harsher. "What I would have hated myself for was treating Hana like her life meant nothing to me. And what I would have hated *you* for was needing me to."

Carole slowly shook her head. "Some fingerprints are indelible," she answered. "What I needed was for you not to love her now. Perhaps, in that way, I wish you were a little more unknowable." She paused, as though reluctant to say more. "If you find out that she lied to you, David, what will you do then?"

David had no answer. Leaving, Carole touched him lightly on the arm, a last reflex. Only then did David see the silver house key on his coffee table.

23

Head raised and eyes narrow, Bryce Martel tasted the rich cabernet, then nodded his approval to their waitress, a young woman whose braided hair came in several colors. When she was gone, he said to David, "You seem to have stirred them up."

They were dining at Bacar, a converted warehouse south of Market Street with high ceilings, brick walls, and an extensive wine list, a chic variant on the more formal dining favored by an older crowd. "How so?" David asked.

"Israel is a wonderful country," Martel answered. "But it's riven by factions and contradictions — religious versus secular, dove versus hawk, the pragmatists who supported Ben-Aron versus the prophets who despised him — all of whom, understandably enough, view politics as a matter of life and death. What you suggested last night on Larry King — that Ben-Aron's murder might in some way be an inside job — would, if true, be turned against whichever faction Israel's various antagonists might find to blame." Martel put down his wineglass. "One night on CNN won't change the government's mind. But you may find that you have some provisional allies, as opposed to friends, once you visit Israel."

"For example?"

"Journalists, supporters of Ben-Aron, opponents of his successor, perhaps those who hope to gain political and electoral advantage by tying his murder to the ultraright." Martel paused to eye the menu. "But you'll find those waters murky and quite difficult to navigate — Israel is not a place that lends itself to easy understanding. For that, you'll need a guide."

David sipped Martel's selection. "I was hoping you'd have a candidate or two."

"One, especially. Zev Ernheit — a historian and archaeologist by training, and a former intelligence officer by profession, now working for himself. There's no nook or cranny of Israeli society where Zev doesn't know someone, and he hears the echoes of the past back to King David and beyond.

"Israel, after all, sits on ancient land, and historic memory is encoded in the DNA of Jews and Arabs alike. Only if you grasp the grievances and divisions of each society can you fully understand the defense you're weaving for Ms. Arif."

"What about the government?" David asked. "Can your man help me there?"

"The *government* will help you, to a point. Not by giving you what you ask, but by providing tidbits here and there, an aura of accessibility, if for no other reason than to keep track of what you're doing. For which one can hardly blame them, given the embers you propose to poke a stick in." Pausing, Martel glanced about, taking in the affluent young professionals with a look that suggested how negligible he found them. "To live in Israel requires an alertness most Americans never learn. If an Israeli takes you to a restaurant like this, he's likely chosen it not for the wine list but for a security system that makes it a tad less likely you'll be blown up before dessert." Martel touched a napkin to his lips. "As to those things the government does *not* want you to know — yes, my friend Zev can help."

"That will be much appreciated," David said. "And what about the West Bank?"

"A different place. And your reasons for going, of course, are different."

David nodded. "I need to explore Saeb's and Hana's lives — their associates, their secrets, whatever our own intelligence people are looking for. The same thing for the suicide bombers, Hassan and Jefar."

"You need context," Martel observed. "Where these men came from, what drove them, who knew how to use them, and on whose behalf. And where all *that* fits into the byzantine relations among the contending forces — Hamas; Fatah, the party of Faras; and Al Aqsa, the militant arm of Fatah. Understanding the crosscurrents of Palestinian politics is the only way to find out who may have planned the assassination, and why."

David found this catalog even more disheartening than the tasks he faced in Israel. "Anything else?" he asked dryly.

"Yes. To have any hope of succeeding, you'll need to penetrate Al Aqsa itself, which has been driven further underground by the Israelis. And, finally, you'll need a line into Hamas."

David shook his head. "Do you know any way of doing that?"

Martel smiled. "Of course. And I also know the people who can help you. That's why you're paying for dinner."

David did not know what Hana had said to her

husband. But while Saeb's affectless demeanor did not conceal his resentment, he allowed Munira to leave with David, his authority preserved by his insistence on the time of her return and, as usual, by the black cloth that shrouded her head and body.

Saeb and Munira had moved to a furnished apartment in Pacific Heights, a cement Bauhaus structure of nine stories that served as refuge for the dislocated — the newly separated or businesspeople on temporary assignment. David knew the building; he had helped a friend whose marriage had broken up move his clothes and books, and he had found the sterile environment, with its motel furniture and department store art, utterly depressing. Now, as he drove Munira to the prison that held her mother, it seemed that much more dismal.

The girl huddled in the passenger seat, curled slightly forward, her posture suggesting the attitude of prayer. He tried to imagine her sense of aloneness and disorientation.

"How are you, Munira?" he asked.

She gave him a sideways glance — shy, or perhaps cautious. At length, she said, "My father watched you on TV the other night."

"Oh? What did he say?"

"He thought I was asleep. So I turned down the volume, and watched you in my bedroom."

David was struck by this image — a father and daughter, separate from each other, watching television in two darkened rooms. "You were good," Munira told him. "I think you're a good lawyer."

David could not help but smile. "Thank you, Munira. That's why your parents hired me."

The girl looked at him askance. "My mother chose you," she said.

This was part of her personality, David thought — like her mother, Munira often stated as fact that which she only suspected. He turned the car onto Gough Street, heading toward the entrance ramp of the bridge.

"The Zionists," Munira ventured. "You challenged them, even though you're Jewish."

"Yes." David paused, wondering how much to say. "You think of Jews as Zionists, and Israel as your enemy. Perhaps, in your experience, that seems so. But Jews have suffered a lot of terrible things, and they worry about people who seem to be *their* enemies. I don't want that to hurt your mother."

The girl's forehead knit in a reflective frown of skepticism. At length she said pensively, "*I* made a mistake."

"What's that?"

"I was mean to her, and now I'm being punished." Munira frowned again, as though confused by her own choice of words. "I can't be with her," she amplified, "to be kind the way I should have."

"Hana knows how you feel," David answered. "She once was your age, and a daughter who I'm sure was less than perfect. But if you worry about these things, maybe this is the day to tell her."

Munira clasped her hands together. "I don't know. Sometimes she confuses me."

David smiled. "Me, too," he answered, and then wondered if the mild joke revealed more than it should. "What's not confusing," he added, "is how much your mother loves you."

Eyes downcast, Munira considered this. "I think I'm why she fights with my father so much."

Her candor surprised David. Then it struck him, more forcefully than before, that Munira had no one to confide in but Saeb, nor even a cell phone to call friends. "I don't know why they fight," David responded. "Or what it might involve. But I know your mother believes in you, and in what you can accomplish in the world."

Munira considered this solemnly. For the remainder of the drive, she and David shared little else, save for what might have been a companionable silence. But at the detention center, as David watched their meeting through a sheet of glass, Munira touched her forehead to her mother's, resting it there as Hana's eyes shut tight.

24

In the early morning hours before the second hearing, David sat at his kitchen table with a legal pad in front of him, too wired to sleep.

Intently, he drafted, scratched out, and then rephrased answers to the questions Judge Taylor might ask, honing each response until it was as succinct as he could make it. In one sense, this thoroughness was an antidote to the worry inherent in any hearing where the stakes were high; on a deeper level, it reflected the consuming tensions of a case where each step might determine whether Hana lived or died. But David's dogged absorption in the lawyer's task served still another purpose: it kept at bay the tangled emotions that otherwise might overwhelm him.

To be in Hana's presence was exhausting, a constant struggle to suppress sympathy, suspicion, resentment, and the fear of manipulation caused by her ambiguous behavior. She was alternately cool, compassionate, angry, and frightened; at times, she hinted at a feeling for him that might be real or contrived. Even his images of Hana were a kaleidoscope of contradictions: the chilly remoteness with which she had passed the polygraph; her elliptical references to their past as lovers; her palpable hurt at his distrust. He even wondered about the moment when, her forehead touching Munira's, Hana's eyes had closed, so evocative of a mother's love and longing. Was this scene intended for him?

And his own motives for defending her remained elusive — he still could not separate principle from pride, remembered passion from the fear of living a life of comfort paid for, in the end, with Hana's death. Whatever the truth, that life was now beyond retrieval, and he had no picture of another life on the far side of this case. Only one thing seemed clear to him: how he would feel about that life would likely rest on what he discovered on the way. Who Hana had become, and whether she was innocent of murder, would matter enormously.

David stared at the kitchen window, a square of darkness, and saw nothing but his tired image gazing back at him. In five hours he must perform as a lawyer, displaying the presence and command that, as much as reason, sometimes tipped the balance. Lawyers have no room for the seeping dread of early morning.

Turning from the window, David honed another phrase.

Sitting at the judge's conference table next to Marnie Sharpe, David felt the hyperalertness that came from too much coffee and too little sleep. Taylor began by addressing Sharpe. "You have a complaint, I gather, regarding Mr. Wolfe's appearance on *Larry King*."

"Yes," Sharpe answered. "Specifically, about Mr. Wolfe's intimation that Israel is concealing information about the death of Amos Ben-Aron. That insinuation was based on highly confidential information the government provided Mr. Wolfe, pursuant to this court's order that he not use such information without its prior permission." Pausing, Sharpe seemed to search Taylor's expression for cues. "Further, Mr. Wolfe's assertions threaten to taint the jury pool with conspiracy theories that are — at best — speculative. For both reasons, we ask this court to bar him from public comment on the case or the various theories through which he may defend it."

Her face inscrutable, Judge Taylor inclined her head toward David. With an air of bemusement, David spread his hands. "We've had a two-month avalanche of publicity unfavorable to Ms. Arif — magazine covers, newspaper headlines, round-the-clock cable news reports, statements by world leaders — millions of words and thousands of hours, all of which blur the distinction between indictment and conviction. But now, in a single hour on CNN, I've tainted a process that, Ms. Sharpe suggests, was *not* previously tainted by her refusal to give Ms. Arif the same polygraph test she gave to the sole witness against her. The problem, Ms. Sharpe asks you to conclude, is *not* the unfairness of her own conduct, but my unfairness in bringing it up.

"There's enough prejudice against my client without muzzling her lawyer to make the prosecution look better than it deserves." David slid a stapled document across the table. "As for my supposed violation of this court's order, we've prepared a transcript of my interview. It's notable for the absence of any reference to confidential documents, as opposed to a truth that makes Ms. Sharpe uncomfortable — that Israel is refusing to provide information potentially vital to defense."

"This 'truth' is based on what? Divination?" The judge's expression became as flinty as her tone. "I don't need to read this — I took the time to watch you. The message was clear enough: you have a reason to believe that one or more members of Ben-Aron's security detail may be implicated in his death. And that reason could only be the information Ms. Sharpe provided you pursuant to my order."

David accepted the rebuke in silence, hoping to cool the judge's anger before it tainted the proceedings. "My order," Taylor continued, "does not allow you to perform the dance of the seven veils on CNN — a tease here, a feint there, a tantalizing hint of the delights to come." The judge's voice became more even. "I appreciate the problem of adverse publicity. So I'm not going to bar you from expressing skepticism about this case — based on the public record. But if you so much as allude to a document subject to my order, you'll be back here to explain why you shouldn't occupy a cell down the hall from Ms. Arif." Judge Taylor stared at David for another moment. "All right. Let's hear about your motion to compel the prosecution to request information from the government of Israel."

David paused to organize his thoughts. "With apologies, Your Honor, I'll start where I left off: with Ms. Sharpe's reliance on her only witness's polygraph examination to prosecute a woman who passed a polygraph examination of her own —"

"Yes," the judge interrupted. "What about that, Ms. Sharpe?"

Sharpe looked momentarily startled. "The examination of Ibrahim Jefar was as much to determine whether he would *take* it as *pass* it."

"And if he'd *failed* it, Counselor?"

Sharpe composed herself. "We would have assessed that result in light of the corroborating evidence suggesting that he was truthful. Once he agreed to take this test, and passed, we had an added degree of comfort."

"Did Ms. Arif's results make you a little less comfortable? Or are some polygraphs more equal than others?"

"In the eyes of the law," Sharpe responded, "they're equally inadmissible. Which means that we're thrown back on the evidence regarding Ms. Arif. All of which — Mr. Jefar's statement and the physical evidence that corroborates it — points to her guilt."

Taylor arched her eyebrows. "All the evidence *available,* you mean?" Turning to David, she asked, "Isn't that your point here, Mr. Wolfe?"

"Exactly. So far, Israel has withheld information that may help Ms. Arif establish that she was framed as part of a conspiracy that may reach within Ben-Aron's security detail. The United States cannot maintain this prosecution while refusing to ask for evidence that may discredit it."

"Tease this out for me," Taylor said. "Suppose that an Israeli abetted an assassination carried out by Palestinians. Would that, in itself, make Ms. Arif any less guilty than the late Iyad Hassan?"

"Let me answer with a not-so-hypothetical scenario," David said. "Whoever leaked the route called either Hassan or, more likely, Hassan's handler. Suppose, as I do, that this second person is *not* Hana Arif?

"Right now, the only *real* witness against Hana is a dead man. But a breach in security would mean that someone in Israel may know far more than Ibrahim Jefar about my client's innocence or guilt — or, at least, may know who does. How can we have a fair trial without trying to unravel this?"

The judge turned to Sharpe. "What's your answer, Ms. Sharpe?"

" 'Unravel this,' " Sharpe echoed. "How? By asking us to arrange depositions of every member of Ben-Aron's security detail, at whatever cost to the national security of another sovereign nation? Israel would never permit it."

"It *was* Israel's prime minister who died, Ms. Sharpe. The Israeli government *is* counting on the United States to prosecute those responsible. And the United States cannot do that without providing Mr. Wolfe whatever he's entitled to."

"Which is whatever the United States possesses, Your Honor — not whatever Israel may have."

"Which Israel can decide to produce — or not." The judge's tone became impatient. "You're mounting a prosecution based on hearsay from Jefar, against a defendant who passed a lie detector test — and whom you nonetheless propose, if successful, to execute. You can't control what the Israelis do. But there's nothing to keep you from presenting them with a choice: give the United States any information in its possession relevant to Ms. Arif's defense or put at risk this entire prosecution."

Sharpe's body, as stiff as her expression, betrayed her resistance to what she saw as David's trap. "Your Honor," she protested, "this court must be aware — as Mr. Wolfe most certainly is — of the Jonathan Pollard case. Pollard was an American Jew turned citizen of Israel who was convicted of stealing secrets from our government. When the United States prosecuted Pollard, Israel refused to identify his handlers at the request of the defense. That's the precise response Mr. Wolfe is expecting here." Sharpe adopted a more even tone. "Despite that, the United States was allowed to prosecute Mr. Pollard. If, as the defense anticipates, the Israelis decline our request on behalf of Ms. Arif, it should not affect our ability to prosecute."

"According to whom?" Taylor rejoined. "I'm in this job for life. Whatever the fate of Ms. Arif, what matters to me is whether I can sleep at night. So here's my order.

"First, the United States will request that the Israelis provide it with any information that tends to exculpate Ms. Arif or is otherwise relevant to her defense. Including," Taylor added emphatically, "Mr. Wolfe's assertion that she was framed.

"Second, if that information warrants depositions of Israeli government personnel, Mr. Wolfe may file a further motion seeking such depositions, setting forth the identity of the deponents and the specific grounds for deposing them."

Startled by his success, David glanced at Sharpe, who appeared too stunned to conceal her dismay. "Third," the judge continued, "I will defer setting a trial date to give the Israeli government time to produce, and Mr. Wolfe time to investigate, any information relevant to the defense." Facing Sharpe, the judge concluded, "Should Israel refuse, this court will consider issues far more fundamental than when this trial might begin. Please convey that by whatever means our government deems appropriate."

Sharpe, it was apparent, could not even muster the formulaic thanks.

"Is there something you don't grasp, Ms. Sharpe?"

"No, Your Honor. Thank you."

Nodding, Taylor turned to David. "Your papers

suggest that you're traveling to Israel. Regardless of its government's response to my order, I suggest you take your trip sooner rather than later." Her tone was cool. "I don't want you coming back to me having done little more than file this motion, which, in all likelihood, you expect will get you nothing except what you really want: grounds for a motion to dismiss. That might suggest a certain cynicism — or even provoke it. Rather like your interview on CNN."

It was a warning, if David needed one, that his own road would be hard, its end uncertain. "Thank you, Your Honor. I'll take that advice to heart."

"So you're going to Israel," Hana said gently. "The homeland you have never seen."

"Yes. And also the West Bank."

Hana nodded, and then gave him a piece of writing paper. "These are the names you wanted, friends and colleagues who know me well." Her smile, though ironic, seemed almost melancholy. "Carefully culled, of course, to eliminate all those who think me capable of murder."

David did not know what to say. Hana rested a graceful finger on the last name she had written. "In the Galilee, there is my cousin Sausan. I've met her only once. But she is a young woman of interesting contradictions, a Muslim whose mother was a Christian and whose grandmother was a Jew — no doubt why she finds herself unmarried, running a school in Israel. She's also very smart and very pretty."

David smiled. "Is that why I should meet her?"

"If you think so." Hana's face was sober now. "But I have another reason for asking. Sausan can show you my parents' village, I think, even the home where they lived. Her father will know where it is."

David was surprised. But the depth of her expression suggested how important this was. "You want me to visit for you?"

"Yes. And for my parents." She spoke more hurriedly, her eyes averted. "I have written how to find them at the camp. This would be yet another favor, David, a side trip to Lebanon. But I have no real way to reassure them, and they have little way to know what has happened to their village. Perhaps you can do both."

David hesitated: some part of him resisted meeting the man and woman so influential in Hana's refusal to marry him, and who, if they knew him as her lover rather than her lawyer, would no doubt turn him away. "I know," Hana said in a softer voice, "this is deeper into my life than you wish to go. Or than, before, I ever wished you to go. But our journey has become much more complex than I imagined. And so I ask."

After a moment, David nodded. Putting the paper in his pocket, he stood.

"David?" Looking up at him, Hana hesitated. "This will be a good trip, I hope. Not just for me, but you. But whatever happens, please come back safe."

For an instant, their eyes met, and then she looked away. "I'll try," David said, and left. When, by instinct, he turned back toward the witness room, Hana was gazing at him through the clouded window.

David went home and packed for Israel.

Part III
The Besieged

1

David took an overnight flight to Tel Aviv.

His seat in business class reclined into a bed. Adjusting his pillow, he glanced around him at his fellow passengers, predominantly middle-aged Israeli businessmen or Hasidic Jews, the women in sober clothes, the men with side curls and black hats and coats. The men tended to be pale, either portly or too thin; in David's estimate, they could have used a few hours in the gym or, at least, in unfiltered sunlight. He felt no more connection with these fellow Jews than if they had all been Muslims.

Closing his eyes, David fell asleep.

Toward dawn, when he awakened, Hasidic men draped in prayer shawls were drifting toward a small corner of the compartment, apparently to seek the first light of morning. They held prayer books; a leather strap was wound around their arms, a small leather box strapped to their foreheads. The box, David discovered in a guidebook, held a parchment inscribed with a portion of the Torah; the purpose of the strap was to bind the body, mind, and heart, the better that the men should act for good, not evil. A worthy goal, David supposed.

From between the seats in front of him, a Hasidic boy of perhaps seven, dressed like his father but with a child's bright-eyed curiosity, peered at David as if at some foreign creature. But when David smiled, the boy grinned back at him, delighted to make contact. At once David thought of Munira, swathed in black, reading the Koran under her father's watchful eye. That any culture imposed a belief system on its children, other than free inquiry and free choice, remained alien to him, he realized, despite the harsh lesson he had learned from Hana.

An hour later, they landed. David had come to Israel at last.

Leaving the plane, he followed the signs to the baggage claim area, his meeting place with Bryce Martel's friend Zev Ernheit.

Ernheit was a broad-shouldered man in his early forties with a graying crew cut, prominent features, and perceptive brown eyes that seemed to take in David with skepticism and a trace of grim amusement, as if to say, What have I got here? It was the expected response, David supposed, of a former Mossad operative to the Jewish lawyer for the accused Palestinian assassin of Amos Ben-Aron.

Ernheit's handshake was firm, his manner direct. "If you're not too tired," he said, "we'll stop for a history lesson on the way to Jerusalem. Martel assures me that anything I tell you will be new."

Even as he spoke, David noticed Ernheit's air of tensile alertness, the way his glance swiftly took in those around them. The loose short-sleeved shirt he wore, David realized, concealed a gun. "Anything," David answered with a smile. "And everything. Including who really murdered Amos Ben-Aron."

Ernheit merely shrugged, his look of amusement gone.

The newly paved roadway from Tel Aviv to Jerusalem ran through a landscape of rocky hills that had once been desert but now was dotted with pines. The early Zionists, Carole had told him, had determined to create an arable land by planting trees — in Hebrew school, Carole and her friends had raised money to support the planting of yet more trees. What David was seeing now, Ernheit told him, was a hundred years of planting, more than two hundred million trees, creating Israel's own small miracle, the only man-made climatic change in human history that was for the better.

"All these trees," Ernheit observed, "are a metaphor. The State of Israel is not only rooted in our history but in the sweat of a million Jews. The land that Palestinians claim as theirs is not the land they left."

The modern houses of Israeli Jews, David saw, tended to be white stucco structures with red roofs, which seemingly had sprung from nothing. Clustered together, they reminded David of the exurbia that typified southern California, with its sense of suddenness, vitality, man's irresistible enterprise. On a nearby hill, David spotted a cluster of sprawling homes above which the dome of a mosque was outlined against blue sky. "An Arab village," Ernheit observed.

David nodded. "The architecture's different."

Ernheit kept his eyes on the road. "The cultures are different," he answered laconically. "Jewish children leave home, Arab sons bring their wives home to live with their families. So the homes themselves just keep on growing."

Quiet, David thought of Hana and her parents.

"About Ben-Aron," Ernheit said abruptly, "our important conversations will take place out-of-doors. You're an intruder here, an unwelcome guest. Take it as a given that your telephone calls will be monitored, your hotel room bugged. You're also likely to be followed."

"For what reason?"

Squinting in the midday light, Ernheit put on sunglasses. "Let us suppose," he said, "that our government believes what you do — that a conspiracy to murder our prime minister included Jews. Assume further that they do not yet know who was involved in the conspiracy, or its dimensions. In which case they are as anxious to know as you are. Perhaps more."

"Why waste time on me?"

"Why not? You may actually stumble across something they want to know. There are some in Israel who, for reasons of their own, may wish to help you."

And whose side are you on, David wondered. He could not be entirely sure, he thought to his discomfort, that Ernheit was not himself a human wiretap. "I'll remember that," David answered.

They stopped on a hill with a distant view of the city of Jerusalem. At its crest, partially shaded by leafy green trees, was an ancient stone building that, but for the Islamic inscription above its entrance, could have been a church. As they approached it on foot, David asked, "What place is this?"

"A good place to start," Ernheit answered. "The church that became a mosque. The burial place of Samuel, perhaps the greatest prophet of the Jews.

One of only three — the others being Aaron and Moses — ever to converse with God."

"Who built the original structure?"

"Crusaders, the scum of Europe. They came to extract holy relics and instead struck Islam at its heart, setting off its ceaseless conflict with the West." Pausing, Ernheit pointed to the inscription. "That's the work of Saladin, the great emperor who reconquered Jerusalem and restored honor to the Muslim world. So this became a holy place for three religions."

David followed Ernheit through the entrance. Inside, the stone building was divided into sections — a mosque where Muslims could pray, a portion of the old church preserved for Christians, and, at its center, two sets of steps, one for men and one for women. Following Ernheit down the stone steps, David saw the tomb of Samuel covered in cloth, beside which three Hasidim sat, their heads bowed, reciting prayers as their bodies rocked slowly back and forth.

Emerging, Ernheit and David sat on the hillside facing Jerusalem. Pointing to an adjacent hill, Ernheit said, "That's where Saul, the first king of Israel, built his palace. But the structure you see is the unfinished palace of Hussein, the Bedouin king of Jordan, abandoned when we conquered it in the war of 1967. You begin to understand, I imagine, what I'm telling you."

David sorted through his sense of shifting boundaries, religious sites built on top of one another, the intertwined histories of contending peoples. "That everything here is complicated," he ventured.

Ernheit laughed softly. "Even truth. In the Middle East, there are at least four versions. For believers there is theology — the written word of God, infallibly true. But for Jews and Muslims, God's truth is different and conflicting." Ernheit hooked a thumb at the structure behind them. "Here, as you have seen, is archaeological truth, the record of men's footprints, to which theological truth does not always conform. Then there is historic truth, combining fact and myth, a narrative of the past as a people wishes it to be.

"Finally, there is political truth — history's first draft, a story of the current day in which religion, archaeology, and history are shaped to the need of the teller. Which is why Arafat insisted, contrary to the Jewish truth, that the Dome of the Rock, the Muslim shrine, is not built on the site where Abraham came to sacrifice his favorite son, Isaac — who, in the Islamic telling, was Ishmael, the precursor of Muslims."

David smiled. "Sibling rivalry."

"Only this one's three thousand years old. In essence, it's a contest between Muslims and Jews over which is the favored people of God, each claiming that He granted them the land to which both have sought to return." Ernheit spoke with resignation. "In Hana Arif's view, she lives in the Occupied Territories, surrounded by Jewish oppressors. But to many Jews, she lives in the biblical land of Judea and Samaria, now occupied by Arab terrorists and anti-Semites — the descendants of those who slaughtered Jewish settlers in the 1920s and '30s, and call our Day of Independence their Day of Tragedy."

"And for you?" David asked. "Where does history start — and end?"

Ernheit pondered this, then pointed at the distant skyline of Jerusalem. "For me, sitting in this place, it starts three thousand years ago." He turned, looking hard at David. "*This* is where the Jewish people were born — not Argentina, or Uganda, or any of the other throwaway places the world suggested we settle after the Holocaust was done and six million of us had died for the lack of a place to go. South America is nothing to us. Africa is nothing to us. Our heritage and roots are here. Jews were a majority in Jerusalem in the early nineteenth century, and a thriving presence in this land ever since the Zionists came here in the 1880s, fleeing the pogroms of eastern Europe. So this is where our history begins, and this is where it will end."

Dead or alive, David thought — there was no mistaking the determination in Ernheit's words. "I need you to understand something," David said at length. "About this trip, and about me. I may be a lousy Jew to some, but that's their problem, not mine. I have no use for suicide bombers, terrorists, or anyone who wants to eradicate this country. If I thought Hana was one of them, I wouldn't be here. There's nothing in this case for me but heartache and ambivalence. And, perhaps, the need to know whatever truth there is to know, like it or not."

Ernheit studied him. "Like it or not," he repeated. "An important qualification. I've read some of your statements about Arif — that she's a mother, that she would never risk her child's future. And I knew at once that you presume to understand too much.

"So let me tell you a story. Two years ago a Palestinian woman, dressed in a long black shroud but obviously pregnant, set off a metal detector at a checkpoint near East Jerusalem." Ernheit's tone was clipped, factual. "The day was blazing hot.

Teary-eyed, she explained to the young Israeli soldier who stopped her that, as a child, she had broken her leg so badly that the surgeon had pieced it together with screws and a metal plate. Because she was Muslim, the woman said, she could not show him the scars on her leg. But he must understand that she was harmless — no mother, Jew or Arab, would sacrifice her child to harm others.

"As I said, the soldier was young. He explained later that she looked close to giving birth. And so, reluctantly, he let her pass. Perhaps thirty yards beyond him was a cluster of Israeli soldiers. He saw the woman approach them, asking for water. As one drew out his canteen, she blew herself and four soldiers to pieces."

"She wasn't pregnant."

"Yes, she was," Ernheit demurred with a sardonic smile. "Eight months pregnant, in fact. But her husband, a Hamas activist, had been in an Israeli prison for twice that time. And so her brother-in-law, also Hamas, gave her a choice: to die at his hands in an honor killing or redeem herself by taking some Israelis with her and her bastard child. She chose the latter course."

David tried to imagine this. "And the lesson?"

Ernheit's smile vanished. "Is simple. Don't ever think you understand this place. And never believe you comprehend your client, or what may have impelled her to murder our prime minister. Because you don't."

2

On the winding road to Jerusalem, David and Ernheit passed Jewish and Arab villages; a British cemetery, the remnant of colonialism; and the modern buildings of Hebrew University, whose founders, Ernheit explained, had reinvented a three-thousand-year-old language in a determined act of cultural resurrection. They stopped again at Mount Scopus, overlooking Jerusalem.

David leaned against the railing of the viewing area. On the sloping hillside beneath them was a Jewish cemetery; the custom, Ernheit explained, was to bury the dead east of Jerusalem, where the prevailing wind blew from the city. Now, carried by that same wind, the haunting sound of a muezzin's call to prayer issued from the Old City of Jerusalem, whose sandstone walls, built by Roman conquerors, surrounded the sacred sites of three civilizations.

The panorama of the city was that of the Middle East, ancient and, David thought, compelling in its sense of spiritual beauty, its mosques, spires, and minarets rising above the wall amid palms and pine trees. Framed against the modern neighborhoods and buildings that surrounded it, the Old City seemed ethereal; even at this distance, David could understand man's desire to possess it. Ernheit pointed out the golden Dome of the Rock, the Muslim holy site; the Church of the Holy Sepulchre, built on the supposed place of Christ's crucifixion; and the black dome of the Al Aqsa Mosque. "For Muslims," Ernheit said, "the Al Aqsa Mosque was the 'end of the journey,' a holy place to come if Mecca was too far away. More recently, it supplied the name of the terrorist group that, his assassin claims, planned the murder of Amos Ben-Aron."

"Do you believe that?"

Ernheit leaned against the railing, his keen expression focused on the city. "Why do you think I'm helping you? If Hana Arif is guilty, as seems likely enough, let the Americans kill her. But she couldn't have put this plan together on her own. And those who helped her are not Al Aqsa."

Ernheit said this last with such conviction that David turned to stare at him. After a time, Ernheit pointed to the rolling landscape beneath the city. "Do you see that line of trees below the wall?"

Gazing out, David saw that the line, even and densely wooded, ran along the length of the horizon. "It's like a border," he said.

"Effectively it *is* a border — the 'Green Line,' we call it, the edge of Zionist planting. After 1948 it became a de facto border, and remained so until the war of 1967. As you see, it does not include the Old City of Jerusalem. And it is very difficult to defend." Turning to the left, Ernheit raised his arm to indicate a green wall, twenty feet high, snaking along the hillside, its construction incomplete. "And that is our new de facto border, at least for the time being — the security barrier, meant to protect us from Al Aqsa, Hamas, Islamic Jihad, and whoever else on the West Bank may send the next

Iyad Hassan to murder us in Jerusalem or Tel Aviv or Haifa.

"Between these two borders is a no-man's-land of fear. Some opponents of Ben-Aron, including the religious, believed that he would give Faras and the Palestinians the sacred ground of the Old City; others believed he would abandon our settlements in the West Bank. All you require to become afraid is to look out at the Green Line, history's illustration of how precarious our existence was and is. And then, perhaps, you could begin to think Ben-Aron a traitor. Leaders have died for less."

"So you believe that Jews helped kill him?"

"I believe that it cannot be ruled out. But the answer to who killed him may also be found in the manifest failures of another leader, Yasser Arafat. And in the murder of still another, Yitzhak Rabin."

David considered this. "Dead leaders," he said. "And missed opportunities."

"Arafat never missed an opportunity to miss one. But sometimes he had outside help." Ernheit wiped his sunglasses, carefully placing them in the pocket of his shirt. "After Arafat returned to the West Bank from his exile in Tunis, Rabin decided that the Occupied Territories were a quagmire for Jews — that he had to find some pragmatic way, through Arafat, to give the Palestinians their own country in exchange for a lasting peace. Which earned Rabin a bullet at the hands of a right-wing Jew.

"You would think his murder might lead to a reaction against the Israeli right, a political uprising for peace. But Hamas, which did not want peace, chose this precise moment to launch a wave of suicide bombers against Israel. The result of *that* was the election of Arafat's most adamant enemy, Benjamin Netanyahu — the candidate of the Israeli right and, some would argue, Hamas. A synergy of extremists on both sides killed the chance of peace."

Behind them, the sunlight of late afternoon cast its failing light across the Old City, causing the tint of the golden dome to deepen. "Whatever our own failings," Ernheit continued with quiet bitterness, "this current mess is, in great measure, Arafat's legacy to us all. Netanyahu was succeeded as prime minister by Ehud Barak, who was prepared to negotiate a lasting peace, with President Clinton as the intermediary. But Arafat lacked the courage, and certainly the desire, to give up the right of return so cherished by radicals like your client's husband. To snarl matters still further, Barak's leading opponent, Ariel Sharon, chose this crucial juncture to visit the Al Aqsa Mosque — supposedly to assert Israeli sovereignty over Muslim holy cities." Ernheit smiled grimly. "If so, the messenger could hardly have been worse: Palestinians view Sharon as the architect of the massacre at Sabra and Shatila. His visit became the supposed flashpoint for more suicide bombings by Hamas, Al Aqsa, and others in what became the Second Intifada."

David noted the qualifier. "Is that what you think?" he asked.

"Not quite. My own belief is that Arafat used Sharon's visit as his pretext — he thought that countenancing terror might give him more leverage with Barak in peace negotiations. In this, as in so many other things, Arafat was a fool. What he got instead was nine hundred dead Jews, three thousand dead Palestinians, and the defeat of Barak by Sharon, Arafat's archenemy, who became prime minister of Israel.

"The upshot is essential to understanding who might have planned the murder of Ben-Aron. After sixty suicide bombings in seventeen months, Sharon surrounded Arafat's compound in Ramallah and pretty much obliterated everything around him, leaving Arafat to rail against 'the Zionists' on his cell phone as the battery died, the media yawned, and his entourage ran out of food." Ernheit shrugged, as if to say that this was only justice. "For the last three years of his life, Arafat was a pariah, humiliated by his virtual incarceration, scorned by America and Israel, forced to look on helplessly as Sharon built a security barrier and unleashed a twelve-day attack on the refugee camp at Jenin, a nexus for terrorists and the home of Ibrahim Jefar, killing fifty-six Palestinians, whom Arafat could only add to his list of 'martyrs.' The man was dead before he died. And he left his people nothing but occupation, violence, an economy in ruins, a string of Israeli settlements on the West Bank — some of them illegal — with a road system reserved for Israelis that connects them like a spiderweb, and, of course, this barrier. As fertile ground for extremism as you'd like. Hence, the rise of Hamas."

"And the death of peace?" David asked.

"I think so. To me, the last hope of peace was a collaboration between Faras and Ben-Aron. Now Ben-Aron has been assassinated, like Rabin; like Arafat, Faras has lost all credibility; much like Netanyahu, our new prime minister has launched fresh attacks on terrorists. And Ben-Aron's dream of peace is as dead as the man himself. So what remains on the West Bank," Ernheit concluded in a tone of quiet fatalism, "aside from Israeli soldiers, presently engaged in wiping out Al Aqsa, is the vacuum that Arafat left behind: a struggle for power between Faras and Fatah — perhaps fatally weakened by the assassination and Israel's response to it — and the extremists of Hamas. The question is who gains from such a vacuum, and from the death of Amos Ben-Aron."

"Easy. Anyone who doesn't want peace between Israelis and Palestinians."

"A very long and contradictory list," Ernheit concurred. "Unfortunately, when it comes to who plotted to murder Ben-Aron, that's your list of suspects."

"No doubt your government is working overtime to sort them out."

"The Shin Bet in particular. It collects intelligence on Palestinian and other terrorist groups, as well as Iranian espionage activities in Israel and the West Bank. Also right-wing extremists such as the Masada movement."

"I saw their leader on television," David said. "Barak Lev. He's insane."

"Perhaps. But one man's psychopath is another man's savior, committed to religious truth. Perhaps that's why the Shin Bet has had the devil's own time cracking the Masada movement. Those men don't talk — except to one another, and to God."

"And God talks only to Samuel," David answered. "And Moses and Aaron."

Ernheit laughed briefly. "You'll make a Jew yet. But if you give God orders, as Lev did, perhaps God answers in His own way. Lev's last request, you may recall, was that God strike Ben-Aron as dead as Adolf Hitler."

"Is there any chance," David asked without much hope, "that the Shin Bet would tell me at least some of what they know?"

"No chance. But there are others, as I said, who may wish — very quietly, and indirectly — to put you on the proverbial long and winding road." Ernheit glanced at his watch. "In fact, we're meeting one of them at the King David, for drinks and a little conversation.

"His name's Moshe Howard. Nominally, he's your legal adviser in Israel, retained to assist you regarding your request for information. Inasmuch as it's hopeless, that would be a foolish waste of money — assuming he ever sent you a bill. Which, given his profound distaste for your client, he would never do."

"So why are we meeting?"

"In four months we elect a prime minister — unless something dramatic happens, it will be the one who just took power, Isaac Benjamin, who is supported by the settlers and the religious, deplored by the followers of Ben-Aron." Ernheit paused to consider his words. "Moshe has an interest in changing the electoral dynamic, and you may serve that interest. For now, let's leave it at that, and hope he decides to trust you."

3

The King David Hotel was majestic, the former headquarters of the British military, a six-story sandstone structure built in the imperial manner. Its palm-shrouded patio, patrolled by waiters in white jackets, looked out on the Old City, a ghostly outline in the dusk. Freshly showered and wearing a newly pressed sport coat and slacks, David sipped red wine with Ernheit and Moshe Howard.

Howard was David's age, slender and fine featured, with short brown hair and inquisitive blue eyes. "The occasion for your visit is uncomfortable," he told David after a few moments' conversation. "But it is necessary that you see the geography we share. This is not Middle America."

David nodded. "One look at the Green Line, and it's easy enough to see why people might feel threatened."

Howard smiled faintly. "My father," he said, "was a Jewish officer in the British army when they helped liberate Bergen-Belsen. It changed him. After he came here, he would often speak of the 'Holocaust syndrome' — a deep trauma in the psyche of Israelis, so that any danger, internal or external, echoes with the threat of extermination.

"Of course, the slaughter of Jews did not begin with the Holocaust — it took place in Europe long before, and in places like Hebron on the West Bank, where Palestinians murdered Jews. So it is inevitable that we fear the Palestinians, who now send their young to kill themselves *and* us — who would not fear people with such disdain for the value of human life? But often we fear each other: Israeli Jews versus the Israeli Arabs, who, many believe, are potential agents of outside enemies like Iran; the secular — including advocates of peace like Ben-Aron — versus the settlers and religious, who fear 'betrayal' at the hands of their fellow Jews."

Listening, Ernheit inclined his head toward David. "We spoke a little of the right of return," he told Howard, "the abiding passion his client's husband, and others like him, rail about incessantly."

"Show me the Palestinian leader who will say to his people there will be no return," Howard responded, "and I will show you a leader with no future. And if the four hundred thousand descendants of refugees in Lebanon, and the half million more on the West Bank, did return to Israel, *we* would have no future."

David looked from Howard to Ernheit. "Isn't the reverse also true?" he asked. "There are three million or so Palestinians in the West Bank. You can't make them part of Israel, nor can you occupy their land forever. Ben-Aron was looking for a way out."

"In 1967," Howard answered in an arid tone, "when our army chased the Jordanians out of the West Bank, it was like Eve biting the apple. Even at the time, most of our leaders understood this. But many religious Jews were enraptured — at last we had reclaimed the land given us by God. And the Jordanians, it transpired, were happy to be rid of real estate filled with Palestinians who, under

Arafat, had disrupted the regime of King Hussein. In short, we couldn't *give* these people away.

"And so, over time, we built settlements on the land we had acquired as a bulwark against invasion, much as the kibbutzim near Jerusalem had slowed the Arab invasion in 1948. It would have been better to put soldiers there; soldiers can be removed to make a peace. But kick out a quarter million Jews who have made their lives there? Not so easy."

"I'll take you to the settlements," Ernheit said to David. "You'll see homes, synagogues, cemeteries, the work of three generations. And you'll understand what has bred a handful of dangerous extremists like Barak Lev."

For a few moments, the three men sipped wine in silence, the patio dimly illuminated, the Old City spectral in the moonlight, the white-jacketed waiters gliding among the tables filled with patrons. "Peaceful," David said at length.

Howard nodded. "And beautiful, too. But Jerusalem is surrounded by cemeteries, and the dead sometimes seem more powerful than the living — King David and Emperor Saladin, still pursuing their own vision of this land. And yet this is still the only place in the Middle East where Christians, Jews, and Muslims have a chance to live together in peace, to create a vision of the future. For one people to own it would be tragic —"

Abruptly, the sound of an explosion shattered the quiet. A woman on the patio cried out; at once, Ernheit was on his feet, hand on his gun, listening intently to the muffled echo, the thin sound of distant shrieks. "The Old City," he murmured.

Remembering the moment of Ben-Aron's assassination, David felt a tremor in his hands. Some of those around them, he saw, had sought shelter beneath their tables. Howard did not move. With a calm deliberation that seemed both studied and precarious, he took out his cell phone and began to dial. All around them, cell phones rang in a nerve-racking cacophony.

Howard listened intently. After a moment, he asked, "The children are with you?"

As David watched, Howard's face relaxed. Ernheit sat down again.

"They're all right, then," David said to Howard.

Nodding, Howard sat back in his chair, arms at his side. It was a long time before he spoke. "A third of us have lost relatives," he told David, "or at least someone we know, to a suicide bomber. My wife used to take a bus home from work. One afternoon, a block before it was to pick her up, it exploded. The bus driver's arm ended up at her feet.

"She never takes the bus now. She tries to keep our children away from crowded places. And when she hears any explosion, anywhere, she calls them." Howard paused, then said tiredly, "Religion may be the death of us all."

David contemplated his wine. "Religious fanaticism, you mean."

"Yes, and it's most dangerous in the Middle East. Start with the Islamic clerical rulers in Iran, who plan to develop nuclear warheads while financing terrorism throughout the region. Move to their natural allies among the Palestinians, including Hamas. Now groups like Hamas and Hezbollah have missiles that can kill us in our towns and cities. And if we have a nuclear Iran, and the West Bank becomes an Islamic fundamentalist state instead of a prosperous trading partner, a security barrier will do *us* no good at all.

"But how do we untangle ourselves from the settlements on the West Bank, so despised by Palestinians? To remove perhaps a quarter million settlers by force, including people like Barak Lev and the Masada movement, could well fragment our own army." Howard looked at David intently. "You claim to believe that the conspiracy to murder Ben-Aron reached inside his security detail. If you are right, the Jews who helped plan his death understood that by placing Isaac Benjamin in power, they were killing the chances of peace."

David nodded. "The night I met Ben-Aron, one of his aides told me there were perhaps two hundred people actively looking for ways to kill him."

"A handful of fanatics," Howard answered. "Those Ben-Aron's plan threatened most live in the settlements that are most exposed or — like Lev's — outside the boundaries authorized by our government. Many are American Jews from places like Brooklyn whose only authority is the God of the Old Testament. For them, the only way to keep their dream of greater Israel alive is for there to be no peace."

The waiter arrived, bringing their dinner and lighting a second candle. The three men watched the flame flicker, then catch hold, casting a circle of light on the white tablecloth. Glancing at the waiter's retreating back, Howard inquired, "Are you familiar with the rodef principle?"

"No."

"Stated broadly, Jewish biblical law holds that a Jew is entitled to kill any man who is trying to kill him. Unexceptional in itself. But run that principle through the mind of a fanatic Jew committed to making a stand outside the boundaries of the State of Israel — a man willing to die before abandoning the home God meant for him — and assassinating Ben-Aron becomes an act of self-defense."

David glanced at Ernheit. "What do you know about Barak Lev?"

"Very little." Ernheit put down his wineglass. "What *is* known is that he has deliberately chosen to create his own Jewish frontier, an illegal settlement outside of any boundary. Four years ago, two of his followers drove a trailer at night to a Muslim village and parked it outside a school attended by Palestinian children. The trailer was filled with plastique timed to blow up as the children were coming to school.

"Our police caught these men as they were deflating a tire — their intent, it seemed, was to make the trailer's presence less suspicious. Only *that* prevented a tragedy which would have inflamed the intifada still further."

David considered this while he ate his pasta. "When Rabin was killed by a Jew," he said at length, "Hamas launched a wave of suicide bombings, effectively changing the electoral dynamic and transferring power to Rabin's opponents. Suppose the murder of Ben-Aron involved the help of Jews but is blamed exclusively on Palestinians. That would accomplish the same thing: discrediting Faras and Al Aqsa, bringing Isaac Benjamin to power, and strengthening hard-liners on both sides."

"Two problems," Ernheit responded. "First, your theory requires the collaboration of someone close to Ben-Aron — some fanatic Jew living in a trailer on the West Bank could not pull it off. Second, it would necessitate close operational cooperation between this person and the Palestinians who carried out the murder.

"It's conceivable that there could be the parallel plots to assassinate Ben-Aron — one by Jews, one by Arabs. But it is hard to conceive how two sides who so hate each other would come together in a seamless conspiracy." Ernheit's smile was fleeting. "While, incidentally, framing the unfortunate Ms. Arif."

David sat back, looking at both men. "Your government has launched a massive inquiry," he said. "But it's buttoned up tight. If right-wing Jews were involved in killing Ben-Aron, and that became public, it would hardly help Isaac Benjamin."

Howard shook his head. "If you're implying that those investigating would deliberately ignore, or cover up, such a possibility, you should think better of everyone involved. Our legal system is at least as honest as yours, and Isaac Benjamin — whatever his faults — would want the murderers brought to justice.

"But before the election? This investigation will proceed carefully, deliberately, and confidentially. Whatever his motives, Benjamin cannot stampede them. Which means, effectively, that he will remain in power."

David studied him. "Unless?"

"You are on a faster timetable," Howard answered softly. "You have a client to defend. Others, deeply interested in the outcome of our election, may also share your sense of urgency. Some may even have sources within the government who quietly hold a similar agenda.

"Perhaps, in time, you will hear from them."

4

The next morning, at the invitation of the Israeli government, David drove to Tel Aviv to meet General Ehud Peretz, head of the Intelligence Bureau for the Israel Defense Forces, the IDF.

The appointment, as Zev Ernheit explained, was Israel's concession to David's request for information. Peretz was a national figure; a heroic young officer in the 1973 war and an adviser to prime ministers on intelligence and terrorism, he was now charged with running counterterrorism activities on the West Bank, including the swift and comprehensive reprisals aimed at eradicating the Al Aqsa Martyrs Brigade. It was only during the 1973 war, Ernheit said, that Peretz's mother had told him she was a survivor of the Nazi death camp at Maidanek. When the war was finished, Peretz had gone there; once he saw, still preserved, the bones and ashes of the dead, he resolved to spend his life in the defense of Israel.

As David worked his way through the security procedures for entry to the massive cement-and-glass structure, Israel's Pentagon, he reflected on this story. The young people bustling in and out of the building, barely out of their teens, bespoke a commitment to military service very different from that in the United States: even in this city on the

Mediterranean, the border between Israel and the West Bank was at most an hour away. For Israelis, obliviousness was not a choice, and national defense not an optional activity. David Wolfe, the American Jew, was an outsider.

Ehud Peretz looked as smart and tough as he no doubt was — crew-cut hair, intent brown eyes, a seamed, rugged face, and a barrel chest, with muscled forearms exposed by a short-sleeved khaki shirt. Though he greeted Wolfe with a firm handshake, his cool expression suggested his distaste for David's visit. Waving David to a chair, he said bluntly, "I am familiar with your theory. But the performance of Amos's security detail is now the business of others. That leaves us to discuss the mythic people known as Palestinians."

Directness was best, David thought. "My client doesn't consider herself mythic."

"Perhaps not. But then her husband is a chief perpetrator of the myth." Despite its flatness, Peretz's tone betrayed a weary sarcasm. "Do you know where Ibrahim Jefar and Iyad Hassan were from? Refugee camps — Hassan from the Aida camp, Jefar the cesspool of Jenin. And why do such places exist after nearly sixty years? Because no Arab countries will take those people, and the Palestinian Authority does nothing to relieve their misery. The camps dramatize our role as 'occupier,' and keep alive this fantasy of return. Most important, they breed hatred of the Jews — and, not so incidentally, suicide bombers.

"Let me show you something." Circling his desk, Peretz sat next to David, angling his computer screen so they could watch together. A film appeared, apparently a mosque filled with men listening to an imam, his speech translated in English subtitles. "This was broadcast on public television in Ramallah — two days before Ben-Aron's assassins departed for America. The imam is a darling of Hamas."

His voice shrill, the bearded young cleric spoke in an angry rush underscored by the rapt attention of his listeners and the poisonous words rendered in the subtitles: *Israel is a cancer,* David read, *and the Jews a virus worse than AIDS.*

"We protested to Faras," Peretz said, "and the imam was taken off the air. But he remains employed by the Palestinian Authority in its Ministry of Religion."

On the screen, the faces of the imam's listeners were intent — some men nodded, and all but a few seemed focused on every word. *In the history of the world, Jews are behind every suffering. The British and the French had to punish and expel Jews. So did the Spanish.*

"That's a fairly perfunctory account of the Spanish Inquisition," David observed.

The Jews provoked Nazism. They encouraged hatred of Germany, and the boycott of goods, as Jewish bankers strangled the German people until they rose up in self-defense. Praise be to Allah for giving us the worst enemy of believers, the verminous Jews.

David felt a visceral outrage. "This was on Palestinian TV?"

Clicking his keyboard, Peretz froze the picture. In one corner of the screen, David saw black arrows touching the heads of two men, one with his head bowed, one staring straight ahead. This was the man David recognized first: Iyad Hassan. The man with the bowed head appeared to be Ibrahim Jefar. "Faras can speak as politely as he likes,"

Peretz said coolly. "But this imam has become the true face of the Palestinian Authority, and these assassins his progeny. What choice does he give us but to kill them?"

David searched the faces of the men imbibing the imam's speech. Hassan's face seemed alive with fervor; Jefar looked down as though, detached from the crowd around him, he was reflecting on something else. One other man caught David's eyes: in profile, his face shadowed, he seemed not to be watching the imam but Jefar.

Nerves suddenly on edge, David leaned closer. The man was slight, smaller than the others. Something about the angle of his head was eerily familiar.

David placed his finger on the screen. "This man. Do you know him?"

"No." Peretz smiled slightly. "But you're wondering if it's Khalid."

"Yes."

"So are we. Whoever it is, he seems to have greater interest in Jefar than in the imam. But we've blown this image up, and there's no way to be certain. Before and after this, he does not appear at all." Peretz gazed at the picture. "In any event, that film suggests why the West Bank is a Garden of Eden for terrorists. Hassan and Jefar are notable only for whom they killed, where they killed him, and what it will cost us all."

"And, therefore, for who sent them."

"In theory, it could have been anyone. There are untold numbers on the West Bank who see terror as their only weapon and believe that Jews have no history but as 'oppressors.' In their schools, even in children's notebooks, you will find photographs of suicide bombers. Men like Hassan and Jefar grew up believing that by killing and dying they will bring honor to their families, redeem their victimhood, and pave the way for the return to the land we 'stole.' That is why there is such an endless supply of 'martyrs.' "

"In the early 1990s," David said, "I understand that Israeli intelligence gave covert support to Hamas, hoping to drain support from Arafat."

Peretz shot him a look of surprise, as though recalibrating his sense of David's knowledge. "A terrible mistake. But then the law of unintended consequences was born in the Middle East."

"And so Arafat encouraged the formation of the Al Aqsa Martyrs," David went on, "to keep Hamas from monopolizing 'armed resistance.' Both Faras and Ben-Aron believed Al Aqsa could be diverted from violence, perhaps by joining a security force that could fulfill one of Israel's requirements for peace — that the Palestinian Authority control Hamas and others. But now you, personally, are directing the eradication of Al Aqsa on the West Bank."

Peretz spread his hands. "What choice do we have? We're confident that Jefar was linked to Al Aqsa. Faras does not control terrorists, and his government, now dominated by Hamas, is little more than armed gangs playing at democracy."

"And when Israel has destroyed Al Aqsa," David asked, "and Faras is reduced to a eunuch, who profits?"

Sitting beside David, Peretz folded his arms, gazing out the window at the skyline of Tel Aviv. "Anyone who opposes peace — on the West Bank, anyone who can pick up the pieces. In particular, Hamas."

"And the Iranians?"

Peretz gave him another look of appraisal. "Yes, the Iranians. We and they have a history. In the early nineties, they struck at us in Argentina; in 2002, we caught them trying to smuggle their most advanced explosives, rockets, and long-range missiles to Arafat on a boat called the *Karine A*.

"The cornerstone of Iranian foreign policy is our destruction. They've funneled money to Hamas, Islamic Jihad, Hezbollah, and Al Aqsa. And they did not like Faras for his overtures toward Ben-Aron."

"Given all that," David asked, "does Iran operate within Israel?"

Peretz's expression became closed. "Yes," he answered tersely. "And in the United States. But through Arabs, not Jews. We have far fewer extremists than the Palestinians, and we take responsibility for controlling them. They could not murder our prime minister, and they have yet to blow up Arab schoolchildren.

"We are not killers, Mr. Wolfe. We are trapped in a cycle of violence, fighting for our own survival. Do you know about the Passover bombing?"

"Only what I read."

"Every year, a group of aged survivors from Auschwitz brought their children and grandchildren to a restaurant in Haifa, to celebrate their families and their lives. Two years ago, as always, they met amid much warmth and laughter, much wonder at their good fortune to be alive. Then, at seven o'clock, a Palestinian entered the room and blew up thirty people, mostly children. The elders who still lived were forced to search among the ruined bodies for the children or grandchildren they cherished all the more for having survived Hitler."

Listening, David envisioned Harold Shorr in

such a gathering, and realized that, in the logic of this fantasy, David, Carole, and their children would be with him. Quietly, Peretz continued: "I am sure Arif and her husband decry our operation in the refugee camp at Jenin — how children died, how indiscriminately we killed the innocent. *I* ordered that operation." He stood, gazing down at David. "The Passover bomber was from Jenin. The group we targeted planned the bombing. I ask you — as a man and as a Jew — what would you do if the choice were yours? And do you, as lawyer for this accused assassin, feel better than if you were in my place?"

In the words, David heard the bitterness of a soldier whose hardest decisions felt inevitable. "I can't answer that," he said.

"Good. Because now you are a part of this." Peretz still spoke quietly. "You cast about for plotters, and convince yourself Arif is innocent. I have read your statements — how can this woman, a lawyer and a mother, also be a murderer? Harsh experience provides my answer. The Passover bomber was a young mother, a lawyer like Arif. As she set off the explosives, she was smiling at a two-year-old, the great-granddaughter of a Holocaust survivor. Her own two children are now orphans.

"Your client was not required to die — or, if Jefar had not survived, even to sacrifice her freedom. So why would a mother do this?" Peretz's tone became steely. "Hatred. Her husband's, and her own, fed by Sabra and Shatila, their own version of Jenin. Don't believe your client is immune to hate. I've read accounts of her classroom lectures. You are now the guest of 'the worst human rights violator in the Middle East,' 'imperialists masquerading as victims,' and Amos Ben-Aron was just another man who 'steals our land and walls off our hopes.' Perhaps, in your client's view, such a man deserved to die."

David maintained his calm. "If you have any evidence against her, tell me."

"None but what you already have. Nor anything concrete against Saeb Khalid, though I sense you'd like that better. Nonetheless, I have spent an hour with you, even though you're playing games with Israel's national security on behalf of a woman who, unless this implausible 'frame' of yours is real, is the killer of Amos Ben-Aron." Abruptly, Peretz's voice softened. "In the army, my mentor and closest friend."

David had no answer. "So now I will ask a favor," Peretz said bluntly. "I want you to meet with survivors of the Passover bombing, at least those who can stand to be in the room with you. I do not want you to leave as untouched as you came."

"I'm not quite untouched," David answered. "But I'll meet with them, of course. No one I love has ever been murdered."

Returning to the hotel, David was far more tired than jet lag could account for.

On his bed, he found an envelope. The typed note sealed inside read: "Visit the Holocaust History Museum at Yad Vashem. There is much you can learn there."

David had been in Israel for twenty-three hours.

5

After setting his alarm, David slept.

He slipped into a dream. He was driving on a busy, rain-slick highway with a woman whose face he could not see. Suddenly he realized that he must swiftly cross two lanes and exit to the right. The highway was crowded and David had only seconds; braking abruptly, he swerved across one lane and then accelerated, trying to slip between two semitrucks onto the exit ramp. The woman gave a soft cry. As the truck behind them clipped his bumper, David lost control . . .

When the alarm jolted him awake, he lay across the mattress amid tangled sheets. It took him seconds to remember that he was in Jerusalem, alone, and that his fifth-floor window framed a view of the Al Aqsa Mosque. He had never felt so isolated, or so adrift, so completely at the mercy of others.

Dressing slowly, as though still in a dream, he readied himself for Yad Vashem.

The starkly modern museum was built on a hillside surrounded by pine trees. The day was bright and clear; around David, young men and women, Israeli soldiers, came and went. Those departing seemed subdued: so that they might better understand their service, Ernheit had explained, the IDF took them to Yad Vashem. The other defining trip, Ernheit had added, was to the desert fortress of Masada, where Jewish rebels had committed mass suicide rather than yield to the Romans. "Once you've finished at Yad Vashem," Ernheit said, "you will understand Masada."

Entering, David was greeted by a collage of black-and-white film footage, showing the normal lives of European Jews before the Holocaust: shoppers at a market, bright-faced children at a school, celebrants observing Passover — all of them oblivious to what awaited. Then, taking a ramp, he descended into the museum.

At the bottom of the ramp was a large photograph from a concentration camp. It was filled with the bodies of adults and children piled on wooden fagots, some with their eyes closed, others with the sightless stare of the dead, their arms and legs at angles seldom seen in life. At the end of the war, the Germans who had run the camp tried to burn the evidence of their crimes; there were so many bodies that the guards, forced to work in haste, could not completely incinerate them all. Beside this was a display of smaller photos retrieved from the half-charred corpses — a family at the beach; smiling couples; boys in athletic uniforms — the only evidence the dead possessed that their lives had once been different.

For some moments, David did not move.

The next room began the path between these two depictions of innocence and death: a film of gleeful Germans throwing books by Jews into a bonfire, as though prefiguring the burning of Jews themselves; a children's board game in which the object was expelling Jews from Germany; beer mugs with anti-Semitic slogans etched above their portraiture; photos of German doctors measuring the heads of Jews, seeking to identify the features that marked them as "subhumans." Then, without warning, David stepped into his parents' living room.

Perfectly preserved, it was that of a Jewish family living in Berlin: austere, entirely secular, its wooden chairs, tables, and mirrors antiques. David had always thought of his parents' chosen decor as an affectation, the efforts of a couple who barely saw themselves as Jewish to appropriate the style of New England Episcopalians; now he perceived that, whether consciously or not, they had replicated the parallel life they might have lived in Germany. Except that, by the time of Kristallnacht, when Nazis had looted and destroyed the homes of German Jews, David's mother and father, children then, were safe from harm in the beautiful American city that their grandparents had chosen.

Your father became a psychiatrist, Bryce Martel had said to David, *because, like many psychiatrists, he wished to understand himself. But whatever he discovered, he did not wish to share. Including how he felt about being a Jew.*

As with sex and death, Philip Wolfe had avoided all mention of the Holocaust.

Past the sprawling pile of shoes taken from those awaiting cremation was a semicircular display, holding records of some of the six million who had perished.

Behind this was a room filled with computers. At each station, visitors could enter the names of their relatives, perhaps learn more about their fate. But David had never known family names beyond those of his grandparents, or even what place in Germany they might have come from. If the Holocaust had touched his ancestors, he did not know it.

He hesitated, then decided to experiment with the past.

"Wolfe," David tapped on the keyboard, followed by "Germany."

He found twenty-one names and several photographs — men, women, and children, perhaps relatives, perhaps not. He scanned the faces but found no clue to consanguinity. Wolfe was not an uncommon name, and for all David knew, it was anglicized from some more unwieldy, less attractive surname.

He tried his mother's name, Schneider, with similar results. Then, out of some vestigial memory — an inscription written in a leatherbound book, he guessed — another surname came to him: Wolfensohn.

He typed the name onto the screen and pushed "Enter."

Several names and faces appeared. The second photograph froze him: Hans Wolfensohn, a surgeon, had perished with his family at Birkenau. It was a face David remembered from childhood, in memory close enough to startle him — his father's father, an estates and trusts lawyer who had taken David to the zoo and tucked him into bed with stories. But never of the past.

Shaken, David stared at the doctor, his grandfather's murdered doppelganger. He thought of his prep school friends, with their ancestral homes and famous progenitors, senators or industrialists, their lives preserved in portraits or biographies. But like Hans Wolfensohn, David's past had been erased.

■■■■

Outside, a man stood waiting for him — bald and fit, sunglasses perched on top of his head, his manner casual. Without preface, he told David, "When the first Jew died in the War of Independence, we did not count from one, but from six million and one. But if you believe that Israel is God's answer to the Holocaust, at least there is a symmetry."

David was too distracted for subtlety. "Who are you?" he asked.

"My name is Ari Masur."

David knew him at once — though still youthful, the former general came from a founding family of Israel, and his father had been a hero in Israel's War of Independence. Perceiving David's recognition, Masur added with an ironic smile, "Some think I wish to become prime minister of Israel. But today I'm simply your driver. I promise that your journey will be less taxing than the one you just completed."

They drove in silence to Jerusalem, taking what seemed to David an elliptical route, Masur glancing at the rearview mirror. "I once headed the Shin Bet," he explained. "Sometimes, for amusement, I practice the art of evasion."

Though his instincts were alive with curiosity, David asked him nothing. The last few hours were too present.

Parking near a public square, they walked down cobbled side streets and then entered a three-story sandstone home. It was five hundred years old, Masur observed, but perfectly preserved. Through the alcove David saw a tree-sheltered patio surrounded by a garden; ascending the stairs, they passed carefully appointed rooms combining sunlight and shadow, rich with a sense of history. The roof garden, shaded by olive trees, afforded a panorama of Jerusalem.

A dark-haired woman, gazing out at the city, turned at the sound of footsteps. She was forty or so, with an erect carriage and aquiline features that caused David to stop where he was.

"I'm Anat Ben-Aron," she told him. "I believe you knew my father."

Startled, David looked into her face, so reminiscent of Amos Ben-Aron's. "I *admired* your father," he said at last. "So meeting you is difficult."

"Yes. I imagine so."

The cool matter-of-factness in her tone and manner left no room for polite evasion. "Whoever killed him," David said, "I don't believe it was Hana Arif."

Ben-Aron gave a curt nod. "This I also understand. So let us sit."

They did so beneath an olive tree at a corner of the roof garden. Ice and bottled water waited on the table; whatever they meant to discuss, Masur and Ben-Aron did not want it overheard by servants. Masur poured water into the glasses with the precision of an apothecary. "I assume we speak in confidence," he said to David.

"Of course."

"All right, then. Anat and I are among the embattled who still believe that peace is possible. By grotesque coincidence, you may become our ally."

Ben-Aron leaned forward on the table, her study of David's face unwavering and keen. "Whether Arif lives or dies," she told him, "is of little concern to me. I care about two things: knowing who planned my father's death, and ensuring that he did not die for nothing. As of now, his death is a weapon for those he despised in life: Arab terrorists and fanatic settlers like Barak Lev."

Trying to find his bearings, David sipped some water. "I've had much the same thought," he ventured.

"We have an election soon," Masur said. "As matters stand, it will complete the transfer of power to Isaac Benjamin and those who define peace as a separation barrier, strengthening Hamas and leaving the West Bank as a festering sore, filled with the angry and impoverished." Once more, Masur glanced at Ben-Aron. "Now, again, we bomb them, this time to wipe out Al Aqsa. And, again, we have no choice.

"But what does it gain us? More power for Hamas. Without the hope of peace, the Palestinian people will turn to them for good. And the only winners will be the haters on both sides of this barrier we're building."

"This is geopolitics," David said. "My interests are different. I'm a lawyer, defending a client who may die —"

"Yes, by suggesting that Jews helped kill my father," Ben-Aron interrupted brusquely. "You recall the murder of Yitzhak Rabin. The radical settlers also hated *him.* In their minds, they were engaged in an underground war with the secular Jews, which they had to win before they could deal with the Arabs." Her lips curled in distaste. "When Rabin was murdered by a Jew, some literally sang and danced. But the great majority of us were sickened, and expected Rabin's policies to continue."

"Until," David added, "Palestinian terrorists, especially Hamas, launched a wave of suicide bombings."

"Not just Palestinians," Masur said. "Iranians."

"Are you saying," David prodded, "that the Iranians were behind the assassination of Rabin?"

"No. I'm saying they exploited it, by fomenting and financing the wave of suicide attacks carried out by Palestinians, destroying the chances of peace and leading to the election of a right-wing government of Israel. And, in doing so, the Iranians learned a valuable lesson for the future.

"By themselves they could not kill Rabin. But a right-wing fanatic could. So they perceived that those who hated them *and* the Palestinians the most — fanatic settlers — were also enemies of the State of Israel."

Ben-Aron gazed at the table, her handsome features set, as though fighting back repressed emotion. "For the worst of the settlers," she said with quiet bitterness, "Israel is not a place of democracy or hope but of land and tombs and sacred sites. This is not Judaism — it's idolatry, and now it's become insane. Throughout history, the insane kill to achieve their dreams."

"Your father's security detail," David responded gently, "was meant to repel the insane."

The statement, and the challenge it contained, prompted a swift glance from Ben-Aron to Ari Masur. "This is a small society," Masur said at length. "With various overlapping spheres of influence, and many connections. And one connection that embraces most Jews."

David reflected on what he knew. "The army?"

"Military service," Masur corrected. "Almost all of us serve, even fanatic 'hill boys' like Barak Lev. The army is a place where disparate men forge bonds for life."

Anat Ben-Aron, David saw, was still contemplating the table. "Also the place," David countered, "from which your prime minister's security detail is drawn. Including the most junior, and therefore perhaps the least reliable. But we're talking in riddles. Which 'disparate' men? And how might they be connected to Iran?"

"Were there such a connection," Masur answered cautiously, "it could traumatize the Israeli people. But in the end, this knowledge might be the saving of us, and of Anat's father's plan. Sooner or later, Mr. Wolfe, everything in Israel leaks. Why not in a good cause?" Once more, Masur smiled. "Whether a plan for peace, or the defense of a former lover."

Astonished, David realized that Anat Ben-Aron was studying him. "For now," she said quietly, "we are done. But you should not leave Israel too soon. With skill and patience, you may start to find some answers to your riddles."

6

In the hills of Haifa, a striking coastal city with commanding views of the Mediterranean, David sat on a patio with four middle-aged Israelis, two widows and a wife and husband, whose families had been shattered by the female suicide bomber from the refugee camp at Jenin.

It had happened, as Ehud Peretz had told him, on the Saturday night of Passover, when four generations — the eldest, survivors of Auschwitz — had gathered to celebrate the regeneration of their families. The restaurant was owned by Arabs: Haifa was a place where Israelis and the descendants of Arabs who had chosen not to flee lived in relative amity. At the moment of the bombing, each of these survivors had just finished a delicious meal and felt suffused with well-being and the love of family.

From Zev Ernheit, who had driven him here, David knew their stories. Shoshanna Ravit, a dark, slender woman of fifty whose mournful gravity evoked for David a Velázquez painting, had come to the restaurant with her husband, Isaac, a retired army colonel turned businessman; her son, David, a keen soccer player and student of architecture; and their daughter, Rachel, a young teacher of students with special needs. Saar Mendel had come with her husband, Mickey, and son, Dov; that night they were celebrating Dov's release from military service. Eli and Myra Landau had attended the celebration with their daughter, Nurit, a high school senior whose raven hair and bright smile were captured in a photograph that gazed back at David from the wooden table around which the four of them had gathered in the twilight.

David struggled for words to bridge the gulf of sorrow and distrust between himself and these grieving parents, wondering as he did so why General Peretz had arranged this meeting. "I'm sorry for your loss," he told them. "I can't claim to know how you must feel. But I want you to know, especially given the reason I've come to Israel, that I hate what you've been forced to suffer."

In the silence, Shoshanna Ravit regarded him. She sat in a wheelchair, her slacks hanging loosely where her feet should be; as with the others, her voice was drained of life. "General Peretz said you came to learn," she told him. "But that you shouldn't be allowed to pick and choose. For our part, we've become used to speaking of our families to keep them alive in memory, along with the hope that others outside Israel will comprehend what we must face."

David nodded.

"So, do you want my memories?" she asked.

In the candlelight, Shoshanna had looked into the face of her daughter. The atmosphere was boisterous, filled with talk and laughter; in the privacy this offered them, Rachel leaned closer and confided, "Two weeks ago, I met this guy . . ."

At the corner of her eye, Shoshanna saw a movement that distracted her: a young Arab woman with dark, soulful eyes approaching a table filled with four animated generations of an Israeli family, the youngest a blond infant on her great-grandfather's lap. His arm, circled around her, showed the tattoo on his forearm.

"Arik's really cute," Rachel was saying. "And so completely smart . . ."

The Arab woman smiled at the infant. When the great-grandfather looked up, returning her smile, she closed her eyes, then exploded with a concussive shudder that lifted Shoshanna from her chair.

When consciousness returned, she lay in a pool of blood, faintly aware of the keening sounds around her, the lack of feeling in her legs. Beside her lay her husband, blood trickling from his mouth. The thought came to her, slowly, that he was dead.

Turning on her stomach, Shoshanna faced the room. It was nothing like before. Where families had been were splintered tables, bodies or pieces of bodies, blood spattered on the wall.

Shoshanna closed her eyes. She must be strong for her children, she admonished herself, and then darkness overcame her.

She awakened in the ambulance as a paramedic was giving her a shot. "What is this for?" she asked groggily.

"Tetanus and hepatitis B."

"Then be sure to give this to my children," she instructed him. "Even though Rachel still cries at shots . . ."

Finishing, she told David, "I used to love to walk along the seashore with my family, feeling the cool splash of water on my feet and ankles. When I awakened from my numbness, I saw that I had no feet or ankles, and realized I also had no family."

■■■■

Unlike Shoshanna Ravit, pain had left Saar Mendel with a look of passive bewilderment, as though she were confronted by a puzzle to which she could not divine the answer.

She had met Shoshanna at a gathering arranged by Eli Landau, spurred by the realization that "normal" people feared to be with them. "We both confided," Saar explained, "that what still haunted us at night was the fear that our children had suffered pain."

Six months after the bombing, resolute but afraid, they had gone to the police and asked to view the photographs of those who had once been their loved ones.

Shoshanna's husband, daughter, and children appeared in the photographs much as she recalled them in life. Saar, however, could not recognize the ruins that were proven by medical science to be what remained of Mickey and Dov; she could identify only Dov, and only by the gold necklace that he wore to contrast with his tan. But the photographs afforded her a terrible consolation — her family could not have suffered for more than a split-second. "If God had let me choose," she told David with moist eyes, "I would have begged to become another photograph. Instead, He cursed me with the role of witness."

Compared to this, Myra Landau explained, the death of their only child was a fluke. "The same nail that struck my elbow pierced Nurit's aorta. Her face was calm, unchanged, as though she were asleep. But when I put my face to her lips, I could feel no breathing."

She turned to her husband, Eli. He was framed by a lush garden at his back and, beyond that, a panorama of the Mediterranean in twilight, the fading glow of sunset becoming a deep purple on the water, the first encroachment of night. It was a stunning view in which David could take little interest, save to wonder whether Eli Landau could ever contemplate this with anything like pleasure.

"Why do you defend this woman?" Eli demanded.

Ari Masur's earlier allusion to his true relationship with Hana still shadowed David's mind. But that knowledge, he had decided, was a result of the surveillance of Saeb and Hana at Harvard. "Because I don't think she did this," he answered. "And because I want to know who did. There are those in Israel who did not care for Amos Ben-Aron."

Eli stared at him. "Palestinians, not Jews, murdered Amos Ben-Aron, and with him our illusions. All our government can do is to build this fence and try to keep out bombers. From what we learned about this woman and where she came from, if the fence had existed then, so might our daughter. Instead our army went to Jenin. After that, Ehud told us, there was no one left to punish."

But there would always, David thought, be someone left to punish. Watching his face, Myra Landau said, "Americans judge us, as does the world. But no one can understand. We are normal people who suffered at random; the only abnormal thing about us, as victims of terror, is that we symbolize the loss of the security and serenity Americans take for granted. At least until Hana Arif helped a suicide bomber kill a Jew in San Francisco." She managed a smile that brought no light to her eyes. "When will you make peace? the world asks us, even after Hezbollah rains missiles on our city. I used to hope for peace, and now I don't. It is like Nurit. One moment you have a child, and then you don't. So you ask yourself, Did I dream that child? All that keeps you sane is to speak of her." Pausing, she added quietly, "Even to you."

In the candlelight, David looked at the faces of four suffering parents, and could find nothing to say. "By heritage," Eli Landau told him, "we are Europeans. But we live surrounded by people for whom life has a different meaning. Arab families murder their daughters in honor killings, send their children to kill our children and themselves. Our own settlers, whatever you may think of them, don't stone their wives and slaughter Arab families."

Listening, David chose not to mention the followers of Barak Lev, who had attempted to blow up a school filled with Palestinian children. "This suicide bomber," he asked, "what *did* you learn about her?"

"Ehud Peretz said that you would ask this. Her name was Farah Abboud." Eli Landau gave him an ironic look. "She was Hamas, the sister-in-law of Iyad Hassan."

Zev Ernheit was parked outside. David got into the passenger seat, drained by the emotion of the evening. Only now did David fully understand why he had come: in exchange for agreeing to the experience of hearing those stories, Ehud Peretz had left for him a nugget of information, the possible connection of Ben-Aron's assassin with Hamas.

"How was it?" Ernheit asked.

"Wrenching." David slumped back in the seat. "I saw a suicide bombing, after all. My imagination may work a little better than they suppose."

Ernheit fished out a cell phone from his shirt pocket and placed it in David's hand. "I've been told to give you this. Once you're alone, listen to your messages."

In his hotel room, David turned on the cell phone and pressed the "1" key.

The man's voice was Israeli, his English faintly accented. Tomorrow, David was to go to the Old City, meandering like a tourist. But at four o'clock he must find himself, as though by chance, in the Assyrian Chapel, deep in the bowels of the Church of the Holy Sepulchre, the place of Christ's crucifixion.

7

Around two o'clock, David entered the Old City of Jerusalem on foot, a map sticking from the back pocket of his khaki slacks.

He paused at the base of the wall built by Romans over two thousand years before, scarred by bullets from the wars of 1948 and 1967; passing beneath an arch designed by Muslims, he followed the path used by Crusaders and entered a vibrant world teeming with tourists, Arabs, Orthodox Jews, students, and professional-looking men and women of varying origins. Reflecting its history, the city was divided into four quarters: Jewish, Muslim, Christian, and Armenian, the last occupied by those whose ancestors had fled slaughter by the Turks. But in many places, these peoples intermingled; taking a narrow cobblestoned street past stone buildings with no space between them, David passed the home of an Armenian family, a mosque, and a young Jewish boy reading a book in his parents' palm-sheltered courtyard. It was hard to imagine any country staking an exclusive claim to this place, although many had tried; David thought of the bomb that had exploded as he ate at the King David, adding to the thousands of people killed in this city over thousands of years.

Pretending to consult his map while registering

the faces around him, he followed a seemingly purposeless path that, in fact, he had committed to memory. He passed another incongruity: in a Roman plaza excavated after 1967, a Jewish girl chattered on a cell phone, reminding him of Munira. A Jewish section became a Muslim shopping area without notice; the alley was only a few feet wide, with Arabic signs for shops offering candlesticks, condiments, pillows, brightly colored rugs, grains, noodles, and olive oil, sold by an Arab man smoking from a hookah. Looking up, he saw police surveillance cameras. There were no garbage cans allowed here, a precaution against terrorists hiding bombs; every evening at five o'clock an army of street cleaners entered the Old City.

David checked his watch.

At two forty-five, he stood atop a stairway above the plaza of the Western Wall. Beyond the wall he could see the golden Dome of the Rock and the severe black dome of the Al Aqsa Mosque, the touchstone for the group that had spawned Ibrahim Jefar. Entry to these places was forbidden to him. Yet the Dome of the Rock was the site on which Abraham had built an altar to sacrifice Isaac, or Ishmael, depending on whether one was Jewish or Muslim. It reminded David of the gulf between Hana and himself, of all the ways people differ over, and kill for, their own conceptions of God.

David looked about him and saw, pasted to the stone walls, a campaign poster for Isaac Benjamin and another, older poster of Amos Ben-Aron, with Hitler's mustache painted on his upper lip. He snapped a couple of random photographs. If someone was following him, he could not detect it.

Descending the steps to the Western Wall, he saw

an Orthodox Jew dispensing paper yarmulkes for the men who wished to pray there. He hesitated, then accepted a yarmulke and took his place among the bearded men at the wall, who were bobbing and bowing so that they might better be seen by God.

David closed his eyes, trying to clear his thoughts of all distraction. Then his mind formed as close to a prayer as he could summon — a remembrance of his father and mother, then of Hans Wolfensohn and his family. Finally, he thought of all who had died, or would yet die, for possession of this beautiful, tragic place.

When he finished, it was a little after three o'-clock.

Consulting the map again as though deciding where to go, David began tracing the path of Jesus on the Via Dolorosa, toward the Church of the Holy Sepulchre.

It was a long climb up well-worn stone steps, with the Stations of the Cross marked by metal plaques engraved with Roman numerals. David passed a wedding party of pretty young Arab women laughing as they hurried by, their dresses and shawls filigreed with gold. Turning as though to look at them, David recognized no one he had seen before.

At last emerging from the narrow alley, David stood in the plaza before the Church of the Holy Sepulchre. He no longer glanced at his watch; he had reached his destination and did not want to suggest that time had meaning for him.

Of Roman design, the church was the oldest in the world, built in the year 330 at the direction of the mother of an emperor who had declared herself a Christian. Inside, the sectarian rivalries pervading Jerusalem reached their apex. The dark and vast interior was divided among various sects, and today each was holding its own procession. David found their discordance at once beautiful, haunting, and disturbing: Franciscan monks in dark robes read aloud from Latin missals as they proceeded by candlelight up the stone stairway, while nearby a group of Armenian Christians, voices raised in competition, sang a hymn of their own. Above them, two chapels, one Catholic and one Greek Orthodox, depicted the crucifixion of their savior according to their own lights; as David descended to the floor beneath, candlelit and redolent of religious mystery, he saw a splinter group of Catholics reciting a Latin mass. Suddenly, he found his path blocked by a congregation of Greek Orthodox priests, kneeling for their separate observance.

Now David had to worry about his deadline. When he looked about him, searching for an alternate route, he saw no one familiar. As time passed with agonizing slowness, he watched until at last the chanting ended, then he resumed his journey with a carelessness he no longer felt.

Minutes later, in the bowels of the church, David entered the Assyrian Chapel. It was small, circular, and dark, occupied only by five Ethiopian women in white veils and cloaks; they made the sign of the cross, then prostrated themselves in the manner of Muslims. When David checked his watch, it was eleven minutes past four.

There was nothing to do but wait.

To his left, through a break in the stone wall, David saw a cave. Peering inside, he heard soft footsteps behind him. "Some believe," a quiet voice said, "that Christ was buried in this cave. That would be consistent with the custom of the times."

Turning, David saw a short man of indeterminate age and origin with a high forehead, slicked-back brown hair, and a smooth face that featured full lips and shrewd, crescent eyes. More quietly yet, the man said, "It seems no one followed you."

"Except you, perhaps," David answered. "And I have no clue who you are."

The man shrugged, as if this detail were trifling. "Let us sit together in Christ's cave," he said. "A couple of Jews can do no harm."

David wondered about this, or even if the man was Jewish. For an instant he had a random, skittish thought: were he to die inside the cave, he had no hope of resurrection. "After you," David said.

The cave was claustrophobic, too confining for David to stand. He knelt beside the stranger, two tourists contemplating the place of Christ's presumptive burial.

"So let me tell you a story," the man said in the casual tone of a tour guide. "Several years ago, two men joined our army — one from Tel Aviv, one an immigrant from America. Both were Orthodox, devotedly religious; both were disciplined and highly motivated. Both were taken into our elite military unit, the paratroopers; both became officers. And both came to think of themselves as brothers." The man's lips formed a smile, as if at the thought of their friendship. "They took leaves together, visited holy sites, formed a mutual interest in archaeology. But when their times of service expired, only one remained in the army. The second man left, having decided to establish a settlement to fulfill the biblical destiny of Jews to populate the land of Greater Israel. Though he was disappointed that his friend chose not to join him, the settler and the soldier remained close, bonded by their shared experiences and common beliefs."

David glanced behind him. The Assyrian Chapel was empty; his companion kept speaking, his tone conversational yet hushed. "The soldier knew an Orthodox woman in Tel Aviv who, he thought, might wish to become part of the new wave of pioneers. The woman traveled to the settlement and met his friend; to the pleasure of all three, the two of them fell in love and decided to marry.

"But then the woman fell victim to the terrible lottery of terrorism. Taking the bus to work one morning, she sat next to a suicide bomber from Hamas." The man shook his head. "Though the explosion killed many, she simply vanished. There was nothing left to bury."

David thought of the photograph of Eli and Myra's daughter, her bright smile and warm gaze. "Stricken by grief," his companion went on, "the settler was consumed by his hatred of Palestinians. The soldier, also grieving, applied for assignment to protect a man he revered as *Israel's* protector, Ariel Sharon." The man turned, gauging David's reaction. "You begin to see the point of my sad story, I think."

"Not until it ends."

"They said you were a cool one," the man responded. "I'll get to the point. Though the settler found a wife and had a daughter, nothing healed his heart. The soldier, after several years, became the protector of the man his settler friend believed to be worse than Arafat, the new prime minister, Amos Ben-Aron. And the settler, whose name is

Barak Lev, became the leader of the Masada movement, the alleged plotter of a bombing of Palestinian schoolchildren, and the father of a murdered six-year-old."

David stared at him. "Let me understand you. Are you suggesting that these two men were complicit in the assassination of Amos Ben-Aron?"

The man picked up a pebble near his feet. "What I'm saying is that Barak Lev would have strangled Ben-Aron with his bare hands, but he would never get that close. His friend the soldier could fulfill his wishes by much more artful means."

"After Ben-Aron's assassination, I assume the soldier was treated harshly."

"On the contrary. You would expect that every member of Ben-Aron's detail would be thoroughly vetted for contacts with anyone like Lev; were there doubts about any individual, he might be subjected to sleep deprivation, polygraphs, or sodium pentothal. But our man remains untouched."

"Don't you think their friendship's already known?"

"We *know* it's known. But this murder, it seems, is quite complicated. Perhaps our government's investigators are simply proceeding with the caution such a matter deserves. Certainly those in power have no interest in taking steps that might be uncovered by the media, and that might suggest, before it's wise to do so, where their inquiry is headed." The man's tone became ironic. "In such a case, political self-interest might be the incidental by-product of sound judgment and discretion. Whatever the reason, the truth — if what we suspect *is* true — may not emerge in time to do your client any good. But that is not my interest."

"What is?"

"The future of Israel. And who will decide that future."

David's knees had begun to ache. "Our interests may coincide," he said with measured impatience. "But so far your story brings me nothing. I need the name of Lev's army friend."

"We understand your legal process, Mr. Wolfe. We know your judge will require a name. Even better, would you like to meet our suspect?"

Astonished, David laughed. "You're joking."

"Not quite so cool now?" The man took a cell phone from his pocket "This is your new cell phone. Sorry if that makes you feel like an assassin, but you need to keep it with you. And be patient — it may be hours, it may be days. But you will get a call. Shabbat Shalom."

Without another word, the man left.

8

The next morning, cell phone at his side, David drove from Jerusalem to Masada.

The place was formidable, sheer cliff surrounded by desert. Taking the cable car to the walled plateau that held the ancient fortress, David could see miles of Judean wasteland, the blue expanse of the Dead Sea. The fortress itself, an ingenious redoubt of storerooms, living spaces, and bathing pools of which ruins still remained, had once served as King Herod's palace. It was here where Jewish rebels, besieged by Romans, had killed their families and themselves, leaving the victors with corpses instead of slaves.

Gazing out at the desert, David considered his own connections to this tragedy. The rebels were an extreme religious sect, the Zealots, who killed other Jews for not adopting their practices; their resistance had precipitated a Roman military campaign that deepened the subjugation of the Jews. In myth and film, David had seen the Jews of Masada portrayed as martyrs; no doubt this heroic symbolism had caused Barak Lev to attach the name Masada movement to his outposts in the West Bank. But what struck David now was that these "martyrs" had begun by killing their fellow Jews and, having drawn their conquerors deeper into the land of Israel, had ended in self-extermination. He could only hope this cycle would not recur.

David descended to the parking lot and headed for the Lower Galilee, from which, sixty years ago, Hana's parents had fled the Jewish army.

The e-mail from Hana's younger cousin, Sausan, had given him precise directions couched in engaging humor. "When the vegetables outnumber the people," she had written, "you'll know you're close."

Two hours later, so it was. The rolling land of the Galilee was ripe with corn, sunflowers, olives, citrus, tomatoes, garlic, chickpeas. This richness was the product of water and irrigation, employed by Jews to transform the land years before the State of Israel was born. Here and there David saw the remnants of Arab culture: a mosque, a distant hillside town where the residents, like Hana's parents, once had grown olive trees but, unlike them, had remained. Among their descendants was Sausan Arif, Muslim daughter to a Christian, granddaughter to a Jew.

The village of Mukeble, where Sausan was the principal of an elementary school, bordered the West Bank. Just before the turnoff was a checkpoint, its guard station protected by bulletproof glass, behind which the IDF was building a fortification with barracks and a watchtower. A wire fence at least twenty feet high separated Mukeble from a field of grass, beyond which David could see the outlines of Jenin, home of Ibrahim Jefar.

Near the entrance to the school, a slender young woman sat expectantly on a bench. At a distance, she looked enough like Hana that David felt his heart stop.

Up close, this illusion was dispelled. The woman

who greeted him had the same swiftness of movement and, David surmised, of thought; her olive skin and straight hair, though lightly tinted with henna, were reminiscent of Hana's. But her eyes, a striking green, formed a crescent when she smiled, giving her a look of slightly skeptical amusement that signaled that, were he lucky, she might include him in the joke. "You must be David," Sausan said, extending her hand. "If there were a new man in the village, I'd have heard it."

"Guilty." David surveyed the village perched on a hill behind the school, many of its houses modern, some constructed to the height suitable for extended Arab families. "You've chosen a pretty place to live."

"It's hardly Tel Aviv," Sausan answered. "But it's unique in this part of the world, as you will find. That is why I stay here."

"And the fence? There was trouble, I imagine."

"Some. In the beginning, the fence was a dilemma for our village — many here have relations in Jenin." Sausan frowned. "But before it was built, terrorists would come here, seeking shelter in our homes. We are a town of Christians, Jews, and Muslims, peaceful with one another, sharing the same schools and governing council. No one wanted problems. Though the fence offended some, once more we live in relative tranquillity. Just as, my father tells me, we did in 1948. That is part of our history."

The last phrase carried a tinge of sadness, and also satisfaction — the catastrophe that had changed so many lives, including Hana's, had somehow passed her family by. Sausan stood closer, looking up at him. "Do you think that Hana will die?"

The directness of her question pierced him. "I hope not."

Sausan inhaled. "I wish they'd stayed," she said at length. "Still my father asks, 'What is their life, trapped in a pile of rubble, treated like dogs by the Lebanese?' "

"They were frightened, Hana says, by the massacre at Deir Yassin."

"That was part of it, I know. The Israelis wanted the Arabs gone, frightening and harassing them and sometimes pushing them out. It is a myth that Arab leaders called on them to leave." Her voice became somber. "But it *is* true that those same leaders refused to accept the U.N. partition that separated Israel from the West Bank, choosing war instead. So there is blame to go around."

David watched her face; already her shifting moods, like Hana's, were not hard for him to follow. Abruptly, she said, "Would you like to see my school?"

Inside, the classrooms were well equipped, with new textbooks and varied displays on the walls. In the art room, David noted a poster showing a menorah, a Santa Claus, and the symbols of Ramadan. "How do your students get along?"

"That's not without its complications. Before the fence, Christian or Muslim Palestinians could sometimes settle in our village. But the children from Jenin were poorer than ours, and had absorbed the violence spawned by the occupation." Sausan stood straighter, her face set in a determined cast. "So we work with them. Without exception, the children who left Jenin much prefer to be here. Over time, their anger begins to subside. That, too, is part of why I stay."

■ ■ ■ ■

Sausan drove him through the village. "What is it like to live here?" he asked.

"For me?" Sausan flashed an ironic smile. "I am single, yet a multiplicity of people all in one. It complicates my life." She adjusted the visor, screening the sun of late afternoon. "My father, Hana's uncle, is Arab. I am Muslim — for better or, as I occasionally think, worse. But my mother is Jewish by birth — *her* mother came from Poland, and married an Arab Christian. So, unlike Hana, I am mired in ambiguity."

Sausan's life here, David reflected, could not be easy. As though following his thoughts, she said, "I am two months short of thirty, a genetic mutt with a master's degree. That last seems to qualify me as something of an intellectual — not a quality prized by all Muslim men." She flashed a grin. "I can't entirely blame them. By my own admission, I lack docility."

David smiled. "You seem peaceable enough."

"I suspect you're not so easily daunted. But in the context of Mukeble, I'm something of a troublemaker."

"How so?"

"When I came here, I organized a forum for Muslim and Jewish women to meet together, unsettling a few husbands. Worse, I organized a rally day for the women to race each other in jeeps, the 'Queen of Galilee Race.' " Sausan smiled again. "In fact, you're driving with the reigning queen.

"That much I could get by with. But then I tried to organize a forum for us to meet with Palestinian women from Jenin. Before the intifada, there was a tradition of cooperation. But now the Palestinian

Authority is collapsing, and the mayor of Jenin is too fearful of Hamas to stick his neck out at the behest of an Arab-Jewish woman." Once more, her tone betrayed regret. "The assassination of Ben-Aron, Hana's supposed crime, has killed this plan for good. We've lost the chance to know each other."

Passing sprawling houses and prosperous villages, they slowed at a bend in a winding dirt road that separated two cemeteries, one for Muslims, the other for Christians. "Recently," Sausan said, "an old Christian woman died. First, there was a service at the mosque, then one at our village's new church, when many Muslims witnessed a Christian service for the first time in their lives.

"Afterward, both Muslims and Christians helped clean and tidy up that old Christian cemetery, her final resting place. Why, I found myself wondering, do people still choose to hate each other? And why has hatred swallowed Hana?"

David turned to her. "Whose hatred, Sausan?"

Frowning, Sausan watched the road. "I've wondered that myself."

They stopped at the church, a sandstone structure with burnished wooden doors. It was Latin Catholic, Sausan explained, obedient to Rome, its services conducted in Arabic, its construction approved by the government of Israel and financed by Arab Christians in England and America. "Of three thousand people in Mukeble," Sausan said, "perhaps one hundred and fifty are Christians. But in a hundred years, only a few new churches have been built in the Middle East. This is one."

Inside, the church was spacious, featuring an altar filigreed with Arab characters and a confessional with two booths separated by a wooden screen. "If you care to confess," Sausan said wryly, "I'll gladly listen. There's so little entertainment here."

David smiled. "Too long," he said. "Too complicated. Anyhow, I'm Jewish."

She gave him a look. "It's not the Jewishness, I think. It's the complexity."

Outside, David checked his cell phone: no messages. Once again, he felt disoriented, the plaything of forces he did not fully comprehend.

Sausan was gazing out at the not-so-distant city of Jenin. "I don't know Hana well," she said after a time. "Still, I admired her. But even before this, to think of her made me sad."

David turned to her. "Why?"

Sausan nodded. "Two years ago, I visited her in Ramallah. She is smart and lovely, and adores her daughter. But not her husband, I think. Between them lies a struggle for Munira. And, perhaps, some deeper trouble."

"Of what kind?"

Sausan looked at him closely. "I think you are more than her lawyer, true?"

"True," David answered warily. "I knew her years ago at law school."

"All right. This next is personal, a woman's instinct. Whatever the cause, Saeb seemed angry at my presence. Perhaps it was my independence; perhaps the very idea of me, the granddaughter of a Jew, offended him. But he seemed little warmer to Munira, more judge than father. When he left for Jordan, four days into my visit, I felt all three of us become lighter — mother, daughter, and me. And I thought, She does not love this man, and he loves neither one of them. Hana is the prisoner of her daughter, and therefore of her husband."

Sorting through his emotions, David chose a lawyer's question. "Do you know why he went to Jordan?"

"To see a doctor. He has some sort of heart problem, though its nature wasn't clear to me. Nor did I understand why he stayed in Amman for a week." Eyes downcast, Sausan hesitated, then added quietly, "Were he not so strict a Muslim, I would have imagined him with a lover. Hana also. Most of us need more than what I saw there."

They spent the next moments in silence. Glancing at the slanting sun, David said, "Is there still time to see where Hana's parents lived?"

"I think so." Then, as if responding to impulse, Sausan continued, "Or we can look at it tomorrow, take more time. I know an inn nearby where we can stay." Suddenly abashed, she added with a smile, "In separate rooms, of course. I *am* Muslim, after all."

Her embarrassment jogged a memory. *We're a shame culture,* Hana had told him, *not a guilt culture.* "Of course," David answered with a smile of his own. "I *am* Jewish, after all."

9

The Upper Galilee, Sausan noted as they drove, was also lushly developed, a legacy of the kibbutzim. But the greenness ended at the border between Israel, Syria, and Lebanon, over which the Golan Heights loomed, its history a reminder of the warfare that ravaged this land, where no border seemed permanent. On the outskirts of a town nestled in a valley that ran from Israel to Lebanon, Sausan pointed out an Israeli outpost, a United Nations observation tower, and — just inside Lebanon — an artillery position once manned by Hezbollah, terrorist client of Iran and Syria, the latter of which held more power in this place than did the Lebanese. "Coming here," Sausan observed, "makes me think of Saeb Khalid, and why he became so bitter."

"It was Sabra and Shatila, I thought."

"In the end. But, as always here, there is a history. Before Saeb was born, some Palestinians in Jordan tried to assassinate King Hussein — another reason, years later, that Hussein was pleased enough when Israel took over the West Bank and its populace.

"But in this case, Hussein was more proactive. He grew weary of the PLO acting as a shadow government, agitating for his overthrow. So Hussein dumped the PLO into Lebanon, lock, stock, and barrel." Sausan turned to him. "Perhaps you know the rest. Arafat began using Lebanon as a base, helping precipitate a civil war between Lebanese Muslims — Syria's surrogates — and Maronite Christians, whose militia was the Phalange. The collapse of order allowed the Palestinians to launch terrorist operations against Israel, here in the Galilee. And so the army of Israel entered Lebanon to put down Arafat and the PLO.

"After that, the murderers of the Phalange became the ally of Israel. So what happened to Saeb and his family at Sabra, as awful as it was, is just another bloody example of history's cause and effect. This is our curse — too much history, too little geography. That's what created Saeb Khalid."

Sausan, David reflected as they drove, was a thoughtful woman; though keenly analytic, she had a somewhat poetic sensibility, as though the contradictions of her heritage, and of the place in which she chose to live, allowed her to see the horror and beauty in the lives of contesting peoples.

In the last village before they reached the inn, David inquired about the roofs of reinforced concrete he saw on several buildings. "Those were built before 1982," Sausan explained, "the year of Sabra and Shatila, when Israel went into Lebanon. Before, the PLO would shell the town; after, when Arafat left for Tunis, the shelling stopped. So the newer roofs are normal. Now, after what has happened with Hezbollah, perhaps the next roofs will be concrete again." Her voice became softer. "There are so many stories, David, so many ways to look at the same thing. At times I envy those with only one truth, like Saeb or Hana. But that's the problem in this place — people do not hear one another's stories. I cannot help but hear them all."

Tucked in his shirt pocket, David's cell phone still had not rung.

Nestled on a hillside, the Auberge Shulamit was an old stone hotel, appropriated as a fortress in 1948, then reborn as a charming inn. Though the location offered a sense of refuge, its commanding views of the Golan Heights and into Lebanon and Syria reminded David of what made this part of the world so treacherous.

"Have you ever thought of living elsewhere?" he asked Sausan.

They sat by a window in the restaurant, candlelit in twilight, and furnished with small wooden tables covered by white tablecloths. Sausan had ordered a glass of red wine; tasting it on her lips, she pondered her answer. "At times," she said. "A city would be exciting. And it is sometimes lonely." She laughed. "Perhaps that is why I kidnapped you."

David smiled. "I'm not sure that's a compliment."

"Oh," she said with rueful humor, "it is. It's just that flattering men jibes so poorly with my temperament. And I'm badly out of practice."

Feeling the first glow of wine, David realized how solitary he had been, and how much he was enjoying Sausan's company. Perhaps, he warned himself, she reminded him too much of Hana. "I don't mind," he answered. "I'll take honesty over flattery." He paused, then acknowledged, "This has been a difficult time for me. The stakes in this case are very high, and a lot of people don't like what I'm doing. Sometimes I feel alone."

Sausan studied him. " 'Sometimes'? Perhaps that is an understatement."

"Perhaps."

"And perhaps, also, you are afraid of losing someone you love."

Discomfited, David looked into her eyes. "Before I took this case, I was engaged. But I already lost Carole weeks ago."

Sausan shook her head. With unnerving directness, she said, "I meant Hana."

David tried a deprecatory smile. "Your cousin's an old friend who became a client. She's also married, however happily or unhappily — not to mention she's Munira's mother. If all that's not enough, she's fiercely Palestinian."

Sausan's smile was at once skeptical and knowing. "So many reasons, so quickly said. I only hope you're better at deception when you're in court. Or pity Hana." Her eyes became serious. "This afternoon, when I was speaking of Saeb and Hana, I watched your face. What I said about their marriage mattered very much to you. Not just as a lawyer, I suddenly knew, but as a man."

There was some relief, David realized, in giving up all pretense. "Am I really that transparent?"

"Perhaps only to me — seeing you, and having met Hana. I'm a woman, after all. For that I need no practice."

The waitress filled their glasses, affording Sausan time to study him. When they were alone, she said, "This must have happened in law school, without Saeb knowing. Or at least so you and Hana must have thought."

The statement disconcerted him still further. "I'm sure Saeb didn't know," David answered. "If he had, he more likely would have murdered her than married her."

Sausan looked down, eyes veiled. "And still you

love her?" she asked.

David turned to the window, gazing at the scattered lights of the Galilee. "Years ago, I taught myself not to think about that. Now I can't — as you suggest, it would be fatal in her lawyer. And how can you love a woman you're not sure you even know, and maybe never did?"

Sausan glanced up at him. Gently, she said, "Especially if you wonder what she may have done."

David's silence, he supposed, was as eloquent as speech.

"As I told you," Sausan said at length, "I don't know Hana well. But certain things I saw. Hana is a mother, Munira the person she loves most in all the world — more than her husband, even more than some imagined country. More, given her circumstances, than she could permit herself to love you." Sausan contemplated her wineglass. "I don't quite know what I'm saying to you. But if Hana were involved in killing Ben-Aron, it would have been for her daughter's sake, not for any cause. However little sense that seems to make."

David pondered this. "It doesn't, really."

Shrugging, Sausan let it go.

By unspoken consent, they left the subject of Hana; eating the flavorful entrées — hers lamb, his rabbit — they talked of their own lives. "From here," she said, "I really don't know what's next. At times I feel ready for an adventure, a dramatic change in a life that feels too settled; at others, I think I'm doing exactly what I'm supposed to, close to family and people that I love." She tilted her head. "What would you do, if you were me?"

"Change." David answered with a smile. "But then I'm American, as your cousin never tired of pointing out. And my advice may be suspect in any case: until now, I avoided change like some deadly disease. So maybe I'm too confused to answer."

"But once you are through defending Hana? What then?"

The question unsettled him; intent on saving Hana, he had suppressed any thought of what lay beyond. "I don't know," he conceded. "The most I can say is that I'm free to choose — the residue of a broken engagement and a political suicide." He smiled wryly. "It's like the old Janis Joplin lyric: 'Freedom's just another word for nothing left to lose.' "

Looking into David's eyes, Sausan returned his smile. "So surprise yourself, David. And then tell me how it feels."

He walked Sausan to her door, a few feet from his. "You didn't kidnap me," he told her. "You're the best company I've had in months."

Suddenly serious, Sausan gazed up into his face. "Thank you," she said. "But I know those months have been hard. I'm only Hana's cousin, who resembles her a little. Not quite so pretty, or so accomplished."

David tried to smile. "You're way too modest."

"Just too honest." Sausan paused, then added quietly, "I like your company, too, David. I hope that's flattery enough."

He watched her unlock the door and disappear inside.

Alone in his room, David lay awake, conscious of the woman on the other side of the wall, the woman awaiting trial in America, the cell phone that did not ring.

10

When David and Sausan met for breakfast, she was quieter than the night before, at times regarding him over the rim of her coffee cup with a quizzical look. Perhaps, David guessed, she was wondering, as he did, whether their rapport had been partly an illusion, an accident of time and place and uncertainty in both their lives. "I enjoyed last night," he finally said. "Quite a lot, actually."

Her green eyes searched his, and then betrayed the hint of a smile. "Yes," she answered. "So did I."

After this, the silence they shared on the drive to Hana's village felt less awkward than companionable.

A few miles short of the village, they stopped at a Jewish cemetery. Some of those buried here, David saw from the tombstones, were lost in the wars of 1948, or 1956, or 1967, or 1973, or, in 1982 and again in 2006 in Lebanon; here was the history of Israel's survival, punctuated by war and death. "Perhaps only in America," Sausan told him, "do people believe they can erase the past. Here we know it's not so simple."

Approaching the land where Hana's father and mother were born, Sausan tried to evoke their world. They, like their neighbors, were olive farmers. Every October, they picked the trees clean and carried the olives on donkeys to an olive press, where they visited with other farmers. After this, they seeded the ground with winter wheat. If the winter was good — if God willed that there be rain enough — the wheat would rise and help feed their family; if it was stunted, it would feed the sheep and goats, which provided milk, cheese, and, for celebrations, meat.

"Like that way of life," Sausan said, "these villages have vanished. The Israelis destroyed some of them; others collapsed on their own. But memory has proven less perishable."

When they reached their destination, David sat for a moment, gazing through the windshield at the landscape farmed by Hana's ancestors, the ruins of a dream.

Sausan led him among stone rubble and untended trees to the remnants of a house at the edge of what had once been a village. The walls were now at most three feet high; the ceilings had collapsed, leaving stones strewn in random piles, both inside and out. The steel beams that had once reinforced the ceiling, Sausan said, had been stolen long ago; the cement that had bound the stones had turned to dust.

"We're in the sitting room," she continued, "used only by Hana's grandfather and his guests. The women cooked on a wood-burning stove outside the house. The water came from a well used by the entire village — perhaps twenty families, two hundred and fifty people in all, many of them cousins or second cousins. Except to press the olives, they rarely left. For them, this was enough."

David looked out at the sweeping view of the

Galilee. The place had a timeless feel, bespeaking a way of life passed from one generation to the next. Amid the rubble, David spotted pieces of glazed clay, the shattered remains, Sausan explained, of a serving platter from which the family had eaten. "Hana says that her grandfather buried money in a metal chest," he told her, "to dig up when they came back."

"No matter. The currency would have been from the British Mandate, quite useless now. Like the ruins of this house."

David felt profoundly sad. He thought of Munira, who could no more return here than engage in time travel. And it was impossible to imagine Hana here, living as a simple village woman. In the perversity of history's cause and effect, the founders of Israel, as much as the murderers of Sabra and Shatila, had made Hana who she was — a feminist and lawyer, uprooted from her family's pastoral traditions, who dreamed of a liberated future for her daughter, the great-grandchild of the olive farmer whose key Hana still wore around her neck. It was the key to a myth; the key to her life. But it had long ago served its purpose, steeling her determination to leave the refugee camp where she was born. It was time, if David could manage to free her, for Hana to put the key aside, and to free Munira from the myth in which Saeb, out of bitterness, meant to suspend her like a fly in amber.

Perhaps he would say as much to Hana. But what he would say to her parents, when the time came, he did not know. "When I visited Hana," Sausan said now, "she did not ask about this place. And so I did not tell her."

David shook his head. "All this misery," he

murmured — to Hana, to Munira, to himself, and, finally, to Sausan, his companion in this moment.

"I know," she answered simply.

As Sausan drove them back to Mukeble, they were quiet. For once in his life, David had nowhere to go. The next hours or days were uncharted until a stranger called or Zev Ernheit, through some alchemy he would not explain, materialized another lead. David could as easily stay in the Galilee as drive back to Jerusalem.

Then, just as they reached Mukeble, the cell phone in his pocket buzzed.

Snapping from his reverie, David pushed the "Talk" button. "There's a room reserved for you at the Dan Hotel in Tel Aviv," the voice said. "There you'll learn how and where to meet the person you are seeking."

It was the voice of the man from the Assyrian Chapel. Before David could speak, his caller broke off the connection.

"What is it?" Sausan asked.

At once, David was filled with anticipation and uncertainty. "Something about Hana's case," he answered. "I have to leave, I'm afraid."

Parking, Sausan was quiet for a moment. "Your visit has been interesting," she said with a wry smile. "If fleeting."

"Too fleeting," he answered. "But thank you."

Sausan looked at him intently. "I wish you luck, David. And please tell Hana that I think of her."

She touched his hand, then left him, walking briskly toward the school. Watching, David had a flash of memory — Hana, in Cambridge, walking away from his car after their respite in New

Hampshire. Sausan, like Hana, did not look back.

Focusing on what he must do, David drove to Tel Aviv.

11

Tel Aviv was less than an hour's drive from the border at Mukeble, another measure of Israel's vulnerability. Yet it was more possible here than in Jerusalem to have the delusion of safety — one saw no fence or, for that matter, many Arabs, nor were there Arab villages in the surrounding hills. The city itself was more secular and cosmopolitan, with traffic jams, high-rises, chic shopping areas, and smartly dressed women along the street. It was here that, despite its insistence on Jerusalem as its capital, Israel maintained the headquarters of the IDF. And it was partly for the same reason — security — that the United States had situated its embassy in Tel Aviv.

Calling from his car, David asked for times when the American ambassador might consent to see him, a courtesy extended to provide at least the appearance of cooperation from a government that, by fiat of Judge Taylor, must press his cause with the Israelis. His assistant promised that she would get back to him — though David's call was expected, the ambassador's schedule was in flux. And so, David thought, was his own.

He reached the Dan Hotel in late afternoon. It was a modern high-rise near the water, as different from the King David as Tel Aviv was from

Jerusalem. Ordering a light dinner from room service, he gazed out at the Mediterranean in twilight, the cell phone at his side. When he answered the knock on the door, expecting dinner, he found a bellman carrying a basket of cheese, fruit, and crackers, bearing a handwritten envelope that read, "David Wolfe" — a welcoming gift, the man said, of the hotel. Tipping the bellman, David opened the envelope.

The message inside was typed. At ten A.M. the next day, David was to meet a taxi in the underground garage. The driver would drop him two blocks from the Café Keret; David should walk to the café and look for a man drinking coffee at the last table in the back. The man was a member of Ben-Aron's security detail; his name was Hillel Markis. Markis was expecting to meet someone from the Shin Bet, the message concluded, and it was up to David to learn what he could before his quarry grasped the subterfuge.

David finished reading the message, his senses fully alert. Markis, he knew, must be "the soldier," Barak Lev's friend from their days together in the army. And if Markis's name was linked in public to Barak Lev's, the legal equation in Hana's case — and the political equation within Israel — might be utterly transformed.

As instructed, David ripped the card up and flushed its pieces down his toilet. A moment later, the telephone rang. It was the embassy; the ambassador would see him for breakfast at eight o'clock, in the dining room of the hotel. The Galilee suddenly seemed light-years away.

David slept badly. He awakened with a feeling of caged restlessness; at two minutes before eight, he was drinking coffee in the restaurant, watching a tractor crawl up and down the beach.

"Mr. Wolfe?"

Standing, David saw a bald, compact man with a broad, pleasant face and shrewd blue eyes, behind whom a watchful security detail stationed itself at various points in the restaurant. Giving David a firm handshake, he said, "I'm Ray Stein — your man in Tel Aviv." He flashed a smile. "At least, sort of."

"All I can ask."

Stein sat across from him. "What's with the tractor?" David asked.

"That's a specially designed backhoe. Every morning it sifts the cans and cigarette butts. Sand's the perfect place to plant a bomb, and trash cans aren't allowed — by afternoon the beach is littered. This is their solution."

"A tough way to live."

"So's what you're doing," Stein answered bluntly. "The other day I met with an editor from the *New York Times.* All *they're* doing is trying to report what's going on here. But if they run a photograph of a grieving mother, it's considered a willful provocation by one side or the other. Objectivity is an offense: Jews say the *Times* is anti-Semitic; Palestinians want it to take Jewish reporters off the beat. And for each new murder, the *Times* is supposed to provide a history lesson, explaining why some faction thinks that particular act of violence is okay." Stein gave him a penetrating look. "Defending Hana Arif is infinitely worse. Either you're a complete idealist, or just insane. Like half the Middle East, I often think."

"I only got nuts recently," David answered. "Before this case, I was fine."

"So I hear. So how's your trip been? Exciting?"

Reluctant to discuss the events that had brought him to Tel Aviv, David described his visit to the village of Hana's family. "No one's ever going back," he told Stein. "That's the sad thing — not just the violence and the hatred, but the sheer futility of it all. The 'right of return' is about psychology, not reality."

"Ben-Aron understood that," Stein answered. "Too bad he's dead. Though I'm not sure how far he'd have gotten. When Palestinian leaders hint in private that they'll compromise the idea of return, I don't believe them for a minute. I won't until they start saying it in public. And you and I will likely be dead by then."

"Do you think there's any hope?"

Glancing up, Stein signaled to a waitress. "There has to be," he answered, "or what's the point? The extreme right in this country, the ones who hated Ben-Aron, see nothing but perpetual war or the threat of war. So why have a country at all? Why not go somewhere safer and hope to be a protected minority, like us Jews in America?

"I don't believe in some great pan-Arab plot against Israel — too many of these countries, like Egypt and Jordan, have better things to worry about. I do believe in specific threats, like Hamas or Al Qaeda or Iran. They're more than enough to deal with, but maybe it can be done." Stein's tone grew quiet. "This is a wonderful country in most ways, something to be proud of. I'd hate to see it dragged into the abyss."

The waitress arrived to take their orders. As she did, David contemplated how much to tell this man, and how far — in spite of Stein's directness — to trust him.

After the waitress left, Stein asked, "So how is it I can help you?"

By instinct, David chose candor. "Suppose I can develop hard information linking the assassination to Barak Lev. Would our government help me back the Israelis to the wall?"

The ambassador stared at him. "Where the hell did you come up with that? And how do you expect me to answer?"

"Like a man who'd rather have me pissing outside the tent than in."

"I guess it hasn't escaped you," Stein said at length, "that we'd rather shift responsibility for the assassination. What I assume you're implying, without quite saying it, is that Lev is linked to this security breach you've been talking about, which our own people think may well have happened."

"Yup."

Stein pursed his mouth. "Well, that would certainly shake things up around here, including the Israeli government. Be that as it may, any prospect of a solution between Israelis and Palestinians serves our interests in the region." Narrow-eyed, Stein contemplated his coffee cup, then looked up at David again. "Tell me, since you seem to be so knowledgeable about the mysteries in the case, who set up the network in the United States? I agree it wasn't Al Aqsa — they don't have the capacity. And I don't believe for a nanosecond that the Mossad, which does, was complicit in the plot against their own prime minister. Leaving us with whom?"

With this question, David knew he was standing on quicksand. "Who else," he parried, "can operate in the United States and Israel?"

"Iran." Stein exhaled audibly. "But people like

Lev and Iranian intelligence don't live in the same universe. The Iranians would have to use cutouts, people you couldn't trace to the Ministry of Security in Tehran."

"You mean like they did when they tried to ship armaments to Arafat on the *Karine A*? Why do I think that nothing I've said comes as a complete surprise?"

Stein laughed softly. "I'll give you this — you've done your homework. The problem is that you're shadowboxing an enemy, or enemies, you can't see. Suspicion's one thing; proof's another."

"What if I can give you something that falls midway between suspicion and proof?"

Stein sat back. "I'll pass on the information you're offering, Mr. Wolfe. Whoever you're dealing with has interests of their own. But I will say that our government has interests beyond convicting your client."

For the first time since coming to Israel, David felt a moment of hope. "I'm glad someone does," he answered.

A few minutes before ten, David took the elevator to the garage.

The cabdriver — a squat man with a closed-off look and a two-day stubble — was parked near the elevator. When David leaned through the open passenger window and said, "David Wolfe," the cabbie motioned him inside.

Exiting the garage, the driver checked his side mirrors. For twenty minutes they drove in silence, taking one turn after the other. The sensation was akin to being kidnapped. David asked no questions. He had no idea where he was.

After a last abrupt turn, the cab came to a stop in

a neighborhood of shops and restaurants. Pointing up the street, the man said in a thick Russian accent, "It is two blocks. Get out now — I am paid already."

The day was sunny but cool. Hands in his pockets, David stood on the street for a moment, gripped by the importance and yet the incongruity of the moment — he was a lawyer in a murder case, adrift in another country, behaving like a spy.

The thunderous boom of a large explosion broke off his thoughts. On the street ahead, brakes screeched and cars began honking, their drivers trying to escape; pedestrians scurried past him, away from the direction of the blast. Suddenly David knew exactly what had happened: the explosion had occurred at the Café Keret. He also knew that he should not be anywhere near it.

For another moment, he simply stood there, listening to the wailing sirens of the ambulances and police cars that were already on their way. Then he turned and walked in the opposite direction.

When he reached the hotel room, the first bulletins were coming from CNN. There had been another suicide bombing, the reporter said, at a sidewalk café in Tel Aviv.

12

Within thirty minutes, David had checked out of his hotel and called Zev Ernheit on his cell phone. Their conversation was terse: David asked to meet at once; Ernheit gave him directions to a place near the town of Qalqilya. As he drove, David checked his rearview mirror; he did not see anyone following him.

When he spotted Ernheit's car, David understood the reason for their meeting place — a large patch of asphalt off the highway surrounded by open fields, it provided no cover for close surveillance. The nearest structures were a thirty-foot concrete wall, from which extended miles of security fence, winding through open fields and over hills, designed to enclose within its boundaries red-roofed Israeli settlements. The wall and fence lent the stark landscape the air of a war zone.

Ernheit leaned back against the car. Still on edge, David asked, "What *is* this place?"

"We're at the de facto border between Israel and the West Bank," Ernheit answered. "Before the intifada, where we're standing was a thriving outdoor market. Palestinian farmers brought their produce here to sell to Israeli buyers — hotels in Tel Aviv would purchase fruit and vegetables by the crate-load. Then it became a place where suicide bombers got explosives from their handlers.

"Now we have a hundred-and-fifty mile security infrastructure: an electronic fence, a ditch, more fence. Where Israelis in their cars or homes are within range of a handgun, the barrier becomes a wall." Ernheit pointed to the barrier as it snaked along a distant hill. "It's designed to pick up Jewish settlements and exclude Palestinian villages. But Palestinians who once could go from one village to another in twenty minutes now may have to travel for five hours. So we started building underground tunnels to facilitate their movement and still allow us to check for bombs and weapons. But commerce between us is dead."

"This is Alice in Wonderland," David said. "Fences, walls, ditches, tunnels."

"It's real enough to the settlers." Ernheit turned to him. "The fence excludes outposts like Bar Kochba, where Barak Lev and the Masada movement are centered. That's another reason why Lev wanted God to strike down Ben-Aron. For them, this barrier dooms their future, and the future of Greater Israel."

David tried to imagine the desperation such men might feel. "A few hours ago," he told Ernheit, "there was a suicide bombing in Tel Aviv. What do you know about it?"

Ernheit showed no surprise. "Enough. Besides the bomber, there was only one death, that of an Israeli drinking coffee by himself. Very unusual — suicide bombers typically try to kill as many people as possible. It's also odd that no one's taken credit for it."

A remark from Moshe Howard came to David: that after the Second Intifada began, he sought out unpopular restaurants, believing that the absence of customers would cause a suicide bomber to move on. "No one will," David said. "It was an assassination. The victim was Hillel Markis, a member of Ben-Aron's security detail, and a close friend of Barak Lev's. I was supposed to meet him."

Ernheit stared at him. "Let's get away from the road," he said. "This is not the day to be standing around with you."

David drove behind Ernheit along the security fence, climbing a hill to a beautifully terraced community of spacious homes. At the top of the hill was a grassy playground where two girls played on swings; at its edge, wooden benches commanded a view stretching all the way to Tel Aviv. Leaving his car, David followed Ernheit to a bench. "From here," Ernheit told him, "the housing and land you see hold four million of the seven million citizens of Israel. Before 1967, this was the site of a Jordanian artillery battery. The settlement behind us, Alfe Menashe, was established to claim a strategic point as ours. After forty years, it's hardly the frontier outpost imagined by most Americans." Pointing to his left, Ernheit said, "That village on the other side of the fence, less than a mile down this hillside, is Arab. Lev and his settlers also live beyond this fence. It's the divide between life and death, they believe."

A muezzin's call to prayer issued from the Arab village, a thin cry in the hot, dry air. Ernheit turned to David. "Before or after the bombing, were you followed?"

"I don't think so."

"It was good you chose to leave at once. You don't want people asking how you happened to be there, and who might have sent you. Although it seems that someone knew."

"I'm no CIA agent, but whoever arranged the meeting was very cautious."

"Not cautious enough." Lines of concentration etched the corners of Ernheit's eyes. "Let's take your theory," he continued. "In San Francisco, the assassins' network disappeared, leaving the Americans with nothing but Hana Arif. In Israel, a member of Ben-Aron's security detail is killed in a 'suicide bombing,' which may leave *you* with nothing but guesswork about Lev. The Israeli link to your 'conspiracy' has been cut."

David allowed deferred emotions to seep through him — helplessness, horror, confusion, fear, and, above all, despair that Hana's fate might have been planned by someone whose presence he could only sense. "Who's doing this, Zev?"

"I'll tell you who's not," Ernheit said brusquely. "The Israeli government. No doubt they're keeping tabs on you. But Israelis believe in the rule of law. At least," Ernheit added with irony, "like the Americans, within the borders of our own country. If the Mossad wanted to do Markis in, they'd lure him to Monte Carlo.

"Our government may not be anxious to share their leads with you — for good reason, given that your interest may have precipitated Markis's death. But our people are at least as curious as you are about how Ben-Aron's security broke down. If they thought this man knew anything at all, they'd very much want him alive."

"And someone else wanted him dead."

"Then start with the bomber — an Arab, by all accounts, though if you're right no one will claim him. The problem with your conspiracy is that it still fails to cohere." Ernheit smiled grimly. "Remember that insane film Oliver Stone made about the Kennedy assassination? In Stone's fever dream, JFK was killed not by Lee Harvey Oswald but by Lyndon Johnson, the CIA, Fidel Castro, right-wing Texas oilmen, and gay cross-dressers from New Orleans. The connections made no sense, and you'd have had to rent a hotel ballroom just to get them all together."

"Oswald," David said, "*could* have acted alone. JFK was riding in a convertible and his route was public knowledge — all Oswald needed was a rifle and an open window. But Hassan and Jefar needed a lot of help in San Francisco to supply the uniforms, motorcycles, and explosives. Even that wasn't enough: they also had to know that Ben-Aron's route had changed.

"The list of groups who could set up that kind of network in the U.S. is very small. So's the list of people who could leak a change in route. I need to understand how they got together, and what their motives were. Somewhere there's an answer."

Ernheit leaned forward, chin propped on his hands as he surveyed the landscape. "But in Israel? Someone just blew up your witness, and you're running out of time. Sooner or later our government will place you near the Café Keret. They'll be very curious. And your invisible helpers will become even more cautious."

"Then I have to hurry, don't I?"

"To do what?"

"Meet Barak Lev."

Ernheit laughed aloud. "Perhaps for lunch? If I follow your rather convoluted logic, someone just killed his coconspirator, making him extremely wary. Or maybe it was Lev who had Markis killed?"

"Not lunch," David persisted. "Just a meeting. I expect you're not without ideas about how to arrange one."

Ernheit shook his head. "Do I really want to be mixed up in this, I wonder? Do you? And what is it you expect from such a meeting? A confession?"

"A conversation. Enough to take to the judge." David's tone became urgent. "I can't wait for your government. Are you really so sure, after today, that whoever is ruthless enough to kill Hillel Markis would have let Hana live if she was guilty?"

After a moment, Ernheit turned to him. Softly, he said, "You're right, of course. I'm not without ideas."

13

Back in Jerusalem, restless but exhausted, David did not leave his room at the King David.

He sat up late into the night, the meaning of what little he knew shrouded in obscurity, certain only that the complexities of defending Hana exceeded his resources. No one called. Fearful of surveillance, he did not seek to contact those few people he could identify — Moshe Howard, Avi Masur, Anat Ben-Aron — who might have set him on the path to the Café Keret.

He had taken that path, and a man had died. The guilt David felt — whatever Hillel Markis might have done — was deepened by the fear that someone, tracing his movements, had ordered this murder to prevent discovery of a complex design that had claimed Amos Ben-Aron. In trying to help Hana, he might have sealed her fate.

His only company was television. The authorities were notably reticent: in public, no one connected Markis's murder to that of Ben-Aron. How long, David wondered, would it take for the government to appear at his door, inquiring about his trip to Tel Aviv?

With Markis dead, David's only lead was Barak Lev; his only hope was to persuade Judge Taylor that Lev was part of a conspiracy David could not define. Lev was a recluse, hostile to outsiders. Except perhaps through Ernheit, David had no way to reach him. After Markis's murder, he was not sure that he should try.

Shortly after nine o'clock the next morning, Ernheit appeared at his door. He, too, seemed uneasy. "I keep thinking about Markis," Ernheit said. "I've looked at his murder six different ways. The only way it makes sense is if you're right. But I'd like to know just what it is you're right about."

Like Bar Kochba, Ernheit explained as they drove, the settlement they were visiting lay outside the security barrier, arousing a deep fear of abandonment among those who lived there. But, like Alfe Menashe, it did not conform to the image of a pioneer outpost, peopled by a few Orthodox Jews and fanatics living on the edge; what David saw instead was a lush hillside town of terraced streets, with brightly hued gardens blooming amid palm and jacaranda trees. The sidewalks were brick, the streets well marked, and the school modern, its playground filled with children. The spacious homes, ranch or Mediterranean in style, had the red-tiled roofs distinctive to modern Israel. It was called Sha'are Tikva, the Gates of Hope.

The man they had come to see, Akiva Ellon, was an intellectual beacon of the settler movement. The editor of a magazine that was the voice of the Israeli right, uncompromising in its purity and rigor, he was also known for his connection, if not his unquestioning allegiance, to members of the Masada movement. But far from being unwelcoming or austere, the white-haired man who led them to his garden had a courtly manner, youthful blue eyes, and a faintly humorous expression. No doubt Ernheit's introduction of David played a role; in his ambiguous description, David was a well-connected American lawyer interested in the settlers' point of view. His defense of Hana Arif went unremarked.

An attentive host, Ellon served coffee in china cups, insisting that Ernheit and David sample his fresh pastries. Troubled by his deception, David reminded himself of his obligations to Hana. "You've made this a beautiful place," he said. "How did you come to live here?"

"Me, personally?" Ellon gave a small, ironic smile. "As with so many of our stories, it began with the Nazis. When I was a fourteen-month-old baby, in the Ukraine, they came to our village with an invitation for all Jews. We were to assemble in the square at daybreak, to be given a loaf of bread, a ration of sugar, and transportation to a 'friendly camp.' My father was already serving in the Russian army; when my mother discovered I had a fever, she refused to expose me to the cold. All the other Jews from our village, of course, were shot.

"What followed is a paradigm of Jewish denial. My mother fled with me, spreading the word to other villages. They refused to believe her — when the Germans came, the Jews followed orders, showing up for transit to that 'friendly camp.' How those Nazis must have laughed."

The story, David understood at once, was defining for Akiva Ellon. "How did the two of you survive?" he asked.

"My mother spoke flawless German; I was a blond, blue-eyed baby, a virtual copy of the picture of the German child published by Rosenberg, Hitler's arbiter of Aryan perfection. So we settled in another village, where no one knew us, masquerading as gentiles. Fortunately, no one but her ever saw me nude." Ellon's voice grew soft. "After the war, my mother told me, 'Every day, I thought you would be my executioner.' But she clung to me, her only child, waiting for my father to return. He never did. And so she brought me here to Israel, our refuge."

David heard a quiet bitterness in Ellon's last words. "And after that?"

"From the first, I gave myself to our new country, body and soul — worked on a kibbutz, fought in the wars of '67 and '73, then moved here to help secure the future of our nation and our people. And now the State of Israel has no use for us."

Ernheit glanced at David. "Tell David how Sha'are Tikva came to be," he suggested.

Ellon spread his hands, a graceful gesture of sadness and self-deprecation. "It is such a typical story, really. Many of us are kibbutniks — for us, settling in this place, the biblical Samaria, was a normal part of repopulating the land of Israel. Nor did we steal this hilltop. A quarter century ago, we simply bought it from an Arab and came here to live in trailers, eight families with no roads or schools or electricity. Now we are eight hundred families, five thousand of us in all, who have no other home. In fact," he added softly, "my mother is buried here."

David paused, taking in the shaded garden, Ellon's freshly painted villa. "The government, Zev tells me, claims Sha'are Tikva would be difficult to defend."

"Defend?" A trace of anger crept into Ellon's tone. "The defense of Israel was why the government encouraged us to come here — we were heroes, the new pioneers, embraced by politicians of every stripe. *We* did not change. Men like Amos Ben-Aron did, bandying about Orwellian phrases like 'the Palestinian people,' as if such a people ever existed." Ellon shook his head in wonder. "And what of *our* people? We are parents who love our children and our neighbors, wanting nothing but to live on the only land God ever gave us, made home to us by our own labors. Yet we may be sacrificed to the Arabs' need for ethnic cleansing. Perhaps Hamas or Al Aqsa will remove us to a 'friendly camp.' "

A thought struck David. Though they had driven past Arab villages, he had seen no Arabs; the bypass road they had taken was for Israelis, rendering the Arabs invisible. "So what would you do," David asked, "with the Arab population of the West Bank? You are a quarter million; they are maybe twelve times that."

Ellon shrugged. "Give them back to Jordan, I suppose — ethnically, that is what they are, Jordanian. It is not simple, I know. But history never gave the Jews a choice between good and bad, only bad and worse. Worst of all would be giving up this land." Punctilious in his role as host, Ellon stood up and refilled David's coffee cup. "Ben-Aron was a tragedy. He began as a soldier and ended as a coward — the pathetic caricature of history's subservient Jew, made the most dangerous man in Israel by the witchcraft of his rhetoric.

"Why this transformation? Like so many others, his mind crumbled under the weight of Jewish history." Sitting again, he looked at David intently. "No other people have been the target of extermination throughout history; no other country wonders how long it can continue to exist. So how do Israelis react to an unbearable reality that, except for the strongest of minds, is psychologically crushing? By inventing 'peace' where there is no hope of peace. By denying that those who dispatch suicide bombers to murder us would kill us all if we let them. And by turning their backs on us, their brothers and sisters. We settlers were to be Ben-Aron's initial sacrifice on the altar of denial."

For this man, David thought, the certainty that his fellow Jews were gripped by a mass delusion must be close to unbearable. "How do you live with this?" he asked.

Ellon gave a wistful smile. "By writing poetry, and translating Shakespeare's sonnets and plays. Anything but *The Merchant of Venice*."

Above Ellon's roses, a small bird hovered in delicate suspension. "But now Ben-Aron is gone," David ventured.

Ellon regarded him closely. "A reprieve," he said at last. "But others like him will arise. Within Israel, the Jewish disease flowers anew — politicians who believe that the Arabs who hate us will be seduced by kindness, intellectuals for whom the suffering people are Palestinians, not Jews. Two years ago, the six-year-old daughter of one of our leaders, Barak Lev, was shot by an Arab sniper. No politician spoke of her, no poet commemorated her in verse. She had become that unremarkable thing, a murdered Jew. Now I look at this barrier and wonder how many more of us will join her among the anonymous dead."

"If that is what your children face, why stay here?"

"Where, in all the history of the world, do we go? Where will this not happen to us?" Ellon's tone hardened. "This is our land. That is why some will take up arms rather than abandon it. If I were younger, I would join them, and fight our enemy to the end. Whether Arab or, God help us, Jew."

David felt a chill — in an hour, in the lovely garden of this civilized, tormented man, he had come far closer to grasping why Ben-Aron might have died. "Perhaps David should meet Barak Lev," Ernheit suggested, "and see Bar Kochba."

Ellon considered this, his eyes shaded. Then he looked at David with a level gaze that, despite his feeling of betrayal, David returned.

"Excuse me," Ellon said courteously. "I will make a call."

14

Driving toward Bar Kochba, the outpost of Barak Lev, David and Ernheit moved deeper into the Occupied Territories. David saw the rubble of an Arab home destroyed by shelling, with a black scar on the wall where the rooms above it had collapsed. The vistas were rugged, sun-baked. Above the terraced hillsides were Arab villages; on the road, controlled by Israelis, David still saw no Arabs.

As the road took them gradually higher, the landscape became even more stark. Turning a corner, they encountered the rudiments of Jewish civilization: trailers, goats, a wine press, a modest synagogue. To David, the settlement of Bat Ein looked like a trailer court in the Mojave Desert, except that it was perched atop a jagged landscape with a harsh and contested history. Following the directions provided by Ellon, they passed a ramshackle school and stopped beside a vineyard with a stirring vista of the Judean hills. In the distance, David could see the wooded Green Line, a measure of how far they had traveled beyond what had once been the border of Israel.

Amid the vines a burly, red-bearded man in overalls leaned against a tractor. As they approached on foot, David saw that he wore a yarmulke, and that a prayer shawl was tucked under his overalls. His gray eyes were keen, his face weathered, and his high forehead had the sheen of sun and sweat. Smiling, he extended his hand to David. "I'm Noam Bartok. You're the American who's looking for Barak."

"That's right."

"I'm his spokesman, as the need arises. I'm also an American — or was." Turning, Bartok gestured at the landscape. "*This* is my home now, a long way from Newark. For all twelve of my kids, there is no other place."

"It's certainly not Newark," David said. "Or like anywhere I've been before."

Bartok smiled again. "Let's sit. You've come a long way, too."

He led David and Ernheit to a bare pine log. Together they sat gazing at the vineyard as Bartok passed a thermos of tepid water. "Most evenings," Bartok said, "just before I go home, I sit and look out at these hills. When Leah and I decided to help redeem the land that is truly Israel, we came to the place that is ours. Not as defined by any government, but by God."

He spoke with the clarity and conviction of a man who had found truth. "I saw the barrier," David said after a time. "It's many miles from here."

"And the Green Line even farther." Bartok gazed down at the red earth. "Men like Ben-Aron mutilate our land with lines of their own devising — drawing 'borders,' telling us what places to live are 'legal' and what are not. As if that's for men to say.

"God gave this land to our people — our children, our grandchildren, and *their* children — for the rest of time. Land is not an office, or a desk." Leaning forward, Bartok lowered his shoulders, as if bearing history's weight. "The only way for Israel to save itself is to return to God. Those who sacrifice His land for 'peace' will only cover it in blood."

Ernheit was watching the settler's face. Almost gently, he said, "I'm Israeli. And still I wonder what happens if the army comes to evict you."

"Then I send away my wife and children." Briefly, Bartok closed his eyes. "If God requires it, I will die here."

David and Ernheit shared his silence. Without looking at David, Bartok slowly exhaled. "I can direct you to Barak," he said at last. "But I don't know that he'll speak to you. He has just lost a friend, he told me — almost a brother. This is a day for him to pray."

The trip to Bar Kochba was like a journey to the end of the earth.

The roads became dirt, the terrain rocky, the barrenness of land without water reflected in the stunted, scrubby oaks. Here and there an irrigated swatch of ground yielded grapes or peaches or cherries. But the hills on which Bar Kochba sat, ringed by Arab villages, were, from a distance, desolate, the only sign of humanity a desultory string of trailers.

At the crest of the first hill, David and Ernheit found a scene surprising in its ordinariness: on a patch of grass overlooking the desert, four young mothers sat watching their children play on a plastic swing and slide. But for the setting, and the fact that the women's heads were covered in scarves, it could have been anywhere in the world. "Let's check our directions," Ernheit suggested.

Parking, they approached the group. A round-faced young woman in glasses glanced up at them with mild curiosity. Ernheit squatted beside her, looking out at the desert. "A remarkable place," he said.

The woman shrugged. "It is our home."

The other women's faces betrayed no understanding; David guessed that they spoke only Hebrew. Nodding toward the children, Ernheit asked, "Which ones are yours?"

For a moment, the woman looked down. "We have only the one," she said softly. "The dark-haired boy with glasses. But I imagine you are looking for someone else."

"Barak Lev."

A shadow crossed her face. "I am his wife," she said at length.

David considered her anew, the mother of a child murdered in this place, the sweet-faced wife of a fanatic who, quite possibly, had facilitated the murder of Amos Ben-Aron. She asked no questions; perhaps she had learned not to. "Just follow this road," she said. "At the end, you will see a man. He will tell you where to go."

The road traced the ledge of a jagged cliff, which plummeted to form one wall of a deep canyon, its wind-seared expanse a multicolored brown. On the other side, a string of trailers squatted on the scarred, rocky earth; far across the canyon, more trailers stood like sentinels. "Grim," Ernheit said. "But this is how Sha'are Tikva began."

Gazing at the cliffsides hewn by the wind, David spotted dark holes in the orange-brown rock. "Are those caves?" he asked.

"Yes. Centuries ago, Benedictine monks dwelt there. This is a good place for ascetics."

David felt his apprehension grow. "Think Lev will talk to us?"

"Maybe. From what I've seen on television, he has his prophetic moods."

At the end of the road a man with an assault rifle stood beside a jeep. Pulling up, Ernheit rolled down his window. "We're looking for Barak Lev."

The man peered inside the car. "Get out," he commanded.

Facing the canyon, David and Ernheit stood beside the car as the man circled behind them. Ahead, a thin trail led through scrubby brush to the edge of the cliff. "Take that path," the man directed. "I'll be at your back. But first give me your handgun."

Expressionless, Ernheit handed over his gun and began walking, David behind him. For all he knew they were walking off the cliff.

Two feet from its edge, Ernheit stopped.

Standing beside him, David saw a wooden platform jutting from the cliffside. At the end of the path, steps had been hacked downward into the side of the canyon. Gingerly, Ernheit took them, then David, conscious that a misstep, or a push from behind, would send them to oblivion. To one side of the last step, David saw, a plateau in the face of the cliff was sheltered by the platform. In its shadow were books, provisions, a bed, an oil lantern, and several boxes of ammunition. To David, it felt less like a refuge than a place to die.

Barak Lev stepped from the shadows, holding a semiautomatic rifle. He was tall and bearded, the austere contours of his face as harsh as the terrain. Though he could not be over forty, he had the fierce aspect of a patriarch, and his gaze was unnaturally bright.

"I know you," he told David. "You have come about Hana Arif."

David waited, saying nothing. Glancing at Ernheit, Lev pointed the rifle at the low stone wall to one side of his redoubt. "Sit," he ordered. "Over there, where I can watch you both."

David sat beside Ernheit. At close range, Lev's eyes seemed to betray a soul more troubled than inflamed. "What is it you want from me?" he asked David.

"To find out who killed your friend."

Lev's eyes flickered. He sat at the end of his platform bed, a few feet from David, gun tacked beneath his right arm with its barrel pointed at Ernheit. "And you think that I know this?"

"Not the name of the bomber, but who sent him. And why." David stared hard into his eyes. "If they came for Hillel Markis, they may also come for you."

Lev did not seem to blink. "*You* came for Hillel," he said in a chill accusation. "Death followed. And now you're here."

"Death followed Amos Ben-Aron," David countered. "Whoever planned his murder killed Markis. I guess they didn't tell you that would happen."

Beside him, David felt Ernheit tautly watching him, then Lev. Softly, Lev answered, "You would have me die in an Israeli prison."

David felt a tense anticipation — at last, were he skillful, he might discover at least one aspect of the truth. "You don't control these people," David said. "You never did. Now you understand the cost, and that they won't hesitate to kill you. Better to die in prison having named the people who killed your friend."

Lev's smile was grim. "And killed Ben-Aron, you

think. That is your interest here — extricating your Arab woman from this conspiracy you think I'm part of."

"That's *my* interest. Yours is in avenging Hillel Markis."

Lev's bark of laughter made David flinch. "My interest is in Greater Israel. This admission you would have me make could well destroy its future.

"Every November in the rump state called Israel, Jews mourn the death of Yitzhak Rabin. *I* celebrate it, and honor the man who killed him. But there are still too few of us, and far too many of the others. Let Ben-Aron's death be the work of two Palestinian students and your whore of a law professor." Lev's smile betrayed a trace of self-contempt. "For all I know she is as guilty, or as innocent, as I. The pawn who thought himself a king."

David felt the truth like a tangible thing lurking in the shadows, just out of sight and reach. "Whose pawn?"

"Even if I knew, I would not tell you. Not even for Hillel." His tone grew quiet. "I have lost a woman, and a child, and now a friend. I can only hope we are all the pawns of God.

"Our destiny is bigger than any one of us, or even all. God demands the destruction of this rotten secular Jewish state, through whatever means there is — enemy or friend. Then the Israel of the Bible can arise, a place free of Arabs and cleansed of this so-called democracy." His eyes became bright again, lit by the reanimation of his vision. "Compared to this, Hillel is nothing, I am nothing, Arif less than nothing. You have wasted your time in coming here."

But David believed that he had not: his dialogue

with Lev, witnessed by Ernheit, might well be sufficient basis to demand more information from the Israelis or even, perhaps, to compel them to produce Lev for a deposition. From there, the outline of a conspiracy involving both Palestinians and Jews, however complex and obscure, might raise more definitive doubts about Hana's guilt. Standing, David told Lev, "Just stay alive. For now, that's all I want from you."

Ernheit stood with him, as did Lev, gazing hard at David. "Tell me this," Lev said. "What is it that makes a Jew trouble himself for the life of an Arab slut?"

"There are Jews," David answered, "and there are Jews. Not all Jews have a psychotic God who tells us who to murder."

The skin around Lev's eyes tightened. With a derisive smile, he pointed to the steps with his rifle. "Go," he ordered, his smile vanishing. "Before God speaks to me again."

Glancing at Ernheit, David turned, feeling pinpricks on the back of his neck. As the two men headed toward the steps, there was a swift, percussive pop, then a sickening spattering sound. David flinched, instinctively ducking, then looked sideways back at Lev.

The top of his head had vanished. Blood and brains and hair were splattered against the rock; eyes rolling backward, Lev toppled to the ground. Ernheit grabbed David's elbow and pulled him down.

"Don't move," Ernheit hissed.

His face inches from Lev's sightless eyes, David quickly turned his head. Catlike, Ernheit crawled forward to the mouth of the redoubt. David felt his shock and fear as a clammy nausea that chilled his skin and gripped his throat and the pit of his stomach. All he could see was the far wall of the canyon, pocked with caves.

David inhaled, then exhaled, face pressed against the ground. He and Ernheit lay like that for endless minutes, Lev crumpled dead beside them.

Finally Ernheit took the cell phone from his pocket and started dialing.

The Shin Bet arrived in helicopters — crime scene investigators, armed officers, and two lead agents, who took Ernheit and David to an empty trailer.

The agents were cool, expressionless, thorough. The sniper was a professional, Ernheit told them with assurance, who had shot from a great distance. His only target was Lev; David and Ernheit knew too little for inclusion in his assignment.

The agents questioned David separately. He told them what he could — that Markis and Lev were friends; that he suspected them of complicity in the murder of Ben-Aron; that he did not know the man who had met him in the Assyrian Chapel. His description of the stranger was sketchy. He did not mention Ari Masur or Anat Ben-Aron.

Toward the end, to David's surprise, Avi Hertz — Israel's liaison to the prosecutor — entered the trailer. Wearily, David said, "I thought you were in America."

"Where you should be," Hertz answered with lethal quiet. "You've accomplished a great deal in the last two days. A death in Bar Kochba and, I suspect, in Tel Aviv.

"You played a dangerous game with us. Now whatever these men knew has died with them. Did you think we were so quiet, and so cautious, just to frustrate your defense? Or can you possibly imagine we had some larger aim in mind?"

"You kept me on the outside," David retorted. "I have a client to save from execution. You might have tried to reconcile our interests."

"Go home," Hertz said softly. "You have done your work in Israel."

15

The next morning, after ascending from a dark pit of sleep, David went to the Western Wall.

This was an act of will — he could not escape the image of a dead man with a shattered skull, or the instinctive fear that the next dead man could be him. So it was necessary, he concluded, not to cower in his room, haunted and disoriented and alone. Near the wall, David saw a cluster of angry demonstrators — Lev's followers, a man explained to him, protesting the inability of the government to protect Jews in the biblical homeland. Nonetheless, the wall seemed as good a place as any for meditation.

Wearing a paper yarmulke, David bowed his head. Three months ago, before Hana's call, he had been living a life of his own design. The only deaths he had known had been natural or accidental; the only mischance, his affair with Hana; the only barriers to his success — the conflicting ambitions of others — a contingency he could plan for and surmount. Then he had thrown it all away, along with Carole and Harold, because of a mixture of principle and passion he still could not untangle. Even then he had been naive; too certain of his ability and nerve, he had misconceived the danger and complexity of the strategy he had designed. Now two men had died, one right before his eyes. It was hard not to see himself as the man who might have fatally impeded, to Hana's detriment, the discovery of how, and by whom, Ben-Aron had been murdered.

And for what? Still he was not sure of Hana's innocence; the ambiguities of her relationship to Saeb, intertwined with the evidence against her, were difficult to unravel. David's only beliefs were contradictory and, for now, beyond proof: that Al Aqsa could not, by itself, have engineered an assassination in America; that Iyad Hassan might have been connected to Hamas; that Barak Lev and Hillel Markis had facilitated the murder of their own prime minister; that the authors of an undefined conspiracy had killed them both; that someone other than the Shin Bet had followed David.

Because of *that* there was nothing more for him to do here. He had not heard from those who, for their own reasons, had tried to help him; the murders of Lev and Markis had no doubt driven them deeper underground, unwilling to deal with a man who had become an albatross. Glancing at the men praying all around him, David wondered who among them might be his shadow.

He had run out of choices now. Whatever his self-disgust at being overconfident and overmatched, he could not quit the case, or forget what he now knew: that the key to Hana's guilt — or, he hoped, her innocence — lay in a conspiracy the dimensions of which he had yet to grasp. To retreat behind the shield of "reasonable doubt" would not be enough to save her. He would go, as planned, to the West Bank.

Turning, David followed the cobblestoned

streets to the edge of the Old City. He made no efforts at evasion, not even to look behind him.

That evening as he packed, David watched CNN. On the screen, he saw the men of the Masada movement bearing Barak Lev on a litter, his ruined head exposed. His wife wept openly; his son, barely five, walked stoically at her side. They buried Lev where he had died.

As the film ended, CNN followed up with a second report: only hours after Lev's funeral, in a village beneath Bar Kochba, someone had shot and killed a teenage Arab girl. Her fatal wound was nearly identical to Lev's.

The next morning David checked out of the hotel. Politely, the young woman at the desk asked, "Where do you plan to visit next?"

"Ramallah."

She blinked, seemingly perplexed. "How far is that?" she asked.

"Ten miles."

His answer seemed to surprise her. As though recounting a rumor, she said, "I hear it is dangerous there."

David was struck by a dual level of irony — not only had he precipitated two murders in Israel, but Ramallah was visible from numerous vantage points in Jerusalem. And yet, for all this young woman knew, he could have been traveling to Zimbabwe: her sole impression was that the place, and its people, were to be avoided.

"I'll be careful," David promised.

16

David met his investigator in front of the hotel. Nabil Ashawi was a former member of the Palestinian security forces; Ashawi's virtues, according to Bryce Martel, included discretion, an eye for trouble, and sometimes shadowy connections that he could use to help David probe the lives of Hassan and Jefar, and even Saeb Khalid. David found him to be quiet and self-contained, a slight man with thinning hair, a soft voice, and perceptive, somewhat melancholy brown eyes. His other attribute, rare for a Palestinian, was that he had a pass to enter Jerusalem.

Settling into Ashawi's van, David told him what the young Israeli hotel clerk had said. Ashawi gave a mirthless laugh. "Thanks to the checkpoints," he responded, "Ramallah might as well be in Zimbabwe. You will see."

Within twenty minutes, David felt the impact of the checkpoint at Qalandiya.

They waited in a single lane of traffic, with a thirty-foot-high security wall on one side and, on the other, a line of Palestinians trudging behind a wire screen toward a checkpoint too distant for David to see. The delay afforded Ashawi time to explain the differences between travel on the West Bank for Israelis and Palestinians. One Israeli bypass road was entirely off-limits to Arabs; the others were protected by more than six hundred roadblocks, which insulated them from Arab cities, leaving the roads used by Israelis unimpeded by obstacles and largely free of Palestinians. It was this, David realized, that had rendered the Arabs invisible even when Ernheit had driven near their villages.

David checked his watch. "How long will it take us to get to Ramallah?"

"It *should* take, at most, a half hour. Today? An hour, two hours. One never really knows." Elbow propped against the window, Ashawi gazed listlessly at the road. "What so many fail to understand is that the checkpoints do not separate Israel and the West Bank, but one part of the West Bank from another. Their purpose, the Israelis say, is to interdict terrorists and weapons. But these checkpoints do not discriminate — because we are all Palestinians, we are all suspects. And so all of us wait."

"How frequent are the checkpoints?"

"Frequent, and unpredictable. There are permanent checkpoints, like this one, and temporary barriers — so-called flying checkpoints — set up to create the element of surprise for terrorists. For the rest of us, we often find it impossible to get home for dinner, or to visit a sick parent." As Ashawi spoke, the line of traffic, at a standstill for minutes, began slowly creeping forward. "The Israelis divide us into zones. The cities are Zone A, in theory controlled by the Palestinian Authority — although at any time the IDF can come in to pursue terrorists, as they did in Jenin. Zone B, the areas immediately around the cities, is jointly administered by the IDF and the Palestinians. And

Zone C, the countryside surrounding A and B, is controlled exclusively by the IDF. So our cities are separate enclaves; for Hana Arif to get from Ramallah to Birzeit University, she must pass through whatever checkpoints the Israeli army wishes to impose." Ashawi gave a fatalistic shrug. "Some days she will make all her classes, some days not. And she will never know which days. Same thing for students such as your assassins, Jefar and Hassan."

"What would you have the Israelis do?" David asked. "From what I've learned, it strikes me as a chicken-egg problem: are there suicide bombings because the occupation continues, or does the occupation continue because there are suicide bombings?"

"There will be suicide bombings," Ashawi answered, "as long as there is hatred and despair. And there will be hatred and despair as long as there is occupation."

"Only until then?" David asked. "For someone like Saeb Khalid, there will be hatred and despair until the Palestinians return to Israel, and Israel does not exist."

His face closing, Ashawi shrugged again. Behind the wire, David saw a Palestinian woman in a scarf walking with her head down, as though on a treadmill to eternity, her slow, unchanging steps bespeaking a deep weariness in the bone and brain, days endlessly the same. At length, Ashawi said, "You wanted me to find out whether Jefar is Al Aqsa or Hamas. I don't know yet. But I did learn something about him that is pertinent to your rumination about chickens and eggs.

"Ibrahim Jefar's oldest sister and her husband

live in a village outside Jericho, closed off by a checkpoint and surrounded by a barricade. A year ago, eight months pregnant with her first child, Jefar's sister began to hemorrhage. Her husband called emergency services and was told that an ambulance would be waiting on the other side of the checkpoint." Ashawi's tone remained factual, as though imparting a commonplace of daily life. "Jefar was visiting. Together the three of them set off in a car. But the checkpoint had stopped traffic altogether. Though it was obvious that she was in excruciating pain, for over an hour her husband and brother pleaded with Israeli soldiers to hurry her through. Finally, her husband told the soldiers that they could take responsibility for the death of a pregnant woman and her child. Only then did they allow her husband and Jefar to leave the car and try to walk her to the checkpoint.

"Just before they reached the ambulance," he continued, "she collapsed. When she awakened in the hospital, the baby had died, and she had undergone a hysterectomy. She has not spoken since." He turned to David. "Her story explains more about Jefar than any label you can put on him. Perhaps the Israeli soldiers who stopped Jefar's sister also impeded a suicide bomber in another car, and saved a Jewish life. But it is they, not Al Aqsa or Hamas, who made Ibrahim Jefar into Ben-Aron's assassin. The cause and effect of occupation is not a mathematical equation."

A half hour later, they reached the checkpoint. With stone-faced indifference — perhaps a mask for fear — a female Israeli soldier armed with an assault weapon took Ashawi's papers and David's passport, and sauntered with ostentatious lassitude to a bulletproof guard post. Two more soldiers, as young as the woman, combed the car and the trunk, edgily glancing at Ashawi as they did so. No one spoke. To David, the moment crackled with tension and distrust.

After ten minutes, the woman returned David's passport and began snapping at Ashawi in Hebrew, jerking her thumb to summon him from his van. When Ashawi turned to David, his jaw was working, his voice taut. "She says that I cannot drive you — my papers are not in order."

David felt alarmed and helpless. "What's the problem?"

"Maybe an American coming to the West Bank. Maybe she's impressing her friends. My papers were fine yesterday, and they'll be fine tomorrow. It's just that this child-bitch of a soldier can do whatever she wants with me." As the soldier continued barking at him, Ashawi added in a lower voice, "When she's not looking, drive the van on through, then stop beside the fruit market. I'll try to catch up."

The woman led Ashawi away. Glancing over his shoulder, David eased the van past the guardhouse, eyes straight ahead. No one stopped him.

On the other side of the checkpoint he spotted a fruit market where Arabs — the women covered, many of the men in kaffiyehs — gathered to shop. Adrift in the Arab world, David pulled to the side of the road.

For over twenty minutes he waited, apprehensive. Then Ashawi climbed into the driver's seat, having blended in with the pedestrians who passed behind the wire. "Welcome to the occupation," he said tersely. "You've now broken Israeli law."

David checked his watch again. He had been on the West Bank for less than two hours, and already he felt tense and angry. Ashawi had gone silent.

Ramallah was a city of opposites: young women in modern dress mingling with their covered Arab sisters; crowded streets whose shabbiness was relieved by bustling fruit stands and sandwich shops with colorful signs in Arabic; and, amid several mosques, a church. Of fifty thousand residents, Ashawi explained, perhaps a quarter were Christians. But whatever their religion, the character of the city was deeply Arab — any Jewish fanatic who imagined "a Greater Israel" that could somehow include or expel these people was, David knew at once, in full flight from reality.

Ramallah was home to Hana and Saeb. It was also the site of Arafat's tomb — formerly his compound and bombed to rubble by the air strikes that had traumatized Munira. It was there, Ashawi explained, that they would meet a friend, a man whose knowledge might be of use to David. Then they would proceed to Birzeit, where David had a meeting with the president of the university, Hana's friend.

Encased by a glass shell, Arafat's black marble tomb was set in an open plaza surrounded by the half-ruined buildings. The tomb was covered in flowers and smiling photographs of Arafat; at its foot was a plaque sent by the children of Sabra and Shatila. Two Palestinian policemen stood stiffly at each side, an honor guard for the father of a would-be country he could not quite summon into being.

David and Ashawi stood in front of the tomb. "He is a symbol," Ashawi said. "He did not build a civil society, and he underrated the strength of the Jews. Some say that he allowed the Palestinian Authority to sink into corruption, indifferent to the needs of the people, and so gave us Hamas. But where would we be without him?"

"Now? Some say you'd have a country, instead of an occupation."

"Then they say too much," Ashawi answered curtly. "The Jews have already taken three-quarters of our homeland and refuse even to discuss our desire to return. Was Arafat supposed to accept all that, and the settlements as well? Did they expect him to buy peace at the cost of all our dignity?"

David did not answer. "Do you remember when Arafat's body was brought here?" Ashawi asked in a quieter tone. "A proper ceremony was planned, but crowds of mourners seized his coffin and gave him a spontaneous burial.

"The rest is little known. At three A.M. that morning some soldiers from the Palestinian Authority dug up his coffin, removed his body, and prepared him for a proper Islamic burial." Ashawi's voice became almost reverent. "The remarkable thing, the soldiers say, is that he looked the same as in life. Death had not touched his face."

Ashawi sounded as though he half-believed it. Quiet, David wondered if those who succeeded Arafat, like Marwan Faras, were doomed by the murder of Ben-Aron, and the violence that had followed, to find no peace with Israel. He doubted that the next Palestinian leader could, even in legend, defy the need for embalming by relinquishing the right of return.

In her way, the woman at the King David had been right. David had entered a different world, the homeland of Hana Arif and Saeb Khalid.

17

Ashawi's friend, Amjad Madji, turned out to be a wiry, soft-spoken peace activist in his late thirties who taught a course in human rights law at Birzeit. Among his former students, it transpired, were Iyad Hassan and Ibrahim Jefar.

"Two different men," Madji said, shortly after joining them. "When I first met him, Ibrahim was searching — still teachable, I thought, someone who could be turned away from violence. Not so Iyad. He was already closed, a missile waiting to be pointed."

As Ashawi drove them from Arafat's tomb, David turned to face Madji. "By whom?"

Though his manner was confident, Madji spoke with a judicious calm that suggested an observant nature tempered by experience. "Not the Al Aqsa Martyrs," he answered. "At least if I'm any judge. Perhaps, to kill Ben-Aron, Iyad might cooperate with Al Aqsa. But his family was Hamas, I think — certainly his sister-in-law, the suicide bomber. And Hamas suited his temperament as I assessed it: puritanical, with a deep contempt for women, a fanatic for whom Islam means hating Jews and Israel. Al Aqsa might serve his ends, but it could never speak to his needs. As for me, I had no chance with him at all." With a shrug of resignation, he said, "Souls like Hassan's are harsh soil for nonviolence."

As was the West Bank, David suspected. Deferring his inquiry about Hassan and Jefar, he asked, "How did you come to believe in nonviolence?"

"In the great tradition of Gandhi and Mandela," Madji answered dryly, "I got myself arrested.

"It's easier than people think, and far less pleasant than the populace of Israel may allow itself to conceive. Justice in the territories is a Gilbert and Sullivan pantomime of law, a shell without substance. Have you had time to master the Israelis' rules of detention?"

"Not yet."

"Too bad," Madji responded with an ironic smile. "From what I read of America's own 'war on terror,' you might someday find this useful to know.

"Here, there are two types of detention, both of which permit the IDF to jail you for up to six months, for no particular reason. Regular detention is based on an accusation by someone else, truthful or not. For the first eighteen days, you may be held without a lawyer if the prosecution asserts that you're an exceptional case — which cases, in fact, are quite unexceptional. If you fail to confess, a prosecutor can apply for one extension, then another, on the basis of secret 'evidence' the prisoner never sees." Now Madji's smile was pained. "The purpose, naturally, is to extract a confession. Problems arise when one has nothing to confess."

At once, David thought of Hana. *I have nothing to give up,* she had told him. *That's the problem with being innocent . . .*

"By contrast," Madji was saying, "administrative detention is reserved for those suspected of something even less specific, about which the suspect need not be told. That was me."

The traffic was slowing. Ahead, David watched soldiers erecting a barrier across the road. Turning back to Madji, David saw the man's eyes narrow, an instinctive flash of worry that aroused his curiosity. "I'd like to hear about it," David said.

Madji had been back from Stanford Law School for less than thirty days when a soldier stopped him at a flying checkpoint between Ramallah and Birzeit.

It was 1996, during the period when suicide bombings shattered the peace of Israel and altered the course of its election. There was a "mistake" on Madji's identification, the soldier said — he must go with him to a compound run by the IDF. "With that," Madji said softly, "I lost contact with the world as I knew it."

The room where they imprisoned him was dark, he supposed. But he could not be sure — the bag over his head prevented Madji from seeing; the rope that bound his wrists behind his back kept him from removing the bag. His ankles were chained to the chair he sat in.

Twice a day, they brought food and allowed him to relieve himself. But mostly he knew his jailers by their voices, especially those who screamed at him when he fell asleep in his chair. He could call no one — not his parents or a lawyer. The burning pain of constricted muscles became excruciating; he vomited much of what he ate until his stomach felt raw. His cell stank of puke and urine.

After a time — he could not tell how long — his grasp of reality began to slip. He would have confessed to anything, named anyone he might have suspected of some crime. But he had been too long in America; he knew too little to fabricate a confession.

The one hint of his problem was a name they kept repeating — "the Palestinian-American Assistance League." But only when they removed the bag, and showed him the scholarship application he had written, did the memory break free: the PAAL was a group of Arab-Americans who offered money to Palestinians studying in the United States. "They finance terrorism," his interrogator insisted.

"I know nothing," Madji said miserably. "They rejected my application."

They put the bag back on his head, and the darkness resumed.

Madji felt himself diminishing in flesh and spirit. When they questioned him, he wept more than spoke.

One day, as every day, he heard the door to his cell open; as always, he flinched, atrophied muscles tightening with fear.

Gently, someone removed the bag. An Israeli he had not seen before knelt in front of his chair, removed the shackles from his ankles, and then unbound his hands. He was a slight man with a scholar's face, and he looked almost as miserable as Madji. "We are sorry," he said simply. "The man we are seeking is not you." Placing a hand on Madji's rope-burned wrist, he offered a smile of encouragement. "We will clean you up, and then you are free to go."

"How long have I been here?" Madji asked.

The man shook his head, as though commiserating. "Forty-two days."

When Madji emerged, he had lost thirty pounds. What the IDF had done to him, he learned, was arguably legal — even the circumstances of his incarceration, one could maintain, were not truly torture but the "moderate physical force" permitted in order to secure confessions. "Perhaps," he told David now, "others held in the same compound gave up information that allowed their interrogators to thwart an act of violence. Perhaps, to the Israelis, I was just a sad mistake, an unfortunate byproduct of their duty to save lives. But they changed my life forever."

Madji gazed at the checkpoint in the distance, his face haunted. "For days I sat in my apartment and relived what had become of me. Again and again, I thought of the Israeli who seemed to have felt almost as soiled as did I. The Israelis were prepared to respond to violence, I realized — they knew how to fight it, and it justified their excesses, even when those excesses spawned still more hatred and violence. But perhaps a broad-based peace movement, grounded in a nonviolent resistance that included women, might force them to confront themselves. Their own conscience was the one enemy Jews could not defeat."

David was both impressed and deeply skeptical. "How long will *that* take?"

"A while, I'm afraid. My own group, Palestinians for Peace, is in its infancy. And nonviolence is still seen as weakness, not resistance. But more Palestinians are beginning to understand that violence has not brought about our return, or even given us our own country." Madji fished a cigarette from his pocket with the deliberate movements of one suppressing a deep desire for tobacco. "The question is who, on each side, wins out. The Israelis are frightened; the Palestinians, humiliated. The psychology of extremists on both sides is much alike. If the murder of Ben-Aron continues this vicious cycle, *they* will be the winners." Looking keenly at David, Madji said, "But that's why you're here. To learn who hoped to gain from this, and pray that they do not include your client."

"In a nutshell, yes."

Madji opened his car door. "We won't be moving for a while. So step outside with me while I smoke. Since my time with the Israelis, I've found it helps me think."

Leaning against the car, Madji took a deep drag on his cigarette. "My assessment of Jefar is that he's truthful. Or, put another way: that, like me, he would be broken by imprisonment and fear. But his confession leaves much obscure."

"In what way?"

Madji drew on his cigarette. "It's easy enough to find 'resistance' groups who wanted Ben-Aron dead — Hamas, Hezbollah, Islamic Jihad. Perhaps some in Al Aqsa wished him dead as well. But actively plotting his assassination?

"Look at the result. Al Aqsa is shattered. Its reason for being — to divert radical support from Hamas to Fatah, Faras's party — has boomeranged. Now that Israel scorns Faras and he can't deliver peace, Hamas will pick up the pieces, and Faras's successor will be a member of Hamas."

David looked toward the flying checkpoint. Cars were inching forward now; walking beside Ashawi's van toward the roadblock, Madji began puffing more quickly, his gaze moving between the harsh, rocky landscape and the barrier across the road, as though searching for some alternate route. "Perhaps," David mused aloud, "Al Aqsa never thought it would be implicated. Would anyone expect Jefar to survive? There was nothing left of Hassan."

Distracted, Madji seemed to be counting his own footsteps. "It's simple enough to trace Jefar to Al Aqsa," he said. "He was among a group of their people I spoke to about nonviolence — without success, it's clear. Later, after what befell his sister, he left school. I never saw him again."

His tone held a weary fatalism. "And Hassan?" David asked. "Do you know anything more that could tie him to Hamas?"

"No. What bewilders me is that, to my mind, Hassan truly despised women — in class, he would barely look at any of his female classmates, especially those who did not cover. He acted as if they were unclean." Madji stopped where he was, inhaling a last puff of his cigarette. "As I understand Jefar's confession, Hassan said that Hana Arif not only gave him his instructions but had recruited him in the first place. It's a little hard to imagine the relationship between Arif and Hassan that would make such a conversation possible." He paused, considering his own statement. "And yet, as I say, I would tend to believe Ibrahim's confession. And why would Hassan lie to him?"

"All good questions. Did you know Hana or her husband?"

"Only by reputation, as two professors who quite openly despised the occupation. Beyond that, nothing."

David glanced at his watch. It was almost three o'clock, and though the president of Birzeit was expecting him any minute, he supposed she knew to wait. The afternoon sun, while not oppressive, had left a sheen of perspiration on Madji's forehead.

"So," David said, "you think that if Al Aqsa is destroyed and Faras loses all credibility, then Hamas will seize total power?"

"Yes. Hamas was always the chief critic of Fatah and Faras — that they're corrupt, that they've compromised with Israel, that they've betrayed a newer, brighter, more honest generation. It's Hamas that set up a network of charities, schools, medical facilities, summer camps, and sports clubs for Palestinians old and young, establishing a shadow government that also promotes and finances suicide bombings and other acts of violence against Jews. Once, in Ramallah, the Israelis found a cache of arms and explosives hidden beneath a Hamas preschool." Madji dropped his cigarette butt, grinding it out with the toe of his black leather shoe. "Within Fatah, Al Aqsa was a recourse for young people who thought Arafat and his people were crooks and frauds. From Israel's perspective, Al Aqsa's surely to be feared — witness Jefar. But by destroying Al Aqsa, Israel is effectively assisting a group of Muslim fundamentalists — Hamas — expressly pledged to its destruction, whose burning contempt for Arafat and his heirs is matched by an open admiration for jihadists like Bin Laden. God help us if Hamas is all that's left."

"Wasn't it part of Faras's strategy on becoming leader of the Palestinian Authority to seduce Hamas into joining the political process?"

Madji lit another cigarette, eyeing the checkpoint as he did. They were now roughly thirty yards from the barrier, and the cars they were walking beside kept creeping slowly forward. "Joining the process is one thing," Madji answered. "For Hamas to win elections was quite another. It now may put Israel to a terrible choice: leave the Palestinian Authority in the hands of Islamic fundamentalists or abolish the electoral process and, effectively, any pretense of Palestinian self-government, extending the occupation for years. Only a man like Iyad Hassan would cherish such a moment." Madji paused, slowly turning his head toward David. "That's another thing that perplexes me. It's certainly possible to imagine a joint operation between Al Aqsa and Hamas. It's happened before: if Hamas has a bomb and Al Aqsa a bomber, it becomes what you might call kismet. But a plot to kill Ben-Aron? The potential consequences to Al Aqsa, and to Faras, seem way too obvious. Deconstructing all this requires a sharper mind than *I* have."

"Or maybe just more information," David proposed. "Is it possible that someone from Hamas could infiltrate Al Aqsa?"

"Someone like Jefar, you mean? Sure. But to what end, and on whose orders? Hana Arif's?" Madji shook his head. "There's too much here I don't understand. Or maybe, as you say, we both know far too little."

Squinting, David put on his sunglasses. "Tell me," he asked, "what happens when you say to Palestinians that they're not returning to the places where their parents lived?"

Madji's face set. "I don't," he answered. "Personally, I've no interest in returning to Jaffa, the old port of Tel Aviv, where my grandfather lived before he was murdered by the Irgun. But I could never face someone living in a refugee camp and tell him he has no right of return."

Then you will have no peace, David thought but did not say. Even between Amos Ben-Aron and

Marwan Faras, the gulf was measured by what Amjad Madji chose not to say.

Fifteen minutes later, still walking beside Ashawi's van, David and Madji reached the checkpoint.

Madji was perspiring more freely now. When the strapping young Israeli soldier took his ID papers, retreating a few paces to call someone on his cell phone as he scanned them yet again, Madji began pacing in small circles, an unlit cigarette twitching between his fingers. "They always do this," he said. "It's pro forma — because we oppose the occupation, the Israelis think my peace movement is their enemy."

He was trying to convince himself, David sensed, that nothing was amiss. But Madji would never pass a checkpoint without remembering the burning of his muscles and the stench of his own vomit. He seemed somehow smaller than he had been.

When the soldier returned Madji's papers and took David's passport, Madji hastily lit his cigarette. Brusquely, the soldier asked David, "What are *you* doing here?"

"Visiting," David snapped without thinking. "What are *you* doing here?"

The soldier kept them for another fifteen minutes.

18

With the president of Birzeit at his side, David stood in Hana's office.

As he had expected, the office was neat: its one photograph, of Munira at an earlier age, showed a smiling child too young to cover her dark, glossy hair. From Hana's second-story window at the law school he could see much of the campus. Situated on a hill surrounded by pines, the buildings were white and modern, and the students looked much like students anywhere, a mix of young men and women smoking and chatting or hurrying from place to place, save that some of the women were covered. On the surface, there was little to suggest the seedbed of radicalism that had produced Jefar and Hassan. But throughout its recent history, Birzeit had been repeatedly closed or encircled by the IDF.

Its president, Fatima Khalil, a stout, handsome woman in her fifties, elaborated for David's benefit. "Between '87 and '91," she began, "when Hana and Saeb hoped to study here, the IDF closed us altogether. When our professors tried to hold classes in their apartments or homes, the IDF raided them. By 2000, they had closed Birzeit fourteen times.

"What has happened since 2000 is no better —

merely different. For a short time in 2002, the IDF imposed a curfew in most of our cities, under which you could not leave your home for more than three to four hours a week. Kids couldn't go to school, or adults to work." Though her demeanor remained calm, Khalil's voice became harsher. "During this time, the IDF killed seventeen people in Ramallah. The hospital staff was forced to keep them in refrigerators and, finally, to dig up a parking lot and bury them beneath it. Even the dead, it seemed, had a curfew."

"And here?"

"The IDF ringed our campus with checkpoints and obstructed access roads with concrete blocks and mounds of earth. At one point they blocked food supplies and cut off our water and telephone communications. We were a hornet's nest of radicals, they claimed, and then proceeded to radicalize still more of us." Khalil's eyes were both angry and sad. "My daughter is such a person. She was a student here, a soft, gentle girl who studied literature and wrote stories. One day, she participated in a peaceful protest against the IDF. Israeli soldiers threw her in a jeep and stomped on her arms and legs until she fainted from the pain. Then they dumped her by the road like garbage."

"Is she all right?"

"She had no permanent damage," Khalil answered simply. "Except in her heart: after this incident, she could not encounter a checkpoint without screaming at the soldiers with a hatred I never knew her to possess. Her father and I sent her to school in Turkey just to keep her out of prison." Khalil walked to the window and gazed out at the students scurrying across the campus between classes. "Among our students, to be sure, are

Hamas, Islamic Jihad, and Al Aqsa. Now we are famous for Hassan and Jefar. But when I look at these young people, what I see is waste and loss.

"While they're here, we assist them financially in every way we can — education is the lifeblood of the nation we hope to build. But after graduation day, where will these young people go? Our economy is a shambles. For the educated intelligentsia — would-be engineers or lawyers forced to become laborers or waiters — the index of despair is still higher. I sometimes think of all these young people — our students and the Israelis sent to be their jailers, both frightened of each other — and imagine them on a tragic collision course from which neither can find an exit. But, except for the soldiers who die here, the young Israelis can leave their nightmare behind. Our nightmare never ends."

Listening, David could sense what the IDF found so combustible in Birzeit: charismatic teachers inflamed by impotence and confinement; thwarted students, their resentment kindled by the sharpening of their minds. "But you didn't come here," Khalil told him with a self-deprecating smile, "to consider problems quite so cosmic. From your e-mail, I know you wish to learn more about Hana and Saeb Khalid. As did the Shin Bet and the IDF, who spent an entire day in this very room."

David turned to face her. "What did they want to know?"

"Much the same as you. For example, that the computers and printers used by all our professors are standard, like the one you see on Hana's desk."

"And the paper?"

"Also standard — any professor or student

could, in theory, have typed and printed the telephone number on the paper given to Iyad Hassan." Khalil smiled wryly. "By training, I'm a lawyer, and so I've tried to think along with you. What I've just said, regrettably, does not explain why Hana's fingerprints are on the paper."

"No. It doesn't." David leaned against the desk. "Who had access to this office?"

"Before Hana was arrested? In theory, anyone." Khalil sat in Hana's chair, looking up at him with curiosity. "Do you know if she locked her office?"

David felt them circling the subject of Saeb Khalid. "Only at night," he answered. "No one else had a key, she tells me."

Khalil nodded. "I know from our records that we gave Saeb and Hana a computer and printer to use at home, the same as these. What paper they used there I'm not sure."

For a moment, David studied the photograph of Munira, wondering what, if anything, was indicated by the absence of a photograph of Saeb, or of husband, wife, and child together. "The fingerprints are problematic," he said at length. "For someone to frame Hana, she would have had to give them the paper herself. Otherwise, they would have had to use a piece of paper they knew already had her fingerprints." He placed a hand on Hana's printer. "This holds about fifty sheets. When Hana refilled it, she might leave prints on the first sheet or the last, but not on those in between. So someone walking into her office to steal a piece of paper couldn't assume that her prints would appear on the top paper. Only the bottom."

"So they would have to be clever."

"Or lucky." *Unless they lived with her,* David thought but did not say.

Khalil folded her hands, pensive. "The Israelis also wanted both of their personal files. And as you did in your e-mail, they asked about Saeb's absences from teaching."

David kept his tone neutral. "He has a heart condition, I was told. I gather he sees a Jordanian specialist in Amman."

Khalil smiled thinly. "The condition must be serious — one leaves the West Bank at one's peril, never knowing if the IDF will allow you to return. That's why I no longer take vacations." Her smile vanished. "During the 1967 war, my brother fled to Amman. They never let him back; thirty-five years later, he was not allowed to attend our father's funeral. Too radical, they said."

"How did Saeb and Hana get back here after Harvard?"

"Good question. Perhaps the forces of international beneficence played a hand, as they did in educating them in America." Khalil smoothed the pleats of her dress. "A better question is why they let Saeb return from Jordan, given how outspoken he's been since coming here. I suppose they reviewed his medical records and did not wish to be accused of murdering a sick man by denying him the care he needs."

"Have *you* seen his medical records?"

Khalil shook her head. "We took him at his word. Does he look well to you?"

"Neither well," David said sardonically, "nor happy."

Khalil laughed softly. "Happiness, I believe, is not in his nature. Nor is he a fount of self-revelation.

"You asked for specific information about his absences, so I went back and checked our records.

He made six trips to Amman, each lasting up to a week, with the most recent being just over three months ago. Two weeks, in other words, before Saeb, Hana, and Munira all traveled to America." Her expression became pensive. "Again, that the Israelis let either of them go is a bit of a surprise. I guess they have more violent people to worry about — or thought they did. Even paranoids have real enemies, and every day they spend here earns them more."

David studied her, then decided to be blunt. "Was Saeb with Hamas?"

Khalil's eyes narrowed. "I make it my business not to know these things, and so I don't. As to Saeb or Hana, I know nothing."

"What about Jefar and Hassan?"

"I know only their backgrounds. Both are from refugee camps: for Jefar, Jenin; for Hassan, Aida — another version of hell. As for whether they're Al Aqsa, you'd have to ask whoever in Al Aqsa is still alive. Not that you'll be able to find them: the Israelis are looking to kill the rest, and meeting with you is too big a risk for Al Aqsa to take."

"What about classes? Did either Jefar or Hassan know Saeb or Hana?"

"I know Iyad Hassan had one class with Saeb. But that means little or nothing. Saeb is very popular; the classes are too large for him to meet or remember every student."

And yet, David reflected, Amjad Madji had remembered Hassan, who was made singular by his anger and his disdain for women. Khalil picked up the photo of Munira. "Such a bright smile," she remarked. "She seems to smile less now, like many of our children.

"One of our teachers tracked five children from

elementary school to age eighteen. The young ones wanted to be artists, or writers, or musicians. By high school, one boy had seen his girlfriend die when the IDF blew up her house, allegedly a terrorist haven; a girl's brother was beaten at a checkpoint; another girl's father was in jail. And their vision of the future had narrowed to hatred of Israelis." Khalil replaced the photograph, still examining Munira's face. "Hana and I spoke of this. Munira was her anchor, I often thought — Hana wanted a better life for her in Palestine, not perpetual war with Israel in the name of some Islamic dream."

"So you don't see her as a murderer?"

Khalil gave him a level gaze. "Hana, like me, is a mother. We would do anything to protect our children. That is why my daughter is in Turkey.

"We don't abandon our daughters, or want them to be martyrs. If someone could prove that Hana involved herself in this assassination to protect Munira from harm — then, yes, I would believe it. Until then, I would tell you it's impossible."

19

That evening David met Hana's closest friend, Nisreen Awad, at Stones, a restaurant in Ramallah.

Stones was not what David expected. A two-level café, all glass and steel beams, it was jammed with young people eating and smoking and drinking at the bar as multinational music pulsed from the sound system. Nor was Nisreen quite what he had imagined: tall, full-figured, and striking, she sat with David, smoking from a hookah and speaking with an insouciance more suggestive of a bohemian than the serious lawyer David knew her to be — Hana's colleague in negotiations with Israel before Hana had quit in anger. "So I'm to be a character witness?" Nisreen said. "I'll try to improve on my character between then and now. A bit like clearing out the Augean stables, some would say." Puffing from the hookah, she looked at David with evident amusement. "You were expecting someone else?"

"Maybe someone a little more repressed."

"I work very hard to avoid that. It probably helps that I'm a Christian, and not married to Saeb Khalid." She waved a hand at the crowd; many people were wearing blue jeans, as was she. "Ramallah is shot full of contradictions. Many of these people are Christians, traditionally more affluent and better educated. But just outside the city is a refugee camp filled with people who don't know that a place like this exists. They are Muslim, and grindingly poor. Needless to say, their women do not come here."

"How do Palestinians handle the contradictions?"

"Not easily. We are a much more open society than many Arab countries — there's more education, and women have a stronger voice. But many Christians have left for the U.S. or Europe, and many Muslims do not believe in a secular democratic government." Nisreen took a deep hit on the water pipe, exhaling smoke in a sinuous stream, which evanesced in the darkness. "Whether these problems heal or fester depends in great measure on whether the Israelis believe their own rhetoric about peace. Hana thinks they don't, which is why she still despises them."

This last remark troubled David — he could imagine Marnie Sharpe teasing out of Nisreen a portrait of Hana that made hatred of Israel central to her recent past. "Because of Munira," Nisreen went on, "it's hard to believe that Hana was involved in killing Ben-Aron. But too many people have heard her call the Israelis imperialists, and Ben-Aron a pious phony." Her voice became emphatic. "A warning, then: if you try to pass her off as Mother Teresa, this prosecutor may jam it down your throat."

David sat back, sipping the sauvignon blanc Nisreen had ordered for them both. "I guess you'd better tell me why Hana quit."

Nisreen took another deep drag on the water pipe. "First, you have to understand the context of Hana's anger — these settlements, and this cynical land grab the Israelis call a security fence.

"In 1993, as part of the Oslo agreements, Israel promised to freeze the settlements. Instead, they kept expanding them, adding territory and population and using more of our water." Nisreen put down the water pipe. "Since 1993, the settlement population has almost doubled, cutting deeper into the West Bank. But almost as bad as the Israelis' geographic expansion is their psychological detachment.

"The settlers live in a bubble. Their bypass roads connect the settlements to one another, dividing the West Bank and enabling Israelis to travel without seeing any Arabs. So they create their own delusion." Nisreen flashed a quick, sardonic smile. "Once we met our Israeli counterparts in a Jewish settlement. Hana pointed out a painting on the wall — a landscape of the surrounding area, totally accurate except that the Arab villages had disappeared. 'You have erased us,' Hana told them, 'just like you erased my parents from the history of the place you now call Israel.'

"That initiated an angry debate. When Hana accused the Israelis of breaking their word by expanding the settlements, one man responded that they had to do this to pacify right-wing Israelis. 'Then truth is a convenience,' Hana said. 'And I should not believe anything you tell me.' " David could imagine Hana's eyes flashing as she upbraided the Israelis.

"Anger is one thing," David said. "Did you ever hear her call for violence against Israel or Ben-Aron?"

Nisreen considered the question. "To the Israelis, she said more than once that they were manufacturing suicide bombers by the score. But we all say these things." Pausing, Nisreen added with obvious reluctance, "Once, to me, Hana said that Ben-Aron would certainly die, and all that mattered was who killed him. I know what she meant: better their extremists than ours. By the time of the trial, I expect this conversation will have faded from my memory. But I hope she did not say as much to others."

The tacit acknowledgment that she would protect her friend by lying, while not surprising, left David uneasy. "What prompted Hana's resignation?" he asked.

"The security wall. Most Israelis and Palestinians know that there must be a two-state solution, with sensible borders. So how could they call it a security wall, Hana asked the Israelis, when it snakes this way and that to pick up settlements, water extraction points, and more Palestinian land? She's right of course — if they complete it as planned, it will block our roads and surround our cities, cutting us off from one another. The whole idea is to create a de facto border that takes as much land from us as possible, while penning up our population in separate enclaves." Nisreen looked at David intently. "Hana comes from people trapped in the refugee camps at Sabra and Shatila, unable to go anywhere. To see us hemmed in by a wall made her heartsick and discouraged. So when Ben-Aron refused to renounce or redraw the wall, she quit. 'It's hopeless,' she told me. 'I cannot take part in this man's charade.' Again and again, the Zionists cannot resist reaching for one more piece of cake.

"After she resigned, she was more depressed than I had ever seen her. It was as though everything — her life, her hopes for Palestinians — was collapsing all around her. A slow death of the spirit." Nisreen's voice grew husky. "My God, I thought, this woman deserves so much more."

"Than what exactly?"

"The life she's facing. She came back from America in a time of hope, believing she could help build a country, and found herself surrounded by death and oppression, with hatred mounting on both sides." Nisreen leaned forward, her voice and manner becoming even more impassioned. "Occupation gives young Israeli soldiers the power of life and death, at the same time exposing them to constant fear, all of which leaves them cynical yet traumatized and, in a certain way, dehumanized. And its constant pressure on the occupied breeds hatred in Palestinians and, in children, a lasting trauma. Seeing this in Munira pierces Hana's heart." Gazing at David, Nisreen continued in a tone of deeper resignation. "Most Israelis refuse to come here. Part of it is fear, but it's also a form of denial. It's ironic, really. The Israelis are a magnet for the guilt of others because of the Holocaust and centuries of persecution. But they cannot reconcile the suffering they've endured with the reality that, under *their* occupation, it is we who are suffering.

"In law school, at NYU, one of my closest friends was a Jewish girl from Tel Aviv. But she won't come to see me in Ramallah, and when we talk on the phone, it is all about suicide bombers, never about occupation — she cannot seem to hear me. And yet she, perhaps more than I, holds the key to our future.

"For Hana, the future has become Munira's future. And what *is* that future, here, exactly?" Briefly, Nisreen scanned the crowd. "What you see is us spending what we have today instead of planning for a tomorrow we do not control. We are voiceless — however we cry out, the world does not hear us."

Throughout this remarkable monologue, David watched the emotions flashing across Nisreen's face: anger, sadness, resignation, the deep need to express herself to someone not a Palestinian. "I know something about Hana," he said. "Tell me about you."

Nisreen gave him a smile of self-deprecation. "Actually, I've been talking about myself all along. Occupation is all I know. But if you want to hear about me, I'll tell you a few stories from my life. I'm to be a witness, after all.

"Unlike Hana, I am native to the West Bank. My mother was PLO. In 1967, she was arrested and my father, her apolitical fiancé, was detained. He would be released, the Israelis told her, if she revealed the names of her associates in the PLO. She refused." Nisreen's tone commingled pride and indignation. "Three years later they released her. She was deaf in her left ear from being slapped on the head. When she married my father, she had to stand to his left in order to hear their vows.

"That's my parents. One of my cousins is serving nine years for being Hamas. My brother served a year for joining Al Aqsa. My sister's fiancé went to Arafat's compound to pick up a friend — also Al Aqsa, though her fiancé was not — and both were killed by Israeli soldiers who were hunting down the Al Aqsa guy." Nisreen's voice hardened. "You might think us an unusual family or, at least, unusually unfortunate. We are not.

"For reasons of traditions and economy, I still live in my parents' home. The woman who cleaned it until recently has eight children, and a marriage that was in trouble — her husband could not find work where they lived and, because of checkpoints, spent most of the week in another village.

"One night he came to our home, looking for his wife. My parents and I could not tell him where she was. Then, while we were talking, we heard her name on television. When we turned to watch, we saw her standing between two Israeli soldiers at a checkpoint. She'd been arrested for carrying explosives." Nisreen shook her head. "We were all astonished — they were not even Muslims, let alone political. Just poor people with eight children to feed.

"It turned out someone from Hamas had paid her to carry explosives through the checkpoint — the raw ingredients for a suicide bombing that might well have killed Israeli children. What's even more jarring is that, in the morning, she had gone to the market and bought clothes for her own children. Then she'd cleaned our house and gone off to the checkpoint. In her mind she was merely taking an opportunity to make money and, I think, express hostility toward her husband for his failure to provide.

"It's absolutely nuts, of course — practically and morally. But it should introduce more complexity into your vision of who carries out acts of terror, and how the occupation distorts our lives."

Listening, David sorted through his reactions. "When Palestinians talk of suicide bombing," he told her, "it often sounds like something thrust on them by the Israelis. But when I was in Israel I saw a tape of an imam speaking to a group of men that included Jefar and Hassan — the worst kind of anti-Semitic crap in which Jews have no more worth than cockroaches. Worse, the imam's little sermon ran on Palestinian TV."

Nisreen waved a dismissive hand. "This is deplorable, I grant you. But no one watches. It's just government propaganda, a reflexive reaction to the fact that the Zionists' lobbies and their sympathizers dominate the world media."

"As a Jew," David cut in, "I don't take it quite so lightly. Neither did Hassan." His voice softened. "In this better world of yours, could Munira marry a Jewish boy? Could you? Or does hatred of Jews go deeper than the occupation?"

For the first time, Nisreen did not look at him directly. She drew on the water pipe, receding into her own thoughts. "At work," she said at last, "an Arab man is dating a Jewish woman in Jerusalem. It is difficult, and not just because of checkpoints. To some of us, it is offensive that he does not date a Palestinian. That is the honest truth." She looked at David again. "My reasons are political. What the others feel, I cannot say.

"For me, it is all about the occupation. All of us, Jew and Arab, need an end to this. That is why I continue to work on negotiations, and why I did not despise Ben-Aron as Hana did." Nisreen spoke in a voice tinged with regret. "With him alive, our people had at least some hope. Now there is only more hatred and reprisal, with the Palestinian Authority crumbling before our eyes. The only winners are extremists on both sides. If this is Munira's future, it seems very bleak.

"For Hana, the occupation is even worse than it is for me. At least I have my parents. Hers are trapped in Lebanon; the Israelis will not let them come to live here. And now her daughter may be trapped as well — not only by the Israelis but by her father's insistence on what an Arab woman should be."

David pondered this. "At Harvard," he observed, "Saeb didn't strike me as a Muslim fundamentalist."

"According to Hana, he wasn't. Otherwise she would never have married him." Contemplative, Nisreen sipped her wine. "My sense is that his turn to Islam mixes politics and psychology. Politically, Hamas is more antagonistic toward Israel, and uses Islam as a kind of ideological glue. Psychologically — and this is where it gets tricky — my guess is that the more friction there is between Saeb and Hana, especially about Munira, the more he is impelled toward a religion whose extremists insist on male dominance.

"I came to view Saeb and Hana's clash over their daughter as symbolic. On the one hand, you have Hana, a fair example of the progressive Arab women who could form a base of support for a girl like Munira." Briefly, Nisreen smiled. "Not that I'm any role model, but, in many ways, Hana would like Munira to live as I do — free to say what I want, date whom I please, go where I like, spend time with whoever interests me, satisfy my ambitions, and stretch my curiosity any way I choose. That can be a hard life: I am gossiped about, and many traditional Palestinians find my attitudes unforgivable. But there are more and more women like me. In Hana's mind, we are the future she desires for Munira."

David flashed on Munira, covered, reciting in a monotone how her father compelled her to study the Koran. In that moment he felt, more keenly than before, the visceral struggle between husband and wife to define the destiny of their only child. "On the other hand," Nisreen was saying, "there is the structured life of a woman embraced by fundamentalist Islam, where she has no relationship with men except for marriage, and that, at its worst, manifests itself in spousal abuse, polygamy, and honor killings. Do you know about those?"

"Generally," David answered. "My understanding is that a woman can be murdered by her family for some real or imagined sexual transgression. In one case, I was told, a married woman who had become pregnant as the result of an affair was forced by her brother-in-law to become a suicide bomber."

Nisreen nodded. "It's not always about sex, or even the woman's conduct. Last year, in Ramallah, a Muslim father killed his daughter for wanting to marry a Christian. In another case, a father raped his daughter, then tried to sell her into prostitution because her honor had been lost. When a group of women tried to intervene, the father simply killed her. Grotesque." Her face softened. "Your story of the female suicide bomber was one Hana and I discussed. It seemed to upset her more than most."

The last remark stirred David's curiosity. "Was there a particular reason?"

With uncharacteristic reluctance, Nisreen contemplated her lap. Quietly, she said, "You are a friend from law school, right?"

"Yes."

Nisreen exhaled. "Hana is a deeply unhappy woman. By this, I mean not only unhappy in her marriage but unhappy in her heart and soul. Beneath her intellect and self-possession hides a terrible solitude."

David felt an answering sadness. "Because of her marriage?"

"Her marriage, and her regrets." Nisreen looked up at him. "I tell you this in confidence, okay?"

"All right."

"In law school, Hana had an affair. Saeb never knew, of course; if he had, he might have killed her — literally. But this lover left his mark."

David felt his skin tingle. "What did she say about him?"

"Very little. Just that he was American — that the whole thing was impossible, but that she had never been able to forget him." Nisreen looked reflective. "We only spoke of it twice, the last time just before Hana left for America.

"She was wondering whether she should try to see him. The pull was very strong, but Hana was frightened of her emotions. Then she said to me, 'Do you know what I've been feeling? That he would have made a better father for my daughter.' " Nisreen smiled sadly. "It was so unlike Hana — magical thinking, impossible in life. If she'd chosen this man, she would have no Munira. And Munira is all to her.

"What it told me was that her sense of loss was so deep, and her worries for Munira so pronounced, that she wished to indulge herself in fantasy. It made me sadder than anything else she could have told me."

David could find no words. He sat there as a series of realizations overcame him, transforming the way he understood every word Hana had said to him, and everything she had done, since the day that she had first called him. Looking at him askance, Nisreen inquired, "You knew this man, perhaps?"

David managed a smile. "You're her best friend, Nisreen. You know how private she can be. Especially about something like this."

Nisreen nodded, satisfied. In that moment,

David understood how she had missed what, to a woman so perceptive, might otherwise have been obvious. Nisreen could not imagine David as Hana's lover, because David was a Jew.

20

In a haze, David checked into the Park Hotel and shut himself in his room.

He lay on the bed for hours, barely moving but unable to sleep. Ever since Hana's plea for help, he had distrusted her — not merely because of doubts about her innocence but because of misgivings about who she had become. It was absurd to care for her after thirteen years, he had argued to himself, and infantile to believe she might still care for him — if, indeed, she had ever cared as much as he. David had been wary, distant, resentful of her impact on his life, uncertain of his judgment as a lawyer and a man. And now Hana's closest friend had transformed his understanding of her.

Vainly, he wished that he could reach Hana — just to hear her voice, and to ask about her confessions to Nisreen. Instead, he reran the tape in his head that had recorded their every meeting — her words, her expressions, her tone of voice. Now her questions about Carole, and even her hesitations, were illuminated. She had loved him at Harvard; she cared for him still; as a wife and mother facing imprisonment or execution, she was at least as conflicted about her feelings as David.

But this new understanding could not change his doubts about her innocence — although, intuitively, Hana's feelings for him put her ability to pass the polygraph in a better light. Yet the evidence against her remained intact, and his chief rebuttal — that, as a mother, Hana would not risk involvement — assumed that her love for Munira necessarily equated with innocence. One fact could change this assumption overnight.

Again and again, David's thoughts returned to the murders of Markis and Lev, and to his own role as catalyst. He was still uncertain of his competence, ignorant of the dimensions or design of the conspiracy he imagined, and fearful that if he came closer to the truth someone else — perhaps he himself — might die. Turning out the light, he knew only that when he awoke he would feel more confused, caught between his doubts about Hana's innocence and his knowledge that the one thing he was certain that she had concealed was her feelings for David himself.

Zahi Farhat, a principal adviser to Marwan Faras, sat with David in the lush garden of his villa in the hills above Ramallah, reflecting the affluence that had settled on the leaders of Fatah and aroused so much resentment among ordinary Palestinians — especially men like Saeb Khalid. "They are soft and corrupt," Saeb had remarked with scorn. "They forget what we brought them back to do." That Saeb had meant not merely the establishment of a functioning government but the extinction of Israel had not been lost on David.

A courtly man whose gray hair and glasses added to his somewhat professorial appearance, Farhat was certainly better company than Saeb. And his importance to David had been emphasized by Nabil Ashawi: if he chose, Farhat might arrange access to leaders of the Al Aqsa Martyrs Brigade. As he poured David tea from a china carafe, Farhat spoke of Ben-Aron's assassins. "These refugee camps," he said with a melancholy expression, "are such a problem. And now these two alumni may have pulled everything down around them — not just Ben-Aron but Fatah, Al Aqsa, and, of course, any hope of peace. While Hamas profits, Marwan Faras and the rest of us are hanging on by our fingernails."

"Satisfy my curiosity," David said. "You've got a million people in these camps, and still more overseas. Some date back to the birth of Israel itself. The Israelis would say that the Palestinian Authority preserves them for the purpose you claim to deplore — breeding violence and resentment of Israel, while diverting attention from your own failures. In short, that Hassan and Jefar are your creation, not theirs."

Farhat gave a wispy smile. "I acknowledge that if we were to dismantle the camps, in the eyes of the world there would be no refugee problem, no reminder of the injustice so many have suffered. We are invisible enough already. But the essential truth is that camps preserve a sense of identity, where refugees divide themselves into communities that commemorate the villages they came from —"

"And where they live in an idealized past," David interrupted, "clinging to the symbols of their expulsion from paradise, while their grandchildren play in open sewers. It's a recipe for the trouble you're in. If there's anything I'm clear on, it's this: neither the Jews nor the Palestinians are going anywhere, and anyone on either side who thinks that could happen, at least without unspeakable displacement and brutality, is insane. So why can't you folks say as much?"

Farhat studied his manicured fingernails. "A leader who told Palestinians they had no right of return would cease to be a leader. Fatah is ready to compromise. But how can we acknowledge Israel's right to exclude all Palestinians from the land of their grandparents, solely on the basis of their religion?

"The very concept of Israel is racist. No other state on earth proposes to maintain a 'democracy' confined to those of a single ethnicity or religion, even while they keep us stateless. The Israelis live in a state of siege, believing anti-Semitism to be a permanent condition of mankind; erecting walls when walls are falling around the world; portraying us as terrorists rather than human beings; and importing Russian Jews by the millions in their desperation to win what they most fear losing — a demographic war." Farhat jabbed the table. "An Israeli general once made the most racist, sexist remark I've ever heard: 'the ultimate ticking bomb is the womb of a Palestinian woman.' And yet they complain about this speech by the imam. Such hypocrisy."

All at once, David had heard enough. "Truly," he responded with sarcasm and anger. "I can't imagine why a people who've suffered three thousand years of genocide and rejection, culminating in the Holocaust, could possibly want a refuge of their own. After all, it's only Palestinians who've been expelled from country after country, only Jews who refuse to recognize someone else's narrative of suffering.

"Aside from these assassins, do you know who *I* think murdered Ben-Aron? All of you. Because you're living on different planets, and *yours* will soon be blissfully free of anti-Semites. Bullshit. Just like the Israeli notion that — whatever you call them — the Palestinians aren't a people. History made them one." David slowed his speech. "I've been here for just two weeks, and already all I can think is 'God help this place.' Assuming that anyone can even agree on who God is. All I can hope for is to get my client out of this fucking mess alive."

Farhat stared at him, then emitted a short laugh. "There is truth in what you say, however rudely. And I acknowledge Israel's legitimate fear of suicide bombers. But you can't oppress and dedevelop a whole society, and then build a wall between yourself and the problems that you've helped create. Only when the occupation ends can we build a civil society. And only then will those suicide bombings we all deplore come to an end."

David shook his head. "How can you expect the occupation to end before the violence stops? How can Israel protect itself without checkpoints and a wall?"

"By leaving us, and quickly, before Hamas takes over completely. You want to know how terrorists are made? Think of Jefar's pregnant sister. Or just be Palestinian for a day. Drive to a checkpoint until traffic stops, get out of the car, and walk a half mile to the barrier. You'll find an Israeli soldier with a cigarette in his mouth and, quite possibly, his gun leveled at one of the two hundred or so people stuck in front of you.

"Perhaps you're a student, unable to get to school. Perhaps you're one of the hundreds of women who've delivered a baby, hopefully alive. Perhaps you're the husband, shamed in front of his family by a soldier as young as his own son." Farhat's voice became almost elegiac. "Perhaps you're just delayed returning home. And what awaits you? Poverty is widespread, unemployment is rampant. Your village is cut off from the next, your children cut off from a future that holds out more hope than does yours. And on the hill above you is a settlement populated by Jews who scorn you, or maybe just this wall.

"As for these 'martyrs,' forget the idea that they receive universal praise — most of us cringe at every dead Israeli. Don't blame religion or ideology alone. To the incitement of the imam you mentioned, add despair, humiliation, and the desire for revenge. It is the occupation, not fanaticism, that spawned Ibrahim Jefar."

"Not to mention," David retorted, "terrorist networks that offer money to families of 'martyrs.' For that, the Israelis hold you accountable, and should. But let's not quibble. It's in your interest to help me before Hamas becomes entrenched."

Farhat propped his elbow on the table, gazing at the multicolored garden that surrounded them. "Before Ben-Aron was murdered," he finally said, "Hamas won control of the legislature. Our strategy had been to keep drawing them into the political process, even at the risk of losing power altogether. We had no choice — any attempt to disarm them would lead to an all-out war between us, which the Palestinian Authority lacks the security resources to win.

"But this was also delicate. To win back the legislature, we needed peace with Israel. In other words, we needed Ben-Aron." His tone became mournful. "Now the Israelis blame us for failing to control his killers; our people blame us for delivering Israeli reprisals instead of peace. That Jefar was Al Aqsa may have sealed the fate of Fatah. Certainly, it ended our ability to bring Al Aqsa into our security forces, which would have strengthened our hand against Hamas.

"This leaves Hamas even more powerful than before. Soon they will launch their own reprisals against Israel. Only if Israel gives us nationhood can we regain power, disarm Hamas, and stop these suicide bombings. Otherwise, Hamas is the Palestinian future."

"And if they are?"

"Then we will have a Muslim fundamentalist state, dedicated to Israel's destruction. Bad for Israel, obviously. Also bad for our educated classes. Especially women like Arif and Nisreen Awad, who would be separated from men at public events and even forced to cover, and whose daughters' educations might become extremely limited. Many secular Palestinians would leave, of course. Democracy here would end."

"All because Ben-Aron is dead," David responded, "and his assassins were supposedly Al Aqsa. Granted that Jefar was. But he was recruited by Hassan. And members of Hassan's family were Hamas — including a suicide bomber in Haifa."

Caution seemed to veil Farhat's eyes. "We've considered all that. But we cannot prove his connection to Hamas. And such accusations sometimes get men killed." Pausing, Farhat stared at the table. "Since Ben-Aron was murdered, we have lost what little control we had."

"And how does that serve Al Aqsa?"

"It doesn't. That is what I find so puzzling. But not all of its members are rational. Even its leaders."

David waited until Farhat looked up again. "I want to meet with them," he said.

Farhat shook his head. "They are dead now," he answered softly. "Or so deep underground that not even Israel can find them."

"Not even you? I'll settle for whoever's alive and brave enough to take the risk."

Farhat raised his eyebrows. "Like Barak Lev? You don't even know who killed him, do you?"

David felt his confidence falter. "True," he acknowledged. "But we're not in Israel now. The leaders of Al Aqsa must be skilled in self-protection, or the Israelis would have killed all of them long ago."

"Even so, why take the chance of meeting with you?"

"Because it might turn out to be a better means of self-defense than remaining underground. Al Aqsa leaders have denied any connection to Hassan, or the plot to kill Ben-Aron. Most people dismiss that as a survival tactic. But I happen to believe it. More specifically, I believe that nothing about this assassination is as it seems — that this was *not* an Al Aqsa operation, that Hana Arif was *not* the handler. And that whoever put this together carefully calculated the consequences, both in Israel and here.

"If I'm right, my defense of Hana may be *your* best hope of survival. I need Al Aqsa's help, and yours, in tying Iyad Hassan to Hamas. From there, maybe I can find out who his handler *really* was, and who the handler worked for. As matters stand, you'll soon have nothing more to lose."

Farhat appraised him closely. "All right," he said at length. "I'll consider what you say."

"Good. Because there's something more I want: the medical records for Saeb Khalid."

Though Farhat's eyes widened, David sensed

that his astonishment was feigned. "For what purpose?"

"In the past few years, Khalid traveled to Amman, supposedly to consult a specialist about a serious heart condition. Maybe he has one. But the last trip was just before Saeb went to America. Like his prior trips, this one took several days, leaving him time for other things. I'm curious about what they were, and who he might have seen."

Farhat regarded him with bleak amusement. "So you wish to substitute the husband for the wife?"

"Only if it works. But if he has no heart condition, or saw a Jordanian doctor only briefly, that would pique my curiosity."

Farhat opened his palms. "But why ask *us* for Khalid's confidential records? Why not the Israelis? Perhaps they, too, have taken an interest in him."

"You know they have," David snapped. "But the Israelis won't help me, so I'm asking you. Saeb Khalid may be a Palestinian, but he is no friend to Fatah. And I'd like to get his records without him, or anyone but us, knowing anything about it." Pausing, David spoke more quietly. "No one knows what happened here. Unless we find out, the Middle East may blow up, and a Palestinian state along with it. Maybe I could live with that. But I don't want Hana executed in the bargain."

Farhat smiled faintly. "As before, Mr. Wolfe, I admire your candor. For today, let that be enough."

21

A morning later, David traveled to Hebron in the company of a stranger.

"You must see conditions in Hebron for yourself," Nabil Ashawi had told him, "and this man may be able to help you in ways that I cannot. Go, and you will see."

His guide, Abu Jamal, was a slight bespectacled man, a former mathematics teacher in his mid-forties, twice jailed in his youth for an alleged association with the PLO. In the back seat of his jeep was body armor as well as perfume, which, Jamal explained, could help ward off the effect of tear gas when combined with cotton balls held to the nose.

At the Qalandiya checkpoint, they stopped again, beginning the process with which David was now familiar — a half-hour delay while tense soldiers checked their papers and searched their trunk and bags for explosives. Once more David felt as though he had entered a dream state that, triggered by some random event, could easily become a nightmare. But he assumed that Jamal had been provided by Farhat, and he hoped that this trip would link him to a leader of Al Aqsa.

In the driver's seat, Jamal gazed at the thirty-foot-high concrete wall that separated Qalandiya from Jerusalem. "The Jewish," he said, "have stolen our homeland, and now are stealing more. If we ever get through this barrier, I will show you the village of Atwani."

Though the landscape around Atwani was rocky and barren, its hills were softened by fig and olive trees and fields where sheep grazed. On the highest of the hills, covered in pine, was a settlement dominated by the Masada movement. "The settlers," Jamal said, "harass these villagers with impunity, killing their sheep, stealing their crops, throwing rocks at their children on their way to school. They are the worst of the Jewish, making trouble so there will never be peace."

Jamal's repetition of "the Jewish," tinged with anti-Semitism, began to chafe David's nerves. "Barak Lev," Jamal said, speaking the name as if it were a curse. "Whoever blew his head off is a hero."

At the foot of a hill where three Palestinians were grazing their sheep, they came to a clinic run by the Christian Peacekeepers Team. Outside were two young people, a brown-haired Canadian man and a fresh-faced blond woman from Minnesota, and their supervisor, a schoolteacher from New York who wore her silver hair in a bun. The blonde had one arm in a sling, and David spotted a bruise along her collarbone.

"That doesn't look much like a skiing accident," he said.

The young woman, Shannon Heath, mustered a smile that went as quickly as it had come. "A few weeks ago," she told him, "some settlers began cutting down the villagers' wheat. Our whole deal is reducing violence and friction — if necessary, by asking the Israeli authorities to intervene. These guys" — she indicated the others with a nod of her head — "weren't here. So I started videotaping the settlers myself —"

"They beat her with chains," her supervisor said tersely. "What you can't see is Shannon's punctured lung."

Arms folded, Jamal stood to the side, smiling grimly. "The Jewish," he said again, as though this were comment enough.

David ignored him. "Is anyone protecting you?" he asked the supervisor.

"In theory, the Israeli authorities. But the settlers stole Shannon's video camera, and she doesn't know the men who attacked her." The woman bit her lip. "A few weeks before, the IDF told the villagers that our reports to the media were causing 'trouble,' and that they would protect the villagers themselves. The village leaders answered that the only reason the Israelis cared at all was because we're here."

"So we're not leaving," the Canadian said.

David watched Shannon's troubled face. "We can't," she affirmed. "Last year the settlers poisoned sheep, this year they stole wheat. Just before he started beating me, I asked one of the settlers — this teenage kid, actually — what right he had to take wheat from the villagers' land. 'I have a deed,' he told me. 'It's called the Bible.' Without us here, I swear to you they wouldn't stop at killing sheep."

Their supervisor pointed up a nearby hill. "Would you like to see the village?" she asked. "One of the leaders speaks English. He can tell you more."

At the top of the hill, David entered another place and time, where shepherds and subsistence farmers lived much as they had for centuries. Women in head scarves and long dresses walked alongside lean, sun-wizened men, carrying sacks of grain into a dark cave they used for storage. The cave dated to the Romans, David discovered; inside, the remnant of a column still remained.

The village leader, a teacher named Khader Mafouz, greeted David courteously. Leading David to his home, Mafouz pointed to the ruins of a mosque. "About twenty years ago, we built this. As soon as we were done, the IDF destroyed it." He stopped, hands on hips, surveying the concrete buildings that formed the village. "The Israelis tend not to give us building permits. So the mosque was an 'illegal' building, as is our school. Whatever we build, they can destroy at any time. And now there is this wall."

David saw a truck filled with IDF soldiers climb a road to the settlement, churning dust. "The wall," Mafouz went on, "will encompass much of the land around us. We say it is ours; they say, 'Prove it.' But we have no deeds. So now we are going back to cemeteries, trying to show that we have lived in this place for centuries."

A quiet despair in his voice hinted that this mission held scant hope. "Once our people lived in caves," he told David. "Sometimes I'm afraid we'll be living in caves again. But we don't want our children to be run off by these settlers, or cut off from their land. It is a great dilemma — to commit violence against them is too big a risk. Instead, with the help of our Christian friends, we persist."

They entered his home, a concrete structure with timeworn carpets scattered across the floor of the main room. David sat on a carpet; beside him, Mafouz squatted, maintaining his balance without apparent effort. As they sipped tea, Mafouz swatted the flies that buzzed around them. "I am sorry," he said. "They are from the settlers." He pointed at the settlement, visible through the open space that was his door. "They bring their garbage down the hill, and make of our village their garbage pit."

David turned to him, thinking to ask a question. But Mafouz kept gazing at the hill. "If I could," he said softly, "I would drive them from this place. And if they refused to go, I would kill them all. When someone comes as they have, to take your land and way of life, to resist them is not terrorism. It's survival."

Driving to Hebron, Jamal and David passed a squalid refugee camp bounded by a twenty-foot wire fence, followed by an Arab village over which an IDF watchtower loomed, as Jamal related Hebron's long and contentious history. Once home to the prophet Abraham and his family, followed by the site from which King David had ruled, Hebron was occupied, in succession, by Romans, Crusaders, and Arabs led by Emperor Saladin. The Ibrahimi Mosque, Saladin's doing, was the fourth most holy site in Islam. That this place was sacred to both Jews and Muslims helped explain why its previous eighty years had been so bloody. In 1929, sixty-seven Jews were slaughtered by Palestinians — but only, Jamal hastened to add, because Jews had slaughtered Palestinians in Jerusalem the day before. "What the Jewish never speak of," Jamal said, "is that other Palestinians saved several hundred more Jews from death."

And what Jamal was failing to speak of, David knew, was that a second massacre several years later had claimed almost all the Jews remaining. "In 1967," Jamal went on, "when the occupation began, hard-line Jewish settlers established a presence in the old city of Hebron, harassing their Arab neighbors under the protection of the IDF.

"Now four hundred and fifty of them, protected by three thousand soldiers of the IDF, rule the heart of a city of one hundred and fifty thousand Palestinians." Jamal smiled bitterly. "It is a special arrangement for these settlers, called the Hebron Protocol. You will soon see how they honor it."

To David, Hebron felt like the heart of the Middle East. Now and then he saw distinct touches of modernity — a chic perfume and cosmetics store, an outlet for CDs, videogames, and DVDs. But the streets leading to the Old Town were choked with peddlers and pedestrians, bringing the cars and yellow taxis to a near standstill. Virtually all of the women David saw were covered, some so completely that only their eyes were visible, suggesting a culture light-years from Ramallah and any life Hana wanted for Munira. Thinking of Hana, then Saeb, David wondered if he was entering the past or the future. It did not surprise him to learn from Jamal that Hebron, traditionally conservative in its observance of Islam, was now a stronghold of Hamas. "The settlers," Jamal said flatly, "have reaped what they have sown."

David's only certainty was that there was little place for Nisreen Awad or Fatima Khalil if Hebron proved to be the future of the West Bank. As a matter of education and outlook, they had more in common with secular Israeli women like Anat Ben-Aron — or Sausan Arif, a mixture of two worlds — than with women whose faces David could not see.

Their only choice, in the end, would be exile; one reason for this would be that the absolutists of two religions had kept women on both sides from making common cause.

"Show me where the settlers live," David said.

At the edge of the Old Town, the two men left the car behind. Eight hundred or so years ago, when Saladin built the Ibrahimi Mosque, the cramped, narrow alleys and cobblestoned streets had sealed the character of this place and, with it, the way of life David felt closing in around him. With difficulty, David and Jamal snaked through a crowded market crammed with peddlers' stands and shops purveying fruits, breads, camel meat, sandwiches, clothes, shoes, and toys — it was so besieged by shoppers that, at times, David found it impossible to move. Now and again young men pushed wooden wheelbarrows filled with more fruit or goods, replenishing the stands. Though fascinated by Hebron's market, David found it odd to be Jewish in this place, so distinctly Arab in its character, and odder still to think that Jews had chosen to settle here.

The marketplace ended with a narrow shopping alley — a souk not unlike that of the Old City of Jerusalem, crammed with merchants and shoppers. But after several blocks, the vibrant character of the souk abruptly ended.

Its architecture was the same. But the shoppers thinned to a trickle; only a few peddlers sat against the wall, as dispirited as their customers. "This is the place of the settlers," Jamal said.

The sense of emptiness was eerie. "Where are they?" David asked.

"It is the Sabbath — they are inside with their prayer books and assault weapons." Stopping,

Jamal pointed at the second-story windows. "That is where they live."

Gazing up, David's view was obstructed by wire mesh on top of which lay heaps of garbage, the remnants of rotting food mixed with cans and bottles and, in one case, diapers. In a crack between the garbage David saw the flag of Israel. With quiet anger, Jamal said, "They come here because, before Islam, the place of the Ibrahimi Mosque was a sacred site for Jews. Now the spiritual heirs of those ancient Jews have returned to dump their waste on Arab peddlers. The wire is the peddlers' sole defense."

The souk went on like this for perhaps a quarter mile, its quiet the only evidence of the settlers save for the insults scrawled on the walls in Hebrew, the stench of garbage, and the steel-and-wire barriers that blocked the side alleys, erected by the settlers. Ahead, David saw a rotating steel gate, operated by remote control from a guardhouse manned by soldiers of the IDF. As he approached, two soldiers aimed their weapons at him, their faces drained of expression. "These are the settlers' guardians," Jamal remarked sardonically. "Of course, they claim to be protecting us. From the settlers or, perhaps, the next Baruch Goldstein.

"You've no doubt heard his name. Goldstein was a doctor in the Israeli army, and a friend to Barak Lev. In 1994, on a Friday much like this, he entered the Ibrahimi Mosque with an assault rifle and began firing at Palestinians as they knelt close together in prayer, their backs affording him a perfect target. He killed twenty-nine Arabs and wounded another hundred before the survivors beat him to death."

As Jamal spoke, he and David passed through the

first gate and headed for the second, also manned by soldiers. "The Israeli government," Jamal went on, "denounced Goldstein's act and compensated his victims. But Yigal Amir claims that shooting Yitzhak Rabin first entered his mind when he saw the hundreds of mourners at Goldstein's funeral. And it was Lev, I'm told, who helped write the epitaph on Goldstein's tombstone." As they reached the second gate, Jamal recited the epitaph from memory: "Here lies the saint Dr. Baruch Goldstein. Blessed be the memory of this righteous and holy man. May the Lord avenge his blood, who devoted his soul to the Jews, Jewish religion, and Jewish land. His hands are innocent, and his heart is pure. He was killed as a martyr of God." With disdain, Jamal added his own coda, "Jews, too, have their martyrs. And now Barak Lev has joined them."

David was thinking not of Lev but of Amos Ben-Aron. "After this massacre," he asked, "what happened in Hebron?"

"A lot of rioting. Twenty-six Palestinians died, and two Israelis. After that, more settlers came to honor Goldstein's memory, protected by more soldiers."

At the third checkpoint, David looked into the stony face of the nearest Israeli soldier. Impatiently, the soldier waved David forward. "I will leave you here," Jamal said abruptly. "Go to the mosque, and wait."

Alone, David reached the final checkpoint, at the foot of the steps leading to the mosque. With a casual insolence, a young soldier demanded his identification. Examining David's passport, he asked curtly, "Why are you here?"

David looked at the soldier coolly. "To see the

mosque. Is there a problem with that?"

The soldier stared at him. Then he handed back the passport, waving David through. He was not in the best frame of mind, David reflected as he climbed the steps. But then not every holy site had soldiers and a metal detector at its threshold, the residue of a massacre. And his last visit to such a site, the Assyrian Chapel, had led to two men's deaths; the images of their murders shadowed David's thoughts as he reached the entrance.

Passing through the metal detector, David crossed the threshold of the mosque. This was the site of the cave where Abraham was entombed, along with his wife Sarah and the sons who personified the contending claims of Muslims and Jews, Ishmael and Isaac. Though the mosque had been built over the cave, for centuries thereafter Arabs and Jews had worshipped here in relative peace. Then came the influx of European Jews inspired by Zionism; then their slaughter by Muslims and expulsion from the city; then the advent of settlers and soldiers; then Goldstein — all moved by their supposed reverence for this place and the God it proposed to honor.

No one approached him. Warily, he wandered through a spare and airy room in which female worshippers knelt on rugs, passing the tomb of Abraham, surrounded by a glass encasement. He entered a vast and ornate sanctuary, its walls richly filigreed, in which a blind man prayed, the unseeing whites of his eyes open and unmoving. At the back was a wall, the legacy of Goldstein, separating the Jewish section of the mosque from that reserved for Arabs; at the front an ornate altar, inspired by Saladin, was scarred with bullet holes, like the walls of the Old City of Jerusalem.

He paused there, alone, and then another man appeared beside him. "The work of Goldstein," the man said, pointing to the holes. "For some, they symbolize not loss but lost opportunity. If his aim had been better, more of us would have died."

David turned to him. He was young, mustached, and handsome, his tension betrayed by the gaze that darted past David's head. "I do not have long here," he said softly. "You are seeking men not easily found. Are you willing to risk dying with them, should the Israelis choose the moment of your visit to end their lives with bombs or bullets?"

David hesitated. "If that's my only choice."

"Then go to the refugee camp at Jenin and ask to see Ala Jabril. He will start by showing you how our people live." The man placed a hand on David's shoulder. "Good luck. And allow yourself some time and patience. These men move from hour to hour, and are best seen at night."

22

That evening, David checked into the Paradise Hotel in Bethlehem.

He went about his normal routine, unpacking, showering, and planning the next day, his thoughts moving between Hana — how she was, what they might say to each other with so much changed — and the risks he was running on her behalf. In itself, Jenin was a dangerous place, and meeting with any leader of Al Aqsa far more dangerous yet. The Israeli practice of targeted killings could not be as surgical as the term implied: bullets fired into a safe house reserved for a clandestine meeting would not choose one participant over another; bombs or rockets would not discriminate at all. But he had little choice — to meet with Al Aqsa was to assume Al Aqsa's risks.

Distractedly, David scanned the *International Herald Tribune.* Near Jenin, two members of Al Aqsa had been incinerated in their car by an Israeli rocket; at the Qalandiya checkpoint, soldiers had arrested a member of Islamic Jihad, also from Jenin, assigned to carry out a suicide bombing on the terrace of the King David Hotel, where, two weeks ago, David had dined with Zev Ernheit and Moshe Howard. Pensive, David went to meet Abu Jamal, the man who would take him to Jenin and who aroused in him such misgivings, even as David wondered at the wisdom of betting his life, and perhaps Hana's, on this man's undisclosed arrangements.

The restaurant, Shepherd's Palace, was inside a Bedouin-style tent, half as long as a football field and as wide, its flooring composed of one ornate carpet after another. Jamal and David sat at one of many tables surrounded by couches, where friends and families lounged while sharing spicy dishes of lamb, beef, chicken, and vegetables, along with plates of bread and hummus. The atmosphere was noisy and convivial: friends hugging and laughing and arguing; children running from table to table. Though the diners, whether Arab or Christian, were mostly secular, at scattered tables the women were covered or even veiled. After the seething caldron that was Hebron's Old Town, David experienced the easy mix of disparate people as a relief. But he could not forget that he was the only Jew in sight.

"A lot of families," David observed to Jamal.

"It is our way of life," Jamal responded. "Divorce is very hard here, and our families are extended ones — cousins, nephews and nieces, aunts and uncles, all with their network of friends. So it is with my family." Scanning the restaurant, Jamal added, "I must know thirty people here, and Bethlehem is not my home. The way our cities are isolated by Jewish checkpoints is a hardship for us all. But not as hard as for Hana Arif, I would think, whose own extended family is trapped at Shatila."

The remark reminded David of how different Hana's culture was from his, how little the small family circle of David and his reserved and private parents had resembled what he saw around him. Watching three generations at a nearby table — grandparents, parents, aunts, uncles, and boys and girls of various ages — David understood, as he had not at Harvard, how culture had divided him from Hana and made his vision of the future so alien to hers.

All this he thought, but could not say. Of this much he was certain: his affair with Hana, and her feelings for him now, would be repugnant to Abu Jamal. "Your families," David observed, "seem to work better than your government. At least by the evidence of the Palestine Authority."

Jamal shrugged, a tacit concession. "That is why there is Hamas. Of course, occupation is our great tradition — the West Bank has been governed in succession by the Romans, the Byzantines, the Saracens, the Turks, the British, the Jordanians, and now the Jewish. As for the Palestinian Authority, I acknowledge it's been corrupt."

"It's been a basket case," David said flatly. "No wonder so many Israelis felt they couldn't trust it, long before the rise of Hamas and death of Ben-Aron. Your security forces are weak and divided, and suicide bombers keep blowing up families like the ones sitting all around us. The only difference is that they're Jews."

"Perhaps we are better at resistance than at governance," Jamal countered. "Our experience at self-rule is so much less. To build a civil society takes time — first we must be free of the Jewish and their oppression."

It was impossible, David thought, for Jamal not to know that he was Jewish, or that their debate was also a surrogate for emotions far more personal. "And so Israel is your excuse?" he asked.

"Are Palestinians so powerless that they have no role at all?"

Jamal's mouth compressed. "You speak of power. America has power. Your Jews have power. Because of the Jewish media and money, the government of the United States created a state for Jews, and continues to arm and finance the racist State of Israel to ensure its survival and its occupation of our land. So do not speak to me of power. Power is the property of the Jewish."

" 'The Jewish,' " David respounded softly, "can be such clever people. But not so clever as to keep from being slaughtered through the ages, whether at Auschwitz or Hebron. If that had happened to Arabs, this restaurant would be close to empty. Perhaps you'd like to guess which of these families would still exist."

"Ah," Jamal interjected with an air of condescension, "at last the Jewish trump card, the Holocaust. A great exaggeration."

David felt his self-control slipping away. "You mean six million dead Jews. How many do you think it is — a pitiful two million? A paltry one million?" He kept his voice soft. "Until recently, I was engaged to a woman whose father survived Auschwitz. I've seen the scars on his chest, and felt the scars on his soul. Someone put them there —"

"The Germans," Jamal cut in. "So why not give the Jewish their own state in Bavaria?"

David managed a brief smile. "Overpopulated, I suppose. And Jews and Germans enjoy a certain history."

"So do we with the Jewish. Until they stole our land, we lived in relative peace. They complain that the Germans wanted to make their country *judenrein,* a nation with no Jews." Jamal jabbed David's arm with a forefinger. “The Jewish brought Nazism to Palestine — their own state, free of Arabs. What hypocrisy. Now it’s the settlements, illegal under international law. But for the Jewish, law does not matter.” Rubbing his fingertips together, he finished, “For the Jewish, it is always about this — money. That is where your power comes from.”

David leaned forward, until his face and Jamal’s were inches apart. “I’ve seen the occupation,” he said, his voice low and hard. “I’d go insane. Obviously, you already have. Nonetheless, I wish you your own country, as ‘the Jewish’ have, in the hope that you don’t devour each other.” Deliberately, David put his index finger on Jamal’s wrist, an echo of Jamal’s own intrusive gesture. “This much I know. If you had the absolute power, you would kill every Jew in Israel or, at least, arrange a large enough ‘return’ to ensure that they lost their Jewish state. And then one of them might decide to blow up your family, just as the Irgun killed so many British. The next Baruch Goldstein would be your own creation.” Quietly, David finished: “Where does it end, I wonder. Listening to you, I think the answer is ‘Never.’ ”

Jamal sat back so that David’s finger no longer rested on his wrist. In a brittle tone, he said, “What do you want from me?”

Briefly, David wondered if his own anger with Jamal was a cover for fear, the subconscious hope that by offending this man in the name of self-respect, he could avoid placing himself at risk. “To go to Jenin,” he said, “as we’ve discussed.”

“And there is also something else you want, yes?”

With this, David knew, the minuet of indirection was coming to an end. “Yes. The medical records for Saeb Khalid."

"Not just that." Jamal's slight smile had a taunting air. "You want them without anyone knowing, and you are not scrupulous how. Just as long as they fall into your lap in some mysterious way."

"Exactly," David answered. "And sooner rather than later. It is, as you say, a matter of Jewish money. For that, this 'Jewish' will gladly pay."

23

Shortly after dawn, Jamal and David headed for Jenin in silence.

The trip was marked by the trappings of occupation: an extension of the security barrier that hemmed in Bethlehem itself; a checkpoint where undocumented Palestinian workers, barred from seeking work in Israel, waited in dispirited huddles; an Arab village, destroyed in 1948, now occupied by settlers; a web of settlements and watchtowers on both sides of the road; a settler walking with a rifle and a Doberman. The landscape became greener, lusher — a valley terraced with olive trees, its bottomland rich with cucumbers, corn, chickpeas, wheat, and grapes. It reminded David of the Galilee, once home to Hana's family, still home to Sausan Arif. But these sights resulted from a detour; because of the current state of siege, the IDF had blocked the main road to Nablus and, therefore, to Jenin.

The delay afforded David ample time to contemplate his dilemma: forced to rely on a man he did not like or trust, he was seeking out a meeting that held dangers he could not predict. Long ago he had lost all illusion of control.

Three hours later they reached the outskirts of Jenin.

The city itself was graffiti-scarred and denuded of trees, its dingy streets and shuttered buildings bespeaking a dire poverty. At the entrance to the refugee camp was an enormous multicolored metal horse, salvaged from the scraps of cars and trucks and ambulances blown up by Israeli rockets. The street beyond was cramped, shabby, and choked with run-down cars, through which a dark-haired child on a battered bike forged a twisted path past two-story concrete buildings caked with dirt and covered with painted slogans. This was not a "camp," David thought — it was a third-world slum in a war zone, haven to Al Aqsa and Hamas, a cousin to the place where Hana was born and Saeb's parents murdered.

They met Ala Jibril outside the community center, a two-story stucco building tucked in a narrow alley. He was a large, almost shambling man with hooded eyes, a somber mien that rarely changed, and a voice that was soft but deep. He helped run the center, Jibril explained vaguely, and it was his task to show David the life his people were forced to live. He said this as though David were a tourist or a social worker, not a Jewish-American lawyer seeking out Al Aqsa.

While Jamal waited outside, David and Jibril entered a rehabilitation clinic for children. Following Jibril down a hallway, David saw posters of Donald Duck and Winnie the Pooh juxtaposed with photos of fighters brandishing weapons. At its end was an open room where three children were stretched out on tables, their atrophied legs exposed, being treated by therapists for the effects of cerebral palsy.

"We have seven such therapists," Jibril told David. "But it is not enough."

"Why so much cerebral palsy?"

Jibril gazed at the children. "The occupation. Children born at checkpoints, or to mothers discouraged from giving birth at hospitals, may not receive sufficient oxygen; mothers take medications without proper medical advice; childhood fevers go untreated. This is the result."

From one of the tables, a bright-eyed child smiled up at David. But her flaccid legs showed little sign of life.

At the school, a brisk, dark-haired teacher named Reem led David to a playroom with carpets depicting hippos, rhinos, and elephants; desks where children drew; and shelves filled with games and toys. It would have seemed quite normal, save that the small boy drawing at a desk wore a prosthesis where his left leg had once been.

Reem followed David's gaze. "The IDF," she said simply. "The boy's father was Hamas. But war is not so easily confined.

"For us, it is devastating to see children maimed by the land mines and grenades the Israelis left behind. And troubling to watch them using the ruins of a tank to play at combat, or repeatedly drawing rockets, bombs, and soldiers, or fighting among themselves." She pointed to the toy shelves. "You will see we have no guns or swords. Our purpose here is play therapy, our goal to relieve the psychological pressures on children traumatized by violence. Our hope, in the end, is to teach them that violence only breeds more violence."

David thought of Sausan Arif, wrestling with the impulses of children who had come to her school from Jenin. It was strange to think of her now, separated from Jenin by fifteen miles and a wire fence.

Nodding toward the boy at the desk, David said, "Would he mind if I looked at his drawing?"

Reem walked over to the child, speaking quietly. When the boy shrugged, she beckoned David to come. His picture was a happy one — the figures of a mother, father, and child, standing at the edge of an ocean he no doubt had never seen. But then, David remembered, the boy's own father was dead. The boy himself did not look up.

Reem walked with the two men as they left the school. The hallway leading to the street was lined with photographs of children. But these children were dead: a girl of six or seven, lying in a pool of her own blood; another dead girl fallen next to her two dead brothers, her features unrecognizable; a dark-haired boy in a coffin. The photographs were meant to evoke both horror and sympathy. But, in David, they also provoked disquiet: what did a child emerging from a playroom stripped of violent toys learn from this tableau of violence and revenge? The last poster suggested an answer: a young Palestinian man with an assault weapon, a portrait of resistance and resolve. Turning to Reem, David said, "Do your children ask about these posters?"

She could not seem to look at him. "When the Israelis leave us in peace," she murmured, "there will be no posters."

On the way to what Jibril called the Martyrs Cemetery, he pointed out damage from the IDF incursion. Next to a row of houses being rebuilt from rubble was the shell of a bombed-out home. "This is where Zacharias Ibaide lived," Jibril told David and Jamal. "Once he attended a camp with our children and Jewish children, the work of a peace activist from Israel. But when he grew older and still there was no peace, he joined Al Aqsa. In its effort to kill him, the IDF instead killed his mother and father.

"Now our children play in the ruins of his home and find the remnants of missiles fired by F-16s, sent to Israel by your country. Those who are older recall the IDF coming in a hail of missiles, tank fire, and bullets." Staring at the rubble, he said more quietly, "The Israelis claim to have killed only 'terrorists.' In the cemetery lie two retarded men, murdered running through the streets because they did not know any better. For them, the 'terrorists' were the Jews who took their lives."

"Welcome to hell," Jamal told David. "A collaboration of the Jewish and the Americans. Who often are the same."

Near the cemetery, they passed another bombed-out three-story house, hollow from its roof to its foundation. In the empty lot beside it was a bullet-riddled car, its windows shattered, its hood bedecked in flowers. "My cousin's," Jibril explained phlegmatically. "He was Al Aqsa, assassinated by a special unit of the IDF."

Set in the bare red earth beside these ruins, the Martyrs Cemetery had begun with fifty-eight graves, dug after the IDF incursion; now it included many more dead. Entering, the three men stood among concrete rectangles inscribed in Arabic, most surrounded by beds of flowers. "To our left are two brothers," Jibril told David, "assassinated by the IDF. To our right is the man who owned the house you just saw, buried without his head. Beside *his* grave lies my cousin.

"The smaller monuments are for children or infants — you can guess their age from the size of their tombstones." Jibril pointed to a monument at the center of the cemetery. "That is for my uncle, seventy years old when we pulled him from beneath the rubble of his house. Long before that he had ceased to be a threat to anyone. As for the children, death deprived them of the opportunity."

"There are others who should be here," Jamal added bitterly. "Our martyrs who died in Israel. But the Jewish refuse to send them back."

The man's obtuseness frayed David's self-control. "Perhaps," he suggested, "they were hard to distinguish from their victims. Body parts tend to look alike." Turning to Jibril, David said, "In Israel, I met three survivors of the restaurant bombing in Haifa. The IDF claims that *this* was its reprisal."

"Not at all," Jibril answered without irony. "This is what the world fails to understand. The bombing in Haifa was our reprisal against the IDF — which four times previously tried to enter our camp — and for the martyrs who died resisting. Don't believe that we are by nature killers and fighters. If we have become that, the Israelis have made us so."

David thought of Shoshanna Ravit, and Eli and Myra Landau, their unfathomable loss and grief. But for so many who had suffered in this land there was no suffering but theirs. Here people died not just from bombs and bullets but from the death of empathy.

"What do you think of this?" Jibril asked David.

David gazed at the cemetery. "I think there are no words that matter."

Shoulders slumped, Jibril seemed to weigh this ambiguous response. Then he nodded. "Tonight you will be my guest for dinner. Later, if you are fortunate, you will meet someone. He may have the knowledge you are seeking."

That night, after dinner at a modest restaurant on the outskirts of Jenin, Jibril led David and Jamal to the back room of another restaurant and then, after receiving a call on his cell phone, into the darkness of the camp.

Jibril took them once again to the Martyrs Cemetery. Silent, they waited in the cool night air. A quarter moon barely illuminated the tombstones, creating dim outlines of varied shapes and sizes. David felt a chill on the back of his neck; warily, Jibril glanced upward, as though expecting gunships from the IDF. No one spoke.

As David glanced around him, the shadow of a tombstone seemed to change shape, growing taller in an eerie apparition. Then a second shadow arose, and David heard soft footfalls as moonlight transformed the shadows into two men in dark clothes and stocking masks, each with an assault weapon cradled in one arm.

The first gunman spoke softly to Jibril in Arabic. Following the two gunmen, Jibril waved David and Jamal forward, passing the bullet-riddled car and walking single file down an alley so dark and narrow that David could barely see. Abruptly, a door opened, expelling a pale light; with hurried gestures, a third gunman in a stocking mask waved them inside. "All of us must stay," Jibril whispered to David. "They wish to have no mistakes."

The third gunman led them through a hallway to a bare center room without windows, illuminated by a single lamp — someone's dwelling, David thought, with a carpet, couch, and chairs. The third man sat in the chair, flanked by the two armed men from the cemetery. With a curt gesture, he indicated that David, Jibril, and Jamal should sit facing him on the couch. Resting the M-16 on his lap, he slowly peeled off the stocking mask, revealing himself as a man of roughly thirty with a two-day stubble, and bright black eyes beneath which David saw the bruises of sleep deprivation.

"I am Muhammad Nasir," the man said, "commander of the Al Aqsa Martyrs Brigade in Jenin." As though feeling David's tension, Nasir gave him an ironic smile. "Forgive this drama. But the IDF means to kill me — I stay nowhere for more than an hour, perhaps less. And your record in Israel is not encouraging."

He spoke with a weary resignation, too tired for bravado or even animation, except that his eyes kept darting to the doorway. For the second time in his life, David felt that he was watching a man condemned to die; like David's father, there was death in this man's face, the difference being that Nasir was awake to see it coming. "Jenin was once my home," he told David, "such as it was. After the bombing in Haifa, the Israelis came with their gunships, tanks, and soldiers, destroying houses, even pissing in our women's cooking pans. Now they blame us for Ben-Aron."

A slender man brought tea in cups — the owner of the house, David guessed, nervously fulfilling his role of host before he disappeared again. After accepting the tea with a courteous nod, Nasir turned to David and said bluntly, "You wish to know the truth about Hana Arif. For better or worse."

David nodded, teacup cradled in both palms. With the trace of a smile, Nasir said, "To her lasting shame, she is not ours."

David felt the release of pressure, the beating of

his own pulse. "You're certain."

"Of course. I have asked our people in Birzeit. As far as they can tell, her entire contribution to the liberation of Palestine is angry words. A cheap commodity." His voice took on an edge. "It is hard to know which is more insulting — that we would be fool enough to assassinate Ben-Aron, or to use this woman to do it. But Ibrahim Jefar was ours, and this is enough for the IDF. And so we are dying for a lie."

"Tell me about Jefar."

Nasir lit a cigarette, puffing with a distracted, fretful quality. "A boy," he said, with a combination of compassion and disdain, "who thought to avenge his sister by becoming a martyr.

"Some in Al Aqsa see a value in this. I do not. When Jefar came to me with the hope of revenge, I tried to convince him that it was better to preserve his life, to see whether Marwan Faras, our leader, could bring us peace and our own state." Nasir took another hasty puff, his next words emerging on a cloud of smoke. "If Faras failed, I told him, better to kill the soldiers of the IDF than to butcher children at a shopping mall."

"How did he react?"

"We have seen how he reacted — by killing the wrong Jew at the wrong time. Perhaps blowing up Ben-Aron was too historic to be missed, even though the cost is the destruction of Al Aqsa." Nasir's voice was quiet but steely. "Whoever used Jefar meant for that to happen. This makes sense no other way."

"Jefar seems to believe he was acting for Al Aqsa."

"Jefar should be dead," Nasir countered with sudden vehemence. "Why did he live? Here is my answer: to tell his make-believe story."

"What if he's telling the truth as he knows it?"

"Then Hassan was lying to him. And Hassan is *not* Al Aqsa."

One of the masked bodyguards, David saw, glanced nervously at his watch, then spoke to Nasir in Arabic. In a clipped voice, Nasir told David, "My friend thinks we should not pass much more time here —"

"Who did Hassan belong to?" David inquired urgently.

"Ask yourself, Who wins by this? Hamas. Al Aqsa supports Fatah and Marwan Faras; our ranks include Christians and the secular; many of us prefer killing Zionists here instead of in Israel. We will even live with a Jewish state if they end the occupation, dismantle their settlements, release our prisoners, and compensate us for expelling our fathers from their land. For us, that is enough." Nasir's eyes burned brighter. "Not for Hamas. They want nothing less than to destroy Israel and establish an Islamic Palestine from the Mediterranean to the Jordan River. Between Hamas and Al Aqsa is a blood feud. First, Hamas wants us eradicated; then they wish to take over the Palestinian Authority; then they will go after the Jews."

David saw a young boy standing on the threshold, gazing at Nasir with shy but obvious admiration. His father came, nervously shooing him away. "If all that's true," David said, "then Hassan must be Hamas —"

A loud pop interrupted him — a gunshot, or the backfire of a car. Without speaking, one of Nasir's bodyguards headed for the door as Nasir touched the trigger of his weapon. "Hassan is from the Aida camp," Nasir said hurriedly. "His brother was

Hamas; his dead sister-in-law — the martyr from Jenin who died in Haifa — was Hamas. Our people in Aida think that Hassan himself was Hamas. His mother lives there still; if she wishes, perhaps she can tell you." Nasir jabbed his half-smoked cigarette into a ceramic plate, grinding it to a nub. "This much I know. Whoever selected Jefar, whether Hassan or someone else, picked a dupe they could deceive, and who might well crack under pressure. That is part of their design."

Beside David, Jibril stirred, betraying his own apprehension. "One more question," David said. "Is Saeb Khalid with Hamas?"

Nasir looked up from the burning stub. "Some at Birzeit believe so," he answered. "But they say he is a deep one, difficult to read. He knows many people. Is a meal with someone a conspiracy, or a discussion among friends? It is hard to know. Perhaps, like his wife, he is nothing but words. Perhaps not."

Returning, the bodyguard spoke to Nasir in a rush of Arabic. "It is time for me to go," Nasir told David. "But there is something I must say to you.

"I have been resisting the occupation since I was fifteen and served four years in prison for throwing a Molotov cocktail at an Israeli tank. Now I know no other life. But I am tired, and we are no closer to a homeland. Many more of us will die; many more Israelis will die like the ones at Haifa, killed to punish Jews for ignoring the misery their soldiers have unleashed." His eyes held David's. "If you find the truth, you must tell it to the world. That's why I risked meeting with you. In a world that hears neither our suffering nor Al Aqsa's denials about Ben-Aron, you may be our only hope. After us there will only be Hamas."

"If peace comes instead, what will you do?"

The question seemed to take Nasir by surprise, causing him to hesitate. "I would have a family," he answered, "and watch my children grow up in the normal way." But this assertion lacked conviction; he could not seem to envision a life, David sensed, beyond the one he led. Or, perhaps, beyond the next few hours or days.

He stood abruptly. "An unusual evening for you," he said to David. "A story to tell *your* children as you tuck them into bed."

Nasir turned to Jibril, embracing him, then placed a hand on Jamal's shoulder, speaking with apparent warmth in Arabic. Jamal stood straighter, his slight body almost vibrating with pleasure at a hero's blessing. A thousand Gandhis, David thought, could not have made this man so proud.

In seconds, Muhammad Nasir had vanished into the night. Feeling the sweat on his forehead, David listened for gunshots. For the moment there was only silence.

24

After Jenin, the Aida camp held few surprises for David. Arriving with Nabil Ashawi, he surveyed the dispiriting environment: a building with a crudely painted mural that depicted the Palestinian flight from Israel; the IDF watchtower at the entrance to the camp; two young boys playing soldier in a dusty street. Thirty yards away, the security wall itself, looming above the camp, was being extended to seal off its inhabitants from the hilltop settlement of Gilo.

"During the intifada," Ashawi said, "Aida was under curfew for thirty-seven days. Twelve died here — some were members of the resistance, some merely bystanders." He pointed to the second story of a school. "Two of them, a student and a teacher, died from Israeli shelling. After that, they filled in the windows with cement.

"Seven thousand people live here, with no health services at all. Unemployment among the men is eighty-five percent. No wonder Hamas is thriving. Iyad Hassan was inevitable — only the name of his victim distinguishes him from others."

David gazed at the security wall. "Did the Israelis question his mother?"

"They tried. But she is in mourning, and despises them. Her daughter says she told them nothing. At least you represent a Palestinian, and are coming with me as your translator. We can do no worse; maybe we'll do better." He gave David a sideways glance. "How did you get on with Jamal, by the way?"

"We bonded."

To David's surprise, Ashawi grinned. "He has a certain point of view. But I suspect he may be helping you, even as we speak."

Three Palestinian boys, perhaps ten or eleven, careened around the wall and into an alley. In a cloud of dust, a jeep filled with armed men in uniforms and sunglasses pulled up in hot pursuit. They jumped out, weapons drawn; their leader, a burly man with a brutish face, barked at David and Ashawi in Hebrew. Curtly, Ashawi answered, shaking his head. The men rushed down the alley, looking from side to side.

"Russians." Ashawi spat the word. "Private security guards for the settlement. No doubt those young criminals threw rocks at them.

"Israel proclaims that no one in this camp can return to where their grandparents lived. But they welcomed one million of the stupidest louts Russia ever puked up, simply because they claim to be Jews. So here they are at Aida. Let's hope to God they don't kill anyone but themselves. At least until we get out of here."

They went looking for Hassan's mother.

She welcomed them in the common room of her shabby dwelling, a small woman shrouded in black that concealed all but her face and hands. Her wrinkled eyelids partially covered eyes that gazed past David toward some indeterminate place that might not exist on earth. Also dressed in black, a thin young woman with a sentinel's protective bearing, Iyad Hassan's sister, sat beside their mother. To David, the windowless room suggested the vistas life afforded them.

David and Ashawi sat on the carpet, facing the two women. Softly, Ashawi offered what sounded like their condolences, as David tried to imagine Iyad Hassan, the obdurate killer of Ben-Aron, growing up in such a place. Though his mother's face was without expression, tears surfaced in her eyes.

At the end of Ashawi's speech, the woman murmured a few words. "She thanks us," Ashawi said without turning from her. "She mourns for her son."

"Does she know why he did this? The example of his sister-in-law?"

Ashawi paused, formulating the question, then spoke a few quiet words. Briefly answering, the woman shook her head. "No," Ashawi translated, "Iyad chose his destiny long before."

"What does she mean?"

Ashawi spoke again. The woman looked down, then began to answer, at first slowly, and then with greater heat. David saw the daughter's hand clasp her mother's wrist. "His sister doesn't like what she's saying," Ashawi explained. "But the mother claims Iyad's journey started at eleven, when he went to an Islamic school. One day she came there to pick him up. A sign on the wall read, 'Israel has nuclear bombs, we have human bombs.' Then she heard Iyad reciting, 'I will make my body a bomb that will blast the flesh of Zionists, the sons of pigs and monkeys.' His zeal scared her."

Abruptly, the woman spoke again, her voice tinged with sorrow. "Iyad began praying constantly," Ashawi interpreted. "He was always at the mosque, late at night and early in the morning. She tried believing that this was normal. But then he became quieter, barely speaking to her. Only later did she learn that he had been watching films of martyrs who had died killing Jews."

"Who were his friends?" David asked.

As Ashawi posed the question, Iyad's sister's eyes narrowed. The mother hesitated, then answered. "They were from the mosque," Ashawi related. "Also Iyad's soccer club. In 1998, the soccer club even went to Jordan, then Iran."

David was instantly alert. "A fundamentalist school, a mosque for martyrs, a 'soccer club' that visits Iran. What does that sound like to you?"

"I know." Ashawi tried to keep his tone matter-of-fact, to avoid unsettling the women. "But if I ask the question, the daughter may cut us off."

"Let's try a diversion, then. Ask the daughter how she feels about Iyad's death."

Turning to the younger woman, Ashawi spoke. She tensed, then emitted a few sharp words. "She is proud of Iyad," Ashawi said. "He was a man of faith, not like the sons of whores who are Al Aqsa, propping up the corruption of Fatah."

David watched the daughter's face. "Can't quite stifle her biases, can she."

"It seems not," Ashawi said. "But I'm surprised that there aren't minders here, to keep either of them from talking to us. God knows what kind of men may be showing up."

"Then we'd better get to the point. Ask who led Iyad to become a martyr."

Ashawi spoke briefly. The daughter shook her head, refusing to answer. With sudden bitterness, the mother said, "Hamas."

Her daughter turned to her, gripping her wrist more tightly. Defiantly, the woman repeated, "Hamas," then continued in an accusatory tone. "It was Hamas," Ashawi translated swiftly. "Hamas ran the school, the mosque, and the club —"

Hassan's sister interrupted, speaking hurriedly. "They know nothing about Iyad's time at Birzeit," Ashawi paraphrased, "or who was involved with him in killing Ben-Aron."

"Ask the mother if there's anything else she can tell us about her son."

Listening, the mother gazed at the floor. Then, breaking from her daughter's grasp, she went to another room and returned with a spiral notebook, which she placed in Ashawi's hands. "Iyad's diary," Ashawi told David. "She hid it from the Jews."

As Ashawi read, Iyad's sister addressed him in a vehement tone. "We can't keep it," Ashawi told David. "Anyhow, this reads like eyewash — a lot of religious fervor without any names or details. Except, at the end, there's a telephone number."

"Memorize it, if you can."

Ashawi stared at the page. Then, speaking softly, he gave the notebook back to Hassan's mother. She answered in a few tired words.

"We are welcome, she says. But it is time for us to go."

Nodding to both women, David followed Ashawi out the door, leaving behind a mother's grief, a sister's anger, and their rupture over a martyr's death.

In the jeep, Ashawi wrote down the telephone number for David, then tapped it out on his cell phone, listening intently when someone answered. Tersely, he said, "That was Birzeit. The School of International Relations."

"Saeb Khalid's school," David answered.

■ ■ ■ ■ ■

At the hotel, David scribbled notes, sorting through what he had learned: the relationship between Hillel Markis and Barak Lev; the unhappiness of Hana's marriage; Saeb's access to her computer at home and in her office; Muhammad Nasir's denial that Al Aqsa was connected to Hana or the plot against Ben-Aron; Saeb's extended trips to Jordan; Iyad Hassan's connection to Hamas and, perhaps, to Iran; Hassan's class with Saeb. In themselves, the facts were tantalizing. But the information to weave these disparate threads into a design, if there was one, remained beyond his grasp.

Mentally exhausted, David began packing. He was traveling to Lebanon, as he had promised Hana, to see her mother and father. Though curious, he did not expect the trip to be rewarding. But he would not be sorry to leave the West Bank, and not only because of the sense, alien before now, that as a Jew he might be the subject of undifferentiated loathing. He also felt the soul-wearing pressure of occupation, of becoming an accidental member of a population whose sole interest to the occupier was that one might be a suicide bomber. The Promised Land, which many on each side believed was promised them alone, might be consumed not merely by hatred and violence but also by the most banal of human faults — a failure to imagine the life of another. The only common denominator of occupation was that it degraded everyone.

What he needed most, David told himself, was sleep.

Stripping off his shirt, he noticed an envelope

that had been slipped beneath his door. Hopeful, he ripped it open. Inside, awkwardly translated into English, were the files of Saeb's doctor in Ramallah.

As he read, David exhaled. If the files were legitimate, Saeb suffered from a serious cardiac arrhythmia, which might, under certain circumstances, become a fatal heart attack. There was a referral to a specialist in Amman; records of examinations to confirm Saeb's visits. By all appearances, Saeb Khalid was a very sick man.

But not so sick, David noted, that his medical examinations in Jordan took more than a day. Then he found a second curiosity: Saeb had asked his doctor in Ramallah to send certain specimens, not otherwise described, to the only lab the doctor knew sophisticated enough to perform the tests required. A lab in Tel Aviv.

Calling Zev Ernheit, David arranged to meet him in Jerusalem. But first David had a promise to keep, in Lebanon.

25

On a hot Tuesday morning in Beirut, David honored his promise to Hana.

By now the refugee camp of Shatila seemed familiar. Even the rubble, preserved for a quarter century, evoked the ruins in Jenin, except that it was more extensive, haunted by more ghosts and the horror of systematic slaughter. He could not help but think of Saeb Khalid, a boy of fourteen, forced to watch the rape of his sister and the murder of his family.

At the community center, David got directions to the home of Hana's parents, located in the section named for the village they had fled as children. It was a concrete rectangle among several others like it that lined both sides of a narrow alley that smelled of sewage. With considerable trepidation, David knocked on the wooden door.

When a white-haired woman answered, David knew at once who she was. Slight and wiry, she had clear brown eyes that contrasted with a face lined with age and care and the harsh simplicity of her life. Maha Arif was like a glimpse of Hana's future had she not left this place and culture — although, David knew, Hana had never wholly parted from it. Maha looked up at him suspiciously while David absorbed the fact that this small Arab woman was Hana's mother.

"I'm David Wolfe," he told her. "Hana's lawyer. She asked me to come see you."

The name Hana drew a sharp, querying look, expressive of fear and hope. David realized that he had overlooked the gulf between Hana and her parents. "I'm American," David said. "Do you know someone who speaks English?"

The woman held up her hand, then disappeared inside the house, leaving the door ajar. David heard voices speaking Arabic, and then a stocky middle-aged man with a dark mustache came to greet him. "I'm Basim," he said, "Hana's uncle."

Once again, David identified himself. "Please," Basim said, opening the door wide.

David followed him into a small sitting room, not unlike that of Iyad Hassan's mother, but with a window to the alley, affording a swath of natural light, which fell on a stunted olive tree in a pot. An older, gray-haired man with a gaunt face gazed at him warily through thick glasses that suggested extreme myopia. "This is Yousif," Basim explained, "Hana's father."

Basim spoke a few phrases to Yousif and Maha while Yousif blinked at David as though he had just dropped in from the moon. David had a painful, incongruous vision of Hana's parents and his own — the Jewish psychiatrist and the professor of English — trying to converse as Hana translated. Eyes fixed on David, Maha Arif spoke in a burst of Arabic.

"She needs to know," Basim translated, "if her daughter will be safe."

Facing Hana's mother, David answered, "For now, she is safe. I promise I'll do my best to free her."

Basim translated this, and then Maha's next interrogation: "Did you go with Hana to the school for lawyers?"

In the life Hana shared with them, David realized, he had never existed. "Yes," he said simply. "I knew her at Harvard."

A film of tears came to the woman's eyes. "Since Hana went to America," Basim explained, "her mother has rarely seen her. Of Hana's child, she has only pictures."

Belatedly, Maha requested that he sit with them on the worn pillows scattered across the carpet, then offered him tea. Abruptly, Yousif Arif spoke in a tone both mournful and harsh. "He prays that his daughter can find justice in America," Basim translated. "There is no justice here."

Since Hana's father was a child, David reflected, this place was all he knew. David thought of Maha's sister — Hana's aunt — buried beneath the ruins of her home. "In America," David said, "there is justice."

"Even for Palestinians?" Basim asked sharply.

"Yes."

When Basim translated, Yousif spoke more vehemently. "Here," Basim said for him, "we are prisoners. There is no work for us, and we are not allowed to be citizens. This poor olive tree you see is all that remains of our real home. And now they may take our daughter's life."

Maha spoke again, her voice urgent. "Are you a good lawyer?" Basim translated.

"Yes," David answered simply, "I'm a very good lawyer."

As Basim translated, the first trace of relief appeared in Maha's eyes. Now she spoke in a quieter voice. "That is what her daughter deserves," Basim explained. "Hana has a fine husband, from a good family. But Saeb is not a lawyer. Now only a lawyer can save her."

Hearing these words, David recalled Hana quoting her mother's warning: *Please do not love anyone in America.* And wished that he could say to her: *If Hana had been free to love me, now she would be safe.* Instead, he merely nodded.

"And how is my granddaughter?" Maha asked through Basim. "Is she afraid?"

David hesitated. "She has her father," he answered. "And like her mother, she is strong, and very smart."

When this was translated, Yousif gave his wife a look, then responded through Basim. "Does she also talk back like her mother?"

"Yes. Hana told me that Munira is your revenge on her."

Yousif made a clicking sound with his tongue, and then his brief smile vanished. This time his voice was guttural. "She did not kill the Jew," Basim said for him.

David was not sure whether this was a statement or a question. "No," he answered. "She did not kill Amos Ben-Aron."

"Then it is all Zionist lies," Basim persisted.

"It is *someone's* lies," David answered. "I mean to find out whose."

When Basim translated this, Hana's mother looked at him dubiously. What went unspoken, he supposed, was her belief in the depth of the Zionists' perfidy, their bottomless disdain for the rights of Palestinians. Choosing to divert the conversation, David passed on Sausan's greetings. "Her grandfather," Yousif answered through Basim, "was my father's brother. But he remained. He was married to a Jew."

This was his only response. Belatedly, Maha said, "We do not know Sausan. He remembers her father only as a child."

Yousif spoke again. "It is unnatural," Basim translated, his expression conveying the sadness of Yousif's words. "Families are cut off from their land, and divided from one another. Yousif sells Maha's sweets from a handcart in the street, a man without his daughter or granddaughter. It is not a life; it is the shadow of a life."

Sitting beside him, Maha touched her husband's sleeve, speaking to him quietly. Basim hesitated, then told David, "They get by, she says."

Yousif did not seem to hear this. "When we fled," he said through Basim, "my parents left our teacups on the table, to show that we would come back to refill them. They did not imagine dying in this place."

As though to affirm her husband's memory, Maha spoke to Basim. "There were olive trees," Basim told David. "Lemon trees, as well. She says she can still smell them."

"Can you?" David asked.

Basim's smile was almost bitter. "Some days I believe I can. But I was born here. My memories are of the Phalange."

At the word "Phalange" Maha's expression darkened. Standing stiffly, Yousif reached into the drawer of a battered table. With swollen fingers, he removed a wrinkled paper, turned sepia by the passage of time, and held it out to David.

To David's surprise, it was written in English. "It is a registered land document," Basim explained, "issued by the British government of Palestine. It proves Yousif's title to his father's home."

David thought of its ruined walls, its shattered

ceramic plates. Yet, to Hana's parents, the house remained as it was when they were children, a place to which they might return, in a time that still existed. This was as impossible for David to imagine as Hana and Munira existing in such a place. Yet Hana wore her grandfather's key, and Munira recited his memories.

Carefully watching David's face, Maha spoke to him. "When you saw Sausan," Basim asked for her, "did she take you to our village?"

David looked into the eyes of Hana's mother. "No," he answered softly. "But it sounds beautiful. I hope you will see it again someday."

As Basim repeated his words in Arabic, Maha's eyes filmed: she seemed to know that she would never return, and that David knew this, too. Reaching out, she touched his wrist, the lightness of her hand a ghost of Hana's. "I just want to hold my daughter," she said. "Please save her from our enemies."

26

On his last night before flying home, David met with Zev Ernheit at Katie's Restaurant in Jerusalem.

Katie's was small and intimate, with candlelit tables and a voluble proprietress, a Moroccan Jew who bantered with Ernheit before bringing their wine. "And so," Ernheit asked of David's time in the West Bank, "what were your impressions?"

"That the occupation's a disaster," David answered bluntly. "For everyone."

Ernheit spread his hands. "What choice do we have? Hours ago, at a checkpoint in Ramallah, we caught a twenty-year-old from Hamas carrying a bomb and an IDF uniform. That's the balance sheet for today — thousands of Arabs inconvenienced, unknown Jewish lives saved from another terrorist. Would you prefer that they died?"

"What I'd prefer is that sane people on both sides find a way out." David put down his wineglass. "What in hell are settlers doing in Hebron?"

"Hebron is at the heart of Jewish heritage," Ernheit countered. "Jews have a right to worship there."

"At what cost?" David asked with real exasperation. "Deploying the IDF to keep a pack of Jewish fanatics free to dump their garbage on Muslim peddlers?

"You know what amazes me, Zev? It's that so many Jews and Palestinians don't give a damn about one another's stories. Too many Palestinians don't grasp why three thousand years of death and persecution make Jews want their own homeland, or how suicide bombings alienate Jews and extend the occupation. Too many Jews refuse to acknowledge their role in the misery of Palestinians since 1948, or that the daily toll of occupation helps fuel more hatred and violence. So both become clichés: Jews are victims and oppressors; Palestinians are victims and terrorists. And the cycle of death rolls on. The two things the extremists have in common is how much they hated Amos Ben-Aron, and a gift for keeping old hatreds fresh." David stopped, then continued more evenly: "In three short weeks I've seen all kinds of suffering, from the families in Haifa to the misery of Hana's parents. But they live in different worlds. Hana has become a bit player in a tragedy that shows no sign of ending. Not for her, or her daughter, or anyone who lives here."

Ernheit studied him coolly. "In the end, David, which side would you choose?"

David's own gaze did not waiver. "I'm a Jew. I feel more at home here; on the West Bank, I heard enough anti-Semitism to remind me of how often Jews have had no choice but to fight or run. So if I had to choose, I'd have no choice.

"The problem is that every day more choices are foreclosed for those who live here. Each day that Jews fight to build more settlements or Palestinians stoke the fantasy of return, they guarantee that someone else will die. And the hatred embedded in the DNA of this region continues to metastasize.

"With Ben-Aron dead, I don't see peace anytime soon. It may not come at all. If it doesn't, you have no choice but to end the occupation anyway, withdrawing behind your security wall into a Fortress Israel that incorporates settlements that never should have existed. On the other side, instead of a diverse and resilient people, you'll see a lot of educated Palestinians fleeing to Los Angeles, leaving a wounded, angry populace on a festering scrap of land, listening to the voices of fundamentalism and the rhetoric of return. You'll get Hamas for good. You've already got Iran."

Ernheit gave him a bleak smile. "And then?"

"This won't be a place for children."

Ernheit clasped his hands in front of him. "There's too much you still don't understand. What you want, most Israelis want. Perhaps most Palestinians. But our extremist settlers do not define our future by murdering Palestinians. It's fanatics like Hamas and Al Aqsa that bring the settlers what power they have, and make the occupation a grim necessity. It was Palestinians who murdered Ben-Aron."

"Not by themselves," David answered quietly.

Ernheit glanced around them at the other patrons, their faces illuminated by candlelight. "Will we ever know?" he inquired. "Perhaps you regret your tactics here."

David drew a breath. "I regret the deaths. And their consequences."

"To your client?"

"To whoever would profit from the truth." Saying this, David felt his own fatigue, compounded by his sense that access to the truth was controlled by others. "There's a sense to all this, if only we could find the key — and that could make a difference far beyond this trial. Someone killed Lev and Markis to prevent us from getting to the heart of this."

"And you learned nothing about those murders during your time on the West Bank."

"If I did, I don't know it yet. But I'm confident Al Aqsa wasn't responsible. And I don't believe that Al Aqsa carried out Ben-Aron's murder in America." David sipped his wine. "What makes sense is that Jefar was a dupe; that Hassan was Hamas; and that whoever directed this meant for Ben-Aron's plan for peace to end, for Israel to wipe out Al Aqsa, and for Hamas to come to power."

"Why would Lev or Markis want Hamas in power?"

David paused. "In the logic of extremists," he answered, "both sides can give each other what they want — perpetual conflict between Israelis and Palestinians. Their only quarrel is about who wins."

Cradling his face in his hand, Ernheit regarded David across the table. "Aside from a lasting peace, what do you want from our government?"

"I'd like to know what Saeb Khalid was doing in Amman. Most of his time wasn't spent with doctors. Perhaps the Mossad knows."

"Perhaps. Whether they'll tell you is something different altogether." Briefly, Ernheit looked perplexed. "But there's also this lab in Tel Aviv where Saeb Khalid sent these unspecified samples you told me about."

"Yes. Maybe it's nothing; maybe it's just about his heart. But the notes in his doctor's files were intriguingly obscure."

Ernheit nodded. "To me, as well. The lab in question is not a medical facility. It's forensic, staffed by criminologists and often used in murder cases."

David's hand froze, his wineglass an inch beneath his lips. "For what?"

"What you'd expect — fingerprints, crime scene evaluations, DNA, studies of gunshot wounds. Certainly not cardiology."

David considered this. "Perhaps your government would be willing to get the records of whatever Khalid had this lab evaluate."

"On what pretext? Just how would you relate this to Arif's defense?"

"I don't know yet. But like Saeb's leisurely stays in Amman, it's odd — if only because there's no obvious explanation."

Ernheit smiled faintly. "I'll see what I can do," he answered. "At least we won't be killing anyone."

Which was the spirit in which, two hours later, they ended their last meal together. After shaking his hand, Ernheit touched David's shoulder. "In spite of everything," he told David, "I wish you luck. At least you're leaving Israel alive."

Back at the King David, David sat at the bar, sipping a Calvados as he sifted through his thoughts, a television droning in the background. The trip had changed him, he was certain, but he had not had time to understand how. He wished that he could talk with Carole, Harold, and, most of all, with Hana. In his heart and mind, the trip had changed her, as well.

What would it be like, he wondered, the next time he sat across from her? Within the next two days he would know . . .

A familiar name broke through David's thoughts: Muhammad Nasir.

As David glanced up, startled, a police photograph of Nasir appeared on CNN. "The IDF," a newscaster said, "announced that it had killed Nasir, a prominent leader of Al Aqsa, in a rocket attack on a home in the refugee camp of Jenin. Through the Internet, Al Aqsa claimed that two innocent civilians, a man and his eight-year-old son, also died in the attack, and vowed reprisals for what they called 'Israeli barbarism.' "

If peace comes, David had asked Nasir, *what will you do?* A foolish question.

It never ends, David thought now. A deep sadness filled him. Finishing his brandy, he drifted to the patio of the King David, gazing for a final time at the outline of the Old City of Jerusalem. Then he went to his room and packed.

■ ■ ■ ■

Part IV
The Secret

■ ■ ■ ■

1

The same white room, bare walls, laminated table. The same guard peering at a lawyer and his client through the bulletproof window webbed with wire. But to David, this meeting felt very different. What he had learned about Hana since he had last seen her made him want to reach out for her, even as he told himself that he had to fight this impulse.

For a moment, Hana gazed at him, as though to verify his reality. "I missed you, David."

Suspended between tenderness and suspicion, David understood that his only refuge was to be professional, as dispassionate and cool as he could manage. "I'm sorry I was gone so long," he answered, "The trip was a bit more complex than I'd imagined."

Hana tilted her head in inquiry. "What did you learn?"

"Many things, from many people. Including Nisreen."

Briefly, Hana glanced down, then looked at him with renewed directness. "Yes?"

"Tell me about your marriage, Hana." Though David's voice was quiet, it was not a request. "This time, leave nothing out. That includes Munira."

Hana watched his eyes. "Where should I start?"

"With where it stood between you and Saeb

when the three of you came here."

Hana's shrug resembled a twitch. "It wasn't good."

"Meaning?"

"There was a distance. It had grown over time."

"My own parents could have said as much. Define 'distance.' "

"We no longer made love." Hana's voice became raw. "Is that what you want?"

"It's a start. When did *that* part end?"

Hana sat back, arms folded. "This is perverse."

"Humor me," David said softly. "I have my reasons for asking."

Arms still folded, Hana looked down. "Six months or so before we came here."

"Was there a reason?"

"So 'distance' is not enough? He stopped wanting me. I didn't complain."

"Why not?"

"Because I'd stopped wanting him long before." Her eyes flashed. "Is this your revenge on me, David? Does extracting these answers make you feel better?"

David waited until the anger in her face melted into confusion. "No," he answered. "It makes me sad that *this* is what we're left with. But I can't get swept up in my own feelings. Or yours, whatever they may be.

"Saeb had access to your office, your cell phone, your computer, and the paper you used. Your husband could have framed you; the man I knew at Harvard never would have. So if he did, something must have happened between you, so visceral that it converted love to hate." His voice became softer. "I need to understand that, Hana. However hard this is for both of us."

Her eyes closed. "The truth is simple, and undramatic. I no longer loved him."

"Why?"

"Many reasons. Some of them we might have surmounted. But more and more Saeb became a man I never wanted to be with — a man who scorned women." Hana looked at him again, and her tone became more level, as though she were trying to recalibrate their conversation. "Over time, our relationship became a battle over Munira. Almost as though she were a surrogate for me."

"When you say surrogate . . ."

Hana gazed at the table, as though striving to put her instincts into words. "When Saeb's family was murdered, I became the one person he looked to, for all the things that most of us seem to need. So it was when we were married. For Saeb, to believe that he was not who I wanted — or wanted to make love with — would cause a death inside him."

And did Saeb believe that? David wondered. Instead, he asked, "What does that have to do with Munira?"

"It was never put into words. Perhaps Saeb blamed my idea of what a woman should be for how I was with him. Perhaps insisting that Munira grow up to be different from me was a form of reprisal. Certainly the more radical he became, the more extreme he became in his religion, the more he tried controlling every aspect of her life.

"Within the last year, after Munira turned twelve, it grew worse." Hana's voice filled with muted anger. "Suddenly there were the *musts* I've told you about — she must cover, she must study the Koran, she must pray five times a day. And *must nots* — no makeup, no blue jeans, no mixing with boys. Over all this we had bitter fights. But the worst was over how Munira would marry."

"In what way?"

"Saeb wanted to arrange it." As she spoke, her fingers became tightly interlaced. "It's enough that I honored our traditions. Let it end with me. But even now, when Munira visits me, I feel her fading away." Her voice trembled. "For my own sake, I do not much care what happens to me. For Munira, I *must* get out of here. Whether I'm dead or a prisoner for life, Saeb will control her future. I could not bear for that to happen to her."

She was close to tears now, and the depth of her feelings jarred David's self-control. Quietly, he asked, "Is that why you told Nisreen that a man you knew in law school would have been a better father for Munira?"

With this, Hana could not look at him. "Such a foolish thing to say. But I wanted a different life for Munira." Her voice caught, becoming lower, softer. "Saeb and I never spoke of you. Perhaps I didn't have to."

There were many things he could have said. Instead, David asked, "What do you know about Saeb sending something to a forensics lab in Tel Aviv?"

Hana looked bewildered. "When did this happen?"

"About nine months ago. I've been wondering if he sent them paper from your printer, to ensure that at least one sheet had your fingerprints, but not his."

Hana bent her head. "These are terrible things to think about, David."

"We have to. Do you know why his visits to Jordan lasted several days?"

"Medical tests, I thought."

"Not true."

Hana looked up again. "You know this?"

"Yes. He also had access to your cell phone, right?"

"Of course. But at midnight?" Hana shook her head. "Whoever the handler was, he or she used another cell phone."

"Which suggests that you were framed." David leaned forward, his face a few feet from her. "This is complicated, Hana. I think at least two Israelis were involved. But both of them were killed before I could find out more."

Hana's lips parted. "Please, you must tell me everything that happened."

He explained as much as he could. "Muhammad Nasir," he concluded, "swore that Al Aqsa didn't plan the assassination, and that you were never a member. Now he's dead, too."

Hana absorbed this, her eyes filling with mute despair. At length, she asked, "Did you go to see my parents?"

"Yes. They're very worried — no doubt they saw me as some sort of martian, and it's hard for them to grasp what's happening except as the work of Zionists. But otherwise, they're well. At least as well as they can be in a place like that."

Slowly, Hana nodded. "At Harvard, there were things in my life that I found hard to convey to you. Shatila was one; my family another. Now you understand much more than I ever thought you would." She paused, then asked, "You also saw Sausan?"

"Yes. I liked her. Very much, in fact."

"I thought you might. And she showed you our village?"

"What was left of it," David amended gently. "Ruins amid the olive trees. All that's left of your grandfather's house is its foundation and fragments of ceramic dishes. The village as you imagine it exists only in your parents' memory."

Hana's face turned somber. "Did you tell them this?"

"I couldn't. Not after your father showed me his grandfather's deed."

"Then you did a kindness." Suddenly, tears welled in Hana's eyes. "I wish you could hold me, David. Just for a moment."

But he could not. Nor, as much as he wished it, could he yet be sure she was innocent. Faced with a trial, he could not lose himself.

"I'm sorry, Hana. It's become my job to free you, not love you."

He clung to that as he left, Hana watching him through the glass.

2

David's next step was to hire a jury consultant, a sleek former marketing executive named Ellen Castle, whose blond mane, chic style, and surgical enhancements belied her keen grasp of trial dynamics.

They sat in his office a half hour after sunrise, drinking coffee while David outlined his tactical dilemma. "I've got two potential defenses," he summarized. "The one I'd like to put on is a conspiracy involving Israelis, Hamas, and maybe Hana's husband. But the judge won't let me go there unless I come up with proof.

"The defense Marnie Sharpe hopes to stick me with is confined to arguing reasonable doubt: that Jefar may be lying or deluded; that the evidence against Hana was planted by someone else. The problem is that I can't offer an alternative explanation that points to Hana's innocence — or at least suggests a conspiracy so complicated that a juror inclined to skepticism might feel sufficient doubt."

Castle flicked back her hair. "If you have to try the case Sharpe's way, can you get the judge to bar Jefar's testimony on hearsay grounds? It seems like his whole story depends on what Hassan told him."

"*If* Judge Taylor keeps him off the stand," David

responded, "then Sharpe's case collapses. I've got a shot at that. But it would take real guts on Taylor's part to kick Hana loose without a trial."

Castle pondered this. "If Jefar testifies," she said at length, "and all Taylor lets you do is harp on reasonable doubt, your client's in deep trouble."

Though David had always known this, to hear it from an expert was depressing. "So far," he told her, "the Israeli government won't tell me what they know. My potential witnesses to a conspiracy are dead. Except in the case of Muhammad Nasir, I can't even claim to know who killed them. All I've got is questions without answers."

Castle frowned at the quandary this presented, then asked, "I assume you want me to pull together a mock jury for you to present your case to, then focus-group their reactions. The question is, Which case?"

David finished his coffee, examining the grounds at the bottom of his cup. "The lousy one," he answered. "Reasonable doubt. That's the only defense I'm sure I've got."

When David listened to his voice mail, there was a message from Zev Ernheit.

It was evening in Israel; David reached Zev in a noisy café in Tel Aviv, sharing dinner with his wife and several friends. "God knows who else is listening to this conversation," Zev said over the chatter. "But let me find a quiet place on the sidewalk, so at least it won't include the people in this room."

David waited, listening as the background noise became the sounds of urban traffic. "So far," Ernheit said in a softer voice, "I've found out nothing about this crime lab. But I do have something on Khalid's visits to Jordan, though I can't tell you where I got it. How does a side trip to Iran strike you?"

David stood. "When?"

"About three years ago. A Palestinian can't fly from Israel to Tehran, but flying there from Amman is no problem."

"How long was he there?"

"Two days. We don't know what he did, or who he saw. But when he came back to the West Bank through Israeli border control, all his passport showed was a stamp from the Jordanians for reentry into Jordan. His entry into Iran wasn't recorded."

David considered several questions, then asked the obvious one. "Then how did they know Saeb was even there?"

"He told them. Flipping through his passport, one of our people noticed he'd entered Jordan twice, three days apart, with no record that he'd ever left. Khalid readily admitted that he'd been to Iran and said he had no idea why they'd failed to stamp his passport. He hadn't noticed it, he claimed, but who knows the ways of bureaucrats."

"Did he explain why he was there?"

"A whim. As a resident of the West Bank, he was prevented by the Israelis from traveling to Iran; as a professor of international relations, he wanted to see Iran for himself. I'm told he was pretty cheeky about it."

"Did your intelligence people buy that?"

Ernheit laughed briefly. "Not entirely. But they could hardly call the Iranian secret intelligence service. So all they could do was keep an eye on Khalid.

"To what end, I don't know. Except that there's no evidence of further trips to Iran. Of course, we don't have the manpower to constantly watch every person who hates us, or hangs out with people who do."

"On the later trips, do we know what he did in Amman besides see a doctor?"

"My anonymous friends may," Ernheit said, "but they're not saying. Whatever he did, no one arrested him for it. Our government even let him travel to America."

David pondered this. "I assume the Iranians are active in Amman."

"Of course," Ernheit answered. "As they are in many places."

"Thanks, Zev. Go back and enjoy dinner."

That afternoon, David and Bryce Martel walked on Baker Beach. It was unseasonably warm, even for October, and families and couples strolled along the sand or waded into the chill, lapping surf in shorts or rolled-up jeans. Ahead, a young couple tossed a Frisbee for a retriever, who snatched it from the waves, shaking the water out of his fur as his owners meandered toward the Golden Gate Bridge, its span bright orange in the distance.

"Would the Iranians assassinate Ben-Aron?" Bryce asked rhetorically. "You know about their operation against Israelis in Argentina. But few people know that, several years ago, we uncovered evidence that the Iranian secret intelligence service was plotting to kill the director of our NSA."

"That takes a lot of nerve."

"Our man had *hit* a nerve by strongly opposing Iran's nuclear program. For a while the director worked in an underground location with Secret Service protection." Martel stopped to peel off his windbreaker, stretching his arms as he did. "I'm getting stiffer every day — rigor mortis by degrees. Old age seems to be God's way of preparing us to die."

David shoved his hands in his pockets. "If the Iranians wanted to kill our NSA director, why not Ben-Aron?"

In silence, they followed the cavorting dog along the water's edge. "Iran has a history of playing geopolitics," Martel responded after a time. "Iran's main connection has been to Islamic Jihad. But it has links to Hamas. And, like Hamas, Iran despises Faras for talking peace with Ben-Aron.

"Given that, I can see the Iranians recruiting someone like Iyad Hassan even without the blessing of Hamas. And if the stakes involve developing nuclear weapons before anyone can stop them, they might take some pretty tall chances."

"Suppose Iran lobbed a nuclear weapon on Tel Aviv."

Martel emitted a harsh laugh. "You've seen Israel. It's a strip of land on the Mediterranean. One or two warheads would kill hundreds of thousands of Israelis in an instant — crushed in buildings, torn to shreds by flying glass, or just incinerated. Others would die in firestorms, or from radiation poisoning. Medical facilities would be overwhelmed, water supplies unusable, housing and shelter unavailable, transportation and communication decimated.

"Normal human society would cease; the balance of nature would unravel. Unburied corpses and untreated sewage would breed typhus, malaria, and encephalitis. Truly, the living would envy the dead. The fact that Israel might also have destroyed Iran would help them not at all." Martel shook his head. "That's why the Iranians desire such a weapon. All they need is to have it, and no one will dare fool with them. They can dominate the Middle East, working to eliminate Israel by less dramatic means. Including an Islamic Palestine."

David stopped walking, struck by how this narrative made Hana seem so small, a bit player in a ruthless game of nuclear politics. "And Saeb?" he asked.

"Might be an Iranian asset. Do you have any proof of that?"

"None. But let's assume further that Saeb recruited Hassan, and Hassan recruited Jefar. Could the Iranians come up with the explosives, uniforms, motorcycles, passports, et cetera they needed in America?"

"Yes. Aside from the ringers in their mission at the U.N., they've got a network of Iranian émigrés. Iran could even work through Hamas sleepers in places like Berkeley. The Iranians would give their individual assets a piece of the project, none grasping what the pieces added up to. Even Hassan may not have known who he was working for. No one would, except a select few people in Tehran."

"That leaves Israel. What's Iran's capacity there?"

"It has agents in place, mostly Arabs. But your thesis requires a connection between Iranian agents and Lev or Markis." Martel resumed walking. "I have no problem believing that they shared a common objective: the death of Ben-Aron. But it's like Mozart meeting Genghis Khan for drinks. They both might like scotch, but who brings them together?

"We've been talking for an hour, David. No doubt everything I've told you is enthralling. But from where you sit, spinning theories is a waste of time. You're a lawyer, and lawyers face the impediment of proof."

Three days later, a group of strangers drove home Martel's last point.

In David's conference room, twelve people recruited by Ellen Castle — mainly students and retirees — gathered to consider the case for, and against, Hana Arif. They listened to opening statements delivered by David's associate, Angel Garriques, in the role of Marnie Sharpe, and David on behalf of Hana; parsed the expected testimony, particularly that of Ibrahim Jefar; and then heard Angel's summation and David's pointed response, dissecting the evidence against Hana. Two hours later, they returned a guilty verdict.

Afterward, David interviewed the jurors. The young woman selected as the foreman, a graduate student whose sympathies David had expected, crystallized the reasons. "You're implying that someone framed your client," she told David. "But you can't give us a person, or even a reason why. If *you* don't know, who does?"

3

Past midnight, nine hours before the last, crucial hearing in the chambers of Judge Caitlin Taylor, David was still awake.

He was as prepared as he could be. But this did not give him peace, or sleep. At length he put on a sweater and windbreaker and, leaving his flat, walked to the marina and then on the path along the bay, wisps of fog dampening his face, the only sound the deep susurrus of the surf. To experience such dark and solitude was strange, but no more so than to absorb how much his life had changed. When he chose a place to sit, it was on the bench where, months ago, Harold Shorr had implored him not to defend the woman who, thirteen years ago, he had loved more than anyone, before or since.

The memory of his conversation with Harold tugged at him; even more acutely than before, David realized that he had also loved Carole's father and, in the deep way that one loves comfort and generosity and the sense of being at home, Carole herself. And now at last he understood why their identity as Jews was so defining. Israel and Palestine had taught him that.

Since his return, he had been immersed in the task before him: preparing for a trial that, if he did not succeed in stopping it, could cost Hana Arif her life. But he could no longer deny the profound effect of his trip to the Middle East, and all that he had perceived. And so for an hour, observing the streaks of moonlight on an obsidian bay, he allowed his soul to catch up with his body.

The stakes were not just Hana's life or freedom but the future of a girl whose life Hana seemed to value more than her own. The unreasoning love of a parent for a child had revealed itself to David; the young woman he had loved at Harvard had not yet known how this would feel. This emotion, too, David had begun to comprehend — partly because of Saeb, but also because he had come to care about Munira. All this made Hana's trial different from any other.

And what of Hana herself? Were she with him now, he might have said much more to her. That he wondered whether she felt for him because the sadness in her life created a space for memories. That were it not for the trial, he might give her the affection she seemed to need, and find out how that felt to both of them. That when he looked at her, he still felt the deep sense, however irrational, that there were feelings between them that transcended where they came from. But now he had seen where she had come from, and he could say none of those things. And as her lawyer, he could not so much as touch her. He could not yet be certain that she was innocent of killing Amos Ben-Aron.

David felt a surge of anger. He hated the choices he had forced himself to make: to be so entwined with Carole and her father and then have their relations so brutally severed was far more painful, he understood, than the loss of his career in politics.

Since law school, he had been determined to protect himself from hurt. But he had hurt himself nonetheless; he had made himself into a more reflective, more deliberate version of his father. Hana had not done this to him — he had done it to himself.

But whom could he say this to?

No one. Right now, it was enough for him to know it. And he realized that just as losing Hana all those years ago had made him an emotional somnambulist, her return had reawakened him, forcing him to define himself by instinct, not calculation. He was not yet certain he was grateful — it was unsettling to be so aware of his flaws, his confusion, the raw edges of his emotions, even the simple truth that life cannot be managed. He had not felt so frightened yet so alive since the night Hana had walked out of his life.

Now she was back, to whatever end. And what that end might be was partly in his hands, and partly in the hands of unknown people who did not blink at murder.

At this thought, he looked about him, abruptly wary. But there was no sound except the bay and the rustling of the pine boughs above the bench. He could not fear for himself; the next few weeks would require all the resources he had.

Standing, he walked back to his apartment, his gaze focused on the path before him, his thoughts refocused on the hearing. In the last hours before dawn, he slept.

For this hearing, as before, David and Sharpe had filed their motions under seal, keeping them from anyone outside Judge Taylor's chambers. David's papers included a narrative of events in Israel and on the West Bank: the connection between Lev and Markis; their deaths and that of Muhammad Nasir; his meetings with Nasir and the mother of Iyad Hassan. They also contained hearsay, potential leads, evocative but inconclusive facts, and theories and suspicions that David could not prove — Hassan's possible connections to Hamas and Saeb Khalid; Saeb's mysterious trip to Iran; Saeb's access to Hana's cell phone, computer, and printer. As glue, he emphasized the Israeli government's continuing refusal to reveal the fruits of its own inquiry. All of which seemed to perplex Judge Taylor without persuading her of what she should do.

When she said as much, David answered simply, "Dismiss the case."

Her eyes reduced to slits, Marnie Sharpe controlled her tension by scribbling notes. From the end of the conference table, Taylor spoke with uncharacteristic heat, a sign of her own nerves. "Based on what *facts,* Mr. Wolfe? I can't dismiss this prosecution on your web of surmise, however disturbing or even shocking some of it may be."

David was prepared for this. "*That's* the precise basis for my motion to dismiss," he replied. "Ms. Arif should not be punished for my inability to go beyond 'surmise.' Ms. Sharpe now concedes the likelihood that Ben-Aron was murdered as the result of a breach in his own security. But how that breach occurred may only be known to the Israelis themselves. And someone — we don't yet know who — killed the men who most likely were involved —"

"One by a suicide bomber," Taylor interrupted, "the other by a sniper. How can I make the prosecution be responsible for *that?*"

"It's not. But the prosecution *is* responsible for

securing from the Israelis information relevant to Ms. Arif's defense, or face dismissal of the case."

"In other words," Taylor shot back, "Israel must tell you what it knows about this breach in security — or else. Even if your inquiry provoked the murders you now cite as a reason for dismissal."

"This court dispatched me to Israel," David answered firmly, "with instructions to go beyond waiting for its government to help me. I had no choice but to do that. I didn't kill these men, Your Honor. Someone else did. Their identity and motives are material to the case against Ms. Arif."

Judge Taylor sat back, gazing at David while she searched for a response. Sharpe's glance moved from one to the other. "Where does that leave your surmise about Hassan?" Taylor inquired more evenly. "Or Dr. Khalid? Am I supposed to require Ms. Sharpe to secure the cooperation of Hamas, Al Aqsa, and the Iranians? And if they fail to confess to whatever they're supposed to know, do I just send Ms. Arif on her merry way? Just how far does your argument go?"

"As far as the Israelis, at the least —"

"And if they *do* cooperate?" Taylor interjected. "Let's suppose the Israelis can confirm that Lev and Markis helped engineer the assassination. In and of itself, their complicity does not absolve Ms. Arif."

David felt his confidence evaporating. "Suppose further," he parried, "that Hillel Markis called the handler for Hassan and Jefar to leak the change of route. The handler either was or wasn't Hana Arif. Which means that Markis knew whether she was innocent."

"Not necessarily — at best, all Markis might know is that someone *else* was also involved." Taylor's tone became insistent. "To repeat, Markis is dead. No one thinks the Israelis killed him. And his murder doesn't disturb the evidence against Hana Arif."

"Such as it is. There are far too many loose ends here."

"Yes. Not least in Tehran."

"For all I know," David said in desperation, "the Israelis know about *that,* as well. Markis aside, how can the United States put Hana Arif on trial without knowing more about what is clearly a very complex conspiracy?"

"How many months would *that* take, Mr. Wolfe? And how can you say with confidence that anything we discovered would help Ms. Arif?" Taylor leaned toward David. "John F. Kennedy has been dead for over forty years. The one thing that seems clear is that Lee Harvey Oswald shot him. Should we now exonerate Oswald because, in some people's minds, the facts surrounding that core truth remain murky?

"You ask a lot, Counsel. But I should allow Ms. Sharpe to have her say."

Sharpe, David thought, was so plainly dressed — black suit, white blouse — that her clothes seemed more like armor; her demeanor was so emotionless that this surely took extraordinary effort. "The court has made my points," she responded. "Ms. Arif's motion to dismiss takes place in a shadowland of conspiracy theories and speculation. This prosecution, by contrast, is grounded in fact.

"*Fact:* According to Jefar, Hassan told him that Arif is the handler.

"*Fact:* Hassan had a piece of paper bearing Arif's fingerprints and cell phone number.

"*Fact:* Hassan's cell phone shows a call to Ms.

Arif's cell phone.

"*Fact:* Ms. Arif can't account for her movements in the critical hour before and during the assassination —"

"What about Dr. Khalid?" Taylor interrupted. "He seems to be Mr. Wolfe's best alternative."

"Based on what?" Though stiff, Sharpe had the composure of an advocate who had scrutinized this problem from every angle. "No one disputes where *Khalid* was during the assassination — with his and Arif's daughter. Despite this, we've questioned Jefar incessantly about Khalid; combed Khalid's phone record and credit cards; mapped out his movements to the hour; inquired through the Israelis into his relationship with Hassan; and looked into why he traveled to America."

"Then what about Arif?" Taylor asked. "According to Mr. Wolfe, the apparent initiative for coming to America wasn't hers."

"*Apparent* initiative," Sharpe emphasized. "Who knows what really happened? Perhaps the suggestion of Ben-Aron's critics that Khalid shadow his appearances in the United States was cover for Ms. Arif, part of Mr. Wolfe's elusive conspiracy —"

"Perhaps," Taylor interjected with the glimmer of a smile, "it was financed by the Iranians . . ."

Sharpe spread her arms in a show of helplessness. "Or murderous right-wing settlers. But why would Khalid frame his own wife? That strikes me as a *very* dangerous thing to do."

This was true, David thought, and it was the obstacle he returned to over and over. "But let's revisit," Sharpe continued, "the core of Mr. Wolfe's motion: that Ms. Arif should go free unless the government of Israel tells him whatever it knows, despite the fact that the murder of two Israelis demonstrated that to do so might threaten its own investigation, and even Israel's national security.

"I concede that I may not know all the government of Israel knows. I concede that they've refused to make their files, or their security personnel, available to the defense. But I'm certain that if the Israelis had information — or even leads — suggesting Khalid's guilt, they would give that to us." The swift glance Sharpe shot David contained a hint of triumph. "A few hours ago," she continued, "the foreign minister of Israel assured our secretary of state that Israel has no such information. We will shortly file a letter from the foreign minister confirming that. I don't know what more we can ask of Israel before commencing a prosecution for the murder of its prime minister."

This last revelation, David knew, might doom his motion. "Israel's inquiry is ongoing," he quickly interjected, "and there are clearly other facts to be discovered. The foreign minister is not omniscient."

"Nor are we," the judge retorted. "As so often in this imperfect world, we are stuck with what the law allows.

"I sympathize with your difficulties, Mr. Wolfe. This isn't a domestic murder, but a transnational case with many complications. Nevertheless, given the evidence against Ms. Arif, complexity alone does not foreclose her prosecution." Taylor modified her tone, a gesture of compassion toward an advocate about to hear a ruling that might doom his case. "If you come up with more concrete information, I'll certainly reconsider. Absent that, this trial will go forward. Motion denied."

A brief silence followed, perhaps the judge's way of allowing David to absorb his disappointment.

"All right," she told him, "your other motion is hardly of lesser moment — your request to bar Mr. Jefar from testifying. Let's hear about that."

"Beyond dispute," David answered crisply, "Jefar's testimony is hearsay. He never met Ms. Arif. He never placed a call to her. He has no idea how Hassan got that slip of paper. By his own account, all he knows is what a dead man told him.

"If Jefar's lying, the jury shouldn't hear from him. If he's telling the truth, he's repeating the story of a terrorist who may have lied about all sorts of things — starting with his supposed allegiance to Al Aqsa, and ending with Hana Arif. How am I supposed to get at *that* — by cross-examining Hassan?

"If this is a frame, it's bulletproof. The court has already turned down my request for more information. If one considers what's left, it's an injustice worthy of Franz Kafka: Ms. Sharpe seeks Ms. Arif's execution without offering a single witness who can even claim to know whether she's innocent or guilty."

For a moment, Judge Taylor let David's words hang in the air, affording herself time for reflection. "What do you say, Ms. Sharpe?"

"That every case of hearsay testimony presents the difficulties cited by Mr. Wolfe. That's why hearsay is generally barred — its credibility cannot be tested on cross-examination. That's also why there are exceptions for testimony like Mr. Jefar's." Sharpe's tone became more confident. "Jefar's statement regarding Ms. Arif admitted his own complicity. That's a classic indication of credibility, falling under the core exception to the hearsay rule: an admission against his own interest, exposing him to punishment."

“What interest?” David asked, his voice incredulous. “Jefar was arrested at the scene with a motorcycle jammed with explosives. A hundred or more witnesses saw him try to blow up Ben-Aron. The only impact of his ‘admission against interest’ is that he *lessened* his punishment by avoiding execution.”

“Jefar’s statement,” Sharpe responded, “need not stand on its own. It’s buttressed by Hassan’s phone call to Ms. Arif’s cell phone, and the slip of paper with her prints on it. Neither of which he conjured up.”

“Could you try the case without him?” Taylor asked.

“I could not,” Sharpe acknowledged. “But that’s not the question. All that’s before the court is whether the rules of evidence allow Jefar to testify. They do.”

Taylor’s air of command had withered; to David, she looked unhappy and trapped. “I must tell you,” she said to Sharpe, “that this is far from the strongest prosecution case I’ve ever seen. That bothers me. I think it should bother you. But with respect to Mr. Wolfe’s motions, the law falls on your side. You’ve got enough for a trial, and that’s what we’re going to have.” Turning to David, she added, “The trial will begin two weeks from now, barring a surprise. You’ve had all the discovery I can give you.”

For the first time in his memory, David could not offer up the formulaic thanks. “Thank you, Your Honor,” Sharpe said for them both.

Listening to David’s account of the hearing, Hana’s lips parted.

“I’m sorry,” he finished.

"I can see that on your face." Hana looked down, absorbing what he had told her. "I, too, tried to hope. But I did not expect you to win. My comfort now is knowing that no lawyer could do better."

David tried to smile. "You haven't seen the other lawyers."

"I don't need to." Hana's face was serious. "Whatever happens in this courtroom, I will feel much better knowing that you're there."

But what about Munira? David wanted to ask. Instead, he absorbed, yet again, the fact that he was forced to defend this woman while constrained by rules most likely to seal her conviction.

"You look like you need a hug," Hana said with a trace of a smile. "But it's become my role to free you, not love you. At least until the trial's over."

Confronted with his own words, David could only smile, even as he wondered what she meant.

4

For days, in a courtroom filled with restive reporters, David and Sharpe picked a jury under Judge Taylor's careful scrutiny.

The lines were clear enough: Sharpe wanted jurors who deferred to the government, believed strongly in the death penalty, and would accept the prosecution's story without probing for its flaws. David searched for those who were skeptical of established authority, concerned with wrongful executions, and willing to consider alternative explanations for the same event. For David, this divide was complicated by the presence on the jury panel of several Jewish retirees whose seeming tendency toward open-mindedness might be countered by outrage at Ben-Aron's murder and a passion for Israel's survival.

Reluctantly, David used his last peremptory challenge to disqualify a retired Jewish executive who spent several hours each week perusing Web sites that praised Israel and excoriated Palestinians; Sharpe used her last such challenge on a disabled former teacher, also Jewish, who had protested the NSA's program of domestic surveillance. One crucial factor favored Sharpe: seeking the death penalty entitled her to disqualify any potential juror who might be reluctant to vote for an execution. It was, to David, a sophisticated form of jury stacking; seven prospective jurors, six of whom David wanted, were disqualified for expressing qualms about the death penalty.

The process took eight days. The twelve finalists included five women — all, to David's satisfaction, mothers and grandmothers. The obvious leaders seemed to be Bob Clair, a former insurance executive, and Ardelle Washington, a fortyish librarian who struck David as the most forceful of the jury's four minority members — two African-Americans, one Hispanic, and a Cambodian who had recently earned his Ph.D. in anthropology. Clair and Washington were, perhaps, most important: David and Ellen Castle, who assisted in assessing the jurors, agreed that one of them would likely become the foreman and, as such, would help shape the deliberations. It was not unlike a lethal variant of computer dating in which the stakes were not a wasted evening but Hana's life.

"You need her daughter here," Castle said to David.

"I know."

"*I* will be there," Saeb said tersely. "That is enough. This trial is no place for Munira."

Since his return, David had barely seen Saeb. Now, sitting across from him in the sterile apartment he shared with Munira, David was struck by the precision of Saeb's movements; the intentness with which he watched David's expressions; the contrast between his eyes, so vividly alive, and a frailty that seemed even more acute. It was true, David thought: this man could die soon. But probably not before his obstinacy — or, worse, his design — helped the government kill his wife.

David struggled to control his tone. "They could *execute* her, Saeb. Her defense is as much emotional as factual — 'Why would a woman who loves her daughter risk abandoning her forever?' But the jury has to *see* their interactions. Those are things I can't put into words."

"Munira is twelve years old," Saeb countered.

"And likely to have a dead mother. She doesn't need you to work so hard."

Saeb tensed, then inquired softly, "What, exactly, do you mean?"

"That this is about Hana, not you. The jurors don't know or care about your paternal prerogatives."

"So for them, Munira must play a Muslim Barbie?" Glancing toward the hallway, Saeb spoke in a tone too quiet to be overheard. "Attending her mother's arraignment was traumatic. Munira is more than a courtroom prop."

"And more than your property. Her mother needs this."

"Her mother is in prison," Saeb's voice became still softer. "You seem to know so much about my wife. Tell me, does Hana wish Munira to choose between a mother and father? Or does she simply not care how this affects her daughter?"

David stared at him. "Over the years," he said at last, "I've thought many things about you. But I never imagined this. Why have you stayed married to a woman you're so willing to let die?"

Saeb's fleeting smile was not a smile at all. "We're very close to the crux of things, aren't we?"

David's nerves felt raw. "Exactly what does *that* mean?"

"In this context, David? That you forget your place. You're only a lawyer. I am Hana's husband,

and so have the rights of a father." Saeb sat back, studying David with the supercilious air of a man humoring a favor seeker. "I will discuss this with my wife. In the meanwhile, the jurors will see me at the trial. Perhaps you can assure them that Hana would never risk separation from her husband by killing Ben-Aron."

This last remark was delivered in a tone so emotionless that David could not decipher it. "I'd at least like to see Munira," he said at length, "if only to find out how she's doing."

"This is not necessary," Saeb said dismissively. "*I* take her to see her mother; I tell Hana how she is. Perhaps were Munira not sleeping . . ."

Saeb finished the sentence with a shrug. David was left to wonder whether Munira was behind the bedroom door from beneath which came a shaft of light. "It's only eight o'clock," he objected. "It's not too late to wake her."

"Perhaps," Saeb replied. "But no doubt you are already tired, and still have much to do. Opening statements begin tomorrow."

David left. He had seldom felt so impotent, or so filled with anger.

The first morning of a murder trial crackles with anticipation. But David had experienced nothing like this — the courtroom crowded with media from around the globe; the building ringed with trailers sent by TV networks from CNN to Al Jazeera; pro-Israeli and pro-Palestinian demonstrators, separated by police, who shouted insults at one another. Settled in the jury box, twelve apprehensive citizens awaited the two women who were missing: the judge and the defendant.

Hana arrived first, escorted by two marshals. She

wore a flowing skirt and rose-colored blouse and looked as composed as she could manage; she glanced at the jury with muted anxiety, then at her husband, positioned behind the defendant's table. Taking the chair beside David, she asked, "No Munira?"

David shook his head. Briefly closing her eyes, Hana murmured, "Perhaps it is for the best."

Glancing toward the jury box, David saw Ardelle Washington look from Hana to Saeb. But Hana could not do what David wished: fabricate a smile for her husband. Restive, David scanned the courtroom and saw Angel Garriques, stationed next to Saeb; Marnie Sharpe, so intent on her own thoughts that she seemed divorced from her surroundings; and Avi Hertz, whom David had not seen since the murder of Barak Lev. And then the courtroom deputy called, "All rise," and Judge Caitlin Taylor assumed the bench, her black robe as crisp as her manner.

"Ms. Sharpe," she inquired. "Are you ready for the United States?"

Sharpe began stiffly. Charm was not her métier; logic was. She seemed rational and meticulous, a person who would wear well with most jurors.

"This is a simple case," she assured them. "We are seeking to do justice for the murder of a world leader who strove to bring peace where there is no peace. But, in the end, this is a case of murder; you must judge the defendant by the same standards as the countless other cases of murder being tried across America. The only difference is her motive: to kill the hope of peace."

Inclining her head toward Hana, Sharpe's tone hardened. "To accomplish this, two men drove motorcycles filled with explosives into the limousine that carried Amos Ben-Aron. Iyad Hassan died instantly; by a grotesque twist of fate, Ibrahim Jefar lived to name the woman who directed this heinous act. The woman you see before you: Hana Arif.

"How does Jefar know that?" Sharpe asked rhetorically. "Because Iyad Hassan told him. According to Hassan, Arif recruited him at Birzeit University, where she taught; directed his lethal activities in San Francisco; and, on that last fatal day, instructed him to carry out this terrible crime." Her voice lowered. "The first suicide bombing in America, a crime so deadly and indiscriminate that it claimed not only the life of its target but an Israeli and an American — both husbands and fathers — charged with his protection."

Beside him, David saw Hana watching as Sharpe looked from juror to juror. "Amos Ben-Aron," she said quietly, "could be identified only by his dental work. But a peculiar feature of a suicide bombing is that the bombers expect the same fate — obliteration. This is what the explosion on Fourth Street did to Iyad Hassan, and what Ibrahim Jefar believed it would do to him."

Several jurors looked bewildered and appalled, as though straining to imagine the state of mind that would embrace such horror. "Jefar's accusation against Ms. Arif," Sharpe told them, "is supported by *other* evidence possessed by Iyad Hassan — a piece of paper with Ms. Arif's fingerprints and cell phone number; a call to that same cell phone recorded on Hassan's cell phone. But that Jefar meant to sacrifice his life is of critical importance. He came here to die, not to lie."

On his notepad, David scribbled "suicide = credibility." Seeing this, Hana drew a breath. "Mr. Wolfe," Sharpe continued, "will try to summon a shadowy conspiracy involving unknown persons. These conspirators may well exist. In fact, it may be true that of all the people in this courtroom, only Hana Arif knows who they are."

This was a clever thrust, David thought, meant to compel him to put Hana on the stand. "Lacking better alternatives," Sharpe added with a touch of scorn, "Mr. Wolfe is forced to argue that these unknown conspirators framed Ms. Arif for unknown reasons. Consider what this theory requires you to believe: that on the instructions of some shadowy mastermind, Iyad Hassan, who expected to die, lied to Ibrahim Jefar, who expected to die. Why? Mr. Wolfe does not know. Who was this mastermind? Mr. Wolfe cannot tell you."

Sharpe, David recognized, was now daring him to name Saeb Khalid as a suspect. But David had no evidence; to accuse Saeb might only condemn his wife, and risk David's own credibility. Glancing at Saeb, David saw that he was as impassive as before. "The reason for this reticence is simple," Sharpe went on. "Mr. Wolfe's supposed mastermind does not exist.

"When all the speculation is done, you must rely on the evidence before you. And the evidence, we will show, can lead to only one conclusion." Pointing across the courtroom at Hana, Sharpe spoke firmly, "Hana Arif plotted the murder of Amos Ben-Aron. Now her work is done, and yours begins: to bring justice to three murdered men, and, by doing so, to redeem the honor of our country."

The opening was simple, David thought, and as effective as he had feared. His touchstone jurors,

Bob Clair and Ardelle Washington, gazed at Sharpe with a somber respect.

Standing, David briefly placed a hand on Hana's shoulder.

He took his time before speaking. In part, this was a tactic, drawing the jury to him. But it also enabled David to rearrange his argument while reining in his own emotions; touching Hana, intended as another piece of courtroom theater, felt like more.

His gaze swept the jury, lighting on Ardelle Washington. "A terrible crime occurred," he told her. "Two men are clearly responsible, and one of them survives — Ibrahim Jefar. But to avoid the ultimate price, he gave the government another name: Hana Arif.

"In one sense, Ms. Sharpe is correct: an ordinary feature of many murder prosecutions is a snitch. And Jefar is an ordinary snitch — unreliable, self-serving, and guilty of a loathsome crime. Except that he is even less impressive."

With this beginning, David saw, he had the jury's attention. "Ms. Sharpe seeks to impress you with Jefar's willingness to die. Then why did he accuse Ms. Arif in order to live? It can't be some problem in their relationship. As Mr. Jefar will tell you, he never met or spoke to Ms. Arif. All that he claims to know is what a dead man told him.

"How convenient. You can never hear from her supposed accuser, Iyad Hassan, or even look him in the eye. But that's just the beginning of the hall of mirrors the government calls its case. To kill Ben-Aron, Hassan and Jefar needed motorcycles, explosives, uniforms, cell phones, false ID, and cash, all provided to them in America. Yet not one scrap of evidence connects Hana Arif to any of these things."

At the corner of David's vision, Saeb gazed down in thought. "How strange," David continued. "How bizarre that a plot that required numerous cell phone calls would yield a record of only one. How peculiar that this law professor would hand an incriminating piece of paper to an assassin. How incredible that this supposed orchestrator of a complex crime would be so unsophisticated. How perplexing that the Al Aqsa Martyrs, Ibrahim Jefar's resistance group, would hand over this assassination to a woman with whom Ms. Sharpe can show no prior connection." Turning to Hana, he invited the jury to appraise her. "And how unbelievable that this responsible wife and mother, so devoted to her twelve-year-old daughter, would risk her life in such a dangerous plot."

As David had instructed, Hana gazed back at the jurors, hoping to establish some human connection. "Yet *this,*" David told them abruptly, "is as good as the prosecution's case will *ever* get: a snitch who knows nothing about whether the defendant is innocent or guilty, and two pieces of 'evidence' that make no sense. Ms. Sharpe's case is so flimsy not because she hasn't tried but because it's all that those who framed Hana Arif could manage to concoct. Yet their plan has one overwhelming virtue: if the woman they framed knows nothing, then we will never know who really planned the murder of Amos Ben-Aron.

"How perfect," David said with real sarcasm. "Ms. Sharpe blames Ms. Arif for the silence of the innocent and her lawyer for not being able to identify the guilty. But only the guilty can speak to this crime. And where it matters most, Ms. Sharpe herself is silent — silent about the questions she hopes you will not ask; silent about the answers she cannot give you.

"It is up to you to demand them. And if she still cannot answer, you must tell her *and* the world that we do not convict a woman of murder because she's all the government has."

Pausing, David studied the expressions of the jurors — puzzled, doubtful, waiting to be persuaded. But he had done all he could. There were two things he could not do: name an alternative to Hana or change the fact that all Sharpe need do was to address Hana's supposed role in the assassination. The trial had begun as he had feared it would.

"Thank you," he said quietly, and sat down beside his client.

5

In search of a dramatic opening, Sharpe called as her first witness James Emmons, head of the Secret Service detail assigned to protect Prime Minister Ben-Aron.

His testimony was as David expected, a recitation of the bombing and its aftermath, delivered with an air of quiet understatement that seemed to emphasize the horror Emmons was describing to the jurors. But Sharpe left nothing to their imagination: over David's vehement objections, she introduced an amateur video of Ben-Aron's last minutes.

In the darkened courtroom, a paralegal from Sharpe's office began to run the video. It had been filmed on Fourth Street, David knew, a few yards from where he and Carole had stood. Soundless images filled the giant screen: Ben-Aron, waving through the window; the black cars gliding past, guarded by police on motorcycles, presenting an image of impregnability and power. Then a motorcycle veered toward the car, Iyad Hassan's. Watching this, David tensed, dreading what he had already seen.

A second motorcycle, Ibrahim Jefar's, glided nearer Ben-Aron's window. Jefar glanced toward Hassan, as though looking for a signal. Without looking at Jefar, Hassan angled his motorcycle toward Ben-Aron's limousine.

In slow motion Hassan was three feet from it, then two. A spray of Hassan's blood and brains rose into the air just before the limousine exploded, vanishing in fire and smoke that spewed pieces of metal in all directions.

Hana gasped softly, grasping David's arm. Amid the flying debris he saw human limbs; Ibrahim Jefar catapulting sideways; his motorcycle tilting, then falling. Iyad Hassan had vanished.

The screen went dark. Still transfixed, David remembered Carole, trembling in his arms. "You need to let go," David whispered to Hana, and her fingers slipped away from his wrist.

The courtroom deputy switched the lights on. Blinking and disoriented, the jurors gazed at the empty screen. Bob Clair's slender face was drained of color.

Sharpe stood where she had before, a few feet from the witness. Emmons regarded her with stoic misery. "Does that film," she asked him, "accurately reflect the bombing as you saw it?"

"Yes."

"So the prime minister's limousine was totally destroyed?"

"It was. And everyone in it — the prime minister, Rodney Daves, and Ariel Glick. There were no bodies, only scraps."

"How well did you know Rodney Daves?"

Though Emmons still looked in Sharpe's direction, his eyes seemed clouded. "I'm godfather to his children, Clay and Amy. I was the one who called his wife."

This was where David would have ended, and where Sharpe chose to finish. With a look of dour satisfaction, she told Judge Taylor, "No further questions."

Taylor silently regarded the jury. David saw the youngest juror, Rosella Suarez, dabbing at her eyes with a twisted piece of Kleenex. "Let's recess for ten minutes," the judge suggested.

Hana and David sat in a stark witness room, drinking coffee. "Emmons's testimony would have done the job," he said. "But Sharpe wanted to horrify the jury."

Hana looked pale. "Because it makes a death sentence easier to get? Or just to make the jury hungrier to convict me?"

David did not answer. "I'll try to make Sharpe pay the price," he promised.

David strolled toward Emmons, hands in his pockets, standing a respectful distance from the witness. In a tone of mild curiosity, David asked, "Do you happen to know, Agent Emmons, how the assassins came to be on Fourth Street?"

Emmons shook his head. "No."

"Then let me see if I understand your procedures. Two days prior to the prime minister's arrival, a small working group of the Secret Service, the Israelis, and the SFPD — acting under your direction — chose his route to the airport."

"That's correct."

"And the route you chose took Market Street to Tenth Street, not Fourth Street."

"That's also true."

David cocked his head. "When did the route change?"

Emmons shifted in the witness chair. "Twenty minutes before Mr. Ben-Aron departed from the

Commonwealth Club. It was just an extra precaution."

"Who was supposed to know about the change?"

"Just the members of our joint protective detail."

Briefly scanning the jury, David saw that they were attentive, seemingly less stricken than before. "Did you personally communicate the change in route?"

"Yes. By secure cell phone to the Secret Service agent driving the lead car; the head of the Israeli detail, Shlomo Avner; and John Russo, head of Dignitary Protection for the SFPD. They were charged with informing their respective people."

"And did they?"

Emmons crossed his arms. "Obviously so. The motorcade turned down Fourth Street."

"Where Hassan and Jefar were waiting."

"Yes."

David summoned a puzzled look. "So who called *them?*"

"I don't know."

"They weren't on the list of people to call, I take it."

"Of course not."

"Nonetheless, someone in the detail — a Secret Service agent, an Israeli agent, or one of the police — must have called them."

Sharpe stood at once. "Objection," she called out. "The question asks for speculation."

As Taylor turned to David, he countered, "There are only so many possibilities, Your Honor. I think we can trust this witness to sort them out."

"Agreed. You may answer the question, Agent Emmons."

"That's one possibility," Emmons told David. "The other is that somehow Hassan and Jefar intercepted our communications —"

"In which case," David interrupted, "they wouldn't have needed a handler — allegedly Ms. Arif — to tell them of the change in route."

Emmons looked momentarily startled. "I suppose not."

David smiled faintly. "In *that* case, we can all go home."

"Objection," Sharpe called out with real heat. "We allege that Ms. Arif recruited Iyad Hassan. And who, I might ask, directed these two men to the explosives?"

"Who indeed?" David asked the judge. "But let me withdraw the question, and ask the witness whether he has any information connecting Ms. Arif to any of the paraphernalia used by the assassins."

Seemingly distracted by the swift exchange, Emmons took a moment to answer. "I do not."

"All right. In addition to the possibility of a communications intercept, did the FBI and the Secret Service — specifically including you — investigate the possibility that someone on the Secret Service detail or the SFPD tipped the assassins to the change of route?"

"We did," Emmons answered. "We interrogated each of our people and the police involved, administered polygraphs, and reviewed their phone and financial records for any peculiarities. We even replicated the background investigations for every one of them. We found nothing that would raise suspicion."

"What about the Israelis?"

Emmons hesitated, clearly torn between his human desire to deflect the blame and his professional obligation to assist the prosecution within the bounds of truth. "We made no inquiries of the members of Israel's protective detail. My understanding is that the Israeli government is carrying out its own investigation."

"Do you know anything about what they've found?"

"Nothing."

"Except, of course, that nothing they've found implicates Ms. Arif."

"Objection," Sharpe said swiftly. "The question has no foundation. If Agent Emmons knows nothing, by definition he can't know *that.*"

"Wouldn't he?" David asked the judge with an air of bemusement. "Wouldn't Ms. Sharpe? It defies belief that the Israeli government would conceal information connecting Ms. Arif to the murder of its own prime minister."

A glint of amusement surfaced in the judge's eyes. "Your argument has a certain logic," she told David. "But Ms. Sharpe can only give us what she has. If her case includes no witness from Israel, that speaks for itself. Please ask another question."

Satisfied, David glanced past the jury at Avi Hertz, so inscrutable he seemed waxen. Casually, David asked the witness, "Have you heard of a man named Barak Lev?"

Emmons's eyes narrowed. "Yes. He is — or was — a settler on the West Bank, the leader of an extremist group called the Masada movement. Their goal is to drive the Palestinians from the West Bank, which they believe was granted to Israel by God."

"Didn't like Amos Ben-Aron much, did he? In fact, didn't Lev prophesy that God would strike Ben-Aron dead?"

Folding his hands in front of him, Emmons considered his answer. "From their statements, Lev and others in the Masada movement believed Ben-Aron would abandon them to the Palestinians. And so they believed that God must kill him."

Hands on hips, David looked at Emmons askance. "Prior to Ben-Aron's arrival, did the Secret Service compile what it calls a 'watch list' of people in America who might pose a serious threat to Ben-Aron?"

Suddenly aware of where David was headed, Sharpe stood reflexively, as though to object, then seemed to think better of it. "Yes," Emmons answered tersely.

"And did the list include American Jews sympathetic to the Masada movement?"

"It did," Emmons responded pointedly. "But primarily in Brooklyn."

David decided to let this go. "Are you familiar with a man named Hillel Markis?"

"Yes." Once more, Emmons hesitated. "He was a member of the Israeli security detail protecting Ben-Aron in San Francisco."

"Are you also aware that Markis and Lev not only served in the army together but were, in fact, close friends?"

Emmons shook his head. "I have no firsthand knowledge of that."

David paused a moment. "I notice that you spoke of Markis in the past tense."

"I did," Emmons answered. "Because he's dead."

"How did *that* happen?"

Plainly aware of David's role in Markis's death, Emmons shot him a look of veiled hostility. "He died in a suicide bombing. In Tel Aviv."

"Do you know whether anyone else was killed or wounded?"

"Just the bomber. Markis was alone."

"When did this happen?"

"About two months ago."

"Has anyone claimed responsibility for the bombing?"

"No."

Abruptly, Marnie Sharpe stood up. "Your Honor, may I approach the bench?"

Following Sharpe, David joined her in huddling before Judge Taylor. "Your Honor," Sharpe said with considerable vehemence, "the last four questions should disqualify Mr. Wolfe from continuing as counsel for Ms. Arif. With an air of innocence, he asks this witness for his secondhand knowledge of two murders witnessed, or nearly so, by Mr. Wolfe himself. He can't be both witness and counsel."

"I don't propose to be," David responded evenly. "We've been over this already. There's no dispute that Lev and Markis are as dead as the prime minister. I wish I'd had no connection whatsoever to these deaths. But there are other witnesses to all three of them, and Ms. Arif wants me as her counsel."

Taylor turned to Sharpe. "I won't prejudge your motion to disqualify Mr. Wolfe, if that's what you're suggesting. We can recess the trial and have this out. But the outcome isn't obvious, and Ms. Arif's desire to have Mr. Wolfe as her lawyer weighs heavily with me. So let me pose a practical question: if I decide to disqualify Mr. Wolfe, are you willing to have a new trial, with new counsel, perhaps months or years away? Or are you content to try the case against Mr. Wolfe?"

Both he and Sharpe, David understood, were staring into a dark hole of uncertainty: though

Sharpe wished to be rid of David, the resulting delay might help Hana's case more than the prosecution's. For an instant, David even hoped that this might happen. Frowning, Sharpe asked, "Can I take this under advisement?"

"Only until nine A.M. tomorrow," the judge said curtly. "In the meanwhile, I'm allowing Mr. Wolfe to continue his cross-examination."

As David walked away, he saw a curious double image: Hana's look of gratitude and worry; Saeb, sitting behind her, watching David's face. Turning back to the witness, David said, "We were discussing the murder of Hillel Markis. Was Barak Lev also murdered?"

"Yes. By a sniper, one day after Markis."

"Then let's summarize: a member of Ben-Aron's security detail, Hillel Markis, was close to the head of the Masada movement, Barak Lev, who wished aloud for God to strike down Ben-Aron. Ben-Aron is killed; then Markis; then Lev. Is all that correct?"

"As I understand it, yes."

"Do you know who killed Markis and Lev?"

"I do not. All I know is that both were murdered in Israel."

Walking to the defendant's table, David stood beside Hana. "Are you aware of any connection between *Ms. Arif* and Markis or Lev?"

"I'm not."

"Then let's return to your watch list of people who might pose a threat to Prime Minister Ben-Aron. To your knowledge, did it include anyone affiliated with the Al Aqsa Martyrs Brigade?"

Emmons shot the quickest of glances at Marnie Sharpe. "Not to my knowledge."

"And yet Ibrahim Jefar claims to have been acting for Al Aqsa."

"So I understand."

David moved closer. "In your estimate, Agent Emmons, was the assassination of Amos Ben-Aron the work of professionals?"

"It was highly professional, yes."

"Do you believe Al Aqsa capable of such an operation in the United States?"

"No. Al Aqsa lacks sufficient infrastructure."

Glancing at the jury, David caught Bob Clair's look of perplexity. "Are you aware of any connection between Al Aqsa and Hana Arif?" David asked.

"I am not," Emmons said emphatically.

The tone of this answer suggested a partial breakthrough: though an official of the government, Emmons seemed troubled by the holes in its case. "As a member of the Secret Service," David asked, "are you aware that other Middle Eastern countries are hostile to the State of Israel?"

"Of course."

"Which of these countries has the capacity in the United States to support a complex operation like this assassination?"

Emmons seemed to stir. "Iran," he said flatly. "Specifically, Iranian intelligence."

"And are you aware of any connection between Ms. Arif and Iranian intelligence?"

For longer than the question merited, Emmons contemplated his answer. Again, David felt a curious duality pervade the courtroom: the jury and the media, unaware of what lay behind David's questions; the witness and the prosecutor, both on edge, fully alert to where David might be heading. Saeb, though expressionless, seemed preternaturally still.

"No," the witness answered. "Not between the Iranians and the defendant."

"Thank you," David said. "I have no further questions."

6

In David's dream, a solitary woman shrouded in a black cloak and hood entered a dark alley in a surreal replica of a refugee camp, her movements tentative and fearful, her head turning from side to side. She was separated from David by a barbed-wire fence: all that he could discern was that the woman was of Hana's size, and that her movements seemed familiar. Though he wished to help her, the shadowy figure, coming closer, filled him with apprehension.

As she passed through the alley, tombstones appeared behind her. David leaned against the wire, its barbs pricking his forehead.

A foot away, the woman reached out with one slender arm, her delicate fingers touching his. "Help me," she said in perfect English.

"Who are you?"

The woman did not answer. As David strained to see her features in the half-light, she slowly drew back her hood, freeing her long black hair.

The woman was a girl: Munira.

Awaking with a start, David saw the red illuminated numbers of his alarm clock.

His mouth was dry. Already, he felt the dream recede into his subconscious, leaving half-remembered fragments. As with other dreams, he could make no sense of it, except as the eruption of emotions he had been struggling to repress.

David closed his eyes, trying to focus on tomorrow.

The day's first witness, Dr. Elizabeth Shelton, was the medical examiner for the City and County of San Francisco. Slender, blond, and crisp in manner, Liz Shelton had become, in her late forties, a nationally respected expert. And, in David's opinion, her testimony served no purpose except to turn the jurors' stomachs.

He had said as much to Judge Taylor, offering to stipulate to the deaths. But Sharpe had insisted on her right to prove, by whatever means she thought best, the most rudimentary elements of a murder case — that those murdered were, in fact, dead. And so Hana sat with David, gazing at the table, as Sharpe led Dr. Shelton in painstaking detail through the ways in which the bomb carried by Iyad Hassan had transformed its victims.

This exegesis was illustrated by slides of fragments of body parts, teeth, and bones, projected for the jury on a screen. The cause of death, Shelton told the jurors, was a massive explosion; the charred remains, such as they were, did not allow examiners to distinguish one victim from another, save through dental records and DNA. Eyes shut, Hana would not look at the projections.

All in all, it took Sharpe and Shelton an hour to kill Amos Ben-Aron, an hour longer than this task had taken Iyad Hassan. When it was done and Judge Taylor called a recess, David felt a light hand on his shoulder. "So," Saeb inquired softly, "do you think Munira should have heard this? Or seen it?"

David merely looked up at him. Saeb gazed at his wife; their eyes met, and then Hana turned away from him, looking at no one.

Approaching the witness, David stopped abruptly, as though struck by a sudden thought. "Tell me, Dr. Shelton, just why is it you're here?"

Composed, Shelton looked toward Sharpe. "Objection," the prosecutor called out. "Not only is the question vague and ambiguous, but it calls for a legal conclusion. Obviously the United States called Dr. Shelton to establish cause of death."

"Is there any doubt," David asked Judge Taylor, "about how the victims died?"

"I hadn't thought so," Taylor said in an arid tone. "But I'm sustaining Ms. Sharpe's objection. Make whatever point you have some other way."

"Thank you, Your Honor." Facing Shelton, he asked, "As far as you know, Dr. Shelton, does the defense dispute that the cause of death was the explosion Ms. Sharpe screened for the jurors only yesterday?"

Shelton's lips compressed; David sensed that she had not appreciated being used as Sharpe's prop, and did not relish becoming David's. Evenly, she answered, "Not that I know of."

"Do you know anything at all about whether Hana Arif is in any way responsible for this explosion?"

Shelton folded her hands. "I don't."

"Other than what you've heard alleged about Iyad Hassan, do you have any personal knowledge whatsoever about *who* might be responsible?"

"No."

"Then let me ask you again: why *is* it that you're here?"

"Objection," Sharpe called out, sounding as annoyed as David had intended. "The *same* objection. This is a waste of time."

"Your Honor," David responded calmly, "it strikes me as incautious for Ms. Sharpe to accuse me of wasting time. Since Dr. Shelton took the stand, all of us are an hour and a quarter closer to being dead, and not a minute wiser as to Ms. Arif's innocence or guilt. It seems only fair that I make that point."

"It seems that you have," Taylor rejoined. "So I'll ask you both not to consume more time with speeches."

Glancing at the jury, David saw Ardelle Washington contemplating Marnie Sharpe with a look of seeming displeasure, and sensed that he had made his second, unstated point — that Sharpe was trying to exploit the jurors' emotions.

"In that case," he said to Taylor, "I'll keep this witness no longer."

During the noon recess, David retreated to his office with Angel Garriques; hastily they gobbled sandwiches while discussing the morning's events. Responding to Angel's encouragement, David told him, "I scored what points I could. But I might as well have 'reasonable doubt' tattooed on my forehead — our defense is all questions, and no answers.

"The only concrete evidence in the entire case points to Hana's guilt. Once Sharpe calls Ibrahim Jefar, all that gore will resonate with the jury. Not to mention help Sharpe argue for the death penalty. That's why she's doing this."

The telephone rang. David hesitated, then picked it up.

His caller was Zev Ernheit. "I'm still waiting on the forensics lab," Ernheit told him without preface. "It's true that the lab received materials from Saeb Khalid, asking for some tests. But all my sources are willing to say is that his purpose wasn't discerning fingerprints — Hana's or anyone else's."

"Shit."

"What they *did* test," Ernheit continued, "I don't know. I can't get the documents."

David glanced at Angel, who was following David's end of the conversation with obvious concern. "Keep trying," he told Ernheit. "I think it may be helpful."

"If the test isn't for fingerprints, David, how could it be useful?"

"I'm not sure. But we're in trouble here. Whatever might help, we need."

Ernheit was silent. David found himself wondering, yet again, what role the Israeli government was playing in Ernheit's efforts. "All right," Ernheit replied at last. "I'll try."

In the afternoon, Sharpe called Special Agent Dante Allegria, an explosives expert from the FBI. With his dark, curly hair, open face, and straightforward manner, Allegria reminded David of the sort of contractor who would remodel your kitchen, finish on time, and send you an honest bill. He was also a skilled and experienced witness; as he testified, Allegria spoke directly to the jury, building a rapport. "The assassin," Allegria told them, "used a plastique explosive known as C-4. It's the American version of an eastern European plastique, Semtex, which is the explosive of choice for terrorists."

Sharpe stood to the side, a bit player in Allegria's

tutorial. "Why, in your opinion, would Hassan choose C-4?"

"Objection," David said without standing. "Lack of foundation. We don't know *who* chose this explosive, but we're pretty sure it wasn't Hassan. According to the indictment, he found it in a container in South San Francisco. All he did was connect the wires."

"Sustained," the judge ruled.

"Why," Sharpe amended with some exasperation, "would *someone* have chosen C-4 to blow up the prime minister's limousine, and Mr. Ben-Aron with it?"

"Because you need a charge sufficient to destroy armor. Most explosives can't do that. But even one saddlebag of C-4, attached to a motorcycle, has an excellent chance of achieving what happened here: totally destroying an armored vehicle. The flying metal alone could have killed the people inside."

Only that wasn't necessary, Allegria did not need to add. More subtly than Liz Shelton, Allegria had enabled Sharpe to resurrect the carnage. "And how did Hassan ignite the C-4?" Sharpe asked.

"It's pretty simple," Allegria said. "The plastique was electronically wired to a toggle switch on the handlebars of both motorcycles. Press the switch, and the C-4 ignites. Technically, all Hassan needed to know was how to wire the C-4 to the switch."

"Is that technique familiar to you?"

"It is. Al Qaeda's used it. In the Palestinian territories, so have Hamas and the Al Aqsa Martyrs Brigade. The only new thing is that this happened in America."

At the mention of Al Qaeda, David saw, Bob Clair raised his eyebrows — with a single question, Sharpe had managed to conjure something alien and terrifying, the shadow of 9/11, while reminding the jurors that the second such horror, the assassination of Amos Ben-Aron, had introduced suicide bombing to the streets of San Francisco.

"Thank you," Sharpe said. "That's all I have."

Approaching the witness, David stood between Allegria and the jurors, forcing him to focus on David. "Were you able," David began, "to determine the specific source of the explosive used by Iyad Hassan?"

"We certainly tried," the witness answered earnestly. "One place we always look at is the military — greedy or disgruntled soldiers, sometimes Al Qaeda sympathizers, who steal explosives and sell them on the black market. But here we just don't know."

"So you've got no idea whatsoever where *these* particular explosives came from, or who procured them, or even who left them for Hassan to find."

Allegria shook his head. "I'm afraid not, no."

"Do you know of any evidence linking Hana Arif to the procurement of those explosives?"

"None."

"All right. Judging from the technique you describe, would you say that the assassination itself was a professional job?"

Allegria considered this, his deep brown eyes regarding David with a look of thoughtful candor. "What I'd say," he allowed, "is that Hassan used a technique favored by those who practice terror as a profession, one that was particularly suitable for eliminating a head of state.

"In other bombings where the objective is blowing up a car, terrorists will often detonate the explosives by remote control. But that's a little less reliable, and may not work on an armored car. In this case, the planners chose the right technique, a suicide bombing; the right plastique, C-4; and the ignition system most likely to do the job."

David cocked his head. "But those choices also require the bomber to know the specific route of Ben-Aron's motorcade, true?"

Allegria hesitated. "True."

"As well as any *change* in route."

"Yes. This wasn't a random bombing."

Having drawn the jurors' thoughts back to the possibility of a security leak, David asked, "Given this technique, would you say that Iyad Hassan expected to die?"

For an instant, the witness looked bemused — as, David saw, did Marnie Sharpe.

"Unless he was delusional," Allegria answered. "Once he pushed the switch, he was gone."

"But not before?"

"No. Until it's detonated, C-4 is very stable. You and I could play catch with it."

"No thanks. From your testimony, I gather C-4 is easy enough to wire."

"Yes."

"Indeed, Hassan wired his bike with great success."

Allegria looked slightly puzzled. "If you mean that Hassan succeeded, obviously so."

"So why didn't Ibrahim Jefar's bike go off?"

For a long moment, Allegria gazed back at David. "I'm not sure," he answered finally. "When I inspected Jefar's motorcycle, the wiring was connected to the toggle switch, but not to the C-4 concealed in the saddlebag."

"Isn't *that* why Jefar's plastique failed to explode?" David asked with mild incredulity. "That's a pretty elementary mistake for Hassan to make."

Judge Taylor leaned forward, clearly grasping David's point. For the first time, the witness looked down, considering his response. "It would be," Allegria answered, "if that's what happened. Perhaps it was jarred loose in the explosion."

"But if Jefar pushed the switch before Hassan — which is what the indictment claims — that didn't happen, did it?"

"I guess not."

"So isn't the most likely explanation either that Hassan failed to wire it properly or that Jefar disconnected it?"

The witness spread his hands. "They're both certainly possible. If it was Hassan, we'll never know."

"That's kind of a problem, isn't it. But let me ask you this: if you assume Hassan wanted Jefar to live, wouldn't he do just what I'm suggesting — not complete the wiring?"

"Sure," Allegria answered, his tone combining perplexity with protest. "But why on earth would he do that?"

On the bench, Taylor gazed up at the ceiling, attempting to conceal a faint smile. "Why don't you leave that one to me," David suggested to Allegria. "Please, answer the question."

Allegria settled back in the witness chair. "Even if what you say is right, Mr. Wolfe, Hassan couldn't be sure Jefar would live. Way too big an explosion; way too many flying pieces."

"Nonetheless, wouldn't you say that whoever disconnected — or failed to connect — the wire substantially enhanced Ibrahim Jefar's chances of surviving?"

Allegria folded his hands. "A lot would depend on luck, and how close Jefar was to the explosion.

But if 'substantially' means going from 'no chance' to 'some chance,' then the glitch in wiring enhanced Jefar's prospects of surviving."

"And, in fact, he did survive."

"Yes."

David skipped a beat. "And therefore," he prodded, "Jefar was alive to repeat Iyad Hassan's story about Hana Arif."

"Objection." Sharpe's voice crackled in the courtroom. "The question piles speculation on speculation."

David did not care — that he had made his point was apparent from the curiosity on Bob Clair's face as he looked from Sharpe to David. "I'll withdraw it," David told the judge with a careless air. "The last few answers were sufficient."

But David's moment of satisfaction was brief. At five o'clock, when the trial recessed, Angel joined him for the beginning of their second eight-hour shift, as they rehearsed, rearranged, and debated his cross-examination of Sharpe's next witness, Ibrahim Jefar.

Toward midnight, David repeated what was obvious to both of them: "All questions and no answers."

7

Even had David been a visitor, he would have sensed that this day in court might tilt the balance of the case against Hana Arif.

Outside the federal building, police cordoned off the streets, and satellite trailers crowded tightly together. A small army of reporters recited live feeds into minicams; demonstrators shouted across the barricades. Inside the courtroom, reporters jammed uncomfortably into the wooden benches; the later arrivals leaned against the walls on both sides, their continuous chatter noisier than before. At the prosecutor's table, Sharpe was flanked by her smart and methodical chief assistant, Paul MacInnis; Victor Vallis, the FBI agent in charge; and George Jennings, the head of the Criminal Division for the Department of Justice. David sat between Hana and Angel Garriques, who, like David, had memorized every fact they could gather about Ibrahim Jefar.

Awaiting the judge, Hana was quiet, filled with thoughts David could only imagine. Their brief conversation had touched on that morning's news reports — the killing by the IDF of two Al Aqsa members in a village near Ramallah; the murder of a Jewish settler living above the souk in Hebron. Softly, despairingly, Hana had murmured, "My country," and lapsed back into silence.

Behind them, Saeb took his place in the first row. Though he appeared self-contained, the thumb and forefinger of his left hand rubbed together, as though he were twisting a piece of paper into a tight ball. Even the jury seemed subdued.

"All rise," the courtroom deputy proclaimed, and Judge Taylor took the bench.

Quiet descended. Folding her hands, the judge scanned the scene in front of her. In a tone that aspired to matter-of-factness but did not quite achieve it, she told the prosecutor, "You may call the next witness, Ms. Sharpe."

Intently, David absorbed his first impression of Ibrahim Jefar. Under her breath, Hana murmured, "I don't think I've ever seen this boy before."

Her accuser was quite thin, with hollow cheeks and a neatly trimmed beard that did not age his unlined face or limpid brown eyes. He looked alien and confused, as though he had arrived here by some cosmic accident, a wrinkle in time or space. And something terrible seemed to have seeped into his gaze: a hopelessness that pervaded his very being, the vision of years and decades spent waiting to die, sealed away from a life that, from now until death, would exist only in his memory. It would have been better, David thought, if Jefar had blown himself to pieces — not just for Hana and David, but for Jefar himself.

After a few preliminary questions, Sharpe asked Jefar to relate the story of his sister's experience at the checkpoint. Even here, his voice sounded hollow and dissociated. "So this is why you joined Al Aqsa?" Sharpe inquired in a neutral tone.

"Yes." Jefar said listlessly. "I wished to redeem

my sister's honor."

"How did you become involved in the assassination of Amos Ben-Aron?"

Jefar, David noted, was unable to look at anyone for very long; his presence here seemed to have deepened his sense of failure. At length, he said, "One day, Iyad Hassan sat down next to me in class. He knew of my sister, and what the Jews had done to her. We talked for perhaps an hour."

"Concerning what?"

"The Zionists." Jefar crossed his legs. "Iyad said that we would never be free until the scab of Israel was removed from all our lands, and we returned to claim what was ours. He said that only cowards shrank from the will of God."

Beside David, Hana studied Jefar with a look of perplexity; if her knowledge of the witness was any deeper than David's own, she showed no sign of it.

"How did you respond?" Sharpe asked the witness.

Jefar looked up at her fleetingly, almost shyly. "From how Iyad was talking, I knew he was more religious than me. But I agreed with him about the Jews."

"Did you discuss Prime Minister Ben-Aron?"

Jefar gazed into the distance, as though recalling the fatal divide between his life then and now. "I called Ben-Aron the abortionist of my sister's baby. The soldiers at the checkpoint were only his assistants."

"After that," Sharpe asked, "did your relationship with Hassan continue?"

Jefar nodded, still addressing some middle distance. "After class, we would meet for coffee and talk about jihad and the occupation. I was very careful — I did not want to reveal that I was with Al Aqsa, or betray Muhammad Nasir, my commander in Jenin." Jefar hesitated, then said rapidly, "But one day I told Iyad that every time I thought of my sister, my blood boiled and I wished to become a martyr — to make the Jews in Israel feel what they made *us* feel."

David glanced at the jurors. Across the gulf of experience and culture, Bob Clair seemed to scrutinize the witness with a muted horror, as if looking at the Arab terrorist of America's nightmares. "How did Hassan respond?" Sharpe asked.

"At first Iyad was quiet. Then he said that God would give me what I sought."

"Did he say how that might happen?"

"Not then. But the next time we met, he asked me to his apartment, for dinner." Jefar sat back, speaking in the monotone of a man narrating into a tape recorder. "I expected there would be others. But Iyad was alone. He showed me pictures he had taken of the Jewish security wall and the barriers the IDF had built around Birzeit. When I expressed my anger, he sat down, looked me in the eye, and asked if I was ready to consider martyrdom."

"What did you say?"

At the neck of Jefar's open shirt, his throat seemed to twitch. "That I was."

Sharpe paused, intent on her witness. "Did Hassan then say what he meant?"

"He said that Muhammad Nasir had assigned him to carry out a special task, and wished for me to join. But that this involved performing my final service."

"How did you respond?"

Jefar, David saw, seemed to look everywhere but toward Hana. "I was scared," he said. "But I was also proud. I had asked Muhammad Nasir for this favor once before. So to Iyad, I said, 'Tell me what

Muhammad asks.' "

As Sharpe nodded her encouragement, David saw Ardelle Washington bite her lip. "And what did Hassan say?" Sharpe asked.

Jefar swallowed, then looked directly at the prosecutor. "It had been decided that revenge on the IDF was not enough. We would show our resolve by cutting off the head of the Jewish serpent, the Zionist who had emptied my sister's womb."

David felt his skin grow cold. Beside him, Hana drew a breath. "And did you agree?" Sharpe asked.

"At first, I was filled with wonder. 'How is this possible?' I asked Iyad. He answered that Muhammad had assured him that the plan was carefully laid out, but that its details would be hidden, even from him. Each step would be revealed to us just before we took it."

"Did Hassan say *how* the plans would be revealed?"

"There would be the tightest operational security. I was not to speak to Muhammad Nasir, or even visit Jenin. All instructions would come to Iyad alone. He would pass them to me."

"Did Hassan say who would pass him the instructions?"

As though in a trance, Jefar merely nodded.

"We need an audible response, Mr. Jefar."

"We needed someone close at hand," Jefar said slowly, "who could also travel to America. Someone whose allegiance to Al Aqsa was not known."

"Did Hassan tell you who that was?"

"In Mexico, I asked him. Iyad hesitated, then swore me to secrecy." Jefar looked down. "It was a professor at Birzeit, he said. A woman named Hana Arif."

Though she should not have been surprised,

Hana appeared stunned, and David saw her skin turning pale. "Did you know Professor Arif?" Sharpe asked Jefar.

"On sight, yes. But only that."

"And do you see her now?"

Hassan blinked. Then, as he had not done before, he looked directly at Hana, pointing as he did so. In a parched voice, Jefar said, "That is her."

On the other side of David, Angel Garriques gripped his pencil with the fingers of both hands. Taylor still regarded the witness. "Mr. Jefar has hours to go yet," she said to Sharpe. "We'll recess for ten minutes."

As Taylor left the bench, Hana turned to David. "For Jefar, this is the truth."

David nodded. Turning, he saw Saeb Khalid, shoulders slumped, staring at the floor.

For the next hour of testimony, Sharpe led the witness through each fateful move toward the assassination: the assassins' departure from Ramallah; their circuitous route to Mexico; their illegal crossing into the United States; their acquisition of new identities; the long drive to San Francisco. Then, step by step, the days spent using and disposing of cell phones; the acquisition of the van; the container filled with the tools of assassination, including a map showing the route of the motorcade. Jefar recited this in a sepulchral tone — except for the moment when they opened the container, when Jefar's face and voice expressed a kind of wonder. Each step, David noticed, seemed to draw the jury deeper into the world of the two assassins; each step was preceded by a cell phone call, involving Hassan alone, after which Hassan referred to his caller as "she" or "her." And each reference caused one juror or another to glance at Hana.

Toward the end of this litany, Sharpe introduced Prosecution Exhibit 62, handing it to David before passing it to the jury. Silent, Hana stared at a slip of paper bearing her own cell phone number.

When Sharpe gave it to Jefar, she asked, "Can you identify Exhibit Sixty-two?"

"Yes. Hassan brought it with him to San Francisco. I saw him throw it in a waste can at the last motel."

"Did he tell you what the number represents?"

"It was the international cell phone number of Professor Arif."

Angel Garriques stirred. "Perfect for NSA surveillance," he whispered to David. "Who'd be that stupid?"

Hana kept watching the witness, awaiting his account of the assassination.

This was not long in coming. Though terse, Jefar's account of the plot's last few hours exerted its own spell; as the witness spoke, David envisioned the assassins dressing in their police uniforms before dawn; driving to an empty lot south of Market Street; pulling the motorcycles from the van as dawn broke; biding time for several hours until, their faces concealed by helmets and goggles, they took up their stations near Market and Tenth, nervously awaiting the motorcade that would mean their own deaths. Iyad Hassan, Jefar recalled, had begun praying under his breath in Arabic. To Jefar, he had murmured, "It is just as she promised."

Then Hassan's cell phone had rung. "As Iyad listened," Jefar told Sharpe, "he became upset. 'That was her,' he told me. 'They've changed the Zionist's route.' "

Bob Clair, David saw, listened to this with a look of curiosity. "What happened then?" Sharpe asked.

"We must go, Iyad said — quickly. So I followed him to Fourth Street."

"Did he keep the cell phone with him?"

"No. He threw it in a trash barrel."

"When you reached Fourth Street, what did you do?"

Jefar inhaled, his eyes half shut. "We went a little way down the block, and waited. After a minute or so, the first limousine turned the corner."

Sharpe moved closer, her quiet tone underscoring the moment. "Did you have a plan, Mr. Jefar?"

"We were to join the motorcade alongside the Zionist's limousine. Iyad would be the first to drive into its rear door and detonate. I was to follow." Jefar's voice was husky. "Even if Iyad failed, I'd blow the Zionist straight to hell."

"Did you follow these instructions?" Sharpe asked.

Jefar's answer held a touch of shame. "We joined the motorcade, but when I saw the Zionist's face, I could not stand to wait."

"What did you do?"

"I pushed the switch."

"What happened?"

"Nothing. Then Iyad turned his motorcycle into the Zionist's limousine . . ."

"And then?"

Jefar looked down. "Everything exploded," he said softly. "Even the air itself."

Sharpe stepped closer still. "Did you expect to die?"

"At the moment I pushed the switch." Pausing, Jefar summoned a kind of dignity. "I did not expect to be here. I do not *wish* to be here now."

There would be more questions, David knew — the moment when Jefar found himself alive; his recuperation; his dealings with the government. But the rest did not much matter. Jefar had made Sharpe's case.

8

As a prosecutor, David Wolfe had been well known for relentless, even ruthless, cross-examinations; in one case the defendant, a stock promoter who had bilked retirees out of pension money, had asked for a recess in order to vomit. But a half day of watching Ibrahim Jefar, combined with the incendiary crime with which Hana stood accused, had confirmed David in a different strategy: a patient attempt to probe any holes in Jefar's account. At its core was the troubling sense that Jefar had told the truth, and that the liar — if there was one — was Iyad Hassan.

On the witness stand, Jefar looked wary and diminished. Approaching him, David stopped a comfortable distance away, hands in his pockets. The manner he chose was factual, dispassionate.

"As I understand it, Mr. Jefar, you never met Hana Arif."

Jefar gave a quick bob of the head. "That's true."

"You never spoke to her about assassinating Amos Ben-Aron."

"No."

"You don't even know whether, in fact, she's affiliated with Al Aqsa."

The witness shifted his weight. "I only know that from Iyad Hassan."

"And it's also true that Hassan is the sole reason you believe that Muhammad Nasir, the former leader of Al Aqsa, wanted you to assassinate Amos Ben-Aron."

A defensive look crept into Jefar's eyes. "That is true."

David paused. "If I told you that Muhammad Nasir claimed that he was not involved in this assassination, and that he asserted that Hana Arif was not a member of Al Aqsa, whom would you believe?"

"Objection." A barely controlled anger jackknifed Sharpe from her chair. "There is no foundation for that question, nor can there be. Muhammad Nasir is dead."

"Nasir wasn't dead when I met with him," David told Taylor swiftly. "I'm probing the basis for the witness's accusation against Ms. Arif."

"With a groundless and unprovable hypothetical —"

"Enough," Taylor snapped. "Both of you. Please approach the bench."

They did so. "All right," Taylor said to Sharpe in a lower voice. "Make your point here. Though I think I know what it is."

"I'm sure you do, Your Honor. In his last few days of questioning, Mr. Wolfe has effectively told the jury that three supposed witnesses have been murdered. This *last* question is based on Mr. Wolfe's self-serving account of a dead terrorist's self-serving statement. It's not only utterly unprovable, it's hearsay —"

"So is Jefar's entire testimony against Hana Arif," David interrupted.

"Mr. Wolfe," the judge said sharply. "We both know what you're up to. You posed an inappropriate question, to which Ms. Sharpe was bound to object, and then followed up with a gratuitous statement couched as argument. Do it again and you're looking at a mistrial."

David bowed his head, feigning a penitence he did not feel. "It's up to you," the judge told Sharpe. "I'll be happy to instruct the jury to ignore Mr. Wolfe's statements about Muhammad Nasir."

Sharpe shot David a look of spite. "Thank you, Your Honor. But I'm afraid that repetition will only serve his strategy."

"All right," Taylor said to David. "No more of this."

"Thank you, Your Honor." Satisfied, David returned to his station in front of the witness. "Let's turn to the assassination plan itself," he said to Jefar. "Did you discuss that plan with anyone but Hassan?"

Jefar seemed to hunch, becoming smaller. "Iyad told me not to — that this was Muhammad's order. So I told no one."

"Do you know whether Hassan lied about *that?*"

Jefar blinked. "I believed him . . ."

"Why?"

"Because he told me."

"To summarize, then, all you ever knew about the plan to kill Ben-Aron was what Iyad Hassan told you."

Jefar fidgeted with his shirt collar. "That is right."

David tilted his head. "This morning, you testified about a prior conversation with Muhammad Nasir in which you asked to become a martyr. Did you tell him specifically what you wanted?"

"That I wanted to die as a bomber in the bastard country called Israel."

"And how did Muhammad Nasir respond?"

Across the courtroom, David saw Sharpe stir, instinctively nettled by the reference to Nasir. But this question, unlike that to which she had objected, was rooted in Jefar's own testimony. And its impact on the witness was so palpable — discomfort and bewilderment — that David knew at once that what Nasir had told him about admonishing Jefar was true. The witness rubbed both temples with his fingertips, as though to ward off a headache. "What Muhammad told me," he finally answered, "was that it was better to kill the IDF soldiers occupying our land than Jewish civilians in the land that they thought was theirs. And that it was more useful for me to live as long as I could."

"Am I correct in understanding that Nasir — and also Al Aqsa — was willing to accept an independent Palestine living in peace with Israel?"

"Under certain conditions — an end to settlements, fair borders, recognition of the great injustice done our refugees."

"Isn't that what Ben-Aron wanted?"

"So he said," Jefar answered bitterly. "But my sister could not hear him."

"And Iyad Hassan," David prodded softly, "knew all about your sister before you ever told him."

Jefar looked down. "Yes."

"Other than Hassan, do you have any reason to believe that Muhammad Nasir, your commander in Al Aqsa, had changed his mind about the effectiveness of suicide bombings?"

"No."

"Or about whether you should become a martyr?"

"No."

In the jury box, Bob Clair raised his eyebrows, as though making a mental note. From voir dire,

David knew that Clair was a linear thinker — he liked things to make sense, and here they did not. Emboldened, David asked Jefar, "Is it possible that Iyad Hassan, knowing about your sister, exploited your hatred of Ben-Aron to enlist you in an assassination planned by people other than Al Aqsa?"

"Objection," Sharpe called out. "This is yet another hypothetical question, lacking any foundation in the evidence."

Holding up her hand for silence, Judge Taylor turned to David. "Mr. Wolfe?"

"The question's not only legitimate," David said firmly, "it goes to another critical aspect of this case: whether the origin of the plot as described by Ibrahim Jefar — *and* by the prosecutor — is fact or fiction."

"I understand," the judge replied. "Perhaps you can frame the question in some other way."

"Thank you, Your Honor." Turning back to Jefar, David asked, "Do you personally know *who* designed the assassination plan?"

"No."

"So Hassan could have been working for anyone, right?"

Briefly, Jefar looked dazed, as though the last solace of his days and nights — that he had carried out a mission authorized by Muhammad Nasir — was being stolen from him. Quietly, he said, "I cannot know."

"This morning you mentioned operational security — the need to keep all details secret. Yet Hassan told you that Hana Arif was his handler. Did you wonder why, in Ms. Arif's case, Hassan breached operational security?"

"I asked him this," Jefar answered wearily. "Iyad expected us to die."

This was the answer David had hoped for. "Did Hassan give you the name of anyone else involved?"

"Only Muhammad Nasir." Abruptly, Jefar added, "About Hana Arif, surely Iyad told me the truth. He had her telephone number on a slip of paper."

"How did you know it was Ms. Arif's number?"

Jefar hesitated. "Iyad told me. But this is true, correct? Iyad called her on that number."

David placed his hands on his hips. "How do you know that, Mr. Jefar?"

Jefar glanced at Sharpe. "From the prosecutor. This was shown on Iyad's cell phone, yes?"

David smiled. "Lawyers, as Ms. Sharpe has been at pains to point out, aren't witnesses. Based on your own personal knowledge, did Mr. Hassan call the cell phone number on that slip of paper?"

Jefar shrugged. "I cannot know."

"And even if Hassan did call, you can't know who — if anyone — answered."

"No."

"Do you know who gave Hassan the piece of paper?"

Jefar paused again. "Iyad said it was Professor Arif."

"We're back to Hassan again," David said more harshly. "Do *you* know, Mr. Jefar, who gave Hassan the piece of paper with Ms. Arif's cell phone number?"

"No."

"You also testified that, just before the assassination, Hassan threw his cell phone in a trash basket. Do you know why?"

"He always got rid of them, every day or two. He didn't want our phone calls traced."

"Twenty minutes from death? Given that Iyad Hassan was blown to pieces, what do you expect would have happened to his cell phone if he'd kept it with him?"

Jefar folded his arms. "Perhaps we would have been intercepted by the police. Who knew what would happen?"

It was an effective answer. David hesitated, then asked, "When Hassan threw the cell phone in the trash barrel, you were on Market Street, correct?"

"Yes."

"And Market Street was lined with people who could have seen him do this."

"I suppose so, yes."

David paused. "That was the cell phone, was it not, on which Hassan had just received a call telling him that Ben-Aron's route had changed."

"Yes."

"Do you know the number of the phone used to place *that* call?"

"No." Jefar hesitated, then asked, "But wouldn't Iyad's cell phone also show that?"

"What exactly would it show?"

Jefar looked bewildered, as if he could not fathom how David could be so obtuse. "A cell phone number," he answered.

"International? Or local — with services confined to the United States?"

"Local. Hassan told me that all the phones we used were local. Something about avoiding U.S. intercepts or surveillance."

"And yet the telephone number on the slip of paper — supposedly Ms. Arif's — had the country code for Israel and the West Bank."

Jefar placed his fingertips together. "That is what I saw, yes."

"Do you know why Hassan would call a cell phone registered to Ms. Arif, for which she received a monthly bill from a Palestinian service provider?"

"I do not know."

David smiled faintly. "Doesn't that strike you as a breach of 'operational security'?"

Once more, Sharpe tensed, apparently searching for an objection. But there was none, and the jurors were plainly interested in hearing Jefar's answer. "I do not know," he said tonelessly.

For a split second, David wished that he could see Saeb Khalid's expression. "Let's back up a little," he continued. "This morning you described entering a storage container at night and finding police uniforms, plastique, motorcycles, and a map showing Ben-Aron's route. Do you have any idea who put them there?"

"No."

"Or who might have *ordered* them to be put there?"

"No."

"Who wired the plastique to the motorcycles?"

"Hassan."

"Is there a reason you didn't wire your own?"

Jefar shrugged helplessly. "I did not know how."

"Did you check the plastique to see if Hassan had wired it properly?"

"No. I would not have known what to check."

"So you don't know when — or how — the wiring became disconnected?"

"No."

David paused for effect. "But you *do* know that it wasn't disconnected by the explosion. Because you pressed your toggle switch before Hassan did?"

"Yes."
"That was contrary to Hassan's order, true?"
Jefar looked away. "Yes."
"Hassan's orders were to let him go first."
"Yes."
"But isn't that effectively what happened? When your motorcycle failed to explode, you stayed back, and then Hassan went for Ben-Aron's limousine and ignited his own plastique. Just as he had planned."
"I suppose so, yes."
"So you're alive because you stayed back — as ordered by Hassan — and because your motorcycle — wired by Hassan — failed to explode."
"Objection," Sharpe said quickly. "Calls for speculation. The witness can't know what would have happened."
"Really?" David retorted. "According to the prosecution's own expert, Mr. Allegria, if Mr. Jefar's bike had exploded he would not be with us. Mr. Allegria also suggested that the witness would have died had he been as close to the limousine as Iyad Hassan."
Sharpe stepped forward. "Mr. Wolfe had his shot with Special Agent Allegria, Your Honor. By his own testimony, Mr. Jefar is not an expert on explosives."
Briefly, Taylor considered this. "I'm going to sustain the objection, Mr. Wolfe. Do you have some other question on this subject?"
"I do." Turning to the witness, David asked, "You were close to the explosion. Why do *you* think you're alive?"
Jefar hesitated. "Because I wasn't next to the car when Iyad struck it."

"And that was consistent with his instructions, right?"

Taking out a handkerchief, Jefar briefly dabbed his forehead. "Yes."

"Okay. A while ago you mentioned the possibility that you and Hassan might be captured, not killed. Did you ever discuss what might happen to you if you lived?"

"One night, in Mexico, Iyad spoke of this."

"What did he say?"

"That the Americans would give us to the Jews, to torture."

Sharpe leaned forward; from her expression, David sensed that Jefar had never revealed this to her. "Did you discuss any other possibilities?" David asked.

Jefar closed his eyes. "Iyad said they might send us to a CIA prison, in Russia. There they could do anything they wanted — remove our fingernails, hold electric wires to our genitals."

This was a fantasy, David knew — any involvement in this assassination would make Jefar and Hassan public figures, far too visible for mistreatment to be possible. But to someone as unsophisticated as Jefar, the prospect might have seemed quite real. "Did what Iyad Hassan tell you about torture influence your decision to cooperate with the prosecution and implicate Hana Arif?"

"Objection," Sharpe said. "The government made no such threats. All we told the witness was that his testimony — if we believed it truthful — entitled him to consideration in whether we sought the death penalty or life imprisonment."

"I understand that," David told Taylor mildly. "My question was whether Mr. Jefar was motivated to accept that deal because he feared being tortured."

Nodding, the judge turned to Jefar. "When you entered your agreement with the prosecutor," she asked him, "did you do so — in whole or in part — because you feared being tortured as Mr. Hassan had described? Either by the Israelis or by the CIA?"

Jefar hung his head. "I was afraid of torture, yes. More than of execution."

Nodding, the judge looked back at David. "Mr. Wolfe?"

David glanced at Jefar. Listless, Jefar sat there, only the crown of his head visible to the jury — a piece of human wreckage, exposed to the world as a potential dupe, his weaknesses and fears stripped bare, and still ignorant of the forces that might have delivered him to this fate. David felt a moment's pity. But this was how he wished the jury to remember Ibrahim Jefar.

"Thank you," he said to Judge Taylor. "No further questions."

Returning to his chair, he saw Hana's look of gratitude, and then Saeb's appraisal of the witness, so chill that he could have been studying a specimen on a slide. An image came to David from the film General Peretz had shown him — a shadowy figure in a mosque, evocative of Saeb, who watched Ibrahim Jefar listen to the diatribe of a radical imam.

Over the break, Sharpe seemed to have pulled Jefar together for redirect.

"Concerning the plot itself," she asked Jefar, "did Iyad Hassan ever tell you anything that wasn't true?"

Jefar shook his head. "No. It all unfolded as Iyad said."

"Did anyone working for the prosecution ever mention Hana Arif before you mentioned her to us?"

"No. Never once."

"Did we ever threaten you with torture?"

"No."

"Or treat you inhumanely?"

"No."

"After Hassan gave you the name of Ms. Arif, did he consistently refer to the person who called with instructions as 'her' or 'she'?"

"Yes."

"As you sit here today, do you still believe that Iyad Hassan was telling you the truth?"

Jefar mustered what remained of his pride, his voice still wan but firmer than before. "I do."

As Sharpe stepped closer, the jurors followed her. Speaking slowly and precisely, she asked Jefar, "Do you know of any reason why Hassan would lie to you about the involvement of Hana Arif?"

"I know of none. Not from anything Iyad did, or anything he said."

And that was Hana's problem, David knew — the great unanswered questions: why, and who? Head bent, Hana touched her eyes, mirroring Jefar.

9

With his heavy eyelids, curved nose, and small, pursed mouth, Special Agent Victor Vallis, Sharpe's final witness against Hana Arif, reminded David of an aging turtle waiting to consume a fly. The fly was Hana; Vallis's role was to anchor the prosecution case while assuring the jury that her defense was based on nothing that would qualify as evidence. Within minutes he had identified the threads of Sharpe's narrative: Jefar's accusation; the piece of paper with Hana's prints and phone number; Hassan's midnight call to Hana's cell phone. Next he coupled Hana's resignation as a member of the Palestinian negotiating team with her fiery denunciation of Ben-Aron. Then, piece by piece, Sharpe and Vallis parsed the evidence.

"With respect to the slip of paper," Sharpe asked him, "did the FBI perform tests to determine where it came from?"

Vallis nodded. "We did. The paper was manufactured in Ramallah, and is of the type used by every professor at Birzeit University — including by Ms. Arif."

"Did the slip of paper bear any fingerprints other than those of Ms. Arif?"

"Only Iyad Hassan's."

David saw Bob Clair nod to himself. Vallis's

manner was calm, dispassionate, systematic — designed by Sharpe to appeal to a meticulous thinker like Clair. "How did you tie the telephone number to Ms. Arif?" Sharpe asked.

"After her arrest, we confiscated her cell phone. Its number matched the number on the slip."

"And once Mr. Jefar confessed, what steps did the FBI take to verify his veracity?"

"To start, we walked Jefar through every element of his confession. We found the van used by the assassins. We found the storage container, and extracted fingerprints belonging to both Jefar and Hassan. We retraced their steps from the day they crossed the border from Mexico — motel bills, meals, rental car fees — all charged to the Visa card Hassan picked up in Texas. Then we interrogated Jefar again to fill in any blanks."

"And what did you conclude?"

"That Jefar was absolutely truthful," Vallis answered firmly. "At no time was there any discrepancy between Jefar's account and the physical evidence."

Beside David, Hana was very still — in her, a sign of tension. "Did you investigate Ms. Arif's movements?" Sharpe asked.

"That was critical to her indictment," Vallis answered. "According to Jefar's confession, Iyad Hassan received a cell phone call informing him that the motorcade route had changed from Tenth to Fourth Street — from a caller Hassan identified as 'she' — approximately ten minutes before the bombing. This matched a call shown on Hassan's cell phone from a cell phone with a San Francisco area code. So it became important to explore Ms. Arif's activities in the time period surrounding the call."

"What did you determine?"

"By her own account, shortly before the prime minister's speech began, Ms. Arif left her hotel room, telling her husband and daughter that she wished to shop alone. A video taken by a security camera in the hotel lobby shows her leaving at eleven fifty-seven A.M., and returning at one thirty-one P.M." Vallis paused, turning to the jury as he recited facts from memory. "Hassan received the call regarding the change of route nine minutes earlier, at one twenty-two. The assassins struck eleven minutes later.

"Ms. Arif could give no specific account of her movements during that entire period of time. She bought nothing, nor do any sales personnel in the Union Square area remember having seen her."

"Did you question Ms. Arif about what she was doing?"

"Yes. In a tape-recorded interview."

Briskly, Sharpe introduced the tape into evidence; remembering Hana's vague responses, David braced himself. Sharpe pushed a button on the tape recorder. Vallis's voice echoed in the courtroom. *Where were you during Ben-Aron's speech?*

Despite her rehearsal with David, Hana had hesitated. The tone of her answer was cool, disdainful. *Wandering. Alone.*

Where?

Around the area of Union Square.

Why didn't you watch the speech with your husband and daughter?

I just didn't feel like it, Hana answered in the same chill voice. *I have heard too many speeches.*

Did you tell your husband you were going shopping?

Yes.
Did you?
No. I didn't feel like shopping, either.

Since this questioning, David reflected, he had learned that there was another way to read these answers: as the responses of a dispirited woman, weary of her marriage and depressed about her future and Munira's — a woman who needed a respite from her family. But its timing was terrible, and Hana's voice on the recording sounded less despondent than indifferent.

Did you go into any stores? Vallis asked.
No. Not that I recall.
What did you do?
As I said, Hana answered, *I wandered. I have no specific memory of where.*

On the tape, Vallis's tone was clipped. *Did you speak with anyone?*

No. At least not that I remember.

In the courtroom, Hana gazed at the table, listening to the echo of her own words. She seemed to appreciate what David understood too well: that her answers fit someone who had needed to make or receive cell phone calls without being seen or overheard. Facing Vallis, Sharpe stopped the tape.

"Was the FBI ever able," Sharpe asked him, "to put together a more specific account of Ms. Arif's movements than the one she gave you?"

"No." Again Vallis looked at the jury. "It was almost as if, for one hour and thirty-four minutes, Hana Arif had ceased to exist." Though quiet, Vallis's voice held an edge of condemnation. "As of the assassination, Ms. Arif had been in San Francisco for a little over forty-nine hours. By her own account, as confirmed by credit card receipts and the hotel security camera, this period was the only time she was not in proximity to her husband or daughter."

Her expression sober, Judge Taylor glanced at Hana; among the jurors, Ardelle Washington raised her eyebrows. "Did you try to determine," Sharpe asked, "whether some other person could have been the handler?"

"We did," Vallis answered firmly. "We did not pick Ms. Arif out of a hat, or ignore other possibilities. But we could find no evidence in conflict with Iyad Hassan's statements to Ibrahim Jefar, or Jefar's confession."

Sharpe nodded her satisfaction. "Thank you," she said. "No further questions." When David glanced at Saeb — an impulse he could not restrain — Saeb's eyes were locked on him, his look cold and accusatory. But whether this reflected Saeb's belief that David had failed his wife or his suspicion that David hoped to offer him up as an alternative, David could not tell.

David's initial approach with Vallis was clinical and linear, a reflection of the witness's own demeanor. "Let's go back to the evidence you cited against Ms. Arif," David suggested. "Start with the call from Hassan's cell phone to her, the one that occurred at 12:04 A.M. on the morning of the assassination. Did Ms. Arif's cell phone reflect any other calls to or from Mr. Hassan?"

"No."

"Or calls to or from any number you can't account for?"

"It did not. But by Mr. Jefar's description, Hassan switched cell phones frequently, to avoid being traced. It's logical that the handler would follow this procedure. Which is why, we believe, the call to

Hassan about the change in route was made from another cell phone."

"A cell phone with a San Francisco area code, correct?"

"Yes."

"Which you can't connect to Ms. Arif?"

"That's true."

David moved closer to the witness, his questions coming faster. "Have you been able to locate that cell phone?"

"We have not."

"Or find any record of who bought it?"

"No. It was purchased for cash, at Teague Electronic in San Francisco. The salesperson can't recall the buyer."

"You're an expert in counterterrorism, Agent Vallis. Is the technique you describe — the use of cell phones, purchased for cash, that are frequently replaced — common to terrorists?"

"Terrorists and drug dealers."

David adopted a look of puzzlement. "Have you ever known a terrorist to make or receive calls on a cell phone registered under his real name, for which he received a monthly bill at his home address?"

Vallis hesitated. "No."

"So in your considerable experience with terrorists, Hana Arif is the only alleged terrorist dumb enough to have done that?"

Vallis crossed his arms. "We assumed this call reflected an emergency."

"You 'assumed' that," David repeated. "Can you recall a case where one terrorist wrote his or her number for another terrorist on a piece of paper?"

"It's not usual — more often, they just call each other, and let the cell pick up new numbers. But

I've seen instances where someone has written down their number."

"Do you remember any where the terrorist *typed* their telephone number?"

"No."

"So you 'assumed,' Agent Vallis, that Hana Arif was stupid enough to use her own cell phone in communicating with Ben-Aron's assassin, having cleverly typed out her own phone number to conceal her own handwriting."

Vallis compressed his lips. "Not everything terrorists do is logical."

"Certainly not in *this* prosecution. According to Iyad Hassan, the plotters used local cell phones to avoid surveillance. Does *that* make sense to you?"

"Yes. Sophisticated terrorists know that calls to or from international numbers can be traced by the National Security Agency."

"Would you say that the terrorists in this case were sophisticated?"

"If you're referring to the ultimate planners, yes."

"Except for Ms. Arif," David said. "I guess no one told her not to use her own international cell phone."

Bob Clair, David noticed, studied Vallis with the ghost of a smile that seemed to reflect less humor than curiosity. Shrugging, Vallis said, "It was only one call. If Hassan's cell phone had blown up with him, we never could have traced it."

This was a good answer, David recognized. "But Hassan threw the phone in a trash can," he said, "where the police were able to find it."

"That's true."

"And tossed the slip of paper in a wastebasket at his motel, where the police were able to find *that,* too. With respect to Ms. Arif, you seem to have caught one lucky break after another."

"*Some* breaks," Vallis allowed. "But I remind you that Ms. Arif's own fingerprints were on that piece of paper. No one could have put those there but her."

This was another adroit response — carefully rehearsed, David understood, to remind the jury of what the defense could not explain. "But can you say," David shot back, "that Professor Arif typed that number?"

"No. The printer used to type the number can't be distinguished from others."

"And the same model printer was issued to every faculty member at Birzeit University, correct?"

"True."

"And it's also true that anyone could have walked in or out of Ms. Arif's office."

"That's my understanding, yes."

"And so anyone could have stolen a piece of paper, or even used her printer to type her number."

"True. But we found no one else's prints on her computer. And an intruder would have had no way to ensure that any individual piece of paper would have her fingerprints on it."

This was the best possible answer, one for which David had no obvious comeback — only an unsupported suspicion, directed at Saeb, that he could not express. He paused, hands on hips. "Outside of this scrap of paper and a single call, is there any evidence that Ms. Arif ever knew, spoke to, or met Iyad Hassan?"

Vallis frowned at one corner of his mouth. "He *was* a student there —"

"*That's* your answer?" David interrupted with mild incredulity. "Did Hassan even take a class from Professor Arif?"

"No." Vallis hesitated, then added, "He did take a class from Saeb Khalid, Professor Arif's husband."

"Are you seriously suggesting that Dr. Khalid introduced Professor Arif to Iyad Hassan, whereupon the two of them commenced a clandestine relationship — undetected by anyone — dedicated to the murder of Amos Ben-Aron?"

"Objection," Sharpe said at once. "No foundation —"

"Overruled," Judge Taylor broke in before David could respond. "I'd like to hear the witness's answer."

"That's one possibility," Vallis responded calmly. "Another is that they were connected by other members of the conspiracy, and arranged to communicate in secret."

"Do you have any evidence that Ms. Arif was a member of the Al Aqsa Martyrs Brigade?"

"No."

"Or Hamas?"

"No."

"Do you have any idea whatsoever as to how she could have become a member of this conspiracy?"

Briefly, Vallis looked down. "No."

David smiled. "By the way, Agent Vallis, who were the other members of the conspiracy?"

Mindful of his demeanor, the witness refocused his gaze on David, responding with an air of seeming candor. "We don't know yet."

"Was it Al Aqsa?"

"We don't know, Mr. Wolfe. All we have is Hassan's statement to Jefar."

"As an expert on terrorism, Agent Vallis, do you believe that this elaborate plot was carried out in

America by the Al Aqsa Martyrs Brigade?"

Vallis hesitated, and then, like any well-schooled expert, conceded another point in order to retain his credibility. "I don't believe they have the assets."

"So who put the motorcycles in the storage container?"

"We don't know. Because it was destroyed in the explosion, we've been unable to specifically identify the motorcycle used by Hassan. The one used by Jefar was purchased through an advertisement on the Internet, for cash, by a man the seller could identify only by a general description."

"Which was?"

"That he appeared to be of Middle Eastern origin. We've been unable to determine who he is."

David paused, letting the jury absorb that — for the first time, a conspirator other than Hana or the assassins had entered the jurors' consciousness. "Do you know the origin of the police uniforms?" he asked.

"No."

"What about the van?"

Vallis remained composed. "Same thing. Purchased through the Internet; bought for cash; the buyer an unknown man who might have been Arab."

"What about the map?" David asked. "Any idea how the map got there?"

"No."

"According to the chief of the Secret Service detail, he designated the original route less than three days before the assassination, and told only a few select members of Ben-Aron's protective detail. Yet that same route appeared on the map found by Hassan and Jefar. Do you have any idea how *that* happened?"

"No."

"Have you at least asked the Israeli government about it?"

For an instant, Vallis looked annoyed — perhaps at the Israelis, or at David, or simply at being forced to repeatedly admit his ignorance. "The Israeli government is conducting its own confidential inquiry. Whatever it may have learned, if anything, is not yet available."

"But aren't you kind of curious? I mean, here you are, prosecuting Ms. Arif for a capital crime, and you don't even know who gave the assassins the original route, or how in the world that person got it."

Sharpe began to stand. Before she could object, Taylor held up her hand, turning to the witness with a look of keen expectancy. "Our investigation is ongoing," Vallis said. "But we believe that the evidence against Ms. Arif speaks for itself."

"She didn't put the map there, did she? You at least know *that* much, right?"

Vallis folded his hands. "We don't assert that she put the map there, no."

"And given what you know about her movements while in San Francisco, she couldn't have."

"Not as far as we can determine."

"And yet," David said with open scorn, "right now you're offering the jury a three-person conspiracy — Hassan, Jefar, and Ms. Arif. One of whom can't testify."

"We know it involved more people —"

"You just don't have a clue who they might be. Are you suggesting that Ms. Arif directed their activities?"

"No."

"Or designed this very complex operation?"

"No."

"Do you know anything in her background that suggests that she's even capable of such a thing?"

"No."

"And you don't have a single name — not in America, not in the Middle East — of whoever might have planned this, or bought the van, or put the explosives in the storage container, or secured the uniforms and motorcycles."

Vallis glanced at Sharpe. But Judge Taylor's attitude had clearly dissuaded the prosecutor from objecting. "No names," he answered. "No."

"Nor do you know who leaked the change in route."

"No."

"You must know something. Any idea who ordered the murder of Ben-Aron's security man Hillel Markis?"

"No."

"Or of his friend Barak Lev?"

"No. *If* they were friends."

David threw up his hands. "Isn't that a whole lot of ignorance to place on the shoulders of a thirty-six-year-old wife and mother with no prior record of terrorist activities?"

At the corner of David's vision, Ardelle Washington turned to Vallis, her silent gaze, newly stern, commanding him to answer. "Again," Vallis said, "we may not know who planned the assassination. But the evidence against Arif cannot be ignored —"

"Didn't you indict her," David snapped, "hoping she could give you the names of those who *did* put this plot together?"

"Objection," Sharpe said. "Asked and answered. The witness has already described the evidence underlying this indictment."

"Such as it is," David said to Taylor. "We're entitled to know whether the government hoped to pressure Ms. Arif into naming others."

"Objection overruled," the judge said. "Go ahead, Agent Vallis."

Narrow-eyed, Vallis composed an answer. "We have the requisite evidence," he insisted. "Of course, it's always our hope that parties to a conspiracy will identify their coconspirators —"

"What if Ms. Arif is innocent?" David interjected. "Then she's got no way out of this trial, and no coconspirators to trade in the hope of avoiding execution."

"Objection," Sharpe said. "No foundation. Finding the answer is what juries are for."

"Sustained," the judge ruled promptly.

Turning to the witness, David searched for a striking way to close. "Beyond what you've already said," David asked, "are you aware of any additional evidence against Hana Arif?"

Vallis shook his head. "Not at this time, no."

"Then don't you think you should have waited until you had more answers?"

Vallis hesitated. "We felt what we had was sufficient to proceed."

"Did you," David said with disdain. "I guess that's what juries are for. No further questions, Your Honor."

Sharpe's redirect was brief. "With respect to the evidence against Ms. Arif," she said, "does the FBI have any reason to believe that it was fabricated?"

"We do not."

Sharpe stepped forward, slowing her speech to emphasize each word. "Do you know of anyone,

Agent Vallis, with a motive for framing Ms. Arif?"

"We know of no one."

"In your experience of terrorism, can you identify any logic behind the theory that someone took an innocent woman and decided to put her in the crosshairs of a conspiracy to assassinate the prime minister of Israel?"

"I can't." Pausing, Vallis shook his head. "That theory makes no sense to me. None at all."

With that, the prosecution's case against Hana Arif came to its end, on a question for which David had no answer.

10

Before the marshals took Hana back to the detention center, David arranged to meet with her in a private witness room. Though an armed marshal guarded the door outside, the cramped room had no window; for a few minutes of solitude, rare since Hana's imprisonment, they were alone and unobserved.

Free of her need to project dignity and self-possession, Hana slumped in her chair. "I'm so very tired," she said softly. "You must be, too."

David felt himself coming down, the adrenaline high of cross-examination evanescing. "This is hard," he acknowledged.

Hana looked up at him. "You were good. I can't imagine anyone better."

Though David could feel no elation, he managed to smile. "That's because no one is."

Unsmiling, Hana watched his eyes. "So tell me the truth," she said quietly. "That's what you want to do, isn't it? Here, where no one can see my face."

This was so precisely right that David had no heart for evasion. "Tomorrow, we start presenting our defense. The problem is that the jury's already heard it.

"I've raised all the questions in cross-examination. The most I can do is reprise them. All we have is a grab bag of suppositions and a theory we can't prove — that you were framed. But by whom? And why?" David softened his tone. "We both know the most plausible 'who.' But if there's a plausible 'why,' I don't know what it is."

Hana shrugged, a twitch of her shoulders.

David studied her face. "I can't go after him, Hana. Not without a motive."

Hana's eyelids lowered, her lashes veiling her abstracted gaze at the table between them. As if speaking to herself, she murmured, "In a week, perhaps two, the jury may find me guilty. The foreman will recite the verdict and, in seconds, my time as Munira's mother will be over.

"I'll never be alone with her. I'll barely be able to touch her — or anyone." Tears glistened on her lashes. "Prison gives me too much time to think, and leaves too little to the imagination. All I need is to take the months I've spent alone and multiply them by a hundred. Death might be a kindness.

"Have I described my cell? I can tell you about every inch. Or shall I describe my fantasies?" Her voice trailed off in embarrassment and irony. "Best they stay my own. Perhaps I can improve on them."

Silent, David worried that her composure might slip away entirely. Instead, she asked, "How did all this happen, I wonder. How did all I hoped for, all I ever felt and wanted, come to this? What happens if Saeb controls her life?"

David had no answer. In a trembling voice, Hana said, "Do I need to ask you, David? After all that's happened to us, it seems like so very little."

It took a moment for David to comprehend her. Then, yielding to instinct, he stood and circled the table. She rose from her chair to meet him. It had been thirteen years since Harvard, thirteen years since he had felt her slender body against his, so strange yet so familiar. She was almost completely still, as though drawing his warmth and closeness into her being. Gently, David stroked her hair.

A tremor ran through her body. Except for her stillness, it was as though they were making love. Then Hana drew back her head, eyes tearless as she looked into his, their mouths so close he could feel the soft exhalation of breath through her parted lips before they formed a wistful smile. "I know, David. You don't need to tell me."

Perhaps she meant that he was still her lawyer; he did not know. She touched his face with cool fingertips, letting them linger there. "I'm all right now."

Before he could respond, Hana turned and knocked on the door, summoning the marshals.

They took her away. David drove home, trying to comprehend the meaning of what had occurred between them. Then he forced himself to focus on the opening witness for the defense, Bryce Martel.

The trial resumed at nine A.M. the next day. When they brought Hana into court, she gave David a faint smile, most apparent in her eyes. Then she looked at her husband, and their light vanished.

David's opening minutes with Bryce Martel elicited a brisk summary of Martel's credentials as an expert in national security, intelligence gathering, and counterterrorism. In itself, Martel's presence lent new credence to what, heretofore, had been David's lonely defense of an accused Palestinian terrorist. But Martel's principal role was to educate jurors like Bob Clair about the ways of terrorists.

"For terrorists and spies," Martel told the jury, "deception and concealment is a fact of life. It can be no other way.

"Take Jefar and Hassan. From the moment they entered the United States, they depended on pseudonyms, false identification, and untraceable cell phone communications. That's completely consistent with the entire plot. Each step was so closely held that not even Hassan or Jefar knew what would happen until the next call from their handler. And the overall plan was so shrouded in security that the government can't even tell you who supplied the explosives, the motorcycles, the map, or the van. The operation simply vanished, leaving four men dead." Martel frowned. "In its grim way, this is a textbook assassination. Except for one anomaly."

"Which is?" David prompted.

"The case against Hana Arif. From a planning perspective, everything else about this crime is flawless. But every piece of evidence against your client reflects flaws I find inexplicable." Adjusting his glasses, Martel addressed the jury in the lucid manner of a gifted lecturer. "Take the obvious: Hassan told Jefar that Hana Arif was his handler and recruiter. That's just not done — if Hassan had mentioned a name at all, it should have been a pseudonym. A male pseudonym, at that."

"Even if they expected to die?"

Martel smiled wryly. "A terrorist can *hope* to die. But even Jefar acknowledges knowing they could be detected and arrested — to Jefar, that's why Hassan threw away the last cell phone. And yet Hassan violated the most basic rule of the 'operational security' he was otherwise so careful to maintain: don't reveal your handler's name." Pausing, Martel once more addressed the jurors. "Then there's the supposed selection of Ms. Arif — a woman known to Hassan from his time at Birzeit — as Hassan's handler. The real handler should be a stranger, whose true identity Hassan would never know."

David glanced at Ardelle Washington, her attention seemingly gripped by Martel's clarity and expertise. "What other anomalies did you find?"

A flash of disdain surfaced in Martel's eyes, the distaste of a perfectionist for human error. "I hardly need dwell on the idea that Ms. Arif would use her own cell phone to further an assassination plot. All I have to say is that it's literally senseless. So is giving Hassan her telephone number on a piece of paper.

"*Of course* it would have her fingerprints. *Of course* someone else might find it. She might as well have tucked her business card in Hassan's wallet. For *that* to make any sense, you have to believe two things: that Ms. Arif is a fool, and that whoever planned this assassination is a bigger fool for using her." Martel paused for emphasis. "Everything we know about this operation tells us just the opposite. Whoever planned the murder of Amos Ben-Aron can stake a claim to genius."

David paused, letting the jury absorb this. "Just to tie up a loose end, Mr. Martel, how *should* a competent handler communicate his telephone number?"

"In the simplest possible way — I tell you the number; you commit it to memory. Then you forget it as soon as you can."

"So is there another way to look at all of these anomalies?"

"There is," Martel said firmly. "Instead of assuming that they make no sense, assume they do. Once you make *that* assumption, these flaws are consistent with the whole — an intricate plan, designed by a very clever mind, to point the finger of blame at a woman who knows nothing." Martel's eyes glinted with something close to admiration. "If that's the case, the fabrication of a circumstantial case against Hana Arif is the ultimate blind alley, leading nowhere. In fact, you might view this prosecution as a cul-de-sac: the government can only go backward, or in circles."

Eyeing the jury, David felt a deep satisfaction: his father's friend had imbued David's theory with substance. Only Marnie Sharpe looked unimpressed.

This was her manner when she rose to cross-examine — crisp, skeptical, and wholly lacking in deference. "I've listened to your theory," she told Martel. "So let's get back to facts.

"According to her phone records, the midnight call to the defendant's cell phone took slightly over five minutes. If Ms. Arif was framed, who was it that answered?"

Though Martel appeared unruffled, he hesitated slightly. "I can't tell you that, Ms. Sharpe. I've been asked to render an expert opinion on the prosecution's case. I'm not a private investigator. Nor am I witness to some unknown fact."

"But you are, it seems, a logician. Logically, the wizard who framed Ms. Arif needed someone else to take that call, correct?"

"So it would seem."

"So how would the person who answered —

whom you can't name — get his or her hands on the cell phone?"

David did not glance at Saeb. But Sharpe's strategy was clear: to force the defense to accuse Saeb Khalid — without sufficient basis in fact or reason — or risk allowing her to make David's theory look utterly implausible. With admirable calm, Martel stated David's objection for him. "Again, that's beyond the scope of my role as expert. I'm an interpreter of fact, not a finder of new facts."

While it was true, that this answer did not satisfy the jurors was clear from Bob Clair's face. "As an 'interpreter of fact,' " Sharpe asked Martel in a faintly derisive tone, "tell me why it wouldn't have been easier for your plotters to stick to what you characterize as the terrorists' normal game plan: using a pseudonym for the handler, rather than taking the risk of falsely accusing a real person."

"Why might the planners name Ms. Arif?" Martel asked rhetorically. "As I said, one purpose could be to mislead you: instead of searching for the handler, you believed you already had her in custody, with your only remaining question in whether she would talk." Pausing, Martel returned Sharpe's condescension with a wintry smile. "But what if Ms. Arif knows nothing? If *that's* true, the most you can accomplish is to literally bury your mistake, while never trying to find the one person whose identity could help you unravel the entire plot. The real handler for Iyad Hassan."

It was a perfect answer, David thought — and the only one Martel could give. "Any idea who that could be?" Sharpe demanded.

"Nothing concrete. And it would be irresponsible for me to speculate."

"Really. So how did your 'framer' get ahold of

computer paper with Ms. Arif's fingerprints?"

Martel shrugged. "There are ways, obviously. People other than the defendant had access to her office."

Sharpe gave him a look of theatrical skepticism. "So *someone* used her phone, *someone* pilfered paper from her office, and *someone* told Hassan to lie. Is that it?"

Martel nodded. "I'm saying that could be 'it.' "

"And coming up with the identity of whoever planned all this is beyond the scope of your assignment."

"Yes."

Sharpe gave him a chill smile of her own. "That's truly disappointing, Mr. Martel. No further questions."

During the noon recess, David returned to his office, preparing with Angel Garriques for the next defense expert. "Sharpe took some of the edge off Martel," Angel said with resignation.

"An expert witness can only do so much," David answered, and then his telephone rang.

It was Ernheit. "I just got the lab test," Ernheit said hurriedly. "The one they ran for Saeb Khalid."

David stood. "What is it?"

"A three-page report. But I can't make any real sense of it, let alone relate it to your case. Maybe you can do better."

"Fax it to me," David said.

"As soon as I get back to my office," Ernheit promised. "Forty minutes or so."

Forty-five minutes later, when David left for court, the fax had not arrived.

The second defense expert, Warren Kindt, was a

former FBI agent with an expertise in bombmaking. David's half hour of direct examination served to make a single point: in its role as bomb, Jefar's Harley-Davidson was doomed to fail.

The crew-cut Kindt looked tough, his manner was casual, his voice soft. "The wiring wasn't connected to the plastique," he said. "Simple as that. Jefar could have pressed the switch all day."

"Do you know why it wasn't connected?" David asked.

"If you mean how it became disconnected, no, I don't. I'm not sure it was ever connected. The wire would probably need to be taped to the plastique. If the tape had simply peeled off, you'd think it would still be in the saddlebag containing the explosives. But I couldn't find any tape, or any residue of tape."

"What does that suggest to you?"

"Either someone had removed the tape or Hassan had never taped the wire in the first place. Take your pick. The only thing I know for sure is that Jefar's still here to testify against your client."

On cross-examination, Sharpe did what she could. "Isn't it possible," she asked, "that Hassan taped the wire to the plastique, and then it fell off while Jefar was riding his Harley?"

"It could have happened like that," Kindt answered. "Only what happened to the tape? It should still be in the saddlebag. But your crime lab folks found no tape."

Sharpe appeared unfazed. "Jefar claims not to have seen how Hassan connected the wire," she pointed out. "So did Hassan need tape? Isn't all that was required was for the wire to touch the plastique?"

"True," Kindt said agreeably. "Hassan could have put the bars of plastique on top of the wire, and assumed that the wire would stay where it was, weighed down by the explosives. One problem though — the wire was barely long enough to reach the saddlebags. With a motorcycle vibrating like a Harley does, a wire that short could come all the way out of the bag.

"That's where the wire was when I looked at it. But whether that happened because of the explosion — or before, or even after — I've got no way of telling."

Sharpe gave him an abstracted look, clearly framing her next question. "For the sake of argument, suppose — as the defense somehow imagines — that Hassan wanted Jefar to live. Would failing to connect the wire guarantee that?"

"Hardly. The blast was meant to be tightly concentrated on its target. But an explosion that essentially emulsified an armored limousine, and everyone inside it, had a genuine likelihood of killing anyone as close as Jefar."

"How?"

"You name it: fire, shards of metal, being thrown off a motorcycle and landing on your head. Even the force of the blast itself might have blown Jefar's head clean off. If one of the sharpshooters didn't do that first." Kindt paused, then added firmly, "What I'm telling you — and all I'm telling you — is that Jefar's own motorcycle was never going to kill him."

"But that's hardly a guarantee," Sharpe pressed, "that even a deliberate failure to connect the plastique would allow Jefar to live."

Kindt nodded his concurrence, more vigorously than David would have liked. "Any way you slice it,

Ibrahim Jefar is a lucky man. Assuming that a life in prison, with death your only exit, is anyone's idea of luck."

Hana, David saw, closed her eyes at the end of Kindt's last answer.

David's redirect was brief and deceptively casual. "By the way," he asked, "have you seen this technique before? That is, C-4 plastique wired to a detonator."

"Sure. At least half a dozen times."

"Name me the most recent."

"It was in Jordan," Kindt answered, just as David had prepared him. "Someone parked a motorcycle next to the car of an Iranian dissident in Amman. When the guy came back to his car, the assassins blew up the motorcycle, and him with it."

"Any idea who the assassins were?"

Sharpe started to rise, David saw. Then she shrugged, signaling her indifference. "Nobody's sure," Kindt told David. "Bombing techniques aren't subject to copyright. But everyone's guess was Iranian intelligence — the mullahs didn't like this man at all."

"Thank you," David said. "No further questions."

When David returned to his chair, he looked at Saeb, raising his eyebrows as if to say, "What do *you* think?" Saeb answered with a stare more expressionless than normal.

"I have no questions," Sharpe told Judge Taylor with ostentatious boredom, confirming for the jurors that they had heard nothing of importance.

It was six o'clock before David reached his office.

Ernheit's fax was on his desk — three pages,

neatly typed. David scanned it hurriedly and then more systematically, his reading slowed by a growing sense of consequence far greater than he ever could have imagined.

But for the surprise it contained, the report should not have taken him that long to grasp. "The client," Saeb Khalid, had submitted three samples of hair and hair follicles for testing: specimen A, specimen B, and specimen C. Each sample of hair was from a different person; "the client" wanted to know if their sources were genetically related. In short, Saeb Khalid had asked for a comparison of three persons' DNA.

David read the results a second time, then a third. The donor of specimen A was not related to the donor of specimens B and C. But donors B and C were, beyond doubt, genetically linked.

David's mouth felt dry.

For a long time — he had no idea how long — he stared at the last page of the report. He could not seem to move.

At length, his hand trembling slightly, David reached for his Rolodex. It took a moment for his awkward fingers to flip to the card he needed. Composing himself, he dialed the number of Diablo Labs in Oakland, willing someone to still be there on a Friday evening.

A man's voice answered. "Steve?" David asked.

"Afraid so — working late again. Who's this?"

"David Wolfe."

"Hey, David." The pitch of Levy's voice rose. "This must be about the Arif case."

David mustered a fair show of calm — at worst, he sounded to himself like a mildly harried lawyer. "I can't say," he said. "But I'm afraid it's a rush."

"It's always a rush," Steve Levy answered. "So

what have you got?"

"I want you to look at the results of a DNA test performed in Israel."

Briefly, David described the report. "Do you have the samples they tested?" Levy asked.

"No."

"Then I can't tell you anything more than what you just told me. I sure as hell can't tell you who these people are, or whatever else it means."

"I think you can," David answered. "I'll send you the report by messenger."

"Why?"

"Because I'm enclosing a fourth sample. I'd like you to compare its DNA to the others."

"ASAP, of course."

"It's about the Arif case." Despite his effort to control it, David's voice thickened. "All I can tell you is that this could help me save a life. But it's Friday, so at least you've got the weekend."

When David got off the call, he stared at his darkened window, motionless. Then he took the scissors from his desk drawer, and cut off a lock of his own hair.

11

David navigated the weekend on autopilot. He caught up with the media — newspapers, cable TV, and the Internet — discovering with mild surprise that the doubts he was raising in the courtroom had begun to permeate the mass consciousness. At a friend's dinner party, he employed his social reflexes to evade a barrage of questions about his defense of Hana while engaging in chatter that, hours later, he had forgotten. Minutes passed with agonizing slowness, or simply vanished. He was living in suspended animation, unreal even to himself.

On Sunday, he met with Nisreen Awad, to rehearse her testimony as a character witness for Hana. Though she greeted him warmly, David remained detached and businesslike, going through the questions and answers with little affect or digression. The question that consumed him was the one he could not ask.

Monday morning found him restless. Arriving in court, he passed through the media gauntlet without pausing, except to murmur, "It's going well." He sat at the defense table in a cocoon of his own thoughts, staring at Judge Taylor's empty bench as the cacophony of spectators grew louder. He ignored Sharpe entirely. When Hana entered and sat beside him, asking how he was, he looked at her in silence, his gaze unblinking and intense.

Her eyes widened slightly. "Is something wrong, David?"

"I don't know yet," he said, and turned away.

As a witness, Nisreen Awad was precise and firm, far less emotive than the woman he had dined with in Ramallah. She had known Hana for a decade, Nisreen told the jury, as a colleague in talks with Israel, and as her closest friend. She had seen Hana under stress, in the quiet of her home, and, most important, as a mother. "Above everything," she told the jury, "Munira is Hana's reason for being."

"Given all you know about Hana Arif," David asked her, "do you believe that Hana is capable of participating in the assassination of Amos Ben-Aron?"

For a long moment, Nisreen gazed toward Hana. "Absolutely not," she said firmly. "So many reasons make such a thing impossible."

"Such as?"

Nisreen spread her hands. "Where to start? For one thing, Hana has come to believe — and has told me many times — that yet more violence is not only pointless but an invitation for Israeli soldiers to stay in the West Bank. Look at what's happened there since this man was murdered — more deaths, more reprisals, more repression. It's utterly predictable, and the last thing Hana wanted.

"She's deeply angry with Israeli policy — that's why she resigned from our negotiating team. But this crime has sent us backward." Nisreen softened her voice. "Once again, we hear the sound of bombs and gunships. These are the sounds that gave Munira the nightmares she still suffers. I remember Hana saying, 'If I could erase her memories of explosions and death, no price would be too great.' More than anything she wishes for her daughter to be healthy in her mind and soul. Everyone else comes second."

For an instant, David had the bitter, intrusive thought that Nisreen Awad might not know just how true this was. "In your observation of Hana's marriage," David asked, "did you learn things that further persuaded you that she's incapable of risking imprisonment or death?"

Listening, Sharpe gave David a look of suspicion and surprise; on the witness stand, Nisreen Awad glanced uncomfortably at Saeb. "As to Munira," she said at last, "there was great disagreement between Hana and her husband. Saeb wished to make Munira an Islamic woman in the most traditional sense — making her cover, not allowing her to go anywhere she might meet boys, arranging her marriage, and even limiting her education. Hana has a visceral aversion to such things: she fiercely wanted for Munira to have the freedom and opportunity to become an independent woman.

"This led to bitter fights. I overheard the end of one — Saeb telling Hana that a cat would make a better mother than a woman who was American in everything but name." Nisreen paused, clearly still troubled by the memory. "Soon after, Hana discovered a lump in her breast and thought she might have cancer. The lump turned out to be benign, but I can still remember the fear in Hana's eyes. 'I cannot die,' she told me. 'I cannot let this man ruin everything Munira is.' "

In the jury box, David saw Ardelle Washington, a divorced mother of three, wince involuntarily. The courtroom felt even more still than usual; Taylor barely seemed to move, as though transfixed by what she was hearing. David had to will himself not to steal a look at Saeb. Softly, Nisreen continued, “Hana could not choose whether to die of cancer. But she could choose not to risk dying for an act of murder, which — in any event — is wholly contrary to her character. The prosecutor could show me far better evidence than this, and I would tell her that for Hana to be guilty is impossible in the deepest fiber of her being. A guilty verdict would separate her from Munira forever. Only her worst enemy could imagine a punishment this cruel.”

David was quiet, letting Nisreen’s last statement echo in the courtroom. “Thank you, Ms. Awad. I have no further questions.”

When he returned to the defense table, looking directly at Hana’s husband, Saeb’s eyes glinted with hatred and humiliation. Hana stared at the table.

“Perhaps you shouldn’t have done that,” she murmured listlessly.

“Perhaps you shouldn’t have married him,” David snapped under his breath. “But maybe that’s your sole defense.”

Hana looked away.

Sharpe cross-examined Nisreen as David would have, her tone dispassionate and ever so slightly belittling. Yes, Nisreen would do anything to save her friend — anything, Nisreen added, but lie. And no, Nisreen conceded, she could not explain the evidence. She admitted that there were no witnesses to the private conversations she had related, and was forced to acknowledge hearing Hana’s angry denunciations of Amos Ben-Aron as a pious hypocrite, talking peace while stealing land and water. By the time Nisreen left the stand, Sharpe had blunted her impact, and David was moving closer to a conclusion filled with risk: that Sharpe was forcing him to call Hana as a witness on her own behalf.

David did not say this to Hana. At noon, he hurried to his office, noting as he left that Hana could no longer look at her husband.

Steve Levy had called. Sitting in his chair, David took a deep breath and then returned the call.

Levy was at lunch. For thirty minutes, David paced his office, pausing to take distracted bites of a pastrami sandwich he could not finish. When Angel knocked on his door, David shooed him away, insisting that he needed time to think.

Minutes before he had to leave, his telephone rang.

It was Levy. "I've run the test," he said.

David sat down heavily. "And?"

"I don't know what you're trying to prove. But the results are clear enough. You already know that B is a genetic match with C, while A is a match with neither." Levy paused, as though gazing at his notes. "The hair sample you sent me — which I'll call sample D — matches neither A nor B. The genetic match is between that person and sample C."

It was seconds before David could ask, "And so?"

"My conclusion, David, is that B and D are genetically reflected in the person represented by sample C. That's really all it could be."

David managed to thank Steve Levy and get off the phone, overcome by how profoundly the meaning of his life had changed. And, if he and Hana could bear it, the trial itself.

David Wolfe was Munira Khalid's father.

Twenty minutes later, Sharpe and David were sequestered in Judge Taylor's chambers, the judge appraising the lawyers from behind her desk. "The jury's waiting for us," she said to David. "You requested this conference."

David felt the tingle of his nerve ends. "I need a recess," he said baldly. "Over the noon hour, I learned about a new piece of evidence, potentially transformative of my client's defense. It also may affect my status as her lawyer."

Taylor's eyebrows shot up. David watched her mentally catalog the possibilities, including that David had just discovered that Hana Arif had lied to him about her innocence. "Can you favor us with a more elaborate explanation?"

"I can't, Your Honor. Not before I discuss it with my client."

Though wary, Sharpe regarded him with the trace of a smile: she plainly suspected, as David would have in her place, that whatever had shaken him so badly could only serve her case. "Ms. Sharpe?" Taylor asked.

The prosecutor shrugged. "On behalf of the United States, I don't want *any* delay. But I suppose we can spare one afternoon."

"That's all I'm giving you," the judge told David. "So meet with your client straightaway."

When David entered the courtroom, the jury was assembled and Hana waited at the defense table. He walked past Saeb without acknowledging his presence.

Hana looked up at him anxiously. "What's happening?"

For all David thought he knew about her, he felt as though he were seeing a different person. Slowly sitting down beside her, he answered, "I've asked the judge for a recess. Her clerk is looking for a witness room, so we can talk."

Worry stole through her eyes. "Concerning what?"

David inhaled. "Thirteen years of deception. Yours, to be precise."

12

The marshals sequestered David and Hana in the same claustrophobic witness room as before, the wooden table between them. She studied him with an even gaze that did not quite conceal her anxiety, as if she felt a danger she could not yet define. Warily, she asked, "What is it we need to discuss?"

"Our daughter."

Hana was still, her eyes widening slightly. "What do you mean?"

"Do not do this." David spoke the words slowly and emphatically. "One more lie, one more evasion, and I'll petition Taylor for leave to withdraw as your counsel. When I tell her why, she'll have no choice but to grant it."

Hana's throat pulsed. "How can you know that you're her father?"

"The same way as Saeb. He had three hair samples tested for DNA — his, yours, and Munira's. I just added mine to the mix."

"Please, I don't understand."

"Oh, I think you do. You've fooled us both, beginning at Harvard. But Saeb's not quite as dense as I am. Though to be fair, he's had thirteen years to live with you, and a daughter who became a walking clue." David's voice was level, relentless. "What would motivate you, I always wondered, to become part of this assassination? But now it all makes sense.

"In Israel, Zev Ernheit told me the story of a married woman who became a suicide bomber. She was pregnant with her lover's child. Her brother-in-law gave her a choice: take some Jews with you or become the victim of an honor killing —"

"I didn't know."

David ignored this. "Saeb must have given you a choice," he continued. "Let him use you as a cutout, or he'd unmask you as the whore whose daughter was fathered by a Jew. So you became his operational protection, insulating him from discovery by communicating with Hassan —"

"Then why would I hire Munira's father as my lawyer?" Hana's voice shook, and tears surfaced in her eyes. "Yes, I wondered. And when Munira grew older, and taller, I was afraid. But that is all."

"Really?" David paused, then quoted her own words back to her, across the years. " 'We're a shame culture, not a guilt culture.' "

Hana stared at him. "Do you really know me so little?"

David gave her a cold smile. "I don't know you at all."

"Saeb never told me, David. I swear it."

David felt no pity. "That's quite a marriage," he said. "I hope you don't feel too misled."

Hana flinched. "I know you're hurt —"

" 'Hurt'?" David echoed. "Another woman might find a less trivial word."

"*Stop* it." Her voice was tight, desperate. "You're so caught up in my betrayal that you can't recognize the truth when it's staring back at you."

" 'The truth'? What is it today?"

"That I had no motive. And that Saeb's motive is Munira. Tell me how long he has known this."

Whatever David suspected, the tremor in her voice had the undertone of discovery, terrible in its consequences. "Almost a year now!"

Briefly, Hana closed her eyes, as though struggling to extract sense from memory. "Saeb must have suspected for years before that," she said slowly. "The more he doubted, the more he turned his own torment — his images of you and me as lovers — into making Munira everything I was not." Hana massaged her temples. "And when Saeb became certain whose daughter she was, he brooded over a way of punishing me more terrible than a bullet in the head. A Muslim honor killing dressed up as an American murder trial.

"An enlightened Arab would divorce me. A traditional man would murder me. Saeb selected a more useful death." Hana gazed at David imploringly. "I'm innocent, David. How many more polygraphs do you wish me to take?"

David was buffeted by emotions too complex to unravel. "Then in your version of the truth, Saeb becomes the handler."

"Yes. He could have taken the paper, and gotten the cell phone from my purse." Hana's voice filled with anguish. "What did he mean to do to her, once all this was over? What *will* he do —"

"Don't use her on me," David snapped. "All I want from you is the truth."

"You can choose what truth to believe: Saeb blackmailed me, or he framed me. But either way, Munira is your daughter. Please, she's not to blame for any of this."

This caused David to sit back, silent. He had a daughter, a young Arab girl who, for much of her life, had been punished in her parents' place. And now that fact — and that girl — were the hidden key to her mother's trial, transforming the inexplicable into a pattern that made its own chilling sense. "What's between the two of us," David said at last, "has to wait. The one decision that can't wait is the role Munira will play in your defense."

Hana's face contorted. "I can't expose her, David. Not in open court."

"I don't want you to. I'll save that revelation for later."

"And tell Munira and the world that Saeb is not her father? Can't you see what that would do to her?"

"It might well be devastating." David answered. "So would you rather be found guilty? Do you think Munira would prefer having a dead mother to having a father who's a Jew?"

David watched the full implication of his question overcome Hana's last reserves. She covered her face, shoulders trembling with sobs he could not hear.

"Who gets to survive, Hana? You or Saeb? You can 'protect' Munira only by protecting the husband you say is trying to kill you. Or you can try to save yourself and our daughter by letting me nail your husband to the wall.

"I've only known that I'm a father for two hours. But now I can put a price on all I've given up for you: Munira's life. No father would leave this girl to Saeb Khalid."

The only sign that Hana heard him was her stillness. After a time, she uncovered her face in what seemed to be an act of will. "Tell me what it is you want."

"For you to testify in your own defense. Not as

the angry Palestinian woman I saw fencing with the FBI but as the one I'm seeing now. And then I want you to sit back and watch me trade your life for Saeb's."

"Even if you think I'm the handler. Even if you think that Saeb blackmailed me into helping murder Amos Ben-Aron."

"Even so," David answered. "Ben-Aron's dead. Munira's still alive."

Hana watched his face. "I'm sorry, David. I know what I've done to you. To be a parent changes everything."

David let her apology go unanswered. "You've got eighteen hours," he said. "Then you have to choose between Munira's feelings and her life. I'm going to spend that time reflecting on the only thing about this maze of lies I know for sure: that Munira is my daughter."

As though in a trance, David returned to his office, coping with details that could not wait, striving to clear the mental space to absorb the fact that, elsewhere in this city, a girl who was part of him lived frightened and alone.

David heard a soft rap on his door. Expecting Angel, he called out sharply, "What is it?" When the door opened, he saw that his visitor was Carole Shorr.

Tentative, she stopped in the doorway, eyes filled with uncertainty. "I was afraid to call," she said.

David touched the bridge of his nose, and then looked up at her. "You could have," he said gently. "I'd never refuse to see you. It's just that this isn't a good day for it."

She stood there, unsure of whether to stay or go. "I've been following the trial. All I wanted to say is that I understand a little better. Maybe when the case is over, we could talk about whether that matters to us."

The word "us" told David more than anything else she could say. He did not know how to respond; all he could feel at this moment was the need for a friend, a way to share his burden. Softly, Carole said, "I've never seen you look this tired."

Perhaps it was the simple word of kindness; perhaps it was the memory of days and nights when Carole was his closest friend, when they talked and listened and planned and argued, each believing, at least hoping, that the only end to their life together would come in their old age. Whatever the cause, David felt the rush of dammed emotions he could no longer quite control. "I'm more than tired, Carole. I feel like my life has been turned inside out, that I've completely lost my balance. You know me — I always felt I was prepared for anything, and could deal with whatever life threw at me. No more."

Carole tried to smile. "Then maybe it's good I came."

David heard a familiar note in her voice, Carole as source of comfort and advice. "If anyone could fix this," he said, "you could. But no one can."

"I could try."

David shook his head. "It's more complicated than you can ever know. And I can't tell you why, because it involves lives other than yours or mine."

Carole shook her head, bemusement combining with persistence. "Please, David. I tried to walk away from you. But I'm finding that I never did, not in my heart. Give me the chance to help you. Please don't shut me out."

"I don't *want* to," David burst out. "You can't

know how much I'd like to talk with you, and how much I don't want to seem like someone who never loved you. Because that's just not true. But what's happened to me is something I can't share with anyone. Because an innocent person could suffer, or worse than suffer. And I can't burden either one of us with that."

Carole watched his face. "Is this about Hana Arif? Please, tell me."

David exhaled. "Hana, and much more than Hana. It's also about me."

Carole stared back at him, and the blood seemed to leave her face. "You still love her, don't you?"

David shook his head. "It's not just about love, or who I love. I can't say any more than that."

Carole looked away. After a time, she said, "Once I thought we were the essence of each other's life. But you don't have a life to give me. Whatever happens, you've given it to her. I could never be more than a substitute for Hana, standing with my nose pressed against the glass." Abruptly, she stood, speaking in a despondent rush. "I'm sorry, but I have to leave now. I have to take my own life back."

She hurried to the door, as if to make it outside before she fell apart. Then she was gone, the door ajar behind her, and all that remained was the rapid click of her heels on the marble floor.

13

By the time he reached Saeb's apartment, David had regained his self-control, though he still felt poised on the edge of a precipice. But when Saeb opened the door, David felt a coolness steal through him.

Hana's husband stared at him, making no move to step aside. "What is it?"

"I came to see Munira. And you."

An emotion akin to irritation, but more edgy, crossed Saeb's face. "Without calling?"

"Hana wants me to talk with her daughter. I was on my way home, and I realized that this is my window of opportunity."

Saeb's eyes hardened. "I lack your sense of urgency. It is not as if Munira's leaving. As you know, we are prisoners of your government."

"Munira's certainly a prisoner. And I'm still standing in the hallway." David kept his voice quiet. "You and I have some things to settle. As for Munira, if you want Hana to get an order giving her lawyer access to her daughter, I'll be back. Or we can just talk now."

A smile of disdain, summoned with apparent effort, flashed and vanished on Saeb's face. "Such theatrics. But I suppose you're tired."

Grudgingly, Saeb admitted him. Glancing about

the stark living room, David looked for Munira and saw no one. He took a chair without invitation.

Saeb hesitated, then sat on the edge of the couch across from him. "Hana will be testifying," David said bluntly. "I want Munira to be there. Professing maternal devotion to a girl the jurors have never seen is no longer an option."

Saeb shook his head. "This is too much stress for her."

"More than a dead mother? I don't see Munira as quite so fragile."

Saeb gave David a long, appraising look. "And if I refuse?"

"I already told you." David still spoke quietly. "I'm not here to ask your permission. I came to take Munira to dinner and tell her what to expect. Alone."

The corners of Saeb's eyes narrowed slightly, as though he was sensing a change in the balance between them. "Hana's on trial. Her needs are paramount, I agree. But it is not for her lawyer to bark orders at me about our daughter."

David inclined his head toward the bedrooms. "I count three doors in that hallway. You can make me open them all, or you can get Munira yourself. I've got no more time to spend with you."

Saeb hesitated and then smiled, a belated effort to evince superiority. "As I said, such theatrics. But soon this will be over, and you and I will part company, as will you and Munira. So enjoy your little moment of transitory power."

Stiffly, Saeb stood, walking past David to the hallway. David did not look over his shoulder; he heard Saeb, speaking in Arabic, then the light voice of his daughter. Only when a door opened did David turn.

Munira stood beside Saeb, glancing in confusion at David, still a girl at the beginning of her emergence into womanhood. But the alteration David saw in her was more than the passage of weeks, and it was all he could do not to show this on his face. With a penetrant gaze, Saeb looked from Munira to David. "I've explained to Munira why you've come," Saeb said. "So take her. You and I will discuss this later."

Side by side, they walked five blocks to the Elite Café, where David could secure a private booth — a lawyer in his business suit, an Arab girl in a dark head scarf and *abaya.* Recognizing David, the hostess ushered them to a table, with a curious look at Munira.

The girl sat across from him, carefully rearranging the folds of her clothing with graceful fingers. "You came to talk about my mother," Munira said worriedly. "Is she all right?"

David nodded, clinging to his role as lawyer. "She's testifying soon. I know, and you know, how important you are to her. I'd like the jurors to see for themselves how important *she* is to *you*."

Munira looked at him from beneath dark lashes. "You wish me to be in court?"

"Yes."

"Then I will be, no matter what he says. I could not stand to lose her."

She spoke the words with such intensity that David's heart went out to her. David imagined her sleepless nights and anxious days, cocooned from the world in a place that held nothing of her own, not even the person David was now certain Munira loved most. "Good," he said. "That will really help her."

Munira nodded gravely. Their waiter came, dispensing menus. "Take a look," David suggested. "You could probably use something to eat."

As Munira considered the Cajun offerings of the menu, David studied her without embarrassment. A few moments of this changed his earlier assessment: she *would* be beautiful, he decided, merely in a different way from Hana, the lines of her face stronger and more chiseled, her eyes less limpid but flashing with intelligence. Still scanning the menu, Munira put a curled middle finger to her lips and rested her index finger on her cheek, and David knew at once where this mannerism had come from. It was his mother, to the life.

David felt as if his heart had skipped a beat. *You're my daughter,* he wanted to say. *Don't you feel it?* Looking up at him, Munira asked, "What is blackened catfish?"

David managed to smile. "I'm not sure you want to know, Munira. How do you feel about spicy seafood?"

He knew nothing, of course, about what his daughter liked or disliked — except, perhaps, Jews. "At home," Munira informed him, "we eat many spicy things."

"Then maybe you should try the gumbo."

Taking their order, the waitress bought David coffee. Munira gazed at the porcelain cup in front of him. "Whenever I see a coffee cup," she said softly, "I remember my grandfather's parents, leaving their teacups on the table when they ran away from the Zionists. They thought they would be back soon."

Gently, David said, "That was almost sixty years ago."

"It doesn't matter," the girl insisted. "I want my

grandfather to have his house back, as beautiful as it was."

How long would it be, David wondered, before the dream of return did not consume the members of Hana's family? Munira was his daughter and yet not his daughter, estranged from him by history and deception. "The most important thing," David told her, "is that you have your own life, and your own dreams. You can't make up to your grandparents, or even your parents, all the things that happened to them."

But this was too abstract, David saw at once. Her face closing, Munira said, "They are part of me. Their struggle is our struggle, the struggle of all Palestinians."

This rote echo of Saeb Khalid jarred David, reminding him of the delicacy of the psychic space he suddenly occupied. He was no different from a surrogate father, except in his intentions — Munira had lived her life with others, oblivious to her power to change *his* life. Awkwardly, he ventured, "I know how hard things have been. I'm wondering if there's some way I can help you."

Munira's brows knit as she considered his offer. Shyly, she asked, "Would it be okay for you to buy me a cell phone?"

Her request was so unexpected that David smiled; then he realized that, for Munira, a cell phone might be the only way of breaking her isolation. "What would your father say?" he asked.

Munira looked down, a young girl caught between her desires and the truth. "He would be angry at you," she conceded. "But my mother wouldn't. She'd just tell me not to lose it."

David cocked his head. "So what should I do?"

Munira looked into his face. "I have to talk with

my friends," she said with sudden fierceness. "I haven't talked to Yasmin since the Zionist was killed."

"Who's Yasmin?"

"My best friend from Ramallah. But she's in America now — Washington, D.C. Her parents work for the Palestinian Authority." Her words came out in an angry rush. "When we came on this trip, my mother said I could call Yasmin every day. But then I lost my cell phone. My mother was sleeping, and I couldn't find her phone. When I borrowed my father's he got so mad I thought he'd kill me."

Sipping his coffee, David gazed across its rim at the outraged girl who was his daughter. "When was that?"

"A long time ago." Pausing, Munira looked at the ceiling, calculating the time of the injustice. "It was the day before, I think."

"Before the assassination of Amos Ben-Aron?"

"Yes."

Carefully, David put down his cup. "Were you able to call Yasmin?"

Munira nodded. "I had to leave a message. But then she called me back, and we talked until the battery died. We'd just got through talking when my father started banging on my door."

"What happened?"

"He was looking for his cell phone. He opened the door and saw it in my hand. He started yelling that I'd stolen it from his coat." Munira looked as bewildered as she sounded. "Sometimes I borrow my mom's. But he said the phone was not to be used by children, and asked me if I'd been calling people."

David kept his tone neutral. "What did you say?"

Munira looked down. "I was afraid of what would happen if I admitted that I'd used it. So I said I never did."

"Did he believe you?"

"He kept asking me if I was lying, or if I was sure. I was too frightened to tell the truth. Instead I told him the battery was dead." Munira shook her head. "But he still won't give me another cell phone. That's his punishment for stealing."

David felt a swift sequence of realizations come to him — that Saeb had kept the FBI from meeting with Munira; that he restricted her contacts with David; that she almost always saw her mother in Saeb's company; that he'd kept her from attending a trial that featured repeated references to cell phone calls and raised the pervasive, lingering question of who else had access to her mother's phone. Which was, perhaps, not quite the right question.

"Just out of curiosity," David asked mildly, "did you even see your dad actually use that phone?"

"I can't remember." Munira looked vaguely troubled, as though disturbed by the aftermath of a nightmare she could no longer quite recall. "He has another one now, I think. I haven't seen the one I took since he got it back from me."

David was momentarily quiet. "I'll talk to your mom about a cell phone," he promised. "Then maybe I'll have a word with your dad."

The next morning, shortly after six A.M. — nine A.M. in Washington — David called the office of the Palestinian mission. When the receptionist answered, he identified himself as the lawyer for Hana Arif. The purpose of his call, he said, was difficult to explain. But he needed to speak to a friend of the Khalid family who worked for the Palestinian Authority — a man or woman he could identify only as the parents of a girl named Yasmin.

At length a woman came to the telephone, her English sibilant but clear. "This is Furah Al-Shanty, mother of Munira's friend Yasmin. And you are David Wolfe?"

"Yes."

"Well, Mr. Wolfe, you seem to be a very able lawyer. Why is it that you're calling?"

"It's complicated and highly confidential. But you may have a piece of paper critical to Hana's defense."

"What it is, I can't imagine. But go on."

"Your daughter Yasmin has her own cell phone, I believe. Do you keep copies of your billing records?"

"For our phones? Definitely, for business reasons. But for Yasmin's I would have to see."

Standing in his kitchen, David began pacing. "Could you look for me — specifically, the bill covering the period before and after the assassination. I need to see if Yasmin received or placed a call to a particular cell phone number."

"All right, then. I can't look until tonight. If I find something, what should I do?"

"Fax it to my office. And if I'm not in, tell my secretary to come get me, even if I'm in court."

When the call was over, David sat back down. He closed his eyes and came as close to praying as he had since he'd stood at the Western Wall.

14

By the time Hana took the witness stand, she and David had rehearsed the degree to which she could intimate — without assigning a motive — that her own husband might have framed her. Though his own conversation with Munira shadowed David's thoughts, he told Hana nothing about it. This testimony would require all the equilibrium she possessed; perceiving her daughter as a potential witness against her husband would only torment Hana further, making Munira's presence in the courtroom close to unendurable. She had enough to absorb already: if Hana had told him the truth, she had only just learned that the daughter who fiercely identified herself as Palestinian was both an Arab and a Jew.

The moment Munira entered the courtroom with Saeb, Hana looked anxious: she had not seen the girl since David had told her that Munira was his daughter, and that her husband knew it. But Saeb did not know that David and Hana had discovered this, and Munira knew nothing at all. In the last moments before the judge's deputy called the courtroom to order, Hana did not look at Saeb. Instead, she smiled at her daughter, her gaze unwavering, as though she were seeing Munira anew.

For David, this moment had an unsettling

doubleness — Hana's obvious pain at being unable to touch her daughter was both genuine and, he hoped, affecting to the jury. Glancing at the jurors, David saw that Ardelle Washington watched intently, her look seeming to combine the compassion of a mother with her curiosity at seeing Hana, the image of modernity, and her child, who, except for her face and hands, was completely shrouded in black. Beside them, Saeb stared at David with such intensity that David wondered if Saeb was sensing the dangers gathering beneath the surface of the trial. Then the deputy called out, "All rise," and David turned again to the task that would determine whether Hana lived or died.

After the many days in court that had preceded it, David sensed that, for Hana, the act of testifying came as a relief. Positioning himself so that Hana faced the jurors as she responded to his questions, David asked simply, "Were you involved — in any way — in the plot to assassinate Amos Ben-Aron?"

For the first time, the jurors heard Hana's voice, soft but firm. "In no way. I know nothing more about the crime than anyone who reads the newspapers. When I heard that the prime minister of Israel had been killed by a suicide bomber, I was horrified."

"Would you have ever considered participating in a plan to kill him?"

"No." Hana shook her head with vehemence. "That is something I could never do."

"And why is that?"

"Where to start?" Gazing at the jurors, Hana paused, as if unsure of how to address the enormity of such a question. "This murder accomplishes nothing but evil. It has caused more violence and suffering for my people. In the world's eyes, it labels us as terrorists. It postpones the day when we will have our own country. And it may condemn our children, and Jewish children, to hate and kill each other as we did, and our parents and grandparents did before us."

For an instant, Hana stopped herself: David could read on her face the truth that must have struck her — that the children on both sides were personified by her own daughter. "I did not love Ben-Aron," Hana conceded. "I did not trust him. But the men who plotted this murder have no vision but the spilling of more blood. Far better for Jews and Palestinians that *they* were dead rather than Amos Ben-Aron."

Her last sentence gave David a chill: perhaps she was speaking of her own husband. "Yet all of that," Hana finished softly, "is nothing compared to the fact that I am Munira's mother. I would never risk our separation, or leave her to be raised by anyone else."

At the prosecution table, Marnie Sharpe watched Hana with a keen but neutral expression. "Is there something in Munira's life," David asked, "that intensifies your worry for her?"

Hana looked down as though trying to frame her answer with the greatest care. "Munira," she said at last, "is a girl facing womanhood, yet a child so traumatized by violence that it still causes her nightmares. I want her to feel joy in life, not terror. I want her to discover how intelligent and strong she is, how capable of acting for herself. I want her to be whole."

Her voice was thick with emotion — even Judge Taylor, who had watched sociopaths weep in the witness box over victims they had murdered without remorse, regarded Hana with an expression softer than before. "Munira," Hana continued, "is where my husband and I encounter the greatest difficulties. It is difficult to say such private things in public, and in front of her. But they are the deepest reason I could never take part in murdering Amos Ben-Aron.

"Saeb would require Munira to cover herself; to be subservient; and, when she is older, to marry a husband of his choosing. I want Munira to become whoever she chooses to be and, *if* she chooses, to find a husband who will respect her as his equal." Her voice filled with quiet determination. "I don't want my daughter buried — not in rubble, and not in a shroud that covers her body and deadens her soul. *She* is who I fight for now. I cannot entrust her future to Saeb."

They had come to the heart of it, David realized. The trial reflected Hana's life — a visceral struggle between wife and husband, now being waged with such ruthlessness that David had insisted on Munira's presence. Beside her, Saeb sat stiffly, his face a rictus of anger and humiliation; Munira's eyes were downcast, her body hunched, as though she wished to disappear. "Without me," Hana said quietly, "there will be no one who can speak for Munira until she can speak for herself." Looking at her daughter, Hana's eyes filled with pain; when she turned back to David and the jury, finishing her answer, her words were wholly unrehearsed. "I look at Munira and see my life reflected. When I was young, I tried to be free. But I was so bound up with family, and the struggle of my people, that it defined my life and who I chose to marry. For that mistake, I am sorry — for Saeb, for Munira, and for anyone affected by my choice.

"I want Munira to feel connected to her people and her family, always. But I want *her* to define for herself the way in which she honors them." Pausing, Hana finished quietly. "Munira is not yet thirteen. As women, she and I have so much to do together. That work does not include killing Jews."

At the corner of his vision, David saw Bob Clair, himself Jewish, studying Hana with an expression that seemed to contain a measure of sympathy. After a pause, David asked, "Why did the three of you come to San Francisco?"

"Saeb was traveling to America — to shadow Ben-Aron and to criticize his peace plan. But that was Saeb's concern. I wanted Munira to see a country very different from her own, in case she someday wished to study here."

"Who suggested that you come?"

"Saeb did." Hana hesitated. "I was surprised. In the past year there has been much tension between us. Most of it over Munira."

The passion in her voice had diminished — the painful necessity of deploying her daughter in her own defense seemed to drain her. His tone even, David inquired, "How did you respond to Saeb's invitation?"

"That I would come only if we could bring Munira. He answered that he did not wish for Munira to experience this 'degrading culture.' "

"How did you resolve this disagreement?" David asked.

"I said that if Munira stayed home, so would I. In the end, Saeb relented."

A sudden thought hit David hard: if Hana had not insisted that Munira come, she would not now be in this courtroom, and her daughter would not have borrowed Saeb's cell phone. Abruptly, David asked, "Have you ever met Iyad Hassan?"

Hana shook her head. "No," she answered firmly. "I don't even recognize his picture."

"Did you type your cell phone number and give it to Hassan?"

"I did not."

"Who else knows that cell phone number?"

Hana glanced at her husband and daughter. "As far as I know, only Saeb and Munira. Life where we are is too violent and unpredictable — shootings, bombings, delays at checkpoints. I never wanted to be out of touch with Munira, or for her to be unable to reach me."

"Do you know how your fingerprints got on the piece of paper?"

"I don't. But there are only two places the paper could have come from — my office or our home."

"Who," David asked, "has access to your home?"

"Other than guests? Just Saeb, Munira, and our cleaning lady."

"What about access to your office?"

"I'm the only one who has a key. But I lock it only when I leave for the night."

They were settling into a rhythm now, constructing an exercise in logic for the jury. "So during the day," David followed up, "who has access to your office?"

"Colleagues, students — anyone can walk in, really."

"So, in theory, anyone could have walked into your office and taken a piece of paper that you'd touched."

"True."

David waited a beat. "But they also would have had to know your cell phone number, wouldn't they?"

"Yes."

"Aside from Saeb and Munira, do you know how anyone else could have gotten that number?"

"I'm sorry," Hana answered softly. "I don't."

The answer, as they had planned, was less an apology than the statement of a disturbing truth. "Tell me," David asked, "did Saeb and Munira know that you reserved this cell phone for them alone?"

Hana hesitated. "I don't think I ever told them that."

Among the jurors, David saw Rosella Suarez cast a sideways glance in Saeb's direction. "Where do you keep your cell phone?" David asked.

"In my purse. Always."

"And who had access to your purse?"

Hana smiled faintly. "No one, if I have anything to do with it. Although Munira sometimes searched it for something she needed."

David paused again. "While you were in San Francisco, did you lend your cell phone to Saeb or Munira?"

"No. Neither of them asked for it."

"At 12:04 A.M. on June 15, the day Amos Ben-Aron was murdered, what were you doing?"

A shadow crossed Hana's face. "By then, I had been asleep for hours."

"At that time, did you receive a call from anyone?"

"Not that I know of," Hana answered. "No one left a message. Let alone this suicide bomber, a man I'd never met."

"Do you know how it happened that Iyad Hassan's cell phone reflected a call to your cell phone?"

Briefly, Hana closed her eyes. "If I knew who to

blame, I wouldn't be here, charged with murder. Someone else would be."

"During Ben-Aron's speech," David said, "you told the FBI you were wandering in Union Square. Why weren't you watching with your husband and daughter?"

"Because I did not wish to hear yet another speech by Ben-Aron, or see my daughter listening to her father's denunciation. Suddenly the hotel room felt too small, and I wanted to be alone."

"Why did you tell your husband you were going shopping?"

"Because it was easier than telling the truth. I did not wish to quarrel in front of Munira."

"During the time you were gone, did you speak with anyone by cell phone or in person?"

"No." Emotion crept into her voice. "I wandered aimlessly, thinking about my life. I could have just as well been sleepwalking."

Deliberately, David paused. "Is it your conclusion that someone arranged the evidence to implicate you in the murder of Amos Ben-Aron?"

Hana seemed to gather herself. "Yes."

"Do you know who?"

Hana could have given many answers. But she gave the one that was literally true, chosen by David to preserve her options and maintain the element of surprise. "No," she said softly. "All I know for certain is that whoever did this must hate me very much."

"Thank you," David said. "No further questions."

During the ten-minute recess before Sharpe's cross-examination, David looked vainly for his secretary, hoping that she had come with phone records retrieved by Yasmin's mother. At the prosecution table, Sharpe methodically scribbled notes, oblivious to the three members of a family that was slowly being torn apart. David gazed at each of them: Hana sat lost in her own thoughts; Saeb stared fixedly at the floor; Munira, looking worried and unhappy, sat perhaps a little farther from the man she still believed to be her father.

When the recess ended, Sharpe was quickly on her feet. "Do you believe, Ms. Arif, that Palestinians have the right to kill Israelis?"

Hana and David had prepared for this. "In the past," Hana answered, "I said that we were entitled to kill those who occupied our land — soldiers, not civilians. But I no longer say such things, or believe them. My daughter has seen too much death."

"Yet you quit the negotiating team that tries to work out disputes with Israel."

"Yes."

"And at the time you called the Israelis in general — and Amos Ben-Aron in particular — thieves and liars."

Hana appraised Sharpe calmly. "I said much more than that, actually. I also said that the security fence was cover for stealing land and water, and that Amos Ben-Aron was a pious hypocrite, not some saintly dove of peace. And I meant every word. But words are not bombs." Her voice acquired a tinge of sarcasm. "If you imprisoned Palestinians for angry words, as the Israelis sometimes do, the IDF would have no one to harass at checkpoints. All of us would be prisoners."

Easy, David counseled her mentally. Sharpe favored Hana with a skeptical smile. "So tell me, Ms. Arif, just who is it that inflicted this terrible injustice by fabricating evidence against you?"

"As I said," Hana answered, "I don't know. Being innocent means that I can't know who is guilty."

"Does it? You have no idea whatsoever how you might have provoked such loathing, or in whom?"

David did not look at Saeb or Munira. On the witness stand, Hana shifted, appearing fretful. "I suppose there must be those who hate me. But as to who did this, I can't tell you."

"Of the nameless people who hate you, how many have access to your office or your cell phone?"

Hana gave a helpless shrug. "As I say, I have no information about this."

"Did your daughter frame you?"

"Of course not."

"You don't think she had a motive?"

Hana composed herself. "That is not a serious question. Munira is twelve years old. Our quarrels are about her homework, and the careless way she sometimes loses things."

Softly, Sharpe said, "I guess that leaves your husband."

Hana began to speak, then did not. "What do you mean?" she finally asked.

Briefly, Sharpe smiled as if at the feebleness of this response. "Let me spell it out for you. Your only explanation for the physical evidence against you is that you were framed. Yet you admit that no one had your cell phone number but your husband and your daughter —"

"As far as I know," Hana protested.

"As far as you know," Sharpe echoed disdainfully. "So aren't you saying that, as far as you know, you were framed by your own husband?"

Hana gazed at Saeb and Munira, her tension palpable; David had brought her to the brink of an accusation, and now Sharpe had called their bluff. "I would like to think," Hana temporized, "that our marital disappointments have not gone quite that far."

"I don't care what you 'would like to think,' " Sharpe snapped. "I care about the physical evidence: a telephone number, a set of fingerprints, and a telephone call. You claim that they were planted. By whom if not your husband?"

Hana looked away. "I don't know how this happened. I can't say who did this."

"Your husband obviously." Sharpe paused, as if struck by a new thought. "Oh, *and* Iyad Hassan. Did Hassan hate you, too?"

"I don't know how he could have. As I have said, I never met him."

"Then why did he tell Ibrahim Jefar that you'd recruited him to assassinate Amos Ben-Aron?"

"I don't know," Hana insisted. "I don't even know *if* Hassan said that to Jefar."

"In that case, can you tell me why your husband and two men you say you never met, Hassan and Jefar, *all* conspired to frame you?"

For a moment, Hana seemed to stare into a void. Among the jurors, David saw, Bob Clair's apparent sympathy was being replaced by a sharp-eyed look of skepticism. "I don't know how this happened," Hana repeated at last.

Sharpe let Hana sit there a moment longer, an object lesson in evasion. "In that case," she said dismissively, "I see no point in asking you anything more at all."

This last, gratuitous comment was beyond David's power to repair. Wondering how to buttress Hana's credibility on redirect without revealing Munira's paternity, David glanced over his shoulder and saw his secretary holding a manila envelope.

"Your Honor," David said to the judge, "I request a ten-minute recess."

15

Alone in the witness room, David spread the telephone records in front of him. To his relief, they listed all the long-distance calls placed to or from Yasmin's cell phone. As Munira's account had suggested, there were two such calls on June 14, minutes apart: the first, brief call to Yasmin's phone was consistent with Munira leaving a message; the second call, from Yasmin's phone, twenty-two minutes in duration, clearly reflected a conversation. Staring at the cell phone number of the person who'd originally called Yasmin — undoubtedly Munira — David felt an emptiness in the pit of his stomach.

The number, (415) 669-3666, had a San Francisco area code. It was the number about which the FBI had interrogated Hana and Saeb; the number, David had learned since, of the cell phone used to warn Iyad Hassan that the route of Ben-Aron's motorcade had changed from Tenth to Fourth Street. Though borrowed by Munira, the cell phone was Saeb's, and it meant that Saeb Khalid — not his wife — might well have been the handler for Iyad Hassan.

David tried to grasp the full dimensions of what he had just learned. Hillel Markis had probably leaked the change of route, and his call had likely been to Saeb. If true, this meant that Saeb must be connected to the ultimate authors of the plot, if only through an intermediary. This made it far more plausible that Hassan had lied to Jefar about the identity of his handler. With this fact, the credibility of the remaining evidence against Hana was tarnished; there was now far less reason for David to doubt Hana's claim of innocence — and less need, save for a lawyer's need for dispassion, to wall himself off from her.

But one wrenching and unavoidable problem remained: all this, and Hana's acquittal, rested on the memory of a twelve-year-old girl, an unwitting witness against the man she believed to be her father. Worse, this man might be, along with his unknown coconspirators, a threat to Munira's life from the moment he learned what she had done. David was caught between two imperatives: to free Hana, and to save their daughter's life.

His ten-minute recess was up.

David rushed to the courtroom, composing his thoughts as swiftly as he could.

He did not have time to tell Hana anything. Nodding to Sharpe, who followed him, David approached the bench.

"What is it?" Taylor asked with a touch of asperity.

"I'd like to dismiss Ms. Arif from the stand, Your Honor, pending the right to recall her. Beyond that, I request that you extend the recess. I've just received a new piece of evidence, one that I believe may completely absolve my client."

"Then let's hear about it, Counselor."

"I can't discuss it yet. Not before I've spoken to my client." At Taylor's look of displeasure, David added quickly, "What I've learned, Your Honor, is deeply personal to Ms. Arif. With her permission, I'll spell everything out in chambers. All I can tell you now is that this involves much more than the outcome of this trial — including a child's life."

Taylor glanced at Sharpe. "Weren't we just here?" the prosecutor asked with some annoyance. "Not twenty-four hours ago, Mr. Wolfe had important new information to discuss with Ms. Arif. All that followed was her appearance here to tell the same old story of mystification and victimhood."

The judge nodded. "Setting aside the characterization," she told David, "what the prosecutor says is true enough."

David felt his stomach clench. "As an officer of the court," he answered, "I promise you that this is not a ploy. If what I've learned isn't handled responsibly among all of us — the defense, the prosecution, and the court — there may be consequences *none* of us would want to live with."

The judge considered him closely. "All right," she said. "We'll adjourn until nine A.M. tomorrow. At that time, we'll either meet in chambers or finish out this trial. So make good use of your time with Ms. Arif."

In the witness room, Hana sat across from him. "I may owe you an apology," David told her softly. "I just found some evidence that actually suggests you're innocent."

Hana looked stunned. "How?"

"Munira gave it to me."

Hana shook her head, as though trying to clear it. "The day before Ben-Aron was killed," David said, "Munira borrowed Saeb's cell phone. When he found out that she'd taken it, he was furious, even though Munira said she'd never used it. What he doesn't know yet is that she lied to him: she'd already used it to call Yasmin Al-Shanty." David covered Hana's hand. "Saeb's cell phone was the one used to call Iyad Hassan. Your husband is the handler, Hana. But only your daughter can prove it."

Hana closed her eyes. "All I would have to do," David continued, "is have Munira tell the jury her story, and then introduce Yasmin's phone records. But in Munira's mind, that would require her to betray her father in order to save her mother.

"That's not the worst of it. Everyone I've located who could have helped me unravel this plot has been killed — Lev and Markis, I'm sure, by the people who designed this conspiracy." David drew a breath. "I've come to think that Saeb hates Munira as much as he hates you. Even more, perhaps, because he looks at her and imagines us together. Once he discovers the rest, I'm not sure that anything would stop him — or them."

Hana stared at him, eyes widening with anguish. "We need to protect her, David. How can I let her testify? Even if Munira isn't killed, we'd have traumatized her for life, causing her to hate herself; and to hate you and me for putting her on the witness stand. I can't betray *her* like this."

"We're talking about *my* daughter, too." David softened his tone. "I won't let you die, Hana. And I won't risk putting our daughter in the hands of someone who may kill her. I mean to postpone this reckoning for a day or two and try to find another way out."

"How?"

"By asking the judge to put Munira in protective custody, and then calling Saeb as a witness."

Tears ran down Hana's face. "You would ask him about Munira?"

"Only if it's necessary," David said. "But I'll do whatever I have to. Thirteen years and four warped lives is enough. If I can end this thing with Saeb, so much the better."

16

After a telephone call to Judge Taylor, followed by a night of broken sleep, David appeared with Marnie Sharpe in the judge's private office. Taylor sat behind her desk, looking expectantly toward David. "You asked for this party, Mr. Wolfe. Just what do you have for us?"

Reaching into his briefcase, David handed Sharpe and Taylor copies of Yasmin Al-Shanty's cell phone records with the two critical calls circled in red ink. "This is the record of a call placed by Munira Khalid to a friend in Washington, and the friend's call to Munira. Ms. Sharpe should recognize the number of the cell phone Munira used."

Taking out her half-glasses, Sharpe looked for the number and then, finding it, stared fixedly at the paper. Looking up at Taylor, she said slowly, "It's the cell phone used to call Iyad Hassan."

Taylor shot a look of surprise at David. "You can explain this, I suppose."

"Munira can. She 'borrowed' this cell phone from Saeb Khalid without his knowledge. When he found her with it, he exploded, and then badgered her about whether she'd used it. Fortunately, she lied." David looked from the judge to Sharpe. "I assume I don't have to spell out the rest."

Sharpe willed her features to be expressionless,

her tone flat. "How do you know all this?"

"Munira told me. But she doesn't understand what any of it means. Let alone that she's become her mother's principal witness."

Sharpe shook her head emphatically. "This doesn't magically make your client innocent. At most, it suggests that her husband is a coconspirator."

The judge turned toward David. "If Saeb's the handler," she told Sharpe, "then Hassan was lying to Jefar. Which suggests that Khalid typed Hana's cell phone number on the slip of paper and took Hana's cell phone from her purse, enabling Hassan to place his midnight call —"

"That doesn't follow," Sharpe interrupted tersely. "The case against your client is independent of any case against her husband. *Both* of them could have been the handlers, operating together."

"You heard Hana's testimony. The two of them can barely stand each other."

"The two of them," Sharpe rejoined, "could be gifted actors, with you their unwitting impresario. If you're angling for me to dismiss this case, forget it."

David turned to Taylor. Slowly, the judge shook her head. "I can't terminate this trial, Mr. Wolfe. Not without more than you've given me."

"Then at least take Munira Khalid into protective custody. Two potential witnesses have been murdered in Israel. Unless Munira's safe, I can't put Khalid on the witness stand. And that's what the prosecution is forcing me to do." Facing Sharpe, he added pointedly, "Unless the government of Israel has other ideas. I don't intend my questioning to be constrained by the national security concerns of *either* government."

"So we're back to blackmail."

"That's getting pretty tired, Marnie. A member of Ben-Aron's protective detail — probably Markis — seems to have called Khalid. And Khalid may be in bed with Hamas or the Iranians. Maybe both. As a prosecutor, I'd think you'd at least be curious; as Hana's lawyer, I believe that I'm entitled to ask the questions."

"You are," Taylor said, turning to Sharpe. "Unless, Ms. Sharpe, you want me to certify an immediate appeal to the circuit court. All I can tell you is that I won't hog-tie Mr. Wolfe, and I don't think the court of appeals will, either. But I can recess the trial, if you want, and let you find that out for yourself."

Sharpe hesitated, her expression sour. "There are people in Washington I have to consult, and people in Israel *they* may want to consult. As Mr. Wolfe well knows, this raises complications."

"Mr. Wolfe," the judge said with a slight smile, "knows that very well. But that still leaves the question of what to do with Munira Khalid. As I understand your request, Mr. Wolfe, you want me to dispatch federal marshals to collect your client's daughter before her father knows what's about to happen to him — which, I must say, is a rather extraordinary thing for me to do. Are you telling me that Khalid might murder his own daughter?"

David paused, considering for a final moment whether to reveal a more incendiary truth. But he had little choice. "There's another reason to worry," he said in the calmest tone he could muster. "It bears on Munira's safety *and* on Ms. Sharpe's suspicion that, rather than being framed by Khalid, Hana is in collusion with him. All I can request of the government and the court is to keep this confidential unless it has to come out in open testimony."

The judge frowned. "Unless I know what it is, I can't make any promises, and I doubt Ms. Sharpe can either. So you'll have to trust our judgment, or keep whatever it is to yourself."

Reluctantly, David nodded. Then he handed Sharpe and Taylor copies of a three-page document. Quickly, Taylor scanned it. "What is this, exactly?"

"A DNA test requested by Saeb Khalid, based on three hair samples he submitted to a lab in Tel Aviv. What it shows is that Khalid is not Munira's father, and that he knows it."

Tight-lipped, Sharpe studied the report. "The samples aren't identified. How do you know that Khalid is sample A?"

"Because there's one more test," David answered, and gave both women copies of the DNA analysis performed by Diablo Labs. "This completes the picture."

Taylor read the report closely. Finishing, she looked up at David, eyebrows raised. "So who is sample D, the father?"

"I am."

The judge sat back, her face hardening as she stared at David. "You're not joking, are you?"

"No," David answered quietly. "I'm not joking."

"My God," Sharpe burst out. "You took the case because Arif and you were lovers. You've been playing games with the government *and* this court, covering up the truth —"

"Wait a minute," David snapped. "I don't owe you an accounting of my personal life, or my reasons for defending Hana. Or Hana's reasons for asking me to." Facing the judge, he said. "If I were

Hana's husband, she could hire me to be her lawyer. There's no ethical rule that bars me from trying to prevent her execution."

"There might be," the judge retorted angrily, "if your illegitimate daughter was a potential motive for Khalid to frame his wife. That makes you a witness in your client's defense, barred from acting as her lawyer." The judge's voice rose. "I can't believe this — you've planted a potential mistrial at the heart of Arif's defense, knowing you could blow up the whole damned trial anytime you pleased. To call that unethical is to be polite. Lawyers lose their licenses for less than this."

David forced himself to maintain a calm he did not feel. "With respect, Your Honor, that's not the case. I didn't know Khalid wasn't Munira's father until five days ago, nor until two days ago that I *was* her father. There are witnesses in Israel and San Francisco who can confirm that. If I had known any sooner, *you'd* have known. And if I'd have known before the trial, I wouldn't be Hana's lawyer.

"But I am. And now you know. This trial is Khalid's contrivance — an elaborate honor killing, and his revenge on Hana and me. *That's* his motive —"

"Then you're a witness," Sharpe cut in.

"I don't think so," David said. "What's relevant here is that Khalid knows he's not Munira's father, not who her father *is*."

"Your Honor," Sharpe protested. "Mr. Wolfe witnessed the assassination of Ben-Aron. Now we know he had an affair with the defendant, and that he's offering their daughter as his lover's chief defense. How much more entangled with the facts does he have to be? The idea of him cross-examining the man he cuckolded is absolutely grotesque."

"If entertaining," the judge said grimly. Turning to David, she said, "How, if I may ask, do you propose to manage *that?*"

"The way I would if Hana and I were strangers to each other. The prosecutor is asserting that I shouldn't be allowed to do this. But if Hana still wants me as her lawyer — which she does — then the *real* question is whether I'm competent to finish the job. Does my work so far raise any doubts about that?"

Taylor's face clouded with doubt. After a long silence, she turned to Sharpe. "I'm at least as unhappy about Mr. Wolfe's disclosure as you are. But do you really want a mistrial? I can't give you one without stating why, which would only warn Khalid. You'd be better off dismissing the case against his wife."

Sharpe frowned. "Without an explanation or a clearer basis in fact? I don't believe the government's prepared to do that."

"Then the truth might be better served by letting Mr. Wolfe have at his friend Khalid. I recognize what a mess this is. But isn't the ultimate point not only whether Arif is guilty but who else was involved in the murder of Amos Ben-Aron?"

Narrow-eyed, Sharpe seemed to contemplate a spot on Taylor's desk. "No response?" the judge asked. "Then here's what I'm going to do.

"I'm recessing the trial for twenty-four hours, in order to give the government time to consider whether to appeal my ruling. The ruling is this: I'm going to let Mr. Wolfe remain on the case and call Saeb Khalid as a witness. Khalid may invoke the Fifth Amendment. If so, we'll deal with that; if not, we all may be enlightened." Turning to David, the judge continued, "As for Munira Khalid, I will instruct the U.S. Marshal's Office to place her in protective custody on the grounds that the court has received confidential information regarding her safety. Given her gender, age, and background, the personnel protecting her should be women."

David felt a rush of relief. "Thank you, Your Honor."

Taylor regarded him closely. "It occurs to me to wonder, Mr. Wolfe, whether Munira knows that Khalid is not her father. Or that you are."

The question sobered David at once. "She doesn't know any of that, Your Honor."

"Then I hope there's some better way for her to find out than in the middle of her mother's trial. I trust you've given that some thought."

"I have. But I can't predict where my questioning of Khalid may have to go. All I know for sure is that I'm grateful Munira won't be there to watch."

"So am I, Mr. Wolfe." Sternly, Taylor added, "If Ms. Sharpe decides we should proceed, do your best. Because you're not coming back for any retrial. This will be your one and only shot at Saeb Khalid."

By the next morning, the government had determined not to appeal Judge Taylor's ruling; the United States Marshal had sequestered Munira Khalid in an undisclosed hotel room; and an angry Saeb Khalid, served with a subpoena to appear as a witness for his wife, was standing before the judge.

Taylor had cleared the courtroom, ensuring that neither the jury nor the media could hear what would transpire. Aside from Sharpe and David, each standing to one side of Saeb, the only others present were the judge's deputy, a court reporter, and two security guards from the marshal's office. If Saeb was frightened, he did not let this show; he addressed Taylor with a clipped and angry precision. "What you call 'protective custody,' " he told her, "is nothing more than kidnapping under the color of law. Tell me how you justify the seizure of my daughter."

The phrase "my daughter" caused no change in Taylor's expression. "The court has information," she answered, "suggesting that Munira's life may be in danger. That fact, combined with Mr. Wolfe's indication that he may call her as a witness in her mother's defense, has caused us to take this temporary measure. If you wish similar protection, you will have it. If you wish to challenge my order, I'm prepared to have a hearing directly after your testimony concludes, or as soon thereafter as you've retained a lawyer. Suffice it to say that I did not take this action lightly, and regret having to do so at all."

Saeb shot a sideways glance toward David, at once questioning and furious. "I don't know how Mr. Wolfe has justified this," he told the judge, "but he did not come to *me* seeking to protect my daughter. How can you usurp the rights of a father on the word of a lawyer? What kind of system is this?"

Taylor's swift glance at David suggested that they shared a common thought — that whatever Saeb suspected, he did not yet perceive that David, or the court, knew of Munira's paternity. To Saeb, she answered, "A fair one, I hope."

Clearly uncertain about how to proceed, Saeb glanced at Sharpe as though seeking her intervention. When Sharpe said nothing, he straightened, standing taller despite his frailty, his eyes alive with the defiance of someone who feels trapped. "I would like for Mr. Wolfe to state the grounds on which he calls me as a witness, and arranges the abduction of my daughter."

In other words, David thought, *you want me to reveal the traps you may be facing.* "Mr. Wolfe," the judge answered, "has represented to the court that he believes your testimony can help him exculpate Ms. Arif. But he isn't required to spell out in advance his line of examination. If you wish to retain counsel to challenge the subpoena or to advise you about your rights as a prospective witness, I'll recess the trial to allow you time for that."

Saeb glanced at David, then rearranged his features for Judge Taylor, adopting the puzzled look of a layperson at the mysteries of law. "Isn't there a marital privilege? And wouldn't my testimony violate that?"

The judge regarded him with the same air of patience. "The marital privilege, Dr. Khalid, exists to prevent one spouse from having to testify against the other. But the privilege can be waived by the subject of the testimony — in this case, Ms. Arif. Your wife has waived the privilege, freeing you to testify." The briefest of smiles crossed Taylor's face. "Mr. Wolfe assures me that his questions are *not* intended to damage his own client. Nonetheless, if you have questions about the marital privilege, you're free to consult counsel before Mr. Wolfe attempts to enlist you in his effort to exonerate your wife."

The last comment, mordant beneath its seeming neutrality, left Saeb without a response. "The other privilege to consider," the judge continued, "is that which protects a witness from giving testimony that may tend to incriminate him. Obviously, I can't anticipate what you might say under oath, or advise you concerning the risks of testifying, if any. But your own lawyer could, and I can fund one at the government's expense. If you need the advice of counsel before facing off with Mr. Wolfe, please say so."

Again the judge's remarks, while legally impeccable, contained a witch's shaft directed at Saeb's pride. Any doubt that Taylor wanted Saeb to testify had vanished: she had always wanted the truth, and now she had a chance to get at it. Eyes glinting, Saeb responded, "I need no protection from Mr. Wolfe. And I am more than ready to protect my wife, no matter how peculiar her lawyer's stratagems may be."

Sharpe, David saw, had a curious expression — nettled that the trial was slipping out of her control; intrigued by what might be about to happen. Conscious of the record, the judge asked Saeb, "Are you absolutely certain about that?"

Saeb folded his arms. "Of course."

To one side, the court reporter entered Saeb's answer. "Very well," the judge told him. "If at any time during the questioning you wish to consult a lawyer or invoke your privilege against self-incrimination, please advise the court and we'll adjourn the proceedings at once. Do you understand that, Dr. Khalid?"

A flicker of disquiet crossed Saeb's face as if, rather than reassuring him, the judge's warnings felt like a trap, binding him to a confrontation with David Wolfe. "I understand," Saeb answered with less assurance than before. The court stenographer could record only his words, not his air of ambivalence. And this was enough for Judge Taylor.

"Open the doors," the judge said to her courtroom deputy, "and bring in the defendant. Then Mr. Wolfe can call Dr. Khalid."

Saeb turned to David, a bitter smile playing on his lips. Though neither had known it, David thought, this moment had been coming for thirteen years. Staring back at Saeb, he could almost feel his own pulse rate lowering, a deliberate coolness seeping through his brain and body.

A marshal brought in Hana. She stopped, looking from her husband to David. Then she walked to the defense table, eyes straight ahead, as though fearing to deepen the psychic disturbance that seemed to permeate the courtroom. The doors opened, and the waiting crowd pushed into the courtroom. Among them, as David expected and intended, was Avi Hertz, guardian of the interests of the State of Israel.

17

The first moments of testimony involved the usual preliminaries: Saeb's name, profession, and residence; his relationship to Hana and, ostensibly, to Munira. David's tone was pleasant, that of a considerate host introducing his guest to an unfamiliar environment. But the jury, remembering Hana's testimony regarding the marriage, seemed to watch the two men almost as closely as Saeb watched David's eyes.

Stay cool, David reminded himself. But he felt more than cool; he felt a cold, concealed anger, the visceral need to protect Hana and Munira from the man who sat ten feet away. He could only hope that this emotion served them well.

"I'd like to begin," David said, "by discussing the prosecution's evidence against your wife. It includes a piece of paper on which someone typed Hana's cell phone number, and which bears her fingerprints and those of Iyad Hassan. Are you familiar with the telephone number shown on that piece of paper?"

"Of course," Saeb said. "It is Hana's number."

"How long have you been familiar with the number?"

"Since Hana bought the cell phone, as she said."

"And you also had access to her office."

"The same access as anyone," Saeb answered with a shrug.

"So, in theory, you could have taken the paper from her office."

"True," Saeb said mildly. "And also paper she used at home, to spare you the trouble of asking that."

"Thank you. So I assume that, also in theory, you could have typed her telephone number on the paper and given it to Iyad Hassan."

Saeb gave him a tolerant smile. "In theory, yes. That's one of the problems with this piece of evidence. Anyone could have ginned it up."

In the areas he could anticipate, David perceived, Saeb would prove to be an adroit witness, adopting the role of David's partner in a common effort to raise doubts on his wife's behalf. In the same pleasant tone, David asked, "You also had access to Hana's phone itself, did you not?"

Saeb nodded. "In the sense that we live together. I recall borrowing it on one or two occasions when my own phone needed recharging. Munira did the same, I believe. As Hana noted, our daughter sometimes loses things."

This, too, was clever — anticipating David, Saeb was trying to create an alternative user of Hana's cell phone. "Are you suggesting," David inquired, "that on June 15 Munira took an early morning call from Iyad Hassan?"

"I suggest nothing. I don't know *what* that telephone call is about — who received it, or who placed it."

"But again, in theory, you could have removed the cell phone from Hana's purse while she was sleeping, gone into the bathroom, taken a call from Hassan, and left the phone on long enough to create the impression of a conversation."

Saeb looked at the ceiling with an air of bewilderment, as though trying to follow the convolutions of David Wolfe's imagination. "I suppose I *could* have," he conceded in an agreeable tone. "Where I get lost is why I would do such an insidious but clumsy thing. Let alone to Hana."

During the first moments of questioning, David had not moved from his post beside the defense table. "Why indeed? By the way, you also brought your own cell phone to San Francisco, right?"

"Yes."

"And that cell phone, like Hana's, had international cell phone service and the 972 country code used by Israel and the Occupied Territories."

"Yes."

"And you turned that cell phone over to the FBI when Hana was arrested, true?"

"True." Saeb conjured a weary smile. "I had to get a new one at my own expense. Your FBI does not issue replacements."

David paused, hands on hips. "Prior to the time that the FBI impounded your phone, did you have another cell phone in your possession?"

Saeb's eyes narrowed slightly. But he did not seem perturbed; the FBI had asked him the same question. "Not that I recall," he answered. "At least in San Francisco."

"You don't recall having a phone with the 415 area code for San Francisco?"

Saeb spread his hands, his expression as matter-of-fact as his tone. "No."

On the bench, Taylor leaned forward, drawn by the spectacle of a witness perched on the edge of a trap. "Can you think of any reason," David asked, "for you to use a cell phone in San Francisco with service that did not allow you to call home?"

Saeb shook his head, still appearing perplexed. "No. None."

His answers, David noted, were becoming less expansive. "So you didn't buy such a phone while you were here, for cash?"

"No." Saeb allowed a note of annoyance to creep into his voice. "Like any experienced traveler, I do not stuff my wallet with cash. For that reason alone, I would not buy a cell phone in this fashion."

This, David believed, was true: this cell phone, like those planted for Hassan, had been bought by someone else. For the moment, Saeb could feel safe; only he knew where he had discarded the cell phone, and no one could ever trace it to him. "So just to nail this down," David said, "you're absolutely confident that, while in San Francisco, you never possessed a cell phone with the number (415) 669-3666?"

Saeb could give only one answer. "That is not a number I recognize," he said brusquely. "Nor do your prior questions spur even a glimmer of recollection."

For the first time, David stepped forward. "While you were in San Francisco, Dr. Khalid, did Munira ever borrow your cell phone?"

Ever so slightly, Saeb blanched, a moment that passed so quickly that had David not been looking, he might have missed it altogether. "I can't recall."

Moving a step closer to Saeb, David felt Sharpe and the jury watching — the prosecutor knowing, and the jury sensing, that the dynamic between witness and interrogator was changing. "Let me be more specific," David said evenly. "On the day before the assassination of Amos Ben-Aron, did you become angry with Munira because you found her with a cell phone she had taken from the pocket of your coat?"

Saeb's eyes widened. With a certain savage pleasure, David watched a series of realizations flash through his antagonist's mind: that Munira had betrayed him to David; that his previous answers, far from being safe, might be demonstrably false; that David meant to expose him on the witness stand. And then he took the only escape route he could find, the one David had left open to him. His brows knit, Saeb impersonated a witness straining to remember. "I seem to recall that something like this happened. But so much has happened to us, and there have been so many shocks. When your wife is on trial for murder, such incidents as you describe recede in memory."

David nodded. "Do you remember taking your cell phone back from Munira?"

Saeb touched his temples. "Perhaps. But this is very vague."

"What cell phone would that have been, Dr. Khalid?"

Saeb flinched. At this moment, Sharpe could have objected — there was arguably no foundation for David's question. But Sharpe was silent; perhaps she was certain, as was David, that Taylor meant for him to have all the leeway he required. Slowly, Saeb said, "You are asking me to speculate about what is, at most, a vestigial recollection. But it could have only been the cell phone confiscated by the FBI." He paused, then seemingly chose to take a gamble. "If Munira used it, that would no doubt show up on the phone itself, or on our phone records. But I seem to recall Munira saying she had not used it."

David smiled, his eyes fixed on Saeb. "Did you believe her?"

The question jolted Saeb more visibly than any other; he seemed to shrink back on the stand, his frame twisting slightly. David could imagine his thoughts: years ago Hana had deceived him, and now, perhaps, so had Munira. "Of course," Saeb answered, his voice hollow. "We raised our daughter to be truthful."

"Kids," David said softly. "You just never know. Suppose I told you that Munira called her friend Yasmin Al-Shanty on the phone she took from you, and that Yasmin called her back. If the telephone used by Munira is *not* the one confiscated from you by the FBI, how would you explain that?"

Saeb stared at him. "I can't."

"Then let me ask the question in another way. How would you explain it if the cell phone used by Munira had the number (415) 669-3666?"

In the jury box, Bob Clair leaned forward against the railing as though he did not wish to miss even the slightest change in expression. "I can't answer these hypotheticals," Saeb parried. "Your questions are phrased so as to disguise the truth beneath a smokescreen of assumptions —"

"Not assumptions," David cut in. "Facts. Yasmin's mother can identify cell phone records showing calls to and from Yasmin involving the number (415) 669-3666. It's also a fact that (415) 669-3666 is the cell phone number used to call Iyad Hassan ten minutes before the assassination of Amos Ben-Aron. My question is why that phone was in the pocket of your coat one day before Hassan blew up Ben-Aron."

Saeb glanced around the courtroom, and then

his eyes lit on Hana. "Perhaps the telephone was Hana's, not mine."

"How gallant," David said coldly. "Are you now suggesting that Hana stole it from your coat pocket?"

"*I don't know,* Mr. Wolfe. I no longer know what to think."

David stood straighter. "On the morning of the assassination, Dr. Khalid, did you receive a telephone call informing you that the route of Ben-Aron's motorcade had changed?"

"No."

"Did you call Iyad Hassan to tell him that the route had changed?"

"Of course not," Saeb shot back. "I was with Munira. It was Hana who was alone."

This was true, and it deepened David's dilemma: if Munira was Saeb's alibi for the day of the assassination, only testimony from Munira could refute this. Saeb sat straighter, as though sensing that at least in this area, David had no angle of attack. Gazing at the witness with an unimpressed half smile, David asked, "So you know absolutely nothing about who planned the assassination, how it was executed, or who helped carry it out."

"That's correct," Saeb answered firmly.

"And you had no reason whatsoever to try to bring about a prosecution that could result in Hana's execution or imprisonment."

For an instant, Saeb glanced toward Hana, then responded with a mixture of scorn and bemusement. "This is the stuff of fantasies. Disagreements about child raising are no basis for your baroque attempt to slander me in the interests of my wife.

"Am I sorry that Amos Ben-Aron is dead? In candor, not particularly. Am I sorry that Hana is charged for this crime? Very much. But I can no more explain that than anything else about this devious plot."

Saeb was regaining confidence, David saw; the shock of Yasmin's phone records was receding, replaced by the hope that this was David's only weapon. Abruptly, David asked, "Do you have a heart condition, Professor Khalid?"

A brief glimmer of uncertainty passed through Saeb's eyes. "Yes," he answered. "My heart is congenitally weak. My condition also includes arrhythmia, which, under extreme conditions, could cause my heart to stop beating."

"And what is the course of treatment?"

"I take medication. And, of course, I have a cardiologist."

David saw the judge's expectant glance and expressions of puzzlement on several of the jurors' faces. "In Amman, Jordan?" David asked.

Saeb gave David a look of offended dignity that did not quite conceal his unease. "I fail to see why my cardiac misfortunes should be of interest to anyone but me. However, yes — I have visited several times in the last three years with a specialist in Amman, Dr. Abdullah Aziz."

"How many times have you visited Dr. Aziz?"

"Several. I have not kept a running count."

"If I said that there were five such visits in the last three years, would you dispute this?"

Saeb shrugged. "I can neither dispute it nor confirm it."

"Can you tell me, at least, how long these appointments lasted?"

"I did not time them. Always with doctors, one waits."

"But if I tell you that the medical records of these

visits show that each trip to Amman shows a single visit to Dr. Aziz, you would have no reason to dispute this?"

Now Saeb looked distinctly guarded, as though recalculating the dangers he was facing. At the edge of his vision, David spotted Avi Hertz watching Saeb with a jeweler's eye. "I've never seen my doctor's records," Saeb finally answered. "Frankly, I would have thought them confidential —"

"Did any of your appointments," David interrupted, "last more than one day?"

Saeb hesitated. "I think not."

"And yet your passport shows that your trips involved a minimum of three days in Jordan and, on one occasion, seven days away from the West Bank."

Saeb summoned a condescending smile. "Which tells you what? Perhaps that it is pleasant to be free of Israeli occupation. It is the only upside of my medical condition."

"So what do you do in Amman when you're not visiting with Dr. Aziz?"

"What anyone would do. See the sights, eat in restaurants, wander and observe the people. Experience what it is to be in a place that, whatever its defects, is at least under the governance of Arabs."

"Did you ever meet with representatives of any foreign government?"

"I met many people. I do not always remember to ask who their employers are."

"Is that a yes, Dr. Khalid? Or a no?"

"Neither." Saeb bristled slightly. "It is an 'I don't know' and an 'I don't remember.' Why don't you just dismiss me, so you can testify yourself?"

"Oh, I'm sure there must be *some* question you can answer. For example, during one of your trips to Amman, did you travel to Tehran, the capital of Iran?"

Marnie Sharpe, David saw, leaned slightly forward at the question. "Yes," Saeb said stiffly. "I did not know this was a crime."

"What did you do while in Iran?"

"I was anxious to see life in an Islamic state, so different from life in a Jewish colony. I recall a pleasant dinner at the home of an Iranian professor."

"While you were there, Professor Khalid, did you meet with any representatives of the Iranian government?"

"Not intentionally. Perhaps at the dinner. But I cannot recall."

"Let's be more specific, then. Did you meet with anyone employed by Iranian intelligence?"

Sharpe stirred, as though considering an objection, and then said nothing. "If I did," Saeb said with an edge of scorn, "they did not announce their affiliation, any more than America's intelligence agents have 'CIA' monogrammed on their shirt pockets. I cannot see what these questions have to do with the charges against my wife —"

"While you were in Tehran," David cut in, "who paid for your hotel room?"

"I did, of course."

"And during your trips to Amman, who paid your hotel bills at the Intercontinental?"

Once more, Saeb hesitated. "Again, I did."

"How did you pay?"

Saeb turned to the judge, palms upraised, as if to ask whether he must answer such foolish questions. When Taylor's expression did not change, Saeb turned back to David and said, "I really can't remember."

"If I told you that you paid each bill in cash, would you dispute that?"

"I dispute nothing," Saeb answered in a clipped voice. "I confirm nothing. Nothing about this is important."

"Really? Then let me quote an answer you gave earlier this morning: 'Like any experienced traveler, I do not stuff my wallet with cash. For that reason alone, I would not buy a cell phone in this fashion.' Do you remember making that statement?"

"Of course."

"So what about a nine-hundred-and-thirty-dollar hotel bill paid two weeks before the assassination of Amos Ben-Aron. Did you pay *that* bill in cash?"

"I don't remember."

"How could you have paid in cash if you dislike carrying cash?"

Saeb's voice rose. "I don't recall my thought processes."

"That was less than six months ago, Dr. Khalid. Do you at least recall whether that cash was given to you by the representative of a foreign government?"

"Of course not." Saeb paused, then added, "At least as far as I know."

"So you *do* recall that *someone* gave you cash to pay that bill?"

In the jury box, Ardelle Washington looked intrigued; though she could not know what David's questions portended, Saeb's growing agitation suggested their importance. Biting off each word, he said, "I do not recall anything specific."

David felt his heart beat faster. "You don't recall

whether you got this cash from your bank account or from an outside source?"

"No."

"But if you got it from your bank, its records would show that, correct?"

A hint of panic surfaced in Saeb's eyes. In that moment, David saw that for the first time his antagonist feared that — as with Barak Lev and Hillel Markis — David Wolfe might bring about his death. His tone less assured, Saeb said, "I cannot tell you the state of my bank records."

"Do you still deny that someone else gave you cash to pay for your hotel room?"

"As before, I'm neither confirming nor denying." Saeb's voice rose in challenge. "Are you suggesting that someone bribed me to implicate my own wife in the murder of Ben-Aron for the price of a hotel room in Amman?"

David smiled briefly. "No, Dr. Khalid, I'm not suggesting that. Are you familiar with a concept called 'honor killing'?"

Saeb crossed his arms. "I do not know how such a question can possibly relate to this trial."

David moved closer. "I do. So does Ms. Sharpe, who, you'll note, is not objecting. I'll repeat the question: are you familiar with a concept called 'honor killing'?"

Saeb looked toward his wife, and then abruptly faced Judge Taylor, speaking in a tone that seemed more shrill than confident. "Must I respond to this nonsense?"

"Yes," Taylor answered evenly. "Unless you believe that the answer may tend to incriminate you. If so, I will give you the opportunity to consult with counsel."

Saeb stiffened, hands braced on the arms of the

witness chair. Without responding to the judge, he spun on David, saying scornfully, "Yes, I am familiar with the concept of an 'honor killing.' "

"Under that concept, Dr. Khalid, is an Arab man entitled to kill a female relative who has brought dishonor to his family or to himself?"

Saeb looked directly into David's eyes. "Yes," he said grudgingly. "Under that concept."

David moved still closer. "What kinds of behavior constitute dishonor?"

Saeb shook his head. "This is too subjective," he protested. "You are asking my opinion on what some generic proponent of honor killings might feel —"

"No," David interrupted, "I'm asking for your understanding of the traditional grounds for an honor killing. For example, is a man entitled to kill his wife for having sexual relations with another man?"

Saeb's eyes hardened. "I have heard of such things."

"Suppose," David ventured in a tone of mild curiosity, "that the woman involved is only his fiancée. Is an Arab man entitled to kill his *fiancée* for having sexual relations with another man?"

Saeb's mouth opened, and his chest shuddered slightly. An awful suspicion crept into his eyes; David knew that Saeb knew about his affair with Hana, and now David intended to hold nothing back. "According to whom?" Saeb answered. "All this is hypothetical."

"Then let me narrow the hypothetical a little. Is an Arab man entitled to kill his fiancée for having sexual relations with a Jew?"

The thin veneer of indifference slipped from Saeb's expression. In a tone etched with venom, he answered, "I cannot imagine a woman so degraded."

"Can't you?" Abruptly, David walked to the defense table, watching Hana's stricken gaze. *I have to do this,* he tried to tell her with his eyes, knowing that, for the three of them, all that had once passed between them and the thirteen years of deception that had followed were coming to a final reckoning. Then David took a three-page document from a manila folder and gave it to the court stenographer. Saeb stared at the document, utterly still, as though unable to speak or move. With a calm he did not feel, David said, "I would like this document marked as Defense Exhibit Number Twenty-three."

The court reporter stamped it. As Judge Taylor looked on, stone-faced, David presented the exhibit to Marnie Sharpe, who flipped its pages and handed it back. David then passed the document to the jurors; as each juror inspected it, David looked across the courtroom at Saeb Khalid.

Saeb stared back at him with an expression that combined dread, humiliation, and enormous rage. But what David felt toward Saeb was a terrible coldness; as with Muhammad Nasir, David had the sudden sense that he was staring at a dead man. He did not care if Saeb died on the witness stand or in a murder intended to silence him, precipitated by David's questions. All that mattered was whether Saeb would force him to take this to the bitter end, exposing Munira's paternity and traumatizing a young girl who was not Saeb's daughter, but David's. Every moment that the jurors perused the lab test, not yet grasping what it meant, brought the two men closer to the moment of Saeb's decision, a moment David dreaded as much as Saeb must.

At last, David retrieved the exhibit from the jury. Crossing the courtroom, he placed it in Saeb's hands. "Can you identify Defense Exhibit Twenty-three?"

Saeb raised his head, the document in his lap almost forgotten, the two men's eyes meeting as at that long-ago lunch in Cambridge, with Hana caught between them. *There is no "way out" for "us,"* Saeb had told him. *In the end, only one of "us" survives.*

Abruptly, Hana's husband turned to Judge Taylor. In a brittle voice, he said, "I ask to see a lawyer. To discuss my rights."

Taylor's expression was opaque. "Very well, Dr. Khalid. We will recess the trial until tomorrow morning. If you cannot find or afford a lawyer, the court will refer you to a federal public defender."

David felt a shudder of relief pass through him. Then he saw the terrible dullness that had surfaced in Saeb's eyes. In that moment, at last, David felt something like pity for Saeb Khalid.

18

Within ten minutes, Saeb Khalid had hurried away; the marshals had escorted Hana back to prison; and David had requested a hearing in the judge's chambers. "*That* was a courtroom moment I won't forget," the judge said to David from behind her desk. "I take it you have a motion."

"I do," David answered. "We request a further recess, to allow us time to renew our request for information from the government of Israel."

Sharpe looked nettled, the judge wholly unsurprised. "What information do you want?" Taylor asked.

"Anything that links Saeb Khalid to Hamas, the Iranians, or the breach in Ben-Aron's security — testimony, documents, phone records. Any connection, direct or indirect, that might tie the Iranians to the Israeli right. Any information about the murder of Hillel Markis and Barak Lev. Any and all information about the operations of the Iranian secret intelligence service in the United States or Israel. Anything relevant to my further cross-examination of Saeb Khalid, assuming he decides to testify." David turned to Sharpe. "And no more polite requests through legal channels, please. I want the Israeli ambassador, or some other suitable official, brought before the court in person. If

Israel continues to refuse discovery, the United States should not be allowed to maintain this prosecution."

The judge angled her head toward Sharpe. "Before you respond, Ms. Sharpe, let me say what troubles me. Thanks to Dr. Khalid, Mr. Wolfe's broader defense — a multifaceted conspiracy — has become less speculative and more germane. In my opinion, his case against Khalid is as good as your case against Arif. Yet the government of Israel may still be withholding evidence pertinent to Khalid and Mr. Wolfe's conspiracy theory, while the United States maintains this prosecution based on the only evidence anyone has against Ms. Arif. If you were presiding over this trial, you might be as uncomfortable with that as I am."

"*This* trial," Sharpe responded, "is about Hana Arif. What we do about Khalid is a separate matter. But the fallacy in Mr. Wolfe's argument is that his direct evidence of Khalid's guilt — which comes down to the grievances of a twelve-year-old girl regarding cell phone use, a girl who so far has not even testified — does not logically equate to his client's innocence. The evidence against *her* remains intact." A note of accusation crept into Sharpe's tone. "Mr. Wolfe resents the term 'blackmail.' But what he's trying to do is end this prosecution — not with a jury verdict, or on the basis of the evidence but by cornering the State of Israel, which says that it has no evidence about Arif herself. Like so much of this defense, it's a cute trick hiding behind a fig leaf of legality.

"As for his factual defense, it comes down to the same tired ploy: blame your client's coconspirator for everything your client did. That hardly justifies a fishing expedition into the national security apparatus and investigative processes of Israel. The court should tell Mr. Wolfe to put his theory of a frame job to the jury, and let *them* decide for themselves." Sharpe held her hands up, palms extended. "Maybe Hassan deliberately lied to Jefar. Maybe he rigged Jefar's motorcycle not to detonate, confident — for some reason that eludes me — that Jefar would survive the explosion. Maybe Khalid managed to keep his fingerprints off a piece of paper that he was certain had Arif's prints. Maybe he sneaked into the closet at midnight so Hassan could call him on his wife's phone. Maybe he informed Hassan about the change of route while watching CNN with Mr. Wolfe's daughter. Maybe the shadowy masterminds who plotted the assassination were more concerned with assisting Khalid's revenge against his wife than with ensuring that *Jefar* blow up Ben-Aron if *Hassan* could not. Maybe Ms. Arif was wandering Union Square by mere coincidence. And *maybe* — given Mr. Wolfe's considerable talents — he can sell this preposterous package to a jury. But this court should make him try."

Sharpe's sarcastic litany rattled David; in essence, he had just heard Sharpe's closing argument, and it was as compelling as anything he could muster — at least without exposing Munira's paternity and calling her as a witness. "That's a well-crafted rebuttal," he acknowledged to Judge Taylor. "But it only works if the prosecutor can wrench facts out of context. Here's the context: did the Israeli mole — no doubt Markis — call Khalid? We don't know; the Israelis may. Did Khalid work for the Iranians? We're not sure; the Israelis may be. What was Khalid's relationship to Hamas? We have intimations; the Israelis may have facts. Did the plotters plan to frame Hana, or did Khalid alter the plot? If the Israelis can put us on the road to finding *that* out, the argument Ms. Sharpe just delivered collapses altogether. And I won't be forced to do what I otherwise will have to do: blow up the world of a twelve-year-old in order to defend her mother —"

"That's not my problem," Taylor cut in brusquely. "Your domestic drama is your own concern. But I remain troubled by the prospect of convicting Hana Arif based on hearsay testimony in which Jefar channels a dead man, Hassan, whom the jury will never see. And now there's one more problem: Khalid's testimony. What should I do if Khalid refuses to continue, and the prosecutor can't cross-examine him for the benefit of the jury?"

"There are only two things the court *can* do," Sharpe said promptly. "Either instruct the jury to disregard Khalid's testimony or, better, declare a mistrial and start the trial all over again with different jurors. Anything else is unfair to the prosecution."

"That may be true," the judge responded with an ironic smile. "Still, 'fair' is the entitlement of both sides. We'll worry about Khalid when the time comes. But in this trial, or a new one, Ms. Arif should have the benefit of whatever relevant information Israel may possess.

"I'll decide what's relevant. But my idea of relevance is very close to Mr. Wolfe's. I'm adjourning the trial for a week. Four days from now, next Monday, I want a representative designated by the State of Israel to tell me whether it possesses any information about Khalid's direct or indirect connection to the Israeli security detail, Hamas, Iran,

Barak Lev — and what, if anything, it is prepared to divulge. And I also want the United States government to produce for the court, under the strictest confidentiality, any information it may have as to whether the Iranians or Hamas were involved in assassinating Amos Ben-Aron.

"Israel can decide what to do. Based on its decision, the court will either dismiss the case or allow the trial to continue. And neither government should assume that this court is bluffing."

As Taylor hesitated, relief cut through David's apprehension and exhaustion. "There's one more thing," he put in quickly. "Khalid. Not only is he a flight risk, but witnesses in this case have a way of getting killed. What I did to him today may have qualified him for indictment *and* put his life in danger. On either ground, the court should place him in protective custody."

"Oh, I intend to," the judge answered. "There are enough missing pieces without missing Professor Khalid. Based on what we saw this morning, it would truly be a shame to lose him."

Two hours later, David was alone in his office, pondering his choices should Taylor keep the trial going and Saeb invoke the Fifth Amendment. A mistrial would allow new counsel to start over, better armed than David had been. But Saeb Khalid was the key to Hana's defense. A new jury would never see him; the current jurors, no matter how sternly the judge instructed them, could never erase him from their minds. And there was a final, painful consideration: a defense where Saeb was not a witness would depend more heavily on Munira — both for her testimony implicating her presumptive father and by exposing who her father really was.

David tried to imagine what Munira was feeling now, guarded by strangers, frightened for her mother, perhaps divining that she must choose one parent over the other. He found it painful to think of her torment and confusion: the protective instinct of a parent for a child, in his case based on little more than biology, was nonetheless stronger than he ever could have imagined.

He was absorbing this with genuine wonder when the telephone rang. "This is Judge Taylor," the judge said in a voice so somber that it jarred him. "I've already called Ms. Sharpe. I need you back in chambers right away."

She did not explain herself, and David did not ask. "I'm on my way," he said.

Dressed in a gray business suit, Taylor sat at the head of her conference room, looking sallow under the fluorescent light. Whatever had happened seemed to have drained the animation from her face and voice.

"I won't string this out," the judge said to David. "Khalid is dead."

A wave of emotion struck David hard, disbelief commingled with a sense of the inevitable, its residue a clammy feeling akin to nausea. Saeb Khalid was dead; David, perhaps, was the agent of his death. "How did it happen?" he managed to ask.

"No one's sure yet," Sharpe told him grimly. "They found him on the floor of his apartment. There's no obvious sign of violence or a break-in. It could have been a heart attack — with Munira gone, there was no one there to help him. Perhaps only an autopsy can tell us more."

David tried to fathom what had happened. "What does this do to your prosecution?" he asked.

"It doesn't end it. As to what position we take about a mistrial, I've asked Washington for instructions. There's nothing more I can tell you."

For once, Sharpe's tone was factual rather than adversarial. All three of them seemed stunned, like the survivors of a natural disaster. "I have to tell Hana," David said finally. "Then I think Hana and I should see Munira."

Nodding slowly, Taylor looked toward Sharpe. "We'll make the necessary arrangements," the prosecutor said.

Bryce Martel sat in David's living room at dusk, nursing a tumbler of single-malt scotch. "Heart attack?" Martel said. "I wonder. If I were you, I'd subpoena the tapes of any security camera in Khalid's apartment building, see who shows up slipping in or out of the entrances or the garage.

"It'd be risky to kill him. But maybe riskier to let him live — if you're right, at the least Khalid could take the plot to the next level, potentially exposing whoever planned the assassination. This way you're cut off again, just like with Lev and Markis."

"True. But Sharpe says there weren't any signs of violence or forced entry."

Martel gave a dismissive shrug. "Maybe Khalid knew them. Maybe someone put a gun to his head and made him take potassium chloride, which can show up as a fatal heart attack. Or sleeping pills to help him 'commit suicide.'

"We may never know. It might have been the Iranians — they've certainly killed dissidents in America. Maybe even the Mossad, though it's hard to divine a motive. Or *you* may well have killed him." Martel's smile was bleak and fleeting. "This morning, I managed to secure a spot in the rear of the courtroom. You emasculated him in public, or were on the verge of doing so. You didn't just want to expose him, David, you wanted to destroy him. But your due bill goes back years, I think." Pausing, Martel inquired softly, "The daughter's yours, isn't she?"

David met his eyes but said nothing.

"There's always an explanation," Martel said matter-of-factly. "Even for the seemingly inexplicable. From the beginning, I wondered." He sat back, the scotch cradled in both hands, his gaze reflective. "He may well have wanted to die. Imagine how soul-shriveling exposure of the truth would have been for a man like Saeb Khalid — cuckolded by a Jew for all the world to see, his best prospect a lifetime spent in an American prison. Each day would have been torture for him."

David felt raw inside. "I had no choice, Bryce. As a lawyer or as a man."

"I know," Martel answered gently. "I never saw Khalid as the only victim, David. I don't envy *you*, either. I don't envy any of you — you, Hana, or Munira. No matter what comes next, you've all begun serving a life sentence of your own. The only question is how well you'll manage to adapt."

19

At ten o'clock that evening, by special dispensation of the United States attorney, David met with Hana in the witness room of the federal detention center and told her that Saeb was dead.

She looked stunned, almost uncomprehending. Her only visible movement was the briefest of shudders.

Softly, David said, "They may have killed him, Hana."

Hana shook her head, as though to clear it. " 'They'?"

"Saeb may have altered the design to implicate you. But other people were the architects."

Hana bowed her head. "I don't know what to think," she murmured. "I don't even know how to feel. It is all too much."

They sat across from each other in silence, lost in their own thoughts. At last she looked up at him. "And you, David? What do *you* feel right now?"

David hesitated, then decided to tell the truth as he perceived it. "That all this has been waiting in time's ambush since the night you walked out of my apartment. That of all of us, only Saeb is free now. And that the person most affected is the only one of us who's innocent."

Hana closed her eyes. "What will we tell her?"

she said wearily. "After all these years, *how* do we tell her?"

David gathered his thoughts. "I've had a few hours to consider that," he answered with deep reluctance. "In some better time and place, we could feel our way through it, saying as much or as little as seemed right for her. But you're on trial for murder, and your defense has two key elements. As to the first — that Saeb, not you, was Hassan's handler — Munira's call to Yasmin makes her the only witness. As to the second — that Saeb framed you — Munira is his motive.

"In four days, the judge will decide whether to resume your trial. Unless you choose to risk what at best would be a life in prison — your husband's final gift to you and Munira — we have to tell Munira everything."

Hana's face was a study in misery. "That we should have to make such choices . . ."

"I know," David answered gently. "But there are only two ways out of this, I'm afraid. One of them, a mistrial, is only temporary, and I don't think we want to take it."

"Why is that?"

"Because it makes things worse for you. If Sharpe moves for a mistrial on Monday — which I believe she'll do — it'll be on the grounds that she can't cross-examine a dead man, Saeb, whose interrupted testimony may have prejudiced her case. She'll be right, of course. Which is why we'll suggest that Taylor simply admonish the jury to ignore what they in fact can't ignore, allow us to call Munira to testify about her phone call, and then climax your defense by proving that Saeb isn't her biological father."

Hana folded her arms, instinctively resistant.

"I'm sorry," David told her. "But even if Sharpe gets a mistrial, you'd be retried in six months — six months more spent in jail, separated from Munira, wondering every day if a mistrial has lessened your changes of acquittal. And all you'd gain for Munira is a six-month reprieve from the truth."

Despairing, Hana stared at the white walls of the witness room. "What is your second way?" she asked.

"That may depend how the Israelis respond to the lousy choice I've given them: reveal whatever they know or risk the judge dismissing the prosecution and letting you go free. That's the only way we can explain this to Munira in the way we think is right." David leaned forward. "But Taylor doesn't have to make that decision now, nor do the Israelis. By dying, Saeb's given both of them — and Sharpe — an out. Instead of putting the Israelis to a choice, the judge can simply declare a mistrial and buy herself and *both* governments six months' time. That's exactly what I think she'll do."

Hana fell silent. David could feel her struggling to comprehend the full effects of a choice made so many years ago: that her husband was dead; that she and David must live with this; that her daughter had suffered and would suffer more, from the consequences either of truth — the shock of learning that David was her father — or of a lie — the possible conviction of her mother. "So how do I best protect her, David?"

"By telling her the truth at last, as gently as you can." David softened his voice. "There are two ways she can look at this: either that she precipitated her father's death or that she saved her mother's life. So learning who I am to her, however hard, may be a kindness."

Hana covered his hand with hers. "But it would be terrible to tell her in this way — so abruptly, at such an age — and then expose her in public with so much at stake. I *know* her. With all she has been through, Saeb's death is too much already."

David shook her head. "Saeb died," he answered, "because all of us were impaled on a lie. Look at how well that served Munira."

Pensive, Hana gazed at her hand on David's. "If the judge gives us no choice," she said quietly, "we will tell her. Until then, I will hope for a better way, and a better time. Not just for her sake, but for ours." She looked up at him. "You may be her father. But no matter whose fault it is, I'm her only parent. You must leave this part to me."

Listening to her mother's words, Munira hugged herself in anguish and then began to cry, emitting a soft keening sound of grief for Saeb Khalid that pierced her real father's heart.

Stricken, Hana embraced her. For himself, David could scarcely comprehend that he was part of this — sitting beside Hana in a strange hotel suite guarded by U.S. marshals, watching a Muslim girl shrouded in black who was his daughter mourn the man whom she believed to be her father.

When at last Munira was able to speak, her face against Hana's shoulder, she whispered, "Why did he die?"

David could see the agony on Hana's face — the question could have two meanings, one far more devastating than the other. Gently, Hana answered, "We don't know. But your father's heart was very bad."

Munira drew back her tear-stained face, looking into her mother's. "He was so angry at me. Maybe he didn't want to live with me anymore."

Touching her daughter's cheek, Hana tried to smile. "Children think they're the cause of everything, Munira. Women know better. And you're nearly thirteen, as close to being a woman as a child.

"We fought over you, it's true. But the fights were about us. We had ceased to love each other, or want a life in common." Tears briefly surfaced in Hana's eyes. "Love turned to anger is a terrible thing to watch. But you are a victim of anger, Munira, not its cause."

As though relieved, if only for this moment, Munira leaned her forehead against her mother's shoulder. To see them together again was, for David, deeply affecting. But he also knew that what Hana had told her was one more lie: for Munira to learn who her true father was would put her at the center of what had happened, the cause of it all. "It will be all right," her mother assured her softly. "Whatever comes, David will help us."

20

For the last few minutes that Hana was free, David left her alone with Munira, exiting the hotel with no plan but to walk aimlessly in the unseasonable warmth of a late-November day, letting his thoughts meander wherever they might. A black town car glided to a stop beside him. David spun, instantly alert, thinking of Saeb's death as the rear window slid down.

"Get in," Avi Hertz instructed him.

David hesitated. Then Hertz pushed open the door, and David slipped into the seat beside him.

Except for Hertz's driver, the two men were alone. "Don't worry," the Israeli said. "The killing is done, I think. Unless you keep groping about like a blind man, attempting to divine the shape of something you can never see."

The car sped away. "Where are we going?" David asked.

"To have one of those conversations that never happened, and that you will never reveal to anyone. Unless you're a far bigger fool than I take you for, one who cares nothing for his client."

David sat back, gazing out the window, preparing himself for the pitfalls of a confrontation he had both feared and hoped for. He would ration his words until Hertz's promises — or threats — showed him what to do.

Their destination, it transpired, was the middle of San Francisco Bay. As the powerboat knifed the chill waters, circling Alcatraz, the Israeli tossed David a slicker to insulate him from the cold. Hertz's chauffeur, now the boat's captain, could not hear them above the thrum of the motor and the churning waves splitting their wake.

Nodding toward the abandoned prison, Hertz said, "Sorry for the chilly setting. But here we are alone, and I rather like the symbolism.

"You've been spinning a story, Mr. Wolfe, in and out of court, trying to spare your client a fate similar to that of the former inmates of this unhappy place. Perhaps you would care for me to join my imagination to yours. The story might make more sense."

"That depends on how it ends."

With a peremptory gesture, Hertz waved David to a padded seat at the stern of the boat. "I can promise nothing. But we will see."

Shrugging, David sat beside him. "Let's start with the assassination," Hertz said. "Among its obvious effects was to discredit Faras and Al Aqsa, ruin the last feeble hope of peace, and cement Hamas's hold on power. It is certainly reasonable to suppose that a man like Saeb Khalid, and Hamas itself, might desire such a result."

A salty spray dampened David's face. "Hamas," he amended. "And others."

"Stay with Hamas, for now. Hamas has a presence at Birzeit. It is also reasonable to posit, as you have, that Iyad Hassan was not Al Aqsa but Hamas, and that he misled Jefar about his true affiliation.

Just as it is possible to imagine that Khalid, not Hana Arif, approached Hassan. I simply do not know, whatever you may wish to believe, and, frankly, neither do you." Hertz placed his hand on David's wrist. "What we both know, and Khalid knew, is that Munira Khalid is your daughter. That seems to have influenced — if not warped — events and given you another interest to protect."

"Which may make me a fool," David answered, "but a very determined one."

"Then for the sake of your newfound family, I will help make you a little less of a fool." Pausing, Hertz spoke with a steely edge. "You may have entertained a fantasy that the Mossad, or some other agency of Israel, had a hand in dispatching Lev and Markis or even, God help us, Amos Ben-Aron. You and Martel may even wonder if we did in Saeb Khalid. But it was *you,* not us, who had a hand in killing them all. You found them, and murder followed.

"The only acquaintance of yours dispatched by *us* was Muhammad Nasir, and only because he was so richly deserving — if not because of Ben-Aron, then for many other deaths. Regarding Nasir, you may console yourself that you extended his life, as opposed to shortening it. Our people in Jenin saw you slip into your meeting with him. If not for your presence, they'd have blown Nasir to little pieces."

Meeting Hertz's eyes, David felt the goose bumps on his skin. "I never thought the Mossad killed Ben-Aron," David said. "But it's clear to me that *Israelis* — including Markis and Lev — helped kill him. Are you telling me *those* men weren't killed by other Jews?"

"So now we are suicide bombers?" Hertz said

with disdain. "That is not our way. But there are some who believe that the anonymous scrap of flesh who killed Hillel Markis took his orders from Hamas, or perhaps Islamic Jihad —"

"Cut the elliptical bullshit," David snapped. "You knew from the beginning that Lev and Markis most likely were complicit. You chose to sit on it, and let Hana twist in the wind. These men died because you encouraged the United States government to proceed with the prosecution, hoping that Hana was guilty and would try to escape the death penalty by giving you the Arab side of the plot. But she's innocent, so all you got out of it was two dead Jews, and a Jewish lawyer to blame it on."

Hertz's elfin face did not change expression. "So who recruited Lev and Markis? Hamas?"

"I haven't worked that out yet."

"Then you and I are free to improvise. Suppose, as you do, that Lev and Markis despised the Palestinians, loathed Ben-Aron as a traitor, and wanted to save the dream of Greater Israel. The extreme Israeli right, like Hamas, had many reasons to wish our prime minister dead. But each side also despises the other." Turning from David, Hertz spoke softly, his profile grim. "So whoever planned this would have had to use a cutout. Someone who appears to be an Israeli Jew, at least with his pants on — or, perhaps, off. And there are Jews living in Iran."

The theory startled David. "Is that what happened?"

The boat lurched abruptly, causing David to shift his weight. "You and I are writing a story," Hertz answered. "All we need is for our story to be plausible. What makes *this* aspect plausible is that Iranian intelligence, with the help of our indigenous

Arabs, operates within Israel."

"And through Hamas," David countered. "With the help Saeb Khalid, who had become an agent of Iran, Hamas could provide a bomber to kill Markis, and a sniper to kill Lev. That eliminates the two Israelis who might link Ben-Aron's assassination to your not-so-fictitious, quasi-Jewish agent of Iran."

"Yes," Hertz responded coldly. "We were hoping to trace that link, slowly but surely. I think we could have done so. But you helped make the plotters — the Iranians and Hamas, in our story — nervous about Lev and Markis. We are not yet certain who put you onto the two Israelis. But if those who did believed they were helping whatever political cause they serve, their plan went badly awry." Scorn seeped into Hertz's voice. "They, and you, might have imagined that there was an official cover-up in progress. Let me assure you that it is difficult to conceal anything in Israel, though there are forces — the extreme right and politicians allied with settlers — who might have wished to do so. As it is, *you* precipitated the only cover-up by helping get two people killed."

Making no effort to wipe the sea spray off his face, David simply stared at Hertz. "I'm willing to share the credit with you, given that you could have helped Hana and chose not to."

"She was never our concern," Hertz answered coolly. "We couldn't trust her, and her agenda had become *your* agenda. So we didn't trust you, either." After a brief pause, Hertz spoke in a lower voice. "This much I can tell you. The leak in Ben-Aron's security was ours, not the Americans'. Someone on our side told Hassan's handler — perhaps Saeb Khalid, perhaps his wife — about the change of route."

"'Perhaps Saeb Khalid, perhaps his wife,'" David echoed. "Come off it. You know about Munira borrowing her father's phone. If you had a scrap of evidence that Hana was connected to Iranian intelligence, Sharpe would have used it."

"We didn't believe she was connected to Iranian intelligence," Hertz replied calmly, "but to her husband. What's to say, for example, that Khalid didn't blackmail Arif into taking a call from Markis on the day of the assassination — using *his* cell phone — and then calling Hassan while Khalid watched CNN with Munira. Maybe Arif handled *all* the calls to Hassan — *that* would make sense of Hassan's statements to Jefar. Even your theory of defense — that Khalid concocted evidence against Arif — doesn't rule out Arif passing information from Markis to Hassan while claiming to wander Union Square in a daze. You can't be sure, and neither can we."

The accuracy of this threw David off balance, subverting his sense that, at least with respect to Hana, he had come to know the truth. Hertz watched him closely. "Perhaps, Mr. Wolfe, you now better understand our reluctance to take you into our confidence. It is quite possible that Munira, while correctly implicating Khalid, was indeed with him at the very time that her mother was calling Hassan."

David chose to say nothing. "But let us continue," Hertz said smoothly, "to one of your more legitimate questions: who had the capacity to plan and carry out this assassination in the United States? Not Al Aqsa, by itself; even Hamas, which has its loyalists among the Palestinian student population in the United States, could not put all this together. The Mossad *could,* but didn't. That leaves the Iranians."

David studied their wake, two stripes of white roiling the aqua waters. "And their reasons?"

Hertz shrugged. "That's a matter of sophisticated speculation. But you guessed at *some* of the reasons. To begin, the Iranian government is run by fanatical clerics and true believers. One of their goals is a nuclear Iran. An arsenal of nuclear weapons would, in effect, immunize Iran from attack, allowing them to continue to fund and assist Hamas, Al Qaeda, Hezbollah, Islamic Jihad, and whoever else they want, expanding their reach in the Middle East and in the world. All while advancing the one goal that unites every one of these groups: the eradication of Israel.

"The Iranians are sophisticated enough to have recruited Lev and Markis without either man knowing that he was working for Iran; to involve Hassan through Saeb Khalid; and to set up the infrastructure in the U.S. needed to equip and support Hassan and Jefar. By killing Ben-Aron, they could kill his peace plan, discredit Faras and Al Aqsa, ensure Israeli reprisals on the West Bank, divert the attention of both Israel and the United States away from Iran itself, and be certain that the next Israeli government would be as adamantly opposed to peace negotiations as is Hamas.

"On the surface, Iran's ultimate reward would be to keep Israelis and Palestinians at each other's throats, thereby extending and inflaming the chief cause of hatred between Israel and the United States on one side and radical Islam on the other." Hertz looked at David intently. "That's *your* theory, and that might be enough for them — after all, it mirrors their purpose in using Hezbollah to provoke us to act in Lebanon. But suppose Iran also believed that Ben-Aron intended to make peace with Marwan Faras, and then attack Iran's nuclear facilities — assuming this were possible — before their nuclear weapons program came to fruition."

Once more, David was surprised. "Is *that* what Ben-Aron intended?"

"There are those who think so. Among them, the Iranians."

"Still," David said, "assassinating Ben-Aron is a risky thing for Iran to do — far riskier than encouraging Hezbollah to fire rockets from Lebanon into Israel. For Iran to be exposed as having murdered the prime minister of Israel could lead to a concerted military operation by Israel, the U.S., and maybe others, intended to bring down the Iranian regime."

"True. So it is also possible that rogue elements within the Iranian secret intelligence service — the most fanatic — did this without the approval of the mullahs or this miserable Holocaust denier who is their figurehead president. It is even possible that they put this together without involving Hamas itself, as opposed to a couple of its sympathizers." Turning, Hertz gazed across the gleaming water at Alcatraz. "As for the locus of the risk — Khalid and/or Arif — they were reasonable choices. Neither was on your Secret Service watch list, or ours. They were just two more opponents of Israel, Khalid seemingly more adamant than his wife —"

"But if Khalid was caught," David cut in, "the Iranians were vulnerable. That's another reason why framing Hana made sense: she knew nothing about her husband, nothing about Iran. She was an absolute dead end, and Saeb — as Iran's operative — had more than sufficient reason to offer her up as the subject of a frame. If she were guilty, she could lead you to Khalid, who could lead you to Iran. But if she's innocent —"

"Yes," Hertz said with the ghost of a smile. "That is why, unlike Sharpe, I do not consider your assertion of a frame to be quite so silly. And the Iranians could not reasonably anticipate that you — the key to Khalid's hatred of his wife — would choose to represent her. Or that Munira would choose to air her complaints about cell phones to you.

"If you're right, perhaps the Iranians planned this frame from the beginning. Or perhaps Khalid tinkered with the plot given him by the Iranians in order to implicate his wife, hoping the United States would execute Arif on his behalf — a dangerous thing to do, knowing the Iranians, as Khalid surely would have understood. But perhaps he didn't much care to live himself." Sitting back, Hertz crossed his arms. "In any case, regardless of whether Arif is innocent or guilty, you managed to put Khalid in the crosshairs, just as you did with Lev and Markis. So now he's dead, and there is much we may never know — including the role played by the mother of your child."

The depressing truth of this enveloped David. For a while, he watched the seagulls gliding in their wake. At length, he said, "So you think Khalid was murdered?"

Hertz put on a pair of sunglasses. "Quite possibly," he said in his most impassive manner. "I can't tell you who, if anyone, was with Khalid when he expired. But there's a fair chance that when the FBI looks at the security tapes in his apartment, they'll see two men getting in an elevator around the time Khalid died, neither of whom are residents. But even if those men are found, they will know nothing of use, except that they were sent to murder Khalid."

Once more, David found himself wondering which elements of Hertz's narrative were supposition and which far more than that. "However it happened," Hertz concluded, "Khalid's death is the final step in the perfect roll-up, an operation that leaves no trace. If it was murder, it is merely a minor adjustment in an otherwise flawless plan. Especially if Arif is as innocent as she claims."

"And yet," David said with real anger, "you remain perfectly willing to watch our government put Hana in prison for life, or even execute her."

Hertz shrugged. "We did not believe her innocent. We do not know it now."

It was his turn, David knew, to make a move in the chess game Hertz had laid out for them. He folded his arms against the cold. "Then let's talk about what matters to you. Once Munira ties Khalid to the same cell phone used to call Hassan, the breach of Israeli security is on the table in a very public way. Perhaps you don't care about the political upheaval that may provoke, or the schism within Israel when I link Ben-Aron's murder to the Israeli right. But is your government willing to have the vulnerability within its most elite security detail exposed for all to see?"

Hertz remained unfazed. "This is the game you've played with us from the beginning. The consequences within Israel might be unpleasant, I'll concede. But not so terrible that we would abet the escape of a known conspirator in the death of our prime minister."

David parsed this answer. "But you don't know if Hana conspired with anyone," he said. "And you have other concerns beyond the simple fact that

Ben-Aron's security was breached. What's really troubling is that — at least according to your theory — the *Iranians* seem to have breached it. That charge, if it's made in public, raises some nasty issues of nuclear geopolitics. And it would force the government of Israel to respond, perhaps before it's ready to do so."

Hertz's expression darkened. "And, of course, you are willing to put us in that position to advance the interests of Ms. Arif."

"Someone needs to look after her interests," David replied. "And even if Sharpe can keep me from raising this at trial, there's nothing to keep me silent once the trial is done. For openers, I'm sure Larry King and the *Today* show would be pleased to have me back for a postmortem."

Hertz stared at David without blinking. "Let me make clear to you, Mr. Wolfe, how dangerous it is for you to play with nuclear matches in this way.

"Put simply, we cannot permit Iran to become a nuclear power. It would trigger a nuclear arms race in the Middle East, provide a shield for Iranian aggression, strengthen the Islamic extremists within Iran, enhance the prospects of more assassinations of any world leader Iran does not like, help Iran further cement Hamas in power, and create the possibility that Iran, like the Pakistanis, would sell its nuclear know-how to other forces just as bad as it is. In short, it would be a catastrophe for Israel and the world.

"But there is no clear path to preventing such a thing. An invasion aimed at toppling the regime might encounter great resistance, while enraging the entire Middle East. An attempt to destroy Iran's nuclear sites is far from certain to succeed — the sites are dispersed, hardened, and located underground. If we moved against Iran militarily, either through the air or on the ground the hatred toward Israel throughout the region would be inflamed. If we merely try to embargo Iranian oil, it would drive world oil prices higher, hurting the U.S. and others and enabling Iran to make a killing on the black market. And trifles like cutting political or cultural ties are just as pathetic as they seem." Hertz's tone became clipped. "The best chance that whatever course we choose will succeed is the absolute support of the United States and Europe and the acquiescence of the U.N. Right now those power centers are divided. The only way to unify them is to develop *proof* — not the mere suspicion — that Iran planned and carried out the assassination of Amos Ben-Aron."

As they continued to circle Alcatraz, David considered his position. He was not sure that Hertz's "story" was not another form of dissembling, concealing facts or motives he did not wish David to know. But whatever the case, playing this out might serve Hana's interests. "I understand what you're telling me," David said at last.

"Then understand *this*." Hertz placed a finger on David's chest, taking off his sunglasses and staring into David's eyes. "We cannot have you, private citizen David Wolfe, running about making charges prematurely, fucking up our investigation, and requiring us to respond in public. As Arif's lawyer, you cannot be allowed to place your clumsy fingers on the scales of history. *Your* concerns are merely parochial — the fate of a possibly guilty woman and the tender sensibilities of a twelve-year-old girl who might be forced to learn, in an untimely way, that her father is a Jew."

Knowing they were reaching the endgame, David

felt his nerves tingle. With mock contrition, he said, "Please forgive my lack of perspective."

"Do not be so smug," Hertz said coldly. "You forget that Sharpe could move for a mistrial, and then *we* could extradite Arif for trial in Israel. You do not hold all the cards."

David had anticipated this. "You can extradite Hana, it's true. But the only way to silence me is a bullet in the head. Unless you try to throw me overboard."

Hertz shrugged. "It's certainly a thought. Though the Iranians might beat us to it."

"Even if I were dead, it wouldn't change anything. The problem isn't me anymore — it's the prosecution of Hana Arif. Based on the record after I cross-examined Saeb Khalid, any competent lawyer will have to raise the question of Iran. What you need is a way out."

"Yes," Hertz said. "I expected you would get to that."

"Not just expected — hoped. So don't patronize me. This prosecution is bad for all of us. I've known that from the beginning, once I saw that my defense of Hana was at cross-purposes with Israel's larger interests in the world. But by stonewalling our requests you forced me to prove it. You may not like the results, but you damn well guaranteed them. The question now is whether you want to stop at three dead witnesses or take this all the way to the end."

To David's surprise, Hertz laughed softly. "You may be an amateur spy, Mr. Wolfe. But you are a very able lawyer. So what is it you want?"

"For Sharpe to dismiss the case."

Hertz merely shrugged again. "That I also expected. But Sharpe and her superior, the attorney general of the United States, do not work for us."

"But they do work *with* you, and it's the death of *your* prime minister that made this case one our government had to bring." David kept his tone dispassionate. "Only Israel can give the U.S. cover. It's not enough for me to have tied Khalid to the murder — Israel needs to say that it has newly discovered information suggesting that Hana Arif is innocent but cannot disclose it for national security reasons —"

"Impossible," Hertz said flatly. "For one thing, it's a lie. We have no information about Arif, one way or the other."

"I didn't know *your* sensibilities were quite that tender," David answered sardonically. "I'll leave it to you and Sharpe to come up with something that allows the U.S. to save face and my client to go free. But at an absolute minimum, the Israeli government will have to tell the world that it can't comply with Judge Taylor's order."

Hertz considered this. "When you say 'go free' —"

"I mean go anywhere she wants. Here, I hope — I want the U.S. to agree to that up front. But wherever she chooses to live, I'd want you to guarantee that you'll never lay a glove on her."

"And if she wants to return to the West Bank?"

The question aroused in David a deep feeling of dismay. "We both may hope she doesn't," he answered. "But 'free' means just that."

Hertz focused his gaze on Alcatraz. "And if I manage to accomplish all these wonders?"

"Then I'm sure you'll want very little from me," David said with quiet sarcasm. "Merely to abandon those in Israel who want peace, and let the Palestinians serve as scapegoats for Iran's little game of geopolitics. At whatever cost to all of them."

"Sadly," Hertz corrected, "I want even more than that, however distasteful it may be to both of us as people. You will tell Hana Arif nothing of this conversation — I don't want to arouse her patriotic fervor, so that she decides to exculpate her fellow Palestinians by blaming Iran prematurely. And all three of you — Arif, you, and your daughter — will be silent, as if your lives depended on it. Which they may.

"So yes, this means that you will have to betray the people who helped you in Israel, as well as many Palestinians more innocent, perhaps, than your client. Otherwise, we will try her in Israel, and the girl will learn the truth. So if we give Arif her freedom without the exoneration you seek, too bad. She'll have to suffer her damaged reputation without complaint or comment, no matter how many people still consider her a murderer. Better that than death or a life sentence."

David was silent. He despised turning his back on those Israelis with whom he sympathized — Moshe Howard, Avi Masur, and Anat Ben-Aron — while consigning Palestinians to the role of scape-goat. But he was, in the end, Hana's lawyer. "We'll have a deal," he said with deep reluctance, "the moment Hana goes free. But not before, and not if you so much as lay a hand on her anytime later."

For a long time, Hertz merely watched David's face, his own expression neutral. "I think we understand each other," he said. "Perhaps, in time, the truth can emerge without us."

Calling out to his driver, Hertz pointed toward the shore. The minutes it took to get there passed in silence. When they reached the St. Francis Yacht

Club, David and the Israeli parted without a word.

David stood alone on the pier, gazing at the commonplace sight of two sailboats tacking with the wind in front of the barren rock of Alcatraz. He could scarcely believe what had just transpired, or the role that fate was forcing him to play. Nor was he certain that Hertz could achieve what David had asked. All he could do was wait.

For a moment, oddly, David's thoughts turned to Ibrahim Jefar, condemned to die in a federal prison. Whatever the truth, Jefar was a plaything of history. But all of them — Hana, David, Munira, Saeb, even Amos Ben-Aron — had become the playthings of history. All that remained was to see what history offered those who remained alive.

21

David spent the next three days willing himself to prepare for the trial as though he had no hope of freeing Hana. But hope kept breaking his concentration, most insistently when he outlined his questions for Munira. His other distraction — the thought that he might be in considerable danger — surfaced most often in public places, and at night. He was not quite as dismissive of this fear as logic told him he should be; the act of killing someone was so foreign to him that he could not quite believe that it was governed by the rules of reason.

But on the surface, little happened. His three days were hermetic, as though he were waiting for some fuller, more human life to resume. He could not stop wondering how Marnie Sharpe was spending the weekend, what discussions were taking place between Israel and the United States. David took no press calls; though the media was filled with speculation, no one came close to the story David and Avi Hertz had crafted in the middle of San Francisco Bay. That story would become "real," David knew, only if Sharpe made it so on Monday. Until then, he tried not to imagine the life Hana and Munira would lead thereafter.

Monday morning dawned bright and crisp. David tried to see that as an omen.

■ ■ ■ ■

At nine A.M., instead of reconvening in a courtroom filled with avid reporters, Judge Taylor summoned David and Sharpe to her chambers. "You wanted to meet in private," she said to Sharpe. "What is it?"

Sitting in a chair beside David, Sharpe seemed composed but quietly miserable, an advocate about to relinquish an obsession — the hope of winning a high-profile trial in which she had invested countless hours and every last particle of her abilities, a trial that would be remembered when every other case she tried was long forgotten. Without looking at David, she spoke in a monotone, as though reciting a statement written by someone else.

"The government," she told Judge Taylor, "wishes to dismiss the case against Ms. Arif, without prejudice to our ability to refile it should new evidence come to light.

"We're far from convinced that she's innocent. But Mr. Khalid's testimony raises questions that his death makes difficult to answer."

Taylor looked at her keenly. "That might be grounds for a mistrial," the judge cut in. "What about the Israeli government? I ordered it to send a representative."

"That's the second factor in our decision," Sharpe said in the same grudging tone. "The government of Israel has authorized us to say that it is aware of information regarding the broader conspiracy — none of which in itself exculpates Ms. Arif, but which is implicated by Mr. Wolfe's defense and this court's order of last Thursday. For reasons of national security, and so as not to jeopardize Israel's ongoing inquiry into the conspiracy to assassinate Prime Minister Ben-Aron, Israel does not wish to provide these materials to the defense."

Could this be over? David thought in wonder.

"I'm also authorized to say," Sharpe continued, "that based on the record and other facts that are not yet public, the Israeli government believes that Saeb Khalid was complicit in the assassination. All *our* government need say is that Israel's position and the events of the trial create sufficient ambiguity to justify dismissal. There's no statute of limitations for murder, and this crime is plainly too serious for us to stop investigating. But that's our position until further notice."

"So Hana is stuck in limbo," David said to Sharpe. "What makes you think the case against her will ever get any better —"

"Don't press your luck," the judge interrupted with a tight smile. "And just so you don't tantalize yourself with the specter of total victory, Mr. Wolfe, the best I'd have done for you is a mistrial." Turning to Sharpe, she added, "But I must tell you, Ms. Sharpe, that I doubt a reasonable jury would convict Ms. Arif unless you come up with more than I think you ever will. So don't stay up nights brooding about how Mr. Wolfe has gamed the system.

"At the risk of sounding cynical, Mr. Wolfe may not be the only one whose sense of the rules is, shall we say, elastic. It occurs to me that Israel may want you to dismiss the case so it can extradite Arif for trial in Israel. I hope they understand that I won't provide a sympathetic venue for an extradition motion."

"The State of Israel," Sharpe responded, "has authorized me to say that it will not seek extradition."

The judge raised her eyebrows. "Someone," she said, "seems to have thought of nearly everything. Are there any other outstanding issues, Mr. Wolfe?"

David nodded. "There *are* some practical considerations, Your Honor. I believe that Ms. Arif and her daughter may be in danger if they return to the West Bank. I'd like them to be able to remain in the United States indefinitely."

Sharpe's repressed annoyance surfaced in her eyes. "Hoping for joint custody?" she asked in mildly caustic tones. "Or just weekend visitation?"

"Now that you've made this personal," David answered coolly, "I'm hoping for a living daughter. I'm also hoping that the government is competent enough to keep the Iranians from killing anyone else in San Francisco —"

"Enough," the judge interrupted tartly. "Do you have a more helpful response, Ms. Sharpe?"

Sharpe paused, her expression glum. "The United States will extend Ms. Arif's visa, and that of Munira Khalid, for one year's time, pending further action by Immigration and the Department of State. During that time, they can petition for permanent residence on whatever grounds they choose."

David felt his body relax, even as he could hardly believe Hana's change in fortune. "Are there any other variations you wish to work on this dream deal?" the judge asked him dryly. "Short of an executive pardon, that is."

"Yes. Protection of Hana and Munira should they choose to stay. At least for the year's period Ms. Sharpe mentioned."

"I think that's reasonable," Taylor told Sharpe. "Saeb Khalid could have used it — which is one reason why we're here."

Sharpe nodded. "We'll work out the details with Mr. Wolfe." Turning to David, she said, "For your part, we expect that you and your client will agree to make no statement about the case, including about who may have authored this conspiracy. No press conferences, no anonymous whispers. Nothing."

So this, David thought, was how Hertz meant to enforce silence: a lifetime gag order in exchange for Hana's freedom. "That's acceptable," he answered, "just as long as Hana isn't charged again. Also that no one on your end talks about Munira's paternity or what she might have learned about Khalid. If not, all bets are off."

The judge looked from Sharpe to David. "Silence isn't enforceable," she said, "but it certainly seems advisable for all of us." Pausing, the judge gave David a slight smile. "*Someone* really has thought of everything, haven't they?"

David gave no answer; the judge expected none. "Let's go to court," she said after a moment. "Then we can kick your client, and your daughter, loose."

Leaving the judge's chambers, Sharpe and David paused in the hallway.

Sharpe summoned a wintry smile. "You've done it," she said. "Just what you intended from the beginning. You played Israel off against the United States and made the cost of prosecuting too high for Israel to pay."

David did not return her smile; on this point, he could feel no elation. "The cost," he answered, "was even higher than I thought."

"Too many deaths, you mean?"

"Too many deaths, too much knowledge." He paused, then added wearily, "Some days, Marnie, I feel like the guy who bit the apple."

She looked at him askance. "So what else *do* you know? Was Munira really with Khalid for the entire time in which the handler called Iyad Hassan?"

"I don't know about that," David answered. "Unless I choose to press Munira, I may never know. But Hana passed a polygraph. And nothing she ever said about this case — to the FBI, to me, or to you — ever turned out to be a lie. Except, perhaps, when it came to protecting Munira."

"That's the question, isn't it?" Sharpe retorted. "Whether Arif helped her husband in order to protect Munira — Khalid's blackmail as opposed to your graymail."

David shook his head. "Once Hana was charged, she would have implicated Saeb before she'd let him raise Munira."

"That's just speculation," Sharpe said dismissively. "Which is pretty much all we're left with." Her tone became more fatalistic than angry. "I hate losing like this — you know that. But now that we're here, I'm not sure how much I'd have liked winning either. I felt too much like a pawn, and I wasn't sure whose. There's no ending that quite satisfies, is there?"

So Sharpe felt it too. "No," David answered. "But this is the only ending I could live with."

Sharpe gave him a last, dubious smile. "Then I hope you get some good out of it," she said and, abruptly turning, marched ahead of David to the courtroom.

Four hours later, David awaited Hana outside the federal detention center.

Flanked by two marshals, she emerged, dressed in the clothes she had worn on the night of her arrest. She stopped for a moment, blinking in the sunlight. Then, leaving the marshals, she walked toward David. A foot in front of him, she stopped again, aware of the media on the other side of the fence. Then she took his hands and looked up into his face.

"Thank you," she said, eyes glistening. "But that is hardly enough. You've given me back my life, and my daughter."

David tried to smile. "That's what you hired me for, isn't it?"

"Yes. And the only one who paid for that was you." Briefly, Hana lowered her gaze. "Whatever happens, David, I have to see you. Not like this, and not in a courtroom or an office."

He could not tell what this meant. Still conscious of the cameras, she stepped away from him and turned to the marshals. Briefly, she looked back. Then the marshals escorted her to the van that would begin her journey to wherever she and Munira chose.

22

The afternoon passed in a blur, David warding off the media with a carefully crafted mantra: Hana was innocent; the dismissal her vindication; her release the beginning of a life she wished to share only with a daughter shaken by the death of Saeb Khalid. Hana had never wanted to be a public figure, David emphasized, and she did not want mistaken charges or unanswered questions about her husband to keep her in the public eye. What she needed was to heal, and this required that she say nothing more — now or ever — than she already had said in court. This chapter of her life was done.

For the most part, the media was disbelieving or offended — reporters were used to functioning as a hall of mirrors through which persons thrust into the spotlight, however accidentally, paraded with a quickly acquired narcissism. That was their expectation of Hana, and of David. They did not know, of course, that his silence was the price of Hana's freedom. Nor would they ever learn, if David could help it, the deeper reasons, buried in the past, that the reticence of both lawyer and client was not merely their desire but their need.

And so when David returned to his flat in the Marina, a man with no clear vision of his future, he ignored the cadre of reporters gathered by his driveway and the ringing of his telephone and doorbell. Four hours later, when he glanced out the living room window, the reporters were gone.

At a little past nine o'clock that night, David heard a soft knock on his door. Rising from the chair where he sat in the semidarkness, he peered through the peephole.

Surprised, David opened the door.

Hana wore jeans and a sweater. She stood on his doorstep, unsure of herself, awaiting his invitation to enter. "I tried to call," she said at last.

David mustered a smile. "I didn't expect to see you quite this soon."

He backed away from the door. Glancing over her shoulder, Hana slipped inside.

They stood in the alcove, looking at each other. "This feels so strange," she said finally. "Sometimes I imagined being alone with you again, a girl's fantasy. But I never believed it would happen."

David tilted his head. "Who's with Munira?"

"Nisreen." Hana hesitated. "Munira is asleep."

David could feel the beating of his pulse. "And if she were awake?"

"There are things I cannot yet say to her. I can hardly say them to you." Her voice was thick with sadness and remorse. "I don't know your feelings, David, and there could be so many. I was selfish when we were young, selfish when I asked you to defend me. I will try to be less selfish now. If it is better that I go, I would understand."

David shook his head. Then, instinctively, he put his arms around her. He could sense Hana closing her eyes as she let her body relax against him. Silent, they held each other, rocking gently. "And what is it you want?" he murmured.

She leaned back, looking up into his eyes again. "To stay," she answered simply. "To have this time with you, however we choose to spend it."

David gazed into her face, so lovely that, this close, it almost hurt to look at her. Then his fingers grazed the nape of her neck, and he bent his face toward hers.

Her mouth was soft and warm, at once strange and familiar. David felt the two of them suspended in time, unconscious of anything else, uncertain whether this was past or present. And then the hunger for her returned, the sense of passion deferred, of years falling away. What this meant no longer mattered.

His lips found the hollow of her neck. Hana shivered, pressing hard against him. Taking her hand, David led her to the bedroom.

As they undressed, their eyes never left each other's. He could feel the beating of his own pulse, see Hana's desire so intensely that it was almost painful. She was even more beautiful than the woman he had remembered against his will.

Transfixed, they slid between cool sheets, her breasts grazing his chest. At once, they were frenzied, less tender than demanding, ripping away the past with equal ruthlessness until both of them cried out.

Afterward, he touched her cheek with curled fingers, looking into the eyes of a woman he could not be sure he knew. "Was this just gratitude?" he asked.

Her eyes filmed with tears. "If you could see inside me, you wouldn't ask. I've had thirteen years to think of you. But I didn't know you anymore. So I've loved how I remembered you, or my imaginings of who you had become." Briefly, she looked away. "I told myself that my memory of desiring you was a trick of the mind — that I could not have lost myself like this. Now I know that I did, and could so easily again.

"But so much has happened to us. You're so much more self-protective than I remembered, perhaps because of me. And all I can do now is feel sorry for all you've lost."

"I tell myself that it's for the best," he answered softly. "Perhaps someday I'll believe it."

Accepting this, Hana nestled her head against his chest. Moments later, David discovered that it was now he who needed her.

This time it was sweeter, more intimate, less the cauterizing of need than the fulfillment of a desire to be closer. Later, filled with wonder, David and Hana were able to smile into each other's faces.

"So," he said with a fair attempt at humor, "we're lovers after all. But where do we go from here?"

"I wish I could see that far." Pausing, Hana looked away. "It was strange for me today — I was looking at Munira and suddenly saw you. And I felt a kind of peace, like different parts of me were at last becoming reconciled.

"But Munira has lived nearly thirteen years without you. Right now, she is a girl who has lost the father she may feel that she's betrayed. I struggle to know what is best for her."

"To stay here," David answered firmly. "It's best for you, and for Munira. Why should she be sacrificed to hatreds she had no part in causing? America could be a safe place for you both. It's a home for people without a home, or for people whose home has become too dangerous. There will be no peace in the West Bank."

"Dreams are not so easy to give up," Hana said.

"How can Munira and I abandon our people in a time when the world makes us pariahs once again? We are needed more than ever, to try to build a country for all of us, not just extremists who would condemn us to narrowness and hatred. However hard, we are still trying to make a homeland, not just a home."

David felt a stab of guilt at what he could not tell her. "For Hamas?" he asked. "Do you imagine Munira as a forty-year-old veiled grandmother? She's my daughter, too — a Jew as well as an Arab, and an American by birthright." David gazed at Hana intently. "Your story — yours and Saeb's — is the story of what happens to people when war and reprisal never end. And after this there's no end in sight. But does this tragedy of Jews and Palestinians have to define Munira? At least we can do better for her than we did for ourselves."

"Than *I* did," Hana amended softly. "But please do not shame me with it. I made Munira Palestinian, and her home and her friends are there. Among my women friends, such as Nisreen, there is support for younger women to grow into their own identity —"

"What identity is that?" David interrupted. "Can you tell Munira who her father is? Can you tell your women friends that her father is a Jew? Or will Munira remain the product of a sin that has to be hidden? Including from Munira herself."

In the pale light of a bedside lamp, Hana looked bereft. "Adolescents are utterly moral people, David, but only in the narrowest sense. They do not forgive their parents' sins, and they have no room for moral ambiguity. To tell Munira the truth now would give her a mother who is a liar and a whore, and a father who her *supposed* father told her she must hate.

"She might reject us both. She might become our worst nightmare — the closed-off fanatic Saeb tried so hard to create." Hana took David's hand. "When she is closer to being a woman, I will tell her. Then she may have some compassion for us. But now it is more than enough for me to help her heal, free from Saeb."

David felt his buried anger returning. "And what's my role, Hana? To send e-mails? To see myself as a sperm donor? This script was tired thirteen years ago." He forced himself to speak more softly. "I have something more to offer her — a life that doesn't bear the fingerprints of history or hatred or unreasoning religion. When I agreed to defend you, I did it because I wanted to believe in you. Now I have a daughter, and what I did in the end was as much for her as for you.

"I'm willing to be patient. I don't see you as my debtor. But the last few months have changed me, and I want to be a part of Munira's life."

Slowly, Hana nodded. "Then that is only fair, to all of us. Somehow we will find a way."

"Only if you live here," David retorted. "There's no place for me on the West Bank, and you know it. Just as you know that you and Munira are safer here."

"Why?" Hana said softly. "Because if I return, those who may have murdered Saeb will kill me for what I know? When they do not, perhaps you will finally know for sure that I am innocent. Otherwise, you can never really love me."

This was so true that it silenced David. "Does that matter to you?" he finally asked.

Moving closer to him, Hana touched his face again. "I'm not American, David. I've never believed in Cinderella endings. Nor can I be sanguine about what the future holds for Palestine. But this much I believe — I could go the rest of my life and never feel with another man the way I do with you. If that is true, another year or so will make little difference to me."

"Thirteen years wasn't long enough?"

"For Munira's sake, no. For us, it's far too long already. You don't deserve to put your life on hold, certainly not for me. Maybe you have no heart for it. If that is so, or if all that has happened is too much . . ." Her voice trailed off, and then she managed to smile. "Then you will always be welcome in Munira's life. And mine."

David felt his throat constrict. "And for now?"

Briefly, Hana closed her eyes. "For Munira and me," she said, "it is time for us to try to resume our lives. We're leaving, David, the day after tomorrow. Will you come with us to the airport?"

With sadness and foreboding, David waited near the security gate for Hana and Munira to check in for their flight through New York to Tel Aviv, from where the Israeli government would escort them to Ramallah. It was before seven o'clock in the morning, and the airport was quiet; only the watchful presence of deputy marshals suggested that these two passengers were unusual. But to David, Hana and Munira were poised on the edge of uncertainty and danger.

After they got their tickets, Hana whispered something to Munira. Munira nodded and then, glancing shyly at David with dark eyes reminiscent of his mother's, she walked toward him, alone.

Munira wore a soft, flowing dress much like Hana's. She was taller than when they had first met, David suddenly realized, her bearing closer to that of a woman than a child. Somewhat formally, she said, "Thank you for helping us."

We might have been a family, David thought, but for the history of two peoples. Instead, his daughter did not know who he was, and she was returning to a place that was alien to him, a place riven by hatred and grievances so ancient they were honored. "I'm not saying good-bye," David told her. "I'm coming to see you, and I'll be sure to help keep you in cell phones. And maybe someday, like your mother, you'll study in America."

Munira's face clouded. For her, David realized, America had been, in its own way, more frightening than a life under occupation or Hamas. Nor could she now imagine her future. But, perhaps out of courtesy, she nodded, extending her hand.

David took it in both of his. "Be well, Munira."

Hana appeared behind her. Softly, she told their daughter, "Let me speak with David for a moment."

Munira walked away. Standing close to him, Hana asked, "So what will you do now?"

"With my life?" David smiled a little. "It seems you've made me famous. I may have found a new career defending the embattled." He paused, then gave her the fuller answer she was seeking. "Before you came I was heading straight into politics; now, that will never happen. Odd, isn't it, that destroying all my plans should make me more myself. But that may be what's happened, however hard."

Hana looked at him with fondness and concern. "You're a gifted lawyer, David. Maybe what you needed was something to lend these gifts more meaning."

Perhaps this was so. But it was not quite the conversation he wished to have. "I don't want to talk about myself," he said to her, "as though I'm some spare part. The world is filled with spare parts. But also with families, some of whose members see each other for who they are, and even tell the truth."

Even as he said this, it again struck David that he had not told the entire truth to Hana, another price of her freedom. But she did not know this. Briefly, her composure slipped, and her voice became husky. "The truth, then. Before we met again, you still lived inside me. But now I am filled with you. Leaving you is even harder than before, and the rightness of it far less clear."

David felt hope collide with his deepening sense of loss. "Nonetheless, you're leaving. But this can't be the end for us. We have Munira."

Silent, Hana touched David's arm, looking up into his face as she once had long ago, her eyes still luminous but a woman's now, their fire tempered by time and understanding. Then she turned before David could reach for her and was off, walking Munira toward security, a slim mother and daughter with the same determined stride, their two dark heads uncovered.

AUTHOR'S NOTE AND ACKNOWLEDGMENTS

The ongoing tragedy of Israel and the Palestinians is the most complex and controversial subject I've taken on. The disagreements between and among Israelis and Palestinians are so emotional and deeply rooted that it is challenging even to find a common vocabulary: for example, the West Bank, which Palestinians routinely refer to as the "Occupied Territories," is, to many Israelis, "Judea and Samaria," part of the biblical land of Israel. And when it comes to the cause and effect of violence, these differences become incendiary.

I admit to one bias: that only a two-state solution aimed at a secure Israel and a viable Palestine holds any hope of freeing both peoples from the past. But my aim in writing this novel was not to pass judgment on the "truth," or to map out a solution, or to make some implicit argument about moral equivalency between one side or faction and another. Rather, my aim was to craft a compelling narrative that interweaves the varying experiences and perspectives of Jews and Palestinians, and suggests why the prospect of a lasting peace remains so elusive. I trust the reader to understand that telling someone's story does not mean endorsing it, and to exercise his or her judgment and discernment.

I have no doubt that many readers will find something in this novel to dislike. Indeed, some partisans on both sides are so committed to their own narrative that they are grossly offended by any deviation. But I believe that acknowledging each other's perspectives is essential to coexistence. A modest example: it should be as possible for Palestinians and their advocates to comprehend why Jews, after centuries of persecution, desire a Jewish state as it should be for Israel and its supporters to acknowledge the aspirations and resentments of stateless Palestinians, including those whose families were dislocated by the founding of Israel. But, for many, this is much harder than it sounds.

A few more observations. First, while the characters are imagined, the history, the context, and the identity of the contending forces depicted in this novel are very real. Obviously, while Amos Ben-Aron and Marwan Faras are imaginary leaders, their predecessors — men such as Ariel Sharon, Yitzhak Rabin, Benjamin Netanyahu, and Yasser Arafat, referred to in the novel, are major figures in this tangled history. The nuclear ambitions of Iran's ruling classes became common knowledge during the writing of this book; the building of the Israeli security wall continues; the actions of Fatah, Hamas, the Al Aqsa Martyrs Brigade, and Islamic Jihad are reported in our daily media. The places, too, are real; not only Jerusalem, Tel Aviv, and Ramallah but Jenin, Aida, Hebron, Qalqiya, the Qalandiya checkpoint, Mukeble, Masada, and the village of Atwani are among the many locations I saw for myself.

Second, while the events of this novel are also imagined, they are rooted in the extensive travel and research I refer to elsewhere in this note. I could not write about the burdens of those who oversee Israel's security without interviewing those responsible in the IDF; or about the Al Aqsa Martyrs Brigade without meeting one of its leaders; or about the victims of suicide bombers without interviewing their survivors; or about right-wing settlers without visiting settlements; or about politics and geopolitics without consulting diplomats and politicians; or depict those, on both sides, who seek peace without soliciting their views. These are merely examples — my aim was to be comprehensive. I recognize that some people will be offended that those I chose to interview included highly controversial figures, including a leader of the Al Aqsa Martyrs Brigade wanted by the IDF. As I conducted my research, my aim was reportorial; limiting my observations would not have served my story or my readers.

Third, my choice of language: in selecting such terms as "Palestinians" and "Occupied Territories," I employ common usage, even though some Israelis would argue that the "Palestinians" are not a people and that the West Bank, however heavily peopled by Arabs, is God's biblical grant to the Jewish people, and therefore cannot be "occupied." Similarly, I do not seek to avoid the anti-Semitic sentiments one encounters on the West Bank. I cannot possibly satisfy the ideologues and purists, and did not try.

Fourth, while too little of what I observed engendered optimism, it was a wonderful experience to immerse myself in this subject and to meet so many interesting, and often admirable, people. I have tried to do the help they gave me justice. But errors of fact and interpretation are inevitable and, where they occur, the responsibility is mine alone.

I also note that for narrative purposes I have simplified the chronology of suicide bombings in relation to the military operations in Jenin, but not in a way that alters the assertion of the IDF that this operation was a reprisal for such bombings.

Finally, a word about events in the Middle East as of mid-July 2006. I finished writing *Exile* in mid-February 2006. Its geopolitical themes — the regional and nuclear ambitions of Iran; the rise of Hamas and the threat of fundamentalist domination of the Palestinian territories; the relationship between Iran, Syria, and Hamas; the role of Iran and Syria in promoting the actions of Hezbollah in Lebanon; and the exploitation of the plight of ordinary Palestinians by Iran and by extremists on all sides — prefigured, rather than reflected, the developments that followed. I make no claim to prophecy; the sad events in the first eight months of 2006 were utterly predictable, requiring me merely to interpolate a couple of lines about Lebanon to the final text. As so often in the past, extremists dictated the course of events, and while I hope publication of this book in January 2007 occurs in a materially better climate, I fear that it will not.

That said, I would like to thank all those who helped me.

In the early stages of the novel, I interviewed a number of Americans with special expertise in the geopolitics of Israel and the rest of the Middle East: Wolf Blitzer of CNN; former National Security Adviser Sandy Berger; former Secretary of Defense William Cohen; former Ambassador to Israel Martin Indyk; Dan Kurtzer, the ambassador to Israel at the time; terrorism expert Matt Leavitt; former Chief Middle East Peace Negotiator Dennis Ross; and Jim Bodner, Danny Sebright, Bob Tyrer, and Doug Wilson of the Cohen Group.

Other Americans helped me flesh out the legal, investigative, and security aspects of the story: Assistant District Attorney Al Giannini and Assistant United States Attorney Phil Kearney; former Assistant United States Attorney Martha Boersch, and defense lawyers Jim Collins and Doug Young. Former Deputy Attorney General Philip Heymann and Jeff Smith, formerly General Counsel of the CIA, enlightened me as to the ins and outs of litigation involving national security and classified information. United States District Judge Susan Illston generously helped me think through some of the thornier trial issues. Bob Huegly of Dignitary Protection for the San Francisco Police Department; Terry Samway, formerly of the Secret Service; Jeff Schlanger of Kroll and Associates; former FBI agent Rick Smith; and explosives expert Dino Zografos of the San Francisco Police Department contributed their insights on security and investigative matters. Special thanks to defense lawyer Dick Martin, formerly an assistant United States attorney, for his insights on many facets of the legal problems presented here.

I was fortunate to have the assistance of the Foreign Ministry of Israel in arranging interviews and helping to facilitate our very rewarding trip to Israel. Many thanks to Hamutal Rogel of the Foreign Ministry and, especially, David Siegel of the Israeli embassy in Washington, D.C., who creatively and tirelessly worked to share his perspectives and to open doors. The Israeli officials who were generous in sharing their knowledge included Ambassador Alan Baker, General Amos Gila'ad, General Yossi

Kuperwasser, Minister of Housing Isaac Herzog; Ambassador Gideon Meier of the Israeli Foreign Ministry, and Judge Eliakim Rubinstein of the Supreme Court of Israel. It was a special privilege to visit with Vice Prime Minister Shimon Peres, twice prime minister of Israel.

Many thanks, as well, to the numerous other Israelis who enhanced my understanding: Abad Allawi, mayor of the divided town at Ghajur; retired admiral and peace advocate Ami Ayalon; educator Sundos Battah; fundamentalist settler Gershon Ferency; political and security expert Michael Herzog; writer Etgar Keret; Professor Moshe Ma'oz; Dahlia Rabin of the Rabin Institute; Professor Avi Ravitsky; journalist Meier Shalev; communications specialist Myra Siegel; and conservative writer Ariel Stav. I am especially gratified for the poignant accounts of survivors of victims of a suicide bombing in Haifa, two of whom not only lost their husbands and children, but were survivors of the bombing itself: Ron Carmit, Rachel Korin, and Nurit and Doran Menchel.

Finally, I want to thank two Israelis who became friends: Ron Edelheit, a wonderful translator, guide, and archaeological expert, whose knowledge and enthusiasm made historic and contemporary Israel equally alive, and Dr. Yossi Draznin, who not only contributed his expertise but commented on the manuscript.

I am just as grateful to those who brought the Palestinian experience into focus, both in America and during our travels on the West Bank: Akram, a community leader in Jenin; Nisreen Haj Ahmad and Zeinah Salahi of the Negotiations Support Unit of the PLO; Khader Alamour, community leader in the village of Atwani; Nidal Al-Azraq and

Nidal Al-Azra, community leaders in the Aida refugee camp; Dr. Hanan Ashrawi, former spokeswoman for the PLO and now a member of the Palestinian legislature; conflicts resolution specialist Amjad Atallah; Muhammad Abu Hamad, Jenin commander of the Al Aqsa Martyrs Brigade; nonviolence advocate Sami Awad; Professor Wafa'a Darwish of Birzeit University; Yasser Darwish of Birzeit University; Faten Farhat of the Sakakini Institute; Said Hamad of the Palestinian Mission in Washington; skilled translator, observer, and guide Ibrahim Jaber; businessman Majdi Khalil and lawyer Jonathan Kuttab, who shared their observations and experiences of detention; businessman and investor Zahi Khouri; guide Issa Loussei; Nabil Mohamad, who vividly described his experiences during the tragedy at Sabra and Shatila; Amer Rahal, who ministers to disabled children in Jenin; Iyad Rdeinah of the Holy Land Trust; guide, translator, and activist George Rishmawi; Basima Zaroor of Jenin; and Reem Al-Hashimy of the embassy of the United Arab Emirates, who was wonderfully evocative in helping me imagine the characters. Thanks also to Kristin Anderson, Diane Janzen, and Kathie Uhler of the Christian Peacemaker Teams, who introduced us to the village of Atwani.

Several Americans helped me shape the characters of Harold and Carole Shorr. Critical were the observations of the daughters of Holocaust survivors: Nadine Greenfield Binstock, Arlene Breyer, Karen Chinka, Sally Cohen, Esther Finder, Lillian Fox, Janice Friebaum, Jenette Friedman, Suzanne Jacobs, Alys Myers, Michele Rivers, Marsha Rosenberg, and Ruth Shevlin. David Kahan, a survivor of the Holocaust, was generous and unflinching in relating his experiences. And my partner, Dr. Nancy Clair, enriched the narrative by suggesting that it address the Holocaust and its impact; read every chapter as I wrote it; and accompanied me to Israel and the West Bank, where her experiences as an international educational consultant made her an invaluable observer.

I also did a lot of reading, including *Occupied Voices* by Wendy Pearlman; *A History of Israel* by Howard Sachar; *The Missing Peace* by Dennis Ross; *Cain's Field* by Matt Rees; *Prisoner 83571* by Samuel Don; *I Saw Ramallah* by Mourid Barghouti; *The Iron Wall* by Avi Shlaim; and articles and writings by Hillel Halkin, Matt Leavitt, Michael Eisenstadt, Neri Zilber, Patrick Clawson, Akiva Eldar, James Bennett, Erskine Childers, Ellen Siegel, Nabil Ahmed, John Kifner, Jill Drew, Jim Zogby, and Benny Morris. I also viewed the following documentaries: *The Accused* by the BBC; *Children of Shatila* by Mai Masri; *Jenin, Jenin;* and a PBS segment on right-wing Israeli settlers.

The manuscript itself benefited from the advice of several discerning readers: my assistant, Alison Porter Thomas, who did her best work ever in commenting in detail on every page; Fred Hill, my wonderful agent, who encouraged me from the beginning; and John Sterling, president and publisher of Henry Holt, who believed in the idea, helped me shape the novel, and shared my belief that popular fiction can both entertain and enlighten — even when it addresses the hardest subjects.

Finally, there are Alan Dershowitz and Jim Zogby, to whom this book is dedicated. As he has with several other novels, Alan gave me critical advice at an early juncture, helping me frame the extensive research that followed, as well as recommending other experts to interview. Equally important, Alan has conveyed his deep concern for Israel and its future in numerous conversations over the years, and I read — and reread — his incisive book *The Case for Israel* in order to ground myself in the essence of the controversies surrounding Israel and the Palestinians. Without Alan's passion and generosity, I doubt I would have been as receptive to Jim Zogby's challenge "Why don't you tackle the Israeli-Palestinian dilemma?" — or, perhaps, have undertaken this book at all.

Dr. Jim Zogby is, of course, the head of the Arab-American Institute, and a gifted advocate for better understanding of Arab-Americans and, more broadly, the diverse peoples of the Middle East. Jim spent many hours sharing his thoughts in the most patient and generous way I could wish; connecting me with those, in the United States and on the West Bank, whose advice would enable me to write this book the way I did; and, finally, imparting his advice on the manuscript itself. I hope the result does justice to both Alan and Jim in the only way I can — by telling people's stories, the better to impart the common humanity of the Jews and Arabs caught in this tragic conflict, as well as the historic, experiential, religious, and psychological barriers that divide them. Certainly, it has been a privilege to try.

RICHARD NORTH PATTERSON
September 1, 2006

ABOUT THE AUTHOR

Richard North Patterson is the author of thirteen previous critically acclaimed novels, including nine consecutive international bestsellers. Formerly a trial lawyer, Patterson was the SEC's liaison to the Watergate special prosecutor, has served on the boards of several Washington advocacy groups dealing with gun violence, political reform, and women's rights, and is currently the chairman of Common Cause, the grassroots citizens' lobby. He lives with his partner, Dr. Nancy Clair, in San Francisco and on Martha's Vineyard.